Robert Ferguson

The Teutonic Name System applied to the Family Names of France, England, and Germany

Robert Ferguson

The Teutonic Name System applied to the Family Names of France, England, and Germany

1st Edition | ISBN: 978-3-75258-569-8

Place of Publication: Frankfurt am Main, Germany

Year of Publication: 2022

Salzwasser Verlag GmbH, Germany.

Reprint of the original, first published in 1864.

TEUTONIC NAME-SYSTEM.

TO

JOHN ANSTER, LL.D.,

FROM HIS FRIEND

THE AUTHOR.

THE
TEUTONIC NAME-SYSTEM

APPLIED TO THE

FAMILY NAMES

OF

FRANCE. ENGLAND, & GERMANY.

BY

ROBERT FERGUSON.

LONDON: WILLIAMS & NORGATE,

1864.

PREFACE.

The present work, though founded on one previously published by me under the title of " English Surnames and their place in the Teutonic Family," is so entirely changed, not only in its general principle but also in all its details, that it cannot be considered in any other light than that of a new work. Even the former title, as inadequately describing its present contents, has necessarily been abandoned.

It is now put forward as an attempt to connect the family names of France, England, and Germany—so far as the ancient Teutonic element in each is concerned—as members of one common family, and to form them into a definite system in accordance with the nomenclature of the old Germans. It undertakes to shew that as the Saxons and other German tribes in the names of England and Germany, so are the old Franks represented in the present names of France. And it further undertakes to shew that in each case this correspondence does not consist merely in the casual resemblance here and there of individual names, but is to be traced in the coincidence of a

viii PREFACE.

complete and connected system common both to the old peoples and the new.

The basis of my theory is the Altdeutsches Namenbuch of Förstemann, in which the ancient names of Germany are collected, arranged, and in most cases explained. Of this work, which I fear is not so well known in England as it deserves, I cannot speak in terms more suitable than those in which Mr. Taylor refers . to the companion volume on the names of places, as a work " which even in Germany, must be considered a marvellous monument of erudite labour."

But Förstemann draws the line of the Old German period sharply at the end of the 11th century, and as has been shewn by Stark in a little work containing some observations and criticisms on the Altdeutsches Namenbuch, an extension of the survey over the three centuries following would throw much additional light upon the subject. From this little work (which I have unfortunately mislaid and of which I am consequently not able to give the precise title) are taken the few ancient names which are of a later date than the 11th century.

A more important supplement to the Altdeutsches Namenbuch will be found in the names which I have introduced from our own early records, and in particular from the Codex Diplomaticus of Kemble, and the Liber Vitæ or list of benefactors to the shrine of St. Cuthbert at Durham. The latter record commences about the ninth and is continued up to the thirteenth century, but the names which I have introduced may be taken to be generally of the early period. For the names of later date taken from the Hundred Rolls drawn up in the reign of Edward 1st I am indebted to the Patronymica Britannica of Mr. Lower.

Though the explanation of Old German names is a subject which has engaged the attention of almost all the leading philologists of Germany, and though conclusions have in many cases been arrived at which have met with general acceptance, there still remains much which is unsettled and obscure. And further—there are many names now for the first time brought to light through the labours of Förstemann, of which in some cases he has offered an explanation and in others not. Though as a general rule I have adopted the conclusions of the German scholars, I have in some instances ventured to express a difference of opinion, and in a still greater number of cases I have been thrown upon my own resources for the explanation of names not dealt with by any other writer.

The English names, with very few exceptions, are taken from the London Directory, the two works of Mr. Lower, and that of Mr. Bowditch. The little work by Mr. Clark called " Surnames metrically arranged," and which, by the way, is executed with no little ingenuity, contains a few names not found elsewhere. The French names are taken from the directory of Paris, and the Modern German names from the works of Förstemann, Pott, and the other writers elsewhere enumerated. It has not always been an easy task to ascertain the nationality of a name, particularly as the directory of Paris does not generally give the christian names, which might be a guide in a doubtful case. The same remark applies to Suffolk Surnames, some of the names of which look very much like German in an English guise. The interchange which has taken place between the respective countries at a comparatively recent period, as for instance the immigration of Frenchmen into England at the Revocation of the Edict of Nantes and of Scotchmen at an earlier period into France, must also be taken into account. This introduces an element of uncertainty which must to a certain extent modify the particular classification of modern names, though not affecting the general theory of their origin.

In the arrangement of the different groups I have taken, first the simple form or the stem-name, and then the various forms which have grown out of, or which have been built upon it. It will be observed that while there are some groups, as at pages 115, 202, 231, 289, 454, which shew the connection between the ancient and modern names in a very complete form, there are many others which exist in a more or less fragmentary state—the system which I have adopted allowing the missing links, as they may turn up,

PREFACE.

to fall into their respective places. It follows, therefore, that a random reference to any particular group might be by no means convincing, and that my theory must be judged as a whole. The dates which I have affixed to the Old German names, and for which I am indebted to Förstemann, shew the earliest period at which that particular form has so far been found—as to the real antiquity of the name of course they are no guide whatever.

In conclusion, while expressing my obligation to the scholars of Germany for the standing point on which to form my theory, I may perhaps not be' thought presumptuous in expressing a hope that I have done at least something to pay off the debt which I have incurred—no such systematic attempt having as yet been made even in Germany to connect the past and the present in men's names as will be found in these pages.

R. F.

Morton, Carlisle.

LIST OF THE PRINCIPAL WORKS CONSULTED.

Altdeutsches Namenbuch, von Dr. Ernst Förstemann. Vol. I., Personennamen. *Nordhausen,* 1856.

Die Personennamen, insbesondere die Familiennamen, von August Friedrich Pott. *Leipzig,* 1853.

Grimm. Deutsche Grammatik. *Göttingen.*

Grimm. Deutsche Mythologie. *Göttingen,* 1854.

Grimm. Geschichte der Deutschen Sprache. *Leipzig,* 1848.

Grimm. Frauennamen aus Blumen. *Berlin,* 1852.

Weinhold. Die Deutschen Frauen in dem Mittelalter. *Vienna,* 1851.

Weinhold. Altnordisches Leben. *Berlin,* 1856.

Graff. Althochdeutscher Sprachschatz. *Berlin,* 1834.

Zeuss. Die Deutschen und die Nachbarstämme. *Munich,* 1837.

Mone. Untersuchungen zur Geschichte der Teutschen Helden sage. *Leipzig,* 1836.

Glück. Die bei C. Julius Cæsar vorkommenden Keltischen Namen. *Vienna,* 1857.

Wassenberg. Verhandeling over de Eigennaamen der Friesen. *Franeker,* 1774.

Fröhner. Karlsruher Namenbuch. *Karlsruhe,* 1856.

Outzen. Glossarium der Friesischen Sprache. *Copenhagen,* 1837.

Islands Landnamabôk, hoc est, liber originum Islandiæ. *Copenhagen,* 1774.

Kemble. Codex Diplomaticus Ævi Saxonici. *London,* 1845-48.

Kemble. Names, Surnames, and Nic-names of the Anglo-Saxons. *London,* 1846.

LIST OF THE PRINCIPAL WORKS CONSULTED. xiii

Liber Vitæ Ecclesiæ Dunelmensis, published by the Surtees Society. *London*, 1841.

Polyptyque de l'Abbé Irminon ou Denombrement des manses, des serfs, et des revenus de l'Abbaye de Saint-Germain-des-Prés sous le regne de Charlemagne.
Paris, 1844.

Polyptyque de l'Abbaye de Saint Remi de Reims, ou Denombrement des manses, des serfs, et des revenus de cette abbaye vers le milieu du neuvieme siècle de notre ère.
Paris, 1853.

Salverte. History of the names of men, nations, and places. Translated by the Rev. L. H. Mordacque.
London, 1862.

Lower. English Surnames. *London*, 1849.

Lower. Patronymica Britannica. *London*, 1860.

Bowditch. Suffolk Surnames, 3rd Edition. *Boston*, 1861.
(Suffolk means Boston and its vicinity, but the work in reality takes in a much wider range.)

Miss Yonge. History of Christian Names. *London*, 1863.

Taylor. Names and Places. *London*, 1864.

Thorpe. Northern Mythology. *London*, 1851.

Thorpe. The Anglo-Saxon poem of Beowulf, the Scop or Gleeman's tale, and the fight at Finnesburg.
Oxford, 1845.

Worsaae. Danes and Norwegians in England, Scotland, and Ireland. *London*, 1852.

Bosworth. Origin of the English and Germanic languages and nations. *London*, 1848.

Talbot. English Etymologies. *London*, 1847.

Halliwell. Archaic and Provincial Dictionary.
London, 1831.

Wedgwood. Dictionary of English Etymology.
London, 1859-62.

Brockie. The Family Names of the Folks of Shields traced to their Origin. *Shields*, 1857.

CONTENTS.

		Page.
Chapter I.		
INTRODUCTION	... ...	1
Chapter II.		
SIMPLE FORMS	... ...	17
Chapter III.		
DIMINUTIVES		20
Chapter IV.		
PHONETIC ADDITIONS	... ...	28
Chapter V.		
PATRONYMICS	... ...	31
Chapter VI.		
COMPOUNDS		34
Chapter VII.		
LETTER CHANGES		44
Chapter VIII.		
OUR NATURAL ENEMIES		50
Chapter IX.		
MAN AS THE TYPE OF POWER		57
Chapter X.		
THE BRUTE AND ITS ATTRIBUTES		67
Chapter XI.		
THE GODS OF THE NORTH		113
Chapter XII.		
THE HEROES OF THE NORTH		145
Chapter XIII.		
THE WARRIOR AND HIS ARMS		161
Chapter XIV.		
THE PROTECTOR AND THE FRIEND		260
Chapter XV.		
ANCESTOR AND KINSMAN		287
Chapter XVI.		
THE NATION AS THE NAME-GIVER		295

CONTENTS.

xv

Chapter XVII.
THE SEA AND THE SEA LIFE 320

Chapter XVIII.
THE RULER AND THE PRINCE 327

Chapter XIX.
WISDOM AND KNOWLEDGE 347

Chapter XX.
THE TRUMPET OF FAME 368

Chapter XXI.
WEALTH AND PROSPERITY 381

Chapter XXII.
THE OUTER MAN 389

Chapter XXIII.
THE INNER MAN 426

Chapter XXIV.
THE STATION IN LIFE 451

Chapter XXV.
ALL FLESH IS AS GRASS 464

Chapter XXVI.
THE STUFF A MAN IS MADE OF 474

Chapter XXVII.
THE CHRISTIAN ERA 482

Chapter XXVIII.
THEY CALL THEIR LANDS AFTER THEIR OWN NAMES 489

Chapter XXIX.
OLD SAXONS AND ANGLO-SAXONS 504

Chapter XXX.
THE SCANDINAVIAN VIKINGS 510

Chapter XXXI.
A CHAPTER OF FRAGMENTS 516

Chapter XXXII.
CONCLUSION 526

ADDITIONS AND CORRECTIONS 529

INDEX 531

CHAPTER I.

INTRODUCTION.

THE Directory of London is perhaps the crowning wonder of that wonderful place. There may have been in ancient times—who knows ?—cities as great. There may be even now an uncounted population as prodigious at Pekin. But was there ever a city so registered, and classified, and chronicled, as is this teeming Babylon of ours ? No poor man in a dark corner can turn his face to the wall and give up the key of his house unnoticed—no petty shop be shut—no humble name be painted out. As surely as the place which knew him knows him no more, ere many months can pass there is a new name in the Domesday of London.

Here it is—the book of the Modern Babylon —bound in her own scarlet too—two thousand two hundred and sixty pages of names! How dreary seems the catalogue, and yet what a world of hidden history is there within the pages of this book ! For of all these thousands of names not one has been given in vain. There are deeds of forgotten valour that are summed up in a word— there are trivial incidents that have named generations of men—there are good Christians that are called after heathen gods—there are gentle women

INTRODUCTION.

that are called after savage brutes—there are names on the signs of Regent Street that were given in the unhewn forests of Germany.

Truly then the question, "Who gave you this name?" if it could be answered rightly—and in many instances it can—would give us interesting records. One might say—"Eight centuries ago an Anglo-Saxon* bravely withstood the Norman usurpation, and so harassed their forces by his stratagems that he was surnamed Præt, or the crafty—therefore it is that I am called PRATT." Another might say—"A Northman had a son mischievous and full of pranks, so that he was called Lok, after the god of mischief. Steady enough our family has become since then. We have produced the most sober of philosophers— one of the most practical of engineers—yet still we bear the name of LOCKE† from the mischief of our ancestor." And a third might say—"See you yon white horse cut on the turf of the southern down—whence came that white horse came my name. The great Roman historian tells us how our ancestors held the white horse sacred. Hence, when the early invaders wrested the soil from its British owner, they stamped it with this as the sign at once of their victory and of their faith. And, unconsciously as the Wiltshire peasant does reverence to the heathen symbol

---

* One of the companions of the Saxon hero Hereward.

† This may obtain in some individual cases, but I do not think, on consideration, that it is the general origin of the name.

INTRODUCTION. 3

when he annually clears away the grass from the outlines of the white horse, as his fathers have done for perhaps a thousand years before him, so do I, good Christian as I am, preserve a record of that same pagan superstition in my name of "HINCKS."*

The etymology of proper names is the only branch then of the subject which can in any sense be called popular; for most men, even of those who care not to enquire the origin of the language they speak, feel some interest or curiosity in knowing the meaning of the names they bear.

In the investigation of this subject tradition gives us little or no assistance. Not but that there are many traditions as to the origin of names, but in almost all cases they are worthless and delusive. Indeed it is rather curious how tradition, in matters of history so often substantially correct, in matters of etymology is generally sheer invention.

Thus I have no faith in such legends as that which derives TURNBULL from a man having turned by the head a wild bull which ran against Robert Bruce. Or in that which derives BULLSTRODE from an ancestor of the family, having, along with his followers, sallied forth to a conflict mounted upon bulls. Or in PURSEGLOVE from a man having found, at a time when he much

---

* HINCKS seems to be a corruption of Hengist or Hingest, which signifies a stallion. Some traditions make Hengist a Frisian, in which language the word is *hingst*, which approaches near to HINCKS. In the names of places Hengist has become changed into Hinks, as in Hinksey, Berks.—Ang.-Sax. Hengestesige.

4 INTRODUCTION.

needed it, a purse of gold wrapped up in a glove. Or in Lockhart, from an ancestor of the family having accompanied Sir James Douglas to the Holy Land with the heart of the Bruce.

Nor do I give much more credit to the German story which accounts for the name of the poet Saphir in this wise. The grandfather of Saphir, a Jew named Israel Israel, being required, in conformity with an ordonnance of the Austrian government, to change his name, expressed his own perfect indifference on the subject, and his readiness to take any name which the authorities might recommend. " You have a very handsome sapphire ring," said the official, " have you any objections to let Saphir be your name ?" " Not the least in the world," replied this accommodating Jew, and so Saphir became his name. Now I cannot take upon myself to say unhesitatingly that this story is a myth, but it is at least suspicious, and a different origin can readily be suggested for the name.

Neither is much value to be attached to the old Latinization of names. When we find the Ang.-Sax. Goodrick rendered " De bono fossato" —Godshall, the Old German Gottshalck, " De casa Dei"—when we find Armine, the glorious old hero Arminius, made into a " Sancta Ermina,— when we find such childish attempts as Dimoak, " De umbrosa quercu"—Salvein, " De salicosa vena," we see clearly that these are simply guesses —perhaps not unworthy of the age in which they

INTRODUCTION.

were formed, but certainly of no account in this.

Archæology and genealogy will do a great deal, and what they will do has been well done by Mr. Lower in his two works on English Surnames, which will always remain standard books of reference on the subject. It is to him that the credit must be given of being the first to bring to bear on the subject the researches of modern science.

The history of Christian names, which, according to my view, is to a great extent the history also of surnames, has received a most valuable contribution in the recent work of Miss Yonge, which does much to place the subject on a more solid basis than heretofore. And from the other side of the Atlantic we have a work, Suffolk Surnames, by Mr. Bowditch, which, though without pretensions to etymological research, contains the most curious catalogue of names that has yet been published.

With respect to the names of France, there is, as far as I know, no work on the subject which does much more than skim the surface. That by Salverte is elegant and philosophical, but does not go much into etymological detail, and is not always to be depended upon when it does.

In Germany, family names have received a large share of attention, and the same system of patient analysis which has raised the character of German philology has been applied to them. The preliminary step has been to collect all the ancient

6 . INTRODUCTION.

names, and arrange them under their respective roots. This gives a firm standing-ground for the investigation of modern names. In this department the *Altdeutsches Namenbuch* of Förstemann is a most complete, solid, and trustworthy work, extremely well arranged, and throwing, indirectly, more light on English names than any other book I know. This, as the latest work, is the best and the most complete, but the works of Graff and others which it supplements, are of the highest value and importance. Grimm, himself, the father of Teutonic philology, has, in his various writings, supplied knowledge upon which all others have drawn. Professor Pott's book on Modern German family names is also one of great learning and research, and the want of an index, which sadly diminished the debt of gratitude on the part of whose who had to consult him, has at length been supplied.

The study of English names embraces a wider field than that of the English language, because we have no longer the same Ang.-Sax. starting point. The dialects of the various tribes who came over to this country were fused into one common language, and that was Anglo-Saxon— but there was no such fusion of their names. In all their dialectic variations the names of those early settlers still stand in the London directory. Certainly there did spring up in after times a nomenclature properly Anglo-Saxon, formed in accordance with the general Teutonic system, but

INTRODUCTION.

7

still having its own distinctive character. But this nomenclature, as I am inclined to believe, never pervaded the mass of the people, who still held on to the old sort of names which they had brought over with them, and which they carried through Anglo-Saxon times up to the present day.

A word then on the antiquity of our English names. How far some of them may remount we cannot even guess. All we know is that when the dim light of history first shows us the German tribes battling in their rude strength against the legions of imperial Rome, the names they bore were such as are current now. Among some of those mentioned by Tacitus are Verritus, a prince of the Frisians, same I take as our WERRITT and VERITY. Sigimer, the father of Arminius, is the same as our SEYMOUR; and Segimund, his brother-in-law, as our SIGMUND and SIMMONDS. Arpus, a prince of the Catti, is the same as our HARP— VIBELLIUS, a general of the Hermanduri, as our WIPPELL. Then there are several compound names, as Inguiomer, Cariovalda, Maroboduus, and Molorix, of which we have the simple forms, which we may fairly suppose to have been the first in use. This leads me to remark that many of our short and simple names are, as being such root-names, among the most ancient that we have. And not a few there are, which in the changes and chances of this mortal life have become of small account, yet which were names of honour

8 INTRODUCTION.

in the days—aye, and long before the days—when
the Redeemer walked the earth. There is a name
in the directory, SIGGS—it has no very distinguished sound, and its owner is but a worker in
tin plate—yet it is older than the Sigimer, and
the Segimund of Tacitus. NIBBS and NOBBS are
not names which command respect, yet they are
probably the parents of the Nibelungs renowned
in German song—of the courtly Nevilles, and,
according to a German writer, of the mighty
Napoleon. Then there are other names apparently honourable—yet thrice honourable when
their meaning is made clear. Thus ARMINGER
has been supposed to be a corruption of Armiger
—that is, " one entitled to bear arms." Entitled
—aye, well entitled to bear arms!—no herald's
college needs to furnish them—for he bears the
spear of Arminius.* Generally speaking, the
names derived from war are among the most
ancient—probably also some of those derived from
animals, as the bear, the wolf, and the boar—and
some of those of which the meaning is simply
" man." Such names as SUN and MOON we must
also include—we do not meet with them before
the fourth or fifth century—but the thought is
an oriental one,—and there are no names which
might more probably have been brought with
them by the wanderers from their ancient eastern
home.

---

* ARMINGER is a compound of Armin (Arminius), and *ger*, spear.

INTRODUCTION. 9

In referring to the high antiquity of some of our English names, it is necessary to call attention to their two-fold origin. They are derived in part from original surnames, and in part from ancient single or baptismal names. The term "baptismal" must be understood in a modified sense, as implying a name bestowed in infancy, and probably with some attendant rite or ceremony, for many of these names are in reality older than Christianity. The former of these two classes of course cannot be older than the period at which surnames became hereditary—a period not earlier than the Conquest, or if earlier, only in some very exceptional cases. The latter— those derived from ancient baptismal names— may remount to the highest Teutonic antiquity. For those names were not, like surnames, coined as the occasion required, but handed down from generation to generation, perhaps even in some cases, as I have elsewhere suggested, without any reference to their meaning. It will be my object to prove, throughout the present work, that a very much larger proportion of English names than has been generally supposed, are from the latter origin.

I have already made the remark that while the dialects of the various tribes who came over to this country were fused into one common language, which was Anglo-Saxon, their names still retained all their dialectic variations. To the period from Anglo-Saxon times to the present

B

day the same principle applies. English names have not shared *pari passu*, with the changes which have taken place in the English language. The reason of this must be obvious to any one who considers the subject. When a word changes, it changes altogether, because there is only one standard of the language. But this is not the case with names ; one man's name is no rule for another's, and each name separately resists innovation on its own account. Names do change— because the same principles of phonetic mutation affect them—but only individually and partially. Hence we have them in all stages, pure Anglo-Saxon, wholly English, and half-way between the two. In our names NAGLE and NAIL, we have the Anglo-Saxon *nægel*, and the English nail—in our names WEGG and WAY we have the Anglo-Saxon *weg*, and the English way—in our names GUM and GROOM, we have the Anglo-Saxon *guma*, and the English groom. And in the names FUGGLE, FUEL, FOWELL, and FOWLE, we have all the stages of mutation from the Anglo-Saxon *fugel* to the English fowl.

In one respect names have been subjected to an influence from which the English language has been exempt ; they have frequently been corrupted from the desire to make sense out of them. Of course all names have originally had a meaning ; I speak of cases in which the ancient meaning has become obsolete. When a name has no approach towards making sense, men are content

INTRODUCTION. 11

to let it alone, but when it is very nearly making some sort of modern sense, it is very apt to be corrupted. Thus, ASHKETTLE is no doubt the Danish name Asketil ; GOODLUCK is very probably a corruption of Guthlac. There is a place in Norwich called Goodluck's close, formerly Guthlac's close. We have the name THOROUGH-GOOD, and we have the name THURGOOD. The latter is a Danish name, and at once suggests to us that the former is a corruption. So also probably GRUMBLE and TREMBLE for Grimbald and Trumbold, HALFYARD for Alfhard, INCHBOARD for Ingobert, GUMBOIL for Gundbald, &c.

This principle, which is indeed natural to man, pervades also Modern German nomenclature. Thus the name of Maria Theresa's minister was corrupted from its original form of Tunicotto into Thunichtgut, which she again, thinking there *was* something in a name, changed into Thugut.* Our friend Todleben, who gave us so much trouble at Sebastopol, and whose name appears to be such a paradoxical compound,† is another example. The name is in fact, as I take it, formed of two words of the same meaning, both implying affection, and would be more properly Todlieben.

It is to be noted, however, that there are not a few cases in which names have come to us in a corrupted form. We have a name, ARCHAM-BAUD, and the French have the same name,

---

* Thunichtgut, " do not good." Thugut, " do good."
† *Tod*, death, *leben*, life.

ARCHAMBAULT. This is a corruption of an old German Ercanbald, but as a corruption it is nine hundred years old, being found in the 10th century in the form of Archembald. And upon the whole, English names are much less corrupted from their ancient forms than might be expected.

Independently of names which have been corrupted to a meaning, it follows almost as a matter of course from my theory that I should believe a large proportion of the apparent meanings of English names to be merely coincidences. This I do to a very considerable extent, both in regard to our own names, and also, as elsewhere stated, to those of France. In many of these cases there is a *primâ facie* probability in favour of the alteration. Thus, when I suggest that BASTARD, PARAMOUR, HARLOTT, WANTON, OUTLAW, SCULLION, COWARD, VASSALL, are not what they seem, but on the contrary ancient names of the highest respectability, the reader, already puzzled to account for the transmission of such disreputable titles, will be disposed to fall readily in with the amendment. Again, when such names as PURCHASE, WEDLOCK, FLATTERY, MELODY, PARDON, POWER, and such as VINEGAR, MARIGOLD, DANDELYON, are referred to ancient compounds, there will not be much objection, because the English meaning is not very satisfactory. But when I go on to argue that PILGRIM is an Old German name, and that it does not mean one who has made a pilgrimage, some of those who have

INTRODUCTION.   13

followed me thus far may begin to draw back.
" Why," it may be said, "meddle with a name
which has already so good a meaning ?   What
can be more natural than that a man who had
visited the holy places, and come back an object
of wonder and reverence to those around him,
should from this, the one great event of his life,
derive a name to be transmitted to his posterity ?"
All this I grant—Pilgrim, in this sense, might
naturally—might very naturally—become a man's
name.   But in the sense which I propose it *was*
a man's name.   And the best of, " might be's" is
not so good as a " was."   Again, the system
which thus explains PILGRIM explains also PILL,
PILLOW, BILLOW, BILKE, BILLET, BILLIARD, and
a number of other names, both English and
French.   Not but that I recognize the possibility, both in this and other cases, of two different origins for the same name.

With respect to the period at which surnames
became hereditary in England I am inclined to
concur with Mr. Lower in the probability of their
being in occasional use before the Conquest,
though I do not feel so sure that the particular
document on which he relies for proof (a grant of
land to the Abbey of Croyland, dated 1050) is
sufficient to bear out the conclusions which he
draws from it.

There is a document quoted from the MSS.
Cott. by Mr. Turner, in his History of the Anglo-
Saxons, in which we find an Anglo-Saxon family

14 INTRODUCTION.

with unquestionably a regular surname. " Hwita *Hatte** was a keeper of bees in Hæthfelda ; and Tate *Hatte*, his daughter, was the mother of Wulsige, the shooter ; and Lulle *Hatte*, the sister of Wulsige, Hehstan had for his wife in Wealadene. Wifus, and Dunne, and Seoloce, were born in Hæthfelda ; Duning *Hatte*, the son of Wifus, is settled at Wealadene ; and Ceolmund *Hatte*, the son of Dunne, is also settled there ; and Ætheleah *Hatte*, the son of Seoloce, is also there ; and Tate *Hatte*, the sister of Cenwald, Mæg hath for his wife at Weligan ; and Ealdelm, the son of Herethrythe, married the daughter of Tate. Werlaf *Hatte*, the father of Werstan, was the rightful possessor of Hæthfelda, &c."

This document, which is numbered 1356 in Mr. Kemble's collection, is without a date, but has every appearance of being earlier than the Conquest, and if so, HATT is the oldest surname we have on record.

But at a much earlier period we may observe a sort of approach to a family name in particular instances. Mr. Kemble *(Names, Surnames, and Nic-names of the Anglo-Saxons)*, refers to the manner in which the first word of a compound is reproduced in some Anglo-Saxon genealogies. "I think it evident that a great family often desired to perpetuate among its branches a noble name, which was connected with the glories of

---

* What a curious name this would be in English—" White Hatt !"

INTRODUCTION. 15

the country, and had been distinguished in the arts of war or peace, by military prowess or successful civil government. . . . Of the seven sons of Æthelfrith, king of Northumberland, five bore names compounded with Os, thus Oslaf Oslâc, Oswald, Oswin, and Oswidu. In the successions of the same royal family we find the male names Osfrith, Oswine, Osrîc, Osræd, Oswulf, Osbald, and Osbeorht, and the female name Osthryth : and some of these are repeated several times." Here Os, which signifies demi-god, is a sort of family title, and contains a claim to a divine lineage. And the various compounds Oslaf, Oslâc, &c., seem to be formed with a view of preserving this title, and at the same time giving distinctive names, by adding to it suffixes in common use.

But in the Polyptyque de l'Abbe Irminon, compiled in the time of Charlemagne, I find still stronger instances of the individual yearning after a family name. Thus a man called Hildebodus gives to his two sons the names of Hildoardus and Hildebodus, and to his daughter the name of Hildeberga. One Nodalricus calls his son Nodalgis, and his two daughters Nodalgrima and Nodaltrudis. In other cases the mother's name shares in the family nomenclature. Thus, a man's name being Ermengardus, and his wife's Sicleverga, one son is called Ermengaudus after his father, and the other Sicledulfus after his mother. In another instance, a man's name being Ercan-

16 INTRODUCTION.

fredus, and his wife's Ermena, the two sons are called·Ercanricus and Ercanradus after the father, and of the two daughters one is called Ercantrudis after the father, and the other Ermenberga after the mother.

CHAPTER II.

SIMPLE FORMS.

As the basis of the etymological system which it is, my object in the present work to construct, must be taken the class of names which consist of a single word, without any other modification than the vowel-ending usual in men's names. This class of names we may presume to be the most ancient of all—perhaps indeed it may have been originally the most common, though in the earliest Teutonic records that we possess, we find a decided preponderance of compounded names. At the same time, the remark of Miss Yonge that Teutonic names " were almost all compounds of two words," is certainly too strong.

These names appear very rarely indeed in ancient times without the ending *a, i,* or *o,* though at present in the family names both of England and Germany, it is very frequently lost. Thus we have variously, with and without such ending, the names ELL, ELLEY, and ELLA, COLL, COLLEY, and COLLA, HANN, HANNEY, and HANNA, MILE, MILEY, and MILO. When I further adduce BILL, BILLY, BILLOW, PILL, PILLEY, PILLOW, as variations of one single name, with and without this ending, it will be seen how great a revolution my theory, if it can be sus-

c

18 SIMPLE ·FORMS.

tained, must create in the received notions on the subject.

In the next place we have to consider what was the value of this termination. We know that the Anglo-Saxon had the property, by the addition of *a* to a noun, of forming another word implying connection with it. Thus from *scip*, a ship, is formed *scipa*, a sailor,—from *hûs*, a house, *hûsa*, a domestic. This principle is more fully carried out in proper names ; by the addition of the Teutonic terminations *a*, *i*, or *o*, a name would be formed out of a noun, or an adjective, or a verb. And it is still a living principle among us. Thus, when we hear a man with a remarkable nose called in vulgar parlance "Nosey," we have a name formed according to Teutonic analogy. Nurse-maids carry it still further, and form a name out of a verb—thus a child given to screaming they would call "Screamy." *This principle lies at the bottom of Teutonic names.* And thus it is that a man from the South is called Southey.

Of these three terminations *a* is the most ancient. It is that found in Gothic names, as Wulfila, Amala, Totila, though in after times it became changed among the High Germans into the weaker form *o*. It also prevailed among the Old Saxons, and descended from them to the Anglo-Saxons. But among both, the weaker ending *i* was also common, and it is evident from the names in Domesday and in the Liber Vitæ of

SIMPLE · FORMS. 19

Durham that there was a large infusion of it among the tribes who settled in this country. In the latter record, for instance, we find such names as Tydi, Bynni, Terri, Betti, Tilli, Cuddi, Cynni, Locchi, every one of which is still existing at the present day. Indeed this is the form which is most in accordance with the genius of the English language.; that is to say, if we had to form names now, we would, as it appears to me, form them in that manner. And as this ending is now much more common in English names than the regular Anglo-Saxon form *a*, it seems to me very probable that the process of change from *a* into *i* may have been still going on. The ending in *o* is also not uncommon in our early history ; in Domesday, for instance, we have Dodo, Baco, Bugo, Odo, Wido, Heppo ; and there are not a few still remaining among our family names.

The termination in *a* sometimes appears in its simple form, as in COLLA, ELLA, Saxon names without change—sometimes in the form of *ay*, as in HANNAY and HAYDAY. The termination in *i* is sometimes *y*, as in BRANDY—sometimes *ey*, as in ATTEY—sometimes *ie*, as in LOCKIE. The termination in *o* appears most frequently in its simple form, as in HADDO, CUTTO, but sometimes in *oe*, as in PARDOE, sometimes in *oh*, as in SCOTTOH, and sometimes in *ow*, as in HADOW.

CHAPTER III.

DIMINUTIVES.

A diminutive in the language implies small-ness. Thus manne*kin* is a little man —stream*let* a little stream—satch*el* a little sack. But in proper names, I take it—at least as the general rule —that the sense is that of affection or familiarity expressed through the medium of smallness.

The English language is not strong in diminutives ; in this respect the Scottish language, which in such a phrase as "wee bit lassie," can string three diminutives together, has much more power of expression. English names, on the other hand, are very rich, both in the number and variety of their diminutives, almost every Teutonic form being represented.

The principal diminutive endings contained in our proper names are, according to my estimate, seven, viz., that in k, that in l, that in *kin*, that in *lin*, that in s, that in *ns*, and that in m. There are certain other endings, elsewhere referred to, which may be in some cases diminutives.

The diminutive in k, *ek* or *ock* is common to all the Germanic branch. Hence from GARE we have GARRICK, from LOVE we have LOVICK, from

DIMINUTIVES. 21

FIZ we have PHYSIC.* From JELLY we have JELLICOE, from SIM we have SIMCO—these have the old German termination in *o*. From MANN we have MANNICO and MANNAKAY, with the two terminations in *o* and *a*; from WILLEY we have WILKIE (Williki) with the termination in *i*.

The French diminutive in *et* appears to some extent in our language to have superseded the Saxon form in *ec*. Thus we use linnet instead of the Ang.-Sax. *linece*. But there is a continual tendency among the uneducated to substitute— or rather to retain—the old form. Thus when our friend Jeames, of immortal memory, contributed to the pages of Punch what he was pleased to call a "sonnick"—he merely substituted one diminutive for another. Let us then forbear contempt when we hear this vulgar form —it is a relic of that stern old struggle which preserved us our glorious language.

The diminutive in *l, el* or *il* is common to both the Germanic and Scandinavian branches. In the latter, as well as in the English language, it is much used in verbs. In all such words as quarrel, wrangle, squabble, scuffle, shuffle, wriggle, higgle, smuggle, grumble, tinkle, tipple, the sense of pettiness is more or less prominent. In this form, from BENN we have BENNELL, from DUNN we have DUNNELL, from HASE we have HASELL.

---

* Here is an instance of the way in which names turn up, and missing links are supplied. In the former edition I had to say "from an old German Fizo we have PHYSICK." But there comes a new directory, and it brings us an English FIZ.

DIMINUTIVES.

From BARR, BARRY, BARROW, we have BAR-RELL, BARLEY, BARLOW.* Grimm refers to an Old German Runilo as a diminutive of Runo ; we have a name, RUNICLES, which seems to be a double diminutive, viz., this and the former combined. This double form obtains sometimes in Old High German.

The diminutive in *kin* is of later growth, and is more common in Modern German than in Old German names. It is not, as has been supposed, cognate with German *kind*, child, but is more probably formed by the addition of a phonetic *n* to the diminutive in *k*. From DUNN we have DUNKIN, from BENN we have BENKIN, from PARR we have PARKIN, from WILL we have WILKIN, &c.

The diminutive in *lin* is probably formed in a similar manner to the preceding by the addition of a phonetic *n* to the diminutive in *l*. Hence we have CATTLIN, TOMLIN, EVELYN, &c., and in the form *ling*, which also appears both in ancient and modern names, BUTLING, WATLING, DOWLING, &c. Neither the diminutive in *kin*, nor that in *lin*, are, like the more ancient forms in *ck* and *el*, found with the endings *a*, *i*, or *o* (except with the first as a female ending.)

The diminutive in *s*, like those in *k* and *l*, is of great antiquity, being found in the name Cotiso, of a Dacian mentioned in Horace. This

---

* The endings in *ley* and *low*, though sometimes from this diminutive, are doubtless in some cases local, from *ley*, a meadow, and from *low*, a mound.

DIMINUTIVES. 23

name—elsewhere referred to—I take to be a High German form of the later name Godizo, and to be still surviving in our GODSOE. From the Old German names Milo, Willo, Walo, Rico are formed with this diminutive Milizo, Wilizo, Walizo, Richizo, whence our MILLIS, WILLIS, WALLIS, RICHES. I think also that this diminutive is frequently represented in our names simply by a final *s*, and that MILLS, WILLS, WALLS, RICKS are probably the same as the above, though an *s* final is no doubt often added only phonetically. With the ending in *i* we find in Domesday Copsi and Brixi (Bricsi), which we still have as COPSEY and BRIXEY. A Saxon bishop of Worcester was called Leofsy, and an archbishop of York Cynsy; these two names still exist as LOVESY and KINSEY. But there enters here an element of doubt on account of these Saxon names sometimes appearing with the ending *si* or *sy*, and sometimes with *sige*, as if from *sig*, victory. Thus the Archbishop Cynsy signs in a charter as Cynsige; Wynsy, bishop of Lichfield, appears as Winsige; Albsi as Ælfsige, &c. Has the guttural been added in the one case, or has it been lost in the other? The former supposition would be most in accordance with analogy, for as diminutives, Cynsy, Wynsy, Albsi, Leofsy would correspond with the Old Germ. names Cuniza, Winizo, Albizo, and Luviz.

Occasionally, though very rarely, the form *s* becomes *sc* in ancient names. More frequently

DIMINUTIVES.

in English names, as BURNISH, MELLISH, VAR-
NISH, for it is in accordance with the character of
the language. Indeed, I am inclined to think
that the diminutive in question is that which we
still use in adjectives, as small*ish* and brown*ish*.

The ending *ns* I take also to be diminutive,
and to be formed by the addition of a phonetic *n*
to the preceding. Hence from an Old German
Custanzo we have CUSTANCE ; from the Old
German Cholensus we COLENSO and COLLINS.

The ending *m*, which I take to be also
diminutive, is supposed by Förstemann, who finds
it to prevail especially among the West Franks,
to be in some cases of other than German origin.
And so, in some present French names, as BON-
AMY and BELLAMY, we can hardly help thinking
of *ami*, friend. And yet, when we find this ending to prevail most extensively at present among
Friesic names, where it can hardly be otherwise
than German, and when we find the names BON-
NEMA and BALLEMA corresponding with the
above, it suggests the possibility, even for these,
of a common German origin. Another instance
of coincidence between the Friesic and the French
is found in the name of the well-known tragedian
TALMA, which corresponds with the Friesic TIAL-
LEMA and TIALMA.

Among English names we have JESSMAY,
WHITMEE, IVYMEY, and WAKEM, which seem to
be from this origin, and to correspond with the
ancient names Gisoma, Widomia, Ivamus, and

DIMINUTIVES. 25

Wakimus quoted by Förstemann. To this source also I am inclined to refer the names YOUNGMAY, MILDMAY,* and CRICKMAY, the first of which corresponds with a Friesic JONGMA, and the second possibly with a Friesic MELLEMA. I before took the ending in these names to be from Ang.-Sax. *mæg*, Old Eng. *may*, maiden, for which there seemed a reasonable probability in each case—the name CRICKMAY being referred to *krieg*, war, and supposed to be connected with the war-maidens of Odin—while the others seemed too natural to require explanation. But the forms in which this ending is found in ancient names seem irreconcileable with this theory. Among other names from this origin may be mentioned that of the Dutch painter HOBBEMA.

The ending *sm*, which is also found in some Frankish names, Förstemann seems more decidedly to consider as not German. But here again its prevalence in present Friesic names seems to me to militate against this opinion. Can it be the Ang.-Sax. *smea*, small, delicate, used like the Danish *lille* as in Tove*lille* (Dovey), Rosa*lilla* (Rosie)? The fact of its being anciently used more especially in the names of women, and of its always appearing in the form *sma*, seem rather in favour of this opinion. And the fact of its being added to *compound* names, as in the case of the scholar HALBERTSMA, stamps it with

---

* Mr. Lower says (*Pat. Brit.*) that "the family are traced to 1147, and the name to Mildmé."

D

26   DIMINUTIVES.

a different character to that of the other diminutives. Among the few English names which seem to be from this source is BALSAM, which compares with the ancient name Balsmus. I have also found in Lancashire the name ERASMUS; it seems not to be a new name in England, for in the *Liber Vitæ* there is an Ærasmus; it seems curious that in both these cases, as well as that of the well-known scholar, the name should be in the Latinized form. I rather think that the French name DOUSSAMY may be from this source, representing the Old Frankish name Teodisma, and comparing with the present Friesic names DIUDESMA, DOYTSEMA.

The termination *et*, as a German ending there is no ground for thinking to be a diminutive. But as a French diminutive it is frequently added to German compound names, as in the French names HENRIQUET, HENRIOT, BERNARDET, &c.

The same rule applies to the ending in *en*, which is often added as a French diminutive to German names. Probably in this manner are formed the French names GIRARDIN, BERNARDIN, GUILLOTIN, LAMARTINE, from GERARD, BERNARD, GUILLOT, LAMART, all likewise French names in use. Pure German names do not thus form diminutives out of compounds—they resolve them first into their simple forms—thus Willi*co*, according to Pott, is a Frisian diminutive of Wilhelm. When therefore we find *en* or *in* added to a compound name, as in GIRARDIN, we may, I think,

DIMINUTIVES. 27

take it to be the French diminutive. But when we find it added to a simple form, as in WALLEN, it must be taken to be from the origin referred to in next chapter.

The ending in *let* may probably be in some cases the French diminutive *et* added to the German *el*. But in other cases it is no doubt the second part of a compound name.

There is no doubt that in the English language *ey* or *ie* is a diminutive form. It is more particularly common in the Lowland Scotch, which has such words as doggie, mousie, lassie, dearie. It is of Teutonic origin, and occurs also in the Dutch and in the Swiss. Hence might be such names as MINNEY, DEARY. But more probably they are only the ending of men's names in *i*.

The ending in *cock*, as in HANCOCK, WILCOCK, is included by Mr. Lower among diminutives. It is found in French names as well as English, as, for instance, in BALCOQ, BILLECOQ, VILCOCQ, VIDECOCQ. But nothing that I have met with in the study of ancient names helps me to throw any further light upon the subject.

CHAPTER IV.

PHONETIC ADDITIONS.

By a phonetic addition we mean something which is added to a word only for the sake of sound, and which leaves the sense exactly where it was before. There are two kinds of phonetic additions common in Teutonic names—one in the middle of a word, and the other at the end, the former occurring only in compound, and the latter only in simple names.

The favourite sound employed at the end of a word is *n*, and thus from the Old German names Godo, Hatto, Lando, Waldo, Aldo, Baldo, are formed Godino, Hattin, Landina, Waldin, Aldini, Baldin; and the corresponding English names GODDEN, HATTEN, LANDON, WALDEN, ALDEN, BOLDEN.

Now as proper names are of course subject to all the tendencies of the language to which they belong, we may expect to find in the popular speech a parallel principle to that which I have assumed for names. Or rather, I should say, it is *because* I find this principle in the popular speech, that I feel warranted in applying it to proper names. Now, if we compare the German rabe with the English raven, and conversely, the English bow with the German bogen, we find that

PHONETIC ADDITIONS. 29

while, in meaning, the two words are in each case perfectly identical, there is an ending added which serves as a finish or rounding off of the word. So also in the provincial word ratt*en* for rat, and many other cases.

A similar office is also performed by the letter *r*. Thus to the simple form contained in the Gothic *wato*, while all the Scandinavian dialects add *n*, as in Swedish *vatten*, all the German add *r*, as in English *water*. We have examples in our own provincial dialect; for, as Mr. Latham observes, "wolfer, a wolf, hunker, a haunch, flitcher, a flitch, teamer, a team, fresher, a frog, are north country forms of the present English." The ending *er* in our names (so far as they are derived from Old Teutonic names), is generally to be referred to Gothic *hari*, warrior, but there are cases in which the form of the ancient name is incompatible with this derivation. At the same time, the phonetic origin of *r* is not so clear when it occurs as an ending, as when it occurs in the middle of a name.

When a phonetic addition is made in the middle of a name, it comes in between the two words of the compound, and generally consists of one of the liquids, *l*, *n*, or *r*. Thus Godulf becomes Godenulf, whence, I take it, our GOODENOUGH. So Godehar becomes Godelhar, whence probably the French GODELIER. Godeman becomes Goderman, whence the French GAUDERMEN; and also Godalmand, whence perhaps our

30 PHONETIC ADDITIONS.

GODLIMAN. Thus when I find the names SYCA-MORE and SICKLEMORE, the former of which corresponds with the Old German name Sicumar, I know how to account for the second, since, though the particular name to correspond does not turn up, I see that the phonetic l is very frequent in the ancient names of that group. So also, finding the ancient name Siginiu, I can at least suggest an origin for SIGOURNEY. The above forms of phonetic addition seem to be found chiefly in Old Frankish names.

CHAPTER V.

PATRONYMICS.

Of the two patronymic forms, *ing* and *son*, the former is more properly German, and the latter Scandinavian. The form *ing* was discontinued about the time of the Conquest, and consequently all the names in which it appears are carried back to Anglo-Saxon times. (In some few cases the termination *ing* may be local, from *ing* a meadow, and not a patronymic.) Many apparently adjective and participial forms, such as WILLING, LIVING, DINING, PANTING, are from this origin, the simple forms being found as WILL, LIVEY, DINE, PANT.

The termination *son* is a characteristic feature of all the Scandinavian countries, while in Germany on the other hand it is of comparatively rare occurrence. So well is this distinction understood that a writer on " Nationality and Language in the Duchy of Sleswick and South Jutland" advances the frequency of names ending in *son*, as an argument for the Danish character of the population. Of the twelve most common names in the directory of Copenhagen, there are only two, Moller and Smidt, that are not patronymics. The most common of all are Jansen, Johnsen, or Hansen, Petersen, Andresen or Andersen, and

32   PATRONYMICS.

Nielsen.   Verstegan, in his "Restitution of decayed intelligence," refers to a tradition "among some of our country people that those whose sur-names end in son, as Johnson, Thomson, Nichol-son, Davison, Saunderson, and the like, are descended of Danish race."   Either he mistakes the tradition, or the tradition overstates the truth. Some of these are no doubt Scotch, and others are German—though the termination itself may be of Scandinavian origin.   Many of our names, however, correspond altogether with current Danish names—as HANSON, NANSON, JEPHSON, ERICKSON, GUNSON, IVERSON, JESSON, HEBSON, HIPSON, LOWSON, ANDERSON, with Hansen, Nan-sen, Jepsen, Ericksen, Gunnesen, Iversen, Jessen, Ebsen, Ipsen, Lauesen, Andersen, names common over the whole of Denmark.   It does not follow that all the above names are exclusively Scan-dinavian, but I do take it that the prevalence in England of names in *son* is a relic of the Danish conquests.

It is to be observed that when a name ends in *s*, we cannot be certain of the patronymic form. Thus JESSON and MASSON may not be JESS-SON and MASS-SON, but JESS-EN, and MASS-EN.

The final *s* so frequently added to names, as Wills for Will, Watts for Watt, Box for Bock, may be sometimes a patronymic form.   It is so used in Frisian names, according to Pott.   In other cases I take it to be a diminutive, see p. 22. But in the majority of cases, and particularly

PATRONYMICS. 33

when it is added to compound names, I take it to
be merely a phonetic addition.

CHAPTER VI.

COMPOUNDS.

Almost all the names which occur in simple forms occur also compounded with other words. The extent to which these compounds are translatable, or in other words, to which they have a meaning, seems to me an exceedingly doubtful point. Some of our highest authorities hold the affirmative opinion. Thus Mr. Kemble, speaking of Anglo-Saxon names, says, "These compound words are translatable, intelligible, in other words their conjoint meaning depends upon the separate meanings of the words which unite to form them." And Mr. Turner, on a similar principle, translates Anglo-Saxon names—thus Æthelwulf, "the noble wolf," Dunstan, " the mountain stone," &c. The earlier German writers, as Wiarda and Beneken, certainly followed the same rule, and I think that the principle is also recognised by the modern school of German philologists. I therefore feel bound to use all deference in suggesting a doubt whether Teutonic compound names are in all cases translatable, and formed with a meaning. I am of opinion, however, that even simple names were in most cases bestowed in ancient times without reference to their meaning. There can be no doubt that the first man who was called

COMPOUNDS. 35

Wulf was named directly after the animal. But of the thousands of men who were called Wulf in the long centuries after, I think that the most part must have been called after *other men.* Much on the same principle, I take it, as that on which baptismal names are given now they were given then—sometimes after a relative or friend, sometimes after a name of popular renown—the word itself becoming in such cases, as regards sense, an abstraction. If this theory be correct, it will follow as a matter of course that compound names must also have been formed without a meaning.

It is true that in many cases a certain sort of. sense may be screwed out of such compounds, yet even to get any kind of a meaning we are often driven to great shifts. Thus though Frithu-ric as "powerful in peace" may be held to have a sufficient meaning, yet Frithu-gar, as "the spear of peace" would have to be explained in a sort of metaphorical sense. Again Frithu-bald, "bold in peace," seems rather satirical. And as to Fride-gunt, "the peace of war," and the Old Norse Snae-frid, "the peace of snow,"* let those find a meaning who can. Mr. Turner appears to see this difficulty when he observes that Anglo-Saxon names are frequently "rather expressive of caprice than of appropriate meaning."

But to my mind the strongest argument against giving a meaning to compound names is not so much the difficulty of making sense in any

36 COMPOUNDS.

particular case, as the fact that there is a certain set of words with which almost all names are compounded. And it does not seem consistent with 'reason to expect that promiscuous words, with all sorts of meanings, should make sense when compounded with a set of a dozen or twenty particular words.

But if compounds were not formed with a meaning, what was their value or intention? One of the principles upon which they might be given may perhaps be traced in Old Norse names. Thus Ketel was a very common Scandinavian name; its meaning can hardly be anything else than English "kettle," and Grimm suggests a mythological origin. Ulf, signifying wolf, and Björn, signifying bear, were also common names. In Ulfketel and in Ketelbjörn, these names are severally joined together. Now there can be no possible sense or meaning in such compounds as these—they are in fact not two *words* joined together, but two *names* joined together. And the principle upon which such names were formed might be the same as that on which a father might now call his son John Henry Smith, combining the names of two relatives, or persons whom he respected. Or it might be for the sake of distinction—Ulf and Ketel both being common names—Ulfketel would, without travelling out of the customary range, be sufficiently distinctive. It seems probable that many German names are, on the same principle, not two words compounded,

COMPOUNDS. 37

but rather two names joined together. Such, for instance, as those which contain the names of two animals, as Arnulf, Ebarulf, Wolfpirin, Wolfraban, respectively " Eagle-wolf," " Boar-wolf," Wolf-bear," " Wolf-raven." All these were common names singly.

Again, perhaps another principle may be traced in such a name as the Old German Zeizolf. This, if we translate it, means " darling wolf." But if we suppose " wolf" to have been used as a common name, and without reference to its meaning, then the idea of darling would attach rather to the child that was called Wolf than to the abstract meaning of wolf.

But that there were compound names with a meaning I do not for a moment doubt, only it seems to me that it was not the universal, nor, perhaps, the ordinary rule.

Again, there are many names which are simply compound words taken bodily out of the language. Thus, GARWOOD is the Anglo-Saxon *garwudu*, " spear-wood," a poetical or pleonastic expression for a spear. And ASKWITH is " ash-wood," a similar expression for a spear—spears being made of that wood. So also SKIPWITH, " ship-wood," a ship. (*With*, as compared with *wood*, is the Gothic form instead of the Saxon.) Again, BONIGER seems to be from the Anglo-Saxon *bon-gar*, a fatal spear. These, then, are not compound names, but compound words adopted as names.

COMPOUNDS.

Almost all the words which appear in compounds are found also as substantive names, and will therefore find their places under the various heads into which I have distributed them. But for the sake of facility of reference, I introduce in this place a list of the principal terminations of those English names, which may be referred to ancient compounds.

Am, Iam, as in WILLAM, WILLIAM, HILLAM, HILLIAM. Ang.-Sax. *helm,* helmet. This was a common postfix, but in our names it is difficult to separate it from the local ending, *ham,* home, and from the ending *m* referred to p. 24. It is probable, however, that more names than are suspected are from this origin. The French generally have it as *aume* or *eaume.* Hence the French ALLAUME, ALLEAUME, are probably the same as our ALLAM, ALLOM, ALLUM.

Aud, Aut as in RENAUD, RENAUT. *Aud,* the Gothic form of Ang.-Sax. *ead,* prosperity. This is very common in French names, but in English, following the Saxon form, it becomes more frequently *et* or *ot;* and is very liable to mix up with other words.

Bert, as in HERBERT. Ang.-Sax. *beort,* bright, illustrious. *Pert,* as in Rupert, is the High Germ. form.

Bold, Ball, Ble, as in RUMBOLD, RUMBALL, RUMBLE. Ang.-Sax. *bald,* bold.

COMPOUNDS. 39

Bull in many cases is the same as the above. Thus our CLARINGBULL is no doubt the same name as CLARINGBOLD.

Bault, in French names, as HERBAULT, GERBAULT, the same as bold.

Brand, as in HILDEBRAND, GILLIBRAND. Ang.-Sax. *brand*, sword, Eng. "brand."

Brown, as in GOREBROWN, PHILLIBROWN. Either brown, *fuscus*, or cognate with Eng. "burn" in the sense of fiery or impetuous.

Burn, as in OSBURN. Old Norse *björn*, Old Germ. *berin*, bear.

Pern, as in ASPERNE, is the High Germ. form.

Butt, Bott, Body, as in GARBUTT, TALBOT, PEABODY. Anglo-Saxon *boda*, Old Norse *bodi*, Germ. *bote*, envoy or messenger.

Cough, Copp, as in AYSCOUGH, WHINCOPP, I take to be Ang.-Sax. *côf*, strenuous.

Day, as in LOVEDAY, HOCKADAY.. Anglo-Saxon *dæg*, day. Grimm suggests the sense of brightness, glory.

Dew, Die, Dy, as in INGLEDEW, PURDIE, ABDY, French ABBADIE. Old High German *dio*, servant.

Er, Ery, as in WARNER, GUNNERY, HILLARY. *Har, hari*, warrior.

Forth, as in GARFORTH. Perhaps Anglo-Saxon *ferhth*, life, spirit. Perhaps in some cases a corruption of *frith*, peace. There is also a root, *farth, faerd*, travel, but it is uncertain whether it occurs as a termination.

40 COMPOUNDS.

Fred, Frey, as in MANFRED, HUMFREY. Anglo-Saxon *frith*, peace.

Gar, Ger, Ker, as in EDGAR, RODGER, HARKER. *Gar, ger, ker,* spear.

Gill, as in HARGILL. Old High German *gisal*, hostage. Or local, from " gill," a ravine.

Good, as in HARGOOD, BIDGOOD. God, deus, good, bonus, and perhaps · Goth · as the people's name, are difficult to separate.

Hard, Ard, as in BERNHARD, BERNARD. Ang.-Sax. *heard*, hard, strong.

Kiss, as in ATKISS, HADKISS, WATKISS, is from *gis*, which Grimm thinks the same as *gisal*, hostage.

Lake, Lock, as in WEDLAKE, HAVELOCK. Probably Ang.-Sax. *lacan*, Old Norse *leika*, to play, in a war-like sense.

Land, Lond, as in GARLAND, DOLLAND. Ang.-Sax. *land*, Eng. land. It is also no doubt sometimes a local termination. And also sometimes a corruption of *lind*, probably shield.

Let, as in HAMLET, HARLOT, may be from Ang.-Sax. *lâd*, Old Sax. *lêd*, in the sense of terrible. In some cases it may be a diminutive.

Love, Liff, as in CUTLOVE, MANLOVE, RATLIFF. Ang.-Sax. *leof*, dear.

Man, as in HARMAN, REDMAN. Ang.-Sax. *man*, Eng. man.

COMPOUNDS.

Mer, More, as in MUTIMER, PHILLIMORE. Goth. *mer,* Ang.-Sax. *mâr,* famous.

Mot, as in WILLMOT, HICKMOT, Old High Germ. *môt,* Mod. German *muth,* courage.

Mond, Ment, as in REDMONT, GARMENT. Ang.-Sax. *mund,* protection.

Nant, Nan, as in REMNANT, PENNANT, QUILLINAN. Goth. *nanthjan,* to dare.

Ney, as in RODNEY, GOLDNEY. Ang.-Sax. *niw,* Dan. and Swed. *ny,* new, in the probable sense of young.

Not, Net, Nut, as in HARNOTT, HARNETT, DILNUTT. Ang.-Sax. *nôth,* bold.

Ram, as in BERTRAM, OUTRAM, INGRAM, seems, from the ancient forms in which it appears, to be a corruption of *hraban,* raven.

Rand, as in Eng. BERTRAND, WALROND. Ang.-Sax. *rand,* shield.

Red Rat, Ret, as in ALFRED, TANCRED, GARRETT. Ang.-Sax. *red,* Old High Germ. *rat,* counsel. Some terminations of *wright,* as ARKWRIGHT, are evidently corruptions of *rat.* But there is also an ancient termination *rit,* apparently of the same meaning as Eng. *ride.*

Rick, Rich, Ridge, Ry, as in FREDERICK, ALDRICH, ALDRIDGE, BALDRY. Ang.-Sax. *rice,* Old High Germ. *richi,* powerful. In some cases *bridge,* as in GROOMBRIDGE, may be from this origin.

F

42 COMPOUNDS.

Ron, Ren, as in WALDRON, CALDERON, CHILDREN. This termination, which is exclusively feminine, Grimm derives from *rûn*, socia, amica. In French names it is often a corruption of *raban,* raven.

Sant, Sent, as in HERSANT, MILLICENT. Old High Germ. *sind,* via. Or perhaps in some cases a corruption of *swind,* vehement.

Stone, Stin, as in FREESTONE, GARSTIN. Ang.-Sax. *stân,* stone, in the sense of firmness.

Thus, Tuss, Tiss, as in MALTHUS, FELTUSS, ANSTISS. Goth. *thius,* servant. See also *dew* and *thew.*

Thew, as in WILLTHEW. Anglo-Saxon *theow,* servant, corresponding with Goth. *thius,* and High Germ. *dio.*

Ulph, Olph, as in BIDDULPH, RANDOLPH, MUSTOLPH. Ang.-Sax. *wulf,* Old Norse *ulf(r),* wolf.

Ward, Wart, as in HOWARD, SEWARD, TEWART. Ang.-Sax. *weard,* guardian.

Wald, as in OSWALD. Ang.-Sax. *weald,* power. The terminations in *old* are from the same origin.

Way, Wick, Vey, Vig, as in HATHWAY, HARVEY, HARVIG. *Wig, wih,* war. The termination in *wick* is probably in most cases local.

Win, Wine, as in BALDWIN, BRIGHTWINE. Ang.-Sax. *wine,* friend.

Wood, With, Weed, as in GURWOOD, ASKWITH, DIGWEED. Ang.-Sax. *wudu,* Goth. *vid(s),*

COMPOUNDS. 43

wood. Förstemann also suggests Old High. Germ. *wit*, wide, which may obtain in certain cases. This ending is no doubt also often local. ·

Out of the above list there are many which do not often occur, and the range of really common terminations is not more than about twenty.

The· terminations *a*, *i*, *o*, are not found in compound names, and such names as Ricardo, Alphonso, Grimaldi, though of German origin, are Italian or Spanish as regards the termination.

CHAPTER VII.

LETTER CHANGES.

The greater part of the letter changes which occur in our names are to be accounted for by the differences of Teutonic dialects, and, in particular, by the variations between High and Low German. The High German prefers aspirated and hard—the Low German soft and liquid sounds. The former may be taken to be represented generally by the present German, and the latter by the present English, though it is to be observed that the standard language of Germany does not present the extreme phases of High German. Take, for instance, the range of names of which the root is Germ. *geban*, Eng. *give*, and from which we have GIEVE, GIBB, GIPP, and KIPP. The two former, GIEVE and GIBB, show the form contained in English and in German, the difference between which is a Low German *v* for a High German *b*. But in the name GIPP we have another point of difference in favour of the High German, viz., *p* for *b*. While the last name KIPP shows the extreme point to which, in that word, the High German can go, by changing *g* into *k*. In addition to the four forms above quoted, we have also four others, viz., JEBB, JIPP,

LETTER CHANGES. 45

KIBBE, and CHIPP, the last form being, I think, Frankish. Nor yet do these eight names exhaust the permutations of this little word—there being also, as will be seen in its place, a vowel change which scarcely comes within the range of the present chapter.

Another of the most common interchanges is that of *d* and *t*. The latter is High German, as in Germ. *laut*, Eng. *loud*, Germ. *bette*, Eng. *bed*. Hence we have DODD and TODD, DANDY and TANDY, DENNISON and TENNYSON, &c.

The High German frequently changes *t* into *s* or *z*, as in Germ. *süss*, Eng. *sweet*, Germ. *salz*, Eng. *salt*. Hence our SUSE and SUSANS may correspond as High German forms with SWEET and SWEETEN. And our name SALT may be the same as the Mod. Germ. name SALZ. So also our GROTE and GROSE may be respectively Low German and High German forms of great.

Another High German form is *sch* for *s*. This is very common in Mod. German names—thus, German Schmidt, Eng. Smith, German Schwann, Eng. Swan, Germ. Schneider, Eng. Snider, Dutch Snyders. This form is very uncommon in English names, because it is of comparatively modern growth in Germany.

These are for the most part the common variations of High and Low German. But there are other peculiarities of ancient dialects which are not without their effect upon our names. In the Frankish dialect of the Merovingian period it is a

LETTER CHANGES.

peculiarity to change *h* at the beginning of a word into *ch*, or sometimes into simple *c*. Hence the names of the Merovingian kings Childibert and Childeric for Hildibert and Hilderic. This seems to be the origin of some of our names, such as CHILLMAN (in the Hundred Rolls Childman), for Hildman—CHARMAN for HARMAN—CHILDREN for Hilderannus or Hilderuna—CHILLMAID for Hildimod, &c.

This peculiarity of the Frankish dialect has had the effect of prefixing *c* to many names beginning with *l* and *r*, in the following manner. Several of these names anciently began with *hl* and *hr* : this *h* was aspirated, or in other words, it had something of a guttural sound. The Frankish dialect, increasing the guttural, made this *h* into a *c*. In English, this guttural sound of *h* at the beginning of a word is altogether lost. On the other hand, when it has been so completely defined as to become a *c*, it has preserved itself by its own strength. The result is that we have in English the same names variously, as CROAD and RODE, CROTCH and ROTCH, CROOK and ROOK, CROAGER and ROGER, CLOUD and LOUD, &c. Hence also the French names CLODOMIR and CLOVIS still existing, and the Christian name CLOTILDE.

Another point to be noticed is that in some German dialects *g* is prefixed to words beginning with *w*. We have an instance of this in the name of our gracious Sovereign, GUELPH for Welp. So

LETTER CHANGES.

we have GWILLAN for WILLAN, GWILLAM for WILLIAM, GWALTER for WALTER, &c. Hence comes, I take it, the name of the Italian painter GUIDO, corresponding with our WIDOW. Perhaps also GUIZOT, if it be the same as a Guizo found in the 11th century in the *Niederrheinisches Urkundenbuch.* The High German prefixing *c* instead of *g*, gives us many names beginning with *q* (which is only *c* added to *w*). Thus we have QUIN for WINN, QUARRELL for WARRELL, QUARRIER for WARRIER, QUILL for WILL, QUILLAN for WILLAN, QUILLIAMS for WILLIAMS. Hence comes QUILLINAN from an Old German Willinant. Hence also QUARITCH, known to bibliophilists, from an Old German Wericho, also found, with the other prefix, as Guerich.

On the other hand, as *g* is sometimes added, so it is much more frequently lost. As a termination this is very commonly the case in English, as in Anglo-Saxon *lag*, English "law," Ang.-Sax. *bog*, Eng. "bow." Hence as names we have WAGG and WAY, BOGUE and BOWE, BUGG and BEW; perhaps BEGG and BEE, BIGG and BYE. But this occurs also in Anglo-Saxon and other ancient dialects. Indeed the *g* in such cases can hardly be said to belong to the root; it does not seem to occur in the parent Sanscrit, but to be a hardening of the sound which has accrued in the Gothic languages. Again, *g* between two vowels, or between a vowel and a liquid, is very commonly dropped. Thus we have MEGEN and

MAYNE, BAGLEY and BAILEY, BEAGLE and BEALE, BUGLEA and BEWLEY, DAGLEY, and DALY. This again is common also in ancient names—thus we have Old German names Meginhard and Mainhard, Reginhard and Rainard, Raganar and Reinher, Ragingar and Raingar. Hence our MAYNARD, RENARD, RAYNER, and RANGER.

Another change of frequent occurrence in Old Frankish names is that of n, before b, p, or m, into m. We may trace the same tendency among the French at present in their change of Edinburg into Edimbourg. The few names that we have in which it occurs, such as GIMBERT for Ginbert, WIMBLE for Winbald, may not, however, always be due to French influence, but to a natural principle of euphony. It is more common, however, in French than in English, as in MASIMBERT for our MASSINGBERD.

The vowel changes are less capable of being reduced to definite rules. But as a general principle the Low German prefers simple vowels, while the High German is partial to diphthongs. Take the German *taube*, English "dove." The difference here is, first, d for t—secondly, v for b —and thirdly, the simple vowel for the diphthong. So our name STRUTT may be the same as the German STRAUSS—*ss* for t, as before noted, and the simple vowel for the diphthong. I have before referred to GROSE and GROTE as respectively High and Low German forms of the same name.

LETTER CHANGES.

But the German *gross*, great, is in some High German dialects *grauss*. So that while GROSE and GROTE are High and Low German, we have another name GROUSE, which may be extra High German.

With regard to the simple vowels, there is in proper names—and has been from the most ancient times—an interchange which it would be difficult to refer to any strict rules.

But Weinhold *(Deutsche Frauen)*, sets forth something of a more definite principle, and supposes that a variation of the vowel was sometimes employed for the perpetuation of a family name. " Thus if the father had a name with a simple sound, the son takes the same name with an augmented vowel. The Germans share this peculiarity with the Indians *(Grimms geschichte der Deutschen sprache* 441.) Thus, if a German mother were called Ada, the daughter might be called Ida; the mother Baba, the daughter Buoba; the mother Tata, the daughter Tuota; the mother Wada, the daughter Wida, &c." I do not think, · however, that this amounted to anything like a general principle.

It is to be observed that the quantity of a vowel often varies in the same name; thus we have GODDING and GOODING, GODMAN and GOODMAN, GODRICH and GOODRICH, GODWIN and GOODWIN, &c. We have only, for an instance of this, to cross the border, and we shall often find Tōm and Bōb for Tom and Bob.

CHAPTER VIII.

OUR NATURAL ENEMIES.

That a large proportion of French Christian names, as Albert, Adolphe, Edouard, Frederic, Guillaume, Henri, Robert, &c., are of German origin, is a point about which there can be no dispute. The extent to which the present family names of France may also be referred to a German origin is a subject which has not hitherto been investigated. A few there are, such as ARBOGAST, ARMENGAUD, CLODOMIR, GRIMAULT, and ISAMBERT, which, as corresponding with names of historical Franks, carry their own origin on their front. It is not difficult, again, to trace in DACBERT and DEGOBERT the name of the Frankish king Dagobert—in FERMOND and FERMENT that of Faramund—in CHARMOND and CHARMONT that of Charimund—or to find in GOMBAULT a form of Gundobald less perverted than our own GUMBOIL. But the names of historical personages are few, and the comparison serves rather to suggest, than to fulfil an enquiry. Nor are the materials of investigation wanting, for in the two Polyptyques whose titles I have elsewhere quoted, will be found a register of thousands of men and women of the Frankish period, and chiefly of that class which history allows to live and die unnoticed. Further, as the Frank and the Saxon, and all the other members of the Teuton race were branches of one common family, cognate in the names they bore as well as in the dialects they spoke, so all such records, of the one or of the other, find their mutual parallels in each other. The result then of the enquiry which I propose in these pages to make, will be to show, as I believe, that a very large proportion, indeed I may almost say the staple, of French, as of English names, is German in its origin. And may not mutual sympathies be encouraged, and mutual antipathies be rebuked, if it can thus be shown that there is more in common between the two races—perhaps even than is suspected by ethnologists—certainly than is present to the minds of people in general. And why, after all, should we be surprised if the French turn out to be—what their name describes them—Franks?

It must not be forgotten, however, that a second Teutonic element, of great political importance to them and to us, has entered into the composition of French nationality. We shall, I think however, be disappointed if we expect to find any strongly-marked Scandinavian element in French names. If that element had been more distinct, it might have remained more conspicuous; as it is, though it may not have been without its effect in modifying the nomenclature, yet it seems essentially to have been absorbed in the predominant element of the Frankish. And thus,

52 OUR NATURAL ENEMIES.

though here and there we find names, such as ODIN, ANQUETIL, RAOUL, which seem more particularly to bespeak a northern origin, yet such names are not sufficient to give a character to the nomenclature.

With very few exceptions, I have taken the modern French names from the *Annuaire de Paris,* and following the analogy of the language, have in all cases adopted the spelling and not the pronunciation.

The Frankish dialect being more nearly allied to the High German than to the Low, the differences between French and English names will, to a considerable extent, be the differences between High and Low German, as referred to in last chapter. Thus, though the French Christian name happens to be fixed as Edouard, yet the form most in accordance with the Frankish language would be Audouard. And AUDOUARD, AUDEVARD, &c., is in fact the form which in French family names is the most common. So also AUDOUIN, AUDIGUIER, and AUDIBERT, prevail rather than Edwin, Edgar, and Edbert.

The most common ending for simple names, among the French, as among the Old Franks, is *o,* or with the usual superfluous letters, *eau.* Thus French COUTEAU corresponds, as I take it, with Eng. COOTE—the same name with the ending and without. And as I have before observed that the ending in *i* is that which is in accordance with the genius of the English language, and that, if we had to form names now, we would give them that ending, so the same remark applies to the French and the ending in *o*.

It has been remarked that names derived from trades are more common in France than in England. I should rather say that it is the termination in *er* which is more common, and that among a multitude of names with this termination there are many which *accidentally coincide* with names of trades. I do not for a moment doubt that there are names derived from trades both in France and England, but what I say is that in a number of cases these names may be accounted for—and often more satisfactorily—otherwise. This view is confirmed by the fact that many French names correspond with *English* names of trades. M. de Gerville has noticed one, French HOUELLEUR, English WHEELER, and he has been driven to the shift of supposing that "it was introduced into Normandy during the thirty-two years occupation by the English in the fifteenth century." Truly the French must have been apt to learn, or the lesson must have been sharply taught. For they have also COLLIER, TANNIERE, MILLER, GLAESER, BRAZIER, KRIER, RINGIER, TASCHER, CARTIER, POTTIER, PACQUIER, corresponding with our COLLIER, TANNER, MILLER, GLAZIER, BRAZIER, CRYER, RINGER, TASKER, CARTER, POTTER, PACKER. Now my theory is that all these are, or may be in some cases, ancient compounds, and as I shall elsewhere show,

54   OUR NATURAL ENEMIES.

we have in almost all cases, both in French and English, names which contain the roots, and names which form other compounds.

Regarded from this point of view, French and English names mutually throw great light upon each other. When I doubt whether our POTTER means a maker of pots, it very much strengthens my suspicion to find not only a French POTTIER, but also POTERIE, with a corroborative termination. So when I doubt whether the French NOTAIRE means a notary, an English NOTTER is at hand to back me out.

In another point of view French and English names throw light upon each other—it often happens that the group is more complete in one language than in the other, and there is always a double chance of a missing link being supplied.

It seems natural to expect that at a transitional period in France there might be a certain mixing up of Teutonic and Romanic forms. And we find accordingly that there are some names which, though they run through a range of Teutonic compounds, do not themselves appear to be of Teutonic origin. Such are *barb*, *dulc*, *just*, which seem to be French or Latin, and yet which are found with the usual German endings, such as *bert*, *hard*, &c., appended to them. So also some words of Christian import, as Crist, Sanct, &c., seem to have been treated in a similar manner, in order to make German names of them. These forms, however, are not very common, and

OUR NATURAL ENEMIES. 55

it is not always certain that the word in question is not German.

This chapter may not inappropriately be concluded by an argument to prove that the present ruler of the French may have a name of German origin—that BONAPARTE in fact may be an Old Frankish name, come back, after long exile, to its native land. The case stands thus. Bonibert in the 7th and Bonipert in the 9th century, appear as Frankish names. In that part of Italy which was subdued by the Franks I find the present Italian name Boniperti—it is—or was—that of a jeweller at Turin—and there is no doubt that it is the same name as the Frankish Bonipert. Now from the same part of Italy came originally also the Bonapartes, and the question is simply this— May not the name Bonaparte be nothing more than an attempt to shape the other name, Boniperti, to something of an Italian meaning? Still, the name may be German, and yet not Frankish, for the Lombards, who held that part of Italy before them, were also Germans, and may have had the same name Bonipert. Curiously enough too, from the other side of the Atlantic the name comes back to us in a Saxon form, for the BON-BRIGHT quioted by Mr. Bowditch—Anglo-Saxon *briht*=Old High German *pert*—is evidently the same as Bonipert.

As to the etymology of the name, it may be taken to be from *bana, bona*, a slayer, and *bert* or *pert*, famous.

56 OUR NATURAL ENEMIES.

A famous slayer indeed was he who called men " food for powder !"

CHAPTER IX.

MAN AS THE TYPE OF POWER.

There are several names of which the etymological meaning is simply Man. And there appear to be some—but generally these are not so certain —of which the meaning is simply Woman. Into many of the names signifying man there enters no doubt something of a higher sense—that of manliness or heroism. And the words appear to be used *par excellence*, as we apply the terms manly and manful. Something of this sense appears in the line of Burns'—

> " A man's a man for a' that."

Still there are cases in which it is difficult to trace any other sense than that of mere sex.

At the head of the list is MANN, which is in a more direct manner connected with hero-worship than the rest, if, as is probably the case, its use as a name is to be traced up to the Mannus of Tacitus, the fabled son of the hero or god Tuisco, and founder of the German nation. We do not, however, meet with the name in after times, at least in its simple form, before the 7th cent., though in a compound form, it is found as early as the 4th. Two other forms are Men and Mon, the latter of which was Anglo-Saxon, and is still used in the Lowland Scotch.

H

MAN AS THE TYPE OF POWER.

SIMPLE FORMS.

Man.
Homo.

Old Germ. Manno, Manni, Meni, 7th cent. Ang.-Sax. Mann, Manni, Mon. Eng. MANN, MANY, MENNE, MENNIE, MENNOW. Modern German MANN. French MANN, MANY, MANEAU, MENNE, MENY, MENEAU, MONNY, MONNEAU. Ital. MANNI.

DIMINUTIVES.

Old German Mannila, Manili, 6th cent.—Anglo-Saxon Mannel—Eng. MANNELL, MANLEY—Manlay, *Roll of Battle Abbey*—Modern Germ. MANNEL, MENNEL—French MANLEY, MENEL. Old Germ. Manniko, Mannic, 9th cent.—English MANNICO, MANNAKAY, MANCHEE, MANNIX—Mod. German MANECKE, MANNECK—French MANEC. Old Germ. Mannikin, Mennechin—Eng. MANCHIN.—Modern German MANNIKIN, MANNCHEN.

PATRONYMICS.

Old Friesic Manninga—English MANNING—French MANINGUE.

COMPOUNDS.

(*Frid*, peace) Old Germ. Manfrit—Eng. MANFRED—Mod. German MANFRIED—French MANFRAY, MONFRAT—Italian MANFREDI. (*Gar, ger, ker*, spear) Old Germ. Mangar, 8th cent.—Eng. MANGER,* MONGER? MONCUR. (*Here*, warrior) English MONERY—French MANNIER, MENIER, MONNIER. (*Liub, leof*, dear) Old German Maualiub, 7th cent.—English MANLOVE. (*Hard*, fortis) Modern German MANHARDT, MANNERT—French MONARD. (*Gold, galda*, virere) Old German Managold, 7th cent.—Eng. MANIGAULT,† MANGLES —Mod. Germ. MANGOLD—French MANGAL. (*Wald*, power) Old Germ. Manold, 8th cent.—French MANALT, MENAULT.

In the former edition I thought that OMAN might be from Old Norse *omannr*, a nobody, *o* negative and *mannr*, a man. But it is more probably the same as HOMAN, from *hoh*, high. (See

---

* If this is pronounced like the English word "manger," it is probably the same as an Old Germ. Meginger.

† MANIGAULT, a South Carolina name, may be of French origin.

MAN AS THE TYPE OF POWER. 59

what it is to drop our h's !) ORMAN again, which I thought might be from the corresponding Ang.-Sax. negative particle *or*, is probably the same as an Old Germ. Oraman of uncertain meaning.

Another word signifying a man, a male, is Ang.-Sax. *carl*, Old High Germ. *charal*. This was a very common name, both German and Scandinavian, and is found as early as the 7th cent., but it does not seem, like most other words, to occur often in a compound form. A notable exception, however, is that of the Frankish king Carloman, the combination in whose name of two words both signifying man, gives, as in the Old Norse *karlmenni*, the sense of hero.

SIMPLE FORMS.

Old Germ. Karol, Carolus, 7th cent. Ang.-Sax. Cearl. Old Norse Karl. Eng. CARL, CARLEY, CHARLES, CARROLL, CARLOSS, CARLESS (Carolus ?) Mod. German KARL. French CAROL, CHARLE. Span. CARLOS. — *Carl. Man.*

A third root signifying man is Ang.-Sax. *gum*, *gom*, Old High German *gomo*, *como*, *chomo*, perhaps cognate with Latin *homo*. Hence comes the Eng. " groom," assuming a phonetic *r*.

SIMPLE FORMS.

Old Germ. Goma, Como, Chomo, 7th cent. Old Dan. Gummi. Eng. GUMMA, GUMMOE, GOMM, GUMM, GROOM, COMBE. Mod. German GOMM, KOMM, KUMM. French GOM, GOMME, COM, CHOMEAU, GRUMAY. — *Gom, Gum, Com. Man.*

COMPOUNDS.

(*Rice, Riche*, powerful) Old German Gumarich, Gomarih, Komerih—English GROOMBRIDGE, COMBRIDGR,* GOMERY,

---

* Hence the Scotch name MC.CAMBRIDGE quoted by Lower.

MAN AS THE TYPE OF POWER

COMRIE—Modern German GUMMRICH—French GOMBRICH. (*Mund*, protection) Old Germ. Gummund, Cummunt—Eng. GRUMMANT, COMONT—Frénch GOMANT, COMONT. (*Leih*, carmen) Old Germ. Gomaleih, Comaleih—English GUMLEY, COMLEY. (*Mar*, *mer*, illustrious) Old Germ. Gummar, Kummar—Eng. GUMMER, COMER—French GOMER, CHAUMER.

Seeing the interchange of *c* and *g* in this root, it may be worth while to enquire whether our word " comely," for which there is no quite satisfactory etymon in the dictionaries, may not be from *gom* or *com*, a man, in the sense of manly beauty.

From the Gothic *aba*, man, Förstemann derives the following group of ancient names. Stark, however, recommends to go back to the root-meaning, as found in the lost verb *aban*, pollere, referred to by Grimm. But if we suppose the sense to be that of man as the impersonation of power, we may, I think, as well take that meaning as the abstract one. Whether the root *ib* should be included also in the group, is not so certain.

SIMPLE FORMS

Ab, Eb, Ib, Man. Old Germ. Abbo, Abbi, Abba, Appo, Appa, Ebbo, Hebo, Heppo, Ibba, Hibba, Ippo, 5th cent. Ebba, queen of the South Saxons, A.D., 678. Ibbe, an Ang.-Sax. (*Kemble.*) Ebbi, a Northman (*Ann. Isl.*) Abo (*Domesday Linc.*) Eng. ABBE, ABBEY, ABBA, APP, HAPPEY, EPP, HEBB, HEPPEY, HIPP. Mod. Germ. ABBE, APPE, HEB, IBE. Mod. Dan. EBBE, ERBA. French ABBÉ, APPAY, HABAY, HABY, HAPPE, HAPPEY, HIPP.

DIMINUTIVES.

Old Germ. Abiko, Eppiko—Eng. APPACH, EBBIDGE— Mod. Germ. ABICH, EBBECKE—French HABICH, HAPPICH·

MAN AS THE TYPE OF POWER. 61

Old German Ibikin, Ipcin—English HIPKIN. Old German Abbilin, Appulin—Eng. APPLIN. Abissa, son of Hengest—Eng. ABBISS, APSEY—French HABEZ.

PATRONYMICS.

English ABSON, HEBSON, IBISON, HIBSON—Dan. EBSEN, IPSEN.

COMPOUNDS.

(Dio, servant) English ABDY—French ABBADIE, HABDEY. (Bert, pert, bright) Old Germ. Ibert—English EBERT, HEBBERT, HIBBERT—Mod. German EBBRECHT—French ABERT, HABERT, APPERT, HAPPERT, EBERT, HEBERT, IBERT, HIBERT. (Wald, power) Eng. APPOLD—French ABAULT. (Wid, vid, wood) Old Germ. Abuid—Eng. HIPWOOD—French ABAVID. (Beado, war) Old Germ. Ibed, Ibet—Eng. ABBOTT, EBBETTS, IBBETT, HIBBITT—French ABBETTE, ABIT, HABIT.

A fifth root signifying man is the Old High Germ. *bar*, which however it is very difficult to separate from Ang.-Sax. *bar*, a bear, with which in its root, it is probably allied. I place the following here.

SIMPLE FORMS.

Old German Paro, 10th cent. English BARR, BARRY, BARROW, PARR, PARRY. Barre, Bary *(Roll Battle Abbey)*. French BARRE, BAURY, BARREAU, BARRÉ, PARRA.

(margin: Bar, Par. Man.)

DIMINUTIVES.

English BARLOW, BARLEY, BARRELL, PARRELL—French BARELLE, PARLY. Eng. PARKIN—French BARACHIN. Eng. BARLING. Eng. BARRAS, PARIS,* PARSEY, PARISH—French BARRISS, PARISSE, PARISEAU.

COMPOUNDS.

(Frid, peace) Old German Barfrid, 8th cent.—English PARFREY. (Wald, power) Old Germ. Baroald, 7th cent.—French BARAULT. (Goth. *thius*, Old High German *dio*, servant) Old German Paradeo, Paradeus—English PARADAY,

---

* Robt. Parys, one of the "good men of London."—Pell Records, *temp*. Ed. 3.

62 MAN AS THE TYPE OF POWER.

PARDEW, PARADISE ?—French PARADE, PARADIS ? (*Man*)
Eng. BARREYMAN, PARMAN—Swiss BARMAN. (*Wine,* friend)
French BAROIN. (*Rat,* counsel) Eng. BARRETT, PARROT—
French BARRATTE, BARRET, PARRETTE.

From the Goth. *faths,* man, Förstemann takes
the following Old Germ. name, which is the only
one that we find. And to the same source we
may perhaps venture to refer the following
modern names.

SIMPLE FORMS.

Old Germ. Fatto, 8th cent. Eng. FATT, FATTY, FADDY,
FETT. French FATH.

COMPOUNDS.

Eng. FATMAN ? FETMAN ?

The names signifying woman are attended
with more difficulty and doubt, owing to the
manner in which men's names intermix, sometimes from the same apparent root. Thus there
are several which appear to be from Ang.-Sax.
wif, Old High Germ, *wip,* Mod. Germ. *weib,* wife
or woman. But among the ancient names there
are some that are those of men,* and Förstemann
thinks that the root of *weban,* to weave, intermixes. Or, I should rather suggest, Old Norse
vippa, to move rapidly, Eng. "whip." Wippo
was the name of a mythical Frankish king,
(*Grimm's Deutsch, Myth.* 277.)

SIMPLE FORMS.

Wibb,
Wipp.
Woman ?

Old German Wippo, Wippa, Wibi. English WHIPP,
WHIPPY, WIBBY. Mod. Germ. WIEBE.

---

* If the principle which I have before suggested be admitted, viz., that
anciently names were often given without reference to their meaning, it would be
quite conceivable that a name of which the literal meaning was woman might, of
course in a masculine form, be borne by a man, and *vice versâ.* At the same time
I think it probable that there is an intermixture of roots in this group.

MAN AS THE TYPE OF POWER.

DIMINUTIVES.

Vibill*ius*, a general of the Hermunduri in Tacitus.—Old German Wipilo.—Old Norse Vifill.—Wivell, Roll of Battle Abbey.—Eng. WIPPELL, WEIBLE, WHIBLEY.—Mod. Germ. WIPPEL, WIBEL—French WIBAILLE. Old Germ. Wiviken—Eng. WIPKIN.—Mod. Germ. WIBKING. Eng. WEBLING.

COMPOUNDS.

(*Dag*, day, or *dio*, servant) Eng. WHIPDAY. (*Wald*, power) Eng. WYFOLDE.

Then we have QUIN and QUEEN. It seems very doubtful whether these are from Goth. *qwina*, Ang.-Sax. *cwên*, a woman, Eng. "queen." For an Old German Quino comes before us as a man's name, and Förstemann takes it to be an aspirated form of Wino, from *wine*, friend. This we have also in many other names, as QUILLIAMS for Williams, &c.

It might seem fair, however, to give women's names the benefit of the converse. For we have a name QUOMMAN, which on the same principle might be an aspirated form of woman. But more probably it is the Gothic form of COMMIN, from Goth. *quama*, *quuma*, Ang.-Sax. *cumma*, guest, stranger.

Then DOLL, DOLLING might be from Old Norse *döll*, a woman (Eng. doll ?) This seems rather probably the meaning of the name of a female serf, "Huna et soror illius Dolo," in a charter of manumission, *Cod. Dip.* 981. But we have several compound names which are evidently

64 MAN AS THE TYPE OF POWER.

from a different source, probably Ang.-Sax. *dolh*, a wound, and these two might be the same.

In the former edition I thought that PEGG and PIGG might not improbably be from Ang.-Sax. *piga*, Dan. *pige*, a virgin, particularly from finding Pega or Pegia as the name of an Anglo-Saxon woman, the sister of St. Guthlac, A.D. 714. But on further consideration I think they are more probably, by the interchange of *b* and *p*, the same as BEGG and BIGG.

So also I thought that FANN, FANNY, FANNING, might be from Friesic *faen*, *fana*, Ang.-Sax. *fæmna*, a maiden. And that FENN, FENNING, might be from *femne*, another Ang.-Sax. form of the same. But the Old High Germ. *fanna*, an ensign, seems, upon the whole, to be an etymon more in accordance with the general character of our names.

There is another name, DISS, which I before thought might be from a female origin, but which is at any rate uncertain. The Old Norse *dis* signified a goddess, but originally, according to Grimm, simply a woman, and in proper names, the sense probably wavered between the two. Dis by itself occurs as a woman's name in the Landnamabok, and it was very common in compounds, one of which was Aldis. Hence I thought might be our names DISS and ALDISS. But there is an Old German Diss, Disso, a man's name, which Förstemann refers to Goth. *deis*,

MAN AS THE TYPE OF POWER. 65

wise—hence may be our DISS. And ALDISS may be Ald-iss, the diminutive form referred to in Chap. 3.

Lastly we have the names VERGE, VIRGIN, and VIRGO—apparently the French *vierge*, Eng. *virgin*, Lat. *virgo*. But these are only a few names out of a group, the root of which I am rather inclined to take to be *wearg*, a wolf, *würgen*, to worry.

Upon the whole then it will be seen that names signifying woman are certainly not common, and in most cases uncertain.

A word as to family names apparently from the christian names of women. These have been supposed to indicate illegitimacy, and if any of them have been given in comparatively modern times, this may be the case. But with regard to such surnames as ANNE, BETTY, MOLL, PEGG, SALL, LUCY, I have elsewhere given reasons for supposing them not to be women's names at all, but ancient men's names. That we have some names of female origin I do not doubt, and in the origin of surnames, I can see no reason why they might not in some cases, without any injurious imputation, be taken from the mother. We find that it was so in the case of christian names, as, for instance, in the *Pol. Irm.*, where a woman is called Scupilia, and her son Scopilius, an instance of the vowel change referred to by Weinhold, p. 49.

I

66 MAN AS THE TYPE OF POWER.

There are one or two names, such as MAN-HOOD and MANSHIP (Ang.-Sax. *manscipe,* man-hood), which seem to contain an abstraction. We have also MAHOOD, which may be either maidenhood or boyhood (Ang.-Sax. *mæg,* Old Eng. *mey,* maiden, Goth. *magus,* puer). But the ending *heid* or *hait* (Mod. Germ. *heit,* Eng. *hood*), is found in many ancient names, particularly among the West Franks, and in the 8th and 9th centuries. Thus we have.Adalheid, = noble-hood, *i.e.,* nobility. So also Williheid, which seems to be equivalent to resolution, and Billiheid, which, according to the meaning of the root suggested by Grimm, would be gentleness.

CHAPTER X.

THE BRUTE AND ITS ATTRIBUTES.

Names taken from animals form a very numerous and important list—many of them being of the highest Teutonic antiquity. Several of them are also closely connected with Northern mythology, for as certain animals were consecrated to certain deities, so we find that these are the animals which were most in favor for the names of men. Thus the wolf was sacred to Odin, the bear to Thor, and the boar to Frey. And the names of these three animals, consecrated respectively to the three principal Northern deities, were among the most honourable and the most common names of men. Indeed Björn, signifying a bear, was one of Thor's own names, and I am very much inclined to think that we have here some vestiges of an older worship, superseded by, and incorporated with the more recent Odinic faith. Throughout the whole of Northern Europe we have traces of a sort of superstitious respect paid to this animal, which, according to a Swedish proverb, has twelve men's understanding and six men's strength.*   Hence

---

* Horrebow, in his natural history of Iceland, gives an account of the bear in which the Icelandic estimate of his mental capacity seems by no means in keeping with the Swedish. If a man, according to his story, is attacked by one of those animals, he has nothing to do but to throw him something to amuse him till he can get out of the way. Nothing is better for this purpose than a glove, " for he will not stir till he has turned every finger of it inside out, and as they are not very dexterous with their paws, this takes up some time, and in the meanwhile the person makes off !"

68 THE BRUTE AND ITS ATTRIBUTES.

one of the heroes of Northern romance, fabled to have been the offspring of a woman and a bear, is described as surpassing other men in wisdom, as well as strength. In the former edition I suggested this as the possible origin of our name BARWISE (*i.e.* " bear-wise"), but retracted it in the addenda, assigning the name to an Old Germ. Berwas, Ang.-Sax. *hwæs*, keen, bold. But I overlooked the fact that there is also an Old German Berois,* which may probably be from *wis*, wise. And the decided form of our name BARWISE claims connection with this rather than with the other. So that, if the compound were formed with a meaning, the reputed wisdom of the bear might be the idea intended to be conveyed.

The king of the Northern forests was much in favour on the Scandinavian peninsula, and also among the Saxons of the continent. But among the Germans generally, and also among the Anglo-Saxons, names from the wolf were much more common.

There are two forms—the simple and older form *ber*, and the extended form *berin*.

SIMPLE FORMS.

Ber, Per. Bear.
Old Germ. Bero, Pero, 6th cent. English BEAR, BEER, PEAR, PEER, PERO, PAIRO. Mod. Germ. BAHR, BEER, BER. French BER, BEER, BIÉRE, PÉRE, PEYRE, PERREAU.

---

* In Old Frankish names, of which this is one, *oa* and *oi* stand for *wa* and *wi*, as indeed is the case also in modern French.

THE BRUTE AND ITS ATTRIBUTES. 69

DIMINUTIVES.

Old German Berila, 8th cent.—Eng. BERRILL, BURLEY, PEARL, PERLEY—French BÉRAL, BERILLE, BERL, BERLY, PEROL, PERRELLE, PERILLA. Old German Berico, Berrich, 9th cent.—English BERRIDGE, PERRIGO—Modern German BÄRECKE—French BERICH, PERICHE, PEROCHEAU. English PERKIN—French BERQUIN, PERICHON. English PURLING—French BERILLON, PERLIN.

COMPOUNDS.

(*Ger*, spear), Old German Bereger, Pereker, 8th cent.—Eng. BERGER—Modern German BERGER—French BERGER. (*Gis*, hostage) Old German Perakis, 9th cent.—Eng. PURKIS, PURCHES, PURCHASE. (*Grim*, fierce) Old Germ. Peragrim, 8th cent.—English PARAGREN, PARAGREEN, PEREGRINE? (*Hart*, hard) Old German Berhard, 9th cent.—Eng. BAREHARD—French BÉRARD, PERARD. (*Here*, warrior) Old Germ. Beriher, Bercher—Eng. BERRIER, PURRIER, PERCHER—Mod. German BIERCHER—French BERRYER, BERCHER, PERRIER. (*Helm*, helmet) Old German Perrhelm, 8th cent.—English PERRIAM, PERRAM—French BERHEAUME. (*Land*) Old Germ. Perelant, 9th cent.—English PURLAND. (*Man*) Old Germ. Berman—Eng. BURMAN, PEARMAN— Modern German BERMANN. (*Mar*, famous) Old Germ. Bermar, 9th cent.—Eng. BARMORE, PARRAMORE, PARAMOUR? (*Mard*, reward?) Old Germ. Beremard—French BERMARD. (*Mund*, protection) Old German Berimund, 5th cent.—French BERMOND, BERMONT. (*Rat*, counsel) Old German Perrat—English BERRET, PERROTT—French BEROT, PERROT. (*Dio*, servant) Old German Biridio, Peradeo, 6th cent.—English PERDUE—French PERODY, PEYREDIEU. (*Wald*, power) Old German Beroald, Berolt, 7th cent.—French BERAULT, PERAULT—Ital. BEROALDUS. (*Wine*, friend) Old German Berewin, 8th cent., Beroin—Eng. PEROWN—French PERROUIN. (*Geltan*, valere) English PURGOLD—French PERIGAULT. (*Ward*, guardian) Old German Beroward, Perwart, 8th cent.—Eng. BERWARD, PERWORT. (*Wis*, wise) Old German Berois, 8th cent.—Eng. BARWISE, PURVIS.

70 THE BRUTE AND ITS ATTRIBUTES.

Perhaps to this root may belong the name of the well-known fanatic BAREBONE, with which may correspond a French BARABAN (*bana* or *bona*, a slayer). Another English form is BEAR-BENN.

The following are to be assigned to the extended root *berin*, with which corresponds the Old Norse *björn*. The Anglo-Saxon *beorn*, chief, hero, may mix up with this root. It will be seen in this and the former, how close a connection there is between the roots of bear and man.

SIMPLE FORMS.

Berin,
Bern.
Bear.

Old German Berno, Berino, Bern, Pern, Pirin, 8th cent. Old Norse Björn, Birna. Ang.-Sax. Beorn. Eng. BIRNE, BURN, BIRNEY, PURNEY, BYRON, PERRIN. Modern German BEERIN. French BERNE, BERNEY, PERNY, BIRON, PIRON, PERRIN. Ital. BERNI.

DIMINUTIVES.

Old German Birnico, 8th cent.—Eng. BURNIDGE—Mod. German BERNICKE. English BURNELL, PURNELL—French BERNELLE, PERNELLE. Old German Berinza, Berniza, 10th cent.—Eng. BURNESS, BURNISH ?—Mod. Germ. BEHRENS.

PATRONYMICS.

Old German Bernuing, 9th cent.—Eng. BURNING.—Mod. Germ. BERNING.

COMPOUNDS.

(*Gar*, spear) Old German Beringar, 8th cent.—English BERINGER, BERRINGER—Mod. German BERRINGER—French BERINGER, BERANGER. (*Hard*) Old German Berinhard, 8th cent.—English BERNARD—Mod. German BERNARD—French BERNARD—Span. BERNARDEZ. (*Here*, warrior) Old German Berinher, Berner, Bernier, Pernher, 8th cent.—Eng. BIRNER,

THE BRUTE AND ITS ATTRIBUTES. 71

PERNER—Mod. Germ. BERNER—French BERNIER, PIRNIER. (*Wald*, power) Old German Berneold, Bernolt, 8th cent.— Eng. BERNOLD—French BERNAULT.

As the bear was sacred to Thor, so was the wolf to Odin, and by his two wolves, Geri and Freki, he is represented as always accompanied. I scarcely know how to account for it that though of all German names this was one of the most common, it is not particularly so in English names, and in French names rather the reverse. As a prefix in our names it generally loses the f, as in WOOLGER for Wulfgar.

SIMPLE FORMS.

Old Germ. Vulf, 5th cent.—Wolf, 8th cent.—$Ov''\lambda\iota\phi o\varsigma$ *Procopius.* Ang.-Sax. Wulf. Old Norse Ulfr. English Wulf, Ulf, WOLF, ULPH, ULP. Mod. Germ. WOLF. French VOLF, Wolf. OULIF.

DIMINUTIVES.

Ang.-Sax. Wolfsi—English WOLSEY (*see p.* 23). Old Germ. Wulfico, 8th cent.—Eng. WOOLFOLK. Old German Vulfemia, 9th cent.—Eng. WOLFEM, VULLIAMY.

COMPOUNDS.

(*Bert*, bright) Old German Wolfbert, 8th cent.—English WOOLBERT. (*Frid*, peace) Old Germ. Wolffrid, 8th cent.— Ang.-Sax. Wulfred—Eng. WOOLFREYS. (*Gar*, spear) Old German Wolfgar, 8th cent.—Ang.-Sax. Wulfgar—English WOOLGAR. (*Gaud*, goth ?) Old Germ. Wulfegaud, 8th cent. —Ang.-Sax. Wulfgeat—Eng. WOOLCOTT. (*Heid*, p. 66) Old Germ. Wolfheid, 8th cent.—Eng. WOOLHEAD. (*Hard*) Old Germ. Wolfhard, 8th cent.—Ang.-Sax. Wulfhard—Eng. WOOLLARD—Mod. Germ. WULFERT. (*Here*, warrior) Old German Vulfhar, bishop of Rheims, 7th cent.—Ang.-Sax.

72   THE BRUTE AND ITS ATTRIBUTES.

Wulfhere—Old Norse Ulfar—Eng. WOLPER—Mod. Germ. WOLFER. (*Hath, had,* war) Old German Wolfhad, bishop of Bourges, 9th cent.—Eng. WOOLLATT—French WOILLOT. (*Helm*) Old German Wolfhalm, 8th cent.—Ang.-Sax. Wulfhelm—Eng. WOOLLAMS—French WOILLAUME. (*Hoh,* high) Old Germ. Wolfhoh, 8th cent.—Ang.-Sax. Wulfheh—Eng. WOOLLEY. (*Mar,* famous) Old German Wolfmar, 8th cent. —Ang.-Sax. Wulfmer—Eng. WOOLMER. (*Noth,* bold) Old Germ. Vulfnoth, 9th cent.—Ang.-Sax. Wulfnoth—English WOOLNOTH. (*Raban, ram,* raven) Old Germ. Wolfhraban, Wolfram, 7th cent.—English WOLFRAM (perhaps of German origin). (*Rice,* powerful) Old German Wulfrich, 8th cent.— Ang.-Sax. Wulfric—Eng. WOOLRYCH—French WULVERYCK. (*Stan,* stone) Old Germ. Wolfstein—Ang.-Sax. Wulfstan— Eng. WOOLSTON.

Though in Old German names this was the most common of all post-fixes, yet it is by no means frequent either in English or French. We have the following.

Wulf, Ulf. Wolf. as a post-fix.

(*Ead,* prosperity) Old German Audulf, 7th cent.—Ang.-Sax. Eadulf—Eng. ADOLPH—Mod. Germ. ADOLPH—French ADOLPHE. (*Beadv,* war) Old Germ. Badulf, 8th cent.—Old Norse Bödolph—English BIDDULPH, BUTOLPH? (*Bardi,* giant?) Old German Bartholf—English BARDOLF. (*Gand,* wolf) Old German Gandulf, 7th cent.—French GANDOLPHE. (*Fast,* firm) Old German Fastulf, 8th cent.—Eng. FASTOLF,* FASTAFF. (*Rand,* shield) Old German Randulf, 8th cent.— English RANDOLPH. (*Rag,* counsel?) Old German Ragolf, Raholf, Raulf—English RALPH—Mod. German RALPHS. (*Hroc,* giant) Old Germ. Rocculf, Roholf, Roolf—Old Norse Hrolfr—Eng. ROLF—Mod. Germ. ROLF. (*Stede,* steadfast) Old German Stadolf, 8th cent.—Eng. STIDOLF. Our name

---

* I do not find this as a present English name, but there was a Sir John Fastolf, the supposed prototype of Shakespere's Falstaff, who belied his etymology by running away from Joan of Arc.

THE BRUTE AND ITS ATTRIBUTES. 73

BALFE, Pott makes a contraction of Badulf. But I think that it is more probably the same as the Ang.-Sax. Beowulf, perhaps from *beag, beah,* bracelet; hence, same as an Old Germ. Baugulf.

Wulf or *Ulf* was the honourable name of the wolf. It was the wolf as the servant of Odin—the attendant on the battle-field—the brave, patient hunter. But the wolf has another character—that of the midnight robber—the ruthless devourer—the curse of the shepherd—the terror of the mother. In this character his name was *wearg* or *varg,* which also means assassin. The wolf himself seems to have had an aversion to this name, for in the old days when animals could speak, he is represented in Northern fable as saying—

"Callest thou me Varg, I will be wroth with thee."

But what was not good enough for a wolf seems to have been good enough for a man, for WEARG was the name of a Solicitor-General in the last century. The names VERGE, VIRGO, and VIRGIN I should also be rather inclined to bring in here—referring them to *wearg,* a wolf, or the verb *würgian,* to worry. However, there is uncertainty about this group; Förstemann finds a root *werk* to which he gives the sense of *opus.*

SIMPLE FORMS.

Old Germ. Wargus, Wergio, 9th cent. English WEARG, WERGE, VERGE, WERK, WORKEY,* VERCO, VIRGO. Mod. Germ. WERCK. French VERGE, VERGÉ.

Werg.
Wolf.

---

* In a charter of manumission, *Cod. Dip.* 981, we find Wurci as the name of a serf. It seems probable that this is a sobriquet, and that it means literally "one who works," *i.e.,* with a will. Perhaps then the above name WORKEY ought rather to be associated with it.

J

74 THE BRUTE AND ITS ATTRIBUTES.

PHONETIC EXTENSION.

Eng. VIRGIN.   French VERGEON, VERGNE.

COMPOUNDS.

(*Hari, her,* warrior) Old Germ. Werchari, Werkher, 8th cent.—Eng. VERGER—Modern German ᵕWERKER—French VERCHÈRE. *(Man)* Eng. WIRGMAN, WORKMAN ? (*Noth,* bold) English WORKNOT—French VERGNAUD, VERGNOT. (*Wine,* friend) French VIRQUIN.

Another name for the wolf in Old Norse was *gandr,* to which Förstemann assigns the root *gand, gant, gent, kant, kent,* in Old German names. To this I add *chand, chant,* as a form common in French names, though *chanter,* to sing, probably mixes with it.*

SIMPLE FORMS.

Old German Gando, Ganto, Canto, Gento, son of the Vandal Geiserich, 6th cent. Old Norse Gandr (surname.) Eng. GANDE, GANDY, GANT, CANT, CANTY, CANDE, CANDY, CHANT, GENT. Mod. Germ. GANTE, KANT, GENT. French GAND, CANDA, CANDY, GENTE, GENTY, CHANTEAU.

Gand, Gant, Cant. Wolf.

DIMINUTIVES.

Old Germ. Gantala, Cantulo, 9th cent.—Eng. GANDELL, CANDALL, CANTELO, CANTLE, GENTLE ? Modern German GENEDL, KENDEL—French GANDELL, GENTIL ? CANDELLE, CANTEL, CHANDEL. English CANDELIN—French GANDILLON, CANTILLON, GENTILLON.

COMPOUNDS.

(*Here,* warrior) Old Germ. Ganthar, 8th cent.—English GANDER, GENDER, GANTER, CANTOR, CHANTER—Mod. Germ. GANTER, KANTER—Swiss GANDER—French GANDIER, GANTER, CANDRE, CANTIER, CHANTIER. (*Rad, rat,* counsel) Old German Gendrad, 8th cent.—French GENDROT, CHANTROT.

---

* As in the names Chanteclaire and Chantoiseau.

THE BRUTE AND ITS ATTRIBUTES. 75

(*Rice*, powerful) Old German Gendirih, Cantrih—English GENTERY, GENTRY, CHANTREY, KENDRICK, KENDRAY—Mod. Germ. GENDERICH—French GENDRY, CHANTERAC. (*Ulf*, wolf) Old German Gandulf, 7th cent.—French GANDOLPHE. (*Wine*, friend) French GANDOIN.

Another word signifying wolf is Old Norse *sâmr*. We find this as a man's name in the Landnamobok, and as a dog's name in the Nial-saga. The root *sam* in Old German names Förstemann refers to Old High Germ. *samo*, Eng. "same," in the sense of "equal." But I think that the above derivation is to be preferred.

SIMPLE FORMS.

Old Germ. Samo, 6th cent. Old Norse Sâmr. English SAM, SEMY. Modern German SAHM, SEMM. French SEMÉ, SEMEY. — Sam, Sem. Wolf.

DIMINUTIVES.

English SAMKIN. French SEMICHON.

The boar, which was sacred to Frey, the third of the principal deities, was also in very common use for the names of men. As the Anglo-Saxon *beorn*, the original meaning of which seems to have been "bear," was used in the sense of prince, hero—so the Old Norse *jöfurr*, signifying boar, was employed in Northern poetry in the same sense. The root of the word seems to be the same as that of the group *ab*, *eb*, p. 60, viz., Sansc. *abhas*, powerful, and the lost Teutonic verb *aban*, pollere. From the Old High Germ. *eber*, Ang.-Sax. *efor* and *ofor*, Old Norse *jöfurr*, are the following.

76   THE BRUTE AND ITS ATTRIBUTES.

SIMPLE FORMS.

Eber, Ever, Over. Boar.

Old Germ. Ebur, 6th cent.   Ibor, Lombard prince, 4th cent., not certain.   Old Norse Jöfurr, Ivar.   English EBER, HEBER, EVER, HEAVER, HEIFER, OVER.   Modern German EBER, EVERS.   French HIVER, HEVRE, OUVRÉ.

DIMINUTIVES.

Old German Euerlin, 8th cent.—Mod. German OBERLIN —French EBERLIN.   English EBORALL, EVERALL, OVERALL —French EBERLI, OBERLÉ, IVOREL.

COMPOUNDS.

(*Hard*, fortis) Old Germ. Ebarhard, Everhard, Everard, 8th cent.—English EVERARD—Mod. German EBERHARD—French EVRARD, EBRARD, OUVRARD.   (*Man*) Old German Ewurman, 8th cent.—Eng. HEAVERMAN—Modern German EBERMANN.   (*Rad, rat,* counsel) Old German Eburrad, 8th cent.—Eng. EVERED, EVERETT, OVERED, OVERETT—French EVRATT.   (*Rice,* powerful) Old German Eburicus, king of the Suevi, 6th cent.—English EVERY, IVORY, OVERY, OUVRY—French EVERICKX, IVRY, OBRY.   (*Ger,* spear) Old German Eburacar, 8th cent.—Eng. OVERACRE ?   (*Mar,* famous) Old Germ. Evremar, 8th cent.—Eng. OVERMORE ?

Galt. Boar pig ?

The Old Norse has *galti*, a boar pig, whence "galt," a word still in use in the North of England.   Galti occurs both as a baptismal and as a surname in the Landnamabok, and hence may be our GALT.   But the root *galt* in Old German names Förstemann refers to *geltan,* valere.

In the former edition, I derived SUGG from Ang.-Sax. *sug,* a sow.   But I now think that this root is both deeper and wider, and have introduced it elsewhere.   HOGG also is not to be referred to the animal, but to Anglo-Saxon *hog,*

THE BRUTE AND ITS ATTRIBUTES. 77

prudent, thoughtful. There was a Thurcyl surnamed Hoga (*Cod. Dip. Ang.-Sax. No.* 743),
which Mr. Kemble explains as " the wise or con-
siderate." So also PIGG is to be connected with
PICK, and by the interchange of *b* and *p*, with
BIGG and BICK, from a root signifying to slash.
The Old Norse *gris*, a little pig, occurs both as a
baptismal and as a surname in the Landnamabok.
Hence might be our GRICE, and the diminutive
GRISSELL. But the Old High Germ. *gris*, grey,
(or perhaps grisly) is more probably the general
root of our names, and also of the French
GRISARD, GRISOL, &c.

The horse seems to have been held in especial
veneration by the Ancient Germans. Tacitus informs us that they kept white horses, which they
regarded as sacred, and by whose snortings and
neighings, when yoked to the sacred chariot, they
prognosticated future events. Some trace of this
worship or respect may perhaps be found in the
use, referred to by Grimm, of white horses in
solemn or state processions. Perhaps also in the
frequency with which they appear as the signs
of inns in Germany and Switzerland, and, though
not to the same extent, in England. In London
alone there are about 50 inns or public houses
with the sign of the White Horse. The eating
of horse flesh seems to have formed a part of
heathen festivals, and hence was coupled by the
Christian missionaries along with any other
idolatrous ceremony, and interdicted as such.

78   THE BRUTE AND ITS ATTRIBUTES.

Nor does the attempted revival, among our somewhat whimsical neighbours, seem to have met with any very signal success.   We do not find that in the Northern system of mythology the horse was dedicated especially to any particular god, but twelve horses, belonging to different deities, and each distinguished by its particular name, are enumerated in the Eddas.

The names of Hengist and Horsa, the leaders of the first Saxon invasion of England, are both derived from the horse.   The former is from Ang.-Sax. *hengst*, Old High German *hengist*, Old Fries. *hingst*, Low Germ. *hangst*, a stallion.   The last word is still in use in some parts of Westphalia to denote a horse in general.   Hengist seems to have been anciently by no means a common name.   It occurs as the name of a Jutish chieftain (identical or not with the above), in the Anglo-Saxon poem of Beowulf.   The only other instance is that of a Hengest in the Monumenta Boica, A.D. 1042.   But Hengst is a name still in use among the modern Frisians.   And it is found in names of places in Germany, as Hengistfeldon and Hengistdorf.   In the names of places in England it is generally corrupted into Hinks, as Hinks. in Hinksey, Berks., Ang.-Sax. Hengestesige.   So Stallion. that our HINCKS may probably be the same name.   We have also HINXMAN and the local HINGESTON.

The word *hors* is common to almost all the

THE BRUTE AND ITS ATTRIBUTES. 79

Teutonic dialects. An Old High Germ. form is *ors*, and an Old Fries. form is *hers*.

SIMPLE FORMS.

Old German Orso, 10th cent. Sax. Horsa, 5th cent. English HORSEY, HEARSE, HERSEY. French ORSAY, HERSE, HERCE.

Horse, Herse. Equus.

DIMINUTIVES.

Old German Orsicin, 10th cent.—English HORSKINS, ERSKINE ? Eng. HORSELL—French ORSEL.

COMPOUNDS.

Old Germ. Ursiman, 7th cent.—Eng. HORSMAN. (There is also an Old German Horscman, 9th cent., *hòrsc*, nimble.)

From the other form *hros* may be the following. But Grimm also suggests a word *ros*, red, which may intermix. And our name Ross may of course also be local.

SIMPLE FORMS.

Eng. Ross. French ROSSI.

Ross. Horse.

DIMINUTIVES.

Roscelin (*Lib. Vit.*)—Eng. ROSLING—French ROSSELIN, ROSLIN. French ROSSEL, ROSLY. Eng. ROSCOE.

COMPOUNDS.

(*Bert*, famous) Old Germ. Rospert, 10th cent.—English ROSBERT. (*Hari, her*, warrior) English ROSSER, ROSIER, ROSERY—French ROSSER, ROSCHER. •(*Man*) Eng. ROSOMAN —French ROSÉMON. (*Kel* for *Ketel ?*) Old Norse Hrosskel —Eng. ROSKELL.

From the Ang.-Saxon *mære, mere*, Old High Germ. *marah*, a horse, Eng. "mare," are probably MARE, MEERS, •MEARING, MÁRA, and perhaps MARY. There may be other names, but it is

Mare. Horse.

80   THE BRUTE AND ITS ATTRIBUTES.

difficult to separate this root from *mar, mer,* illustrious.   One or two compounds, such as MARYMAN or MERRIMAN, which would correspond with HORSMAN, HINXMAN, seem more naturally to belong to this.

From the Old High Germ. *marah, march,* a horse, Förstemann derives the root *marc* in Old Germ. names, observing that *marka,* a boundary, may also intermix.   MARK may of course also be in some cases Scriptural.

SIMPLE FORMS.

Mark,   Old German Μαρκιας, Gothic leader in Procopius.
March.   Marco, 8th cent.   Anglo-Saxon March, *Cod. Dip.* No. 971.
Horse.   Eng. MARK, MARKEY, MARCUS, MARCH.   Modern German MARK, MARCH.   French MARCQ, MARC, MARCUS, MARCHÉ.

DIMINUTIVES.

Old German Marclin, 9th cent.—French MARCILLON. Eng. MARKLILE.†   French MARCOL.

COMPOUNDS.

(*Here,* warrior) Old German Marcher—Eng. MARKER, MARCHER—Modern German MÄRKER—French MARCHIRE, MARQUERY.   (*Mar,* illustrious) Old German Marcomer, 2nd cent. *(Aurel Vict. de Cæs.)*—Marcamar, Frankish prince, 4th cent.—Eng. MARRAMORE.*   (*Leif,* superstes) Old Germ. Marcleif, Marclef, 6th cent.—Eng. MARKLOVE—Mod. Germ. MARKLOFF.   (*Ward,* guardian) Old Germ. Marcuard, 8th cent.—Modern German MARKWARDT—French MARQUARD. (*Wig, wic,* war) Old German Marcovicus, 6th cent.—English MARKWICK.

---

† Can this be the Danish diminutive *lille,* as in Tove*lille,* North. Eng. *lile?* The name is found in the Danish county of Lincolnshire.

* Several Old German names from this root appear both as Marah and Mark Thus Marahsind and Marcsind, &c.   The High Germ. *h,* however, must be taken to represent something of a guttural sound.

THE BRUTE AND ITS ATTRIBUTES. 81

I do not think that STALLION is from the animal, but, along with the French STALIN, from *stahl*, steel, which enters into some Old German names.

PALFREY seems also doubtful. It may be from the Old Germ. Baldfred or Paldfred—*fred* in Eng. generally making *frey*, as in Godfrey and Humfrey. But PALFRIMAN cannot be so explained.

COLT is, I doubt not, the High Germ. form of GOLD. So also COLTMAN corresponds with GOLDMAN and COLDMAN. Other compounds are COLTER, COLTART, &c.

These four animals then, the bear, the wolf, the boar, and the horse, all possess obvious attributes which would make them in favour for the names of men. The bear, with his power, his tenacity, his secretiveness, and his imputed wisdom—the wolf, with his ferocity, his endurance and his discipline—the boar, with his vindictive sturdiness—have always been favourite types for the Teutonic race : the horse, with his noble and generous spirit, has had an attraction for all men in all time.

But the cow—the innocent and ungainly cow —what is there in her useful and homely life that could inspire sentiments of reverence in a fierce and warlike people ? The honour which was paid to her was from a more ancient and a more deeply-seated source. From the time when Israel, tainted with Egyptian superstition, set up a

THE BRUTE AND ITS ATTRIBUTES.

golden calf and said "These be thy gods, which brought thee out of the land of Egypt"—and from who can tell how many ages before that time, the cow, as the type of the teeming mother earth; has been an object of human idolatry. In the Northern system of mythology she is not, like the bear, the wolf, or the boar; sacred to any particular divinity, but appears—in what seems to be a fragment of a more ancient myth—as mysteriously connected with the first cause and origin of all things. Grimm has remarked (*Deutsch. Myth. p. 631*), that the Sanscrit root *gô* signifies both ox or cow, and also earth, country, district. Hence, on the one hand the Old High German *chuo*, Ang.-Sax. *cû*, English cow—and on the other Gr. γᾶ, γῆ, earth, German *gau*. He further remarks upon the connection which *rinta*, the earth, and Rindr, wife of Odin, may have with Germ. *rind*, ox.

Both of the above two words, *gow* or *cow*, and *rind*, are found in our names, and we have the choice of the above two meanings. But, upon the whole, the meaning of land, country, seems more in accordance with the general character of Teutonic nomenclature.

I do not take BULL to be from the animal, though, as elsewhere stated, I am not certain, while preferring a different derivation, that it is not from the same root.

There is a root, *ur*, found in several Old Germ. names, which Förstemann refers to Ang.-

THE BRUTE AND ITS ATTRIBUTES.   83

Saxon, Old High German, and Old Norse, *ûr*, buffalo.

SIMPLE FORMS.

Old Germ. Urius, Uro, 4th cent.   English URE, URIE, HURRY.   Modern German UHR.   French OURY, HOUR, HUREAU, HUREY, HURÉ, HEURÉ.

Ur. Buffalo.

DIMINUTIVES.

Eng. HURREL—French HUREL - French HUREZ.

PATRONYMICS.

Old German Urinch, 10th cent.—English YOURING.

COMPOUNDS.

(Hard) Old Germ. Urard, 11th cent.—French HURARD. *(Here*, warrior) French URIER, HURIER. *(Wald*, power) Old German Urold, 9th cent.—French HURAULT. *(Wine*, friend) Eng. URWIN. *(Wig*, war) Eng. URWICK.

Calf was not an uncommon name among the Northmen; there are several men called Kalfr in the Landnamabok and elsewhere. The Old Norse *kalfr*, though primarily signifying the young of the cow, was applied in a more extended sense to the young of various animals. And there is a Northman in the Landnamabok with the name of Selakalfr (seal-calf.) Förstemann has one Old Germ. name Calpho, which he takes to be a transposition of Claffo (name of a Lombard king). But I do not feel at all certain that this, along with a seemingly English name KALVO in the London directory, and a French name CALVO, are not to be referred to the Goth. *kalbo*, calf. We have also CALF and the Germans have KALB and KALFS, which Pott, though I

84   THE BRUTE AND ITS ATTRIBUTES.

think unnecessarily, supposes to be a contraction of some compound name ending in *leib* or *leif*.

There are very few names derived from the dog. DOGGETT, which I before classed under this head, I must now withdraw, as I think it belongs to the root of Ang.-Sax. *dugan*, to be of use or value. Also BICK, and the more *prononcé* name BITCH found in Bowditch, which I take to be from *bicken*, to slash.

Hund, Hunt. Dog.

HUND and HUNDY, corresponding with an Old Germ. Hundo, 8th cent., are probably from *hund*, a dog, Eng. "hound." HUNT, Mr. Lower derives from "hunt," a chase or hunting ground, as a local name. And Mr. Arthur from "hunte," used by Chaucer for huntsman. It is possible that both these derivations, and particularly the latter, may obtain in some cases. But as the general rule I think that HUNT, corresponding with an Old German Hunto, Mod. Germ. Hundt, is only the High Germ. form of HUND. In a roll-call of German officers given by Mameranus, A.D. 550, are the names Hundt, Huntus, and Hontus, the last of which is explained "Georgius canis seu Hontus." Hence HUNTING, French HONTANG, as a patronymic form, belongs more certainly to this last. The Hundings (Hundingas), are a people mentioned in the Scôp or Bard's song, and are supposed to have been the people of Hundland, which the editors of the Copenhagen edition of the Edda place in Jutland.

THE BRUTE AND ITS ATTRIBUTES. . 85

Though the fox was much mixed up with the Fox.
popular superstitions of the Middle Ages, it does Vulpes.
not seem to have been common in the names of
men.   Indeed no ancient names come before us,
and the word appears first in the Hundred Rolls
as a surname, Le Fox.

DEER might be from the animal, though perhaps rather in the wider sense of the German
thier, signifying any wild animal.   But it is impossible, even in the ancient names, to separate it
from *dear*, carus, Germ. *theuer*, which I take to.
be the preferable sense.

RAIN might be in some cases from Old Norse
hreinn, a rein-deer, the name of three Northmen
in the Landnamabok.   But as a name of German
origin it is to be referred to Goth. *ragin*, counsel.

Of other names I take STAGG, BUCK, HART,
GOAT, RAM, EWE, to be derived otherwise than
from the animals.

Lamb was not an uncommon name among Lamb,
the Northmen—little suited as it may seem for Lamp.
those ferocious warriors.   It occurs twice as a Agnus.
baptismal name, and thrice as a surname, in the
Landnamabok.   There was also an Erik Lamb,
King of Denmark, A.D. 1139.   The High Germ‘
form of *lamb* is *lamp*, and there is an Old Germ.
Lampo, 10th cent., but Förstemann thinks lamb,
agnus, an improbable root, and suggests Old
Norse *lempa*, moderari, or Ang.-Sax. *limfan*, Old
High Germ. *limpan*, evenire, convenire.   But in
the face of the above Scandinavian names, I hardly

86 THE BRUTE AND ITS ATTRIBUTES.

think that his objection can be maintained. It seems probable, however, that there may be an intermixture of another root, Old Norse *lemia*, to beat, whence in the Cumberland dialect "lam." Again, there are some names, such as LAMBERT, in which *lam* is a corruption of *land*. * But upon the whole I think that the following may come in here.

SIMPLE FORMS.

Lamb.
Agnus.

Old Germ. Lampo, 10th cent. Old Norse Lambi. Eng. LAMB,* LAMBEY, LAMP, LAMPEE. Modern German LAMPE, LAMM. Dan. LAMPE. French LAMBIE, LAMY, LAMPY.

DIMINUTIVES.

Old Germ. Lampulo, 9th cent.—Eng. LAMBOLL—Modern Germ. LAMLE—French LAMBALLE, LAMBLA. Eng. LAMELIN —French LAMBELIN, LAMBLIN. English LAMPKIN—French LAMBQUIN.

PATRONYMICS.

Eng. LAMPSON. Eng. LAMPING.

COMPOUNDS.

(*Frid*, peace) Old German Lempfrit, 8th cent.—English LAMPREY ?—French LAMFROY ?†

The noblest animal with which the Teutonic nations were familiar was the bear ;—if they came in contact with the lion, it must probably have been some inferior animal of the species. Yet names from this origin, though not very common, are of considerable antiquity, being found as early as the 6th cent. There are two forms—the

---

* Perhaps we may also bring in here LUMB, LUMP, LUMPY, and LUMPKIN (*Bowditch.*)

† Or might be, as Pott has it, from Landfred.

THE BRUTE AND ITS ATTRIBUTES. 87

simple root *leo, lew, low,* (Old High German and Old Saxon *löwe, leo,* Old Fries. *lauw,*) and the extended root *lion, lewon.* These I take separately.

SIMPLE FORMS.

Eng. LEO, LEW, LEWEY, LOWE, LOWY. Modern German LEUE, LAUE. French LÉO, LEWY, LOUÉ.

Lew, Low. Lion.

COMPOUNDS.

(*Wald,* dominion) Old Germ. Leoald, 6th cent.—Modern German LEWALD—French LIOULT, LOUAULD. (*Wolf*) Old Germ. Lewolf, 8th cent.—Eng. LEOWOLF.

EXTENDED ROOT *leon, leuon.*

Old Germ. Leon, Leuan, 9th cent. Eng. LEWEN, LION, LOWEN. French LION, LOUIN.

Leon, Lewen. Lion.

DIMINUTIVES.

Old Germ. Leonza, 9th cent.—Eng. LYONS ? LOWANCE—French ? LIONTZ.

COMPOUNDS.

(*Hard*) Old German Leonard, 6th cent.—Eng. LEONARD, LENNARD—Modern German LEONHARD, LENHARD—French LEONARD—Ital. LEONARDI.

LEOPARD I take to be the Old Germ. name Liubhart, Leopart, Leopard (*liub,* love, and *hart,* hard.) And PANTHER, along with PANTER, PANDER, BANTER, and perhaps PAINTER, I refer to the root *band, bant, pant,* (Ang.-Saxon *bænd,* crown.)

It is probable that our LINK, LYNCH; the French LINK; and the Mod. German LINCK; are from Old High German *linch,* lynx. There is an Old German Linco, 8th cent., which Graff and Förstemann refer to this origin. The Ang.-Sax.

Link. Lynx.

88   THE BRUTE AND ITS ATTRIBUTES.

word is *lox*, whence may be our LOSH, while from the form *luchs*, found in Mod. Germ., may be our LUSK and LUSH, and the Mod. Germ. LEUCHS.

Among the names derived from beasts of prey must be included that of our gracious Sovereign —Guelph being a dialectic form of Welph, Eng. "whelp," signifying the young of beasts of prey.

SIMPLE FORMS.

Welp, Welf. Whelp. Old German Huelp, Hwelf, Welf, 9th cent., Guelf, 11th cent. Welp, *Domesday Yorks.* English WELP, GUELPA,[*] VALPY ?   Mod. Germ. WELF.   French VELPEAU, GELPY ?

DIMINUTIVES.

Old German Walpulo, 9th cent.—Eng. WELPLEY.   Eng. WELLFLIN.

COMPOUNDS.

(Hard) Old German Welfhard, Welfart, Welfard, 7th cent.—English WALFORD, WELFORD—French VALFORT, WALFERDIN *(dimin.)*

Oliphant. Elephant? Upon the whole I take OLIPHANT to be, as generally supposed, from the animal.   Both the two forms, *elifant* and *olifant*, are found in High as well as in Low German.   The former I have never met with in English names, but a writer in *Notes* and *Queries* adduces an ÆNEAS ELIPHANT from a list of the society of writers to the signet in Edinburgh for 1711.   The name in this form is found in Germany as early as the 8th cent.   At least I take it that the Old German names Helfant, Helphant, Eliphand, Eliphant are from

---

[*] A Boston surname, but whether of English origin or not Mr. Bowditch does not say.

THE BRUTE AND ITS ATTRIBUTES. 89

that origin. I once copied from a Wiesbaden visitors' list an "Eléphanty, aus London,"—a name which looks like French.

I do not think that CAMEL is from the animal. There is a root *gamal* or *camal*, found in several ancient names, and which is probably from Ang.-Sax. *gamal*, old.

Ass, for which Mr. Lower has authority as an English name, and which corresponds with a French ASSE, may perchance have to be elevated from a donkey to a demi-god. It may be the Old Norse *ás*, Anglo-Saxon *ôs*, semideus, whence Old Germ. names Aso and Asi, Old Norse Asa. Or if it be the same as HASS, it will correspond with Old Germ. names Hasso and Hassi, of which the meaning is probably Hessian.

HARE I take not to be from the animal, but either to be classed along with HARRE, HARRY, HARROW, from *hari*, warrior; or with AIR, AIRY, from Goth. *ara*, eagle. And HASE I take not to be from the Germ. *hase*, hare, but along with an Old Germ. Haso, from *hath*, war.

RABBIT, along with the French RABOT, RABOTTE, I take to be a corruption of an Old Germ. Radbot, or Ratbod. As an ancient name this appears variously as Radbod, Rabbod, Ratpot, Rappot. There is a Rabbod mentioned as a "duke of the Frisians" in Roger of Wendover's Chronicle.

BADGER I take to be either a compound of *bad*, war, and *ger*, spear; or of Ang.-Sax. *beag*,

L

90   THE BRUTE AND ITS ATTRIBUTES.

Eng. "badge," and *hari,* warrior.   Another name,
BADGERY, is more evidently the latter compound.

I also doubt BROCK, which corresponds with
French BROCQ and BROCA, being from "brock,"
a badger.   Even if from the same root, the derivation seems too narrow.   In Ang.-Sax., Old Norse,
and Old Eng., the word signified a husbandry
horse, which sense obtains in the North of
England at the present day.   The origin seems
to be Old Norse *brocka,* to go with a heavy and
jolting gait.   Brock was the name of a dwarf in
Northern mythology, and he being a wonderful
worker in metals, the above derivation may
perhaps suggest a comparison with the lame
Vulcan.   The name then might have a mythological origin, but I think on the whole that it may
be better accounted for.   Förstemann has nothing
to throw light upon it, but Stark supplies the
deficiency, and produces Old German names
Bruocho and Bruogo, and Ang.-Sax. Brôga, with
compounds Brôcardus and Brôchard, all of which
he refers to Anglo-Saxon *brôga,* terror.   I think,
however, that there may be also a root *broc,*
from Ang.-Saxon *brocian,* to afflict, persecute, a
sense quite in accordance with the character of
ancient names.

It seems rather probable, upon the whole, that
BEAVER is from the animal.   No doubt there is
a root *bef, bif, biv* (Old Norse, *bif,* movement),
which enters into a number of names, and of
which it might be a compound.   But the forms

THE BRUTE AND ITS ATTRIBUTES.   91

in which it appears seem to be too extensive and complete to be thus accounted for. There are three forms—the Low German *bever*, the High Germ. *biber*, and the Old High Germ. *pipar*, all represented in our names—there is also a mixed form *pever*.

SIMPLE FORMS.

Biber (*Hund. Rolls*). English BEAVER, BIBER, PIPER, PEFFOR, PEEVOR. Modern German BEVER, BIEBER, PIPER. French BEVAIRE, BIBER, PIPRE, PIEFER, PIVER.

Bever, Biber, Pipar. Beaver.

DIMINUTIVES.

English PEVERALL—Pevrell, *Roll. Batt. Abb.*—French PEUVRELLE.

I do not think it probable that OTTER is from the animal. There are Old Germ. names Other, Oddar, Mod. Germ. Oder, which Förstemann refers to *aud*, prosperity, and there is an Old Norse Ottar, which he classes along with these, but for which I prefer the derivation of Haldorsen, from Old Norse *ótta*, to strike with fear.

The cat, from the earliest times, seems to have been connected in the Teutonic mind with magic and witchcraft. The Icelandic Sagas relate that Thorolf Skegge, a celebrated magician, had twenty large black cats, which came to his assistance in time of need, and were each nearly a match for a man.

It seems certain that the Northmen had names derived from the cat. Weinhold (*Altnordisches Leben*), refers to the names of two brothers, Kött and Kisi, as both having this meaning. Kött

92 THE BRUTE AND ITS ATTRIBUTES.

again appears as a surname in the Landnamabok. In the Eyrbiggia Saga there is an account of a witch called Katla, a name which seems probably from a similar origin, and which, but that we find it borne by several other women, we might be disposed to connect with her magical character. But as in Northern mythology the chariot of the goddess Freyia is represented as drawn by two cats. this might be the most probable reason for its adoption in proper names.

We do not find any Old Germ. names which can with certainty be referred to this origin. The word *cat* in some very ancient names, as Catumer and Catualda, though by some writers supposed to be from the cat, is referred by Grimm to *hath,* war. And with respect to our own names, and those of France ; though I think it probable that such may occur, yet in all cases there are other roots which present themselves, and render it more or less doubtful.

RATT and MOUSE are both English names, and RATTE and MOUSSE appear also in the directory of Paris ; I have placed both of them elsewhere.

Lastly, we have MOLE, which along with MOLL, and the French MOLE and MOLL, I refer to Old Norse *mola,* to beat, English "maul." And now, having run the quadrupeds to earth, I. must turn to the birds.

BIRD itself seems doubtful, and there are two other roots which I think more suitable than bird,

THE BRUTE AND ITS ATTRIBUTES. 93

avis. One is Old Norse *byrde*, German *bürde*, an extended root of which is Ang.-Sax. *byrthen*, Eng. "burden." The idea of strength seems to have been associated with this root. In Old Norse, *burdir*, *(plur.)*, signified strength, vires, and *burdalaus* signified weak. This might be a sense present in proper names. Another, and perhaps a still better derivation, is Old Norse *burdr*, Anglo-Saxon *byrd*, birth, which obtained anciently a sense precisely similar to that which it has at present in such a phrase as "a man of birth."* And there appear to be other roots with similar meaning in proper names. In some few cases, however, *bird* is no doubt a corruption of *bert* (famous). And there is one name, BURDEKIN, which I am rather inclined to take to be from the bird.

From the Goth. *fugls*, Ang.-Sax. *fugel*, Germ. *vogel*, fowl or bird, are the following.

SIMPLE FORMS.

Old German Fugal, 9th cent. English FUGGEL, FUEL, FOWELL, FOWLE, VOWELL, VOWLES. Mod. Germ. VOGEL. French FAUCIL ? FOULLEY ?

Fugel, Fowl. Avis.

DIMINUTIVES.

Old German Fukelin, Fugaling, 11th cent.—English FAULLON—French FOCILLON. French VOULQUIN.

FAIRFOUL, as Mr. Lower observes, seems paradoxical. But spell it FAREFOWL, and its mean-

---

* Since writing the above, I find that Stark, referring to an Old Germ. name Burdo, not explained by Förstemann, proposes the latter of the two meanings which I have suggested.

94 THE BRUTE AND ITS ATTRIBUTES.

ing is explained at once, "bird of passage." Such names were common among the Northmen. A Summerfugl and a Winterfugl, "Summer-fowl" and "Winter-fowl," are among the names on the coins minted by Scandinavian coiners at York, *(Worsaae, Danes and Norwegians.)* SOMMER-VOGEL is found at present in the directory of Paris, and if French, may be a legacy of the Northmen. A similar sort of name is our SUMMERSELL, the Sumersul in the Domesday of Yorkshire, which appears to be from Old Norse *sula*, explained by Haldorsen as a sort of pelican. In the genealogy of the kings of Northumbria occurs a Sæfugel, which name we still have as SEFOWL.

The eagle, as the king of birds, is at the head of the list, and furnishes by far the greatest number of names. But EAGLE itself is uncertain—it may be the same as an Old German Agil, Egil, Ang.-Sax. Aegel, elsewhere noted. So also the French AIGLE and AIGUILLÉ, the latter corresponding with an Old Germ. Aigila.

There are two forms, the simple root *ar*, (Old High German *aro, ar*, Old Norse *ari*)—and the extended root *arin* (Ang.-Saxon *earn*, Old Norse *arn, ern*, Old High German *arn, erni*). The former is apt to mix up with another word, *hari*, warrior.

SIMPLE FORMS, *ar, aro.*

Ar. Old German Ara, Aro, 7th cent. English AIR, AIREY,
Eagle. EAREE. Mod. Germ. AAR, AHR.

THE BRUTE AND ITS ATTRIBUTES.   95

DIMINUTIVES.

Old German Arila, 8th cent.—English ARIELL, ARLE—French ARIOLI.

COMPOUNDS.

(*Fast*, firm) Ariovistus,* leader of the Helvetii,. 1st cent. B.C., Arefastus, 11th cent., Arfast, Bishop of East Anglia—Eng. HARVEST?—French ARRIVETZ? (*Hard*) Old German Arard, 8th cent.—Eng. EARHEART—Mod. German ERHARDT—French ERARD. (*Had*, war) Old German Arahad, 8th cent.—Eng. EARRATT, ERRATT. (*Ward*, guardian) French EROUARD, EROUART. (*Wald*, power) Old German Arawald, 9th cent.—French AYRAULT, ARRAULT. (*Wig*, war) Eng. EARWIG?

SIMPLE FORMS, ARN, ARIN.

Old Germ. Arin, Arno, Arn, 8th cent.—Old Norse Arni. English ARN, ARNEY, ARNO, HARNEY, EARNEY, HERNE. French ARAN, ARNOU, ERNIE, HERNY.

Arin, Arn.
Eagle.

COMPOUNDS.

(*Here*, warrior) Old Germ. Arnheri, 9th cent.—English HARNOR. (*Wald*, power) Old German Arnoald, 7th cent.—Old Norse Arnalldr—Eng. ARNOLD—Mod. Germ. ARNHOLD, ARNOLD—French ARNAULT, ARNOULD, ARNOLD, ERNOULT, HARNAULT. (*Helm*) Old German Arnhalm, 9th cent.—Eng. ARNUM. (*Man*) Eng. ARNAMAN, HERNIMAN. (*Ger*, spear) Old German Arnger, 9th cent.—French ARRANGER. (*Hard*) English HARNARD. (*Bert*, famous) Old German Arnipert, Arembert, 7th cent.—French ERAMBERT. (*Dio*, servant) Old Germ. Arindeo, 8th cent.—French ARRONDEAU. (*Wulf*) Old German Arnulf, 5th cent.—Eng. ARNULPHE—French ERNOUF.

The Mod. German *adler* is formed from *ar*, eagle (or perhaps large bird in general), by the

---

* Förstemann considers the Germanhood of Ariovistus uncertain. The German writers in general seem, however, to consider it Teutonic, but the older explanation of *heerfurst*, "army leader," is, I think, inadmissible. Diefenbach appears to give some sanction to the above placing of mine. Arfast, the bishop, as a chaplain to William the Conqueror, was, I apprehend, a Norman.

96 THE BRUTE AND ITS ATTRIBUTES.

prefix *adel*, noble. But as a name, Adler is more probably from the Old German Adalhar (*hari*, warrior.) The Dutch form is *arend*, which we find as a name of the 14th century, and whence may be our ARREND.

Hawk. Accipiter. HAWKE (Ang.-Sax. *hafoc*), I do not find as an ancient name. In the *Pell Records* it occurs as a surname, Bene Havekin, the falconer. Hence seems to be our HAWKEN.

GOSHAWK is the Anglo-Saxon *gos-hafoc*, a "goose-hawk," *i.e.*, a hawk powerful enough to strike the wild goose. And SPARROWHAWK is a name dating from Anglo-Saxon times. There was a Sperhafoc elected Bishop of London, A.D. 1050, but ejected before consecration.

Next to the eagle, the raven, as being sacred to Odin, was of all birds the most common in the names of men. Particularly so among the North-men, whose war-standard he formed—there being seventeen persons called Rafn in the Landnama-bok. Among the Germans the name was not universally common, being scarce among the Goths and Saxons. In proper names, particularly as a termination, it often becomes *hramn*, *ram* or *ran*. The Ang.-Saxon has similar forms, *hræm*, *hrem*, *hremn*, for *hræfen*. The Old Frankish dialect, increasing the initial aspirate, makes *hramn*, *hram*, *hran*, into *chramn*, *cram*, *cran*. Hence Chramnus, son of Clothar 1st, Chrannus, (genealogy Merovingian kings.)

THE BRUTE AND ITS ATTRIBUTES. 97

SIMPLE FORMS.

Old Germ. Rabanus (Archbishop of Mayence, 9th cent.), Rapan, Ravan, Ramno, Ram, Chramnus, Chrannus. Old Norse Rafn. Eng. RABAN, RABONE, RAVEN, CRAM? RAMM? Mod. Germ. RABEN. Dan. RAFN. French RABAN, RABON, RABINEAU, RAPIN, RAPINEAU, RAVANNE, RAVON, RAVENEAU, RAFFIN, CRAMM?

Raban, Ram, Ran. Raven.

COMPOUNDS.

(*Bert*, famous) Old Germ. Hrambert, Rambert, 7th cent. French RAMBERT. (*Hari*, warrior) Eng. RAVENOR—Modern German RABENER. (*Rice*, powerful) Old Germ. Ramnerich, Ramerich, 10th cent.—Eng. RAMRIDGE.

LOCAL NAME.

Eng. RAVENSHEAR. (Ravnsöre, "Raven's point," on the Humber?)

Crâwe was the surname of an Anglo-Saxon lady, *Cod. Dip.* No. 685. And I do not find anything to indicate a different origin for our CROWE. Unless indeed it be CROWSON, which however is not certain, as it may be an extension of a root *crose*, and not the patronymic of CROWE.

Crow. Corvus.

The Old Norse *krakr*, Suio-Goth. *kraka*, a crow, occurs frequently in Scandinavian names, and seems to have been generally, though not invariably, a surname. Weinhold (*Altnordisches Leben*) refers to two brothers called respectively Hrafn and Kråk (raven and crow) as instances of names of similar meaning given in a family. Craca also appears as a simple name in the *Liber Vitæ*. Hence may be our CRAKE, CRAIK, CRAIG, CRAIGIE, and CRAKELL as a diminutive.

Crake. Crow.

M

98 THE BRUTE AND ITS ATTRIBUTES.

There are some names, CORBY, CORBIN, COR-
BETT, which we probably have from the French,
and which all appear in the Roll of Battle Abbey.
For these the French corbeau, corbin, raven,
Scotch "corbie," crow, naturally suggests itself.
But there is a Corbus, son of the Frankish king
Theoderic, 7th cent., for which Förstemann pro-
poses Ang.-Sax. ceorfan, to cut, carve, in a war-
like sense. We have, however, scarcely sufficient
data on which to form an opinion.

It may be doubted whether ROOKE is from
the bird, as there is a group of ancient names
with which it would fall in, though in any case
it is probably from the same root.

The swan seems a more natural type of
woman than of man. Yet, though it was more
common in female names, it was not exclusively
so used. Swane appears on the coins minted by
Scandinavian coiners at York. It occurs again
in the Domesday of Yorkshire, and is still a name
well known in that county. Mr. Worsaae remarks that "names of birds appear on the whole
to have been often assumed in the old Danish
part of England." The earliest name on record
from this origin is that of Swanahilda, wife of
Charles Martel, 6th cent. Weinhold (Deutsche
Frauen) observes, in reference to its use in the
names of women, that along with the beauty of
the swan, was contained a warlike sense derived
from the swan-plumage of the maids of Odin.
Two other forms are swen and swon, the latter
Anglo-Saxon.

THE BRUTE AND ITS ATTRIBUTES. 99

SIMPLE FORMS.

Old Germ. Soana, 9th cent. Suanus, *Lib. Vit.* English Swan, Soan. SWANN, SÓANE? Modern German SCHWANN. French Cygnus. SOULN? SUIN?

DIMINUTIVES.

Old Germ. Suanucho, 8th cent.—Eng. SWANNACK—Mod. Germ. SCHWANECKE—French SAUNAC. Old Germ. Suanila, 7th cent.—English SWANNELL, SWONNELL.

COMPOUNDS.

(*Bert*, famous) Old German Soanperht, Soamperht, 8th cent.—French SOMBRET. (*Burg*, protection) Old German Swaneburgh, 11th cent.—Eng. SWANBERG. (*Hard*) Old German Suanehard, 9th cent.—French SOINARD. (*Hari*, warrior) French SOINOURY. (*Wig*, war) English SWANWICK. (*Rat*, counsel, or *rit*, ride) Eng. SWENWRIGHT.

The nobility of the goose is not so obvious as that of the swan. Yet it was in ancient and honorable use as a man's name, if Genseric, the name of the great Vandal chief, is rightly referred by Grimm to *gänserich*, a gander. But it was no doubt the wild goose which gave the name, and if we consider, we shall see that this bird has some qualities calculated to command the respect of these early roving tribes. A powerful bird, strong on the wing, taking long flights to distant lands, marshalled with the most beautiful discipline of instinct, it formed no inapt emblem of those migratory plunderers who renewed their unwelcome visitations with each succeeding spring.

But I doubt very much whether GOOSE itself is from the bird. It corresponds with a French GOUSSE, and I have elsewhere placed them both

100 THE BRUTE AND· ITS ATTRIBUTES.

to an Old German Gauso. So also GOSLING, and the French GOSSELIN I include in the same group. GANDER I have already referred to a different origin, p. 74. The only two names that seem with any certainty to be from this origin are WILDGOOSE and GRAYGOOSE, Ang.-Sax. *græg-gôs,* a grey or wild goose.

Swan was usually—if not invariably a baptismal name—Goose sometimes a baptismal, and sometimes a surname, but Duck always a surname. There was a Northman surnamed Oend in the Landnamabok, and an Anglo-Saxon lady surnamed Enede in Flor, Wig. Our name AND might be from the Dan. and Swed. *and,* corresponding with the Old Norse *önd,* Ang.-Sax. *enede,* a duck. But we have also ANDOE, and this is very evidently the Old German Ando, 7th cent., from *anda,* zeal, spirit. So that AND may be more probably the same. DUCK again is not by any means certain—the Modern German DUCKE, Förstemann refers to Ang.-Sax. *dugan,* to be of use or value. So that DUCK may go along with DUGA, DUGGIN, TUCK, and other names elsewhere noticed, while DUCKLING will correspond with an Old Germ. Dugelin from the same root.

DRAKE again, along with DRAGE, and the French DRACHE, DRACQ, is most probably from a root *drac, drag, trag,* found in many Old Germ. names, and which Förstemann refers to Goth. *tragjan,* to run.

THE BRUTE AND ITS ATTRIBUTES. 101

It is not at all probable that the French CANARD signifies duck. It comes in its place as one of several compounds from a root *gan* or *can*, and it interchanges with another French name GANARD, which again corresponds with an Old Germ. Ganhart.

Thus it will be seen that though there were ancient surnames from the duck, there is no name at present, in French or English, which can with any certainty be referred to that origin.

From the Goth. and Anglo-Saxon *hana*, Old Norse *hani*, Mod. Germ. *hahn*, which signify the male of all birds, but particularly of the hen, may be HANN, HANNA, HANNY, HANNELL, &c. But it is rather more probable that this is only another form of *an*, which is from a different root.

The names derived from the peacock must probably have been bestowed on account of the magnificence, or perhaps the ostentation of the individual. There was an Icelandic chieftain of the tenth century, named Olaf Pâ (Anglo-Saxon *pawa*, Old Norse *pá*, pea-fowl), the splendour of whose dwelling is commemorated in the Laxdæla-saga, and who probably owed his surname to this cause. Hence might be PEA, PAY, POE, the Mod. Germ. PFAU and our PEACOCK and POCOCK, all of which I take to have been originally given as surnames.

Pea. Peacock.

Among the names which I think are to be otherwise explained are COOTE, same as COODE and GOOD—TEALE same as DEAL (Anglo-Saxon

102   THE BRUTE AND ITS ATTRIBUTES.

deal, illustrious) QUAIL, an aspirated form of
WALE—BUNTING, the patronymic of BUNT—
BUSTARD, BUZZARD, MALLARD, and PARTRIDGE,
which I take to be ancient compounds—and
GROUSE, referred to at p. 49.

OSTRICH I have elsewhere taken to be from
the Old Germ. name Austoric. In an Ang.-Sax.
charter Ostrich also occurs as a corruption of the
female name Ostrith.

SNIPE I cannot think to be from the bird,
though it is not improbable that it may be from
the same origin, Dutch and Dan. *sneb*, beak.
Compare an Ang.-Sax. Cnebba, "he that hath a
beak," (Kemble,—*Names, Surnames, and Nic-
names of the Anglo-Saxons.*)

Names derived from small birds enter into a
different category. They seem in most cases to
have been *sobriquets*—perhaps often pet-names,
given especially to women. So the Romans
employed *columba, pullus*, and *passer*—" my
dove," "my chick," "my sparrow." The same
prevails very much at present among ourselves;
indeed birds, with their pretty ways, seem a
natural emblem of woman.

None more so than the dove, which appears sometimes as a pet-name, as in the case of Tovelille
(little dove), the name of Valdemar of Denmark's
mistress, and Dyveke (dovie), that of the German
mistress of Christian the Second. Sometimes
apparently as a baptismal name, though Förstemann proposes Old Norse *dubba*, to beat, in pre-

THE BRUTE AND ITS ATTRIBUTES. 103

ference. However, I am inclined to place the following here, viz., to Goth. *duba*, Anglo-Saxon *duva*, Old High Germ. *tuba*, Dan. *tove*, dove. A rather common name among the early Danes in England seems to have been Tofi or Tobi.

SIMPLE FORMS.

Old Germ. Dubi, Tuba, Tupa, 9th cent. Old Dan. Tofi, Tobi. English DOVE, DOVEY, DOBIE, TUBB, TUBBY, TUPP, TOVEY, TOOVEY, TOBY. Modern German TAUBE. French DUBEAU, DUVEAU, DOBBÉ, DOUBEY, TOUVY, TOUVÉE.

Dove. Columba.

DIMINUTIVES.

Eng. DOBEL—French DOBÉL. English DOBLIN—French DOBELIN. Old Germ. Tubinso, 8th cent.—Eng. DUBBINS.

We have also TURTLE, corresponding with the name Tyrthell, of a bishop of Hereford, A.D. 688. This may be from Ang.-Sax. *turtill*, a turtle-dove, but it may be a question whether we should not look somewhat deeper. For we find the simple form Turta, a woman's name of the 8th cent. This seems to interchange with other women's names Truta and Trutta, and men's names Truto and Trut, 9th cent. May not then the Old High German *trût*, beloved, *trûten*, to caress, be the common origin of all these names, and also of that of the turtle-dove ?

It seems probable that THRUSH, TRUSH, and THROSSELL are from the bird (Ang.-Saxon *thrisc*, *throsle*.) There are, however, two Old German names, Traostilo and Trostila, 9th cent., which Förstemann refers to Old High German, *trôst*, comfort. But the Old Norse *thröstr*, Dan. *trost*, thrush, appears in the name (Thröstr) of three

Thrush. Turdus.

104 THE BRUTE AND ITS ATTRIBUTES.

Northmen in the Landnamabok, which makes the former derivation more probable.

A name which I take to be pretty certainly not from the bird is LINNET. We can trace this name from an Old German Linheit, through a Saxon Liniet, to our LINNET, French LINET, LINOTTE. It is a compound from the root *lin* (probably Old Norse *linr*, mild), with *heit*, state, "hood."

Fink.
Finch. FINK and FINCH, French FINK, seem to be probably from the bird (Ang.-Saxon *finc*, finch). This we find as a surname in Anglo-Saxon times; there was a Godric Finc (*Cod. Dip.* 923.)

Some other names from small birds, as BULFINCH, GOLDFINCH, CHAFFINCH, NIGHTINGALE, TITMUSS, which cannot reasonably be otherwise explained, have probably also been surnames. I do not class WREN along with these, for I think that it is the same as RENN, RENNIE, RENNO, French RENÉ (probably *rân*, rapine.)

Spar.
Sparrow. Spörr (sparrow), is found as a surname among the Northmen. And to the same origin I am disposed to refer our SPARROW, SPAR, SPARLING, and SPERLING (Germ. *sperling*, sparrow.)

There is some doubt about SWALLOW, though the type would not be an inapt one in ancient times, and though there is a Modern German Schwalbe to correspond. But we have also SWALE, and we find an Old German Swala, 9th cent., along with different compounds. So that our SWALLOW might be the same name, varying

THE BRUTE AND ITS ATTRIBUTES. 105

the termination. A probable etymon seems to be Anglo-Saxon *swélan*, to burn (North. Eng. "sweel"), *swol*, heat, fire.

It is not easy to see upon what principle the cuckoo and the owl should have given us names. Yet Gaukr (Old Norse *gaukr*, cuckoo), appears as a baptismal name in the Landnamabok of Iceland, and seems to be the origin of our GOWK and GOOK. We have also CUCKOO and GOUGOU —the Germans have KUCKKUCK, and the French have CUCU and CUQU. The Old Norse *gaukr* had a contemptuous sense similar to that which obtains in the North of England at the present day, where *gowk* signifies both cuckoo and also simpleton. Either this, or the peculiar habit by which this bird evades parental responsibilities, might account for its origin as a *sobriquet*, but not as a baptismal name, of which, however, I find no other instance than the above.

Gowk.
Cuckoo.

The owl is found more frequently in baptismal names, unless some other origin can be suggested for the following group than the Old High Germ. *ula*, Ang.-Sax. *ule*, owl.

SIMPLE FORMS.

Old German Ουλίας, Procop. 6th cent. English OWLE, OWLEY, HOOLE, HOWLE, HOWLEY. Modern German UHLE. French HOULIÉ.

Ule.
Owl.

DIMINUTIVES.

French ULLIAC. Old German Ulit—English HOULET, HULETT—French HOULET, HULOT.

COMPOUNDS.

(*Bert*, famous) Old German Ulberta, 8th cent.—English HULBERT—Modern German ULBRICHT—French HULBERT.

N

106 THE BRUTE AND ITS ATTRIBUTES.

(*Hard*, fortis) French HOULARD. (*Hari*, warrior) Old Germ. Ουλίαρις, Procop. 6th cent.—Eng. OWLER, ULIER—French HOULLIER. (*Man*) Old Germ. Ουλίμοῦν, Procop. 6th cent. —Eng. ULMAN—Mod. German ULLMANN—French OULMAN, ULMAN. (*Mar*, famous) Old German Ulmar, 8th cent.— Ulmerus (*Domesday*)—Eng. ULLMER.

It will be seen from the foregoing pages that while the number of names derived from birds is very considerable, a large proportion of them have been originally *sobriquets*, while others are found only as isolated baptismal names, and that the number of these which have been adopted into what I may call the regular Teutonic name-system is only three or four.

Of the whole tribe of fishes I do not think that there is one which is to be found with certainty in our names. FISH itself, and FISK, are certainly not from fish, pisces, though they might be from Ang.-Sax. *fisca*, fisherman. But I have elsewhere given a reason for proposing Welsh *ffysg*, impetuous, as obtaining at least in some cases.

Of other names BREAM is the Anglo-Saxon *brême*, famous, BURT is the same as BRIGHT, SMELT is the Ang.-Sax. *smelt*, mild, gentle, and TROUT is Germ. *traut*, beloved. TUNNY and MINNOW are TUNN and MINN with the endings *i* and *o* (*Chap.* 2)—HADDOCK is a diminutive—STURGEON is STURGE with a phonetic ending (*Chap.* 4)—HERRING and WHITING are patronymics—COD is another form of GOD ; PERCH and TENCH of BIRCH and DENCH (*Chap.* 7).

THE BRUTE AND ITS ATTRIBUTES. 107

There may remain a few names, originally *sobriquets*, derived from, or connected with fish. I lately met with the curious name ROTTEN-FYSCHE, like the name ROTTENHERYNG found by Mr. Lower in an ancient record of the town of Hull. There is a Northman in the Landnamabok with the not very elegant surname of Hwalmagi (whale-belly.) Mr. Lower produces a similar English name WHALEBELLY.

With the exception of the serpent, I doubt whether reptiles or insects have contributed to our nomenclature. Perhaps, however, another exception may be WASP, which would not be an unnatural etymon. Mr. Lower, moreover, adduces from a Sussex subsidy roll for 1296, a "Roger le Waps," (Ang.-Sax. *wæps*, another form of *wæsp*.)

Owing, as we may presume, to its supposed wisdom or subtlety, the serpent was anciently a common type in the names of men. In the names of women still more so, at least among the Germans. Weinhold *(Deutschen Frauen)* classes the snake and the swan together as the two types most peculiarly feminine. Respecting the former he waxes almost poetical—" Our ancestors had a different idea of this animal to that which we have ; they not only thought it beautiful, but from its insinuating and entwining habits, a type of the living woman. Moreover the mysterious power and magic craft that was attributed to it reminded them of the like mysterious subtlety

108 THE BRUTE AND ITS ATTRIBUTES.

and power of woman, and thus the name Linda had nothing of that hateful sound which our word snake conveys, but everything of insinuation and. enchantment that can be put into a word." I cannot but fear, however, that the original idea may have been a shade more prosaic.

From the Ang.-Sax. *wurm*, Old Eng. *worm*, Old Norse *ormr*, serpent, I take the following. Ormr was a very common name among the Northmen, there being twenty-four men so called in the Landnamabok. It does not seem to be a common name at present in Denmark.

SIMPLE FORMS.

Worm, Orm. Serpent. Old Germ. Wurm, 11th cent. Old Norse Ormr. Eng. WORME, ORME. Mod. German WURM. Mod. Dan. ORM. French WARMÉ?

COMPOUNDS.

(*Bold*, audax) Eng. WORMBOLT.* (*Wald*, power) Eng. WORMALD.

Snook, Snag. Snake? The next group, SNOOK, SNAKE, SNAGG, SNUGG, is not quite so certain. They might be from Ang.-Saxon *snôce*, Old Norse *snôkr*, *snâkr*, Dan. *snog*, snake. But the Old Norse *snâkr*, *snôkr*, as well as another word, *snöggr*, also means active, nimble, in a derived, or secondary sense. There is also a verb *snugga*, increpare, which might be the origin of SNUGG. There is a Snocca, whose name is signed to a charter of

---

* Or this may go along with the Mod. Germ. WARMBOLD, which Pott makes the same as WARNEBOLD, from the stem, *warin*, *warn*, elsewhere noticed. Indeed I am not quite sure that the name WORMBOLT itself is not of German origin.

THE BRUTE AND ITS ATTRIBUTES. 109.

Cadwalha of Wessex, comparing with our SNOOK.

From the Old Norse *lingvi, lingormr*, serpent, I am inclined to take the following, though Graff and Förstemann refer to German *gelingen*, to prosper. Lingi was the name of a king in the Norse Volsungasaga.

SIMPLE FORMS.

Old Germ. Lingo, 11th cent. Old Norse Lingi. Eng. LINGO, LING. French LINGE, LINGÉ.

Ling. Serpent.

PHONETIC EXTENSION.

Old Germ. Linguni. Eng. LINGEN.

COMPOUNDS.

(*Hard*, fortis) Eng. LINGARD. (*Hait*, state, condition) Old Germ. Lingeeid—French LINGET.

Of a similar meaning may be lind, Old High German *lint*, snake, basilisk, "lindworm." But there are other words which are also suitable, and while Weinhold proposes the above, Grimm refers also to *lind*, fountain, and Förstemann thinks of *lind*, gentle. The older writers again propose *lind*, the lime-tree, the wood of which was used for shields. It is probable that there may be an admixture of these different meanings, or of some of them. As a termination, in which it is only used in the names of women, *lind*, gentle, seems to me to be a very suitable meaning. In such more modern names as English LINDEGREEN, which seems to be from the German, the sense is no doubt that of the limetree. But there is a name LENDORMI in the directory of

110   THE BRUTE AND ITS ATTRIBUTES.

Paris, which seems clearly to be from the snake, and to mean lind-worm.

SIMPLE FORMS.

Lind.   Old Germ. Linto, 8th cent.   Eng. LIND, LINDO, LENT.
Serpent.   Mod. Germ. LINDE, LENDE.   Swed. LIND.   French LENTÉ.

COMPOUNDS.

(*Hari*, warrior) Eng. LINDER—French LINDER, LENDER. (*Man*) English LINDEMAN—French ? LINDEMANN.   (*Orm*, serpent) French ? LENDORMI.

Of names apparently from insects, MOTH and MOTE may be taken to be from Old Saxon *môd*, Mod. German *muth*, courage.   EMMETT is from Ang.-Sax. *emeta*, quies, an ill-fitting derivation for poor Robert Emmett.

Lastly—we have BUGG, and an unpleasant name it seems.   Yet there may be crumbs of etymological comfort for the BUGGS—indeed I think a good case may be made out to show that it is a name of reverence rather than of contempt. It is at all events of respectable antiquity, for Mr. Kemble (*Names, Surnames, and Nicnames of the Anglo-Saxons*), mentions an Anglo-Saxon lady, Hrothwaru surnamed Bucge, which he thinks can be derived from nothing else than the name of the odious insect.   The opinion of Mr. Kemble is not lightly to be gainsayed.   Still I should like to know whether there is any other proof that there were bugs in Anglo-Saxon times, or whether there is any other trace of the word in ancient Teutonic dialects.   For I have heard it maintained that the bug is one of the many importations—good and bad—that we have received

THE BRUTE AND ITS ATTRIBUTES. 111

during the last few centuries. In Old Eng. the word meant a spectre—" Thou shalt not be afraid of any bugs by night," in an old version of the Scriptures, referred to an imaginary, and not a real horror. The lady in question, Hrothwaru, surnamed Bucge, is described as " Abbatissa et sanctimonialis"—she was an abbess and a holy person. Now in some ages of the church a per-verted self-mortification did make *un*cleanliness next to godliness, and I could not undertake to say that it was never so in Anglo-Saxon times. Yet still it does not seem very likely that the feeling of reverence, amounting often to super-stition, which prevailed among that simple-minded people, would allow them to apply to a holy lady a term which could not be otherwise than one of contempt. Might not then Bucge be classed with several other ancient names, Buga, Buge, Buggo, referred to in another chapter, and probably, if it be taken to be a surname, having the meaning of bowed or bent, as with age or in-firmity? In that case nothing can be more natural than that the venerable abbess should be called by a name which would at once bring to mind the reverend years,—the cares of her high office—and the self-mortification which had com-bined to bow down her frame.* And even if it

---

* This stands as I had it before. But I now doubt whether Bucge was a sur-name at all. It seems to have been another—and perhaps more probably—her original name. I find that Mr. Haig, in some brief, but very judicious remarks on Anglo-Saxon names appended to a treatise on the cross at Bewcastle, has taken the same objection to Mr. Kemble's opinion.

112 THE BRUTE AND ITS ATTRIBUTES.

were perfectly clear that this lady derived her name from the bug and nothing else—other BUGGS, as I have elsewhere shown, may wear their name with a difference, and have no occasion to change it to Howard.

Having now gone through the names of animals, beginning with the bear, and ending with the bug, we may conclude this part of the subject with a general observation. We find that the names of the nobler quadrupeds, and of the nobler birds, have generally been assumed as baptismal names. That the names of the inferior quadrupeds, and of the smaller birds have been generally conferred as surnames. That any names that may be derived from fishes—and whether there are any is very doubtful—were also probably surnames. That—with the exception of the serpent—names from reptiles and insects, of which I know only one at all probable, were also probably surnames. And, in the exception of the serpent we may perhaps find a trace of that widely-prevailing worship or respect which was paid to that animal as the representative of evil throughout the world.

NOTE TO CHAPTER X.

To *eber* or *ever*, boar, we may put (*wacar*, watchful) Old German Eburacer, 8th cent.—Eureuuacre, *Domesday*—English EARWAKER. The only Old German name which has been distinctly recognised as having this termination is that of Odovacar, and it is creditable to the discernment of Förstemann to have suspected the same form in Eburacer—his judgment, it will be seen, being confirmed by the Domesday name of Eureuuacre (Evrewacre.) Both our own name and the Domesday are quoted from Lower. I must therefore amend the derivation of OVERACRE, and make it same as above.

CHAPTER XI.

THE GODS OF THE NORTH.

The names or titles of their deities have, among various nations and from the earliest period, been assumed as the names of men. Thus we read that Daniel was called by Nebuchadnezzar Belteshazzar, "according," as the king says, "to the name of my god." In this respect the Teutonic nations were not an exception, though, as it seems to me, the practice was more common among the Scandinavians than among the Germans. But it is to be borne in mind that the Scandinavian mythology is the only one which has come down to us in its integrity, and that of the corresponding Germanic mythology we have only fragments. There was a general, but by no means an exact coincidence between the two systems, and we are therefore not so well able to judge how far the names of their deities, the whole of which are not preserved, were assumed by the Germans as the names of men.

Before, however, entering upon the traces of the Northern pantheon, I must refer to two words signifying divinity, and both very common in Teutonic names, whose roots may go down deeper than the Odinic mythology, and perhaps even reveal to us a glimpse of an older and a purer faith.

o

114   THE GODS OF THE NORTH.

One of these is the same as our own word God, Goth. *guth*, Old Norse *gaud*, Ang.-Sax. *god*, Friesic *goad, guad*, &c., Old High German *goth. god, cot* (the last the oldest form.) Various derivations have been suggested for its origin, as that of Pott, from a Sansc. word signifying to hide, as found in *gûdha*, mystery, and that of Eichhoff, from Sansc. *guddha*, pure. The word occurs first—if we set aside the fabled Gothic king Gothila mentioned by Jornandes—in the name, as I read it, of a Dacian referred to by Horace,—

"Occidit Daci Cotisonis agmen."

Mr. Talbot says "The name of this Dacian, Cotison, appears to mean *Gottes sohn*, or Dei filius." Such a name, however, would be quite out of keeping with Old German nomenclature ; and, moreover, I take the nominative of Cotisonis to be, not Cotison, but *Cotiso*. This brings it in at once as an Old German name, corresponding with a later Godizo—*cot*, as Diefenbach observes, being the oldest High German form—and connects it with the present names GODSOE, GODSO, &c.

The word is very apt in Teutonic names to mix up with the adjective, *guot, god*, bonus, which may be from the same root, and also with Goth, the people's name, a word likewise perhaps allied in its root. But the most of the forms I think come in under this head. As an ending, however, I agree with Förstemann in preferring the people's name.

THE GODS OF THE NORTH. 115

SIMPLE FORMS.

Old Germ. Godo, Goddo, Goda, Gotti, Gudo, Guta, Cot, **God.**
Cotta, Cudo, Coutus, 6th cent. Ang.-Sax. Goda. Cudda, **Deus.**
Cuddi (*Lib. Vit.*) English GOD,* GODDY, GOOD, GOAD,
GOODEY, GOODDAY, GOTT, GOTTO, GUT, CODD, CODY, COODE,
COOTE, COTT, CUDD, CUDDY. Modern German GÖDE, GUDE,
GUTTE, KOTT, KUDE. French GODDE, GODEAU, GUDE,
GOUDEAU, GOUT, GOUTÉ, COUDY, COUTY, COUTEAU, COTTE,
COTTEY, COTTA, COTÉ, COTEAU, CUDEY, CUIT.

DIMINUTIVES.

Old German Godaco, 4th cent.—Mod. Germ. GÖDECKE—
French GOUDCHAU. Old Germ. Godila, Gudila, Coutilo, 7th
cent., Gothilas or Gudilas (*Jornandes*, mythical king of the
time of Philip of Macedon).—English GOODALL, COTTLE,
CUTTELL—Mod. German GÖDEL, GOTTEL, GÜTTEL—French
GOUDAL, GODEL, GUTEL, COTEL. Old Germ. Gotichin, 10th
cent.—Eng. GÖDKIN †— French GODQUIN, GAUDUCHON. Old
German Godelenus, Godelin, 6th cent.—English CODLING
—French GODILLON. Old German Cotiso (*Horace*), Godizo,
10th cent.—Eng. GODSOE, GOODESS, COUTTS—Mod. German
GÖTZE—French COUTZ. Old German Chotenza—French
COTTANCE, COUTANCE, COUTANSEAU. Old German Godemia,
9th cent.—Eng. GODDAM, COTTAM—French COUTEM.

PATRONYMICS.

Old Germ. Goding, 8th cent.—Eng. GODDING, GOODING,
CUTTING—Modern German GÖTTING, KOTTING—French
GOTTUNG.

COMPOUNDS.

(*Bald*, bold) Old German Godebald, 8th cent.—Godebol-
dus, *Domesday*—Eng. GODBOLD, GODBOLT. (*Bert*, famous)
Old Germ. Godabert, 7th cent.—French GAUDIBERT. (*Frid*,
peace) Old Germ. Godafrid, 7th cent.—English GODFREY—

---

* John God, the name of a writer who lived about the 17th century.

† Pott, in accordance with his general system of contractions—which, however, I cannot help thinking an erroneous one—makes our name GODKIN, as well
as GOAD and GODDEN, an abbreviation of Godard or Godfrey.

116 THE GODS OF THE NORTH.

Mod. German GOTTFRIED—French GODEFROID, GODEFROY, GODFRIN (French dimin. ?) (*Ger*, spear) Old Germ. Cuotker —Eng. GOODACRE. (*Gisil*, hostage) Old German Godigisil, Godesilus, Burgundian King, 5th cent.—English GODSELL, GOODSALL. (*Heid*, state, condition) Old Germ. Gotaheid, 9th cent.—English GODHEAD (*Manchr.*) (*Hard*) Old German Gotahard, Godehard, 8th cent.—Eng. GODDARD, GOODHEART, GOTHARD—Mod. German GODEHARD, GOTTHARDT—French GOUDARD, COUTARD, COUDERT, COTTARD. (*Hari*, warrior) Old German Godehar, Goter, 8th cent.—English GODIER, GOODEAR, GOODYEAR, GOODAIR, GOATER, COTTER—Modern German GOTTER, GUTER, KUTTER—French GOUTHIERRE, COUTIER, COUDER. (*Gifu*, gift) Ang.-Saxon Godgifu—later Godiva—English GOODEVE—French GAUDIVEAU. (*Lef*, superstes) Old Germ. Godolef, 6th cent.—Old Norse Gudleif —Eng. GOODLIFFE—Mod. German GOTTLEIB. (*Lac*, play) Old German Godolec, 9th cent.— Eng. GOODLAKE, (*Land*) Old Germ. Godoland, 8th cent.—Godland (*Lib. Vit.*)—Eng. GOODLAND. (*Man*) Old German Godeman, 8th cent.— Godeman, *Domesday*—Eng. GODMAN, GOODMAN, GUTMAN, COTMAN—Modern German GUTTMAN—French GOUTMANN, GUTMAN. (*Mar*, famous) Old Germ. Godomar, Cuthmar, 5th cent.—English CUTMORE. (*Mund*, protection) Old German Codemund, 9th cent.—Ang.-Saxon Godmund—Old Norse Gudmundr—Eng. GODMUND—French GOUDEMANT. (*New*, young) Old German Godeniu, Cotini, 8th cent.—Old Norse Gudny—Eng. GOODNOW—French CODINI. (*Ram*, raven) Old Germ. Godramnus, 8th cent.—Eng. GOODRAM. (*Rat*, *red*, counsel) Old Germ. Gotrat, Cuotarat, 8th cent.—Eng. GOODERED—French GAUTROT, CODERET, COUTROT, COTERET. (*Rit*, ride) Old .German Guderit, 6th cent.—Godritius, *Domesday*—English GOODWRIGHT, CUTRIGHT. (*Run*, companion) Old German Goderuna, Guterun, 7th cent.—Old Norse Gudrun—French GUTRON, CODRON, COTHRUNE. (*Rice*, powerful) Godricus, *Domesday*—English GOODRICK, GOODRIDGE, GODRICK—French GODRY, COUTRAY. (*Scalk*, servant) Old Germ. Godscalc, 7th cent.—Eng. GODSKALL, GODSCHALL

THE GODS OF THE NORTH. 117

(*Ward,* guardian) Old German Godoward, 8th cent.—Eng.
GODWARD. (*Wine,* friend) Old German Goduin, Codoin, 5th
cent.—Ang.-Sax. Godwine—Eng. GODWIN, GOODWIN—Mod.
German GUTTWEIN—French GOUDOIN, COUDOIN. (*Wealh,*
stranger) Ang.-Sax. Cudwalh—Eng. GOODWILL.

PHONETIC ENDING.

Old German Godin, Godino, Gudin, Cotini, 7th cent.—
Cotten (*Lib. Vit.*)—English GODDEN, GOODEN, COTTON,
CUDDON. French GODIN, GODINEAU, GUDIN, GUTTIN,
COUTIN.

PHONETIC INTRUSION OF. *n, r, l,* see *p.* 29.

Old Germ. Godenulf, 8th cent.—English GOODENOUGH.
Old German Godelher, 8th cent.—French GODELIER. Old
Germ. Godalmand, 6th cent.—Eng. GODLIMAN ? Old Germ.
Goderman, 9th cent.—Eng. GUTTERMAN*—Modern German
GÜTERMANN—French GAUDERMEN.

It is striking to observe how the names of the
Deity, in the three great languages of Europe,
show forth, each for itself, some one or other of
his attributes. The Romanic *Dios, Dio, Dieu,*
from a root signifying brightness, tells of his
glory—" He dwelleth in the light whereunto no
man can approach." The Germanic *God, Got,* if
we take the meaning of Eichhoff,† speaks of his
purity—" He is of purer eyes than to behold
vanity." If we take that of Pott, it refers to his
impenetrability—" Canst thou by searching find
out God ?" The Slavonic *Bog,* from a root ex-

---

* Perhaps this, along with some other names found in Suffolk Surnames,
may be a German name anglicized.

† Diefenbach, however, seems to distrust both these derivations. Grimm
observes (*Deutsch. Myth.*) that " the root-meaning of this word is a subject upon
which we require to be further enlightened."

118. THE GODS OF THE NORTH.

pressive of abundance, speaks of his bounty—
"He giveth us richly all things to enjoy."

But there is another, and a remarkable word
which was used by our Scandinavian forefathers,
and which is also found, though in a sense seemingly already somewhat debased, among their
German kinsmen, the Old Norse *as*, Ang.-Saxon
ôs, Goth. and High Germ. *ans*. The word does
not seem to have any immediate co-relatives in
the Northern speech—can we venture to connect
it with the Sansc. *as*, to be, giving it the meaning
of the self-existing, and comparing it with the
great "I am" of Scripture? In Old Norse *as*
was a general title prefixed to the names of all
the principal gods—thus Thor is called Asa-Thor,
Brag Asa-Brag, while Odin is called by pre-
eminence The As. In the Anses of the Goths
the sense seems to be a little lower, and more
that of demi-god, while the Ang.-Sax. *ôs* is rendered by Bosworth, perhaps rather under its
meaning, as hero. It is probable that in the
first instance the prefix *os* was confined to the
names of those who claimed to be descendants of
Odin, though in after times it might come to
be more generally assumed. All the founders of
the Anglo-Saxon kingdoms claimed a descent
from Odin, but it was only in the names of the
Northumbrian branch that the word was common.
Mr. Kemble observes "This word is nearly
peculiar to the royal (god-born) race of Northumberland, and occurs rarely in the south of

THE GODS OF THE NORTH.   119

England ; and when it does it is rather of Jutish or Angle than Saxon character."

It will be seen that there is in our names a considerable mixture of the two forms *as* or *os*, and *ans*; it is probable that most of the latter have come to us through the French. The roots *haz* and *hass* are rather liable to intermix with some of these forms.

SIMPLE FORMS.

Old Germ. Anso, Aso, 9th cent.··Old Norse Asa. Eng. ANNS, HANCE, ASAY, ASSEY? ASS? French ANCEAU, HANS, HANNZ, ASSE?

Ans, Os.
Divus.

DIMINUTIVES.

Old Germ. Ansich, Esic, 8th cent.—Eng. ENSCOE—Mod. German ESSICH—French ESSIQUE. Old German Ansila, Ansilo, Ensilo, Asilo, 5th cent.—Ang.-Sax. Esla—English ANSELL, ANSLOW, ONSLOW, ENSELL, ESSELL—Modern Germ. ENSLE, ASEL—French ANSEL, ANCEL, ASSELL. Eng. ASLIN, ESLING—French ANCELIN, ANSELIN, ENSLEN, ASSELIN, OSSELIN.

COMPOUNDS.

(*Bern*, bear) Old German Osbern, Aspirn, 8th cent.— Ang.-Sax. Osbeorn—Old Norse Asbiörn—English OSBORN, ASPERN. (*Bert*, bright) Old Germ. Anspert, Aaspert, Aspert, 7th cent.—French AUSPERT, ASPERTI. (*Berg*, protection) Old German Asbirg, 9th cent.—Eng. ASBRIDGE, ASBERREY. (*Gund*, war) Old German Ansegunde, 7th cent.—Fr. ASSEGOND. (*Gaud*, Goth) Old German Ansegaud, 9th cent.— Ang.-Sax. Osgot—English OSGOOD. (*Hard*) Old German Ansard, 8th cent.—English HANSARD—French ANSART. (*Hari*, warrior) Old Germ. Ansher, 8th cent.—Ang.-Saxon Oshere—Eng. ANSER, ENSER, ENZER, OSYER—Mod. German ANSER, ASSER—French AUSSIÉRE, ESSER. (*Helm*) Old Germ. Anshelm, 8th cent.—Eng. ANSELME, HANSOM—Mod. Germ. ANSELM—French ANSELME, ANCEAUME. (*Lac*, play).

120 THE GODS OF THE NORTH.

Old German Ansalicus, 7th cent.—Ang.-Saxon Oslâc—Old Norse Asleikr—Eng. ASLOCK, HASLUCK. (*Man*) Old Germ. Asman, Osman, 9th cent.—Asseman *Hund. Rolls.*—Eng. ASMAN, OSMAN—French ANSMANN. (*Mar*, famous) Old Germ. Ansmar, Osmer, 8th cent.—Osmer, *Domesday*—Eng. OSMER. (*Mund*, protection) Old Germ. Ansemund, Osmund, . 6th cent.—Ang.-Saxon Osmund—English OSMOND—French ANSMANT, ANCEMENT, OSMONT. (*Wald*, power) Old German Ansovald, Ansald, Oswald, 7th cent.—Ang.-Sax. Oswald—Eng. OSWALD—Modern German OSWALD—Ital. ANSALDI. (*Waru*, inhabitant) Old German Ansverus, Assuerus? 8th cent.—French ASSUERUS? (*Wine*, friend) Ang.-Sax. Oswine—Eng. OSWIN. (*Ulf*, wolf) Old German Asulf, Osulf, 7th cent.—French OZOUF.

Of Odin or Woden, the father of the gods, there are but few subsequent traces in the names of men. In the genealogies of the founders of the Saxon kingdoms, for instance, all of whom claimed descent from Woden, the name is never reproduced as is so generally the case with that of a distinguished ancestor. Perhaps it might be deemed presumptuous to assume the name of the father of the gods. "It seems," says Miss Yónge, "to have been avoided as Zeus was in Greece, and, to a greater extent, Jupiter in Rome." We find, however, one Old Germ. name Wotan, 9th cent., which seems to be from this origin. Possibly also our name WEDDON, which corresponds with the form the word has assumed in Wednesday, and in names of places, as Wednesbury, &c., may also come in here. The Scandinavian form Odin is rather more common. It is found among the names of Danish coiners in

THE GODS OF THE NORTH. 121

England, and it occurs twice in Domesday. The English name ODEN ·is adduced by Mr. Lower, and I find three persons called ODIN in the directory of Paris. The name does not occur in the directory of Copenhagen, nor do I find the corresponding German form in that country.

One of the principal titles of Odin in the Scandinavian mythology, was Oski, from Old Norse *ósk*, a wish, and which is supposed to signify " one who listens to the prayers or wishes of mankind." Grimm *(Deutsch. Myth.)* refers, in connection with the above, to the manner in which the German minnesingers of the 13th cent. personified the *wunsch* or wish. He gives a number of examples, on which he remarks :— " In the greater number of these instances we might put Deity instead of Wunsch. . . In the first example from Gregory, the Wunsch seems almost to be ranked as a being of the second order ; a servant or messenger of the higher deity." Pott remarks that we seem to have here " a trace of the German Cupid." From the above title of Odin seems to be Osk, a Scandinavian female name in the Landnamabok. Also the Mod. German name WUNSCH and the English WISH or WHISH, showing the respective High and Low German forms of the same word. The *Edinburgh Review* for April, 1855, suggests that the surname WISHART (*hart,* hard) may also have been formed from it. It may, however, perhaps rather be the same as the name Wisu-

P

122   THE GODS OF THE NORTH.

cart, Wisigard, of the wife of the Frankish king Theodebert. But WISHER and WHISKER, corresponding with a German WÜNSCHER, rather seem to belong to it. Possibly also WISHMAN and WHISKEYMAN (*Bowditch*.) The only Old Germ. name from this root seems to be a Wiscolo, 11th cent.

On two different occasions Odin appears in a sort of trilogy ; at the creation of the world in conjunction with Vili and Ve ; at the creation of mankind in conjunction with Hœnir and Lodur. These beings do not seem to have had an independent existence, but to denote, as Mr. Thorpe observes, "several kinds of the divine agency." The name Vili is from Old Norse *vili*, Anglo-Saxon *willa*, English " will," and may perhaps have here the meaning of creative impulse. According to Grimm the Anglo-Saxon *willa*, Old High Germ. *willo*, Old Norse *vili*, denote not only inclination, " voluntas and votum," but also " impetus and spiritus," the power that sets will in motion. From the personification of the will in this title of Odin, like that before referred to of the wish, may be the word *will*, so common in proper names. Miss Yonge, generally so trustworthy, has fallen into what I cannot but consider a grave error in following old Camden instead of the German philologists, and making *bil* and *fil* other forms of *will*.

SIMPLE FORMS.

Will. Voluntas, Impetus. Old Germ. Willo, Willa, Wilia, Guila, 5th cent. Eng. WILL, WILLOE, WILLEY, GUILLE, QUILL. Modern German

THE GODS OF THE NORTH. 123

WILLE, QUILE. Dan. WILLE. French VILLE, VILLY, VILLÉ, GUILLE, GUILLIÉ, QUILLÉ.

DIMINUTIVES.

Old Germ. Willico, Willic, 9th cent.—Uillech, *Lib. Vit.* —Eng. WILLOCK, WILKIE, WILKE, QUILKE—Mod. German WILLICH, WILKE—French QUILLAC. Old Germ. Willikin, 11th cent.—Eng. WILKIN—French VILLACHON, GUILLOCHIN. Old Germ. Willizo, 10th cent.—Eng. WILLIS, WILLS—Mod. German WILLIEZ, WILZ—French GUILLES. Old German Williscus, 9th cent.—Modern German WILLISCH—English QUILLISH.

PATRONYMICS.

Old German Willing, Willencus, 9th cent. English WILLING, WILLINK. Mod. Germ. WILLING, QUILLING.

PHONETIC ENDING.

Old German Willin, 11th cent. English WILLAN, GUILLAN. French VILLAIN, GUILAINE, GUILLON.

COMPOUNDS.

(*Bald,* bold) Old German Willabald, 8th cent.—French VILBAUT, GUILBAUT. (*Bern,* bear) Old German Wilbernus, 10th cent.—Eng. WILBOURN. (*Bert,* bright) Old German Willibert, Guilabert, 8th cent.—French GUILBERT. (*Brod,* dart) Old Germ. Willebort, 11th cent.—Ang.-Saxon Willibrord—French WILBROD. (*Burg,* protection) Old German Williburg, 8th cent.—Vilburg, *Lib. Vit.*—Eng. WILBUR*— Modern German WILLBERG. (*Gom, com,* man) Old German Willicomo, 9th cent.—Uilcomæ, *Lib. Vit.*—Eng. WILCOMB, WELCOME—Mod. German WILLKOMM. (*Fred,* peace) Old Germ. Wilfrid, 8th cent.—Anglo-Saxon Wilfrid—English WILFORD, WILFRED (*Christian name.*) (*Ger,* spear) Old German Williger, Williker, 8th cent.—French VILLEGRI, VILCÈRE. (*Gis,* hostage) Old Germ. Willigis, 5th cent.— *Ang.-Sax. Wilgis—Eng. WILGOSS. (*Hard*) Old German

---

* Hence the local name WILBRAHAM, originally Wilburgham. Pott certainly must have been napping when he derived it from Will (William), and Abraham !

124 THE GODS OF THE NORTH.

Willihard, Willard, 8th cent.—Eng. WILLARD—Modern German WILLERT—French WILLARD, VILLARD, GUILLARD, QUILLARD. *(Heid, state, condition)* Old German Williheid, Willibeit, 8th cent.—Eng. WILLETT—Mod. Germ. WILLET —French VILLETTE, GUILET, QUILLET. *(Hari, warrior)* Old German Williheri, Willeri, Willer, 6th cent.—English WILLER—Mod. Germ. WILLER—French VILLERIE, VILLER, GUILHÈRY, GUILER, QUILLERI, QUILLIER. *(Helm)* Old Germ. Willihelm, Guilhelm, 8th cent.—Ang.-Sax. Wilhelm, *(sixth from Woden in the genealogy of the kings of the East Angles)*—Eng. WILLIAMS, QUILLIAMS, GUILLAUME—Modern German WILHELM—Dan. WILHJELM—French VILLAUME, VILLIAME, WILLAUME, GUILLAUME, GUILHEM. To the last Förstemann places also Old German Willermus, Villerm, Guillerma, 10th cent., to which correspond French WILLERME, VILLERM, GUILHERMY; but *orm*, serpent, seems to me a possible origin, though we do not find it elsewhere as a termination. *(Man)* Old German Williman, Wilman, 9th cent.—Eng. QUILLMAN—Mod. Germ. WILLMANN—French WILLEMIN, VILLEMAIN, GUILLEMAIN. *(Mar, famous)* Old Germ. Willimar *(Swiss priest)*, 7th cent.—Eng. WILLMER— Mod. Germ. WILMAR—French VILLMAR. *(Mand, joy)* Old Germ. Willmant, 8th cent.—French GUILLEMANT. *(Mot, courage)* Old Germ. Willimot, 8th cent.—English WILLMOTT —French WILLEMOT, VILLEMOT, GUILLEMOT. *(Mund, protection)* Old German Willimund, Guilemund, 8th cent.— Uilmund, *Lib. Vit.*—Eng. WILLAMENT—French VILLEMONT, GUILLEMONT. *(Nand, daring)* Old Germ. Willinant, 6th cent.—English QUILLINAN. *(Rat, counsel)* Old German Willirat, 8th cent.—French VILLERET, QUILLERET.

Among the many titles of Odin—no fewer than 49 of which are enumerated in the Eddas— one of the principal was Grimr, from Old Norse *grima*, mask or helmet. To this origin Grimm, and, following him, Leo, place the ancient names of the following group, and though it is highly

THE GODS OF THE NORTH. 125

probable, as Förstemann suggests, that *grim*, sævus, intermixes, yet it is impossible to separate them, for the quantity of the vowel is no sufficient guide.

SIMPLE FORMS.

Old German Grimo, Grim, 7th cent.   Old Norse Grimr.   *Grime. Helmet.*
Eng. GRIM, GREAM, GRIME, CREAM, CRYME.   Mod. German GRIMM.   French GRIM, GREMÉ, GREMEAU.

DIMINUTIVES.

Old Germ. Grimila, 5th cent.   Eng. GRIMLEY.   Modern Germ. GRIMMEL.   French GRIMAL.

PATRONYMICS.

Eng. GRIMSON, CRIMSON.

COMPOUNDS.

(*Bald*, fortis, Old German Grimbald, 8th cent.—English GRIMBOLD,* GRIMBLE—French GRIMBLOT.   (*Bert*, famous) Old Germ. Grimbert, 7th cent.—French GRIMBERT.   (*Heit*, state, "hood") Old German Grimheit, 8th cent.—English GRIMMET.   (*Hari*, warrior) Old German Grimhar, Crimher, 8th cent.—English GRIMMER, CREAMER ?—Modern German GRIMMER, KRIMMER—French GRIMAR.   (*Mund*, protection) Old German Grimund, 9th cent.—Eng. GRIMMOND—French GRIMONT.   (*Wald*, power) Old Germ. Grimoald, 7th cent.—French GRIMAULT—Italian GRIMALDI†—Spanish GRIMALDO. (*Wine*, friend) Old German Grimoin, 8th cent.—French GRIMOIN.   (*Ward*, guardian) Old German Grimwart, Grimoard, 8th cent.—French GRIMOARD.

The following names, though perhaps more immediately connected with superstitions of a later date, may in their remoter origin be traced to Nikar, a title of Odin, in which he appears as a water spirit or dæmon.   Throughout Germany

---

* Of the 16th cent.   I do not find it at present.

† Hence the naturalized Eng. name GRIMALDI.

126 THE GODS OF THE NORTH.

and Scandinavia popular superstition has preserved some trace of him in this form. Iceland and the Faroe islands have their Hnikur, Norway and Denmark their Nök, Sweden its Neck, and Germany its Nix and Nickel. All these are water dæmons, appearing generally in the form of a horse, and usually obnoxious to mankind. England has its Old Nick, in which he appears directly in the form of the evil one. As the early Christian missionaries found it difficult to get rid of him altogether, they seem to have changed him into the devil. The following root Förstemann takes to be from this origin.

Nick, Neck.
Water Spirit.

SIMPLE FORMS.

Old German Niko, Neccho, 11th cent. English NICK, NECK, NEX, NIX, NIXIE. Modern German NICK. French NICK, NICAISE. *(The last name seems to be the Old High Germ. nichus, whence by contraction the Mod. Germ. nixe.)*

DIMINUTIVE.

English NICKLEN.

COMPOUNDS.

(Aud, prosperity) French NICAUD. *(Hard)* French NICARD.

EXTENDED ROOT=THE OLD NORSE *HNIKUR.*

Old German Nickar, 8th cent. English NICKER(SON). Dutch NECKAR. French NICOUR.

I am not sure that the father of the gods has not contributed to the commonness of the name of BROWN, for Brûni, from the Old Norse *brûn,* the brow, was one of the names of Odin, and a probable meaning seems to be that of having marked or prominent brows, which is considered to give power and dignity to a countenance.

THE GODS OF THE NORTH. 127

This is what Tennyson is generally understood
to mean by—

"The bar of Michael Angelo."

There are several Northmen called Brûni in the
Landnamabok, and one of them was surnamed
"The White," shewing clearly that at any rate
his name was not derived from dark complexion.

The name of Thor, the second of the gods,
from whom we have Thursday, seems also, like
that of Odin, to have been uncommon as a man's
name in its simple form. Finn Magnusen (*Lex.
Myth.*) states that though he could reckon up
about sixty compound names, he knew no instance
of the simple form.

We have, however, instances of its use in our
own district; there was a Thor, surnamed the
Long, an Anglo-Saxon or Northman of some note
about the time of the Conquest, and who was so
surnamed to distinguish him from another Thor
who had possessions in the same part of the
country.

The name Tor occurs several times in Domesday; this is the Scandinavian pronunciation, as
in Torsdag for Thursday, but it is not clear to
me that this name, as well as our own TORR and
TORRY, is not from another root, probably Old
Norse *döerr*, spear. Thor does not occur in the
directory of Copenhagen, though the patronymic
THORSEN is common.

Grimm thinks that Thor is only a contracted
form of Anglo-Saxon *thuner*, Old Norse *thonar*,

128 THE GODS OF THE NORTH.

thunder. And, in fact, Thuner was another Ang.-Sax. form of his name, as found in Thunresdæg for Thursday. There was an Anglo-Saxon named Thuner, a "limb of the devil," A.D. 654, (*Rog. Wend.*) And we have still the name THUNDER, though uncommon.

The High German form is Donar, as found in Donnerstag for Thursday. This occurs, though not frequently, as a proper name in Germany ; there was a noble family on the Rhine called Donner von Lorheim (*Grimm's Deutsch. Myth.*) Our names DONNOR and TONNOR I apprehend to be the same. There are also some Old German names compounded with it.

Names compounded with Thor were very common among the Northmen, and we have several corresponding. They seem also to have occurred, though rarely, among the Germans, and one or two are to be found in French.

COMPOUNDS OF THOR.

Compounds of Thor. (*Bar*, bear) Thurbarus, Goth. leader 3rd cent.—Eng. THUR-BER. (*Biörn*, bear*) Old Norse Thorbiörn—English THOR-BURN. (*Gar*, spear) Old Norse Thorgeir—Eng. THURGAR. (*Gaut*, Goth) Old Norse Thorgautr—Turgot (*Domesday*)—English THORGATE, THOROUGHGATE, TARGETT ? THURGOOD, THOROUGHGOOD—French TURGOT. (*Kettle*†) Old Norse

---

* Probably from the sacred bear by which Thor was accompanied. Hence THORBURN is similar to OSBURN, p. 119.

† According to Grimm, from the famous kettle which Thor captured from the giant Hymir for the gods to brew their beer in. (*Deutsch. Myth.*) Ketill itself was a common Scandinavian name, and hence Eng. KETTLE. The name THUR-KETTLE then corresponds with another Eng. name ASHKETTLE, Old Norse Aske-till, Ang.-Sax. Oscytill. The French have QUETIL and ANQUETIL, probably for Ansquetil. In Denmark I only find the patronymic KETELSEN, KJELDSEN, KJELSEN.

THE GODS OF THE NORTH. 129

Thorketill—Eng. THURKETTLE—French TURQUETIL. (*Kell*, a contraction of *Ketill*, according to Grimm) Old Norse Thorkell—Eng. THURKLE. (*Man*) English THORMAN. (*Môd*, courage) Old German Thurmod, 9th cent.—Old Norse Thôrmôdr—English THURMOTT. (*Stone*) Old Norse Thôrsteinn—Eng. THURSTON. (*Wald*, power) Old Norse Thôrvalldr—Eng. THOROLD—French TOURAULT? (*Vid*, wood) Old Norse Thôrvidr—Eng. THOROUGHWOOD.

The name of this god in all its three different forms appearing to be synonymous with thunder, it may not be amiss to enquire whether there are any other names which, as perhaps also signifying thunder, may contain other forms of his name. There seems indeed to me a considerable probability that the name of this god, or rather of some god wielding the thunder, is of older date than the rest of the Odinic mythology. There is a root *dun*, which in the opinion of Förstemann, is at least as probably from Old Norse *duna*, thunder, as from Ang.-Sax. *dunn*, brown. Along with this may be included *din* and *don*, Old Norse *dyn*, Ang.-Sax. *dýne*, Belg. *don*, all having the same meaning of thunder. This, however, must be taken for nothing more than a conjecture, though an Old German name Dunitach (=Thunder-day, like Thunresdæg, Thursday?) seems rather to give a colour to it.

SIMPLE FORMS.

Old German Duno, Duna, Dono, Dina, Tunno, Tunna, Tinno, 7th cent. Anglo-Saxon Dun, Dunna. Eng. DUNN, DINN, DONN, DONNEY, DONNO, TUN, TUNNO, TUNNAY, TUNNY, TON, TINNEY. Mod. Germ. DONN, TONNE. French DONNE, DONAY, DONNÉ, TONNE, TUNNA, TINÉ.

Dun, Don, Din.

Thunder?

Q

130 THE GODS OF THE NORTH.

DIMINUTIVES.

Old Germ. Dunila, Donnolo, Tunila, Tinnulo, 7th cent. —Eng. DUNNELL, DONNELL, TUNNELL, TUNALEY, DINELEY, TINLEY—French TONNELLÉ, TINEL. Eng. DONELAN, TINLING—French DONNELLAN.

PATRONYMICS.

Ang.-Sax. Dunning. Eng. DUNNING, DINNING, DINING. TINNING.

COMPOUNDS.

(*Ger*, spear) Eng. DUNGER—Fren. DONCKER. (*Stan*, stone) Anglo-Saxon Dunstan—Eng. DUNSTONE, TUNSTAN. (*Wine*, friend) English DUNAVIN.

According to Grimm, a name under which traces of Thor are still to be found in Germany is Hamer, and which is derived, no doubt, from the celebrated hammer or mallet which he wielded. Hence may probably be the following.

SIMPLE FORMS.

Hammer.
Malleus.
Old German Hamar, Hamari, 8th cent. Eng. HAMMER, HEMMER, AMOR? AMORY? Mod. Germ. HAMMER, HEMMER. French HAMOIR, AMORY?

The name of Bragi or Brag, the god of poetry, seems unquestionably to have been borne by men. Finn Magnusen says "Nomen Bragi sæpe viris, et non raro poetis celebribus in Septentrione contigit." There was among others a celebrated Icelandic bard named Bragi Skalld (Bragi the poet.) The English BRAGG, and the French BRAG may be from this origin, but the Eng. BRAGGER seems uncertain.

The name of Baldur, the Apollo of the Germans, seems to occur in one Old German name Baldor. Another, Baldro, 9th cent., (our

THE GODS OF THE NORTH. 131

Boldero ?) seems less certain. There was also an Old German name Baldher, from a different origin, to which, as being more common, our Balder, and the French Baltar, may more probably belong.

The name of Tyr, son of Odin, in its Gothic form Tius, may perhaps be found in Teias, a Gothic leader of the 6th cent., and with which our Tyas and Tyus seem to correspond. But the Goth. *thius*, minister, an allied-word may put in a claim.

It does not seem probable that Lôk or Lôki, who represented the evil principle in the Northern mythology, would be much in favour for baptismal names. I find it only as a surname in the Landnamabok, and it might have been given for mischievousness or malignity of disposition. The group of names which we have, viz., Eng. Locke, Lockie, French Loque, Locque, Loch, &c., might, however, be from the same root, Old Norse *lokka*, to deceive, seduce. A title of Lôki was Loptr or Loftr, " the aerial ;" this was a common Scandinavian name, and hence possibly may be Eng. Loft. The corresponding deity among the Saxons was Sæter, from whom we have Saturday, and whose name seems to have the same meaning, Ang.-Saxon *sætere*, a seducer. I have found Satter as an English name, though very uncommon.

Mr. Lower *(Pat. Brit.)* makes a suggestion respecting the name of Flint, which I reproduce, without, however, being able to throw any

132   THE GODS OF THE NORTH.

further light upon it. "Our Ang.-Sax. ancestors had a subordinate deity whom they named Flint, and whose idol was an actual flint-stone of large size. The name of the god would readily become the appellation of a man, and that would in time become hereditary as a surname. Such it had become, without any prefix, at the date of the Hundred Rolls (1273), and even in Domesday we have in Suffolk an Alwin Flint. The town of Flint, in North Wales, may however have a claim to its origin."

The following group Förstemann connects with the name of the goddess Frigga or Frikka, wife of Odin. The Ang.-Sax. *frec*, Mod. Germ. *frech*, bold, is also a probable root.

SIMPLE FORMS.

Frigga or Frikka. Wife of Odin. Old Germ. Fricco, Frich, 8th cent. Ang.-Sax. Freok, *Cod. Dip.* 971. English FRICKE, FRICKEY, FRECK, FREAK. Mod. German. FRICK, FRECHE. French FRICQ, FRECH.

COMPOUNDS.

(*Here*, warrior) Old German Fricher, 8th cent.—English FRICKER—Mod. Germ. FRICKER—French FRIKER.   (*Wald*, power) French FRICAULT, FRECAULT.

There are some roots which seem to be connected with the names of certain deities, though there is scarcely sufficient reason for supposing that they are derived from them. Thus the root *had, hath*, war, Grimm thinks is connected with the name of the god Hödr, a son of Odin. And the root *sib, sif*, friendship, with the goddess Sif, wife of Thor. Also the root *nand, nan*, with the goddess Nanna, wife of Baldur. And the root

THE GODS OF THE NORTH. 133

fraw, fri, expressive of freedom or authority, with the goddess Freya. But if the Odinic mythology be, as some think, of no very profound antiquity—if Odin were a real personage, the founder of a kingdom and of a dynasty, it is possible that the names may have been those of men before they were those of gods.

The names of some of the Valkyrjur, maidens of Odin appointed to select the victims in battle, seem, as elsewhere noticed, to have been common in the names of women. One of these is Hrist, probably from Old Norse *hrista*, to shake (perhaps to brandish as a sword), whence seem to be Eng. and French Rist. In connection with this name a suggestion occurs to me. There is a root *crist* found in Frankish names from the 7th to the 9th cent., and which Förstemann takes to be from the name of our Lord. But some of the compounds, as those with *hild*, war, savour rather of a heathen sense, and it now occurs to me as possible that *crist* may be nothing more than the Frankish form of *hrist*, the aspirated *h* forming *c* as noticed at p. 46. To this then may belong English Christ, Christo, Christy, Chrystal; Mod. Germ. Christ, Christel; French Christ, Christy, Christel, or some of them. It may be objected to this theory that all the Frankish names in question occur in Christian times, but on the other hand it is from Christian records that most of the Frankish names known to us are derived. However, I only throw this out as

134 THE GODS OF THE NORTH.

a suggestion, but the fact that as well as CHRIST we have also RIST and GRIST seems rather to suggest a common origin for the three.

There is a race of dwarfs or elves which frequently come before us in the Northern mythology, and the names of many of which are enumerated in the Eddas. The root *alb, alf, elf* is very common in Teutonic names, among the Anglo-Saxons as well as others ; the older German writers referred it to the mountains of the Alps, and the words connected therewith ; but Grimm and Massmann connect it with these mythological elves. Some of these beings seem to have been noted for their wisdom, and others for their mechanical skill, and this may perhaps be the idea present in some of these names, as for instance, Alfred (*rêd,* counsel.)

Alb, Alf.
Elf.

SIMPLE FORMS.

Old Germ. Albo, Alpho, Albi, 8th cent. Eng. ALVEY, ALPHA, ALP, ELBOW, ELVE, ELVY, ELPHEE. Mod. German ALF, ELBE. French ALBO, ALBY, AUBÉ.

DIMINUTIVES.

Old German Albecho, 11th cent.—Ælfech, *Domesday*— Eng. ELPHICK, ELVIDGE. Old German Albizo, Aluezo, 8th cent.—Albsi, *Lib. Vit.*—Eng. ALVIS, ELVIS, ELVES—French AUBEZ. Old Germ. Albila, 6th cent.—Mod. Germ. ALBEL —Fr. AUBEL.

PHONETIC EXTENSION.*

Old German Alfan, Elbenus, Albini, Alpuni, 8th cent. Eng. ALBAN, ALBANY, ALPENNY, HALFPENNY ? Modern Germ. ELBEN. French ALBIN, AUBIN, AUBIGNY, AUBINEAU.

---

* The Latin root may intermix in these names.

THE GODS OF THE NORTH. 135

PATRONYMICS.

Old Germ. Albinc, 8th cent.   French ALBENQUE.

COMPOUNDS.

(*Ger*, spear) Old German Alfger, Halbker, 8th cent.—
Ang.-Sax. Alfgar—Eng. HALFACRE?   (*Haid*, state, con-
dition) Old German Albheid, 8th cent.—Eng. HALFHEAD?
(*Hard*) 'Old German Alfhard, Albheid, 8th cent.—English
ALVERT—French AUBARD.   (*Hari*, warrior) Old German
Alfheri, Albheri, 8th cent.—English ALVARY, ALBERY,
ELVERY, AUBERY—French AUBIER, AUBERY.   (*Man*) Old
German Alpman—Eng. HALFMAN?   (*Red*, counsel) Old
Germ. Alberat, 8th cent.—Anglo-Saxon ``Älfred—English
ALFRED—French ALBARET, ALFRED, AUBRIET.   (*Run*, com-
panion) Old German Albruna,† *Tacitus*, Albrun, 10th cent.
—Fr. AUBRUN.   (*Wer*, defence?) Old German Albwer, 8th
cent.—French AUBOUER.   (*Wine*, friend) Alboin, Lombard
king, 6th cent.—Fr. AUBOUIN.

As well as the dwarfs or elves there was a
race of giants 'which figure in the Northern
mythology as at continual enmity with the gods
—the foundation of the myth (if not a relic of a
still more ancient one), being perhaps to be traced
to the subjugation by Odin and his followers of
the older and less civilized races with whom they
came in contact.   But I do not know that there
are any names in which the sense can with sufficient reason be taken to mean more than large
stature.

Many of the names derived from the weather
appear to have a mythological origin.   Thus
Frosti was the name of one of the dwarfs or elves

---

† A woman mentioned by the historian as highly venerated by the Germans
for her wise counsels.   Among the various readings of the name, this is most in
accordance with ancient nomenclature.

136 THE GODS OF THE NORTH.

before spoken of; the meaning, according to Finn Magnusen, is "gelidus vel gelu ac frigora efficiens." Our nursery hero, Jack Frost, may possibly have his origin in the old northern mythology. Frosti occurs as a Scandinavian name in Saxo; and we have FROST and the diminutive FROSTICK. Frost occurs frequently in the Hundred Rolls, temp. Edw. 1. Mr. Lower observes *(Pat. Britt.)* that "one Alwin Forst was a tenant in Co. Hants, before Domesday, and his name by a slight and common transposition would become Frost." This is true, but the converse might also apply, for *forst* is an Ang.-Sax. form of *frost.* In another name, however, FROST-MAN, given by Mr. Bowditch, I should take the proper form to be Forstman.

One of the Valkyrjur was called Mist, which must be from Anglo-Saxon *mist,* English "mist." There is an Old German name Mistila, 9th cent., which Weinhold takes to be a diminutive of the above. We have MIST, and MISTER, which may possibly be a compound.

Of the same meaning and from a similar source to Mist might naturally be supposed to be FOG and FOGGO. This, however, is less certain; there is a root *foc,* for which Förstemann proposes Old Norse *fok,* flight, to which they might be put.

The name of an old, probably a mythical king of Denmark was Snio (snow.) It enters into some Old German names, and hence may be our SNOW.

THE GODS OF THE NORTH. 137

I thought before that SNOWBALL might be a compound (*bald*, fortis), but on the whole I now think that Mr. Lower's derivation from a feudal tenure *(Pat. Britt.)* is to be preferred.

It seems probable that something of a mythological origin may be assumed for the English RAINBOW, the German REGENBOGEN, and the French RAINBEAUX and REGIMBEAU—the two latter names appearing to bespeak for themselves a considerable antiquity.

The system of personification which pervaded the Northern mythology, and which, extending its influence deep into the middle ages, has left its traces on the popular mind of Europe to the present day, extended to the earth, the sun, the moon, day and night, summer and winter. The sun in Northern mythology was reckoned among the goddesses, being feminine in all Teutonic languages except our own. The moon, on the other hand, was masculine, being the brother of the sun. In some parts of Germany the peasantry still give the sun and moon the title of *Frau* and *Herr*—Mrs. Sun and Mr. Moon.

I thought before that the names signifying sun and moon might be derived from this personification of Northern mythology, but I am now inclined to think that as the worship of the heavenly bodies is probably a relic of an earlier creed, so the names too may be of a date anterior to the Odinic system. From the Goth. *sauil*, Old Norse *sól*, the sun, may be the following.

138-   THE GODS OF THE NORTH.

SIMPLE FORMS.

Old German Sol, Sola, 8th cent.   Also probably, as it
Sole. seems to me, though Förstemann places them elsewhere,
Sun. Σαούλ " Dux barbarorum," *Zosim.* 4th cent., Saul, 9th cent.
Sol, Saul (*Domesday*). Sola, *Lib. Vit.*   Eng. SOLE, SOLEY,
SOUL, SAUL.   Mod. Germ. SOHL.   French SOL, SOLE, SAUL,
SOULE, SOULÉ.

COMPOUNDS.

(*Burg*, protection) Old German Solburg, 9th cent.—Eng.
SOLBERRY.   (*Hari*, warrior) French SOULERY, SOLIER.
(*Hard*) French SOLARD.   (*Rat*, counsel) French SOLERET.

Of the same meaning, according to Förstemann, is the name Sunno, of a Frankish prince of
the 4th cent., and with which may correspond
Eng. SUN.

The moon, in Old Norse *máni*, figures in
Northern mythology as the brother of the sun.
Máni occurs as a Scandinavian name in the
Landnamabok, but I do not find any trace of it
as an ancient name among the Germans.   Perhaps
from this origin may be English MOON, MOONEY,
and MAWNEY.

There is a root *lun*, which Förstemann, finding
names of a similar sort, thinks may be from Old
High Germ. *luna*, Mid. High Germ. *lune*, change
of the moon.   He holds the word to be related
to the Latin, but not borrowed from it.   Luno is
mentioned in Ossian as a Scandinavian armourer,
and the maker of Fingal's sword.   But the
name, at least in that form, could hardly be
Scandinavian.   None of the ancient names given
by Förstemann correspond with the following.

THE GODS OF THE NORTH. ·139

Lun.
Moon change.

SIMPLE FORMS.

Eng. LUNE, LOONEY.   French LUNEAU.

DIMINUTIVE.

French LUNEL.

COMPOUNDS.

(*Aud*, prosperity) French LUNAUD.   (*Hard*) French (or Ital. ?) LUNARDI.

Some other names, such as English SUNRISE, SUNSHINE, German MONSCHEIN, Germ. MORGENSTERN (morning-star), ABENDSTERN (evening-star), MORGENROT (morning-red), ABENDROT (evening-red), &c., may be from a similar origin. Abendrot was the name of a spirit of light (*Grimm's Deutsch. Myth.*)   I do not know what to say of such names as FAIRWEATHER and FINEWEATHER, except that the Germans have similar —*e.g.*, SCHÖNWETTER, BÖSEWETTER, &c.

The worship of the goddess Hertha (the personified earth) was no doubt of remote antiquity among the Germans.   She is reckoned among the goddesses in the system of Northern mythology, but this, I take it, is a relic of a more ancient myth.   A root *jord*, which seems to be from Old Norse *jörd*, terra, comes before us in some ancient names, and we seem, as below, to have it both in this and the Saxon form *eorthe*.

SIMPLE FORMS.

Jord.
Earth.

Eng. EARTH, EARTHY, JURD.   Modern German ERD. French JORDY, JOURDY, JOURDE.

COMPOUNDS.

(*Hari*, warrior) French JORDERY, JOURDIER.

140 THE GODS OF THE NORTH.

EXTENDED ROOT.

Old German Jordanes,. Jordanus, 5th cent.*—Jordan' Jurdan, *Lib Vit.* Eng. JORDAN, JORTIN. Modern German JORDAN. French JOURDAN.

The name of Rinda, one of the wives of Odin, is derived by Grimm from Old High Germ. *rinta*, Ang.-Saxon *rind*, Eng. "rind," and explained as signifying the crust of the earth. From this source may be our names RIND, RINDLE, RINDER, though *rand*, shield, is liable to intermix. There is one Old German name Rindolt, which Förstemann brings in as above.

The Old High German *himil*, heaven, occurs frequently in ancient names, where it is probably from a mythological origin. We have the corresponding Saxon word in our name HEAVEN, but it may be, as Mr. Lower thinks, only a cockney form of Evan. HIMMEL is a Mod. Germ. name and HIMELY is a French name.

From a similar mythological personification may be our names SUMMER and WINTER. These have been supposed to be derived from persons having been born at these seasons. But it seems to me that though a man might naturally enough be called Friday because he was born on a Friday; or Christmas, Noel, or Yule, because he came into the world at that festive season; yet to call him Summer because he was born in all summer, seems rather wide. The names at any rate are of great antiquity. In Neugart's *Codex*

---

* Förstemann thinks that some of these names may be derived from the sacred river Jordan.

THE GODS OF THE NORTH. 141

Diplomaticus Alamanniæ there are two brothers.
called respectively Sumar and Wintar, A.D. 858.
And Winter was the name of one of the companions of the Anglo-Saxon Hereward. With
the English SUMMER correspond Mod. Germ. and
Danish SUMMER, French SUMMER and SOMMAIRE.
The French has also SOMMERARD, which seems
to be a compound. Winter is likewise a Modern
German, Danish, and French name, but there is
another word, elsewhere introduced, which is apt
to mix up with it.

The Eng. name TROLL and the French TROLY
may be from Old Norse *tröll*, a demon. There
was a Danish family named Trolle, of great importance in the 15th or 16th cent., who bore in
their coat of arms a headless troll or demon. The
name and the arms were assumed in commemoration of an exploit of their ancestor in decapitating
a troll-wife, which, sooth to say, he seems to have
done in anything but a chivalrous manner, while
she was presenting him with a drinking horn
(*Thorpe's North. Myth.*) Trollo was also an Old
German, and Trolle is a Mod. Germ. name. Our
name TRAIL is supposed (*Folks of Shields*) to be
a corruption of Troll, though etymologically it
would go better to another root.

The following root Förstemann derives from
Goth. *alhs*, Old High Germ. *alah*,* Anglo-Saxon

---

* The *h* was no doubt in this and similar cases strongly aspirated, like the
Mod. Germ. *ch*.

142 THE GODS OF THE NORTH.

ealh, temple. An intermixture with *halig,* holy,
is easy—indeed the two roots seem to be cognate.

SIMPLE FORMS.

Alk, Elk. Temple. Old German Alach, Elachus, 8th cent. Allic, Alich *(Domesday).* Eng. ALLICK, ALLIX, ELK. French ALIX, ELCKÉ.

COMPOUNDS.

(Hard) Old German Elkihard, 8th cent.—Anglo-Saxon Alcheard, *Cod. Dip.* 520.—English ALLCARD—French AUCHARD. *(Here,* warrior) Old German Alcher, 8th cent. —English ALKER—French ALQUIER. *(Ward,* guardian) Eng. AUKWARD ?†

According to the tradition of Northern mythology the first man and woman were created out of two pieces of wood left by the waves upon the beach. The man was called Askr, which means " ash," and we may presume has reference to the wood out of which he was formed. Many men in after times were called after the Teutonic Adam, as, for instance, Æsc, son of Hengist. We have ASK, ASH, and various compounds, but I am inclined to think that the warlike sense derived from the spear (which was made of ashwood), is stronger than the mythological.

The first woman was called Embla, the meaning of which is not very clear. According to Grimm, it is derived from Old Norse *aml, ambl,* assiduous labour, a derivation which, however, seems open to considerable doubt. The name of the Teutonic Eve is still found in the Christian names of women, as Amelia, Emily, and Emmeline, though

---

† Though this seems a natural compound, yet we find no ancient name to correspond, and it may be only a corruption of ALLCARD.

THE GODS OF THE NORTH. 143

perhaps the Latin Emilia may intermix. The word, however, was by no means confined to the names of women, being found in the name Amal, of one of the Anses, or deified ancestors of the Goths. It was most common among the West Goths; scarce among the Saxons.

SIMPLE FORMS.

Amal, Emel.

Old German Amala, Amelius, Emila, Almo, names of men, 5th cent. Amalia, Ambla, Emilo, names of women, 8th cent. Eng. HAMMILL, EMLY, EMBLOW. Mod. German EMELE, EMMEL. French AMAIL, EMMEL.

DIMINUTIVES.

Old German Amalin, Amblinus, men's names, 9th cent. Amelina, woman's name, 11th cent.—Amelina (woman?) *Lib. Vit.* English EMLYN, EMBLIN, EMBLEM? French AMELIN, EMELIN.

PATRONYMICS.

Old German Amalung, 5th cent. English HAMLING, HAMBLING. Mod. Germ. AMELUNG. French AMELING.

COMPOUNDS.

(*Gar*, spear) Old German Amalgar, Emelgar, 7th cent.— English ALMIGER, ELLMAKER. (*Hard*, fortis) Old German Amalhart, Amblard, 9th cent.—French AMBLARD. (*Hari*, warrior) Old German Amalhari, Amalher, 5th cent.—Eng. AMBLER, EMELER. (*Man*) Eng. AMBLEMAN, AMPLEMAN— Mod. German HAMELMANN. (*Rice*, powerful) Old German Amalaricus, West Gothic king, 6th cent., Almerich, 10th cent.—French ELMERICK.

Lastly—I do not think that any of the names which seem to be derived from the classical deities are so in reality. There are indeed MARS, BACCHUS, VENUS, CUPID, and PAN; also French MARS, JANUS, MINERVE, and German PALLAS, but not " ut sunt divorum." BACCHUS is the

144 THE GODS OF THE NORTH.

same as BACKHOUSE, which seems local, like the Modern German Backhaus and Backhof. VENUS is also local, as shown by Mr. Lower—"Stephen de Venuse, Miles, temp. Edw. 1st." CUPID I put along with CUBITT and CUPIT. MARS corresponds with an Old German Marso, 7th cent., which Förstemann refers to the German tribe of the Marsi. And the French name MINERVE I take to be local, from a place called Minerbe, in North Italy, though I apprehend that the place is named after the goddess.

CHAPTER XII.

THE HEROES OF THE NORTH.

In the dim morning of the history of our race, when we first find the German tribes wrestling in their rude strength against the power of imperial Rome—there stands out—drawn by the hand of an immortal historian—one taller by a head and shoulders than the rest. Foiling in their own science Rome's trained legions—baffling by his singleness of purpose her crafty policy— resisting by his honesty her fatal blandishments —we find in him, the hero, the patriot Arminius, the first embodiment of that principle of unity which Germany has yet fully to learn. With what generous appreciation the great historian describes his country's foe—with what elegant irony he points his description. *" The deliverer of Germany without doubt he was, and one who assailed the Roman state, not like other kings and leaders, in its infancy, but in the pride of imperial elevation; in single encounters some-times victorious, sometimes defeated, but not worsted in the general issue of the war; he lived thirty-seven years; twelve he was in possession of power; and amongst barbarous nations his memory is still celebrated in their songs; his

---

* Tacitus, "Annals." Oxford translation.

S

146 THE HEROES OF THE NORTH.

name is unknown in the annals of the Greeks, who only admire their own achievements ; nor is he very much celebrated among us Romans, whose habit is to magnify men and feats of old, but to regard with indifference the examples of modern prowess."

And yet how few are there at the present day who know even the name of this first great man of our race ; another Arminius, the founder of one of the *isms*, is probably of much more extensive reputation.

The name of Arminius, Armin, Ermin, or Irmin, is not, as some writers have supposed, the same as Herman ; this opinion, as Förstemann observes, is to be considered as now completely set aside. It is a simple, not a compound word ; its root is *arm, erm, irm*—the ending *in* being only phonetic ; its meaning, as Grimm observes, is altogether obscure. Many names compounded from it occur in the genealogies of the kings of Kent and Mercia, as Eormenric, Eormenred, Eormengild, &c. There are traces of Irmin as the name of a deity in the ancient -German mythology.

SIMPLE FORMS.

Armin.
Irmin.
Old German Arminius, leader of the Cheruski, 1st cent., Ermin, Irmino. English ARMINE, ARMENY, ERMINE, HARMONY. Mod. German ERMEN. French ARMENY. Italian ERMINI.

COMPOUNDS.

(*Ger*, spear) Old German Irminger, 8th cent.—English ARMINGER, IREMONGER ? (*Gaud*, Goth) Old German Ermin-

THE HEROES OF THE NORTH. 147

gaud, 8th cent.—French ARMINGAUD. (*Dio*, servant) Old
Germ. Irmindiu, Ermenteo, 7th cent.—French ARMANDEAU,
ARMENTÉ. (*Deot*, people) Old German Irmindeot, 8th cent.
—French ARMANDET.

"The older and the simple form of Irmin,"
says Förstemann, "runs in the form Irm, Erme,
Irim." To this I place the following.

SIMPLE FORMS.

Old Germ. Ermo, Irma, 8th cent. Eng. HARME. Mod. Erm, Irm.
Germ. HERM. French HERMÉ, HERMY.

DIMINUTIVES.

Old German Irmiza, 10th cent.—English ARMS.—Modern
German ERMISCH—French ARMEZ, HERMES. Old German
Hermulo, 9th cent.—Mod. Germ. ERMEL—French HERMEL.
Old Germ. Ermelenus, 7th cent.—French HERMELINE.

COMPOUNDS.

(*Gar;* spear) Old German Ermgar, 5th cent.—English
ARMIGER. (*Gis*, hostage) Old German Ermgis, 8th cent.—
French HERMAGIS. (*Geltan*, valere) Old Germ. Ermegild—
Eng. ARMGOLD. (*Had*, war) Old Germ. Ermhad, 9th cent.
—Eng. ARMAT—French ARMET. (*Hari*, warrior) Old Germ.
Ermhar, 8th cent.—Hermerus, *Domesday*—Eng. ARMOUR;
ARMORY, HARMER—French HERMIER. (*Rad*, council) Old
Germ. Ermerad, 8th cent.—Eng. ORMEROD.

But for the most part the heroes of the North
are legendary rather than historical. At the
same time it must not be overlooked that legends
and traditions are the most ancient vehicle of
history, and that as a general rule we may accept
the existence of the hero, whatever amount of
faith we may be disposed to place in the story of
his achievements.

The most ancient heroic poem in the Teutonic
language at present discovered is probably the

148   THE HEROES OF THE NORTH.

Ang.-Saxon lay which recounts the achievements of Beowulf the Scylding.   The Scyldings (in Ang.-Sax. Scyldingas, in Old Norse Skiöldungar) were an illustrious race, the descendants of Scyld or Skiöld, a name which respectively in Anglo-Saxon and Old Norse signifies "shield."   The Danish traditions make their Skiöld the son of Odin and first king of Denmark, but the Anglo-Saxon genealogies make their Scyld an ancestor of Woden.   Beowulf, as the son of Scyld, was *the* Scylding by pre-eminence, though all his people are called Scyldings.   Our names SHIELD, SKELD-ING, SCOLDING, SKOULDING, I have taken to be from this origin.   As to the name Beowulf, if we could suppose the right form to be Beahwulf, it would be from Ang.-Sax. *beag, beah,* ring, crown, bracelet, and would correspond with an Old Germ. Baugulf.   Or it might be, as Bosworth has it, a contraction of Beadowulf.   Mr. Kemble, however, and following him, Miss Yonge, derive it from *beo,* harvest.

According to the Ang.-Saxon genealogy the father of Scyld was called Sceaf, which signifies sheaf: and whence perhaps the English name SHEAF.

The legend, as related in the Anglo-Saxon chronicles is that, as an infant and asleep, he was brought by the waves in a small boat, with a sheaf of corn at his head, to an island of Germany called Scani or Skandza.   The inhabitants, struck by the apparently miraculous nature of the circum-

THE HEROES OF THE NORTH. 149

stances, adopted him, gave him the name of Scef, and eventually making him their king, he reigned in the town which " was then called Slaswic, but now Haithebi"—the locality marking the legend as probably an Angle one. Very poetically in the poem of Beowulf (though the legend is by mistake transferred to his son Scyld), he is represented, at the close of his long and prosperous reign, as placed by his own last command in a ship, surrounded by the arms and ornaments of a king, and again committed to the waves which had laid him as an infant on the shore. The story is so poetical, both in sentiment and expression, that I may be excused in quoting a part of it from the translation of Mr. Thorpe, again remarking that Scef, and not Scyld, should have been the hero.

> " Scyld then departed
> at his fated time,
> *the* much strenous, to go
> into *the* Lord's keeping.
> They him then bore away
> To *the* sea-shore,
> his dear companions,
> as he had himself enjoined.
>
> * * * *
>
> There at the hithe stood
> *the* ring-prowed ship
> icy and eager to depart,
> *the* prince's vehicle.
> *They* laid then
> *the* beloved chief,
> *the* dispenser of rings,

150 THE HEROES OF THE NORTH.

in *the* ship's bosom,
the great *one* by the mast :
there were treasures many
from far ways
ornaments brought
I have not heard of *a* comelier
keel adorned
With war-weapons
and martial weeds.

*   *   *   *

Men cannot
say for sooth,
councillors in hall
·heroes under heaven,
who that lading received."

Does not this warrior's funeral, in the oldest heroic poem of our language, remind us somewhat in its tone of Tennyson's ode on the funeral of Wellington ?

Among the heroic romances of Germany the most notable is the *Nibelungen-lied*, or lay of the Nibelungs. The name Nibelung is a patronymic or a diminutive of the name Nibel, which the German writers refer to Old High German *nibul*, Modern German *nebel*, a mist. Mone, in his *Heldensage*, has with great labour collected examples of this name from all parts of Germany, as well as the countries into which the Germans have imported it. From the following list of Lombard names, it will be seen that he makes the name Napoleon identical.

Neapoleo de Ursinis, 1306—Napolio Spinula, naval captain of the Gibellines at Genoa, 1336—Nevolonus, a con-

THE HEROES OF THE NORTH.   151

fessor at Faenza, 1280—Neapolion, head of the Gibellines at
Rome under Fred. 2nd—Napolione Visconte di Campiglia,
1199, &c.   .

He further remarks, though in language somewhat wanting in clearness, " The name seems to
have come to the Lombards through two causes.
When we find the Napoleons in alliance with the
Gibellines (more evidences thereof would be desir-
able), the question arises whether or not this is
accidental.   Napoleon is the older "name* and
more nearly expresses the correct form.   I cannot
account for its transmission to Italy except
through the Frankish conquest of Lombardy.†
But as yet I have not been able to meet with any
ancient examples."

I do not find the form Nibelung, except in the
name NEFFLEN quoted by Mr. Bowditch, and
which looks like an English name, though there
are several examples of the simple form Nibel as
below.

SIMPLE FORMS.

Old Germ. Nivalus, Nevelo, Novol, 6th cent.   English Nibel, Nivel.
                                                       Mist.
NIBLOE, NIVOLEY, NEVILLE, NOVELL, NOBLE? Mod. Germ.
NEBEL, NIBEL.   French NIBELLE, NIVELLEAU, NOVEL.

The German hero-book refers to a king
Orendel or Erentel, whom it describes as the
greatest of all heroes, and whose wife was the
most beautiful among women.   In the story of
his shipwreck and subsequent adventures Grimm
traces a close resemblance to the story of Ulysses.

---

* Older than Neapoleon I suppose is all that he means.
† Why not by the Lombards themselves?

152 THE HEROES OF THE NORTH.

The origin of the name appears to be Ang.-Sax. *earendel*, a beam of light, a star. An Ang.-Sax. hymn to the Virgin Mary in the *Cod. Ex.*, seems to apostrophize her under this title.

> " Eala Earendel, engla beorhtast."
> O star, brightest of angels !

Arendel. Star. The names Aurendil, Orendil, Orentil, occur frequently in the 8th and subsequent centuries ; among others was a count of Bavaria. In the old metrical romance of Sir Bevis of Hamptonn, his " good steed" is called by the name of Arundel, which has been presumed, though I think without sufficient reason, to be a corruption of *hirondelle*, a swallow. ARONDEL is not uncommon as a French name ; there are five persons so called in the directory of Paris. In Holinshed's copy of the *Roll of Battle Abbey* is an Arundel, but it is not in all the others. The English name ARUNDEL may be in all, or in some cases, from the place.

Of Weland, the wonderful smith, the Vulcan of Northern mythology, many traces are to be found in this country. There is a place in Berks, called Wayland's Smithy, which retains its name from Ang.-Sax. times. And our names WELAND and WAYLAND are, I take it, derived from him. The etymology of the name I have elsewhere referred to.

The father of Weland is called in Ang.-Saxon Wada, in Old Norse Vadi, in Old High German Wato. He was the son of the celebrated king

THE HEROES OF THE NORTH. 153

Vilkinr or Wilkin, by a mer-wife, and was a hero of gigantic size. Some traces of him are to be found in our early English poets ; Chaucer celebrates Wade's boat called Guingelot. In the Scôp or Bard's Tale we are told that "Wada ruled over the Helsings," a Scandinavian tribe of whose name memorials are to be found in Helsingor (now Elsinore), Helsingfors, in Finland, and perhaps in one place in England, Helsington in Cumberland. As to the meaning of his name, Grimm says "I think that it is derived from his having, like another Christopher, with his son upon his shoulders, *waded* over the nine-ell-deep Grœnasund, between Seeland, Falster, and Moen." Our names WADE, WADD, WATT, &c., elsewhere introduced, I have hence derived.

The brother of Weland was called in Anglo-Saxon Aegel, in Old Norse Egil. As Weland was celebrated as a smith, so was his brother as an archer, and precisely the same legend is related of him as of the Swiss Tell. Having been commanded by the king Nidung to shoot an apple off the head of his son, and having taken two arrows from his quiver, the king demanded his reason for so doing, and received the same bold reply that was given to the tyrant Gessler. The same myth re-appears elsewhere with slight variations and different heroes ; whether the legend of Aegel is the foundation of all the others, or whether it is to be traced back to a still more ancient source, we cannot say. The following

T

154 THE HEROES OF THE NORTH.

group of names are to be referred to this origin, but the meaning of the word is obscure. The form *ail* for *agil* seems, as Förstemann observes, to be more particularly Saxon.

SIMPLE FORMS.

Agil, Ail. Old German Agila (king of the West Goths, 6th cent.), Aigil, Egil, Ailo, Aile. Eng. EAGLE, EGLEY, AYLE, ALE, AYLEY, OILEY. Mod. Germ. EGEL, EYL. Fren. AIGUILLÉ, EGLE, EGLY, AYEL, AILLY.

DIMINUTIVES.

Old Germ. Agilin, Aglin, Ailin, 7th cent.—Eng. AGLIN, EAGLING, AYLING—French EGALON.

COMPOUNDS.

(*Bert*, bright) Old German Agilbert, 7th cent.—Anglo-Saxon Aegelbeorht—French AJALBERT. (*Ger*, spear) Old Germ. Egilger, Ailger, 8th cent —Eng. AILGER. (*Hard*) Old German Agilard, Ailard, 7th cent.—English AYLARD—French AILLARD. (*Hari*, warrior) Old Germ Agelhar, 8th cent.—Eng. AGUILAR.* (*Man*) Old Germ. Aigliman, 6th cent.—Eng. AILMAN, ALEMAN. (*Mar*, famous) Old German Agilmar, Ailemar, 8th cent.—Eng. AYLMER. (*Rat*, counsel) Old German Agilrat, Eilrat, 8th cent.—French AILLERET. (*Ward*, guardian) Old German Agilward, Ailward, 8th cent. —Eng. AYLWARD. (*Wine*, friend) Old German Agilwin, Eilewin, 8th cent.—Ang.-Sax. Aegelwine—Eng. AYLWIN.

The son of Weland was called in Ang.-Saxon Wudga, in Old Norse Vidga, in Old High Germ. Wittich, and in an unpublished Low Germ. poem referred to by Grimm, Wedege. The name, according to Grimm, signifies *silvicola*, being a diminutive from the root *wudu, witu, vidr*, wood. Corresponding English names are WEDGE, VETCH, WITTICH, WHITTOCK.

---

* This name is, I believe, immediately derived from Spain.

THE HEROES OF THE NORTH. 155

Other heroes of the Nibelungen Leid were Gunter or Gunther, Hagan, Hildebrand, and Hawart. The German Gunter corresponds with the Old Norse Gunner of the Volsungasaga ; the etymon is *gunn, gund,* war, and hence our names GUNTER, GUNTHER, GUNNER, &c., introduced in another place. Hagan, according to Lachmann *(Kritik der sage von den Nibelungen),* is " more than heroic." The name comes in a group else-where noticed ; according to Grimm its meaning is *spinosus,* thorny. Hawart is described as a king of Denmark, and I think that our corres-ponding names (HAWARD, HOWARD, &c.) are more particularly of Scandinavian origin. Never-theless, according to Mone, there are many in-stances of the name Haward or Hawart in Southern Germany during the 12th and two following centuries.

It is to be remarked that in the poetic legends of various countries we frequently find something uncommon or supernatural attaching to the birth or to the rearing of the hero. Sometimes he is the offspring of a mortal and a divinity ; some-times of a mortal and one of the nobler animals, as the bear or the wolf ; more frequently he is only reared or suckled by one or other of these animals. Grimm has remarked *(Deutsch. Myth.)* that something of the heroic character frequently attaches to one not born in the natural manner, but cut untimely from his mother's womb. Such, among many other instances, was the Scottish Macduff.

156 THE HEROES OF THE NORTH.

Macbeth—I bear a charmed life, which must not yield
  To one of woman born—
Macduff—   Despair thy charm ;
  And let the angel whom thou still hast served
  Tell thee—Macduff was from his mother's womb
  Untimely ripped—
Macbeth—Accursed be the tongue that tells me so.
  . . . I'll not fight with thee.

The title of *ungeborne*, "unborn," is given to some of the heroes of German romance, and the corresponding one of *ôborni* occurs in the Scandinavian Eddas. From this latter I before took to be our name OBORN ; it might, however, be properly Hoborn, from the root *hoh*, *hoc*, celsus.

It is also to be noted that the wearing of the hair long, or curled, or fastened up in a peculiar manner, was held among the ancient Germans as a badge of the hero. To this I have alluded in another chapter.

It is to be remarked that among the Anglo-Saxons and other Teutonic races there was a sort of nobility arising from connection with a distinguished ancestor. The whole of the descendants of such a man frequently took his name, with the addition of *ing*, giving the meaning of "descendant of," not as their own individual name, but as a family or clan name. Thus as well as being a simple patronymic, in the manner referred to at p. 31, *ing* is often applied as the badge of a family or tribe. Thus from the name of Uffa, king of East Anglia, his posterity were called Uffings (Uffingas.) In the life of St. Guthlac mention is made of a Mercian nobleman who is said to have

THE HEROES OF THE NORTH. 157

been "of the 'oldest race, and the noblest that was named Iclingas." In the genealogy of the Mercian kings there is an Icil, who most probably was the founder of the Iclings. The names HICK, HICKLING, &c., elsewhere introduced, I have referred to this origin.

The Billings were a powerful and celebrated family in North Germany during the 10th and 11th centuries, and there is some trace of them a hundred years further back. *(Grimm's Deutsch. Myth.)* We seem to have a still earlier trace of them in the Scôp or Bard's song, where we are told that " Billing ruled the Werns" (the Verini), a people on the Elbe. There was also a noble family named Bille in Denmark. The Billings seem, from the names of places, as well as from the names of families, to have made considerable settlements in England. The etymology is elsewhere referred to.

The Harlings (Herelingas) are another people mentioned in the Scôp or Bard's song. Their locality was on the banks of the Rhine. There is a castle of Alsatia called Brisach, from which all the adjacent country is called Brisach-gowe, which is reported to have been anciently the fortress of those who were called Harlungi *(W. Grimm's Held. Sag.)* We have the names HARLING, HARLE, referred to in next chapter.

Sometimes *ing* has the still wider sense of nationality. Thus from Skiöld the son of Odin, and first king of Denmark according to Danish

158   THE HEROES OF THE NORTH.

tradition, the Danes were called Skiöldungar (Skiöldings).

The Hokings are a people mentioned in the Scôp or Bard's song—"Hnæf ruled the Hokings." These seem to have been a Frisian people, and to have derived their name from a Hoce mentioned in the poem of Beowulf. Mr. Kemble observes *(Archæological Journal)* that Hocè is "a really mythical personage, probably the *heros eponymus* of the Frisian tribe, the founder of the Hokings, and a progenitor of the imperial race of Charlemagne." The etymology and the names we have corresponding are referred to in another place.

It would seem that a *surname* acquired by some distinguished man was often conferred on others as a baptismal name, probably on no other ground than that of hero worship. Thus Magnus, king of Norway, acquired the name of Barfot (bare-foot), on account of having adopted the kilt when in Scotland. And Barfot ever since has been a common name in the Scandinavian countries. BAREFOOT is also an English name. Probably also on the same principle it is that we have the name of IRONSIDE. There was a celebrated Norwegian pirate named Olver, who, setting his face against the then fashionable amusement of tossing children on spears, was christened by his companions, to show their sense of his odd scruples, Barnakarl or Barnakal, "babies' old man." Hence possibly may be our name BARNACLE.

THE HEROES OF THE NORTH. 159

There is yet another name which I have reserved as a worthy conclusion to this chapter. Very famous in early English romance was the Danish hero Havelok, of whom some traces are still to be found in the local traditions of Lincolnshire. There is a street in Grimsby called Havelock Street; and there was, according to the "History of Lincolnshire," a stone, said to have been brought by the Danes out of their own country, and known as "·Haveloc's stone," which used to form a land-mark between Grimsby and the parish of Wellow. That the Danes would take the trouble of bringing a stone out of their own country is not very probable—but it is possible. The stone in question may have been a bauta or memorial stone ; and some Northman, from a motive of superstition or pious friendship, might wish to consecrate the shores of his new home with the memorial of a revered ancestor.

Havelok was not a common Danish, as it is not a common English name. Its proper Scandinavian form I should assume to be Hafleik, from *haf*, the sea, and *leik*, sport. War being the game of heroes, the termination *leik* or *lac* is frequently coupled with a prefix of that meaning. But there was another pastime in which the Northmen pre-eminently rejoiced. To them the sea was " a.delight," and there were bold Vikings who could make the boast that they had " never slept under the shelter of a roof, or drained the horn at a cottage fire." Thus then the name

160 THE HEROES OF THE NORTH.

Havelok, "sea-sport," would be a name than which we could find no more appropriate for one of the wild sea rovers.

And among the many brave men raised up in our time of great need, let us acknowledge with thankfulness and pride the dauntless valour of the old Danish hero, tempered by a christian spirit, in our own gallant HAVELOCK.

CHAPTER XIII.

THE WARRIOR AND HIS ARMS.

In an age when war was—if not the "whole duty," at least the main business of man—names taken from the pastime in which he delighted, and the weapons in which he trusted, were as natural as they were common. And, directly or indirectly—from words signifying war, battle, death, slaughter, victory—from words signifying strength, valour, and fierceness—from words signifying arms and warlike implements—or from words signifying to wound, to slay, to strike, to crush—there are probably as many names from this source as from all other sources put together.

Of such ungentle origin were the names of women as well as men. Indeed two of the principal words signifying war, *hild*, and *gund* or *gunn*, are more especially common in the names of women, and sometimes, as in the Norse Gunhilda, and the Old German Hildigunda, these two words are joined together. They are still retained in some female christian names, as in the Danish Hille and Gunnila; in our Matilde, French Mathilde; and in the French and Ital. Clothilde. The reason for the particular use of these two words in the names of women is to be found in Northern mythology, where Hild and Gunn are

162 THE WARRIOR AND HIS ARMS.

the names of two of the Valkyrjur, maidens appointed by Odin to select the victims in battle, and also to wait upon the heroes in Valhalla.

Our name HILL has been generally supposed to be local, from residence on or near a hill. But I think it will be clear, from the place which it takes in the following group, that it is, at least in some cases, from *hild*, battle, which, even in ancient names, appears often as *hill*. The Frankish form *child* was common in the names of the Merovingian period, and we have a few in which it occurs, but it is rather singularly wanting in the names of France.

SIMPLE FORMS.

Hild, Hill. War. Old German Hildo, Hilt, Hillo, Childi, Chillo, 7th cent. Eng. HILT, HILL, HILLY, CHILD, CHILL, CHILLY. Modern German HILD, HILT, HILL.

PATRONYMICS.

Old Germ. Hilding, 8th cent.—English HILDING. Eng. HILLSON.

COMPOUNDS.

(*Ber, per,* bear) Old German Hiltiper—English HILBER—French HILBER. (*Bert,* bright) Old German Hildebert, 6th cent.—Mod. Germ. HILBERT—French HILPERT. (*Brand,* sword) Old Germ. Hildebrand, 7th cent.—Eng. HILDEBRAND—Mod. Germ. HILDEBRAND—French HILDEBRAND. (*Ger,* spear) Old German Hildigar, 6th cent.—English HILGERS—Modern German HILGER—French HILGER. (*Hard*) Old Germ. Heldiard, 8th cent.—English HILDYARD, HILLIARD. (*Here,* warrior) Old Germ. Hildier, 8th cent.—Eng. HILDER, HILLYER, HILLARY, CHILDERS—Modern German HILLER—French HILLER, HILAIRE. (*Ram, ran,* raven) Old German Childerannus—English CHILDREN.* (*Man*) Old German

---

* The female name Childeruna (*run*, companion) might also put in a claim.

THE WARRIOR AND HIS ARMS. 163

Hildeman, 6th cent.—Childman, *Hund. Rolls*—Eng. HILL-MAN, ILLMAN, CHILLMAN—Mod. German HILTMANN, HILL-MANN—French CHILMAN. (*Mar*, illustrious) Old German Hildimar, 6th cent.—Eng. HILMER, HELLMORE—Mod. Germ. HILLMER, HELMAR. (*Mod*, courage) Old German Hildimod, 8th cent.—Eng. CHILLMAID ? (*Rad*, counsel) Old German Hildirad, 8th cent.—Eng. HILDRETH—French HILLAIRET. (*Rice*, powerful) Old German Hilderic, Goth. king, 4th cent.—Eng. HILRIDGE.

LOCAL NAME.
(*Drup*, *trup*, corruption of *thorp*, a village) English HILLDRUP—Mod. Germ. HILTRUP.

As a termination *hild* was extremely common, particularly among the Franks. But as in modern names it would change into *hill*, it becomes confounded with the diminutive ending *el* or *il*.

From the Ang.-Sax. *guth*, Old High German *gund*, *gunt*, Old Norse *gunn*, are the following :—

SIMPLE FORMS.
·Old German Gundo, Gonto, Cund, 9th cent. English GUNDEY, GUNN, CONDY, CUNDY, COUND, COUNTY, COUNT ? Modern German KUNDE, KUNTE, KUNTH. French GONDE, GON, CONTÉ, CONTI.

Gund, Gunn. War.

DIMINUTIVES.
Old Germ. Gundicho, 8th cent.—Eng. GUNDICK—Mod. Germ. KUNTKE. Old Germ. Gundila, Cundilo, 7th cent.—English GUNNELL, CUNDELL—Mod. Germ. GUNDEL—French GONDAL, GONDOLO, GONELLE. Old German Gunzo, Gonzo, Cunzo, Conzo, 7th cent.—English GUNS, COUNTZE—Modern German GUNZ, KUNZ—French GONSSE, KUNZÉ. Old Germ. Gunzila, 8th cent.—Eng. CONSELL, COUNSELL—Mod. Germ. GÜNZEL, KÜNSEL—French KUNTZLÉ, CONSEIL—Span. GON-ZALES. Old Germ. Guntiscus, 7th cent.—Eng. GONDISH.

PATRONYMICS.
Eng. GUNNING, GUNSON.

164 THE WARRIOR AND HIS ARMS.

COMPOUNDS.

(*Bald*, fortis) Old German Gundobald, Burgundian king, 5th cent., Gumbald, 9th cent.—English GUMBOIL—French GOMBAULT. (*Hard*) Old German Gundhard, 8th cent.—French GONDHARD, GONTARD. (*Here*, warrior) Old German Gunther, Gonthar, Cuntaher, Cundher, 8th cent.—Old Norse Gunnar—Ang.-Sax. Guthere—English GUNTHER, GUNTER, GUNNER, COUNTER, CONDER—Mod. Germ. GÜNTHER, KONTER —French GONTHIER, GONTIER, CONTER, CONTOUR. (*Lac*, play) Anglo-Saxon Guthlac—Eng. GOODLAKE, GOODLUCK.* (*Nand, nant*, daring) Old German Gundinand, 5th cent.—French CONTINANT. (*Ram, ran*, raven) Old German Gundram, Condramnus, 6th cent.—Eng. CONDRON. (*Rat*, counsel) Old German Gundrat, 8th cent.—French GONDRET. (*Rice*, powerful) Gundericus, Gothic chief, 3rd cent., Vandal king, 5th cent., Gunderih, 8th cent.—English GUNDRY, GUTHRIE, GUNNERY, CONDRY. (*Wine*, friend) Old Germ. Gondoin, 7th cent.—French GONDOUIN. (*Steinn*, stone) Old Norse Gunsteinn—English GUNSTON. (*Salv*, anointed ?) Old German Gundisalvus, Gonsalvus, 9th cent.—Span. GONSALVO.

A third word signifying war is Ang.-Sax. and Old High German *wig*, Old Norse *vig*, which, losing the guttural, becomes in many cases *wi*, both as a termination, and also in the middle of a word. In other cases it assumes a prefix of *g* or *c*, as referred to at p. 46.

SIMPLE FORMS.

Wig, Wick. War.

Old German Wigo, Wico, Wihho, 9th cent. Wig, genealogy of Cerdic, king of the West Saxons. Wiga, Domesday Yorks. English WIGG, WICHE, WICK, WICKEY, VICK, QUICK, WYE, QUY. Modern German WICK, WICH, WEIH. French WIGY, VIGÉ, VICQ, VIEY, GUICHE, GUIEU, QUECK, QUYO.

DIMINUTIVES.

Old German Wigilo, 8th cent.—Eng. WIGLE, QUIGGLE,

---

* Might also be from another root, p. 116.

THE WARRIOR AND HIS ARMS. 165

QUICKLY, WHICHELO—Modern German WEGEL, WIEGEL, WIGGELE—French VIGLA, VICEL. Old Germ. Wikelin—Mod. Germ. WEGELEIN—French VICLIN.

PATRONYMICS.

Old German Wiking, 8th cent.—Eng. WICKING. Eng. WIGSON, WICKSON.

COMPOUNDS.

(*Bald*, bold) Old Germ. Wigibald, Wibald, Guibald, 8th cent.—French GUIBALD, GUIBAUD. ,(*Bert*, bright) Old Germ. Wigbert, Wibert, Guibert—English VIBERT—Mod. Germ. GUIBERT—French VIBERT, GUIBERT. (*Burg*, protection) Old Germ. Wigburg, 11th cent.—Wiburch, *Lib. Vit.*—Eng. WYBERG, WYBROW. (*Hard*) Old Germ. Wighard, Wicard, Wiart, Vichard, Guiard, 7th cent.—Uigheard, *Lib. Vit.*—Eng. WYARD—Mod. Germ. WIGGERT, WICKARDT—French WICART, WIART, VICART, VICHARD, VIARD, GUICHARD, GUIARD. (*Here, heri*, warrior) Old Germ. Wigheri, Wiger, Wiccar, Wiher, 8th cent.—Uigheri, *Lib. Vit.*—Old Norse Vikar—English WICKER, WITCHER, VIGOR, VICARY, WIRE, GWYER, QUIER—Mod. German WEIGER, WEIHER—French VIGIER, VIGERIE, VICAIRE. (*Had*, war, or *ead*, prosperity) Old Germ. Wicod, Wihad, Guichat, 8th cent.—Ang.-Saxon Wigod—Eng. WIGGETT, WICHETT, WYATT—French WICOT, VIETTE, GUICHOT, GUIET. (*Helm*, helmet) Old German Wighelm, 8th cent.—Uighelm, *Lib. Vit.*—English WHIGAM. (*Ram*, raven) Old German Wichraban, Wigram, 8th cent. —English WIGRAM. (*Man*) Old German Wigman, 8th cent.—Eng. WIGMAN, WICKMAN, WYMAN—Modern German WICHMAN, WIEMANN. (*Mar*, famous) Old Germ. Wigmar, Wimar, 7th cent.—Uicmer, Wimar, *Lib. Vit.*—English WIGMORE, WYMER—Mod. Germ. WIEMER—French VIMAR. (*Rat*, counsel) Old German Wigarat, 8th cent.—French VICHERAT, QUICKERAT, QUIEROT. (*Rice*, powerful) Old Germ. Wigirich, 7th cent.—Eng. VICKRIDGE—Mod. Germ. WEGERICH. (*Wald*, power) Old Germ. Wigold, 11th cent. Modern Germ. WEYGOLD—French VIAULT.

166 THE WARRIOR AND HIS ARMS.

A fourth word signifying war is Goth. *badu,* Ang.-Sax. *beado.* I apprehend that the French names BADOU, BATTU, PATTU, &c., contain simply the Gothic word. There are no such ancient forms in Förstemann's list, but it will be seen that they do occur in the *Liber Vitæ.*

SIMPLE FORMS.

Bad, Bed. War. Old German Bado, Batto, Patto, Bedo, Beddo, Betto, Beto, Betho, Peto, Petto, 6th cent. Saxon Bieda, A.D. 501, Peada. Betti (*Bede's* Ecc. Hist.)—Bada, Badu, Bettu, *Lib. Vit.*—English BAD, BATT, BATTY, BATH, BATHO, PADDY, PATTE, PATTIE, BEDE, BED, BEDDOE, BEATH, BEATTY, BETTY, PEEDE, PEAT, PEATIE, PETT, PETO, PETTY. Mod. German BADE, BATH, BEEDE, BETHE, BETTE, PATHE, PÄTHE. French BADY, BADOU, BATTÉ, BATTU, PATTE, PATÉ, PATAY, PATY, PATTU, PATHE, PATHI, BEDÉ, BEDEAU, BEDU, BETTE, BETOU, BIED.

DIMINUTIVES.

Old Germ. Baducho, Patucho, Bettika, 8th cent.—Ang.-Sax. Beadeca—Baduca, *Lib. Vit.*—Eng. BADOCK, BIDDICK, PADDICK, PETHICK, PIDDUCK, PITTOCK—Modern German BADICKE, BETTACK, BETHKE, PATTKE, PETHKE—French PATOCHE, PETTEX. Old Germ. Bettikin, 10th cent.—Eng. BADKIN, BATKIN, BETKIN. Old German Baduila, Patilo, Bedilo, Betilo, Pettilo, Pettili, 6th cent.—Eng. BADDELEY, BATLEY, BATTLE, BEADLE, BEETLE, BETTELL, BETHELL, BEATLEY, BETTELEY, PADLEY, PADDLE, PATTLE, PATULLO, PEDLEY, PETLEY—Mod. German PADEL, PÄTEL, PEDEL—French BADEL, BATEL, BATAILLE, BEDEL, BETILLE, BETAIL, PATAILLE, PETEL.

PATRONYMICS.

Eng. BATTING, BEDDING—French BEDENC.

COMPOUNDS.

(*Hari,* warrior) Old Germ. Bathari, 6th cent.—English BADDER, BATHER, BEATER, PEDDER, PETHER, PETTER—Mod. German BADER, BÄDER, PETTER—French BADER, BADIER,

THE WARRIOR AND HIS ARMS. 167

BEDIER, BETHERY, PADER, PATHIER, PETTIER. *(Hard)*
Beadheard, *Lib. Vit.*—English BEDDARD—French BATARD,
BEDARD, PATARD, PETARD. *(Mar, famous)* Eng. PADMORE,
PATMORE—French BEDMAR. *(Man)* Badumon, Betmon,
Lib. Vit.—English BADMAN, BEADMAN, PADMAN, PATTMAN.
Dutch BETHMAN. *(Rice, rich, powerful)* Old Germ. Baturich,
Paturich, Paturih, Betterich, 6th cent.—English BETHRAY.
BETTERIDGE, BITHREY, PATRIDGE, PATRY, PETRICK, PETRIE
—French BATHREY, PETRY, PATRY. • *(Wine, friend)* Old
Germ. Bettwin, 7th cent.—French BEDOUIN. *(Wald, power)*
French BATAULT, BIDAULT, PIDAULT. *(Ulf, wolf)* Old Germ.
Badulf, ·8th cent.—English BIDDULPH. *(Hild, war)* Old
Germ. Bad·hilt, wife of Chlodwig II., 7th cent.—French
"BATHILDE, *Mme., Superieure de la maison des dames de
St. Clotilde*"—Christian or surname ?

A fifth root signifying war is Goth, *hath*, Old
High Germ. *had*, Ang.-Sax. *heatho*, Old Frankish
chad. There is also a form *cat*, as found in the
Catumer and Catualda of Tacitus, which Grimm
holds to be the most ancient form of this root.
And in the Celtic *cad* or *cath*, war, we trace a
corresponding form of the Aryan tongue—the
Old Celtic name Cathmor being, as Gluck ob-
serves, the precise equivalent of the Old German
Catumer, and the more recent Hadamar, and the
Old Celt. Caturix of the Old German Hadurich.
Grimm connects the name of the god Hoedhr in
Northern mythology with the above root signify-
ing war, as a Scandinavian form.

SIMPLE FORMS.

Old Germ. Hatto,* Haddo, Hatho, Chado, Hed, Heddi, Had, Hat, Chad, Cat. War.
Hetti. Names of Anglo-Saxons, Had or Hath, Dux, in a

---

* The legend of the hard-hearted bishop of this name who was devoured by
rats is well known.

168 THE WARRIOR AND HIS ARMS:

charter of Athelstan ; Hedda, Hædda, or Chad, Bishop of Wessex, A.D. 676.—Hada, *Lib. Vit*—Eng. HATT, HADOW, HAEDY, HEATH, HEAD, HEDDY, HODD ? HETT, CHAD, CATT, CATTEY, CATTO, CATO.—Mod. German HATT, HEDDE, KATT. French HATTÉ, HEDOU, CAT, CATAU, CATTY, CATU.

DIMINUTIVES.

Old German Chadichus, 7th cent.—English HADDOCK,* HETTICH, CHADDOCK, SHADDOCK ?—Mod. Germ. HÄDICKE. Old German Heddilo, Hetilo, Hathli, Catla—Eng. HADLOW, HADLEY, HATLEY, HEDLEY, HETLEY, HOADLY, CATTLE, CATTLEY—Mod. German HÄDEL—French HADOL, CATAL, CATALA. Old Germ. Hadalin, Chadalenus, 7th cent.—Eng. CATTLIN—French HEDELIN, CATILLON, CHATELIN ?

PATRONYMICS.

Old German Hettinc, 10th cent.—Eng. HEADING—Mod. Germ. HADANK—French HADINGUE.

COMPOUNDS.

(*Bald,* bold) Old German Hadubald, 8th cent.—English SHADBOLT—French CHABAULT ? (*Beado,* war) Old German Chadbedo, Chabedo, 7th cent.—Eng. CHABOT—Fr. CHABOT. (*Bern,* bear) Old German Hadabern, 9th cent.—Eng. CHADBORN. (*Gis,* hostage) Old Germ. Hadegis, 9th cent.—Eng. HADKISS. (*Man*) Eng. CHADMAN. (*Mer,* famous) Catumer, Prince of the Catti, 1st cent., Hadamar, 8th cent.—English CATOMORE,† CATMUR, HATTEMORE—French HADAMAR. (*Not,* bold) Eng. HADNUTT—French CHADINET. (*Rat,* counsel) Old German Hadarat, 8th cent.—English HADROT—French HADROT. (*Rice,* powerful) Old Germ. Hadaricus, 8th cent. —English HATRICK, HEADRICK, SHADRAKE (apparently not Jewish)—Mod. Germ. HEDRICH—French CHADIRAC. (*Wig, wi,* war) Old Germ. Hathuwic, Hathuwi, Hathwi, Haduwi—

---

* The curious name HEADACHE quoted by Mr. Lower is no doubt a slight corruption of Headick.

† May be derived directly from Catmere in Berks, but the name of the place is simply that of a man. It was originally Catmere's gemære. "Catmere's boundary" the inconvenient length of which has caused all to be dropped but the name of the man.

THE WARRIOR AND HIS ARMS. 169

Eng. HATHAWAY, HATHWAY, HADAWAY, CHADWICK, CHATA-WAY. (*Wald*, power) Old German Catualda, *Tacitus*—Ital. CATALDI. (*Wine*, friend) Old Germ. Hadawin, Chaduin, 7th cent.—Eng. HADWEN, CHADWIN—Fr. HEDOUIN. (*Walah*, stranger) Sceadwala, father of Beowulf, *Flor. Wor.*, Cadwalha, king of Wessex—Eng. CADWELL, CHATWELL.

The root *haz* Förstemann takes to be another form of *had* or *hath*, while Graff proposes *haz*, hatred, in the sense, perhaps, of hostility. So that in any case the names will come under this head. There is also a root *az*, but the separation, even in the ancient names, seems to me so doubtful that I have included them together.

SIMPLE FORMS.

Old German Hazo, Azo, Azzo, 8th cent. English HAZE. Mod. Germ. HETZ. French AZE.

Haz.
War.

DIMINUTIVES.

Old German Hezilo, Azzilo, 8th cent.—English HASELL, HEZEL—Mod. German HETZEL—French AZILLE. French AZEMA.

PHONETIC ENDING.

Eng. HAYZEN. French AZAN.

COMPOUNDS.

(*Bert*, famous) French AZIBERT. (*Hard*) Eng. HAZARD —French HAZARD, AZARD. (*Man*) Old Germ. Hazaman, Azaman, 10th cent.—English HAYSMAN—French AZIMON (*Mar*, famous) French AZÉMAR.

There is a root *san*, for which Förstemann supposes a Goth. *sanja*, in the sense of beauty, traces of such a word appearing to be found in *seltsâni*, precious, and *unsâni*, deformed. Instead, however, of this hypothetical word, I would suggest the Old Fries. *san*, strife, *sania*, to combat, as containing a meaning suitable for the purpose.

V

170 THE WARRIOR AND HIS ARMS.

SIMPLE FORMS.

San. Combat. Old Germ. Sano, Seno, 6th cent. Mod. German SANN, SENNE. French SENÉ.

DIMINUTIVES.

Old German Senocus, 8th cent.—French SENOCQ, SENAC, SENECA ? Old Germ. Sanilo, Senila, 9th cent.—Eng. SENLO —French SENELLE. French SENILLON.

COMPOUNDS.

(*Gund,* war) Old Germ. Senegundis, 9th cent.—French SANEGON, SENNEGON. *(Hard)* Old Germ. Senard, 8th cent. —Mod. Germ. SENNERT—French SENARD. (*Hari,* warrior) Eng. SANER—Mod. Germ. SENNER—French SANNIER.

Another root for which Förstemann's derivation seems to be still more unsatisfactory is *criech, crieh,* as found in the names Criecholf, Crieholf, Crea, which he appears to refer to the name of the Greeks, but for which the Mid. High Germ. *krigen,* Old Fries. *kriga, krija,* New Fries. *kryen,* to make war, seems to me very appropriate.

SIMPLE FORMS.

Krieg. War. Old German Crea, 9th cent. English CREECH,* CREAK, CREAH, CREE, GREEK, GREGG? GRIGG? Modern German KRIEGK. French CRIA, GRIGI ?

DIMINUTIVE

*English CRICKMAY—*See p.* 25.

COMPOUNDS.

(*Hari,* warrior) English CREAKER, CRYER, CREER, GRIER, GREER—Mod. German KRIEGER—French KRIER, GREHIER, GRIÈRE. (*Wald,* power) French GRIGAULT.

From the Goth. *sakjo,* Old High Germ. *sach,* Anglo-Saxon *sac, sec,* war, we may take the following.

---

* There is a word *creagh, creich, crick,* &c., occurring in names of places, and probably from a Celtic origin, which might intermix in these names.

THE WARRIOR AND HIS ARMS. 171

SIMPLE FORMS.

Old German Sacco, Sahho, 8th cent.   Eng. SACK, SAGO, SAY.   Mod. Germ. SACKE, SACH.   French SAQUI, SAY.

DIMINUTIVES.

Old Germ. Sacquila, 8th cent.   Eng. SATCHELL.

PHONETIC ENDING.

Old Germ. Sachano.   French SACQUIN.

COMPOUNDS.

(*Hari*, warrior) Eng. SACKER, SAGER, SAYER—Modern Germ. SAGER—French SACRE, SACAREAU, SAYER.   *(Man)* Eng. SACKMAN.   (*Wald*, power) Eng. SACKELLD.*

From the Old High Germ. *strit*, Mod. Germ. *streit*, war, are probably the following.

SIMPLE FORMS.

Eng. STRIDE, STREET.   Mod. Germ. STREIT.

DIMINUTIVE.

Eng. STRETTELL.

PHONETIC ENDING.

Eng. STREETEN.

COMPOUNDS.

(*Hari*, warrior) Old Germ Stritheri, 9th cent.—English STREETER—Mod. Germ. STREITER.

From the Ang.-Sax. *camp*, *comp*, Mod. Germ. *kampf*, war ; Ang.-Saxon *caempa*,, *cempa*, combatant, whence the North. Eng. *kemp*, champion, are the following.

SIMPLE FORMS.

Old German Campo, Cempho, 8th cent.   English CAMP, CHAMP, KEMP.   Modern German CAMPE, KEMP.   French CAMPY, CHAMPY, CHAMPEAU.

DIMINUTIVES.

Eng. CAMPLIN, CAMPLING, KEMPLEN—French CHAMPLON. Eng. CAMPKIN.

An eleventh root is *bag*, *back*, *pack*, Old High Germ. *bagan*, to contend.

---

* A Boston surname, but perhaps only a corruption of SALKELD.

172 THE WARRIOR AND HIS ARMS.

SIMPLE FORMS.

Bag, Back, Pack. To contend. Old Germ. Bago, Bacco, Pago, 8th cent. English Bagg, Back, Pack. Baga, Bacca, *Lib. Vit.*—Mod. Germ. Backe, Bage, Packe. French Bague, Bac, Bacque, Bacqua, Bach.

DIMINUTIVES.

English Baguley, Bagley, Bailey—French Paquel, Pacilly, Pagelle, Bailly. Eng. Baglin—French Baglan.

COMPOUNDS.

(*Aud*, prosperity) Old German Bacauda, 5th cent.—Eng. Baggett, Packett—French Baccaud, Pacaud, Bacquet. (*Hard*) Eng. Packard—French Bagard, Paccard. (*Hari*, warrior) Eng. Backer, Packer—French Bagier, Bagary, Pacquier. (*Man*) English Packman. (*Mund*, protection) French Bachiment, Pacquement. (*Wald*, power) French Pacault. (*Ward*) French Bacquart.

From the Ang.-Sax. *sige*, Old Norse *sigr*, Old High Germ. *sigu*, victory, are the following.

SIMPLE FORMS.

Sig, Sic. Victory. Old Germ. Sigo, Sico, Seggi, Secki, 4th cent. Ang.-Sax. Sig, Sigga. Old Norse Sigi. Eng. Seago, Seage, Sike, Sea. Mod. Germ. Sieg, Sigg, Sieke, Sick. French Sège, See.

DIMINUTIVES.

Old Germ. Sigilo, Sigili, 9th cent.—Eng. Sigley, Sickle —Mod. Germ. Sigel, Sigle, Sickel—French Siegel, Siglé, Sichel. Old German Sigilina, Siclina, 8th cent.—English Sicklen, Sickling—Mod. Germ. Siglen. Old Germ. Sigizo, 10th cent.—Eng. Siggs ? Sykes ? Old Germ. Sigunzo, 9th cent.—Eng. Sickens.

COMPOUNDS.

(*Bold*) Old German Sigibald, Sicbold, Sibold, 8th cent. —Ang.-Sax. Sigebald, king of Essex—Eng. Sibbald—Mod. Germ. Siebold—Fr. Sicbel, Sebault. (*Aud*, prosperity) Old German Sigaud—French Segaut. (*Bert*, bright) Old German Sigibert, Sibert, 6th cent.—Ang.-Saxon Sigebert—

THE WARRIOR AND HIS ARMS. 173

Eng. SIBERT—Mod. Germ. SIEBERT—French SIBERT. (*Bod*, messenger) Old German Sigibodo, Siboto, 9th cent.—Modern Germ. SEBODE—French SIBOT. (*Fred*, peace) Old German Sigifred, Sieffred—Ang.-Sax. Sigefred, Bishop of Chicester—Eng. SEYFRIED, SEFFERT—Mod. Germ. SIEGFRIED, SEYFRID —French SEYFFERT. (*Hard*) Old Germ. Sigihard, Sigard, Sicard, 9th cent.—Mod. Germ. SIEGHARDT, SICHERT—French SEGARD, SICARD. (*Here*, warrior, or *gar*, spear) Old German Sigger, Sicker, Sier, 8th cent.—Siggær, genealogy of the Northumbrian kings, Sigar, bishop of Wells—Old Norse Siggeir, king of Gothland in the Volsungasaga—Eng. SEGAR, SIGGERS, SECKER, SEDGER, SIER, SEARE—Mod. Germ. SIEGER, SICHER, SEYER—French SEEGER, SEGUR, SEGUIER. (*Man*) Old Germ. Sigiman, 8th cent.—Eng. SICKMAN—Mod. Germ. SIEGMANN. (*Not*, bold) Old Germ. Sigenot—French SIGNET. (*Rat*, counsel) Old German Sigirad, 8th cent.—French SÉGURET, SECROT. (*Mar*, famous) Old German Sigimar, brother of Arminius, 1st cent., Sicumar—Eng. SYCAMORE, SEAMER, SEYMOUR—Mod. Germ. SEYMER—French SIEMERS. (*Mund*, protection) Old Germ. Sigimund, Burgundian prince, 5th cent.—Old Norse Sigmundr—Eng. SIGMUND, SIMMONDS —Mod. Germ. SIEGMUND, SIMUND—French SIMOND. (*Wig*, war) Old Germ. Sigiwic, 9th cent.—Eng. SEDGWICK. (*Wine*, friend) Old Germ. Sigiwin, Seguin—Seguin, *Roll. Batt. Abb.* —Eng. SEGUIN—French SEGUIN.

PHONETIC INTRUSION OF *l* and *r*, see p. 30.

Old German Sicumar—Eng. SICKLEMORE. Old German Siginiu—Eng. SIGOURNAY.

We have a name SIGRIST, and there is a corresponding French SIEGRIST. Rist was the name of one of the Valkyrjur, maidens of Odin, among whose duties it was to dispense victory. In this sense the compound seems a natural one, and I do not know of any other way in which the name can be explained.

174 THE WARRIOR AND HIS ARMS.

Another root with the meaning of victory may be *gagan, gain.* This root, which is found in several Old German names, Förstemann refers to *gagan*, contra, which in the sense of opposition, hostility, would not be unsuitable. But I think that a still better meaning is found in English "gain," French *gagner*, and the Old Norse *gagn*, which had the direct sense of victory.

SIMPLE FORMS.

Gagan, Gain, Victory. Old Germ. Cagano, 8th cent. English GAGAN, GAHAN, GAIN, GAINEY, JANE, CAHAN, CAIN, CANEY. Mod. German CAHN. French GAGIN, GAGNE, GAGNÉ, GAGNY, GAGNEAU, GAIN, CAGIN, CAHEN, CAIN.

DIMINUTIVES.

Old Germ. Kaginzo. Eng. GAINS, JANES, CAINS.

COMPOUNDS.

(*Aud*, prosperity) French GAIGNAUD. (*Hard*) Old Germ Gaganhard, Caganhard, 8th cent.—French GAGNARD, CAGNARD, GAINARD. (*Hari*, warrior) Old Germ. Geginheri, 9th cent.—Eng. GAINER, JANUARY ?—French GAGNER, GAGNIÈRE, GAGNERY—Ital. GAGNERI.

Then there is another class of names from verbs signifying to wound, to slash, to strike, to kill, to devastate, to spoil, or else from nouns signifying death, havoc, slaughter.

From the Ang.-Saxon *bana*, a slayer, are probably the names in the following group. In the Scôp or Bard's song, an ancient Saxon poem professing to be an account given by a wandering minstrel of the different countries he had visited we are told that "Becca ruled the Bannings." We know nothing further of this people, but their name seems to indicate that they were a warlike tribe.

THE WARRIOR AND HIS ARMS.   175

SIMPLE FORMS.

Old German Panno, 11th cent.   English BANN, BANNY, PANN. French BANLÉ, PANAY.

Pan, Ban. Slayer.

DIMINUTIVES.

English PANNELL—French BANNIELLE, PANEL. English BANNICK? French PANISSE—Ital. PANIZZL ?

COMPOUNDS.

(*Here*, warrior) Eng. BANNER, PANNIER—French BANNIER, PANNIER. (*Ger*, spear) Old Germ. Panager, 9th cent.—Eng. BANGER (if not local)—Modern German BANGER. (*Hard*) English BANYARD—French PANHARD, PANART. (*Ward*, guardian) Mod. Germ. BANNWART—French BANOUARD.

Another form of Ang.-Saxon *bana*, a slayer was *bona*. The root *bon* occurs especially in Old Frankish names, and the Latin *bonus* may perhaps intermix in the simple forms. I have suggested, p. 55, that Bonaparte may be an Old Frankish name in an Italianized form. It will be seen from the following list that the name has representatives, both in French and English.

SIMPLE FORMS.

Old German Bonus, Bono, Pono.   Eng. BONNY, BONEY, PONY. Mod. German BONN, BONNE, BOHN.   French BON, BONNE, BONNI, BONNY, BONNAY, BONNEAU, BONNO, PON.

Bon, Pon. Slayer.

DIMINUTIVES.

Old Germ. Bonila, 8th cent.—English BONNELL—French BONNELL, BONNELYE, PONNELLE.   Old Germ. Bonigo, 10th cent.—Eng. BONNICK—Mod. German BONNECKE.   English BONKEN—French BONICHON.   Old German Bonizo, 10th cent.—Anglo-Saxon Bonsig, *Cod. Dip.* 810—Eng. BONSEY— French BONASSEAUX, BONZÉ, BONYS.

PATRONYMICS.

Eng. BONNING—French BONNINGUE, BONINC.

COMPOUNDS.

(*Aud*, prosperity) French BONNAUD, BONNYAUD.   (*Bert*, famous) Old Germ. Bonibert, 7th cent., Bonipert, 8th cent.

176 THE WARRIOR AND HIS ARMS.

—Eng. BONBRIGHT—French BONPARD, BOMPART—Italian
BONIPERTI, BONAPARTE? (*Fûs, funs,* prompt, eager) Old
Germ. Bonafusus, Bonafusse,* 11th cent.—French BONNA-
FOUS, BONNEFONS, BONIFACE? BONFILS? *(Gar,* spear) Eng.
BONIGER, BOMGAR(SON). (*Here,* warrior) Old Germ. Bonàrius
—Eng. BONAR, BONNER—Modern Germ. BOEHNER—French
BONNAIRE, BONIER, BONNERY, BONHEUR? (*Man)* English
BONNYMAN—French BONNEMAIN. (*Mund,* protection) French
BONNEMENT. (*Hard)* Old Germ. Bonard, 8th cent.—Mod.
German BOHNHARDT—Fr. BONNARD, BONARDI, BONNARDET
(*French dimin.*) (*Sind,* way) Old German Bonesind, 9th
cent.—French BONNISSENT. (*Wald,* power) Old German
Bonoald, Bonald, 9th cent.—French BONALD (Archbishop of
Lyons)—Ital. BONOLDI.

.From the Anglo-Saxon *ben,* a wound, in the
sense, with the ancient termination, of a wound-
inflicter, may be the following. I am inclined to
think, however, that this, and the preceding
groups *ban, bon,* are in reality only different forms
of the same word.

SIMPLE FORMS.

Ben, Bin. Wound. Old Germ. Benno, Benni, Ben, Penna, 8th cent.—Bynni,
Lib. Vit.—Eng. BENN, BENNEY, BINNEY, PENN, PENNY, PINN,
PINNY, PINO—Mod. German BEHN, BIHN, PENN. French
BENA, BINA, BINEY, BINEAU, PENY, PIN, PINEAU, PINAU.

It appears also that Benno, Penno, *was sometimes used
anciently as a contraction of* Bernhard, Benedictus, *and*
Pernger.

DIMINUTIVES.

Old Germ. Benico, Bennic, 9th cent.—Benoc, genealogy
of Ida, king of Bernicia—Eng. BENNICKE, BENNOCH, PEN-
NICK, PINNOCK—Mod. Germ. BENICKE, BINNECKE, PENNICKE
—French BENECKE, BENECH, BINOCH. Old Germ Βενίλος,
Procopius, 6th cent., Benilo, 11th cent.—English BENNELL,

---

* There is also an Old Germ. Bonafuisset, 10th cent. Is not this the French
diminutive added, as in the Old French name Charlemainet ?

THE WARRIOR AND HIS ARMS. 177

PENNELL—French PENEL, PINEL. English BENKIN—Mod.
Germ. BENEKEN—French PENNEQUIN. Old German Benzo,
Penzo—Eng. BENNS, BENSE, BINNS—French BENCE, BENZ,
BINZ, PENCE, PINSEAU. Old German Benimius, Benimia,[*]
8th cent.—Fries. BONNEMA—French BONAMY, BONOMÉ.

PATRONYMICS.

Old Germ. Benning, 9th cent.—English BENNING—Mod.
Germ. BENNING.

COMPOUNDS.

(*Ger*, spear) Old Germ. Benegar, 8th cent.—Eng. BENGER
—French BINNECHER. (*Gaud, got*, Goth) Old Germ. Bene-
gaud, 8th cent.—Eng. PENNYCAD—Fr. PENIGOT, PENICAUD.
(*Hard*) Old German Benehard, Benard, 9th cent.—Modern
German BENNERT—French BENARD, BINARD, PINHARD
(*Here*, warrior) Old German Beneher, 9th cent.—English
BENNER, BYNNER, PENNER—Fr. BENIER, BINIER, PENIÉRE.
(*Aud*, prosperity) French PENAUD, PINAUD. (*Bert*, bright)
French PENABERT. (*Man*) Eng. PENMAN—Mod. German
BENNEMANN. (*Mar*, famous) Eng. BENMORE, PENNYMORE.
(*Nant*, daring) English PENNANT—French BINANT, PENANT.
(*Wald*, power) Mod. Germ. BENNOLD—French PINAULT.

From the Mid. High Germ. *bicken*, Old High
Germ. *pichan*, to slash, Förstemann derives a root
big, bic, pig, pic, to which I place the following.

SIMPLE FORMS.

Old German Bicco, Bigo, Picco, Pigo, Picho, 8th cent. Big, Bick.
Eng. BICK, BITCH, BIGG, PICK, PIGG. Mod. Germ. BIECK, Pig, Pick.
BIGGE, PICK, PICH. French BIGÉ, BIGEY, PICK, PICQUE, To slash.[*]
PICHI, PICHOU, PIGEAU.

DIMINUTIVES.

Eng. BICKLE, BICKLEY, BIGELOW, PICKELL—Mod. Germ.
PICKEL—French BICAL, BIGLE, PICAL.

---

[*] Benimius and Benimia occur as Old Frankish names both of men and
women.

W

178 THE WARRIOR AND HIS ARMS.

COMPOUNDS.

(*Aud*, prosperity) French PICAUD, PICHAUD, BIGOT?
PIGEAT? PICQUET?—Eng. PICKETT? PIGGOTT? (*Hard*)
Eng. PICKARD—Mod. Germ. PICKHARDT—French BICHARD,
BIGEARD, PICKARD, PICHARD, PIGEARD. (*Here*, warrior)
English BICKER, BIGGAR, PICKER, PITCHER—French BIGRE,
BITCHER, PICHER, PICHERY, PICORY, PIGEORY. (*Man*) Eng.
BIGMAN, PICKMAN. (*Ram, ran*, raven) English PIGRAM—
French BICHERON, PIGERON. (*Wald*, power) Old German
Bigwald, Picoald, 7th cent.—French PICAULT, PIGAULT.

I am inclined to think that the following
group are formed by a phonetic *n* from the preceding, and that they correspond with the Old
Eng. *pink*, to pierce, to stab.

SIMPLE FORMS.

Pink.
To pierce.

English BINGEY, PINGO, PINK, PINKEY, PINCH—French
BING, BINGÉ.

PHONETIC ENDING.

Pinceon, *Lib. Vit.*, Eng. PINCHEON. French PINGEON,
PINCHON.

COMPOUNDS.

(*Hard*, fortis) Eng. PINKERT—French PINGARD.

From the Goth. *malvjan*, Old Norse *mola*,
contundere, Eng. "maul," we may take the following.

SIMPLE FORMS.

Mall.
Moll.
To beat.

Old German Malo, 8th cent. Moll, "also called Ethel-
wold," king of Northumbria. Maule, Maulay, *Roll Batt. Abb.*
Eng. MALL, MALLEY, MAULE, MÖLL, MOLE, MOLLEY. Mod.
German MAHL, MALLE, MOHL. French MALLE, MALLÉ,
MALO, MOLL, MOLLÉ, MOLE, MOLAY, MAULL.

DIMINUTIVES.

English MALLOCK—French MALLAC, MALECO, MOLIQUE
Eng. MALKIN—French MALAQUIN.

PATRONYMICS.

Eng. MALLING, MOLLING. French MALINGUE.

THE WARRIOR AND HIS ARMS. 179

COMPOUNDS.

(*Bert*, famous) Old German Malpert, 10th cent.—French MALAPERT. (*Bot*, envoy) Old Germ. Malboto, 8th cent.—French MALBOT. (*Hard*, fortis) Old German Mallard, 7th cent.—Maularde, *Roll Batt. Abb.*—Eng. MALLARD, MOLLARD —French MALLARD, MOLLARD, MOUILLARD. (*Rad*, council) Old Germ. Malrada, 8th cent.—French MALARET, MALRAIT. (*Rice*, powerful) Malorix, Frisian Prince, 1st cent., Malarich, prince of the Suevi in Spain, 6th cent.—English MALLORY—French MALORY. (*Thius*, servant) Old German Malutheus, in a Gothic record at Naples, 6th cent.—English MALTHUS, MALTHOUSE. (*Ulf*, wolf) Old German Malulf, 6th cent.—Eng. MALIFF.

It appears to me that *mel* and *mil* are different forms from the same root, and corresponding directly with Old Norse *melia*, English "mill," which is still used in the sense of pugilistic encounters. Förstemann calls this a yet unexplained root, "ein noch unerklärter stamm," and refers to "mild," also to a Slavonic root. But it appears to me that there is no occasion to go further than the above.

SIMPLE FORMS.

Old Germ. Milo, Mello, 10th cent. Μέλων, a Sigamber in Strabo, 1st cent., Grimm makes the same as the above. English MILO, MILEY, MILLIE, MELLO, MELLOW. French MILLE, MILL, MILEY, MILLY, MILLAUX, MELLÉ, MELAYE.

Mell, Mill. To beat.

DIMINUTIVES.

Old Germ. Milike—Eng. MILLIGE, MILK—Mod. Germ. MIELECKE, MILCKE, MILCH—French MELICK, MÉLIQUE. Old German Milizzo, 8th cent.—English MILLIS, MELLIS, MELLISH—Fr. MILISCH. Eng. MILLIKIN. Fries. MELLEMA —French MALAMY, MILHOMME?

PATRONYMICS.

Eng. MILLINGE—French MILLANGE.

180 THE WARRIOR AND HIS ARMS.

COMPOUNDS.

(*Dio*, servant) Old German Mildeo, 9th cent.—English MELLODEW, MELODY, MELLOWDAY, MALADY. (*Hard*) Old Germ. Milehard, 7th cent.—English MELLIARD, MILLARD—Mod. Germ. MIELERT—French MILLARD, MILORD. (*Hari,* warrior) Eng. MELLER, MILLER ?—Mod. Germ. MILLER ?—French MELIER, MILLER, MILLERY. (*Sind*, expedition) Old German Milesinda, Milissent—English MILLICENT—French MILSENT.

It is rather probable that the word *mald, malt, mold,* which seems to be a derivative of the previous root *mal,* has also the meaning of hostile collision. The prefix *meald* occurs in several Anglo-Saxon names, as Mealdhelm, &c., and Ettmuller supposes an Ang.-Saxon *meald,* in the sense of confrictio. The most natural meaning to give to this seems to be that of mingling in battle fray. The form *malz,* which appears in some French names, may be another form of the same.

SIMPLE FORMS.

Mald. Fray. Ang.-Sax. Malte, charter of Edward, A.D. 1060. Maald, Mald, *Lib. Vit.* Eng. MALT, MOULD, MOULT. Mod. Germ. MALDT. Dan. MALTHE. French MAULDE, MALTEAUX ?

DIMINUTIVES.

Eng. MOULDICK. Dan. MOLTKE. French MALZAC.

PHONETIC ENDING?

Old Germ. Maldra,* king of the Suevi, 5th cent. Eng. MOULDER. French MALTAIRE, MALZAR.

PATRONYMICS.

Eng. MOULDING. French MALSANG ?

COMPOUNDS.

(*Bert*, famous) Old Germ. Maldeberta, 7th cent.—French MAUBERT ? (*Gar*, spear) Old German Maldegar—French

---

* Called in another chronicle MASDRA.

THE WARRIOR AND HIS ARMS. 181

MAUGER ? *(Man)* Eng. MALTMAN—French MAUDEMAIN.
(*Vid, with,* wood) Ang.-Sax. Maldvit—Maldwith, *Domesday*
—Eng. MALTWOOD—French MAUDUIT.

From the Old Norse *basa,* to strive, contend,
Förstemann derives the root *bas* in Old German
names. And from the Old Norse *bisa,* to strive
fiercely, a word no doubt cognate, he also derives
a root *bis.* It seems to me, however, that the two
words are too closely connected to be separated.
Thus we find that the Thuringian king Basinus
was also called Bisinus.

SIMPLE FORMS.

Old German Baso, Basso, 7th cent., Biso, Piso, 9th cent.
Bass, a "Mass-Priest," *Ang.-Sax. Chron.* Bassason, a Bas,
Northman, *Ann. Isl.* Bisi, bishop of the East Angles, 7th Bis.
cent. Bysey, *Roll Batt. Abb.* English BASS, BESSY, BISS, Strife.
PASS, PASSEY. Mod. German BASS, BESE, PASS. French
BASSE, BASSEÉ, BASSO, BESSE, BESSAY, BISEAU, BISSAY,
PASSE, PASSY.

DIMINUTIVES.

Old German Bassac, 9th cent.—Eng. BASEKE, BASK,
BISCOE—Mod. Germ. BÁSKE, BASCH. Old German Basulo,
6th cent.—Eng. BASSIL, BESSEL, BESLEY, BISSELL—Modern
German BÄSEL, PESEL—French BESLAY.

PHONETIC ENDING.

Basinus or Bisinus, Thuringian king, 5th cent. Basina,
wife of the Frankish king Childerich, and daughter of the
above. Pisin, 9th cent. Basin, *Dom sday.* Eng. BASIN,
BISNEY. French BAISSIN, BESSON, BESSONEAU, BESSONA,
BISSEN, PISSIN.

COMPOUNDS.

(*Gaud,* Goth) Eng. BISGOOD, PEASCOD ?—Fr. BASSAGET.
(*Hard,* fortis) French BESSARD, BISARD, PASSARD, PISSARD.
(*Mar,* famous) Eng. BESSEMER, BISSMIRE, PASSMER. *(Man)*
Eng. PASSMAN—Mod. Germ. BASSMANN.

182 THE WARRIOR AND HIS ARMS.

I am not sure that BISHOP is not in some cases from this root. No doubt it might be derived from the office, for even in ancient times such names seem to have been given baptismally, and there is an Old German Piscof, 8th cent., which Graff so derives. But there is a Biscop in the genealogy of the kings of the Lindisfari, who of course must have been a heathen. Possibly it may be from the above root *bis*, with Anglo-Saxon *côf*, strenuous, which apparently occurs sometimes as a termination in Saxon names.

There are several words signifying to beat, some of which are still in use in the English language, or in provincial dialects. One of these is *bang* or *bank*, Old Norse *banga*, Danish *banke*, Eng. " bang," Exmoor dialect " bank," to beat.

SIMPLE FORMS.

Bang, Bank. Eng. BANG, BANK, BENCH, PENK. Mod. Germ. BANCK,
To beat. BANG. French BANGY, BANC.

DIMINUTIVES.

French BENGEL. French PANCKOUKE.

COMPOUNDS.

(*Gaud*, Goth) Old German Bancgot, 9th cent.—English PENKETT. (*Aud*, prosperity) French PANCHAÜD. (*Hard*) English BANGHART,* BANKART—Modern German BENCKERT. (*Here*, warrior) Eng. BANCKER, BANKIER—French PENQUIER.

Another word signifying to beat, Old Norse *beystá*, North. Eng. " baste," may perhaps be the root of the following. This group is constructed on a purely hypothetical principle, as I have as yet found no ancient names to correspond.

---

* A Philadelphia name, possibly of German origin.

THE WARRIOR AND HIS ARMS. 183

SIMPLE FORMS.

Eng. BASTE, BASTOW, BEST, PASTE, PEST. Mod. Germ. BESTE. French BASTA, BASTIE, BEST, PASTÉ, PASTY, PASTEAU, PESTY.

Baste.
To beat.

DIMINUTIVES.

Eng. BASTICK. French BESTEL, PESTEL.

PATRONYMIC.

Eng. BASTING.

COMPOUNDS.

(*Hard*, fortis) Eng. BASTARD—French BASTARD. (*Here*, warrior) Eng. BASTER, BASTRAY, PESTER—French BASTER, BASTIER, PASTIER, PASTRÉ, PESTRE. (*Wald*, power) French BESTAULT.

A third root signifying to beat is Old Norse *klappa*, Old High Germ. *klaphôn*.

SIMPLE FORMS.

Old Germ. Claffo, Lombard king, 6th cent., Clapho, Clep, Cleb, Cleph. Clappa, son of Ida, king of Bernicia. Osgod Clapa, Danish nobleman at the court of Canute. English CLAPP, CLAVEY. Modern Germ. KLAPP. French CLAVEAU, CLAVÉ, CLAVEY.

Clap, Claff.
To beat.

DIMINUTIVES.

Eng. CLAPLIN. French CLABBEECK. French CLAVEL.

PATRONYMICS.

Eng. CLAPSON. French CLAPISSON.

COMPOUNDS.

(*Aud*, prosperity) French CLABAUT. (*Hari*, warrior) Eng. CLAPPER—Modern German KLABER—French CLAPIER, CLAVIER, CLAVERIE, KLEBER. (*Ron*, raven) Fr. CLAPEYRON. (*Rat, red*, counsel) French CLAVROT, CLAPARÈDE.

From the Old High Germ. *bliuwan*, to strike, to kill, Förstemann thinks may be a Goth. name Blivilas of the 5th cent. There are a few names mostly French, which may perhaps be referred to this origin.

184 THE WARRIOR AND HIS ARMS.

SIMPLE FORMS.

Blaive.
Verberare.

French BLAIVE, BLÈVE.

PHONETIC ENDING.

Eng. BLEVIN, PLEVIN. French BLAVIN, BLEVANUS.

COMPOUNDS.

(*Hard*, fortis) French PLIVARD. (*Hari*, warrior) French BLAVIER, PLOUVIER.

The following root seems to be referable to Old Norse *dolgr*, foe, Ang.-Sax. *dolg*, vulnus.

SIMPLE FORMS.

Dolk.
Vulnus.

Old Germ. Tulga (West Gothic king, 7th cent.), Tulcho. Eng. TULK. Mod. Germ. DULK.

PHONETIC ENDING.

Old Germ. Toleon, 10th cent. Eng. TOLKIEN, TOLKEN. Mod. Germ. DULCKEN.

COMPOUNDS.

(*Fin*, people's name ?) Old Norse Dolgfinnr—English DOLPHIN. (*Hari*, warrior) Eng. TOLCHER.

Then there are several roots signifying to break, subdue, crush, and in which the meaning probably often mixes with that of the former class. From the Goth. *brican*, Ang.-Sax. *bracan*, *brecan*, Old High German *brechan*, *brehhan*, *brihhan*, *prehhan*, to break, crush, Eng. "bray," Cumb. "brake," to beat violently, I take to be the following. There are but few ancient names, and Förstemann does not give any explanation.

SIMPLE FORMS.

Brack,
Brick.
To beat

Old Germ. Brachio, Thuringian king, 6th cent., Briccius, 5th cent. English BRACK, BRAKE, BREACH, BRICK, BRIGG, BRIDGE, BRAY, PRIGG, PRAY. Mod. German BRACH, BRY. French BRACQ, BREOK, BRIQUÉ, BRAHY, BRAY, BRÉAU, BRÉE, PRAY, PRÉAU.

THE WARRIOR AND HIS ARMS. 185

DIMINUTIVES.

Eng. BREAKELL, BRICKELL, PRICKLE. Brixi, *Domesday Notts.*—English BRIXEY, BRIX, BRIGGS ? BRIDGES ?—French BRACK ? PRAX ? French BRAQUELONNE, PRÉCLIN.

COMPOUNDS.

(*Aud*, prosperity) French BRIGAUD, BRAYOUD, BRIOUDE. (*And*, life, spirit) Eng. BRIAND, BRIANT—French BREGAND, BRIANT. (*Hard*) French BRACHARD, BRECHARD, BRÉGEARD, BRICARD, BRICHARD, BRÉARD, BRIARD. (*Here*, warrior) Eng. BRACHER, BRICKER, BREAKER, BREECHER, BRIDGER, BRAYER, BRIER, PREACHER—French BRACHER, BRAYER, BREGERE, BRICAIRE, BREYER, PREYER. (*Man*) English BRAKEMAN, BRAYMAN, BRICKMAN, BRIGMAN, BRIDGEMAN—Mod. German BRACKMANN, BRÜCKMANN—French BRAQUEMIN, BRECHEMIN. (*Wine*, friend) French BREGEVIN. (*Wald*, power) Old Germ. Briceold, 9th cent.—French BRAULT, PREAULT.

PHONETIC ENDING.

Eng. BRAGAN, BRIDGEN, BRAIN, PRAIN. French BRICON, BRAINNE.

PHONETIC INTRUSION OF *n*.

Eng. BRAINARD. French PREGNIARD.

Another root signifying to break may be *brit*, Ang.-Sax. *britian*, whence Eng. "brittle." But the Ang.-Sax. *brytta*, ruler, prince, may come in for all or part. Förstemann also proposes Ang.-Sax. *Bryt*, a Briton, and *brid*, as the root of bridle.

SIMPLE FORMS.

Old German Briddo, Britto, 9th cent. Brette, *Roll Batt. Abb.* Eng. BRETT, PRITT, PRETTY, PRIDE, PRIDDY. French BRET, BRETEAU, PRETÉ, BRIDE, BRIDEAU.

Brit. To break ?

DIMINUTIVES.

Eng. BRETTELL, BRITTELL—French BRETEL. Fr. BRETOCQ.

COMPOUNDS.

(*Here*, warrior) Old Germ. Brittharius, Thuringian, 6th cent.—English BRITTER, PRETER—French BRETAR, PRETRE ? (*Hard*) French PRÉTARD. (*Man*) Eng. PRETTYMAN ?

X

186 THE WARRIOR AND HIS ARMS.

Another root of similar meaning I take to be found in Anglo-Saxon *brysan*, Old Eng. *brise*, French *briser*, Old French *bruiser,* English " bruise." The following names show the Teutonic origin in French as well as English.

SIMPLE FORMS.

Brese, Bruse.
Eng.
"bruise."
Old German Briso, Priso, 8th cent. Old Norse Bresi. English BRISE, BRISSEY, BREEZE, BRESSEY, BREWES, BRUCE, PRISSEY, PRUSE. Modern German BRESE, BREIS, PREISS. French BRISE, BRISAY, BREYSSE, BRESSE, BRESSEAU, BRESSY, BRUCY, BROUSSE.

DIMINUTIVES.

English BRISLEY, PRISLEY—French BRESSEL, BREZOL, PRUZELLE. Old German Brisca, 11th cent.—Eng. BRISCO, BRISK, BREYSIC, PRISSICK—French BRISAC. Eng. BRESLIN, PRESLIN—French BRESILLON, BRUZELIN.

COMPOUNDS.

(*Aud*, prosperity) English BRUZAUD—French BRISSAUD. (*And*, life, spirit) English BRUZAND—French BRESSAND. (*Hard*) English. BREAZARD—French BRISSARD, BRIZARD. (*Man*) Eng. BRISMAN, PRISEMAN. (*Here*, warrior) French BRESSER, BRUEZIER.

Then we have several roots signifying to plunder, to devastate, to overthrow. From the root *rob* (Goth. *rauban*, Old High German *raupan*, Old Sax. *roven*), are a number of names, many of which have been supposed to be contractions of Robert. The word has not a pleasant sound to English ears, but it must not be understood in the petty larceny modern sense, but in the respectable ancient sense of burning down a village, slaughtering the men, and carrying off the goods and chattels, women and children.

THE WARRIOR AND HIS ARMS. 187

SIMPLE FORMS.

Old Germ. Ruabo, Rubbo, Rubo, 8th cent. Eng. ROBB, Rob, Rub. ROBBIE, ROFF, ROFFIE, ROAF, ROOF, ROUGH, RUBB, RUBY, To plunder. RUFF, RUFFY, ROPE, ROOPE. Mod. Germ. RÜBE. French ROBBE, ROBI, ROUBO, RUBIO, RUBÉ, RUBY, RUPP, ROUFFE, ROUVEAU.

DIMINUTIVES.

Old Germ. Rupilo—English ROBLOW, ROBLEY, ROUPELL, RUFFLE—French RUBELLE, ROUVEL. English RUBIDGE— French ROBIQUET (*double dimin.*) Old German Ruopilin, 10th cent.—English ROBOLIN—French ROBLIN, ROVILLAIN. French ROBQUIN, ROBICHON.

COMPOUNDS.

(*Here*, warrior) Eng. ROPER, ROOPER, RUBERY—French RÓBIER, RUBIER, ROUVIER. (*Rice*, powerful) Fr. RUPRICH.

Then there is another root *rab, rap, raf,* which I take to be most probably another form of the last, Old High Germ. *raban*, Ang.-Saxon *reafan*, Old Norse *hrapa*.

SIMPLE FORMS.

Old German Rabo, 9th cent., Raffo, 11th cent. English RABY, RAPP, RAVEY. French RABY, RABA, RABEAU, Rab, Raf. To plunder. RABOU, RAFFY, RAPP, RAPÉ, RAVEAU, RAVOU.

DIMINUTIVES.

English RAFFELL—Modern German RAFFEL—French RAPHEL, RAPILLY, RAVEL. English RAPKIN. French RABILLON, RAFFLIN.

COMPOUNDS.

(*Aud*, prosperity) French RÁVEAUD. (*Hard*) French RAFFARD, RAFFORT, RAVARD. (*Here*, warrior) Eng. RAPER —French RABIER, RAVIER. (*Got*, Goth) French RABIGOT. (*Wald*, power) Old Germ. Raffolt, 8th cent.—Eng. RAFFOLD —French RAVAULT. (*Wine*, friend) French RABOUIN. (*Ulf*, wolf) Old Germ. Rafulf, 9th cent.—French RABEUF.

Another form of the same root signifying to rob is I think, *reb, rev, rip, riv,* Ang.-Sax. *refan,*

188 THE WARRIOR AND HIS ARMS.

rypan, Eng. "rifle," (diminutive). Förstemann proposes Ang.-Sax. *ripe,* English "ripe" in the sense of mature, a less probable root, as it seems to me. Some of the Old German names beginning with an aspirated *h,* it is possible that *crib, crip,* may be Frankish forms from this root, as at p. 46.

SIMPLE FORMS.

Rib, Rif. Old Germ. Hripo, Hriffo, 9th cent. Eng. RIBB, RIFF,
To plunder. CRIBB ? Mod. Germ. REIBE, REIFF. French REVU, RIBOU, RIF, RIVAY, RIVÉ, RIVAU, CREPY ? CREPÉ, CREPEAU ?

DIMINUTIVES.

Eng. RIBBECK, REPUKE, RIPKEY. Eng. REFFEL, REVILL, REAVELL, RIPLEY—Rivell, *Roll Batt.·Abbey*—Mod. German RÜPPELL, RIFFEL—French RIBLE, RIBAIL, REBEL, REVEL, REVEIL, CREPELLE ? French REBILLON, REVELIN, RIVELIN.

COMPOUNDS.

(*Aud,* prosperity) French RIFFAUD, RIPAUT, RIVAUD. *(Hard)* French REBARD, RIPARD, RIVARD, REVERD. (*Here,* warrior) Old Germ. Ripher, Riper, 8th cent.—Eng. RIPER, REVERE, RIVIERE, RIVER, CRIPER ?—Ripere, Rivers, *Roll Batt. Abb.*—Mod. Germ. REIBER—French RIBIER, RIBIÉRE, RIVIERE, CRIBIER ?—Spanish RIBERA. (*Wald,* power) Old German Ribald, Rippold, 8th cent.—French RIBAULT, REBOLD, RIFFAULT, RIPAULT—Ital. RIVOLTA ?

PHONETIC ENDING.

Old Germ. Rifuni, 8th cent. English RIPPIN, CRIPPEN ? French RIBUN, RIBONI, RIVAIN.

Another root of similar meaning may be *ran, ren,* from Old Norse *ræna,* spoliare, *rån,* rapine. But this is difficult to separate in many cases from *ragin,* counsel, which is frequently contracted into *rain,* as at p. 48. Förstemann also refers to Rån, the wife of Oegir in Northern mythology.

THE WARRIOR AND HIS ARMS.   189

SIMPLE FORMS.

Old Germ. Rano, 9th cent.   Eng. Rann, Rannie, Renn, Ran, Ren. Wren, Rennie, Renno.   Modern German Rahn.   French Rapine. Ranoe, Renny, René.

DIMINUTIVES.

Old Germ. Ranila, 7th cent.   Eng. Rennell.   French Renel.

PATRONYMICS.

Eng. Rennison.   French Renesson, Rennecon.

COMPOUNDS.

(*Gar*, spear) Old German Rangar—Eng. Raniker, Ranger ?

Another root of the same meaning is *dil, til,* which Förstemann refers to Old High German *tilen*, Ang.-Sax. *dilgian*, diruere, destruere. To the few ancient names of his list I add several others from our own early records.

SIMPLE FORMS.

Old Germ. Dilli, Tilli, Thilo, 8th cent.   Tilli, *Lib. Vit.* Dil, Til. Dill, Tilly, Tillé, *Hund. Rolls.*   English Dill, Dilley, To Destroy. Dillow, Till, Tilley.   Modern German Dill, Till, Tilo. French Dilly, Dillé, Tilly, Tillé.

DIMINUTIVES.

Ang.-Sax. Tilluc (*found in Tilluces leâh, Cod. Dip.* 436.) Eng. Dillick, Dilke, Tillick, Tilke.   French Dilhac.

PATRONYMICS.

Eng. Tilling.   Mod. Germ. Dilling.

COMPOUNDS.

(*Ger*, spear) Ang.-Sax. Tilgâr (*found in Tilgâres dîc, Cod. Dip.* 714)—Dilker, *Hund. Rolls.*—Eng. Dilger, Dillicar. *(Hard)* Eng. Tilleard—Mod. German Dillert—French Tilliard.   (*Here*, warrior) Ang.-Sax. Tilhere, bishop of Worcester—English Diller, Tiller, Tillier—French Dillery, Tillier.   (*Et**) English Tillott—French Dillet,

---

* Many ancient endings, as *aud* or *ead*, prosperity, *had*, war, *hait*, "hood," converge in modern names into *et*.

190 THE WARRIOR AND HIS ARMS.

TILLOT. *(Man)* Ang.-Sax. Tilmann (*found in Tilmannes den, Cod. Dip.* 379)—Tilmon, *Lib. Vit.*—Tileman, *Hund. Rolls.*—Eng. DILLMAN, TILLMAN, TILGMAN, TILEMAN—Mod. German DILLEMANN, TILLMANN—French TILMAN. (*Mar,* famous) Old German Tilemir, 8th cent.—Eng. DILLIMORE. (*Noth,* bold) English DILNUTT. (*Wine,* friend) Tiluini, *Lib. Vit.*—Eng. DILLWYN. (*Mund,* protection) Anglo-Saxon Tilmund (*found in Tilmundes hô, Cod. Dip.* 663)—French TILMANT.

PHONETIC ENDING.

Eng. DILLON. French DILLON, TILLON.

Another root of similar meaning is probably *turn,* which is found as early as the 6th cent., and which Förstemann supposes to be from Old High German *turnan,* Eng. "turn," in the sense of overthrowing, or in the later sense of tilting. He has five ancient names from this root, but none corresponding with ours.

Turn.
To overthrow.

SIMPLE FORMS.

English TURNEY, TOURNAY? French TOURNE, TOURNAY? DURNEY.

DIMINUTIVES.

Eng. TURNELL, TURNLEY—French TOURNAL, DOURNEL. French TOURNAILLON. French TOURNACHON.

COMPOUNDS.

(*Here,* warrior) Turnerus, Capellanus, in a grant to the monastery of Croyland, A.D. 1051—Eng. TURNER—French TOURNEUR, TOURNAIRE, TOURNERY.

Another root with this meaning may be *strude, strut,* Ang.-Saxon *strudan,* to devastate, destroy, along with which, as a High Germ. form, we may class *struz.*

Strude,
Strut.
To destroy.

SIMPLE FORMS.

Old German Strodo, Strut, Struz, 8th cent. English STRUDE, STRUTT. Mod. Germ. STRAUSS.

THE WARRIOR AND HIS ARMS. 191

COMPOUNDS.

(*Here*, warrior) English Struthers.   (*Wig*, war) Eng. Strudwick.

Another root of similar meaning may be Ang.-Sax. *scathan, sceathan*, Old Norse *skêdia*, Old High German *scadan*, Mod. German *schaden*, to injure, plunder, destroy.   There is also another root proposed by Förstemann, and which might intermix—Goth. *skadus*, Old High Germ. *scato*, shade, in the older sense of shelter or protection. And a third might be Old Norse *skati*, rex, vir munificus, from *skattr*, tribute, whence Skati, a name in the Landnamabok.

SIMPLE FORMS.

Old German Scato, 9th cent.   English Skate, Shade, Sheath, Skeet.   Mod. German Schat, Schade. French Scat, Scatti.

Scate, Skeet. To destroy.

COMPOUNDS.

(*Here*, warrior) Eng. Sheather, Shether.   (*Lac*, play) Eng. Scadlock.   (*Leof*, dear) Eng. Skatliff.   (*Wealh*, stranger) Sceadwala,* father of Beowulf (*Flor. Wor.*) Eng. Shadwell.

PHONETIC ENDING.

Old Germ. Scattani (*Genit.*), 9th cent.   Eng. Scaddan.

Some other words of hateful sound to Christian ears are no doubt derived in a warlike sense.   Such is the root *bal, bale, pale*—Goth. *balv*, Old High German *palo*, Ang.-Saxon *bealo*, bale, woe, calamity, in the sense of one who inflicts calamity upon others.   This root is apt to mix up with another of very different meaning, *bil*, lenitas, placiditas, as explained by Grimm.

---

* Or this name might be put to the root, *had, chad*, war, as at p. 169.

192 THE WARRIOR AND HIS ARMS.

SIMPLE FORMS.

Old German Ballo, Pallo, 8th cent.   Paley or Paling,
Danish Jarl in the time of Ethelred.   Eng. BALL, BALLEY,
BAIL, BAILEY,* PAIL, PALEY, BELL, BELLY, BELLOW, BELLEW,
PELL, PELLY, PELLEW.   Mod. Germ. BALL, PAHL, BEHL.
French BALLE, BALAY, BALLY, BALLU, BAIL, BAILLA, BAILLY,
BAILLIEU, PAILLE, PAILLEY, PALLU, BELLÉE, BELLEAU,
BELLI, BELLU, PELLE, PELLÉ, PELLU.

Bal, Bale, Pale. Calamity.

DIMINUTIVES.

Eng. BALLOCK—French BALLOCHE.   English BALAAM,
BELLAMY—Fries. BALLEMA—French BELLAMY, BELHOMME?

PATRONYMICS.

Eng. BALLING, PALING.   French PALLANQUE, PELLENO.

COMPOUNDS.

(*Fred*, peace) Old German Palfrid—English PALFREY.
(*Hard*) English BALLARD, PAILLARD—French BALLARD,
BAILLIARD, PAILLARD, PAILLIART.   (*Here*, warrior) Eng
BALLER, BALYER, PALER—Fr. BAILLIÈRE, BALERY, PAILLEUR,
PAILLERIE.   (*Mer*, famous) Old Germ. Ballomar, 2nd cent.,
Belimar, 8th cent.—Eng. BALMER, BELLMORE, PALMER?—
French BELLEMARE, PALMIER?   (*Ret*, counsel) English
PALAIRET—French BALLERET.

Then there are some roots which signify fear,
loathing, horror, in the sense, with the ancient
termination, of " one who is a terror to others."
Thus a warrior in Saxo describes himself—

> Bessus ego sum,
> Fortis in armis,
> Trux inimicis,
> Gentibus horror.

Hence I take to be the root *og*, Old Norse
ôga, abominari, whence Oegr, a name in the
Landnamabok.   This seems to be the root of our

---

* Or some of these might be put to the root *bag*, as at p. 172.

THE WARRIOR AND HIS ARMS. 193

words "ugly" and "ogre." Förstemann, however, places *og* to the root *hug*, thought, reason, which may indeed intermix—the difference between *og* and *hog* not being much to build upon.

SIMPLE FORMS.

Old Germ. Ogo, 9th cent.   Old Norse Oegr.   Eng. Ogg.
French Og, Ogé.

Og. Horror.

COMPOUNDS.

(*Bern*, bear) Eng. Ogborn.   (*Here*, warrior) Eng. Ogier, French Ogier, Oger.

A root cognate with the above seems to be Goth. *agis*,* Old High Germ. *akiso*, *ekiso*, horror, which is found in several Old German names, none however corresponding with the following.

SIMPLE FORMS.

English Aggis, Aggas, Akass.   French Agis, Agasse, Aguesse, Ajasse, Egasse, Egaze.

Agis, Akis, Ekis. Horror.

DIMINUTIVE.

Swiss Agassiz ?

A third root with the same meaning may be *broke*, *brook*, which Stark refers to Old High Germ. *bruogo*, *pruoko*, Ang.-Saxon *bróga*, terror. There might also be a root *brock*, from Ang.-Sax. *brockian*, to afflict, oppress, but a separation would be difficult.

SIMPLE FORMS.

Old Germ. Bruocho, Bruogo, 11th cent.   Anglo-Saxon Bróga.   Eng. Brock, Broke, Brook, Brew.   Mod. Germ. Bruch, Brocke.   French Broc, Breucq.

Broke, Brook. Terror.

PATRONYMICS.

Eng. Brooking.   Eng. Brookson.

---

* May not this be the origin of Eng. "aghast," formerly spelt *agazed* ?

Y

194 THE WARRIOR AND HIS ARMS.

COMPOUNDS.

(*Here*, warrior) English BROKER, BROOKER, BREWER ?—Modern German BROCKER—French BRUGIÈRE, BRUHIÈRE. (*Man*) Eng. BROCKMANN, BROOKMAN—Mod. Germ. BRUCK-MANN, BROCKMANN, BROOCKMANN. (*Hard*) Old German Brocard, 11th cent.—Eng. BROCARD—Mod. Germ. BRUCH-HARDT—Fr. BROCARD.

Ott.
Terror?
There is another root which may come in here, *ott*, from Old Norse *ótta*, terrere. Hence Haldorsen derives the Scandinavian name Ottar, in the sense of metuendus, "one to be feared," and hence, I take it, the Eng. name OTTER. But whether OTT, OTTEY, OTWAY, are also to be placed to the same root, may be doubtful.

Another word of similar meaning is Old High Germ. *leid*, Old Sax. *léd*, Ang.-Sax. *láth*, hateful, loathly, in the sense, like the preceding words, of one who is a terror to others. But it seems to me probable that there is an intermixture of another root, not noticed by Förstemann, Ang.-Saxon *lédan*, to lead, *láteow*, *latheow*, *ládman*, leader.

SIMPLE FORMS.

Old Germ. Lethu, Lombard King, 5th cent., Laitu, Ledi, Letus. English LAID, LADY, LATE, LATHY, LEATH, LEETE.
Laith, Late.
Loathly
Mod. Germ. LETHE, LETTE, LEYDE. French LAITY, LAITIÉ, LETHO, LEDÉ, LEDO, LEDOUX, LEDIEU, LETTU.

DIMINUTIVES.

Old Germ. Ledila, 9th cent.—Eng. LATHALL, LEATHLEY, LETLEY—French LÉTALLE, LETAILLE, LÉTOILE. Old Germ. Ledoc, 8th cent.—French LEDUC, LETAC, LETOCQ.

PATRONYMICS.

Old German Leiting, 9th cent. English LEEDING, LATHANGUE. Mod. Germ. LEDING. French LETANG.

THE WARRIOR AND HIS ARMS. 195

COMPOUNDS.

(*Ger*, spear) French LEDAGRE. *(Hard)* Old German Lethard, Letard, 9th cent.—English LEATHART—French LATARD. (*Here*, warrior) Old Germ. Leither, Letar, Lether, 8th cent.—Ang.-Sax. Lethar (*Episcopus, Cod. Dip.* 981)— Eng. LATER, LEATHER, LEADER—Modern German LEDER, LEITER—French LEDIER, LE THIÉRE? *(Man)* English LAIDMAN, LADYMAN. (*Rice*, powerful) Old Germ. Letoerich, 8th cent.—French LAEDERICH. (*Ramm, ran*, raven) Old Germ. Lethramnus, 9th cent.— French LADURON, LETTERON. (*Rat*, counsel) Old German Laidarat;'(Archbishop of Lyons, 8th cent.)—French LADRET, LATERRADE. (*Ward*, guardian) Old German Lethward, 8th cent.—English LATEWARD.

There is another root very difficult to separate from the above, Goth. *lathon*, Old High German *ladon*, to invite, in the sense, according to Förstemann, of challenge. So that in any case the names come under this head.

SIMPLE FORMS.

English LADD, LATH, LATTEY, LATTA. French LADÉ, LATTE.

<small>Lad, Lath. Challenge</small>

COMPOUNDS.

(*Here*, warrior) Eng. LATTER—French LATRY, LATOUR. (*Leof*, dear) English LATLIFF. (*Mar*, famous) Old German Lathomar, 7th cent.—Latomer, *Roll Batt. Abb.*—Latimarus, *Domesday*—Eng. LATIMER.

From the Goth. *driugan*, Ang.-Sax. *dreogan*, militari, we may take the following.

SIMPLE FORMS.

Old German Drogo, Drugo, Trogo, Trugo, 7th cent. Drogo, *Domesday*. English TROKE, TROW, TRUE, DREW. Mod. Germ. DROGE, TROCHE, DRUE. French TRUC, TROU, DROU, DRUEY.

<small>Drog. Drew. Militari.</small>

DIMINUTIVES.

Eng. DREWELL, TROWELL—French TRUELLE. French DROULIN.

196 THE WARRIOR AND HIS ARMS.

PHONETIC ENDING.

English DRUGGAN, DROWN. French DRUGEON, DROUEN, DROUYN (de Lhuys.)

COMPOUNDS.

(*Bert*, famous) French TRUBERT. (*Hard*, fortis) French DROUARD. (*Hari*, warrior) Old German Truogheri, 9th cent.—English DREWERY, DRUBY, TROWER—Mod. German DRUCKER, TRÜGER—French DRUCQUER. (*Man*) English TRUEMAN—Mod. Germ. DRUMANN.

The following seem to be from Anglo-Saxon *grillan*, ad litem provocare. There is only one Old Germ. name, which Förstemann thus derives.

SIMPLE FORMS.

Grill.
Challenge
Eng. GRILL, GREELE, GREELY, CRILLY, CREALEY—French GRILL, GRILLY, GREEL.

COMPOUNDS.

(*Hari*, warrior) French GRELLIER. (*Man*) Old Germ. Grilieman, 10th cent.—Eng. CREELMAN.

From the Goth. *draban*, Ang.-Saxon *drepan*, to hew, slash, wound, are probably the following.

SIMPLE FORMS.

Drab.
To slash.
Old Germ. Drebi, 8th cent. Eng. TRAPP, TRIPP. Mod. Germ. TRAPPE. French TRAPPE, TRIBOU.

DIMINUTIVES.

Old Germ. Trebel, 10th cent. Eng. DRABBLE, TRAVEL, TREBLE. French TREBOUL, TREFFIL.

COMPOUNDS.

(*Wald*, power) Old German Trapold, 9th cent.—French TRABOLD, DREVAULT.

In an age of hand-to-hand conflict, when every man had to depend on the strength of his own arm and the temper of his own steel, a tried and trusted weapon was naturally regarded with a feeling something akin to veneration.

THE WARRIOR AND HIS ARMS. 197

We find, both in the Celtic and Teutonic myths, that the sword of a celebrated warrior was often distinguished by a proper name, and that magical or peculiar properties were not unfrequently attributed to it. Thus the celebrated sword called Sköfnung, which belonged to the Icelandic warrior Hrolf Kraki, and which was afterwards carried away out of his grave, could not, as related in Scandinavian myths, be drawn in the presence of women, or so that the sun shone upon the hilt, without losing something of its virtue.

The sword of Roland was called Durenda, a word which also occurs frequently in the names of men, where it is probably derived, at least in many cases, from the weapon of the renowned champion. In France, at the present day, the name is extremely common.

SIMPLE FORMS.

Old German Durand, Duorant, 9th and following centuries. Durandus, *Lib. Vit.* Eng. DURAND. Mod. Germ. DORAND, DURAND. French DURAND, DURANDEAU, DURANT. Ital. DURANDY, DURANTO.

Durand. Sword of Roland.

COMPOUND.

(*Hard,* fortis) French DURANDARD.

Names derived from weapons are extremely common, but not, as it seems to me, at least as the general rule, in any metaphorical sense, but rather on the principle referred to p. 18. That is, in simple forms, the ancient termination gives the sense of "one having a sword," "one having a spear," &c.

198 THE WARRIOR AND HIS ARMS.

Sword itself is not common ; it is found in an Old Germ. Sueridus, 4th cent.—in the name Swerting, of a Goth mentioned in Beowulf—and in Svertingr, the name of four Northmen in the Landnamabok.

SIMPLE FORMS.

Old Germ. Sueridus, 4th cent. Eng. SWORD. Modern Germ. SCHWERDT. French SOURD, SOURDEAU, SERDOU, SERT.

Sword.
Ensis.

COMPOUNDS.

(*Here*, warrior) Eng. SWORDER, SORTOR—Fr. SOURDIÈRE. (Or else the same as Old English ." sworder," swordsman ?) (*Wal*, stranger) Eng. SORTWELL—French SOURDEVAL.

A more common word is *brand*, Old Norse *brandr*, signifying literally a torch, a burning, but metaphorically a sword, from its shining, in which sense it is still used in poetry. Graff gives it the former meaning in proper names, but Förstemann, more reasonably, as I think, the latter. It was common among the Lombards, and among the Northmen, but not among the Saxons, nor, except as a termination, among the Franks. Another form in Ang.-Sax. and Old Fries. is *brond.* The Brondings are a people mentioned in Beowulf, also in the Scôp or Bard's song.

SIMPLE FORMS.

Old German Brantio, 9th cent. Old Norse Brandr, Brandi. English BRAND, BRANDY, BRANT, BROND, BRENT— Mod. German BRANDT—French BRAND, BRANDY, BRANDAU, BRANDAO, PRAND.

Brand,
Brond.
Sword.

DIMINUTIVES.

Old Germ. Brandila, 5th cent.—Eng. BRANDLE—Modern Germ. BRANDEL—French BRANDELY, BRONDEL. Old Germ.

THE WARRIOR AND HIS ARMS. 199.

Brandalenus, 8th cent.—Eng. BRANDLING—Modern German BRÄNDLEIN. Eng. BRANDIS,* BRANDISH—Modern German. BRANDEIS—French BRANDÈS.

COMPOUNDS.

(Hard) English BRANDARD. *(Here,* warrior) English BRANDER—French BRONDER (or same as Old English "sworder," swordsman.) *(Ram,* raven) Eng. BRANDRAM. *(Rêd,* counsel) Eng. BRANDRETH—Mod. Germ. BRANDROTH. *(Rice,* powerful) Eng. BRANDRICK.

As a termination I find it in three English names, GILLIBRAND, SHIERBRAND, and HILDEBRAND. And in five French, ALBRAND, AUDEBRAND, CHABRAND, GHEERBRANT, and HILDEBRAND. Perhaps we may find another in MALIBRAN. The name of the Dutch painter, REMBRANDT, comes in here.

Another word signifying a blade, sword, is Old Fries. *klinge,* Germ. and Dan. *klinge,* Dutch *kling.*

SIMPLE FORMS.

Cling, Clink. Sword.

Old Germ. Chlincho, 9th cent. English CLING, CLINGO, CLINK, CLINCH, CLENCH. Modern German KLING, KLINK, KLENCKE.

COMPOUNDS.

(Hard) Eng. CLINKARD—Mod. Germ. KLINKHARDT—French CLENCHARD.

There is considerable probability that in proper names, spade (Ang.-Sax. *spada,* Old High German *spata*), had the meaning of sword. Förstemann observes that this sense obtains in the Romanic languages and in Polish. And the

---

* Perhaps, rather, the ending in these names may be, as Pott has it, from *eis,* iron. And thus BRANDIS, &c., may be the converse of the Old Germ. names Ysbrand, Isanbrand, "Iron-sword."

200 THE WARRIOR AND HIS ARMS.

probability is increased by the fact that plough, as hereafter noticed, had sometimes the meaning of spear.

SIMPLE FORMS.

Spaqe,
Spate.
Sword?
Old German Spatto, 9th cent. English SPADE, SPADY, SPEIGHT. Mod. Germ. SPAETH, SPÄT. French SPADA.

COMPOUNDS.

(*Man*) Eng. SPADEMAN. (*Here*, warrior) Eng. SPADER. (Or perhaps more probably same as " sworder," swordsman.)

A fourth word for a sword is Goth. *meki*, Ang.-Sax. *meche*. There is a Meaca mentioned in the Scôp or Bard's song, as ruling the Myrgings (the people of the Old Nordalbingia), whose name seems to be from this origin. This root is very difficult to separate from another, *mic*, probably meaning great.

Meek,
Meech.
Sword?
SIMPLE FORMS.

Old German Meco, 9th cent. Meaca, *Scôp or Bard's song.* Eng. MEEK, MEEKEY, MEECH.

PATRONYMIC.
English MEEKING.

COMPOUND.
(*Here*, warrior) Eng. MEEKER.

From the Ang.-Sax. *seax* or *sex*, a dagger or short sword, it is supposed by some writers—and this theory I think has the greatest probability —that the Saxons have derived their name. Hence in proper names the meaning may sometimes be that of the nation, and sometimes that of the weapon.

Sax, Sex.
Dagger.
SIMPLE FORMS.

Old Germ. Sax, Saxo, 7th cent. Sæxa, *genealogy of the East Saxon kings.* Eng. SAXE, SEX, SEXEY, SIX. Modern Germ. SACHS, SAX. French SAX, SIX.

THE WARRIOR AND HIS ARMS. 201.

DIMINUTIVE.	COMPOUND.
English SAXL.	(*Mer*, famous) Eng. SEXMER.

The father of the above Sæxa was called
Sledda. This seems to be from Old Norse *sledda*,
a faulchion or curved sword. We seem to have
here one of the instances of the earliest attempts
at a family name. The father being called by a
name signifying a sword, the son is called by a
name perfectly different in sound, yet having the
same meaning; so as, without any confusion, to
connect him with his father. The following
names come in here.

SIMPLE FORMS.   Slade.
Sledda, Gen. East Sax. kings. Eng. SLADE, SLATE, SLIGHT. Faulchion?

PHONETIC ENDING.   COMPOUNDS.
Eng. SLADEN.   (*Here*, warrior) Eng. SLADER, SLATER ?

A very ancient name is Knife, which appears
in the name Cniva, of a Gothic king of the 3rd
cent. in Jornandes. Two centuries later we find
in the same author a Gothic name Cnivida.
This has the same meaning, " knife-wood," a
poetical or pleonastic expression for a knife.

SIMPLE FORMS.   Knife.
Old German Cniva, 3rd cent., Gniva. English KNIFE,   Oulter.
KNIPE, CANNIFFE (*Manch.*) Mod. Germ. KNIEP. French
CANNEVA, CHENEVEAU. Ital. CANOVA ?

COMPOUNDS.
(*Vid*, wood) Old German Cnivida, 5th cent.—English
KNYVETT—French CANIVET, GANIVET.

We see how in the English *knife* and in the
French *canif*, the awkwardness of the initial *k*
has been variously got rid of—in the one case by
dropping it in the pronunciation altogether, and

z

202 THE WARRIOR AND HIS ARMS.

in the other by the introduction of a vowel, so as to make it a dissyllable, as is the case in some of the above names. The latter course we have ourselves adopted in the 'name of the English king Canute, properly Cnut or Knut.

There are more names derived from the spear than from the sword. One of the most common of all roots is Ang.-Sax. *gâr*, Old Norse *geir*, Old Sax. and Old Fries. *gêr*. Förstemann thinks that *ger*, avidus, and *garo*, paratus, may mix up with this root. The Old Frankish forms *char* and *car*, of *har*, army, are also often difficult to separate.

Gare, Geer, Gore. Spear.

SIMPLE FORMS.

Old Germ. Gero, Kero, Caro, 7th cent. Old Norse Geir, Geiri. Eng. GARE, GAREY, GARROW, GEERE, GEARY, GORE, GURR, JARY, JEARY, CARR, CAREY, CAREW, CORE, CORY, KERR. Mod. Germ. GEHR, GÖHR, KEHR. French GARAY, GARRÉ, GAREY, GAREAU, GERY, GERAY, GIRY, GIROU, GORRE, GUERRE, GUERRY, GÖER, JAYR, JARRY, CAREY, CARRÉ, CAREAU, CORA, CORU.

DIMINUTIVES.

Old Germ. Gericho, Kericho, 8th cent.—Eng. GARRICK, GERICH, CARRICK, KERRIDGE—Mod. Germ. GERICKE, GÖRICH —French GUERICO, CORICH. Old German Gerlo, Kerilo, Cherilo, 8th cent.—Eng. GARELL, GIRL? KERLEY, KERRELL, CHERRILL—Mod. Germ. KERHLE—French GAIREL, GARIEL, GARREL, GARELLA, GUEUREL, CAREL, CORALLI. English GARLING, CARLING, CARLEN, GIRLING—French GARRELON, GARLIN, CARLIN. English GARRAS, GERISH—French GÉREZ, GOREZ, GORISSE, CARRAZ. Eng. GERKIN—Modern German GHERKEN—French CARQUIN.

PATRONYMICS.

Old Germ. Gering, 8th cent.—English GARING, GORING, GEARING—Mod. Germ. GERING, GÖRING.

THE WARRIOR AND HIS ARMS. 203

COMPOUNDS

(*And*, life, spirit) Old Germ. Gerand, 8th cent.—French GARAND, GERANDE, GERENTE, GORAND, GUÉRAND. (*Bad, bet,* war) Old Germ. Kerpato, 8th cent.—Eng. GARBETT—French GERBET, GUERBET. (*Bald*, bold) Old Germ. Garibald, duke in Bavaria, 6th cent., Kerbald—Eng. GORBOLD, GORBELL, CORBOULD—French GARIBAL, GERBAULT, GIRBAL—Ital. GARIBALDI, GERBALDI. (*Bert*, bright) Old Germ. Garibert, 7th cent., Gerbert—Mod. Germ. GERBERT—Fren. GERBERT. (*Brand*, sword) Old German Gerbrand, 9th cent.—Eng. GARBRAND, 17th cent.—French GHEERBRANT. (*Brun*, bright ?) Old Germ. Gerbrun—Eng. GOREBROWN. (*Bod, but,* envoy) Old German Gaerbod, 8th cent.—Gerbodo, *Domesday Yorks.*—Eng. GARBUTT—Mod. Germ. GERBOTH—French GERBAUD, GERBAUT. (*Hard*) Old German Garehard, 7th cent., Gerhard, Gerard, Girard—Eng. GARRARD, GERARD—Modern German GERHARD—French GERARD, GIRARD, GIRARDIN (*French dimin.*) GUÉRARD. (*Hari*, warrior) Old German Garaheri, Caroheri, Gerher—Eng. CARARY, CARRIER—Mod. Germ. GEHRER, KEHRER—Fren. GARRIER, GERRIER, GIRIER, GUERRIER, JARRIER, CARRIÉRE. (*Lac*, play) Old German Gerlac—Eng. GARLICK—Mod. Germ. GERLACH. (*Land*) Old Germ. Gerland, 9th cent., Jerlent, 11th cent.—English GARLAND, CARLAND—French JARLAND. (*Man*) Old Germ. Garaman, Caraman, German—Ang.-Sax. Jaruman, bishop of Mercia—English GARMAN, GERMAN, GERMANY, GORMAN, JARMAN, CARMAN, KERMAN—Mod. German GERMANN, KARMANN—French GERMAN, GERMAIN, CARAMAN. (*Mund*, protection) Old German Garimund, Germund, 7th cent.—Old Norse Geirmundr—English GARMENT—French GERMOND, GUERMONT, CARMENT. (*Not*, bold) Old Germ. Garnot, 8th cent.—Eng. GARNETT—French GARNOT, GUERNET, CARNOT. (*Rod*, red) Old German Kaerrod, 8th cent.—Old Norse Geirraudr—English GARROD—French GIROD, CAROD. (*Laif,* relic) Old Germ. Gerlif—Old Norse Geirleifr—Eng. GERLOFF. (*Ferhth*, life, spirit) Gerferth, *Lib. Vit.*—English GARFORTH. (*Stin*, stone) Old German Kerstin, 11th cent.—Old Norse Geirstinn—English GARSTIN. (*Wald*, power) Old German

204 THE WARRIOR AND HIS ARMS.

Garivald, Garold, Gerwald, Gerald—English GERHOLD, GARROLD, JARROLD, JERROLD—Modern German GERHOLD, GEROLD—French GARAULT, GERAULT, GIRAULD, GUEROULT. (*Ward*, guardian) Old German Garward, Geroard—French GIROUARD. (*Was, vas*, courageous) Old German Gervas— Eng. JERVIS—French GERVAISE. (*Vid*, wood*) Old Germ. Gervida, 7th cent.—English GARWOOD, GURWOOD, JERWOOD. (*Wig, wi*, war) Old Germ. Geravig, Gerwi, 8th cent.—Eng. GARRAWAY, GORWAY, GARVEY, JARVIE, CARROWAY. (*Sind*, way, journey) Old German Gersinda, 8th cent.—French GARZEND, GUERSANT. (*Wine*, friend) Old German Girwin, Garoin, Caroin—Eng. CURWEN—Modern German GERWIN, KERWIN—French GARVIN. (*Wan*, beauty ?) Old German Geravan, 11th cent.—Eng. CARAVAN.

PHONETIC ENDING.

Old German Garino, Gerin, 7th cent. English GOREN. Mod. German GÖREN. French GARIN, GUERIN, GUERINEAU.

The oldest form of *gar*, as found in the Gothic, is *gais*, which shows the identity of the word with the old Celt. *gais*, weapon, the *gæsum* of Cæsar, a sort of javelin used by the Gauls, and the Greek γαισος. Förstemann finds a difficulty in the fact that the word is found in personal names long after Gothic times, as late as the 10th cent. But the theory which I have elsewhere proposed as to the adoption of names in many cases simply as having been borne by men who had gone before, is, I think, sufficient to account for this. Such names would generally— but not invariably—follow the changes of the language. The name of the great Vandal king Genserich, is in some readings, Gaiserich, and would come in here.

---

* Ang.-Sax. *gar-wudu*, spear-wood, a spear.

THE WARRIOR AND HIS ARMS. 205

Gais.
Spear.

SIMPLE FORMS.

Old Germ. Gaiso, Geeso, 6th cent. Eng. GAZE, GEAZEY, CASE, CASEY, KAYS. French GAZE, CAZE, JÈZE.

DIMINUTIVES.

English GAZELLE, CAZALY—French GAZEL, GAZELIUS, CAZEL. French CAZALONG.

COMPOUNDS.

(*Hard*, fortis) Eng. GAZARD—French GAISSARD. (*Here*, warrior) Casere, Gen. kings of the East Angles—English CAYZER? (*Mund*, protection) Eng, CASEMENT? (*Raud*, red) French JAZERAUD.*

From the Celt. *gais*, weapon, the Gaelic tongue forms *gaisge*, bravery. And probably from some German form of the same word comes Eng. *gash*, to cut. Whether of these two meanings is to be found in the following group I cannot say, as the German character is not very strongly marked, and as I find no ancient names to correspond. Perhaps also, as Pott suggests, the French GASC may be the same as Gascon.

Gash.
Vulnerare?

SIMPLE FORMS.

Eng. GASH, CASH, CASHOW, CASK, CASKY. Mod. Germ. KASCH, KASKE. French GASC, GASCHÉ.

DIMINUTIVE.

English GASKELL.†

COMPOUNDS.

(*Man*) English CASHMAN? (*Hari*, warrior) English GASHRY?

Another form from the same root as *gar* and *gais*. is *gaid*, English " goad," to which I put the following.

---

* Seems to correspond with the Old Norse Geirraudr. This termination I have taken to be generally from another word, *hród*, glory.

† Or according to Mr. Arthur, from Gael. *Gaisgeil*, valiant.

206 THE WARRIOR AND HIS ARMS.

Gaid.
Dart.

SIMPLE FORMS.

Old German Gaido, Caide, 9th cent. English GADE, GATE, CADE, CATE, CATO. Mod. German GAIDE. French GAIDE, GAITTE, GAYTTE.

COMPOUNDS.

(Bon, fatal,) Eng. GADBAN—French GATTEBON. *(Gar,* spear) Eng. GATAKER—French GATECHAIR. *(Hari,* warrior) English GAITER, CATER. .

The root *sp* forms many of the words signify-ing a weapon or sharp instrument, and forms them perhaps in two different senses. One sense may be that of darting or shooting forth, as found in *spew, spout, spirt, speed*—the other that of diminution, as found in *spare, speck, split, spin* (to draw out or attenuate), *sparrow, spink* (small birds), *sprat* (small fish), &c.,—this gives the sense of a fine or sharp point.

In the latter sense I take it is formed the word spear, Ang.-Sax. *spere*, Old High German and Old Sax. *spêr*, cognate with Latin *sparus*, &c. It is by no means a common word, either in ancient or modern names.

Spear.
Hasta.

SIMPLE FORMS.

Old German Sperus, 8th cent. English SPEAR, SPYER. Mod. German SPEER. French SPIRE, SPIRO.

PATRONYMICS.

English SPEARING, SPIRING. Mod. Germ. SPÖRING.

COMPOUNDS.

(Man) Eng. SPEARMAN. *(Wine,* friend) Eng. SPERWIN.

From the same root as spear comes spit— Old Norse *spiot*, Dan. *spyd*, Dutch *speet*, Ital. *spiedo*, Old High Germ. *spiz*, Mod. Germ. *spiess*, all having the same meaning of dart or spear,

THE WARRIOR AND HIS ARMS. 207

and no doubt closely allied to the word *spade*, p. 200. I do not find any ancient names to correspond with the following.

SIMPLE FORMS.

Eng. SPITTY, SPITTA, SPITE, SPEED, SPICE. Mod. Germ. SPIESS.

Spit. Spear.

A third form from the same root is spike— Old Norse *spik*, falcicula, Dutch *spijk*, pike, Lat. *spica*, point, &c. The Old Norse *spekia*, philosophari, *spakr*, wise, *speki*, wisdom, might intermix in the following names.

SIMPLE FORMS.

Spech, *Domesday*. Eng. SPEAK, SPECK, SPIKE. Mod. German SPECK. French SPICQ.

Spike. Point.

COMPOUNDS.

(Man) English SPEAKMAN, SPIKEMAN. Mod. German SPECKMANN.

From the root *sp* above referred to, and probably in the former of the two senses, is formed Ang.-Sax. *spreot*, *sprit*, which has the double sense of sprout, branch, twig, and also of dart or spear. In the latter sense might be taken the English names SPROUT, SPROAT, SPRATT, &c., but there is another sense allied to that of sprouting, viz., that of vigour, activity, "sprightliness," to which, on the whole, I have thought it better elsewhere to place them.

Another word for a spear was Old Norse *doerr*, probably from the Sansc. root *tar*, to penetrate, to which Förstemann places the following ancient names. The word *durand*, *durant*, p. 197, I take also to be from this origin.

208 THE WARRIOR AND HIS ARMS.

Dar, Dor.
Spear.

SIMPLE FORMS.

Old German Tarro, Terra, Torro, 9th cent. Terri, *Lib. Vit.* English DARR, DARROW, DOOR, DOREY, DURRE, TARR, TARRY, TERRY, TORRY. Mod. German DOOER. French DARY, DARRU, DOR, DORÉ, DORY, DOREAU, DURR, DUREY, DUREAU, DURU, TARÉ, TERRAY, TERRE.

DIMINUTIVES.

Old German Darila, 9th cent.—Eng. DARRELL, DARLEY, DORRELL, DURELL, DURLEY, TURRELL — French DOREL, DUREL, TARLAY, TURELL.

PHONETIC ENDING.

English DORAN. French DORIN, TORIN,

COMPOUNDS.

(Bon, fatal) Eng. DORBON*—French TARABON. *(Gaud,* Goth) Eng. DARACOTT—French DARGAUD. *(Gund,* war) Old Germ. Taragun,† 9th cent.—Eng. DARRIGON, DARGAN —French TARAGON, TARGANT, DARGENNE. *(Here,* warrior) Eng. TARRYER, TERRIER—Fren. DARIER, TERRIER, TERREUR, *(Gis,* hostage? comrade?) Eng. DARKIES—French DORCHIES; TURGIS. *(Man)* English DORMAN, DURMAN—Mod. German DORMANN. *(Mar,* famous) Old German Terrimar, 9th cent. —English DORMER—Mod. Germ. DORMEIER—French DOER-MER. *(Not,* bold) Old German Ternod, 9th cent.—English TERNOUTH—French TARNAUD, DARNET. *(Wine,* friend) Old Germ. Daroin, 8th cent.—English DARWIN. *(Wald,* power) Old Germ. Derold—Mod Germ. DAROLD, TURHOLD—French DARRALDE, DORVAULT.

From the above root *dar* I take to be formed Ang. Sax. *darêth,* English *dart,* found in two or three ancient names.

SIMPLE FORMS.

Dart.
Jaculum.

Old German Daredus,‡ Tarit? 8th cent. Eng. DARDY,

---

* Förstemann has no examples of *bon* as an ending. But it evidently occurs in some of the words signifying spear, as in GADBAN, p. 206.

† Förstemann seems to think this name corrupted. Only, I presume, in so far that it has lost the final *d.*

‡ Förstemann does not place either of these two names here. Daredus, he suggests, may stand for Dagredus; and Tarit he places to the root *dar,* with an ending probably phonetic. But from the root *dar* with such an ending may not the word *darêth, dart,* be formed?

THE WARRIOR AND HIS ARMS. 209

DART, DEARTH, TART, TARRATT ?· · French DARTE, DARD, DARDIE, TARD, TARDY, TARDU; TARIDE ? TARRATTE ?

PHONETIC ENDING.

Eng. DARTON. French DARDENNE. DARIDAN.

COMPOUNDS.

(*Hari*, warrior) Old German Dirodhar, 8th cent.—Eng. DARTER, TARTER—French DARDIER, ·TARATRE, TARTTER, TARTARY.

From the Old High Germ. *ecca*, Mod. Germ. *ecke*, Ang.-Sax. *ecg*, edge, sharpness, cognate with Lat. *acies*. &c., and from the root found in Sansc. *ag, ac,* to pierce, I take the forms *ag, ac, eg, ec,* widely spread in proper names. And I also include the forms *hag, hac,* though Old Norse *hagr,* handy, useful, might be suitable. Grimm, however, explains the name Hagen as "spinosus." Still it must be admitted that the varied forms of the group suggest the probability of an admixture of roots.

SIMPLE FORMS.

Old German Ago, Acco, Hago, Hacco, Ego, Eggo, Ecco, Hego, Hecco, Aiko, Aio, Eyo, 4th cent. Old Norse Haki. English AGG, AGUE, ACHE, AKE, AKEY, HAIG, HAGGIE, HACK, HAW, HAY, EGG, EGO, EDGE, EYE, HEGGIE, HECK, HEDGE. Mod. German ACKE, EGGE, ECKE, HACKE, HEYE. French HACQ, HACHE, HAGE, HAYE.

·Ag, Ack, Eck. Acies.

DIMINUTIVES.

Old Germ. Hagilo, Hachili, Eccila, 9th cent.—Ang.-Sax. Hagel, Ogd. Dip.—Eng. HAGEL, HECKLE, HAIL—Modern Germ. HÄCKEL—French HECKLÉ. Old German Hacchilin, Echelin, 8th cent.—Eng. ACHLIN, HAILING—Mod. German HÄGELEN—French EGALIN.

· COMPOUNDS

(*Hard*, fortis) Old German Agihard, Achard, Aicard, Eckhard, Heccard, 8th cent.—English ACHARD, HAGGARD—

A 2

210 THE WARRIOR AND HIS ARMS.

Mod. Germ. ECKARDT, HÁGART, HACKERT—French ACART, AYCARD, HAGARD. (*Hari*, warrior) Old German Agihar, Agar, Aichar, Aiher, Egiher, Hager, 8th cent.—Eng. AGAR, ACRE, AYER, EAGER, HAGAR—Mod. Germ. ACKER, AICHER, EGER, HAGER, HAYER—French ACAR. (*Ram*, *ran*, raven) Old German Agramnus, Agrannus, 8th cent.—Eng. ACRON, ACORN ?—French AGRAM,. AGRON. (*Lac*, play) Old German Ekkileich, 9th cent.—French ACLOCQUE. (*Leof*, dear) Old Germ. Ailiv, 9th cent.—Old Norse Eylifr—Eng. AYLIFFE. (*Mar*, famous) Old German Agomar, Aimar, 7th cent.— French AYMER. (*Man*) Old German Egiman, 9th cent.— Eng. AIKMAN, HACKMAN, HEDGMAN, HAYMAN—Mod. Germ. HACHMANN, HECKMANN, HAYMANN—Fr. HEYMEN. (*Mund*, protection) Old Germ. Agimund, Ekimunt, 9th cent.—Old Norse Agmund, Aamund.—Agemund, *Domesday*.—English HAMMOND—French AGMAND, EYMOND, AYMONT, ECHEMENT. (*Not*, bold) Old German Eginot—French AGENET. (*Rat*, counsel) Old German Egered, Accarad, 7th cent.—English ACROYD ?—French EGROT, EYRAUD. (*Wald*, power) Old Germ. Agiovald, Agold, Ekkold, 7th cent.—Mod. German ECKHOLDT—French AGOULT, ACCAULT. (*Ward*, guardian) Old Germ. Eguard, 11th cent.—Fr. ECHIVARD, HACQUART. (*Wine*, friend) Old German Agiwin, 8th cent.—French AIGOIN. (*Ulf*, wolf) Old Germ. Achiulf, a Wern, 5th cent. —Eng. ACHUFF.

The root *ig* or *ic*, which Förstemann considers obscure, I should rather take to be another form of *ag* or *ac*, as found in Old Fries. *ig*, point, edge, sword, Lat. *ico*, &c.

SIMPLE FORMS.

Ic
Cuspis. Old Germ. Igo, Ico, 8th cent. Iccius, Belgic name in Cæsar? Eng. IGO, HICK. Mod. Germ. ICKR.

DIMINUTIVES.
Old Germ. Ikiko, 10th cent.—Eng. HICKOCK.

COMPOUNDS.
(*Ulf*, wolf) Old Germ. Igulf, 8th cent.—French IGOUF.

THE WARRIOR AND HIS ARMS. 211

From the root *ag* or *ac* is produced by a phonetic termination the form *agin* or *akin*. The only appellatives that I find are the Old High Germ. *agana*, Goth. *ahana*, Old Norse *ögn*, stalk, stem, spike, North Eng. *awn*, the beard of barley, from which we may assume for proper names the meaning of spear or weapon.

SIMPLE FORMS.

Old Germ. Agino, Eggino, Achino, Hagino, Haino, 7th cent. Eng. AGAN, ACKEN, AIKIN, HAGEN, HACON, HAIN.* Mod. Germ. HAGEN, HEYNE. Fr. AGON, EGON, EYCHENNE, HAGENE, HACQUIN, HAIN.

Agin.
Cuspis.

COMPOUNDS.

(*Bert*, famous) Old German Aganbert, Agembert, 8th cent.—Eng. AGOMBAR ?—French ECHANBARD. (*Fred*, peace) Old Germ. Aganfred, Ainfred, 8th cent.—French HAINFRAY. (*Hari*, warrior) Old Germ. Agenar, Haginer, 7th cent. —Old Norse Agnar—Mod. Germ. HAGNER—French HAGUENOER. (*Hard*, fortis) Old Germ. Eginhard, 8th cent.—Mod. Germ. HEINHARDT—French ECHINARD, IGNARD.

From the same root *ag* or *ac*, is also probably formed *agil;* p. 154, which may have a kindred meaning. I have there referred to the word as obscure, but I am inclined to think that it comes in here, and that it corresponds with Ang.-Sax. *egl*, a point, *eglan*, to pierce.

From the root *ag* or *ac*, as a nasalized form comes *ang* or *anc* (Old High Germ. *ango*, Ang.-Sax. *onga*, goad, prick, point), to which I put the following. There are several other names, particularly French, which would seem to come in

---

* A form Ain appears to be found in names of places, as Ainsley and Ainsworth.

212 THE WARRIOR AND HIS ARMS.

here, but a comparison with the Old Frankish names shows the original form to have been *ing*. At the same time I feel by no means sure that the root *ing*, except as a termination, is not often the same as *ang*.

SIMPLE FORMS.

Ang.
Prick.
Point.

Old Germ. Anco, Hanco, 8th cent. Eng. ? ANG, HANG *(Bowditch)*. Mod. Germ. ANKE, HANKE. French ANGÉ, ANGUY.

COMPOUNDS.

(*Wine*, friend) Old German Ançoin, 8th cent,—English ANGWIN—French ANGEVIN.

As *agil* from *ag*, so *angil* seems to be formed from *ang*. The appellative corresponding is Ang.-Sax. *angel*, a hook, but in proper names I should rather suggest the meaning of a barbed spear. The theory which derives the Saxons from their *seax* or knife, the Lombards from their *bart* or axe, and the Franks from their *franca* or javelin, derives the Angles also from their *angel* or hook. In proper names then we may hesitate whether to take the weapon, or the people's name, or, if we accept the above theory, the one as derived through the other. Förstemann also proposes the Lat. *angelus*, as a word of Christian introduction, with an admixture of *ingil*, as an extended form of the root *ing*. My own impression—taking all the above groupings together, and finding in them one common root—is in favour of the prevailing meaning of weapon.

Angil.
Hook.
Barb.

SIMPLE FORMS.

Old German Angilo, Engilo, Ingilo, 7th cent. English

THE WARRIOR AND HIS ARMS. 213

ANGEL, ANGLEY, ANGELO, ENGALL, INGLE, INGELOW. Mod. German ANGELE, ENGEL, INGEL. French ANGEL, ENGEL, INGEL.

DIMINUTIVES.

Old Germ. Angelin, 9th cent.—Eng. ANGLIN—Modern Germ. ENGELIN, ENGLEN—French ENCELAIN.

COMPOUNDS.

(*Bert*, bright) Old Germ. Angilbert, 'Engilbert, 8th cent. Eng. ENGLEBURTT—Mod. German ENGLEBRECHT—French ? INGHELBRECHT. (*Haid*, " hood") Old Germ. Anglehaidis, 9th cent.—Fr. ANGLADE. (*Hard*) Old German Angilhart, Engelhart, 8th cent.—English ENGLEHEART—Mod. German ENGELHARDT—French ANGLARD. (*Here*, warrior) Old Germ. Angelher, Engilher, 8th cent.—Eng. ANGLER—Mod. Germ. ENGLER—French ANGELIER. (*Land*) Old Germ. Ingaland —Eng. ENGLAND. (*Man*) Old Germ. Angilman, 8th cent. —Eng. ANGLEMAN—Modern German ENGLEMANN. (*Mund*, protection) Old German Angelmund, 8th cent.—French ANGLEMENT. (*Dio*, servant) Old Germ. Angildeo, Engildiu, 8th cent.—Anglo-Saxon Angeltheow—English INGLEDEW. (*Sind*, via) Old Germ. Ingilsind, 9th cent.—Eng. INGLESENT.

Another root with the probable meaning of spear or sharp instrument is to be found in Ang.-Saxon *staca*, stake, spear—*sticca*, stick, spike—*stician*, to pierce—Old Norse *sticki*, dagger, &c.

SIMPLE FORMS.

Stack.
Stick.
Cuspis.

Old Germ. Stacco, 9th cent., Stucchus, 8th cent. Eng. STACK, STAG, STICK, STOCK, STUCK, STUCKEY. Mod. Germ. STACKE, STICH, STOCK, STUCKE. French STACH, STOCQ.

COMPOUNDS.

(*Here*, warrior) Old German Stacher, 9th cent.—English STAKER, STICKER, STOKER, STOCKER—Mod. Germ. STECKER. (*Hard*) Eng. STACKARD—Mod. Germ. STECKERT, STICHERT, STÖCKHARDT. (*Man*) Eng. STACKMAN, STAGMAN, STICKMAN, STOCKMAN—Modern German STACKEMANN, STEGEMANN, STOCKMANN.

214 THE WARRIOR AND HIS ARMS.

From *staca, sticca,* a sharp point, is formed, perhaps as a diminutive, Old High German *stachilla,* cuspis, Old Norse *stickill,** a sharp point. .

Stackel.
Stickel.
Cuspis.

SIMPLE FORMS.

Eng. STAGGALL, STEGGALL, STICKLE, STOCKILL. Modern Germ. STICKEL, STÖCKEL.

COMPOUNDS.

(*Here,* warrior) Eng. STACKLER, STICKLER, STOCQUELER— Mod. Germ. STIEGLER.

A nasalized form of *stac* or *stic* I take to be *stang, sting* (Ang.-Saxon *stæng, styng,* pole, or as Förstemann suggests, spear, *stingian,* to pierce, stab). None .of the ancient names in Förstemann's list fall in with this group. · ·

Stang.
Sting.
Spear?

SIMPLE FORMS.

Eng. STANK, STING. Mod. Germ. STANG. Mod. Dan. STANGE, STINCK ?

COMPOUNDS.

(*Hari,* warrior) Old Norse Stangar—English STANGER, STINGER. (*Man*) Eng. STINCHMAN.

As spade in some ancient dialects was used in the sense of sword, so plough (Ang.-Saxon *plog,* Old High Germ. *ploh*), had in a similar manner the sense of spear. This obtained in Old High German, and Stark gives that meaning to the following three ancient names.

Plough.
Spear?

SIMPLE FORMS.

Old Germ. Bloc, 11th cent. Plucca, *Lib. Vit.* English PLUCK, PLUGG, PLOUGH, BLOCK, BLOCKEY, BLOGG, BLUCK, BLOW. Mod. German PLÜGGE, BLOCK. French PLOCQUE, PLOU, BLOC.

---

* Hence the summit called Stickle Pike in Cumberland, and the German Stackelberg.

THE WARRIOR AND HIS ARMS.   215

DIMINUTIVES.

Old German . Plugelo, 13th cent.   French BLOCAILLE, BLOQUEL.

PHONETIC ENDING.

Old Germ. Pluckone, 13th cent.   Eng. BLOWEN. · French PLOQUIN, PLUQUIN, PLOUIN.

COMPOUNDS.

(*Helm*, helmet) French PLOUGOULM.   (*Hari*, warrior) Eng. BLOWER—Modern German PLUCKER, PLÖGER—French PLOYER, BLOQUIÉRE.   *(Man)* Eng. PLOUGHMAN—Modern Germ. BLOCKMANN.   (*Not*, bold) Plukenet, *Roll Batt. Abb.*— Eng. PLUCKNETT.*

Tacitus tells us that the Germans were generally armed with a short spear, adapted either for close or distant fighting, and which was called in their language *framea*.   From this word, apparently . allied to the Modern German *pfriem*, Förstemann derives the following ancient names, which are mostly Frankish.

SIMPLE FORMS.

English FRAME, FREEM.   French FRÉMY, FREMEAUX, FROMMÉ, FORME.

Fram. Spear.

DIMINUTIVES.

·Eng. FREMLIN.   French FROMILLON.

PHONETIC ENDING.

Old Germ. Fermin. Ferminus, *Lib. Vit.*   Eng. FERMIN. French FREMIN, FREMINEAU, FERMIN.

COMPOUNDS.

(*Bald*, fortis) Old German Frambold, 8th cent.—French FRAIMBAULT.   (*Hari*, warrior) Old German Frammier, 9th cent.—French FREMIER, FREMERY, FERMERY.   (*Man*) Old German Framan, 9th cent.—French FROMAIN.   (*Mund*, protection) Old Germ. Framund, 8th cent.—Eng. FROMUNT, FREMONT—French FRÉMONT, FROMENT.

---

* Perhaps, as a slight corruption, PLUNKET.

216 THE WARRIOR AND HIS ARMS.

PHONETIC INTRUSION OF *n*.

(*Gar*, spear) Old German Framengar, 8th cent.—English FIRMINGER—French FREMUNGER, FREMANCOUR?

From the Gothic and High German *ast*, branch, also spear (cognate with Lat. *hasta?*), Förstemann takes the following root.

SIMPLE FORMS.

Ast.
Spear.
Eng. ASTE, ESTE, ESTY. French ESTE, HESTEAU.

DIMINUTIVES.

Eng. ASTLE, ESTLE—French ASTEL, ESTELLE. French ESTOCQ.

COMPOUNDS.

(*Hari*, warrior) Old German Asthar, 8th cent.—English ASTOR, ASTRAY—French ASTIER.   (*Ric*, power) Old Germ. Astericus, 9th cent.—Mod. Germ. ESTRICH—French ASTRUC —Ital. ASTRICO.   (*Ward*, guardian) Old German Asduard, 9th cent.—French ESTAVARD.   (*Wood*) English ASTWOOD (*like Garwood p.* 204.)

Perhaps allied in its root to the last word is Ang.-Sax. *æsc*, the ash tree.   The Ang.-Sax. *æsc* also signified a spear, on account of spears being made of ash-wood. For the same reason it likewise signified a ship or a boat. There is a third sense derived from Northern mythology (*see p.* 142), which might obtain in proper names. But on the whole I prefer to take as the general sense that of the weapon.

SIMPLE FORMS.

Asc.
Spear.
Æsc, son of Hengist. Old Norse Askr.   English ASH, ASK, ASKEY. Mod. Germ. ASCHE, ESCH.

DIMINUTIVES.

Old German Askila, 4th cent.—Eng. HASKELL—French ASCOLI, ESQUILLE.   Old German Ascelin, 11th cent.—Eng. ASHLIN—French ESCALIN.

THE WARRIOR AND HIS ARMS. 217

COMPOUNDS.

(*Bert*, famous) Ang.-Sax. Æscbyrht (found in Æscbyrhtæs geat, *Cod. Dip.* 1091)—Eng. ASHPART. (*Hari*, warrior) Old Germ. Aschari, Eskere, 8th cent.—Anglo-Saxon Æschere—English ASHER—Modern German ASCHER, ESCHER—French ESCARÉ. (*Bald*, fortis) Eng. ASHBOLD. (*Man*) Old Germ. Ascman—Aschman, *Hund. Rolls*—Eng. ASHMAN—Modern German ESCHMANN—French AESCHIMANN. ·(*Mar*, famous) Ang.-Sax. Æscmêr—Eng. ASHMORE (or local). (*Ric*, power) Old Germ. Eskirich, 8th cent.—Mod. German ESCHRICH—French ESCAYRAC. (*Wid*, wood) Old Germ. Asquid—Ascuit, *Domesday*—Eng. ASQWITH,* ASHWITH, ASHWOOD. (*Wine*, friend) Old Germ. Ascwîn, 8th cent.—Ang.-Saxon Æscwine —Eng. ASHWIN. (*Ulf*, wolf) Old Germ. Ascolf, 9th cent.— Eng. ASCOUGH.

Another word signifying dart or spear is Goth. *uzd*, Ang.-Saxon and Old Fries. *ord*, Old High Germ. *ort*, Old Norse *oddr*, to which I put the following. Most of our forms in *od* seem, however, rather to be from *aud*, prosperity, than from the above Old Norse word.

SIMPLE FORMS.

Old Germ. Ort, 8th cent. Old Norse Oddr, Oddi. Eng. ORD, ORTH, HORD, HORT, ODDY. Mod. Germ. ORT, ORTH. French ? ORTH, HORTUS ?

Ord
Dart.

DIMINUTIVES.

Old Germ. Ortila, 9th cent.—Eng. HURDLE—Mod. Germ. ORTEL—Ital. ORTELLI. Mod. German OERTLING, ORTELN—French ORTOLAN. Eng. ORDISH—French HOZDEZ (*Gothic form.*) French HORDEQUIN.

COMPOUNDS.

(*Gar*, spear) Old Germ. Ortger, 8th cent.—Eng. ORGAR ? —French ORTIGUIER. (*Hari*, warrior) Old Germ. Ortahar,

---

* Some of these names might be local.

B 2

218 THE WARRIOR AND HIS ARMS.

8th cent., Hortarius* (prince of the Alamanni), 4th cent.—
Eng. HORDER. (*Liub*, love) Old Germ. Ortliub, 11th cent.—
Modern German ORTLIEB—French HORTELOUP. (*Ward*,
guardian) Old German Hordward, 11th cent.—English
ORDWARD. (*Wig, wi*, war) Old Germ. Ordwig, 9th cent.—
Eng. ORDWAY.

From the above root *ord* or *odd* seems to be
formed, by a prefix, the Anglo-Saxon *brord*, Old
Norse *broddr*, spear, dart, Old English *brode*, to
prick. To this Stark places the following Old
German names.

SIMPLE FORMS.*

Old Germ. Broda, 13th cent. Ang.-Sax. Brorda. Old

Brod.
Dart.
Norse Broddr. Broth, *Roll Batt. Abb.* English BROAD,
BRODIE. French BROT, BROET, BRAUD, BRODU, PROTEAU,
PROT.

PHONETIC ENDING.

Eng. PROTYN. French BRODIN, PRODIN.

COMPOUNDS.

(*Had*, war) Old German Prothadius, 7th cent.—English
BRODHEAD—French PROTHAUT. (*Hari*, warrior) Old Germ.
Brothar,† Broter, Produrius, 8th cent.—Brother, King of
Denmark, Brother, Danish king of Dublin—Eng. BROTHER,
PROTHEROE—Mod. German BRUDER. (*Ric*, power) English
BRODERICK.

From the Ang.-Sax. *pil*, Old Norse *pila*, dart,
arrow, I take the following. And I do not feel
at all sure that many other names placed elsewhere to *bil*, *pil*, lenitas, placiditas, ought not to
come in here.

---

* Grimm's derivation of this name (*Gesch. d. Deutsch. sprach.*), from Anglo-
Saxon *corther*, troup, company, seems by no means a satisfactory one. But we
must remember that this great scholar wrote without the full data which the
Altdeutsches Namenbuch now affords.

† I take it that brother, frater, intermixes in these names.

THE WARRIOR AND HIS ARMS. 219

SIMPLE FORMS.

Eng. PEEL. Mod. Germ. PIEHL, PEEL. French PIELLE, PIELLA, PIOLÉ.

Peel. Dart.

PATRONYMICS.

Eng. PEELING. French PIOLENC.

COMPOUNDS.

(*Bon*, fatal) French PELABON. (*Hard*) Modern German PIELERT—French PIELARD. (*Beam*, shaft, handle) English PILBEAM.*

As the Ang.-Sax. *dareth*, dart, from the root *dar*, p. 208, so may, I take it, the Old Norse *billdr (biledr ?)*, dart, be formed from the root *bil* or *pil* (Gr. βαλλω ?) To this we may place the following, though *bald*, audax, is apt to intermix.

SIMPLE FORMS.

Old Germ. Pilde. French PILTÉ, PELTÉ, BILLOTEAU ?

Bild. Dart

COMPOUNDS.

(*Hari*, warrior) English BILLITER, BUILDER—French BELLETTRE, PELTIER, PELTZER. (*Rat*, counsel) Old German Bildrad, 8th cent.—French PELTRET, PELLETERET.

From the Old Sax. *scapt*, Anglo-Saxon *scaft*, *sceft*, spear, shaft, arrow—literally, that which is shaped or smoothed—we may take the following.

SIMPLE FORMS.

Eng. SHAFT, SHAFTO. French CHAFT, CHAPT.

Shaft. Spear. Arrow.

COMPOUNDS.

(*Hari*, warrior) Old Germ. Scaptarius, 6th cent.—Ang.-Sax. Sceafthere—Eng. SHAPTER—Fr. SCHEFTER, CHEFTER. (*Wald*, power) Old Germ. Scaftolt—Eng. SCAFFOLD.

From the Ang.-Sax. *flân*, dart, arrow—that which is flown or flung—we may probably take the following.

---

† Like the Ang.-Sax *garbeam*, spear handle. But probably in both cases the word is only used as a pleonastic form of spear or dart.

220   THE WARRIOR AND HIS ARMS.

Flan.
Dart.
Arrow.

SIMPLE FORMS.

Eng. FLANE, FLAWN.   French FLAN, FLANNEAU, FLOHN.

COMPOUNDS.

(*Bert*, famous) Old Germ. Flanbert, Flambert, 8th cent.
—Eng. FLAMBARD—French FLAMBERT.   (*Gar*, spear) Old
Germ. Flanigar, 9th cent.—French FLAMMGAR.

There is a word *nagal* found in a few ancient
names, which I think may come in here. Förstemann refers to *nagal*, unguis, remarking at the
same time that the sense does not seem a
particularly suitable one for names. But *nagal*,
clavis, in the sense rather of a sharp point, spike,
spear, appears to me to be sufficiently appropriate.
Nor does it seem necessary to take it, as
suggested by Mone (*Heldensage*), in connection
with the mythological smith Weland.

SIMPLE FORMS.

Nagal.
Clavis.
Cuspis.

Old German Nagal, 9th cent.   Old Norse Nagle, Eng.
NAGLE, NAIL.   Mod. Germ. NAGEL, NAHL.   Dan. NAGEL.
French NAGEL, NEÉL, NÉLY.

COMPOUNDS.

(*Hard*, durus) Old Germ. Nagalhard, 8th cent.—French
NALLARD. (*Bert*, bright) French NALBERT. (*Hari*, warrior)
Eng. NAYLOR*—Modern German NAGLER—Dan. NAGLER—
French NÉOLLIER.

There is a curious set of names derived from
the above word *nagal*, nail—to all appearance of
comparatively modern origin—and found both
in English and in German. Such is English
TUFFNELL, on which Mr. Lower remarks—" In
the 17th century this name was spelt Tufnaile,
and I am therefore rather inclined to take it

---

* Of course these names, with the exception perhaps of the French, might
be from the trade.

THE WARRIOR AND HIS ARMS. 221

au pied de la lettre, and to consider " tough nail"
as its etymon. I believe that in this case Mr.
Lower has " hit the nail on the head." Not so,
however, in the case of HORSENAIL (the name,
by the way, as he tells us, of a Kentish farrier),
which he seems to have been beguiled into thinking a corruption of Arsenal. I take it that this
name, corresponding with the Germ. ROSNAGEL,
is also nothing else than what it seems. We
have also HARTNELL corresponding with a Germ.
HARTNAGEL, COPPERNOLL with a Germ. KUPFER-
NAGEL, and HOOFNAIL with a Germ. HUFNAGEL.
And we have ISNELL (iron-nail), BRAZNELL,
CRUCKNELL, HOCKNELL, BRADNELL, DARTNELL,
PRANGNELL (Germ. *prangen*, to glitter ?) BRIT-
NELL (German *breit*, broad), SCARNELL, COURT-
NELL (Dutch, Dan. *kort*, short.) The Germans
have THÜRNAGEL (door-nail), RECKNAGEL (rack-
nail), SCHINNAGL (plate-nail), BLANKENNAGEL
(white-nail), RODNAGEL (red-nail), RUNDNAGEL
(round-nail), WACKERNAGEL,* and several others.
This curious class of names, standing very much
by themselves, must I think have had some
peculiar origin.

From the Old High German *barta*, an axe, I
take to be most probably the following. Words
also suitable are *bart*, beard, and Old Norse
bardi, giant. And the root *bert*, bright, famous,
is also liable to intermix.

---

* Germ. *wacker*, noble, stout, brave. Pott's suggestion that *wacker* is an
epithet applied, not to the nail, but to a man called Nagel, hardly helps us much,
seeing the number of other similar names.

222 THE WARRIOR AND HIS ARMS.

SIMPLE FORMS.

Bard. Axe.

Old Germ. Bardo, Barto, Pardo, Parto, 9th cent. Eng. BARD, BARDY, BARTIE, PART, PARDOE. Modern German BARDE, BART, BARTH. French BARD, BARDÉ, BARDY, BARDEAU, BARTEAU, PARTY.

DIMINUTIVES.

Old German Bardilo, 9th cent.—English BARDOULEAU, BARDELLE—Modern German BARDEL—French BARDELLE, BARTEL. French BARDILLON, PARDAILLON.

PHONETIC ENDING.

Old Germ. Bardinus, 8th cent. Eng. BARDIN, PARDON. Mod. Germ. BARTEN. Fr. BARDON, BARDONNEAU, PARDON.

PATRONYMICS.

Old Germ. Barding, 9th cent. Eng. BARDING, PARDING.

COMPOUNDS.*

(*Hari*, warrior) Eng. BARTER, PARDAR, PARTER—Modern Germ. BARTHER. (*Man*) Eng. BARTMAN—Modern German BARTHMANN. (*Ulf*, wolf) Old German Bartholf—English BARDOLPH.

From the Ang.-Sax. *becca*, axe, might be the following. But I think, now too late, that they ought not to have been separated from the root *big, bic*, to slash, p. 177.

SIMPLE FORMS.

Beck. Axe.

Old Germ. Becco, Begga, Becca, 7th cent. Eng. BECK, BEGG, BEACH, BEECHEY, PEAK, PEACH, PEACHEY. Modern Germ. BECKH, PECK. French BEC, BECK, BECQUEY, PECH.

DIMINUTIVES.

Eng. BEACALL, PECHELL—Mod. Germ. BECKEL—French BECKLÉ. Eng. BEAKEM ?—French BECQUEMIE.

COMPOUNDS.

(*Had*, war ?) Eng. BECKETT, PECKETT—French BÉCHADE, BECQUET, PECQUET. (*Hari*, warrior) Eng. BEECHER, PECKER —French BECKER, PECQUERY. (*Man*) English BECKMAN, BEACHMAN—French BECHMAN.

---

* I do not include here BARTLETT and BARTRAM, for I think that they are rather from *bert*, famous.

THE WARRIOR AND HIS ARMS. 223

There is a word *score*, found in two or three ancient names, which Stark refers to Old High Germ. *scora, schora*, spade, shovel, supposing, as in former cases, the meaning to be that of weapon. This word, and another, *scar*, which Förstemann assigns to Old High Germ. *scara*, acies, I include together in the general sense of cutting, as shown in Ang.-Sax. *scearian, sceorian.*

SIMPLE FORMS.

Old German Scarius, 9th cent., Scoro, Scori, 13th cent. English SCARR, SCARROW, SHEER, SHERRY, SCORE, SHORE, SHOREY, SCURRY, SHUREY. Modern German SCAR, SCHAR, SCHEER, SCHURR. French CHERI? CHEREAU? CHOREY?

Scar. To cut.

DIMINUTIVES.

Old Germ. Scherilo, 9th cent.—Eng. SHERRELL.

COMPOUNDS.

(*Brand*, sword) English SHIERBRAND—Modern German SCHEURBRAND. (*Man*) Old German Scureman, 14th cent. —Eng. SCARMAN, SHARMAN, SHERMAN, SHORMAN—Modern German SCHIERMANN, SCHÜRMANN.

I am inclined to the opinion that *wood* in proper names has sometimes the sense of spear, or at least of a weapon. We find a peculiar use of this word in Anglo-Saxon ; thus *gar-wudu* is "spear wood," a spear—hence the Old German name Gervida, our GARWOOD. The same is no doubt the sense in the Old German Asquid, our ASQWITH—"ash-wood" in the sense of a spear, and probably in our ASTWOOD, p. 216. An Old Frankish name Bonavida, 9th cent., " fatal wood," is probably also a figurative expression for a spear. So also the Gothic name Cnivida, our

224. THE WARRIOR AND HIS ARMS.

KNYVETT, is "knife-wood," a knife. It seems to me probable that wood of itself may sometimes have the same sort of meaning. There is an Old German name Widolaic, our WEDLAKE and WEDLOCK, from *lacan*, to play. This compares with the Anglo-Saxon *æsc-plega*, "ash-play," i.e., play of spears. A similar mode of expression is by no means uncommon even in English. Thus, in a sense more or less poetical, we use steel for a sword, and gold for money. Hence also in sacred poetry, such an expression as "fatal wood" for the cross. And the poetical element, it must be observed, enters largely into the composition of ancient names.

From the Ang.-Sax. *boga*, Old High German *bogo, pogo, poco*, English bow, arcus, I take the following. But there is another word from the same general root signifying to bend, viz., Gothic *baugs*, Old High Germ. *bauc*, Anglo-Saxon *beág*, ring, bracelet, which I think also enters into the composition of men's names, and which it is extremely difficult to separate from the present group.

SIMPLE FORMS.

Bog.
Bow.
Arcus.

Old Germ. Bocco, 9th cent. ? Ang.-Saxon Boge. Old Norse Bogi. Eng. BOGG, BOAG, BOGIE, BOHY, Bow, BEAU, BOOK ? Mod. Germ. BÖGE, POGGE, BOCK ? French POGÉ, BOCH ?

DIMINUTIVES.

Ang.-Saxon Bogel *(found in Bogeles pearruc)**—Eng. BOGLE, BOWELL—Mod. German POGGEL—French POGGIALE.

---

* Bogel's paddock.

THE WARRIOR AND HIS ARMS. 225

COMPOUNDS.

(*Hard*, fortis) Eng. BOGARD—Modern German BÖGERT—French BOCHARD, BOHARD, POCHARD. (*Man*) English BOGMAN, BOWMAN—Mod. Germ. BOCHMANN? (*Mar*, famous) Anglo-Saxon Bôcmêr, Bôhmêr (*found in Bôcmêres stigele, Bôhmêres* stigele*)—English POGMORE, BOWMER—French BOCHMER, BOIMER.

From the extended form found in Modern Germ. *bogen*, may be the following.

SIMPLE FORMS.

Eng. BOGGON, BOWEN. Mod. German BOHN? French BOCHIN, BOIN, BOHNÉ.

(margin) Bogen. Bow.

COMPOUNDS.

(*Hard*, fortis) English POIGNARD?—Modern German BOGENHARDT—Fr. BOGNARD, POIGNARD? (*Hari*, warrior) Eng. BODGENER—Mod. German BOGNER—French BOGNIER.

A common word in ancient names was *helm*, helmet. We have very few names at present in which it can be traced, but as it is apt to change into *hem* or *em*, and so to mix up with other words, it is probable that many more names may exist in a disguised form.

SIMPLE FORMS.

Ang.-Saxon Helm (*found in Helmes treôw,†* Cod. Dip. 1266.) Eng. HELM. Mod. Germ. HALM, HELM.

(margin) Helm. Galea.

COMPOUNDS.

(*Burg*, protection) Old German Helmburg, 9th cent.—English HEMBERG, HEMBERY, HEMBROW. (*Ger*, spear) Old German Helmger, 8th cent.—Eng. ALMIGER (*or to amal, p.* 143.)

Another word signifying helmet is Ang.-Sax. *col*, Old Norse *kollr*. This seems to have been

---

* Bohmer's style. These two names seem to be the same.
† Helm's tree.

C 2

226 THE WARRIOR AND HIS ARMS.

common in Anglo-Saxon and Old Norse names, but, judging by Förstemann's list, not generally in Old German names.

SIMPLE FORMS.

Coll. Helmet. Old Germ. Colo, 9th cent. Ang.-Sax. Cola, Colo, Cole. Old Norse Kollr, Koli. Eng. COLLA, COLLEY, COLEY, COLE. Mod. Germ. KOHL, KOLL. Dan. KOHL. French COLLE, COLI, COLLEAU.

DIMINUTIVES.

Old Germ. Colaicho, 8th cent.—Eng. COLLICK, COLLEGE —Mod. Germ. KOHLIG. French COLLICHON. Old German Cholensus, 8th cent.—Eng. COLENSO, COLLINS.

PATRONYMICS.

Eng. COLLING. Mod. Germ. KÖHLING. Dan. KOLLING. French COLLANGE.

COMPOUNDS.

(*Bert*, bright) Old German Colobert, 8th cent.—English COLBREATH, COOLBREATH—Fr. COLBERT. (*Brand*, sword) Ang.-Sax. Colbrand—Eng. COLBRAN. (*Biörn*, bear) Old Norse Kolbiörn—Eng. COLBURN. (*Hard*) Eng. COLLARD— Modern German KOHLHARDT—French COLLARD. (*Hari*, warrior) Eng. COLLIER, COLLAR—Modern German KOLLER— Dan. KOLLER—French COLLIER, COLLERY, COLÉRE. (*Man*) Old Germ. Coloman, Colman, 9th cent.—Colman, Bishop of Lindisfarne, A.D. 663—Eng. COLMAN, COLEMAN—Modern Germ. KOHLMANN—French COLLMAN. (*Mar*, famous) Ang.-Saxon Colomôr (*found in Colomôres* sic, Cod. Dip.* 509)— Eng. COLLAMORE, COLMER—Mod. Germ. KOLLMEYER.

PHONETIC INTRUSION OF *n, m.*

(*Bert*, bright) French COLOMBERT. (*Hard*) French COLINARD.

" Until something better shall be found," Förstemann places the following to Old High Germ. *hûba*, Ang.-Sax. *hûfe*, Mod. Germ. *haube*,

---

* "Colomore's syke." Syke, a word still used in the North of England, signifies a runner sometimes dry.

THE WARRIOR AND HIS ARMS. 227

cap, crest, or, most probably, helmet. As I cannot say that I am able to suggest anything better, I continue them under the same head. The root of the Saxon names Offa or Uffa may be, however, liable to intermix.

SIMPLE FORMS.

Old German Hubo, Huba, Hufo, 8th cent. Hobbesune, *Domesday*. Eng. HUBE, HOBY, HOOP, HOPE, HOOF. Mod. German HAUBE, HUPE. French HOUBE, HOUPPE, HUPPÉ, CHOUPE.

Hub. Helmet.

DIMINUTIVES.

English HUBBACK, CHUBBACK—Mod. German HOBBEKE, HÖPKE—French HUBAC. English HOPKIN—Mod. German HÖPKEN. Eng. HUBBLE—French HUBEL. Eng. HOBLIN—French HUBLIN, HOUPLON, CHOBILLON. Dutch HOBBEMA.

COMPOUNDS.

(*Hard*) English HUBBARD—French HUBARD, CHOPARD. (*Man*) Eng. HOBMAN, HOPMAN, HOOFMAN—Mod. German HOPPMANN, HOFFMANN?

There is a name COPESTAKE or CAPSTICK, which in the previous edition I completely mistook. It is evidently the German *kopfstück*, head-piece.

From the Ang.-Sax. *scyld*, Old High German *scilt*, Old Norse *skiöld*, English *shield*, there are not many names, though as noted p. 148, it was anciently a name of honour.

SIMPLE FORMS.

Scyld, ancestor of Woden (*Anglo-Saxon Gen.*) Scyld (*found in Scyldes treow, Cod. Dip.* 436.) Skiöld, mythical king of Denmark. English SHIELD, SKELT. Mod. German SCHILDT.* French? SCHILTE.

Shield. Scutum.

---

* Hence ROTHSCHILD, " red shield," adopted, as it is said, by the founder of the family from the sign of his place of business, and certainly not an improvement upon his original name of ANSHELM, "divine helmet."

228 THE WARRIOR AND HIS ARMS.

PATRONYMICS.

Old Sax. Sciltung, 9th cent. Eng. SKELDING, SCOLDING, SKOULDING.

A more common word in men's names is *rand,* rim, in the sense, according to Förstemann, of shield, and to which, as a High German form, I put *rans.*

Rand.
Shield.

SIMPLE FORMS.

Old Germ. Rando, Rento, 4th cent. Eng. RAND, RANCE, RONDEAU, ROUND ? Mod. German RAND. French ROND, RONDY, RONDEAU, RONCE, RONZE.

DIMINUTIVES.

English RANDLE, RENDEL, RENTLE, RUNDLE ?—French RONDELLE. English RANTEM, RANSOM.

COMPOUNDS.

(*Hari,* warrior) Old German Ranthar, 8th cent., Ranzer, 10th cent.—Eng. RENDER, RENTER—Mod. German RANTER, RENTER—French RANDIER, RONZIER, RONCERAY. (*Mar,* famous) Eng. RENTMORE, WRENTMORE. (*Wine,* friend) Old Germ. Randuin, 8th cent.—French RANDOUIN. (*Ulf,* wolf) Old Germ. Randulf, 8th cent.—English RANDOLPH—Modern German RANDOLFF.

An allied form of *rand* is Old High German *ramft,* Mod. Germ. *ranft,* which seems to occur in a few names.

Ramft.
Shield.

SIMPLE FORMS.

Old Germ. Rampo, 9th cent. Mod. Germ. RAMPF.

DIMINUTIVE.

English RAMPLING.

COMPOUNDS.

(*Hari,* warrior) Eng. RAFTER, RAFTERY. Fr. RAFTIER.

A third root signifying shield is Ang.-Sax. *bord,* Old High Germ. *bort,* which, though Förstemann only has it as a termination (as in Heribord, Hiltiport, &c.), evidently occurs in the following.

THE WARRIOR AND HIS ARMS. 229

SIMPLE FORMS.

Bord. Shield.

English BOARD, PORT. French BORDE, BORDA, PORT, PORTA.

COMPOUNDS.

(Hari, warrior) Eng. BOARDER, BORDER—Fr. BORDIER, BORDERY. *(Man)* English BOARDMAN, PORTMAN—French ? BORDMANN. *(Wine,* friend) Eng. BOARDWINE, PORTWINE—French PORTEVIN.

A fourth word signifying shield—but of which I find no trace in ancient names—may be Ang.-Sax. *disc*, Old High Germ. *tisc*. This had the meaning of dish, plate, flat surface, but I think that like *rand* and *bord*, the most probable meaning in men's names is that of shield.

SIMPLE FORMS.

Disk. Shield.

English DIX ?* DIXIE ? Mod. German DISCH. French DIESCH,† TISCI.

COMPOUNDS.

(Hari, warrior) Eng. DISHER—Mod. German TISCHER—French DISCRY, TIXIER. *(Man)* English DISHMAN—Modern German DIXMANN.

From the Ang.-Sax. *hring, hrinc,* Eng. *ring,* in the sense of ring-armour, coat of mail, Förstemann derives a word *ring* in ancient names. And from the Old High Germ. *ringan,* luctari, *rang,* battle, Ang.-Sax. *rinc,* combatant, he also derives a form *rang, rank, renk.* But as the separation, in the ancient names even, is doubtful, and in the modern impracticable, I take them together— the sense being in either case a warlike one.

---

* In Ang.-Saxon *sc* and *x* frequently interchange. Thus Bosworth gives the plural of *disc* as *discas* and *dixas*.

† Or, as seems to be the case in another name, DIETSCH, this may only be a corruption of Deutsch.

230 THE WARRIOR AND HIS ARMS.

Ring.
Mail.

SIMPLE FORMS.

Old Germ. Rincho, Renco, 9th cent. Eng. RING, RINK.
Mod. Germ. RANKÈ, RINGE, RINCK.

DIMINUTIVES.

Old Germ. Ringilo—English WRINKLE—Mod. German
RINGEL—French RINGEL.

COMPOUNDS.

(*Hard*, fortis) Old German Renchard, 6th cent.—Modern
German RINGERT—French RINGARD, RANGHEARD. (*Hari*,
warrior) Old German Rincar, Ranchar, 9th cent.—English
RINGER, RANCOUR—Mod. Germ. RINGER, RENCKER—French
RINGHER. (*Wald*, power) Old Germ. Ringolt—Ang.-Saxon
Hringwold (*found in Hringwoldes beorh, Cod. Dip.* 1117.)
—Eng. RINGGOLD—Mod. Germ. RINGWALD.

The root *sar*, *ser*, for which Förstemann proposes Old High German *saro*, Ang.-Saxon *searo*,
armour, enters into a great number of names.

Sar, Ser.
Armour.

SIMPLE FORMS.

Old Germ. Saro, Sario, Sarra, 8th cent. English SARE,
SARAH, SEAR. Mod. German SAHR, SEHR, SERRE. French
SARRE, SAR, SARRA, SARI, SERRE, SERRA, SERÉ, SERY, SERIEU,
SORRÉ, SORIEU.

DIMINUTIVES.

Old German Serila, Serlo, 6th cent.—Old Norse Sörli,
Sölli —Eng. SAREL, SERRELL, SERLE, SORLIE, SOLLY—French
SERAIL, SOREL.

COMPOUNDS.

(*Bot*, envoy) Old Germ. Sarabot, 9th cent.—Eng. SERBUTT
—French SORBET. (*Hard*) French SERARD. (*Here*, warrior)
French SERRIER. (*Ger*, spear) French SARGER. (*Gaud*,
Goth) Old German Saregaud, 8th cent.—English SARGOOD.
(*Man*) Old Germ. Saraman, 8th cent.—Eng. SERMON—Mod.
German SAARMANN—French SARAMON, CÉRÉMONIE? (*Rat*,
counsel) Old German Sarrad, Sarrat, 9th cent.—English
SARRATT—French SARETTE. (*Wald*, power) Old German
Serald, 9th cent.—French SARRAULT. (*Wine*, friend) Old
Germ. Saroin, 8th cent.—French SARRION, SEROIN.

THE WARRIOR AND HIS ARMS. 231

From the above root *sar*, according to Diefenbach, is formed Old Norse *serkr*, Ang.-Sax. *syrice, syrce*, shirt, North. Eng. *sark*. To this may be put the following names, the meaning of course being taken to be that of a shirt of mail.

SIMPLE FORMS.

Old German Saracho, 10th cent. Serc, *Lib Vit.*—Eng. SARCH, SEARCH, SHARK, SHARKEY, SHIRK, SHIRKEY.

Serk. Shirt of mail.

DIMINUTIVES.

Old German Sarchilo, 10th cent. Eng. SHARKLEY.

One of the most common of all roots in Teutonic names is Goth. *hari*, Ang.-Saxon *here*, Old Norse *her*, army. Grimm suggests that the original meaning may rather have been soldier, which would consist better with the use of the word as a post-fix. Other roots which may intermix are *ara*, eagle, and Ang.-Sax. *heor*, Old Norse *hiör*, sword, both found in ancient names.

SIMPLE FORMS.

Old German Herio, 8th cent. English HARRE, HARE, HARRY, HARROW, CHARIE, CHERRY. Mod. German HEHR, HERR, HEER. French HARO, HARRY, HERR, HÉREAU, HERRY, HEROU, CHAREY, CHARIO, CHARUE.

Har, Her. Army.

DIMINUTIVES.

Old German Haric, Herico, 8th cent.—Eng. HARRIDGE, HERRIDGE, HERRICK—Modern German HÄRICKE, HARKE—French HÉRICHÉ. Old Germ. Heril, Herilo, Herili—Eng. HARRAL, HARLE, HARLEY, HARLOW, HEARL, HEARLY—Mod. German HEREE, HERL, HERRLE, HÄRLE—French HAREL, HARIEL, HARLAY, HARLÉ, HEREL. Old German Herelin, 11th cent.—Eng. HARLING—Mod. Germ. HÄRLIN—French HERLAN. Eng. HARRIS, HARRIES, HERRIES—Fr. HERIEZ, HERRISSÉ.

232 THE WARRIOR AND HIS ARMS.

PATRONYMICS.

Old Germ. Herinc, 9th cent. Eng. HEARING, HERRING. Modern German HARRING, HERRING, HEERING. French HARANG, HERINCQ, HERING.

COMPOUNDS.

(*And*, life, spirit) Old Germ. Heriand, 9th cent.—French HARAND. (*Bat, pat, path*, war) Old German Heripato, 9th cent.—English HEREPATH, HERBET—French HERBETTE. (*Bald*, bold) Old German Haribald, Herbald, 8th cent.— French HERBAULT. (*Ber*, bear) English HARBAR, HARBER, HARBOUR—Mod. Germ. HERBER—French HERBER. (*Bert*, bright) Old German Hariberaht, Frankish king, 6th cent.— Aripert, Lombard king, 7th cent., Heribert, Herbert—Eng. HARBERT, HERBERT—Mod. Germ. HARPRECHT, HERBERT— French HERBERT. (*Bord*, shield) Old Germ. Heribord, 11th cent.—Eng. HARBOARD, HARBORD. (*Bod*, envoy) Old Germ. Herbod, 8th cent.—English HARBUD—Modern German HERBOTHE—French HERBUT. (*Ger*, spear) Old German Hariger, Hariker, Harker, Chargar, 7th cent.—English HARKER, CHARKER—Mod. Germ. HERGER. (*Gaud*, Goth) Old German Haregaud,* 6th cent.—Eng. HARGOOD. (*Gisil, gil*, hostage) Old German Charegisil, 6th cent.—English HARGILL. *(Hard)* Old Germ. Hariard, Herard, 7th cent. Fr. HÉRARD. (*Here*, warrior) Old Germ. Harier, 9th cent.— French CHARIER. (*Laith*, terrible) Arlot, *Lib. Vit.*—Eng. HARLOT?—Fr. HARLET? *(Land)* Old Germ. Hariland, 8th cent.—Eng. HARLAND. (*Man*) Old Ger. Hariman, Harman, Herman, 7th cent.—English HARRYMAN, HARMAN, HERMON, CHARMAN—Modern German HARMANN, HERMANN—French HERMAN, HERMAIN. (*Mand*, gaudium) Old German Herimand, Herimant, 10th cent.—Fr. HARMAND, HARMANT, HERMAND. (*Mar.* famous) Old German Herimer, Harmar, 6th cent.—English HARMER—French HARMIER, HERMIER. (*Mot*, courage) Old Germ. Harimot, 8th cent.—Mod. Germ.

---

* Perhaps also, with a phonetic *n*, the Old German Heringaud, English HERINGAUD. But Förstemann takes it to be rather the same as Aringaud (*arin*, eagle.)

THE WARRIOR AND HIS ARMS. 233

HERRMUTH—French HERMET, CHARMOTTE. (*Mund*, protection) Old Germ. Herimund, Charimund, 5th cent.—Eng. HARMOND—French CHARMOND, CHARMONT. .(*Nand*, daring) Old German Herinand, 10th cent.—Spanish HERNANDEZ. (*Sand*; envoy) Old German Hersand, 11th cent.—English HERSANT—French HERSENT. (*Wald*, power) Old German Cariovalda,* prince of the Batavi, 1st cent., Heroald, Hariold, 8th cent.—Old Norse Haraldr—Eng. HAROLD—Mod. Germ. HEROLD—French HEROLD, HEROULT. (*Ward*, guardian) Old Germ. Hariward, Herward, Heroard, 8th cent.—Ang.-Sax. Hereward—Old Norse Harvardr—English HARWARD, HARVARD—Mod. German HARWARD—French HEROUARD. (*Vid*, wood) Old German Ervid, 7th cent.—Eng. HARWOOD. (*Wig*, *wi*, war) Old German Heriwig, Hairiveo, 7th cent. —Eng. HARVEY—Mod. German HERWIG—French HERVY, HERVIEU, CHARVEY, CHARAVAY. (*Wine*, friend) Old Germ. Harwin, Charivin, Charoin, 8th cent.—Eng. HARWIN—French HEROUIN, CHARVIN, CHAROIN. (To this Old Germ. Erwin, Ervin—Eng. IRWIN, IRVIN ?)

The above word, *hari*, warrior, was one of the most common post-fixes in Old German names. It appears variously as *har, hari, her, heri*, and forms many of our endings in *er* and *ery*, and of the French in *ier*. In certain cases, however, the ending *er* appears to be phonetic, as noticed at p. 29.

From the Ang.-Sax. *fana*, Old High German *fano*, Mod. German *fahne*, Old French *fanon*, an ensign, of which, however, there is but a slight trace in ancient names, I take the following. Another word *fagin, fain*, joyful, is apt to intermix.

---

* As *cat* of *had*, p. 167, so *car* is the oldest form of *har*.

D 2

234 THE WARRIOR AND HIS ARMS.

SIMPLE FORMS.

Fan.
Ensign. Eng. FANN, FANNY, FENN. Mod. Germ. FAHNE. French
FANO, FANÉ.

DIMINUTIVES.

English FENNELL—French FENAILLE. English FANLINE,
FENLON—French FENELON.

PHONETIC ENDING=OLD FRENCH *fanon* ?

Eng. FANNON. French FANNON.

COMPOUNDS.

(*Hari,* warrior) Eng. FANNER, FENNER—Modern German
PFANNER—French FANNIÈRE (or same as Old High German
fanner, standard-bearer.)

Cumber.
Standard From the Anglo-Saxon *cumbor,* standard or
ensign, appears to be the name Cumbra, of an
Ang.-Sax. chief, A.D. 756 *(Rog. Wend.)* Also of
a Cumbro in the *Traditiones Corbejenses.* And
hence may be our CUMBER and CUMPER. The
names CUMBERBEACH, CUMBERBATCH, CUMBER-
PATCH, all no doubt variations of the same word,
may possibly contain the Ang.-Sax. *beág,* English
badge.

Banner.
Vexillum. BANNER, though it might be, as at p. 175, a
compound of *ban,* might also be from *banner,* an
ensign. There was a noble family of Banners in
Denmark, whose founder, according to Saxo, was
a Dane named Tymmo, who assumed the name
of Banner for some exploit, probably capturing a
standard, at a battle between Canute and
Edmund of England.

From the Lombard *bandu,* ensign, standard, as
the most appropriate derivative from *bindan,* to
bind, Förstemann derives the root *band, bend.*
But the Ang.-Saxon *bænd, bend,* crown, chaplet,

THE WARRIOR AND HIS ARMS. 235

from *bendan,* to bend, appears to me to be a word that might at any rate intermix. In addition to the above, Förstemann also suggests the Old Sax. *bant,* pagus, and its High German form *panz.* I am also inclined to include in the group the forms *bond, bund,* for, though the derivation from the Ang.-Sax. *bonda, bunda,* husbandman, seems at first sight the most natural, it does not appear to receive much sanction from the ancient names. Nevertheless, it is very probable that there may be some intermixture of roots. In the comparative table of patronymic forms appended to " Words and Places," Mr. Taylor finds Bondings in Bondingham *(Somers),* and in Bontigny *(Lorraine).* I also add Bansings as found in Bensington *(Oxf.),* anciently Banesinghas.

SIMPLE FORMS.

Old German Bando, Bant, Pando, Penta, Ponto, Panzo, Benzo, Penzo, 6th cent. Ang.-Sax. Penda, king of Mercia. Benza, Pinda, *Lib. Vit.* Eng. BAND, BENDY, BENT, BOND, BUNDY, POND, BANCE, BENCE, BONSEY, BUNSE. Mod. Germ. BANSE, PANSE, BENTE, BENSE, BUND, BUNTE. French BENDA, BINDA, BANCE, BENCE, BENZ, BONDY, BONDEAU, BONTÉ, BONZÉ, PANTOU, PANTHOU, POND, PONT, PONTI, PONTEAU, PONTHIEU, PANSU, PENSÉ, PINSEAU, PONCEAU.

Band. Vexillum.

DIMINUTIVES.

Eng. BANTOCK, BUNDOCK—Modern German BANDKE, PANTKE—French PANTICHE. Ang.-Sax. Buntel *(found in Bunteles pyt, Cod. Dip.* 1102*)*—Eng. BENDLE, BENDELOW, BENTALL, BUNDLE, BONSALL, PENDALL, PENTELOW—Mod. Ger. BANDEL, BENDELL, BENZEL—Fr. PANTEL, BUNZEL, PONCEL. Old German Benzlin, 10th cent.—Benzelinus, *Domesday.*— Eng. PANTLIN—French BANCELIN.

236 THE WARRIOR AND HÍS ARMS.

PHONETIC ENDING.

English BANTON, BENTON, BINDEN, BENSON,* BUNTEN, PANTON, PENTIN, PENSON, PONSON. Mod. German BUNSEN. French PANSIN, PINSON, PINSONNEAU, PONSON.

PATRONYMICS.

Eng. BANTING, BENDING, BENTINCK, BUNTING, PANTING. Mod. Germ. BENTINGCK, BÜNTING.

COMPOUNDS.

(*Hard,* fortis) Old German Pantard, 9th cent.—English PINDARD—French BANSARD, PENSARD, PINSARD, PONSARD. (*Hari,* warrior) Ang.-Sax. Pender *(found in Penderes clif, Cod. Dip.* 1266*)*—Eng. BANDER, BENDER, BINDER, BONTER, BONSER, BUNTER, PANTER, PANTRY, PANTHER, PENDER, PINDER, PONDER, PUNTER—Mod. Germ. BENDER, BINDER— French BENDER, BINDER, PONTIER, PONSERY. (*Rat,* counsel) Old Germ. Bandrad, Pantarat, 6th cent.—Eng. BANDERET, BENTWRIGHT, PENDERED. (*Ulf,* wolf) Old Germ. Pandulf, prince of Capua, 11th cent.—Ital. PANDOLFIO.

Then there are some names of a different class derived from weapons, such as SHAKESPERE, SHAKESHAFT, DRAWSWORD, &c., which are of less, though still of considerable antiquity, and which do not enter into the Teutonic name-system; on these it is not necessary for me to dwell further, as all that can be said upon them is to be found in the last work of Mr. Lower.

We now come to another class of names of warlike origin—those derived from words signifying courage and valour. One of the most common roots is the Old High Germ. *môt, muat,* Old Sax. *muod,* Ang.-Saxon *môd,* Modern German *muth,* courage. Along with this I follow Förstemann

---

* BENSON, BUNSEN, &c., might be patronymics But I am more inclined to take the form as Bens-on, Buns-en.

THE WARRIOR AND HIS ARMS. 237

in classing *moz, muoz,* though Weinhold *(Deutsche Frauen)* refers it to Old High German *muoza,* moss.

SIMPLE FORMS.

Old Germ. Mot, Moata, Muato, Moda, Moza, Muozo, 6th cent. Ang.-Sax. Moda *(found in Modingaham, "the home of the sons of Moda," now Mottingham).* Mote, *Hund. Rolls.* Eng. MOTT, MOTTOW, MOTE, MOAT, MOUAT, MOTH, MOUTH, MODE, MOOD, MOODY, MOSE, MOSEY, MOSS, MOUSE, MUZZY. Mod. German MODE, MUTH, MOTH, MÜTZ, MUSS. French MOTTE, MOTTÉ, MOTEAU, MOITIÉ, MOTHU, MOUTIE, MOSSY, MOUSSE, MOUSSY, MOUSSU, MUSSEY.

Mot. Mode. Courage.

DIMINUTIVES.

Old Germ. Motilo, Mutila, Muezill, 7th cent.—English MOUTTELL, MUTLOW, MOTLEY, MODEL, MUDDLE, MOUSELL, MUSSELL—Mod. Germ. MODEL, MÜDEL, MÜTZELL—French MOTELLE, MUTEL, MOUSSEL. Old Germ. Mudilane, Motilane, 8th cent.—Eng. MUDLIN, MOSLIN—Mod. Germ. MÜSLEIN— French MODELONDE ? Eng. MUDDOCK, MUSICK—Modern Germ. MUSHACKE—French MOUSAC.

COMPOUNDS.

(*Bert,* famous) Old German Mutbraht, 9th cent.—Eng. MUSPRATT. (*Hard,* fortis) Old Germ. Moathart, 9th cent. —Eng. MUSSARD—Mod. Germ. MOZART, MUSHARD—French MOTARD, MOUTARD, MOUZARD, MUSARD. (*Hari,* warrior) Old German Muatheri, Motar,† Modar, 8th cent.—English MOUTRIE, MODER, MUTTER, MOSER, MOUSER—Mod. Germ. MODER. MÜTTER—Fr. MOUTRY, MOITRY, MOUTIER, MOITIER. (*Helm*) Old German Moathelm, 9th cent.—Eng. MOOTHAM ? (*Man*) Eng. MUDDIMAN, MOSSMAN. (*Ram, ran,* raven) Old Ger. Moderannus, 8th cent.—Eng. MOTTRAM—Fr. MOTHERON, MOUSSERON. (*Red,* counsel) English MODERATE. (*Ric,* dominion) Old German Modericha,‡ 11th cent.—English MUDRIDGE—Mod. Germ. MUTHREICH.

---

* Mr. Taylor finds the same name in Mutigny in France.
† It is very probable that *mother,* mater, intermixes.
‡ Hence perhaps the town of Motrico in Spain.

238   THE WARRIOR AND HIS ARMS.

PHONETIC ENDING.

Old Germ. Moatin, Muatin, 8th cent.   English MOTION, MUTTON, MOUZON.   Fr. MOUSON, MOSSON, MOZIN, MUSSON.

I am rather inclined to class along with the above a group of names ending in *st*—either by transposition for *ts, tz* (as for instance Must = Mutz)—or by a simple phonetic hardening of the termination.   The latter is in accordance with a common tendency—for instance, a number of *Punch* is before me in which an Irish game-keeper comforts an unlucky sportsman with " Shure, yer honner, you do it very *nist*."

SIMPLE FORMS.

Must.
Courage ?

Eng. MOIST, MUST, MUSTY, MUSTO.   Mod. Germ. MOST. French MOUSTY.

DIMINUTIVES.

Eng. MUSTILL.   Mod. Germ. MOSTHAL ?   Fr. MUSTEL.

COMPOUNDS.

(*Hard*, fortis) Eng. MUSTARD.   (*Hari*, warrior) English MUSTER—Mod. Germ. MOSTER—French MOUSTIER.*   (*Ron*, raven) Eng. MOSTRAN.   (*Ulf*, wolf) Eng. MUSTOPH.

Another word signifying valour or courage is Goth. *aljan*, Old High German *ellan*, Ang.-Sax. *ellen*, cognate probably with Gael. *allanta*,† fierce, to which may be placed the following.

SIMPLE FORMS.

Allan.
Ellen.
Courage.

Old German Alyan, 8th cent.   English ALLAIN, ALLAN, ELLION, ELLEN.   Mod. German ALLEHN.   French ALLAIN, ALLIEN, HELLION.

---

* Pott makes the French Moustier a contraction of Monastier, and if the name stood by itself, that derivation might be accepted.

† ALLAN, as a Christian name is more probably from the Gaelic.   So may also be some of the above simple forms.

THE WARRIOR AND HIS ARMS. 239

COMPOUNDS.

(*Bert*, famous) Old German Ellinbert, 9th cent.—French ELAMBERT. (*Burg*, protection) Old Germ. Ellinburga, 8th cent.—Modern German ELLENBERG—French HALINBOURG. (*Ger*, spear) Old German Ellanger, 11th cent.—French ALLENGRY. (*Hari*, warrior) Old Germ. Ellanher, 9th cent. —Eng. ELLENOR—Mod. Germ. ALLNER—French ALLONIER. (*Man*) Eng. HALLINGMAN.

A third root with the meaning of valour or daring is *nan, nant,* from the Goth. *nanthian,* audere.

SIMPLE FORMS.

Old German Nando, Nanno, 5th cent. English NANN, NANNY. Modern German NANNE, NÄNNY, NENNE. French NANT, NANTEAU, NANTA.

Nand. Nan. Daring.

DIMINUTIVES.

Old Germ. Nandilo, 8th cent.—Mod. German NENDEL— French NANTEUIL. Old Germ. Nanzo, 8th cent.—English NANS, NANCE—Mod. Germ. NANZ—French NANCY ?*

PATRONYMICS.

Old Germ. Nandung, Nending, 8th cent.—Mod. Germ. NÄNING—French NENNING. Eng. NANSON—Dan. NANSEN.

COMPOUNDS.

(*Hard*, fortis) Old German Nanhart, 11th cent.—French NENARD. (*Hari*, warrior) Old Germ. Nanthar, 9th cent.— Eng. NANNERY, NENNER—French NANTIER.

The word *nod, not,* rather common in personal names, is referred by Förstemann to Goth. *nauths,* Mod. Germ. *noth,* English *need,* with a probable admixture from Old High Germ. *hnôton,* quassare, or Goth. *knôds,* genus. But as the ending of Ang.-Sax. names, in which it was rather common,

---

* May of course be from the place. Can the place be from the personal name? Mr. Taylor refers it, along with Nantes, to Celt. *nant,* a valley.

240 THE WARRIOR AND HIS ARMS.

Bosworth derives it from Ang.-Saxon *nôth*, bold, daring, *nêthan*, audere, which is certainly a preferable sense for names.

SIMPLE FORMS.

Noth.
Daring.
Old Germ. Noto, Noti, Not, Nuti, 8th cent. Eng. NOTT, NOTHEY, NOAD, NUTT.* Mod. Germ. NOTH, NUTT. French NAUD, NAUDEAU, NAUDY, NODÉ, NOTTE.

DIMINUTIVES.

Old Germ. Nothicho, 9th cent.—Eng. NOTTIDGE. Eng. NODDLE, NUTTALL—Mod. Germ. NÖTEL—French NOTTELLE.

PATRONYMICS.

Old Germ. Noding, Noting, 9th cent. English NODING, NUTTING. Mod. Germ. NUDING.

COMPOUNDS.

(*Hari*, warrior) Old Germ. Nothar, 10th cent.—English NODDER, NUTTER, NOSER ? NUSSER ?—Mod. Germ. NOTTER, NÜTZER—Fr. NAUDIER, NODIER, NOTRE, NOTAIRE, NOZIÈRE. (*Hard*, fortis) Old Germ. Nothart, 8th cent.—Eng. NOTHARD. (*Man*) Noteman, *Hund. Rolls.*—Eng. NOTMAN, NUTTMAN.

PHONETIC INTRUSION OF *l.*

(*Hari*, warrior) Old Germ. Nodalhar, 8th cent.—French NODLER.

The most common of all words with this meaning in men's names is the Ang.-Saxon *bôld*, Old High Germ. *bald*, audax, fortis. The form *baltz*, *balz*, which runs through the formation, I take to be High German. This word is apt to mix with *bal*, p. 192.

SIMPLE FORMS.

Bald.
Balz.
Fortis.
Old German Bald, Baldo, Baudo, Pald, Belto, 4th cent. Eng. BOLD, BALDEY, BOLT, BELT, BAUD. Modern German

---

* The Danish Knut (Canute) might intermix. The name was derived, as I have read, from a wen upon his head, but I cannot find the authority again. The name KNUTH is still found in Denmark, and the patronymic KNUDSEN is very common.

THE WARRIOR AND HIS ARMS. 241

BALD, BOLDT, POLTE. French BALDÉ, BALDI, BAUD, BAUDEAU, POLD. Old German* Baldzo,* Balzo, Palzo, 9th cent.—Eng. BALLS, PALSY—Mod. Germ. BALTZ, BALZ.

DIMINUTIVES.

Eng. BALDICK, BALTIC—Mod. Germ. BOLTCHE—French BALZAC. Old Germ. Baldechin, 9th cent.—Eng. BALCHIN.—French BAUDICHON—Ital. BALDACHINI. Old Ger. Baldemia, Balsemia, Balsmus, 8th cent.—Eng. BELDAM, BALSAM—Mod. Germ. PALDAMUS—French BALSEMINE *(French dimin. ?)*

PATRONYMICS.

Old Germ. Balding, Palding, 8th cent. Eng. BOLDING, BOULTING, PAULDING. Mod. Germ. BALDING.

COMPOUNDS.

(Hard, fortis) Old German Baldhard, 8th cent.—French BALTARD, BALTAZARD (=Baltzard.) *(Hari,* warrior) Old Germ. Baldher, Balther, Paldheri, Paltar, 8th cent.—Ang.-Sax. Baldhere—Eng. BOLDERY, BALDER, BOLTER, POULTER, POWTER, POWDER—Mod. Germ. BALTZER—French BALTAR, BAUDIER, PAULTRE. *(Had,* war) Old Germ. Balthad, 8th cent.—Eng. BALDHEAD? *(Ram, ran,* raven) Old German Baldram, Baldrannus, Paldhram, 8th cent.—Eng. BELTRAM —Modern German PELLDRAM—French BAUDRON—Italian BELTRAMO. *(Mund,* protection) Old Germ. Baldmunt, 8th cent.—French BAUDEMENT. *(Rat,* counsel) Old German Paldrat, 8th cent.—French PAUTRAT. *(Rand,* shield) Old German Baldrand, 9th cent.—French BAUDRAND. *(Ric,* dominion) Old Germ. Baldarich (Thuringian king), Baldric, Baldrih, 6th cent.—Ang.-Saxon Baldric—Eng. BALDRIDGE, BALDRY, BOWDRY—French BAUDRY. *(Rit,* ride) Old Germ. Baldrit, 9th cent.—French BAUDRIT. *(War,* defence?) Old Germ. Baldoar, 8th cent.—Eng. BOUGHTWHORE?†—French BAUDUER. *(Wine,* friend) Old Germ. Baldwin, 8th cent.—

---

* It is not easy to say how these should be classed—Förstemann places them as diminutives—i.e., Baldzo=Baldizo, as Willizo from Willo, p. 23. I have taken them, however, only to be High German forms

† An early freeman of Connecticut *(Suffolk Surnames)*. He has certainly contrived to spell his name with the utmost amount of unpleasantness.

E 2

242 THE WARRIOR AND HIS ARMS.

Ang.-Sax. Baldwine—Eng. BALDWIN—Dutch BOUDEWYN—French BAUDOUIN—Ital. BALDOVINO. (*Vid*, wood) Old German Balsoidis, 9th cent.—Eng. BOLTWOOD. (*Ulf*, wolf) Old German Baldulf, 8th cent—Mod. German BALD'AUF*—French BAUDEUF. (*Wig*, war) Old Germ. Balduig, 7th cent. —French BALDEVECK.

PHONETIC ENDING IN *n*.

Old German Baldin, Paldeni, 11th cent. Eng. BOLDEN, POLDEN. Modern German BALDENIUS, PÖLTEN. French BAUDIN, BALSAN.

PHONETIC ENDING IN *r*.

Old Germ. Baldro, 9th cent. Eng. BOLDERO, BOUDROW† —French BAUDRO.

From the Goth. *thras*, fierce, swift, vehement, Old Norse *thrasa*, to contend, Förstemann derives the following ancient names. The name of the Vandal king Thrasamund comes from this root which is probably cognate with Irish *treas*, combat.

SIMPLE FORMS.

Trass.
Fierce.
 Old Germ. Thraso, Traso, Treso, 9th cent. Eng. TRASS, TRACE, TRESS, TRAIES, TRACY, DRAYSEY. French TRAYS, TRESS, TRACY, TRENS, DREYSS.

COMPOUNDS.

(*Hard*, fortis) French TRASSARD, TRESSARD. (*Wald*, power) Old German Trasuuald, 7th cent.—Modern German TRASWALT—Ital. TRESOLDI.

PHONETIC ENDING IN *n*.

Old Germ. Drasuno, 9th cent. French TRESSAN.‡

PHONETIC ENDING IN *r*.

Old Germ. Trasarus, 9th cent. Eng. TRAISER, TREASURE, ·DRESSER. French TERSEUR ?

---

* Pott, taking this name *au pied de la lettre*, explains it as *bald auf*, "early up."

† See p. 130.

‡ Pott's derivation of Tressan from "*tres sain*" is, I think, very unhappy.

THE WARRIOR AND HIS ARMS. 243

The Ang.-Sax. *trum*, firm, strong, courageous, appears to be found in a few* names. The *Altdeutsches Namenbuch* has only one name, Tromolt, 8th century, corresponding with a Trumuald in the *Lib. Vit.* In addition to the Saxon Trumhere below cited, there was also a Trumwine, bishop of Whitherne. The placing of Turnbull here is in accordance with a suggestion of Mr. Charnock in *Notes and Queries.*

SIMPLE FORMS.

Eng. DRUM, DRUMMEY, TRUMP, TRUMPY. Mod. German TRAUM.

Trum.
Firm.
Strong.

COMPOUNDS.*

(*Bald*, fortis) English TRUMBULL, TREMBLE, TURNBULL. (*Here*, warrior) Anglo-Saxon Trumhere, bishop of Mercia— Eng. TRUMPER, DRUMMER ?—Mod Germ. TRUMMER—French DROMERY.

From the Old High Germ. *hwas*, Ang.-Saxon *hwœs*, Old Norse *hvass*, sharp, keen, fierce, rather than from the verb *wasjan*, pollere, suggested by Graff, I take the following, though it is likely enough that there may be an intermixture. And I also think that *wat* is in some cases from *hwœt*, another Ang.-Sax. form of the same word. Thus the Old German names Kerhuuas, Gerwas,† Kerwat (*ger*, spear) all seem evidently to mean "spear-sharp." At the same time, except as a termination, I do not find sufficient ground for bringing it in here. As I have at p. 238 taken·

---

* The Eng. DRUMMOND, French DRUMOND, might be placed here, but I rather prefer the suggestion of Pott, who refers them to an Old Germ. Drudmunt.

† I have, p. 204, taken the secondary sense of boldness, but in connection with the spear the direct sense of sharpness seems on the whole the best.

244 THE WARRIOR AND HIS ARMS.

must to be the same as *muss,* so owing to the same cause—the unsatisfying sound of *s* final—I bring in here some forms in *wast* and *wash.* We have an instance of the latter in the name of Washington, Ang.-Sax. Wassingatun, " the town of the Wassings."

SIMPLE FORMS.

Wass.
Keen.
Bold.

.Old German Oasus, Waso, 9th cent. Ang.-Sax. Wasso, *Cod. Dip.* 971. Old'Norse Hvassi *(surname.)* Eng. Wass, Wash, Quash, Waste. Modern German Wass. French Vasse, Vassy.

DIMINUTIVES.

Eng. Wassell, Wastell, Vassall—Modern German Wessel—French Vassal. Old Germ. Wascelin, 11th cent. • —French Vasselin.

COMPOUNDS.

(Hard, fortis) French Vassard, Guessard. *(Hari,* warrior) Eng. Vasser, Washer—French Vasseur, Vessier. *(Man)* Old Germ. Wesmannus, 11th cent.—Eng. Wasman, Washman—Mod. Germ. Wassmann.

PHONETIC ENDING.

Old Germ. Huasuni, 8th cent. Eng. Wesson. French Vasson, Quezin.

There is a root *jug,* which is referred by Stark to Goth. *jukan,* Old High German *juhhun,* to combat, Goth. *jiuka,* Ang.-Sax. *geóc,* courage, fierceness. The root is probably the same as the Sansc. *yug,* to dart forth.

SIMPLE FORMS.

Jug.
Combat.

Old German Jugo. English Jugg, Judge, Jew, Juo.*
French Jauge, Jaugey, Juge, Jue, Jué, Jui.

DIMINUTIVES.

Old Germ. Jugaz, Jugizus—Eng. Jukes, Juggs, Jewiss—French Jouisse. Eng. Juggins. Eng. Jeula, Jewell—French Jugla, Julia ? *(homme de lettres.)*

---

* A Boston surname—English ?

THE WARRIOR AND HIS ARMS. 245

COMPOUNDS.

(*Aud*, prosperity) French JOUGAUD, JOUHAUD, JOUET—Eng. JEWETT, JOWETT. (*Bert*, famous) French JOUBERT. (*Hard*, fortis) French JAUGEARD, JOUARD. (*Hari*, warrior) Eng. JEWERY ?*—French JUGIER, JUÉRY. (*Mar*, famous) Old German Jugumar, 9th cent.—French JOUMAR. (*Wald*, power) French JOUAULT.

PHONETIC ENDING.

Eng. JEWIN. French JUQUIN, JUIGNÉ, JUIN ?

From the Ang.-Saxon *starc*, *sterc*, Old High German *starh*, strong, rough, fierce, are the following.

SIMPLE FORMS.

Old Germ. Starco, Staracho, 8th cent. English STARK, STARKEY, STIRK, STORK ? STURGE. Modern German STARK, STERK. French STAAR ?

Stark. Strong. Fierce.

COMPOUNDS.

(*Hari*, warrior) Old Germ. Starchar, 8th cent.—English STARKER, STERICKER, STRAKER—Modern German STERKER—French ? STRICKER. (*Man*) Old Germ. Starcman, 8th cent. —Starcman, *Hund. Rolls.*—English STARKMAN—French STERCKEMAN.

In the Ang.-Sax. and Old High German *snel*, Old Norse *sniallr*, there mingles with the sense of swiftness or celerity sufficient of that of boldness or fierceness to bring them under this head.

SIMPLE FORMS.

Old German Snello, Snel, 8th cent. Old Norse Sniallr. Eng. SNELL. Mod. Germ. SCHNELL.

Snel. Brave. Active.

PATRONYMICS.

Old Germ. Snellung, 8th cent. Eng. SNELLING.

COMPOUNDS.

(*Gar*, spear) Old German Snelger, 8th cent. English SNELGAR.

---

* Or local, from *jewerie*, a district inhabited by Jews (*Halliwell*).

246 THE WARRIOR AND HIS ARMS.

Snar.
Fortis.
Celer.

From the same root as *snel* comes Ang.-Sax. *snear*, celer, fortis, which is found in two Old Germ. names, Snaring and Snarholf. Also in a Snearri in the *Liber Vitæ*, and in English SNARE and SNAREY.

Also I think in a warlike sense are to be taken the names derived from the Old.High Germ. *funs*, Old Norse and Ang.-Sax. *fûs*, eager, impetuous, a word which we still retain in the degenerate sense of *fuss*. In ancient names we find it more frequently as a termination, as in Hadufuns (*had*, war), Valafons (*val*, slaughter), Bonofusus (*bon*, slaughter), &c.

SIMPLE FORMS.

Funs.
Fus
Impetuous.

Old Germ. Fonsa, Funso, Fussio, 6th cent. Eng. FAUNCE, FUSS, FUSSEY, FOSS ?* FOSSEY ? French FOUSSE, FUSY, FOISSY, FOSSE ? FOSSY ?

DIMINUTIVES.

Fussel, *Hund. Rolls.*—Eng. FUSSELL—French FUSIL— Ital. FUSELL. English FOSSICK—French FOISSAC—Span. ? FONSECA.

COMPOUNDS.

(*Hard*, fortis) Eng. FUSZARD—Fr. FOUSSARD, FOSSARD. (*Hari*, warrior) French FOUSSIER, FUSIER, FOSSIER, FONCIER ?

It seems to me rather probable that the following contain an allied form to the above. Graff, 3.733, has some trace of a root *fiz*, in the sense of movement.

SIMPLE FORMS.

Fiz.
Impetuous?

Old German Fizo, 9th cent. English FIZE, FIZ, FEES. French FIZEAU, FESSY.

---

* Besides the local word, the Low Germ. *foss*, fox, might come in.

THE WARRIOR AND HIS ARMS. 247

DIMINUTIVES.

Eng. FEASAL—French FIZEL. English PHYSICK. Old Germ. FIZILIN, 9th cent.—Eng. FISHLINE?

COMPOUNDS.

(*Hard*, fortis) Eng. FIZARD—French FISSART, FESSARD.

There are two unexplained words, *fisc* and *fusc*, occurring in Old Germ. names, which I think may be formed out of the preceding—the Swed. *fiaska*, Old Eng. *fisk*, to bustle about, showing the related Teutonic words, and the Welsh *ffysg*, impetuous, which I take to be also cognate, preserving most closely the sense. The form *fisc* is only found in one Old Germ. name Fisculf; the form *fusc* in the following. From the frequent interchange of *sc* and *x*, it is probable that *fix* (= fisc), and *fox* (= *fosc*), may in some cases come in here.

SIMPLE FORMS.

Old Germ. Fuscias (*a Vandal*), 6th cent., Fusco, Fusca (*Franks*), 9th cent. Eng. FUX? Fox? FOSKEY, FISK, FISH, FIX. Mod. Germ. FISCH, FIX. French FUSCH, FIX, FISQ, FIESCHI.

Fusc. Impetuous?

DIMINUTIVES.

Old Germ. Fusculo, 8th cent.—Eng. FOXELL?—Modern Germ. FÜCHSEL?—Ital. FOSCOLO.

PHONETIC ENDING.

Eng. FOXEN, FISKEN, FIXSON. French FIXON.

COMPOUNDS.

(*Hari*, warrior) Old German Fuscari, 8th cent.—English FOXERY—French FIXARY—Ital. FOSCARI. (*Hard*, fortis) Mod. Germ. FISCHART. (*Hild*, war) Old German Fuscildis, 8th cent.—Ital. FUSCALDO.* (*Ulf*, wolf) Old Germ. Fiscolf, 8th cent.—Mod. Germ. FISCHHOF?

---

* Corresponds more nearly with *wald*, power, though *hild* and *wald* are liable to intermix. The name Fuscildis is Frankish.

248 THE WARRIOR AND HIS ARMS.

From the Ang.-Sax. *câf, côf,* strenuous, seem to be the following. There are but slight traces of this root in Old Germ. names, but it frequently occurs among the Anglo-Saxons. There was a converted heathen priest named Coifi, who on the reception of Christianity by the people of Northumbria, undertook the demolition of the ancient shrines. It has been asserted that this is not a Saxon but a Cymric name, and that it denotes in Welsh a druid ; but Mr. Kemble has shown good reasons for believing that it is from the Ang.-Sax. *côf,* active, strenuous. It also appears in the form *cuf,* as in the names Blethcuf and Wincuf, Cod. Dip. 981. The Old High German *kop,* Mod. Germ. *kopf,* head, perhaps in the sense of helmet, is a root liable to intermix.

SIMPLE FORMS.

Cof. **Strennons.** Old German Cuppa, a Frank, 6th cent., Coppo, 9th cent. Ang.-Sax. Coifi. Eng. COFFEY, COVEY, COPP, COB,* CUFF, CUFFEY, CUBBY. Modern German KAUP, KOPP, KUBBE. French COFFY, COPEAU, CUFAY.

DIMINUTIVES.

Old Germ Cuffola, 8th cent.—English CUFFLEY, CUBLEY, COPLEY, COVELL—Mod. German COPPEL—French COVILLE, COPEL. Cofsi, Copsi, *Domesday*—Eng. COPSEY—Modern German KOPISCH—French COPPEZ. English CUBBIDGE, COPPOCK. Eng. COPELIN, CUFFLIN.

COMPOUNDS.

(Hard) English COVERT, COPPARD—French COFFARD, COIFFARD, CAFFORT. (*Et,* p. 189, *note*) Eng. CUBITT, CUPIT. *(Man)* Old Germ. Coufman,† 9th cent.—English COFFMAN, COPEMAN, CUFMAN.

---

* Job Cob, one of the quaintest of names.

† "One of the very few ancient names," Förstemann remarks, "that is derived from a trading origin." I take it, however, to be by no means certain that it is so.

THE WARRIOR AND HIS ARMS. 249

PHONETIC ENDING.

English COFFIN, COPPIN, COVENY. French COFFIN, COFFINEAU.

From the Old Norse *fika*, North. Eng. *feek*, Eng. *fidget*, are probably the following, but the sense I take to be rather that of warlike ardour and impatience.

SIMPLE FORMS.

Fick.
Impetuous.

Old German Ficcho, 9th cent. Figge, *temp. Edw. 3rd.* Eng. FIGG, FIDGE. Modern German FIEGE, FICK. French FIGEAU.

DIMINUTIVES.

Eng. FICKLIN, FICKLING.

COMPOUNDS.

(*Hari*, warrior) Eng. FICKER—French FIGUIER, FICHER.

From the Goth. *driusan*, Ang.-Sax. *dreòsan*, cadere, ruere, we may get also a sense of impetuosity suitable for the purpose.

SIMPLE FORMS.

Druce.
Impetuous.

Old German Drauso, Drooz, Drusa, Tṛuozi, 6th cent. Eng. DRUCE, TRUCE, TROWSE, TRUSS. French TROUSSEAU, TROSS, DROZ.

DIMINUTIVES.

Eng. TRUSSELL. French TROUSEL.

PHONETIC ENDING.

Old German Drusun, Trusun, 11th cent. Fr. TRUSSON.

The Ang.-Sax. *thrist*, bold, daring, appears to be found in Thristlingaden, "the valley of the Thristlings," *Cod. Dip.* 570. And to this, rather than to Fr. *triste*, sad, I put Eng. TRIST, TRISTER, perhaps TRISTRAM (*ram*, raven) though a Celtic origin may be upheld.[*]

Trist.
Bold.

---

[*] History of Christian Names, 2.145

F 2

250 THE WARRIOR AND HIS ARMS.

The word hard (Goth. *hardus*, Old High Germ. *hart*, Anglo-Saxon *heard*), so common, particularly as an ending, in men's names, may be taken to comprise some sense both of *fortis* and *durus*, and to betoken endurance, vigour, and courage. The older derivation of Bernard, &c., from ard, art, kind, sort, nature, is certainly erroneous, but it is very possible that there may be an intermixture of *hard* or *ard*, not in the sense of fortis or durus, but as an ending like that in coward, drunkard, and many other words both in the Teutonic and Romanic languages, as noticed by Grimm *(Deutsch. Gramm.*, 2.339.)

SIMPLE FORMS.

Hard, Hart. Strong, Hardy. Old Germ. Hardo, Herti, 9th cent. Eng. HARD, HARDY, HERD, HART, HEART, HARTIE, HEARTY, CHARD, CHART. Modern German HARDT, HARTZ, HERDE, HERTH. French HARDI, HARDY, HART, ARTUS.

DIMINUTIVES.

English HARTELL—Modern German HAERTEL—French HARDELÉ, ARTEIL.

PATRONYMICS.

Old Germ. Harding, Arding. Eng. HARDING, ARDING, HARTING. Mod. Germ. HARTING, HARTUNG.*

COMPOUNDS.

(Gar, spear) Old German Hartker, 8th cent.—English HARDACRE. *(Hard,* reduplication) Old German Hartart, 10th cent.—French HARTARD. *(Helm)* Old Germ. Arthelm, 9th cent.—Eng. HARDHAM. *(Hari,* warrior) Old German Artheri, Hardier, Charterius, 6th cent.—English HARDER, HARDYEAR, HARTER, ARTER, CHARTER—Modern German HARDER, HÖRDER—Fr. HARDIER, ARDIER, ARTUR, CHARTIER.

---

* The Eng. name HARTSTONGE may not improbably arise out of a misconception of Hartung.

THE WARRIOR AND HIS ARMS. 251

(*Land*) Old German Artaland, 8th cent.—Eng. HARTLAND. (*Man*) Old German Hartman, Hertman, 8th cent.—English HARDMAN, HERDMAN—Mod. Germ. HARTMANN, ERDMANN—French HARTMANN. (*Mund*, protection) Old Germ. Hartomund, 3rd cent.—Eng. HARDIMENT. (*Nagal*, nail) Old Germ. Hartnagal, 9th cent.—Eng. HARTNALL—Mod. Germ. HÄRTNAGEL. (*Nid*, strife) Old Germ. Hartnid, Hartnit, 9th cent.—Eng. HARTNETT. (*Rat*, counsel) Old Germ. Hartrat, 6th cent.—English HARTWRIGHT—Mod. German HARTROT. (*Rice*, powerful) Old Germ. Harderich, Hertrih, 5th cent.—Eng. HARTRIDGE, HARTRY—Modern German HERTRICH—French ? HERTERICH. (*Ulf;* wolf) Old Germ. Hardulf, 8th cent.—Eng. HARDOFF. (*Wald*, power) Old German Artald, 9th cent.—Mod. Germ. ARTELT—French ARTAULT. (*Wig, wic*, war) Old Germ. Hardwic, Hartuih, 8th cent.—English HARDWICK, HARDWIDGE, HARDAWAY—Modern German HARDWECK. (*Wine*, friend) Old Germ. Hardwin, Hardoin, 7th cent.—English ARDOUIN—French HERDEVIN, HARDOIN, HARDOUIN, ARDOUIN.

PHONETIC ENDING.

Old German Hardini, Hardin, 8th cent. Eng. HARDEN, HARTON, ARDEN. Mod. Germ. HERDEN. French HARDON, CHARTON.

From the Old High Germ. *fasti*, Ang.-Saxon *fæst*, firm, unyielding, I take the following, which I think may come in here.

SIMPLE FORMS.

Old German Fasta, Feste, *Hund. Rolls.* English FAST, FEAST, FIST. Mod. Germ. FEST. French FASTOU, FESTE, FESTU.

Fast. Firm.

PHONETIC ENDING.

Old Germ. Fastun, 8th cent. Eng. FASTIN.

COMPOUNDS.

(*Burg*, protection) Old German Fastburg, 8th cent.—French ? FISTEBERG. (*Hari*, warrior) Old German Fastheri,

252 THE WARRIOR AND HIS ARMS.

9th cent.—Eng. Faster, Fester, Feaster, Fister—Modern German Fäster—French Fastier, Fastré, Fester. (*Ulf,* wolf) Old German. Fastulf, 8th cent.—Eng. Fastaff.

From the Ang.-Sax. *stide, stith,* firm, steadfast —the latter also having the meaning of severus, asper, we may take the following. I also include the form *stad,* which Förstemann refers to *stadt,* town, but which—referring to Old Norse *staddr,* constitutus, *stedia,* firmare—I take to be only one of the forms of this root.

SIMPLE FORMS.

Stid.
Stad.
Firm.

Eng. Stitt, Stith, Stead, Steady, Steed, State, Stand, Stent. Mod. Germ. Stade.

PATRONYMICS.

Old Germ. Stiding, Stinding, 9th cent. Eng. Standing. Mod. Germ. Steding.

COMPOUNDS.

(Man) English Stedman, Steedman—Modern German Stedmann. (*Ulf,* wolf) Old German Stadolf, 8th cent.— Stithuulf, *Lib Vit.*—Eng. Stidolph.

Probably in something of a warlike sense is to be taken the following group, the root of which seems to be the Sanscrit *kruc,* vociferari, whence a number of words of similar meaning in the Aryan languages. Then in the Old Norse *hroki,* pride, insolence, *hrôkr,* vir fortis et grandis, also insolens, the sense seems to approach to that of defiance, which is suitable for proper names.

SIMPLE FORMS.

Rock, Ruck.
Stridere.

Old German Rocco, Ruccho, Roho, Roo, Crucus, Crocus (king of the Alamanni, 4th cent.) English Rock, Rockey, Roake, Roach, Ruck, Rugg, Rook, Rue, Crock. Modern

THE WARRIOR AND HIS ARMS. 253

German ROCKE, RÜCKE, RAUCH, ROGGE, RUHE. French·
ROCQUE, ROCHE, ROGUE, ROGÉ, ROGEAU, CROCO, CRUQ,
CROUÉ.

DIMINUTIVES.

Old Germ. Rocula, 7th cent.—French ROUCOLLE. Old
Germ. Roccolenus, 6th cent.—French ROCQUELIN, ROGUELIN.
Eng. ROCHEZ—French ROGEZ, ROQUES.

COMPOUNDS.

(*Bert*, famous) Old German Rocbert, 8th cent.—French
ROQUEBERT. (*Et*, p. 189, *note*) English ROGET, ROCKETT,
CROCKETT—French ROGET, ROQUETTE, CROCHET. (*Hard*,
fortis) Old German Ruchart, Hrohhart, 9th cent.—Modern
German RÜCKERT—French ROCHARD, ROHARD, CROCHARD.
(*Hari*, warrior) Old German Roacheri, Ruachari, 9th cent.—
Eng. ROKER, ROOKER, RUCKER, CROKER, CROCKER—Modern
German RÜCKER—French RAUCOUR, ROCHER, ROUHER.
(*Man*) English RUGMAN. (*Ulf*, wolf) Old German Rocculf,
Roholf, Roolf, 8th cent.—Old Norse Hrolfr—Eng. ROLFE—
Mod. Germ. ROHLOFF. (*Wald*, power) Old Germ. Rochold,
Rouhold, 8th cent.—French ROCAULT, ROCAULD, ROHAULT.
(*Ward*, guardian) French CROQUART.

In a similar sense I take the root *imm*, which
Förstemann considers obscure, and which Abel
takes to be a contraction of *irmin*. The root
meaning seems to be noise, as in Old Norse *ymia*,
stridere. Hence Old Norse *ymr*, clash of arms,
and *ŷma*, battle. The name of the giant Ymir in
Northern mythology is from this root—the sense
being primarily that of loud voice, which suggests
that of huge stature.

SIMPLE FORMS.

Old Germ. Immio, Ymmo, Emmo, 7th cent. Old Norse
Ymi. Eng. YEM ? Modern German IMM, IHM. French
EME, EMY.

Im, Em.
Stridere.

254 THE WARRIOR AND HIS ARMS.

DIMINUTIVES.

Old Germ. Ymizo, 11th cent.—English EAMES, HYMES, EMMS—Modern German IMSE—French IMBS. Old German Imico, 8th cent.—Eng. IMAGE—Mod. Germ. IMMICH.

COMPOUNDS

(*Bert*, famous) Old German Imbert, 7th cent.—English IMBERT—French IMBERT. (*Bald*, fortis) French IMBAULT. (*Hard*, fortis) Old Germ. Emehard, 8th cent.—Mod. Germ. EMMERT—French IMARD. (*Hari*, warrior). Old German Emaher, Emheri, 10th cent.—Eng. EMBER, EMERY—French IMER, EMMERY. (*Ric*, dominion) Old German Emrich, 8th cent.—Eng. EMERICK—Modern German EMERICH—French EMERIC, EMERICQUE.

PHONETIC ENDING.

Old German Imino, 8th cent. Anglo-Saxon Immine. Eng. EMENY. French EMMON.

Probably in something of a warlike sense are to be taken the following, which seem to be from Old High Germ. *ritan*, Ang.-Sax. *ridan*, English ride.

SIMPLE FORMS.

Ride. Eng. RIDE, RIDEY, WRITT, WRITE. Mod. Germ. RITT.
Equitare. French RIDEAU, RIDDE, RIETTE.

DIMINUTIVES.

Eng. RIDDELL—Modern German RIEDL—French RIDEL, RIEDLE. Old Germ. Ridelenus, 8th cent.—Eng. RIDLON—French RIEDLING. Eng. RIDDICK.

PATRONYMIC.

Eng. RIDING, RIDDING.

COMPOUNDS

(*Ger*, spear) Old German Rideger, 10th cent.—English RIDGER. (*Hard*) English RIDHARD. (*Aud*, prosperity) French RITAUD, REDAUT—Eng. RIDEOUT, REDOUT. (*Hari*, warrior) Eng. RIDER, WRITER, WRIGHTER—Mod. German RITTER, RIDDER—French RIDIÈRE.

THE WARRIOR AND HIS ARMS. 255

From the Goth. *neiths*, Ang.-Sax. *nith*, malice, hatred, strife, Förstemann derives the following.

SIMPLE FORMS.

Old Germ. Nid, Nitho, Nitto, Nizo, 8th cent. English KNITT, NEATE, NEED, NIESS, NICE? Mod. German NIED, NIETE, NITZE, NIZZE. French NIZEY.

Nith. Strife.

COMPOUNDS.

(*Bald*, fortis) Old German Nithbald, 9th cent.—Modern German NIPPOLT—French NIBAULT. (*Bert*, famous) Old Germ. Nidperht, 8th cent.—French NIBART. (*Bod*, envoy) Old Germ. Nidaboto, 9th cent.—Eng. NIBBETT, NISBET?—Mod. Germ. NIEPOTH—French NEBOUT. (*Goz*, Goth) Old Germ. Nidgoz, 9th cent.—Eng. NEGUS.* (*Hard*, fortis) Old German Nidhard, Nihard, 9th cent.—Modern German NIEDHARDT, NITZERT—French NIZARD, NISARD, NIARD. (*Hari*, warrior) Old Germ. Nither, 8th cent.—Mod. German NIEDER—French NIÉDRÉ, NETTER. (*Had*, war) Old Germ. Nidhad, 8th cent.—Ang.-Sax. Nithhad—French NITOT.

The following group, which are rather apt to mix with the preceding, I connect with a word *nadal*, very common in Frankish names, and which Weinhold refers to Old High German *nadala*, acus, in a supposed poetical allusion to the snake. This, however, I think very far-fetched, and simply class the word along with others of the same sort already introduced in this chapter. The root is *nad*, which, as Mr. Wedgwood has shown, has the sense of piercing, and from which are formed needle (Old High Germ. *nadala*, Ang.-Sax. *nedl*)—nettle† (Ang.-Sax. *netl*, Mod. Germ. *nessel*)—and as he thinks,

---

* Hence the name of the beverage, from its inventor, one Colonel Negus.

† The Lat. *urtica* may be from a root of similar meaning—cnf. *ord, ort*, p. 217.

256 THE WARRIOR AND HIS ARMS.

the Ang.-Saxon *nœddre*, Eng. adder. I include the form *nestle* on the principle referred to p. 238 —the Norwegian *naestle*, nettle, is a case in point. And for an example of the converse we have Eng. *nest*, Lat. *nidus*, Welsh *nyth*.

SIMPLE FORMS.

Nadal.
Acus.

Old Germ. Nadal, Nadala, 8th cent. English NADALL, NEEDLE, NETTLE, NESTLE. Modern German NADELL, NEIDL, NESSEL. French NIDELAY, NIZOLLE, NESTLÉ.

DIMINUTIVES.

Old German Nadalina, Natalinus, 8th cent.—English NESTLING—Modern German NÄDELIN, NIEDLING—French NESTLEN.

COMPOUNDS.

(*Hari*, warrior) Old Germ. Natlahar, 8th cent.—English NEEDLER, NALDER*—Modern German NADLER, NESSLER—French NESSELER. (*Rat*, counsel) Old Germ. Nadalrad, 8th cent.—Eng. NALDRETT—Mod. Germ. NESSELRATH ?

Another name which I take also to be from a weapon is SNEEZY. This, along with an Old German Snizolf (*ulf*, wolf) may be referred to Ang.-Sax. *snœs*, spear.

And there are a few names overlooked in their proper place in this chapter, which may be referred to Old High Germ. *fehd*, Mod. German *fehde*, Ang.-Sax. *fægth*, *faeth*, Eng. feud.

SIMPLE FORMS

Faid.
Feud.

Old Germ. Feito, 9th cent. Eng. FAED, FAITH, FAITHY. French FEYDEAU, FEYTOU.

PHONETIC ENDING.

Old Germ. Fedane, 7th cent. Eng. FEDDON.

I take the above to be from the same root as the Germ. *fechten*, Ang.-Sax. *feohtan*, Eng. fight.

---

* Either by transposition for Nadler, or perhaps containing the Dutch form *naald*, needle.

THE WARRIOR AND HIS ARMS. 257

The name FECHTER seems to be of German origin, but FICATIER in the directory of Paris looks like the same name in a more thoroughly French guise. Or we might connect it with Germ. *fichte*, the pine-tree, whence Pott derives the German name FICHTE.

From the Old Sax. *werod*, Ang.-Sax. *weorod*, host, army, we may take the following.

SIMPLE FORMS.

Old German Werot, 9th cent. Verritus, Frisian prince in Tacitus, 1st cent.—here? English WERRETT, VERITY? VIRTUE? French VIROT, VÉRITÉ, VERTU?

Werod. Army.

From the Goth. *slahan, slohun*, Anglo-Saxon *slagan, slean*, Eng. *slay*, Old English *sle, slow*, occidere, rather than from the Old High German *slou*, Mod. Germ. *schlau*, Eng. *sly*, as proposed by Förstemann, I take the following. The name SLYBODY, found in Sussex in the 17th century, might have been included here, but as the name Slytbody is found in the same county at an earlier date *(Pat. Brit.)*, we may rather refer it, along with our name SLIGHT, to Anglo-Saxon *slitta*, contention, and explain Slytbody as a messenger of strife, or perhaps rather in the higher sense as a herald of war.

SIMPLE FORMS.

Old German Slaugo, Slougo, Sliu,* 8th cent. English SLAGG, SLEGG, SLACK, SLAY, SLEWEY, SLOW, SLOWEY, SLEE, SLY. Mod. Germ. SCHLAUCH, SCHLECH.

Slag. Slaughter.

---

* Grimm *(Frauennamen aus blumen)*, derives this (female) name from Old Norse *sly*, conferva palustris—a very doubtful derivation, as it seems to me.

G 2

258   THE WARRIOR AND HIS ARMS.

COMPOUNDS.

(Man) English SLEWMAN, SLOWMAN, SLYMAN, SLEEMAN. (*Ulf*, wolf) Old German Slougolf, Sliholf, 8th cent.—English SLYOFF.

There is a word of yet more hateful sound which appears to come before us in men's names, viz., the Old High Germ. *mort*, Ang.-Sax. *mord*, *morth*, Old Scotch *morth*, *murth*, Eng. *murder*, Old Eng. *mort*, Lat. *mors*, death. The meaning is probably nothing more than that of slayer, so common in the names of this chapter. There are but few names in the *Altdeutsches Namenbuch*, and Förstemann does not·give an opinion upon them. Pott suggests the above meaning in the case of the Germ. names Mordt and Mordtmann, but the German Martyrt and the French Mortemart he explains, unsatisfactorily, as I think, as *mors martyrum*.

SIMPLE FORMS.

<small>Mort.
Mors.
Slaughter.</small>   Old German Morto. English MORT, MORDE, MORDAY, MORDUE, MURT, MURTA, MURTHA, MORSE. Mod. German MORDT, MÖRTZ. Fr. MORT, MORTIEU, MORDA, MOURCEAU.

DIMINUTIVES.

Murdoc, *Domesday*—Eng. MURDOCK—Modern German MORTZSCHKE—French MORDAQUE. Eng. MORTAL, MYRTLE, MORSEL, MURSEL—French MOURZELAS ? Fr. MORSALINE.

COMPOUNDS.

(Hard, fortis) Eng. MURTARD—Mod. Germ. MARTYRT ? —French MORDRET (for Mordert ?) *(Ram*, raven) Old Germ. Mordramnus,*.Maurdrannus (Abbot of Corvey), 8th cent.—Eng. MORTRAM. *(Hari*, warrior) English MORTART†— French MORTIER, MORZIÉRE. *(Mard*, fame) French MORTE-

---

* Wrongly placed by Förstemann.

† Or the extended form, as found in Eng. *murder*.

MARD, MORTEMART.* *(Man)* MORTIMAIN, *Roll Batt. Abb.*—
Eng. MORSMAN—Mod. Germ. MORDTMANN.

In concluding this chapter we may remark
how the one thought of war seems to have been
at the bottom of the hearts of our forefathers.
We have seen how everything long and straight
seems to have been, *par excellence*, a spear—
everything broad and flat, *par excellence*, a
shield.   And so, in proper names, a song may
have been the song of victory—an ornament may
have been the reward of valour.   Thus there
may be in reality a number of other names at the
bottom of which is a war sense, but in which the
expression is not sufficiently prominent to warrant
their introduction here.

---

* Might be local—there being two places so called in France.   At the same
time I believe, as elsewhere stated, that many names of places in France are simply
names of men.

CHAPTER XIV.

THE PROTECTOR AND THE FRIEND.

It is a long list of fierce and cruel names that we have just been considering. These—with scarcely an exception—must have been given in the cradle—it was a war baptism, so to speak. The innocent babe on his mother's breast was called by a warlike name, in the hope that his sword would one day make other babes orphans, and other women childless. Even the gentler sex had the same ungentle names, for war was the religion of the day.

It is a pleasant change then to turn to names which speak of peace and good-will, of love, friendship, and affection—even though in some cases we may have to put a ·certain limitation upon the sense. We can scarcely suppose, for instance,•that *frid* or *frith*, peace, so common in ancient names, was used in that sense of peace on earth and good-will towards men, which had no place in the fierce religion of our forefathers. The idea, if applied to their own tribe, might be rather that of protection or security—if applied to their enemies, that of conquest or subjugation. This root was widely spread over all the German tribes, but it is by no means so common in French and English names as might be expected. In many cases, both as a prefix and as a termination, it changes into *frey* or *free*.

THE PROTECTOR AND THE FRIEND. 261

SIMPLE FORMS.

Old Germ. Friddo, Fritto, 9th cent. Eng. FRID, FRED, Frid, Frith. FREAD, FRITH, FREETH, FRETHY. Modern German FRIED, Peace. FREDE. French FRIÉDÉ, FRÉDEAU, FRETÉ, FRETEAU.

DIMINUTIVES.

Old German Fritila, Fridila, 8th cent.—Ang.-Sax. Fridla —Mod. Germ. FRIEDEL—French FREDOILLE, FRITEL. Old German Fridulin, 9th cent.—English FREELING?—French FRÉLON?

COMPOUNDS.

(*Bad*, war) Old German Fridibad, Suabian Prince, 5th cent.—Eng. FREEBOUT—French FRÉPAT. (*Bald*, bold) Old German Frithubald, 6th cent.—French FREBAULT. (*Bern*, bear) Old German Fridubern, 9th cent.—Friebernus? *Domesday*—Eng. FREEBORN? (*Birg*, protection) Old Germ. Fridubirg, 8th cent.—Eng. FREEBOROUGH? FREEBRIDGE? (*Bod*, envoy) Old German Frithubodo, 9th cent.—English FREEBODY. (*Hari*, warrior) Old Germ. Fridehere, 9th cent. —Mod. German FRETTER—French FREDIÈRE. (*Dag*, day) Old Germ. Frittag, 9th cent.—Eng. FRIDAY—Mod. German FREITAG. (*Lind*, gentle) Old German Fridulind, 9th cent. Frelond, *Hund. Rolls.*—Eng. FREELAND? (*Liub*, love) Old German Fridiliuba—Eng. FREELOVE? (*Rice*, powerful) Old Germ. Frithuric, 5th cent.—Old Norse Fridrekr (Icelandic bishop)—Eng. FREDERICK—Mod. Germ. FRIDERICH—French FREDERICK. (*Stan*, stone) Ang.-Saxon Frithestan—English FREESTONE?

·Another word with the meaning of peace—but into which there enters more of the sense of friendship and relationship—is Anglo-Saxon *sib*. Hence the name, according to Grimm, of the goddess Sif, wife of Thor in Northern mythology.

SIMPLE FORMS.

Old German Sibja, 6th cent., Siffo, Sivo. Anglo-Saxon Sib, Sip. Sibba, bishop of Elmham. · Eng. SIPP, SEAVY. Mod. Germ. Friendship. SIEBE, SEPPE. French SIVE.

262 THE PROTECTOR AND THE FRIEND.

DIMINUTIVES.

Old Germ. Sibico, 8th cent.—Eng. SIBBICK—Mod. Germ. SIEBECKE. Old German Sevila? 7th cent.—English SIBEL, SIBLEY—Mod. German SYBEL—French SEVILLA? SYBILLE? Eng. SIFFKEN—Mod. German SIEVEKING. English SIPLING. French SEBILLON, DE SEVELINGES.*

PATRONYMICS.

Eng. SIBSON. Eng. SEPPINGS.

COMPOUNDS.

(*Hari*, warrior) Eng. SIBERY, SIEVIER—French SIPIÈRE, SIÉVER. (*Leis*, learned) Eng. SIPLESS? (*Ric*, power) Old Germ. Sivracus, 8th cent—Eng. SIVRAC, SHIVERICK—French SEVRY? (*Rat*, counsel) Eng. SIEVEWRIGHT?

LOCAL NAME.

(*Thorp*, village) Eng. SIBTHORP, SIPTHORP.

Another root of similar meaning may be *sem*, *sim* (Anglo-Saxon *seman*, to mediate, appease; *sema, syma*, a peace-maker.) There is only one Old Germ. name from this root, which Förstemann does not class. The word *sam*, p. 75, is apt to intermix.

SIMPLE FORMS.

Sem, Sim. Old Germ. Simo, Syme, 9th cent. English SYME, SIMM.
Mediation. French SEMEY, SEMÉ, SEM, SIMUS.

DIMINUTIVES.

Eng. SIMCO. English SIMMILL—French SEMEL, SEMELÉ, SIMIL. Eng. SIMKIN—French SEMICHON.

COMPOUNDS.

(*Gis, kis*, hostage) Eng. SIMKISS. (*Hari*, warrior) French SIMIER. (*Hard*) French SIMARD, SIMART.

Friend. There are a number of words of which the
Amicus. meaning is friendship and affection. Friend itself

---

* This looks as if it were formed on the same principle as the Italian names referred to by Salverte, originating in the family feuds of the middle ages. "A man did not call himself *Tibaldo Capuletti*, or *Salvino Armati*, but *Tibaldo dé Capuletti, Salvino degl' Armati*—one of the Capuletti, one of the Armati."

THE PROTECTOR AND THE FRIEND. 263

is an ancient name, though not common. We find an Old Germ. Friunt, 8th cent., Eng. Friend, Modern German Freund, French Friand and Friant. Then we have Friendship, corresponding with an Old Germ. Friuntskap, 9th cent., of which Förstemann observes that it is " a name standing altogether by itself." But we seem to have one or two similar names, as probably Winship, from *wine*, friend.

The last word *wine*, is the most common of all words with this meaning, occurring most frequently as a termination. It frequently, and especially in French, takes the prefixes *g* and *q*, as noticed at p. 47. It is probable that Ang.-Sax. *win*, strife, war, intermixes.

SIMPLE FORMS.

Old German Wino, Win, Wina, Wini, Winni, 8th cent., Guuine, 8th cent., Quino, 11th cent. Ang.-Sax. Wine, 3rd bishop of London. Eng. Winn, Winney, Wine, Wheen, Whenn, Vine, Viney, Quin, Quiney, Queen, Gwynn? Mod. Germ. Wein, Winne, Quin. French Vinay, Guenée, Gueneau, Guenu, Quenay, Queneau, Quin, Quineau.

Wine. Friend.

DIMINUTIVES.

Old Germ. Vinnilo, 9th cent.—English Winlo, Vinall, Quennell—French Quenelle. Eng. Quinlin. Old Germ. Winicho, Winika—English Winch—Mod. Germ. Winecke, Winke—French Vincke, Vinche. Old German Winizo, Winzo,* 8th cent.—Ang.-Saxon Wynsy, bishop of Lichfield —Eng. Quince, Quincey—French Vincey, Quincey.

PATRONYMICS.

Eng. Winson—French Vinson, Quenessen. Old Germ Wininc, 8th cent.—Eng. Winning—Mod. Germ. Winning.

---

* Förstemann—less reasonably, as it appears to me—places these two names to the root *winid, wend* (Vandal.)

264 THE PROTECTOR AND THE FRIEND.

COMPOUNDS.

(*Bald*, bold) Old German Winibald, 8th cent.—English WINBOLT, WIMBLE—French GUIMBAL. (*Burg*, protection) Old Germ. Wineburg, 8th cent.—Eng. WINBRIDGE ?—Mod. German WEINBERG—French VINBOURG. (*Cof*, strenuous) Ang.-Sax. Wincuf, *Cod. Dip.* 981—Eng. WINCUP—Modern Germ. WEINKOPF. (*Drud*, dear) Old Germ. Winidrud, 8th cent.—Eng. WINDRED. (*Gaud*, Goth) Old Germ. Winegaud, 8th cent.—Eng. WINGOOD, WINGATE. (*Gar*, spear) Old Ger. Winiger, Vinegar, 7th cent.—Eng. WINEGAR, VINEGAR— Mod. Germ. WEINGER. (*Hard*) Old Germ. Winihart, 8th cent.—Mod. Germ. WEINHARDT—Fr. QUENARD, QUINARD. (*Hari*, warrior) Old Germ. Winiheri, Winier, 8th cent.—Eng. WINER, QUINER—Mod. Germ. WINHEER—French GUINIER, GUINERY, QUINIER. (*Laic*, play) Old Germ. Winleich, 8th cent.—Uinilac, *Lib. Vit.*—English WINLOCK. (*Man*) Old Germ. Winiman, 7th cent.—Ang.-Sax. Winemen—English WINEMAN, WINMEN, WHENMAN—Mod. German WEINMANN. (*Mar*, famous) Old German Winimar, 8th cent.—French QUENEMER. (*Rat*, counsel) Old Germ. Winirat, 8th cent.— French GUÉNERAT. (*Stan*, stone) Anglo-Saxon Wynstan— Eng. WINSTON. (*Wald*, power) Old German Winevold, Guinald, 8th cent.—Modern German WEINHOLD—French GUENAULT, QUENAULT, QUINAULT.

PHONETIC ENDING.

Old Germ. Vinin, 8th cent. Eng. VINEN. Mod. Germ. WEINEN. French WINNEN, GUENIN.

The Old High Germ. *liub*, Ang.-Saxon *leôf*, dear, is also very common in proper names. There are, however, other roots very liable to intermix, as Goth. *laifs*, superstes, and Old High Germ. *lôp*, praise, both found in ancient names.

SIMPLE FORMS.

Lib, Lif.
Lov, Lop.
Dear.

⁕ Old Germ. Liuba, Liuf, Leupo, Liebus, 6th cent. Ang.-Sax. Leof. Old Norse Liufa. English LIEF, LIFE, LOUP,

THE PROTECTOR AND THE FRIEND. 265

Lipp, Leap, Luby, Love. Mod. Germ. Lieb, Lippe, Lubbe.
French Livio, Leppe, Lieppe, Lovy, Loup, Louva, Louveau,
Luppé.

DIMINUTIVES.

Old German Liuvicho, Libicho, 8th cent.—Old Danish
Livick—Eng. Livick ,Lovick, Lubbock—Modern German
Liebich, Liebig, Leppoc, Lubbecke—French Libec, Lubac,
Leppich, Levêque? Levick. Old German Lieuikin, 10th
cent.—Eng. Lovekin—Fr. Liefquin. Old Germ. Liubilo,
8th cent. —Eng. Lovell, Levell—Modern German Liebel,
Lippel—French Louvel. Old German Liebizo, Luviz,
Liubisi *(genit)*—Ang.-Saxon Leofsy, bishop of Worcester—
Eng. Libbis, Loveys, Livesey, Lovesey—Modern German
Lepsius—French Liboz, Lips.

PATRONYMICS.

Old German Liubing, 8th cent. Anglo-Saxon Living,
Archbishop of Canterbury. Lufincus, *Domesday*. English
Living, Loving, Levinge.

COMPOUNDS.

(*Dag*, day) Old German Liopdag, 10th cent.—Luiedai,
Domesday—English Loveday. (*Frid*, peace) Old German
Liupfrit—Eng. Lefroy? (*Hard*) Old German Liubhart,
Leopard, 7th cent.—Eng. Leopard, Liberty?—Mod. Germ.
Liphard, Lippert, Liebert—French Libert, Lippert.
(*Hari*, warrior) Old German Liubheri, Libher, Lipher, 8th
cent.—Eng. Lepper, Lover, Lever—Mod. Germ. Lieber—
French Liebherre, Levier, Louvier. (*Lind*, gentle) Old
German Liublind, 8th cent.—English Loveland? (*Man*)
Old German Liubman, 8th cent—Eng. Loveman—Modern
Germ. Liebmann. (*Mar*, famous) Old German Leobmar,
10th cent.—English Livemore. (*Ric*, power) Old German
Liubrich, 7th cent.—Ang.-Saxon Leofric—Eng. Loveridge.
(*Trut*, dear) Old Germ. Lipdrud, 8th cent.—Eng. Liptrot—
Mod. Germ. Liebetrut. (*Wald*, power) Old Germ. Lupoald,
7th cent.—Ang.-Sax. Leofweald—French Libault.

H 2

266   THE PROTECTOR AND THE FRIEND.

Another word of similar meaning is probably *minn*, from Old High German *minna*, Ang.-Sax. *myn*, love, affection.

SIMPLE FORMS.

Minn. Old German Minna, 9th cent.   English MINN, MYNN,
Love. MINNEY, MINNOW.   French MINNE, MINÉ.

DIMINUTIVES.

Old Germ. Minigo, 9th cent.—Eng. MINOCH, MINKE— French MINICH.   Old German Miniul, 11th cent.—French MINEL.   Eng. MINCHIN—French MINACHON.   Eng. MINNS, MINCE.

COMPOUNDS.

(*Hait*, hood) Eng. MINNETT—French MINNETTE.   (*Hard*) Old German Minard, 11th cent.—English MINARD—French MINARD, MINART.   (*Hari*, warrior) English MINER—French MINIER, MINEUR ?   (*Rat*, counsel) French MINERET.

The word *sweet*, dulcis, in the various forms of Old High German *suaz*, Mod. Germ. *süss*, Old Sax. *sôt*, Anglo-Saxon *swêt*, *swês*, appears to be found in some ancient and modern names.   The few Old Germ. names which I have ventured to put here are not explained by Förstemann, and the existence of the word is more clearly shown by the names found in our own early records. The Ang.-Sax. *swith*, vehement, may be liable to intermix, as well as a word *swed* found in some names, and referred by Förstemann to Old High German *swedan*, cremare.

SIMPLE FORMS.

Old German Suoto, Soto, Suto, Suzo, Swiza, 9th cent.
Sweet.   Suet, *an under-tenant before Domesday.*   English SWEET,
Suss.   SWEAT, SUIT, SUETT, SUSE, SAUCE.   Modern German SAUSE,
Dulcis.' Süss.   French SUASSO, SOUSSI, SUSSE, SOTO, SUET.

THE PROTECTOR AND THE FRIEND. 267

PATRONYMICS.

Sueting, *Domesday.* Eng. SWEETING.

COMPOUNDS.

(*Man*) Ang.-Sax. Swêtman, *name of the minter on one of the coins found at Alfriston, Suffolk*—English SWEETMAN—Modern German SUSMANN—French ? ZOUTMAN. (*Leof*, dear) English SWEETLOVE, SUTLIFF ? SUTCLIFF ?

The root of *sweet* is *su*, the primitive meaning of which seems to be *liquescere,* and whence also the words *suck, sugar,* &c. The particle *su* or *sug* is found in several Old Celtic names, as Sucarius, Sucaria (*Gruţ,* 742.3), which Gluck—taking the Old Celt. *sucar* as the equivalent of the Welsh *hygar*—explains as amabilis. The same word comes before us in some Old German names ; I take it to be from Old High German *sugan*, Ang.-Sax. *sucan*, Eng. *suck*, and suppose the meaning to be the same as that of the above word *sweet*.

SIMPLE FORMS.

Old German Zucho. Anglo-Saxon Sucga, Succa, *found apparently in Sucgangrâf, Succanscylf, Cod. Dip.* 441, 1232. Souch, *Roll Batt. Abb.* English SUGG, SUCK, SUCKEY, SUCH, SEW, SEWEY. Mod. Germ. ZUCK. French SOUCHAY, SUE.*

Su.
Sug.
Sweet.

DIMINUTIVES.

Old German Zuchilo, Lombard king, 6th cent.—English SUCKLEY—French SUCHEL. SUCKLING, *Domesday*—English SUCKLING.

COMPOUNDS.

(*Aud*, prosperity) French SUCCAUD, SUQUET, SOUGIT—Eng. SUGGETT. (*Hard*) Mod. Germ. ZUCKERT, SUCKARD—French SOUCHARD. (*Man*) Eng. SUCKMAN. (*Rat*, counsel) French SOUCHERAD, SOUCHERET.

---

* Pott's suggestion of *sang-sue*, leech, hardly needs to be considered.

268 THE PROTECTOR AND THE FRIEND.

EXTENDED FORM=ENG. *sugar*, GERM. *zucker* ?

Old Germ. Suger.* English SUGAR, SUCKER. Modern Germ. ZUCKER. French SOUGÈRE, SOUCHERRE.

COMPOUNDS.

(*Hard*) French SOUCHERARD. (*Mar*, famous) English SUCKERMORE. (*Man*) Eng. SUGARMAN (*Suff. Surn.*)

Between *dear*, carus, and *deer*, the animal, it is impossible to distinguish even in ancient names. The former is the preferable sense, though it is probable that there may be an admixture of the two. The larger proportion of the ancient names are those of women.

SIMPLE FORMS.

Dear. Carus. Old Germ. Dioro, Diura, Teor, 8th cent. Anglo-Saxon Diora. Old Norse Dîri. English DEAR, DEAREY, TEAR, TEAREY. Mod. German DIEHR, THIER, THEUER. French THIRY, THIERRY, THIERRÉ, TIREAU.

COMPOUNDS.

(*Leof*, dear) Ang.-Sax. Deorlaf, bishop of the Magasætas —Eng. DEARLOVE. (*Bert*, famous) Eng. DEARBIRD. (*Man*) Dereman, *Domesday*—Eng. DEARMAN. (*Wald*, power) Old Germ. Deorovald, Deorold, 7th cent.—Mod. Germ. DÖRWALD —French THIRAULT. (*Wine*, friend) Ang.-Sax. Deorwyn (*Mss. Cott.*)—Eng. DERWIN—French THIROUIN.

There is a word *bil*, common in ancient and modern names, and which Grimm (*Deutsch. Myth.*) explains to mean "lenitas, placiditas."† Bil was the name of one of the minor goddesses in Northern mythology.

---

* Förstemann makes this a corruption of Swithger. There seems, however, sufficient ground for taking it as it is. Compare the Celtic name Sucarius.

† This root may, however, sometimes intermix with another *bal, bale*, as suggested at p. 191.

THE PROTECTOR AND THE FRIEND. 269

SIMPLE FORMS.

Old Germ. Bilo, Billa, 9th cent. English BILL, BILLY, BILLOW, PILL, PILLEY, PILLOW. Mod. Germ. BILLE, BILA. Dan. BILLE. French BILLE, BILLEY, PILLE, PILLEY.

Bil.
Pil.
Gentleness

DIMINUTIVES.

Old German Bilicha, Pilicho, 9th cent.—Eng. BILKE—Mod. Germ. BILKE, BELKE, PIELKE—French BILCO, BELAC, BELLOC. Old Germ. Biliza, Piliza, Peliza, 11th cent.—Eng. BILLIS, BELLISS, BELSEY—French BILLEZ, BELAIZE, BELZ, PELEZ, PILLAS. French BILKEN, BILLEQUIN.

PATRONYMICS.

Old Germ. Billung, Billing, Pillunc, 8th cent. English BILLING, BILLINGAY. Modern German BILLING. French BILLING.

COMPOUNDS.

(*Bold*) French BILBAULT. (*Frid*, peace) Old German Bilfrid, Pillfrid, 8th cent.—Eng. BELFRY, PILFORD. (*Gat*, union ?) Old German Piligat, 9th cent.—French PELLAGOT, PELLECAT, PELCOT. (*Gard*, protection) Old Germ. Beligarda, 9th cent.—Mod. German PELEGAARD—French BELLIGARD, BELICARD. (*Ger*, spear) Modern German BILGER—French PÉLIGRI. (*Grim*, fierce) Old German Biligrim, Pilgrim, Pilegrin—English PILGRIM—French PELLEGRIN. (*Heit*, state, hood) Old Germ. Biliheid, 8th cent.—English BILLET, BELLETT, PELLETT, PILOT—French BILHET, BILLET, BELET, PILETTE, PILOT, PILATE. (*Hard*) Eng. BILLIARD, BELLORD—Modern German BILHARDT—French BILLARD, BILIIARD, BELLART, PELLARD, PILLARD. (*Hari*, warrior) Eng. BELLER—Mod. Germ. BILLER—French BILLIÉRE, BELLIER, PELLIER. (*Helm*) Old German Bilihelm, 9th cent.—Eng. BILLHAM, PELHAM—French BELHOMME. (*Man*) English BILLMAN, BELLMAN, BELLMAIN, PILLMAN—French BELLEMAIN, PELMAN. (*Mar*, famous) Old German Belimar, 8th cent.—English BILLAMORE, BELLMORE—Modern German BILMER—French BELLEMARE. (*Mund*, protection) Old Germ. Pilimunt, 8th cent.—English BELLMENT—French BELMENT. (*Not*, bold) Fr. BELLENOT, BELNOT. (*Sind*, via) Old Germ. Belissendis,

270   THE PROTECTOR AND THE FRIEND.

11th cent.—French BELISSENT.   (*Wald*, power) English
BILLYEALD—French BILLAULT.   (*Ward*, guardian) English
BELWARD.   (*Wine*, friend) French BELLAVOINE.   (*Wig*, *wi*,
war) French PELVEY.

PHONETIC ENDING.

Old Germ. Pillin.   Eng. BILLIN, PILON.   Mod. German
BELLIN.   French BELIN, BILLION, PILLIEN, PELLIN.

Smelt. The Ang.-Sax. *smelt*, mild, gentle, is found as
Gentle. the name of a priest, *Cod. Dip.* 822, and we have
an Eng. SMELT.   I find no other trace of it as an
ancient name, and it is possible that the one in
question may have been conferred on account of
character, superseding his ordinary name.

Another word of similar meaning may be
found in Old High German *trût*, Modern German
traut, Low German *drûd*, dear, beloved.   But
the name Thrudr, of one of the Valkyrjur, is
supposed by Weinhold (*Deutschen Frauen*), to
come in, which is probable, more particularly
when the word is used as a termination, in which
case it is found only in the names of women.*
And perhaps for this reason, though it was very
common in Frankish names, we find at present
only scanty traces of it in French.   Another root
liable to intermix is Gothic *drauht*, Old Norse
drôtt, people.

SIMPLE FORMS.

Drud, Trut. Old Germ. Drudo, Trudo, Truto, Truut, Trut, 8th cent.
Dear. Eng. DROUGHT, DROWDY, TROOD, TROUT, TROTT.   Modern
Germ. DRUDE, DRUTE.   French DRUDE, TROUDE, TRUTEY,
TROTE, TROTTÉ.

---

* It is still retained in some christian names of women, as Gertrude and
Mildred.

THE PROTECTOR AND THE FRIEND. 271

COMPOUNDS.

(*Hari*, warrior) Old Germ. Trudhar, 8th cent.—English TROTTER ?—Modern German TRÖDER—French TROTTIER ? (*Man*) Old German Trutman, 8th cent.—Troteman, *Hund. Rolls*—Eng. TROTTMAN—Modern Germ. TRAUTMAN. (*Rat*, counsel) French TROTROT ?

PHONETIC ENDING.

Old German Trutin, 9th cent. English TROUGHTON, TRODDEN. French TRUDON, TRUTIN.

Another word of similar meaning is *tate* (Old Norse *teitr*, Old High Germ *zeiz*), which denotes, according to Mr. Kemble, " gentleness, kindness, and tenderness of disposition." Perhaps something of cheerfulness may enter into the sense, the Old Norse *teitr* being expressed by "hilaris." It was not unfrequent in Anglo-Saxon times, but seems to have been more especially common among the Northmen. There are rather an unusual number of churchmen with this name ; thus, out of eleven Northmen called Teitr in the Annales Islandiæ, there are five, viz., one bishop, one prior, one deacon, and two priests. We might almost be disposed to think that · it was sometimes a name of endearment bestowed upon a beloved pastor, to the superseding perhaps of his ordinary name.

SIMPLE FORMS.

Ang.-Sax. Tata, Minister—Tata, Presbyter—Ethelberga, "otherwise called Tate," daughter of Ethelbert, king of Kent—Tate Hatte, *Mss. Cott.* Old Norse Teitr. English TAIT, TATE, TATO, TEAT, TITE. French TÊTE, TATÉ.

Tate. Amiable.

Upon the whole then it will be seen that TAIT is a very good name for a bishop. And there is a very good bishop for the name.

272 THE PROTECTOR AND THE FRIEND.

The following names may perhaps be referred to the Old High Germ. form *zeiz*, corresponding with Old Norse *teitr*.

SIMPLE FORMS.

Zeiz.
Amiable. Old German Zeizo, 8th cent—Eng. SIZE. Mod. German ZEIZ. French SIESS, CIZA.

DIMINUTIVES.

Old Germ. Zeizilo, 8th cent.—English SISLEY?—French SEYSSEL, CÉZILLE. French SISCO, CESAC.

COMPOUNDS.

(Hard) French CÉZARD. *(Hari,* warrior) Old Germ. Zeizheri, 9th cent.—English SIZER—Modern German ZAISER —French CICERI? *(Lind,* gentle) Old Germ. Zeizlind, 9th cent.—English SIZELAND.

PHONETIC ENDING.

Old German Ceizau, 9th cent. English SIZEN. French CEYSSON.

Another root having the meaning of affection or fondness may be *dod, tod, tot.* In the former edition I referred to the Friesic *dod,* a blockhead, and to the two Old English words *doddypate* and *dodipol,* of the same meaning, quoted by Halliwell. Also to the name of the curious and extinct bird the dodo, which I suppose to have been so named by the Dutch from its well-known stupidity. But there is another sense, no doubt allied, and perhaps from the same root, which I think more suitable for proper names— that of fondness. We see the connection in our own word " dote"—to be foolish and to be fond. Förstemann speaks of the root as obscure, and refers to Old High German *toto,* patrinus, *tota,* admater, which may perhaps however only be

THE PROTECTOR AND THE FRIEND. 273

derived senses —the root lying deeper. Another root very apt to intermix is *deot*, people.

SIMPLE FORMS.

Old German Dodo, Doddo, Doda (wife of the Frankish king Theodebert), Todo, Totta, Tozo, Tozi, 6th cent. Ang.-Sax. Dodda, Dudda, (bishop of Winchester), Totta,* (bishop of Leicester). English DODD, TODD, TODDY, TOTTEY, DUTT, DUDDY, DOZY. Modern German DODE, TODE, TOTT, TODT. French DODO, DODÉ, DOTHÉE, TOTY.

Dod, Tod. Dear.

DIMINUTIVES.

Old Germ. Totilas, Goth. king, 7th cent.—Eng. TOTTELL, DOZELL, DUDDLE. Eng. DOTCHIN.

COMPOUNDS.†

(*Hard*) French DODARD. (*Hari*, warrior) Old German Dothari, 9th cent.—Eng. TOZIER—Fr. DOZIÈRE. (*Man*) Old German Totman, 9th cent.—English DODMAN, TODMAN, TOTMAN—Modern German TÖDTMANN—French DODEMAN. (*Ric*, power) Old Germ. Dotrih, 9th cent.—English DOTRY, DODDRIDGE, DOTTRIDGE.

PHONETIC ENDING.

Old German Dodlin, Todin, 8th cent. English TOTTEN. French DODIN, DOTIN, DOZON.

Along with the above, and in accordance with the classification of Förstemann, I bring in a group containing a dipthong as below.

SIMPLE FORMS.

Old German Duodo, Tuoto, Touto, Tooza, 8th cent. Eng. DOWD, DOWDY, DOODY, DOUBT, DOUBTY, TOOT, DOWSE. Fr. DOUDEAU, DOUTEY, TOUT, TOUTAY, DOUSSE, TOUZEAU, TOUZÉ.

Dowd. Dear.

---

* This bishop was also called Torthelm, and Mr. Kemble considers Totta nothing more than an abbreviation, which may be the case.

† The German name Todleben seems to be formed upon an Old German Totleib. I have taken this, p. 11, to be from *lieb*, dear ; however, the form is rather that of *laib*, superstes.

I 2

274 THE PROTECTOR AND THE FRIEND.

DIMINUTIVES.

Old Germ. Toutilo—Eng. DOWDLE, TOODLE, TOOTALL—French DOUDELLE, TOUZEL. Old German Duodeliu, 11th cent.—French DOUSSOULIN, TOUZELIN. Old Germ. Tuoticha—Eng. TOOTHAKER?—French TOUSAC. Eng. DOWDIKEN.

PATRONYMICS.

Eng. DOWDING, DOWSING.

PHONETIC ENDING.

English DOWDEN, DOUDNEY, DOWSON. French DOUDAN, DOUSSAN, TOUTAN, TOUZIN.

From the Old Norse *linr*, Old High German *leni*, mild, we may perhaps take the following. The Old Norse *linni*, snake, may, however, put in a claim.

SIMPLE FORMS.

Linn, Line. Old German Lino, 9th cent. Eng. LINN, LINNEY, LINE, Mild. LINEY, LEAN. Mod. German LINN, LEINE. French LENÉ, LINNÉE.

DIMINUTIVES.

French LENIQUE. Eng. LINNELL.

PATRONYMICS.

Eng. LEANING, LINING.

COMPOUNDS

(*Heit*, "hood") Old Germ. Linheit—Ang.-Sax. Liniet, *Mss. Cott.*—Eng. LINNET—Fr. LINOTTE. (*Hard*) French LINARD. (*Ger*, spear) Eng. LINNEGAR—French LENÈGRE.

From the Goth. *ansts*, Old High Germ. *anst*, gratia, Förstemann derives some ancient names.

SIMPLE FORMS.

Anst. Old Germ. Ansteus?* Eng. ANSTEY.
Gratia.

COMPOUNDS.

(*Hari*, warrior) Old German Anster, 9th cent.—English ANSTER.

---

* Forstemann derives this name from *ans*, semi-deus, and *thius*, servant.

THE PROTECTOR AND THE FRIEND. 275

Another root of similar meaning may be *nad, nat,* which Förstemann refers to Old Norse *náth,* gratia, Old High German *ganáda.* However it seems to me very doubtful whether it is not a simpler form of *nadal,* acus, p. 256.

SIMPLE FORMS.

Nad, Nat.
Gratia.

Old Germ. Natto, Nado, 8th cent. Eng. NATT. Mod. Germ. NATH. French NATTE.

DIMINUTIVES.

Eng. NATKINS. French NATIEZ.

COMPOUNDS.

(*Aud,* prosperity) French NADAUD. (*Hari,* warrior) French NATIER, NATTER: (*Wald,* power) Eng. NADAULD—French NADAULT.

Then there are several words with the meaning of help or protection. Help itself was by no means uncommon in ancient names, though it will be seen that we have a very scanty list at present.

SIMPLE FORMS.

Help.
Auxilium.

Old Germ. Helpo, leader of the Saxons, 10th cent. Eng. HELPS. Mod. Germ. HELF.

COMPOUNDS.

(*Hari,* warrior) Eng. HELPER. (*Ric,* power) Hilpericus, Burgundian king, 5th cent., Frankish king, 6th cent., Helfrich, 8th cent.—English HELFRICH—Modern German HELFRICH.

A very common word, particularly as a termination, is Old High Germ. *munt,* Ang.-Sax. *mund,* protection. The earlier German writers —as English writers still do sometimes at present —translated *mund* by mouth—thus Rosamund, " rosy mouth."

276 THE PROTECTOR AND THE FRIEND.

SIMPLE FORMS.

Mund, Munt.
Protection. Old German Mundo, Munt, 6th cent.—English MUNDY, MUNDAY, MOUND, MOUNT—Modern German MUND, MUNDT, MUNTZ—French MONDE, MONDO, MONTÉE—Span. MONTES.

DIMINUTIVES.

Old German Μουνδίλας, *Procopius*, 6th cent. English MUNDELL—French MUNDEL, MONTEL.

PATRONYMICS.

Old Germ. Muntinc. Eng. MUNTING. Modern German MUNDING.

COMPOUNDS.

(*Hard*) French MONDEHARD. (*Hari*, warrior) French MONDIÈRE, MONTIER. (*Wald*, power) Old Germ. Mundoald —French MONTAULT.

PHONETIC ENDING.

Eng. MUNDEN, MOUNTAIN. French MONDIN, MONTAGNE, MONTAGNY.

As a termination, *mund* in English becomes frequently *ment*, as in WILLIMENT, ELEMENT, GARMENT, HARDIMENT, ARGUMENT, which are probably from the Old Germ. names Willimund, Elemund, Garimund, Hartomund, Argemund. Another similar name may be MONUMENT, from an Old German Munemund.

Another word having the meaning of protection is *gard, gart*, with its High Germ. forms *card, cart.*

SIMPLE FORMS.

Gard, Card.
Protection. Ang.-Sax. Carda (*found in Cardan* hlæw, Cardan stigele, Cod. Dip.* 427,570.) English GARD, GARDIE, CARD, CART, CARTY. French GARD, GARDEY, GERDY, CART, CARTEAU.

DIMINUTIVES.

Old German Gardilo, 8th cent.—Eng. CARTELL—French GERDOLLE. English GERDUCK.

---

* Carda's *lowe* or mound (probably a grave-mound), and Carda's style.

THE PROTECTOR AND THE FRIEND. 277

COMPOUNDS.

(*Hari,* warrior) Old German Cartheri, Karthar, Gardar, 8th cent.—English GARTER (16th cent.), CARDER, CARTER—French GARDÈRE, CARTIER, CARTHERY. (*Rat,* counsel) Old German Gardrad, 11th cent.—Eng. CARTWRIGHT ?—French CARTERET. (*Ric,* power) Ang.-Sax. Gyrdhricg (*found in Gyrdhricges ford, Cod. Dip.* 369.) English CARTRIDGE. (*Dio, thew,* servant) Old Germ. Cartdiuha, 8th cent.—Eng. CARTHEW. (*Wald,* power) French CARTAULT. (*Wealh,* stranger) Eng. CARDWELL ?

PHONETIC ENDING.

Old Germ. Gardin, 11th cent. Eng. GARDEN, CARDEN, CARTON. Mod. Germ. KARTHIN. French GARDIN, CARDON, CARTON.

Another word 'of similar meaning is *ward, wart,* (Ang.-Sax. *weard,* Old High German *wart,* guardian.)

SIMPLE FORMS.

Old Germ. Warto, Wardo, Ward, 6th cent. Ang.-Sax. Wearda (*found in Weardan* hyl, Cod. Dip.* 1101*,*), Weard, (*found in Weardesbeorh, now Warborough, Oxf., Cod. Dip.* 343.) Eng. WARD, VARDY. Mod. Germ. WART, WARTH. French VART, VERDIÉ.

Ward, Wart. Guardian.

DIMINUTIVES.

Eng. WARDELL. French VERDEL.

COMPOUNDS.

(*Hari,* warrior) Eng. WARDER, WARTER—Fr. VERDIER, VERDERY. (*Man*) Old German Wartman, 9th cent.—Eng. WARDMAN—Mod. Germ. WARTMAN.

For the word *war,* Förstemann proposes no fewer than five different derivations, viz., *wari,* defence, *wâr,* true, *wâron,* servare, *war,* domicilium, and *wer,* man. To these I add Anglo-

---

* Wearda's hill and Weard's barrow—Weardan and Weardes, as the respective genitives of Wearda and Weard, following the rules of Anglo-Saxon declension.

278 THE PROTECTOR AND THE FRIEND.

Saxon *wær*, bellum, as a root liable at any rate to intermix, though I am inclined to take as the general meaning the first of those proposed by Förstemann.

SIMPLE FORMS.

Ware, Defence. Old German Wero, 8th cent. English WARE, WARRE, WARRY, WEIR, WEAREY, QUARRY. Mod. German WEHR. French VARÉ, VARAY, VÉRO, VERRY, WARO, WARRE, WARÉE, QUERREY.

DIMINUTIVES.

Old Germ. Varacco, 8th cent.—Eng. VARICK—Modern German QUARITCH—French VARACHE. English WARRELL, VARRELL, QUARRELL—French VARRALL. Old German Waralenus, 8th cent.—English VERLING—Modern German WEHRLEN—French VERILLON. French VARICHON.

PATRONYMICS.

Old Germ. Warinc, Waringa, 8th cent. Eng. WARING, WARRING. French VARENGUE, VIAREINGUE, WARENGUE.

COMPOUNDS.

(*Bald*, fortis) Old Germ. Warbald, Warbalt, 8th cent.—Eng. WARBOLT. (*Burg*, protection) Old German Warburg, 8th cent.—Eng. WARBRICK—Mod. Germ. WARBURG—Fren. VERBRUGGÉ. (*Ger*, spear) Old German Warger, 8th cent.—Eng. WARRAKER, WARWICKER—French WAROQUIER. (*Goz*, Goth) Old German Werigoz, 9th cent.—Eng. VERGOOSE.* (*Hari*, warrior) Old German Weriheri, Warher, 8th cent.—English WARRIER, QUARRIER—French VERIÈRE. (*Laic*, play) Old Germ. Warlaicus, 8th cent.—Warloc (*Hund. Rolls*)—Eng. WARLOCK—Mod. German WARLICH. (*Man*) Old German Waraman, Warman, 8th cent.—English WARMAN, QUARMAN—Modern German WEHRMANN—French VERMON. (*Mar*, famous) Old German Werimer, 8th cent.—English WARMER. (*Lind*, gentle) Old German Waralind, 7th cent.—Eng. WARLAND. (*Nand*, daring) Old German Werinant, 8th cent.—French VARINONT.

---

* Suffolk Surnames.

THE PROTECTOR AND THE FRIEND. 279

PHONETIC ENDING.
Eng. WARREN. French VARAINE.

Another word of similar import in names may be *burg*, to which Förstemann gives the meaning of condere, servare. In female names, in which, as a termination, it was most frequent, the meaning may perhaps be rather that of chastity or maidenhood. It was most common in Frankish, and is still in French names.

SIMPLE FORMS.

Old German Burgio, 9th cent., Purgo, Burco, 5th cent. Burg, Burk. Eng. BURGE, BURKE. Mod. Germ. BURKE. French BERGE, Protection. BERGEAU, BOURG, BURC, BURQ, PERJEAUX ?

DIMINUTIVES.

Old Germ. Burgizo, 10th cent.—Eng. BURGESS—French BOURGES. Eng. BURCHELL—French BURGAL, BURCKEL.

COMPOUNDS

(Hard) Old German Burghard, 8th cent.—Burchard, *Domesday*—Eng. BURCHARD—Mod. Germ. BURCKHARDT— French BURGARD, BOURQUARD, BURCHARD. *(Hari,* warrior) Old Germ. Burghar, 8th cent.—Eng. BURGER—Mod. Germ. BURGER, BÜRGER—French BERGER, BERQUIER, BOURGERY. *(Rat,* counsel) Old German Burgarad, 8th cent.—French BERGERAT. *(Rand,* shield) French BERGUERAND. *(Wald,* power) Old Germ. Burgoald, 7th cent.—English PURGOLD— Mod. Germ. BURGHOLD—French BERJEAULT. *(Wine,* friend) Eng. BURGWIN—French BURVEVIN.

The word *hud, hut* Förstemann refers to the Old High German *hutta,* hut, or to *hût,* hide. Perhaps, however, we might rather take the sense which is at the root of both of the above, that of covering, hiding, or protecting, as in Old High German *huotan,* Mod. Germ. *hüten,* Eng. hide.

280 THE PROTECTOR AND THE FRIEND.

SIMPLE FORMS.

Hud, Hut. Protection. Old Germ. Hudo, Hutto, 8th cent. Eng. HUDD, HUDDY, HUTT, HUTTY. Modern German HÜTTE. French HUDE, HOUDE, HUTTEAU.

DIMINUTIVES.

Old Germ. Huodilo—English HUDDLE—Modern German HÜTHEL—French HUDELO, HOUDAILLE. Eng. HUDKIN.

PATRONYMIC.

English HUTTING.

COMPOUNDS.

(*Bert*, famous) Old German Hudipert, 7th cent.—French HUDIBERT, HAUDIBERT. (*Burg*, protection) French HAUDE-BOURG. (*Hard*, fortis) Eng. HUDDERT—French HOUDART. (*Man*) Old German Hutuman, 9th cent.—Eng. HUTTMAN—Modern German HUDEMANN. (*Mar*, famous) Old German Hudamar—French HOUDEMARE. (*Wine*, friend) Old Germ. Huuduin, 8th cent.—French HOUDOUIN. (*Wald*, power) French HUDAULT.

A somewhat doubtful word is *bol, bul*, which Ettmüller places to Ang.-Sax. *bôl*, dormitorium, but for which Förstemann proposes Mid. High German *buole*, brother, friend, consort. This word, which is evidently allied to the Old Eng. *bully*, comrade, seems to me to be upon the whole the best, but there are other derivations which might be proposed. First, *bull*, taurus, as a symbol of strength. Secondly, the root of Eng. *bully*, which is, first loud noise, then bluster, intimidation, similar root-meanings being found at pages 252-3. Thirdly, the sense of bigness, as found in *boll, ·bulk*, and other words derived from the sense of swelling.

Bol, Bul. Friend. Comrade.;

SIMPLE FORMS.

Old Germ. Bolo, Buolo, Bollo, Boli, Puolo, Pollo, Poulo, 8th cent. Eng. BOOL, BOWL, BOULLY, BULL, BULLEY, POOLE,

THE PROTECTOR AND THE FRIEND. 281

Pooley, Pole, Pollo, Polley, Pull, Pulley. Mod. Germ. Bohl, Boll, Buol, Buhl, Bull. Norw. Bull. Fr. Bola, Bollé, Boll, Bolley, Bouillé, Bouilly, Boulay, Boulo, Boulu, Bulle, Bulla, Bully, Bulleau, Poulle, Pol, Polý, Polleau, Pulle.

DIMINUTIVES.
Eng. Bullock, Bulck, Pollock—Mod. Germ. Bölicke, Bölke—French Bollack, Bouillac, Boulloche, Polac. Eng. Bulliss—French Boulas, Buloz, Pollisse.

PATRONYMICS.
Eng. Boling, Bulling, Pulling. Mod. Germ. Böhling.

COMPOUNDS.
(*Gar*, spear) Old Germ. Pulcari, Pulgar, 9th cent.—Eng. Bulger, Bullaker—Mod. Germ. Polgar. (*Gaud*, Goth) French Bouligaud. (*Hard*) Pollardus, *Domesday*—English Bullard, Pollard—Modern German Bollert, Pohlert—French Bouillard, Boullard, Bulard, Poullard, Polart. (*Hari*, warrior) Old Germ. Bolheri—Eng. Buller, Bowler, Pullar—Mod. Germ. Buhler, Pöhler—French Bouillier, Bouillerie, Boulier, Boullery, Boler, Bullier. (*Man*) Eng. Bollman, Bulman, Pulman, Poleman—Mod. German Bollmann, Buhlmann, Pohlmann. (*Mar*, famous) Anglo-Sax. Bulemære (*found in Bulemæres thorn, Cod. Dip.* 533.) English Bullmore, Bulmer—French Boulmier. (*Wine*, friend) English Polwin. (*War*, defence) English Bulwer —French Polffer ?

PHONETIC ENDING.
English Bollin, Bullen. Bullion, Pullan. French Boulan, Bouillien, Poulin, Poulain, Pulin.

From the Goth. *hulths*, Old High Germ. *holt*, Ang.-Sax. *hold*, Old Norse *hollr*, faithful, friendly, Förstemann derives the word *huld, hold, hul, hol*, found in Old German names. To this I put the following, though there may be an admixture of Ang.-Sax. *holt*, Old High Germ. *holz*, wood, in the sense of spear or shield.

J 2

282 THE PROTECTOR AND THE FRIEND.

SIMPLE FORMS.

Hold. Faithful, Friendly.

Old German Holda, 9th cent. (Old Norse Hollti, more probably in the other sense.) Holle, *Hund. Rolls.* English HOLT, HOLL, HOLE, HOOLE, HULLAH. Mod. Germ. HULDE, HOLD, HOLT, HOLLE. French HAULT, HOLE.

PATRONYMICS.

Old Germ. Hulling. Eng. HOLDING.*

COMPOUNDS.

(*Ger*, spear) Eng. HOLKER—French HOLACHER. (*Hari*, warrior) Old Germ. Huldear, 11th cent.—English HOLDER, HOLTER, HOLLER—Mod. Germ. HOLDER, HOLLER—French HOLLIER. (*Lind*, gentle) Old Germ. Holdelinda, 10th cent. —Eng. HOLLAND ?—French HOLLANDE ? (*Man*) Old Ger. Holzman ? 9th cent.—Eng. HOLTMAN, HOLEMAN—Modern German HOLLMANN. (*Rad*, counsel) Old Germ. Holdrada, 10th cent.—Eng ? HOLDERRIED (*Suff. Surn.*)

From the Gothic *auths*, Ang.-Sax. *eath*, mild, gentle, Förstemann derives the stem *euth*, with which, however, *aud, ead*, prosperity, is very apt to intermix.

SIMPLE FORMS.

Euth. Mild, Gentle.

Old German Eudo, *duke of Aquitania, 8th cent.*, Heudo, 11th cent. Eng. UDY, YEWD, YOUD. French EUDE, UDE, HEUDÉ.

DIMINUTIVES.

Old Germ. Eudila, 6th cent.—Fr. HEUDEL. Old German Eutilina, 8th cent.—French EUDELINE.

PHONETIC ENDING.

Old German Eodin, 7th cent.—Eng. YOWDEN—French HEUDIN.

COMPOUNDS.

(*Bert*, famous) Old German Eutberta, 8th cent.—French HEUDEBERT. (*Hari*, warrior) Old Germ. Euthar, 8th cent. Eng. ETHER ?—Fr. HEUDIER, (*Ric*, dominion) Eutharicus, *a Goth, son-in-law to Theodorich the great,* 5th cent.—Eng. ETHERIDGE ?

---

* And HOLLING, as found in HOLLINGSWORTH, "Hollings farm or estate."

THE PROTECTOR AND THE FRIEND. 283

The Ang.-Sax. *mild*, gentle, is found in three female names, Mildthrith, Mildburh, and Mildgith in the genealogy of the kings of Mercia. And in two names, Milta and Miltunc, the former of which is also that of a woman, in the *Altdeutsches Namenbuch.*

SIMPLE FORMS.

Old Germ. Milta. Mod. Germ. MILDE. French MILDÉ.

DIMINUTIVES.

Mildmé, 12th cent. Eng. MILDMAY.*

COMPOUNDS.

(*Thrith*, woman) Ang.-Sax. Mildthrith—Eng. MILDRED, MILDERT (*the former also a Christian name.*)

Mild.
Mitis.

I am rather inclined to think that *arm, armin*, p. 146, may also have the meaning of mild or gentle. The German *arm*, so far back as we can trace it, seems to have had, as at present, the meaning of poor. But the Celtic *araf*, which I take to be from the same root, has the meaning of gentle, and in river names I have elsewhere taken *arm* to be its equivalent. At the same time, the root-meaning of *arm*, poor, may be found in Sansc. *arv*, to desolate, and thus Arminius may signify vastator.

From the Anglo-Saxon *æmeta, emeta*, quies, Förstemann derives the following ancient names. The Old English *amese*, to calm, quoted by

---

* I before took this name to be from Ang.-Sax. *mæg*, Old Eng. *mey*, maiden. Such a name would be in accordance with ancient practice, and it would be the equivalent of the Ang.-Sax. Mildthrith. But I have found no trace whatever of the word in ancient use as an ending. I have suggested, p. 25, comparing it with the Friesic Mellema, that the *d* may be intrusive. However, of course the converse would equally apply. Pott, as usual, taking it *au pied de la lettre*, makes it "mild May," i.e., born at that season.

284   THE PROTECTOR AND THE FRIEND.

Halliwell, indicates that that form must also have prevailed in Anglo-Saxon, and points to the sense in proper names as probably that of peace-maker. The emmet (contracted ant), German *ameise*, is probably hence derived, in reference to its supposed rest during the winter.

SIMPLE FORMS.

Emet.
Emez.
Quies.

Old German Ammatas, Emita, Amizo, Emez,* 5th cent. Eng. AMETT, EMMETT, AMISS, EMUS. Mod. German AMEIS. French AMETTE, AMADE, AMÉDÉE ? AMIS.

COMPOUND.

(*Ulf*, wolf) French AMADEUF.

In the same manner the stem *lol*, *lul*, referred by Graff to Old Norse *lolla*, segnities, may rather be taken in the sense of Eng. "lull," to calm, in the sense probably of peace-maker.

SIMPLE FORMS.

Lul.
Soothe.

Old Germ. Lullo, Lul, Lolla, 7th cent.   Ang.-Sax. Lula *(found in Lulan treow, Cod. Dip.* 18*)*, Lull *(found in Lullesbeorh, Lulleswyrth, Cod. Dip.* 374,714.*)*   Eng. LULL, LULLY.   Modern German LÖHLE.   French LULLY, LOLLY, LAULHÉ, LAULL.

PATRONYMICS.

Ang.-Sax. Lulling *(found in Lullinges treow, Cod. Dip.* 227.*)*   French LULING.

COMPOUNDS.

(*Hard*, fortis) Eng. LOLLARD ?   (*Man*) Eng. LULMAN.

Perhaps on the whole most appropriately in this chapter will be introduced the names having the meaning of liberality or munificence. Though it may be uncertain in some cases whether the

---

* Hence Basingstoke, in Anglo-Saxon Embasinga stôc, the place of the Embasings, properly Emasings.

THE PROTECTOR AND THE FRIEND. 285

idea is not rather that of the prince than of the friend. " Bracelet-giver," in the sense of a rewarder of valour, is an expression of Anglo-Saxon poetry.

From the Old High German *geben*, Modern German *geben*, dare, Förstemann derives the following Old German names, which he observes are found both with the root-vowel as *gab*, and with the vowel-change of the present into *gib*.

SIMPLE FORMS.

Old German Gabo, Gebbo, Geppo, Givo, Jebo, Kyppo, Chippo, 8th cent. Eng. GABB, GAPP, GAFF, GAVEY, GIBBY, GIBB, GIEVE, JEBB, JEFF, KIBB, KIBBEY, KIPP, CHIPP. Modern German GABE, GAPP, GEPP, KÄBE. French GABÉ, GAPY, GAVEAU, CABÉ, GIBOU, GIF, JAFFA, JAPY, CHEVY?

Gab, Gib. Give.

DIMINUTIVES.

Old Germ. Gabilo, 9th cent.—English GABLE, GAVELLE, CABLE, KEBEL, KEPPEL—Mod. Germ. GABEL, GAVEL, GEBEL —French GAVELLE, JAVEL, GEBEL, CAVEL—Span. GAVILA. Old German Gibilin, 9th cent.—English GIBLEN, KIPLING— French GIBLIN. Old Germ. Gebizo, 11th cent.—Eng. GIBBS? GIPPS? GIPSY—French GIBOZ, GIBUS—Belg. GEEFS.

PHONETIC ENDING.

Old German Gebino, Givin, 8th cent.—English GAFFIN, GIBBON, GIVEN, GIFFIN, CHIPPEN—French GABIN, GIBON.

COMPOUNDS.

(*Bert*, bright) Old German Gibert, 9th cent.—English GIPPERT—French GIBERT—Italian GHIBERTI. (*Arn*, *ern*, eagle) Eng. GIBERNE—French GIVERNE, GIVERNY, GAVARNI. (*Hard*) Old German Gebahard, Givard, Gifard, 9th cent.— English GEBHARD, GIBBARD, GIFFARD—Modern German GEBHARDT—French GIFFARD, CHIPPARD. (*Hari*, warrior) Old German Gebaheri, 9th cent.—Old Norse Giafar— Eng. GAFFERY, CHIPPER, CHEEVER—Mod. Germ. GEBER,

286   THE PROTECTOR AND THE FRIEND.

KEBER,—French GIBORY, CHIPIER. (*Rat*, counsel) Old Germ. Geberat, 8th cent.—French GABARET. (*Man*) Eng. CHIPMAN. (*Wald*, power) Old German Gebald, Givold, 6th cent.—Mod. German GABOLD—French GABALDA, GAVALDA, GAVAULT, GIBAULT. (*Wine*, friend) Old Germ. Ghiboin, 7th cent.—French GIBOIN.

From the Ang.-Saxon *unna*, dare, may be the following, though Förstemann takes the negative particle *un* to intermix.

SIMPLE FORMS.

Un.   Old Germ. Unno, Unni, Una *(female)*, 9th cent.   Eng.
Dare.   UNNA.

COMPOUNDS.

(*Nid*, strife) Old German Unnid, 8th cent.—Eng. UNIT ?
(*Wine*, friend) Eng. UNWIN.*

---

* We do not find an ancient name to correspond, but there is an Old Germ. Unwan, 9th cent., and an Ang.-Sax. Unwona (3rd bishop of Leicester) ; to which perhaps may be put our UNWIN. The meaning of *wan* is not very clear; Förstemann suggests Goth. *wéns*, opes, which seems to suit in this case.

CHAPTER XV.

ANCESTOR AND KINSMAN.

Of the names derived from relationship, some have probably been surnames and nothing more. Others, in the first instance surnames, may have subsequently been adopted as baptismal, on the principle to which I have already referred. In one or two cases, as in the names signifying father, the idea may have extended somewhat beyond mere relationship. "My father," said his servants to the Syrian king, "if the prophet had bid thee do some great thing, wouldest thou not have done it?" So also in the case of names having the meaning of ancestor there is no doubt present something of that sense of nobility which is always attached to ancient descent. Words with both of the above meanings seem to run through the range of the Teutonic name-system. The most common word with the former meaning is *ad* or *at*, which Förstemann and other writers refer to Goth. *atta*, Old Fries. *atha*, *etha*, father. The stem *had* or *hath*, war, p. 167, is, however, likely to intermix, as well as in some cases *ead*, prosperity.

SIMPLE FORMS.

Old Germ. Atto, Ati, Adi, Atha, Etti, 7th cent. Atta, *Lib. Vit.* Eng. ATTOE, ATTY, ADDY, ETTY. Mod. Germ. ADE, ETTE. French ADDE, ADÉE, ETHÉE, ETEY.

Ad, At. Father.

288 ANCESTOR AND KINSMAN.

DIMINUTIVES.

Old Germ. Atacho, 8th cent.—English ATACK, ATKEY. Eng. ADKIN, ATKIN. English ADDIS, ATTS—French ATYS. Old German Attalus,* (rex. Germanorum, *Aurel. Vict.*) 3rd cent.—Ang.-Saxon Attila—Old Norse Atli—Eng. ATTLE, ATLEY.

COMPOUNDS.

(*Gis, kis,* hostage) Old Germ. Atgis, 8th cent.—English ATKISS. (*Got,* Goth) Old Germ. Adogoto, 8th cent.—Eng. ADDICOTT *(Hard)* Old Germ. Adohard, 9th cent—French EDARD—Ital. ATTARDI. (*Hari,* warrior) Old Germ. Adohàr, Adoar, 8th cent.—English ADIER—French ADOUR. (*Lef,* superstes) Old German Adlef, 8th cent.—French ATLOFF. *(Man)* Old Germ. Adiman, 9th cent.—English ADMANS— French ADMANT. (*Mar,* famous) Old German Adamar, 9th cent.—Eng. ATMORE ?—French ADHEMAR—Ital. ADIMARI. (*Ric,* power) Old German Aderich, 6th cent.—Anglo-Saxon Ætheric *(found in Ætherices hlype,†* Cod. Dip. 813, *and elsewhere)*—Eng. ATTRIDGE, ETRIDGE. (*Rid,* ride) Old German Atharid, 4th cent.—Ang.-Sax. *Æthered (found in Ætheredes haga,‡ Cod. Dip, 595, and elsewhere)*—Eng. ATTRIDE. (*Wid,* wood) Old German Adhuid, 8th cent.—English ATTWOOD ? (*Wolf*) Old Germ. Athaulf, Goth. King, 5th cent.—English ADOLPH §—Mod. Germ. ADOLF—French ADOLPHE.

There is a root *an*, for which Förstemann proposes Old High Germ. *ano*, Mod. Germ. *ahne,* avus, but suggests also an intermixture of another word *ann*, from Ang.-Sax. *ann*, favere. In the female names the latter seems the more probable derivation. There may also possibly be an intermixture of another word, Ang.-Sax. *hana*, Germ *hahn*, cock, which is not unsuitable for proper names.

---

* The name of Attila, the renowned leader of the Huns, Grimm holds to be German and not Hunnish.

† Ætheric's leap, probably in commemoration of some feat.

‡ Æthered's hedge.

§ This, as a surname, is, as Mr. Lower observes, of recent introduction.

ANCESTOR AND KINSMAN.   289

SIMPLE FORMS.

Old Germ. Anna, Anno, Enno, Hanno, Henno, 5th cent. Ang.-Sax. Anna, king of the East Angles. English ANNE, HANN, HANNA, HANNEY, HENN, HENNEY. Modern German HANNE, HENNE. French ANNE, ANNÉ, ANNÉE, HANNE, HANNO, HANY, HENNE, HENNO, ENNE.

An, En. Avus.

DIMINUTIVES.

Old German Annico, Ennico, 8th cent.—English ENOCH, ENOOK, HANKEY?—Mod. German HANNICKE, HENNICKE—French HANNICQUE, HENIQUE, HENOC, ENIQUE. Old Germ. Analo, 8th cent.—English HANNELL, HENNELL—French HENNEL. Old Germ. Hennikin, 11th cent.—Eng. HANKIN —Mod. Germ. HANNEKEN—French HANNEQUIN, HENNEQUIN. Old German Ennelin, 11th cent.—Eng. HANLON. English ANNISS, ENNISS, HENNIS, HENNESSY—Mod. Germ. HANISCH —French HENNECY.

PATRONYMICS.

Old Germ. Anninc, 8th cent. Eng. ANNING, HENNING. Mod. Germ. HENNING. French HANNONG, HENNING.

COMPOUNDS.

(*Bert*, bright) Old German Anibert, 8th cent.—French HANNEBERT, HENNEBERT. (*Fred*, peace) Old Germ. Anafred, Enfrid, 8th cent.—Eng. HENFREY—French ANFRAY, ENFRÉ. (*Gard*, protection) French HENNECART. (*Ger*, spear) Old Germ. Anager, Eneger, 8th cent.—Eng. HANGER, HENNIKER —French ANICKER. (*Grim*, fierce) Old Germ. Anagrim, 8th cent.—English ANCRUM. (*Hard*) Old German Henhart— Mod. German HENNERT—French ENARD, HENARD. (*Hari*, warrior) French HANNIER, ANERY. (*Man*) Old German Enman, 9th cent.—Eng. HANMAN, HENMAN—Mod. Germ. HANNEMANN, HENNEMANN. (*Mar*, famous) Eng. HANMER. (*Red*, counsel) Old Germ. Henred, 9th cent.—Eng. HANROTT, ENRIGHT. (*Wald*, power) Old German Anawalt, Ennolt— Eng. ANHAULT—Mod. Germ. HANEWALD, HÄNELT—French ENAULT, HENAULT. (*Ulf*, wolf) Old Germ. Anaolf, *Gothic leader*, 5th cent.—Eng. ENOUGH—French ENOUF.

K 2

290 ANCESTOR AND KINSMAN.

There is a root *aw*, *av*, which Förstemann thinks may be from Goth. *avo*, grandmother, but, no doubt, like the Lat. *avus*, in the wider sense of ancestor. Graff refers to Old High German *awa*, river.

SIMPLE FORMS.

Aw, Av.
Ancestor.

Old German Avo, Ovo, Ouo, 8th cent. English OVEY. French AVL.

DIMINUTIVES.

Old German Avila, 6th cent.—English AVILA, AVILL. Old German Avelina, 11th cent.—Eng. AVELINE, AVELING, EVELYN—French AVELINE.

COMPOUNDS.

(*Hard*) Eng. HAVARD—French AVART. (*Hari*, warrior) Eng. AVERY, AVER, OWER—French AVARE, AUER. (*Land*) Old Germ. Auiland, 9th cent.—Eng. HAVILAND. (*Man*) Old German Ouwaman, 11th cent.—Eng. HOWMAN ?—Mod. Germ. AVEMANN.

From the above stem *av* comes apparently an extended form *aviz*, found in the following.

SIMPLE FORMS.

Aviz.
Ancestor?

Old Germ. Aveza, 11th cent. Eng. AVIS, AVIZ. French AVISSE, AVISSEAU, AVIZEAU.

COMPOUNDS

(*Hard*, fortis) Eng. EVEZARD. Fr. AVIZARD, AVIZART.

A word of rather uncertain meaning in proper names is *bab*, respecting which Förstemann observes that it is " of a very ancient stamp, and approaching, as it seems, the nature and expression of children's speech ; according to Müller (*M.H.D. Wörterbuch*), the original meaning seems to be that of mother."

SIMPLE FORMS.

Bab,
Pap.
Parent?

Old Germ. Babo, Bavo, Pabo, Papo, 7th cent. Anglo-Saxon Babba (*found in Babbanbeorh, Cod. Dip. 623.*)

ANCESTOR AND KINSMAN.

291

John Babi, *member for Bodmin*, A.D. 1302. English BABB, BABE, BABY, BAUGH, PAPE, PAVEY. Mod. German BABE, PAPE, PAPPE. French BABEAU, BABÉ, PAPE, PAPAU, PAPY, PAVY.

DIMINUTIVES.

Old Germ. Babilo, 6th cent.—Ang.-Sax. Babel *(found in Babeles beorh, Cod. Dip. 618)*—Eng. BABELL—French BABULEAU. Old Germ. Bauika, 10th cent.—Eng. BABBAGE. Old Germ. Babolenus, Papolenus, 6th cent.—Eng. PAPILLON —French BABOULÈNE, BABLIN, PAPILLON.

PHONETIC ENDING.

Eng. BABIN, BAVIN. French BABIN, BÁBONNEAU, PAPIN, PAVIN.

COMPOUNDS.

(*Hard*, fortis) Fr. BAVARD, BAFFERT, PAPPERT, PAVARD. (*Hari*, warrior) English BABER, PAVIER—French PAPER. (*Wald*, power) Fr. BABAULT, PAPAULT. (*Ward*, guardian) French BABOUARD. (*Ulf*, wolf) Old Germ. Babulf, 8th cent. —Fr. BABEUF.

Perhaps with something more of certainty the root *tat* may be taken to mean "father." Diefenbach quotes many ancient and widely spread forms with this meaning (as English "dad," &c.)

SIMPLE FORMS.

Old German Tatto (Lombard king), Tado, Daddo, Dadi, Datto, Deddo, Tedo, Tazo, 6th cent. Eng. DADD, DADDY, Dad, Tad. DADE, DATE, DATT, DAZE, DAZEY, TADD, TADDY, TEDD. Father? Mod. Germ. DATE, DETTE, TADE. French DADO, TAZÉ.

DIMINUTIVES.

Old Germ. Tadilo, Tatila, 8th cent. Ang.-Saxon Tatel, *name of moneyer on a coin of Burgred, king of Mercia, found at Southampton.* English TADLOO, TATTLE, TETLOW. Mod. Germ. TADDEL.

COMPOUNDS.

(*Hard*, fortis) Old German Tethard, 9th cent.—French TETARD. (*Hari*, warrior) Old German Tether, 8th cent.—

292   ANCESTOR AND KINSMAN.

Eng. TEDDER, TEATHER. *(Man)* Eng. DADMUN, TADMAN, TEDMAN. *(Luc,* play) Eng. TATLOCK. (*Wine,* friend) Old Germ. Daduin, 8th cent.—Eng. TATUIN.

It is probable that the stem *ing, inc,* though its etymology is not yet explained, has the meaning of son, offspring, and is cognate with Eng. "young." As an ending in patronymic forms like Dunning and Billing, this is of course certain, but in other cases it is apt to mix with *ang,* p. 212. Ingo was one of the three sons of Mannus, the mythical founder of the German nation, as related by Tacitus.

SIMPLE FORMS.

Ing, Inc.
Descendant.
Old Germ. Ingo, Hingo, Hincho, Engo, 7th cent. Ingi, King of Norway. Incge (Beowulf.) English ING, INGOE, INCH, HINGE, HINCH, HINCHEY. Mod. Germ. ENGE, HINCK. French INGÉ, HINGUE, HINQUE, ENG.

DIMINUTIVES.

Old German Ingizo, 9th cent.—Eng. INCHES—French INGISCH.

PATRONYMIC.

English INKSON.

COMPOUNDS.

(*Bald,* fortis) Old Germ. Ingobald, Incbald, 8th cent.— Eng. INCHBALD—Fr. ANJUBAULT. (*Bert,* famous) Old Germ. Ingobert, 7th cent.—Eng. INCHBOARD—French ANGIBERT. (*Bod,* envoy) Old Germ. Ingobod, 7th cent.—Fr. ANGIBOUT. (*Hard*) Old German Inghard, 8th cent.—Modern German ENGERT—French ENGUEHARD. (*Hari,* warrior) Old Germ. Inguheri, 7th cent.—Eng. INGREY—Mod. German ENGER— French INGER, INGRAY. (*Ram, ran,* raven) Old German Ingram, Ingranna, 8th cent.—English INGRAM—French INGRAIN—Ital. INGHIRAMI. (*Leof,* dear) Eng. HINCHLIFF, HINCHCLIFF. (*Wald,* power) Old German Ingold, 7th cent. —Old Norse Ingvald—Eng. INGOLD—Mod. Germ. ENGWALD

ANCESTOR AND KINSMAN. 293

—French INGOLD. (*Ward,* guardian) French ANGOUARD (*Wis,* sapiens) Old Germ. Inguis, 9th cent.—Eng. ANGUISH.. (*Wolf*) Old Germ. Ingulf, 8th cent.—French INGOUF.

Then there are some other words of similar meaning which are found both in ancient and modern names, but which do not appear, like the foregoing, to enter into the Teutonic name-system. Grimm observes that "in Old Saxon records Fadar, Brothar, Modar, Suster, appear not unfrequently as simple proper names." Förstemann has Fader, Fáter, &c., of the 8th and following centuries—Mothar, Moder, &c.— Brothar, Broter, of the same period—Suester, Sustar of the 9th cent. The origin of these names is not, however, always certain—Mothar for instance is sometimes a man's name, and other words may intermix—see pp. 218, 237.

We have FATHER, MOTHER, BROTHER, SYSTER ; also FETTER and FETTERMAN, apparently from the Ang.-Sax. form *feder*. The Germans have VATER, VETTER, FEDER and FETTER ; MUDDER and BRUDER, also the diminutives VETTERLEIN, MÜTTERLEIN, BRÜDERLEIN. Pott has not Suestar, though according to Outzen SÖSTER or SÜSTER is a common name in Friesland. The French have SISTER, SESTER, and SESTIER—also SYSTER-MANN, which, however, seems to be of German origin, and which means a sister's husband. We have also BROTHERSON and SISTERSON, meaning a nephew respectively by the side of the brother and of the sister.

294 ANCESTOR AND KINSMAN.

I do not include the name UNCLE in this place. It seems rather to be the same as an Unculus, 8th cent., and a Hunchil in *Domesday*; Förstemann proposes *unc*, snake.

I doubt also the derivation of COUSIN from *consobrinus*—first, because such a relationship seems scarcely sufficient to mark a name—and secondly, because it falls in with a group else-where.

CHAPTER XVI.

THE NATION AS THE NAME-GIVER.

Names derived from nationality have probably been in many cases originally surnames. A stranger coming among men to whom his name might have an unfamiliar sound, would be very apt to be. called instead by the name of his nationality. And such names, once established, might afterwards come to be used baptismally. But it is also probable that names of this class might be bestowed baptismally in the first instance from a feeling of national pride; and it is not difficult to conceive how even in the present day, if the choice of names were open, many a father might delight to call his son an Englishman. Other causes have no doubt combined to give names of this sort—causes which though in most cases beyond our ken, are sometimes open at least to a conjecture. Thus, whereas it might seem strange that the name of the Picts should be given to Anglo-Saxons, yet when we find that two of the men who bore it, Pehthelm and Pehtwine, were bishops in the territory of the Picts, it seems natural to suppose that the name was assumed, perhaps as auspicious, on the occasion. Once become a name, it might be adopted by other men, as we find afterwards Pectuald, Pectgils, &c.

296 THE NATION AS THE NAME-GIVER.

In the sense of *advena* we may take the following, which seem to be from the Goth. and Old High German *gast*, Ang.-Sax. *gæst, gest, gist*, Eng. " guest."

SIMPLE FORMS.

Gast, Gest. "Guest." Old German Gasto, Cast, 8th cent. Old Norse Gestr. Eng. GAST, GUEST, GIST, KEAST. Mod. Germ. GAST, KAST. French GASTÉ, GASTY, CASTY, GESTE.

DIMINUTIVES.

English CASTLE, CASSELL, CASTLEY, CASTELLO—French GASTAL, CASTEL, GESTELLI. English GUESTLING—French GASSELIN.

PATRONYMICS.

Eng. GASTING, CASTANG. French CASTAING, CHASTAING.

PHONETIC ENDING.

Old Germ. Gestin, Kestin, Castuna, 8th cent. English GASTIN, GASTINEAU, CASTON, KESTEN. French GASTINE, GESTON, CASTAN.

COMPOUNDS.

(*Hard*, fortis) Old Germ. Gastart—Ang.--Sax. Gisteard (*found in Gisteardeswyl, Cod. Dip.* 595)—French GASSART ? (*Hari*, warrior) English GASTER, CASTER—French GASTIER, GUESTIER, CASTIER. (*Lind*, gentle ?) Old Germ. Gestilind—French GASLONDE ? (*Rat*, counsel) Old German Gastrat, Castrat, 8th cent.—French CASTERAT. (*Ric*, power) Old German Castricus, 6th cent.—French CASTRIQUE. (*Wald*, power) Old German Castald, 9th cent.—French (or Ital. ?) CASTALDI.

From the Goth. *quuma,* Ang.-Saxon *cumma*, advena, we find some names, which are however, apt to mix with *gum,* man, p. 59.

SIMPLE FORMS.

Cumma. Advena. Ang.-Sax. Cumma, name of a serf, *Cod. Dip.* 971. Eng. COMBE ? French CÔME.

THE NATION AS THE NAME-GIVER. 297

PHONETIC ENDING.
Old German Coman, 8th cent. Eng. COMMIN, QUOMMAN
(*Gothic form.*) French COMMUN, CUMON, COMMENY.

PATRONYMICS.
Eng. CUMMING. French CUMENGE.

The above word occurs more commonly as an
ending, and in some of the names, particularly
those compounded with words of affection, we
may perhaps rather find a reference to the "little
stranger" for whom an auspicious journey through
life is invoked.

(*Ead*, happiness) Old German Otoquim, 9th cent.—   Cumma.
Eatcume, *Lib. Vit.* (Old High Germ. *zit*, Ang.-Saxon *tid*,   Advena.
time—in the sense of seasonable?) Old Germ. Zitcoma, 8th   As an
cent.—Tidcume, *Lib. Vit.*—Eng. TITCOMB. (*New*, novus or   Ending.
juvenis) Neucum (*Domesday*)—Nequam (*Gothic form*)
English monk, 13th cent.—Eng. NEWCOME. (*Will*, in the
sense of desire or pleasure) Old Germ. Williquema, 8th cent·
—Uilcomæ, *Lib. Vit.*—English WELCOME*—Mod. German
WILLCOMM.

In the sense of *advena* we may also take
English NEWMAN, German NIEMANN, French
NEYMAN. We find it in England in the 13th
cent., but I take it to be more ancient. But the
stem *new* in general is taken by Grimm and
Weinhold to have, like the Greek *νεος*, the meaning of young, and I have introduced it elsewhere.

From the Old High Germ. *walah*, Ang.-Sax.
weahl, stranger, foreigner, variously with and
without the aspirated *h*, as *wallack*, *walk*, *wall*,
we may take the following. But the Ang.-Sax.
wœl, strages, seems a very likely word to intermix.

---

* I have put this, p. 123, but I think wrongly, to *gom*, man.

L 2

298 THE NATION AS THE NAME-GIVER.

SIMPLE FORMS.

Walah. Old Germ. Walah, Walach, Walco, Walch, Walo, Wal,
Stranger. Gualo, 7th cent. Ang.-Sax. Wala. Eng. WALLACK, WALK,
WALKO, WALKEY, WALL, WALE, WALEY, QUAIL, QUALEY.
Mod. German WALKE, WALLICH, WAHL, WALL. French
VALCI, VALIÈ, VALLÈE, OUALLE, WAL, GUALA.

DIMINUTIVES.

Old Germ. Walezo, 11th cent.—Eng. WALLISS, WALLACE,
WALLS, VALLIS—French VALLEZ, VALLS, WALLES, WALZ.
Old German Valahilo, 8th cent.—Eng. VALLELY, WALKLEY.
Walchelin, *Lib. Vit.*—Eng. WALKLIN.

PATRONYMICS.

Old German Walunc, 9th cent. English WALLING.

COMPOUNDS.

(*And*, life, spirit) Old German Waland, Valand, 8th
cent.—Eng. WALAND, VALIANT—French VALANT. (*Frid*,
peace) Old Germ. Walahfrid, 8th cent.—Eng. WALLFREE—
French VALFROY. (*Hard*, fortis) Old German Walhart, 9th
cent.—Fr. ? WALLART—Mod. Germ. WAHLERT. (*Hari*,
warrior) Old Germ. Walachar, Walchar, Walaheri, Walhar,
7th cent.—Ang.-Sax. Walchere, bishop of Lindisfarne—
Eng. WALLIKER, WALKER, WALLOWER, WALLER, VALLER—
Mod. Germ. WALCKER, WAHLER, WALLER—Fr. VALLERY,
VALLIER, VALHÉRE. (*Had*, war ?) Old Germ. Wallod, Valot,
7th cent.—Eng. WALLET, QUALLET—Fr. VALET. (*Raven*,
ram, ran, corbus) Old ·German Valerauans.* (*Jornandes*)
Walarammus, Walerannus, 8th cent.—Walrafan, *Lib. Vit.*—
Eng. WALLRAVEN (*Suff. Surn.*)—French VALLERAN. (*Man*)
Old Germ. Walaman, 8th cent.—Eng. WALKMAN—Mod.
Germ. WAHLMAN. (*Mar*, famous) Old German Walahmar,
(*king of the Ostro-Goths,*) Walmar, 6th cent.—Mod. Germ.
WAHLMAR—French VALMER. (*Rand*, shield) Old German
Walerand—Walerandus, *Lib. Vit.*—Eng. WALROND—French
VALERAND, VALERANT.

---

* This Gothic name (=Valeravan) must be of an older date than the 8th cent.

THE NATION AS THE NAME-GIVER. 299

From the Goth. *alja*, alius, in the sense of peregrinus, foreigner, Graff and Grimm derive the following stem.

SIMPLE FORMS.

Old Germ. Alj, Ello, Ella, 7th cent. Ang.-Saxon Ella. Al, El. Foreigner.
Eng. ELL, ELLEY, ELLA.

DIMINUTIVES.

' ' Old Germ. Alikin, Elikin, 10th cent. English ALLCHIN, ELKIN.

COMPOUNDS.

(*Brand*, sword) Old German Aliprand, 9th cent.—French ALBRAND. (*Bud*, envoy) Old Germ. Ellebod, 10th cent.— English ALLBUTT. (*Gar*, spear) Old German Elger, 5th cent.—English ELGAR, ELLIKER. (*Gaud*, Goth.) Old German Eligaud, 8th cent.—Eng. ALLGOOD, ELGOOD, ELLACOTT. (*Hard*, fortis) Old German Eleard, 10th cent. —English ELLARD—Mod. German ELLERT. (*Hari*, warrior) Old German Alier, Elier, 9th cent.—Eng. ELLERY. (*Mar*, famous) Old German Alimer, 9th cent.—Eng. ELMORE— French ELMIRE. (*Man*) Eng. ELLIMAN. (*Mund*, protection) Elmund, *Domesday*—Eng. ELEMENT. (*Wine*, friend) Old German Eliwin, 9th cent.—Elwinus, *Lib. Vit.*—Eng. ELWIN —French ELLOUIN. (*Wis*, wise) Eluis, *Lib. Vit.*—French ELLUIS. (*Wood*) Elwod, *Lib. Vit.*—Eng. ELLWOOD.

From the above root *al* or *el*, is formed, in the same meaning as I take it, the extended form *alis* or *elis*. So from Gr. ἐιλω comes ἐλισσω, verso, volvo, a word which may indeed have some relationship to the one in question. The river-names of Germany, Ilse, Elz, Alass, Elison (now the Lise), may compare with the Ilissus and the Helisson of Greece. Grimm refers this stem in proper names to the German tribe of the Elysii (*Tac. Germ.*) But the tribe may derive from a word signifying stranger, wanderer, faintly traced

300 THE NATION AS THE NAME-GIVER.

in the Old High Germ. *alis*, Ang.-Sax. *elles*, Eng. *else*, aliter. The scriptural name Elias may, as Förstemann remarks, be liable to intermix ; in the *Liber Vitæ*, however, it seems invariably to be recognized as distinct.

SIMPLE FORMS.

Alis, Elis. Peregrinus.
Old Germ. Eliso, Elis, 8th cent. Aluso, Elesa, *genealogy of the kings of Northumbria.* Aliz, Alis, Elsi, *Lib. Vit.* Eng. ALLIES, ALICE, ELLIS, ELLICE, ELSE, ELSEY—French ALLAIS, ELLIES.

COMPOUNDS.

(*Gar*, spear) Old German Alsker, 11th cent.—English ALSAGER. (*Gaud*, Goth.) Eng. ELSEGOOD.

Probably the same meaning of stranger may be found in the following, which seem to be from Goth. *anthar*, alius, but with which, in the simple form, the scriptural Andrew is very apt to mix up.

SIMPLE FORMS.

Ander. Alius.
Eng. HENDER ? Mod. Germ. ENDER ? French ANDRO ? ANDRY ?

COMPOUNDS.

(*Aud*, prosperity) Old German Andriaud, 9th cent.— Fr. ANDRAUD. (*Berg*, protection) Old Germ. Andreberga, 8th cent.—Mod. German ANDERBURG. (*Gais*, spear) Old Germ. Andragais, 4th cent.—Fr. ANTRAYGUES, ENTRAGUES.

Names from the points of the compass, as North, South, East, and West, may be included in this chapter. The ancient terminations, *a, i, o,* (which it will be seen are in some cases still preserved), would give them the force of " one from the north," " one from the south," &c.

SIMPLE FORMS.

North. Borealis.
Old Germ. Nordo, Nordi, Nord, 9th cent. Eng. NORTH, NORTHEY, NORRIE. Mod. German NORD, NORTH. French NORY, NAURY.

THE NATION AS THE NAME-GIVER. 301

DIMINUTIVES.

Old German Norlinc, 8th cent.   English NORLAN.

COMPOUNDS.

(*Bert*, famous) Old Germ. Nordbert, Norbert, 7th cent.
—French NORBERT.   (*Gaud*, Goth.) Old Germ. Northgaud,
Norgaud, 9th cent.—Eng. NORTHCOTT ? NORGATE ? NORCOTT?
NARROWCOAT ?—French NOURIGAT.   (*Gast*, guest) Old Germ.
Norigas, for Norigast, 8th cent.—Eng. NORQUEST.   (*Hari*,
warrior) Old German Nordheri, Nortier, 8th cent.—French
NORTIER. (*Man*) Old Germ. Nordeman, Norman, 8th cent.
—Eng. NORMAN—Mod. Germ. NORDMANN, NORMANN. (*Mar*,
famous) Old Germ. Nordmar, 9th cent.—Eng. NORTHMORE,
NORRAMORE—Mod. Germ. NORDMEYER.   English NORFOR =
north-faring ? Eng. NORTHEAST ?—French NOREST ?

From the Old High Germ. *sund, sunt*, Ang.-
Sax. *sûth*, Eng. *south*, we may take the following.
The Ang.-Sax. *sund*, sea, is a word that might
intermix.

SIMPLE FORMS.

Old Germ. Sundo.   Ang.-Sax. Sunt or Sunta *(found in*
Suntinga gemaero, the boundary of the Suntings, Cod. Dip.
445).   Ang.-Sax. Sûth* *(found apparently in Sûtheswyrth,*
Cod. Dip. 314). English SOUTH, SOUTHEY, SUNDAY.   French
SOUDAY, SOUTY.

Sund.
South.

COMPOUNDS.

(*Hard*, fortis) Old German Sunthard, 8th cent.— English
SOUTHARD.† (*Hari*, warrior) Old German Sunthar, Sum-
thahar, 7th cent.—English SUNTER, SUMPTER, SUTHERY—
French SOUDIER.   (*Ulf*, wolf) Old Germ. Suntulf, 7th cent.
—French SOUTIF.

PHONETIC ENDING.

Suthen, *Lib. Vit.* English SOUTHON, SUDDEN.   French
SOUDEN.

---

* There are other traces of this word as a personal name in the Cod. Dip.,—
for instance, Southling, found in Southlingleäh, Cod. Dip. 382, and comparing
with a Mod. German SUNDELIN—Sûthberht, found in Sûthberhtingeland, Cod.
Dip. 1,032.

† May be a corruption of another name SOUTHWARD.   Again—Southward
may be only a mistaken attempt to rectify Southard.

302 THE NATION AS THE NAME-GIVER.

EXTENDED FORM IN *er*

English SOUTHER. French SONDER.

COMPOUND.

(Ulf, wolf) Old Germ. Sundarolf, 8th cent. Mod. Germ. SÜNDREHOFF.

Names derived from the east were most common among the Franks, which, as Förstemann observes, is to be accounted for by their being the most west-lying of the German peoples, and of course having, for the most part, come from the east. Among the Saxons, whose course was northward, he observes that these names were almost entirely wanting. Nevertheless—at present it seems to me that they are more common in English than in French.

SIMPLE FORMS.

Ost, East. Old German Osta. English OST, HOSTE, OWST, YOST,
Orientalis. EAST, EASTY, EASTO. Mod. German OST.

DIMINUTIVES.

Old Germ. Aostilo, 8th cent.—Eng. OSTELL, AUSTELL.

COMPOUNDS.

(Man) Eng. EASTMAN—Mod. Germ. OSTMANN. *(Mar,* famous) English EASTMURE—Dan. OSTMER. *(Rad,* counsel) Old German Austrad, 8th cent.—Mod. Germ. OSTERRATH—French OSTARD *(or to hard).*

The extended form *oster* or *easter* is more common than the simple form *ost* or *east.* It is possible that in some cases there may be a reference to the goddess Ostara or Eastre, but I think in general that it is only the same word as *ost* or *east.*

SIMPLE FORMS.

Oster, Old Germ. Oster. Eng. EASTER, OYSTER. Mod. Germ.
Easter.
Orientalis. OESTER. French OUSTRIA.

THE NATION AS THE NAME-GIVER. 303

COMPOUNDS.

(*Burg*, protection) Old German Ostarpurc, 9th cent.—Eng. EASTERBROOK. (*Dag*, day) Eng. EASTERDAY*—Mod. Germ. OSTERTAG. (*Gos*, Goth.) Old Germ. Austrigosa, *wife of the Lombard king Wacho*—French ASTORGIS. (*Mar*, famous) Old Germ. Austrimir, 9th cent.—Eng. OSTERMOOR —Mod. German OSTERMEIER. (*Man*) Old German Austremonius, 6th cent.—English OYSTERMAN†—Mod. German OSTERMANN. (*Ric*, rule) Old German Austoric, 10th cent.—English OSTRICH.

Names derived from the west seem to have been the least common of all.

SIMPLE FORMS.

English WEST, VEST, VESTY. French VISTO?

*West.
Occidentalis,*

DIMINUTIVES.

English WESTALL, VESTAL.

COMPOUNDS.

(*Man*) English WESTMAN. (*Rat*, counsel) Old German Westrat, 9th cent.—French ? VESTRAETE. Eng. WESTFALL —Mod. Germ. WESTPHAL = Westphalian.

EXTENDED FORM.

English WESTER. French VESTIER.

COMPOUNDS.

(*Dag*, day) English WESTERDAY, YESTERDAY.‡ (*Man*) Old German Wistremand, 7th cent.—English WESTERMAN, VESTERMAN—Mod. Germ. WESTERMANN.

We now come to names derived from those of ancient German tribes, and of the races which bordered upon them. But here an important question suggests itself. Are the names of men derived from those of the nation—or may not

---

* Might be supposed to be from the Christian festival, but it rather seems to be the same as an Old German Ostdag. Compare also the name WESTERDAY.

† A New York name, but perhaps only a corruption of the German Ostermann.

‡ YESTERDAY might be a corruption either of EASTERDAY or WESTERDAY.

304 THE NATION AS THE NAME-GIVER.

both, at least in some cases, be from the same ancient origin? Thus, if Jute signifies giant—if Friese (or Frisian) signifies *comatus*, curled—if Wend signifies wanderer—may not the names of men be carried back to the same ancient source, and have the same meaning? This is a difficult question to answer, and I think that in fact both ways do probably obtain.

From the ancient tribe of the Suevi, Suavi, Suebi, or Suabi (whence the present Swabia), may be the following. Zeuss refers the name to Old High German *suipan*, ferri, Mod. German *schweben*. I also suggest Old Norse *sveipr*, a curl or lock of hair, because the whole of the Suevi, who comprehended several tribes, were noted, according to Tacitus, by a peculiar way of fastening the hair up into a knot.

SIMPLE FORMS.

Swab.
Swablan. Old German Suabo, Suap, Suppo, 8th cent. Swæppa, Ang.-Sax. geneal. Eng. SWABB, SWABEY, SWAAP, SWEEBY. Mod. Germ. SCHWABE, SCHWEPPE, SUPPE? French SOUPE, SOUPÉ, SOUPEÁU.

DIMINUTIVES.

Old German Suabilo, Suapilo, 8th cent.—Eng. SUPPLE—Mod. German SCHWÄBLE—French SOUPLY, SUPPLY, SOBBEL.

COMPOUNDS.

(*Hari*, warrior) Old Germ. Suabheri, 9th cent.—English SOUPER—Fr. SOUPIR. (*Wald*, power) Old Germ. Suapold, 9th cent.—French SOUPAULT.

From the Varini, Werini, Warni, or Werns, whose name Zeuss derives from Old High Germ. *warjan*, to defend, may be the following. Graff places the names to the above Old German stem, but Förstemann proposes also the people's name.

THE NATION AS THE NAME-GIVER. 305

SIMPLE FORMS.

Old German Warin, Guarin, Warno, Weruo, Wern, 7th cent. English WARREN, WARNE, VERNEY. Mod. German WAHREN, WERNE. French WARIN, GUÉRIN, GUERNE, VARIN, VARINAY, VERNEY, VERNAY, VERNEAU.

Warin, Warn. Wern.

DIMINUTIVES.

Old Germ. Wernicho—Eng. WARNOCK—Mod. German WARNECKE—French VARAGNIAC. Old German Werinela, 9th cent.—Eng. VARNELL—French WERNLÉ, VERNEL. Old German Werniza, 11th cent.—English VARNISH—French VERNAZ.

COMPOUNDS.

(*Aud*, prosperity) French VERNAUD. (*Burg*, protection) Old German Werinburg, 8th cent.—English WARRENBURY. (*Gaud*, Goth.) Old German Warengaud, 7th cent.—French VARANGOT. (*Hard*) Old Germ. Wernhart, 8th cent.—Mod. German WERNERT—French VERNERT. (*Hari*, warrior) Old German Warenher, Warner, Werner, Guarner, 7th cent.— English WARRENER, WARNER, WERNER, VERNER—Modern German WARNER, WERNER—French OUARNIER, WARINIER, VARNIER, VERNIER, GUERNIER. (*Had*, war) Old German Warnad, 8th cent.—English WARNETT—French WARNET, VERNET. (*Red*, counsel) Old Germ. Werinred, 9th cent.— French VERNERET.

From the tribe of the Jutes Förstemann and Zeuss derive the following ancient names.

SIMPLE FORMS.

Old German Judo, Juto, Judda, Jutta, Yuto, 8th cent. English JUDD, JOOTH, YETT. Mod. German JÜDE, JÜTTE. Dutch JUT. French JUDEAU, JUDE, JUTEAU.

Jud, Jut Jute.

DIMINUTIVES.

French JUTTEL. English JUDKIN. French JUDLIN.

PATRONYMICS.

Old German Judinga, 8th cent.—Ang.-Saxon* Ytting (*found in Yttinges hláw, Cod. Dip.* 1,114, *and elsewhere.*) Eng. JUTTING. Eng. JUDSON, JUTSON.

---

* The Ang.-Sax. form Yta, Iota, Jute.

M 2

306 THE NATION AS THE NAME-GIVER.

COMPOUNDS.

(*Hari*, warrior) French JUTIER. (*Man*) Eng. YEATMAN. (*Rat*, counsel) Old Germ. Jutrad, 8th cent.—French JOTRAT. (*Wine*, friend) Old Germ. Joduin, 11th cent.—Eng. JODWIN, JEUDWINE—French JOUVIN.

From the name of the Franks may probably be derived the following. Though common in its simple form, this does not often occur in compounds, which may perhaps be attributed to the more recent origin of the name, it having been given to a confederation of different tribes.

SIMPLE FORMS.

The Franks. Old Germ. Franco, Francio, Frenko, 5th cent. English FRANK, FRANCO, FRANCE? FRENCH? Mod. Germ. FRANCKE, FRANK. French FRANC, FRANQUE, FRANCO, FRANCHE, FRANCIA, FRANCE, FRANCEY, FRANZ.

DIMINUTIVES.

Old Germ. Francula, 5th cent.—English FRANKEL. Old Germ. Francolin, 8th cent.—Eng. FRANKLIN—Mod. Germ. FRANKLIN—French FRANQUELIN, FRANCILLON.

PHONETIC ENDING.

Old German Franchin, 8th cent. French FRANQUIN. Ital. FRANCONI?

COMPOUNDS.

(*Hard*) Old Germ. Francard, 6th cent.—Eng. FRANCOURT —French? FRANKAERT.

I find no ancient names to throw any light upon the following group, which I think may perhaps be derived from the tribe of the Chauci or Cauci.* The commonness of these names in French would be accounted for by this being one of the tribes which formed the Francic confederation. However, I only bring forward the subject as one for further enquiry.

---

* There was also another tribe called the Chauci.

THE NATION AS THE NAME-GIVER. 307

SIMPLE FORMS.

English CHALK, CHALKEY, CAULK.   French CHAUSSY; The Chaucl, CHAUSSÉE, CAUCHE, CAUCHY, CHOQUE. or Caucl.

DIMINUTIVE.   PATRONYMICS.

Eng. CHALKLEN.   Eng. CALKING, CAULKING.

COMPOUNDS.

(*Hard*) French CHASSARD, CAUCHARD.   (*Hari*, warrior) English CHALKER, CHAUCER—Mod. Germ. KALKER—French CHAUSSIER, CHOQIER.   (*Man*) Eng. KALKMAN.

From the Falii or Falians, (whence the name of Westphalia,) Förstemann derives a root *fal, falah*, in ancient German names.

SIMPLE FORMS.

Old German Falho, Fal.   English FALL, FALLOW, FAIL, The Falil, FELLOW?   Mod. Germ. FAHL.   French FAULLE, FAULEAU, or Fallians. FALLOU, FAILLE.

EXTENDED FORM=FALIAN.

English FALLON.   French FAULON.

From the name of the Hessians is probably the following stem, which is, however, very difficult to separate from another, *haz*, p. 169.   Also from *ans, as*, semideus, p. 119.

SIMPLE FORMS.

Old Germ. Hasso, Asso, Hessi, 8th cent.   English HASS, Hass, Hess. HESSE, HESSEY.   Mod. Germ. HASS, HESS.   French HASSE, Hessian. HESSE, HESZ.

EXTENDED FORM=ENG. "HESSIAN."

Eng. HASSAN, HESSON, HESSION.   French HASSAN.

There is a stem, *sal, sel*, rather common in ancient names, for which Förstemann proposes *salo*, dark, (Eng. "sallow"), *sal*, hall, or Goth. *séls*, benignus.   I think it probable, however, that at least a portion may be placed to the name of the Salii, a tribe of Franks (whence the Salic law in France).

308 THE NATION AS THE NAME-GIVER.

SIMPLE FORMS.

Sal, Sel. ˙ Old German Salo, Sallo, Salla, Sella, 5th cent. Salla,
Salian. *Lib. Vit.* Eng. SALE, SALA, SELL, SELLEY. Mod. German
SAHL, SELLE, SELLO. French SALLE, SALLÉ, SALA, SAILLY,
SELLE.

DIMINUTIVES.

Old German Salaoo, 6th cent.—English SELLICK—Mod.
German SELKE. Old German Saliso, 9th cent.—English
SALLES, SELLIS—French SALESSE, CELESSE, CELS.

PATRONYMICS.

Old Germ. Salinga, *wife of the Lombard king Wacho,* 6th
cent. English SELLING.

COMPOUNDS.

(*Bald,* bold) Old German Salabald, 9th cent.—French
SELABELLE. (*Frid,* peace) Old German Salafrid, 9th cent.—
French SALFRAY. (*Fast,* firm) French SAILLOFEST ?* (*Got*
Goth.) Salgot (Saxo.)—French SALIGOT. (*Hari,* warrior)
Old German Salaher, 8th cent.—English SELLAR, SAILOR—
Fr. SALLIER, SELLIER, CELLIER. (*Hard*) French SAILLARD,
SALARD, CELLARD. (*Man*) Old German Salaman, Saleman,
Seliman, 8th cent.—Eng. SALAMON (apparently not Jewish),
SALMON, SALEMAN, SELMAN—Modern German SALLMANN—
French SALMON. ˙ (*Ram, ran,* raven) Old German Salaram,
9th cent.—French SALLERON, SELLERIN, CELLERIN. (*Wig,
wi,* war) Old German Selwich—English SALLAWAY, SELWAY.
(*Dio, thiu,* servant) Old German Saladio, 8th cent.—French
SALATHÉ.

EXTENDED FORM="SALIAN."

Ang.-Saxon Salenn. English SELLON. French SALIN,
SALIGNY, SELIN.

COMPOUND.

(*Fast,* firm) French SAILLENFEST.

It is probable that there are many names from
the Goths, but the root is a very difficult one to
deal with, mixing up with *good,* bonus, and
perhaps with *got,* deus. GOTH itself (a Yorkshire
name), might be supposed to be most certainly

---

* We have no sure instance of this word as an ending. Compare Ariovistus,
p. 95.

THE NATION AS THE NAME-GIVER. 309

from the nation. Yet Förstemann refers the Old German names Gotho and Goth, 8th cent., to the other stem, while at the same time—not quite consistently, as it seems to me—he derives the Mod. Germ. names GOTHE and GÖETHE from the nation. I will not attempt to divide the two stems, but I bring in here the form *goz*, which Grimm, Graff, and Förstemann concur in making another form of *gaud*, Goth.

SIMPLE FORMS.

Old Germ. Gozo, Gauso, Gauz, Gossa, Jozo, Cozo, Cauzo, 8th cent. Goza, *Lib. Vit.* English Goss, GOOSE, GOOSEY, GOOZE, CAUSE, CAUSEY, COSE, COSSEY, COOZE. Mod. Germ. GAUSE, GOSE, GÖSS, KOSS. French GAUZEY, GOSSE, GOUSSE, JOSSE, JOSSEAU, JOSSU, JOZEAU, JOUSSE, COSSE, COSSÉ, COZE, COZZI, COUSSY, CAUSSE.

Goz.
Goth.

DIMINUTIVES.

Old German Gozekin, 11th cent.—Eng. JOSKYN—Mod. Germ. GÖSEKEN, GÖSCHEN—French COSQUIN. Old German Gauzilin, Gozlin, Joscelin, 8th cent.—Gozelin (*Domesday*)—English GOSLIN, GOSLING, JOSLIN—Mod. German GOSLING—French GOSSELIN, JOUSSELIN, JOSSELIN. Old Germ. Gaozaich, 8th cent.—Eng. COSSACK—French CAUZIQUE, COZIC.

PHONETIC ENDING.

Old German Cozzuni, 8th cent. Cosin (*Hund. Rolls*)- Eng. GAUSSEN, COSSON, COUSIN. French GOSSIN, GAUSSEN, JOZAN, COSSIN, CAUSIN, COUSIN, COUZINEAU.

COMPOUNDS.

(*Bald*, bold) Old German Gauzebald, 8th cent.—English GOSBELL, GOSPELL. (*Heid*, state, condition) Old German Caosheid, 9th cent.—English GOSSET ?—French CAUSSADE, CAUSSAT, GOSSET ? JOSSET ? (*Hard*) Old German Gozhart, Gozart, Cozhart, 8th cent.—Eng. GOZZARD, COSSART—French GOSSARD, GOSSART, CAUZARD. (*Hari*, warrior) Old German Gauzer, Cozhere, 8th cent.—Eng. GOZAR, COSIER, CAUSER—French GOUSSERY, JOSSIER. (*Helm*) Old German Goshelm,

310 THE NATION AS THE NAME-GIVER.

Jozzelm, 8th cent.—French Gossiome, Josseaume. (*Ram, ran,* raven) Old Germ. Cozram, 8th cent.—Eng. Gosheron—French Gaussiran. (*Leih,* carmen) Old Germ. Gosleih, 8th cent.—Eng. Goslee. (*Lind,* gentle) Old German Gauzlind, 8th cent.—English Gosland, Josland (or from *land,* terra). (*Man*) Eng. Gooseman—Mod. German Gossman—French Cosmène. (*Mar,* famous) Old Germ. Gozmar, 8th cent.—English Gosmer—Mod. Germ. Cosmar. (*Niw,* young) Old German Cozniw, Cozni—French Cosne, Cosnuau. (*Rat,* counsel) Old Germ. Cozzarat, 9th cent.—French Cosseret. (*Rand,* shield) French Josserand, Jousserand. (*Wealh,* stranger) Old German Coswalh, 9th cent.—Eng. Goswell. (*Wald,* power) Old German Gausoald, 8th cent.—English Goswold.

Zeuss refers the following stem to the name of the Danduti, in which Graff and Förstemann also seem to agree.

SIMPLE FORMS.

The Danduti? Old German Dando, Dendi, Tando, Tanto, 9th cent.; Danzo, Tanzo, 8th cent. Ang.-Sax. Daunt *(found perhaps, in Dauntesbourn, Cod. Dip.* 384). Dando, Dandi (*Hund Rolls*). English Dand, Dando, Dandy, Dendy, Dainty, Daunt, Tant, Tent, Tandy, Dance, Dancey, Tansey. French Dandou, Danty, Dentu, Tandou, Danse, Tencé. Ital. Dante ?

DIMINUTIVES.

Old Germ. Tantulo, 8th cent.—Eng. Tendall, Tansell—French Danzel—Ital. Dandolo. Old German Dantlin, Dentlin, 10th cent.—Eng. Dandelyon—French Denullein, Tenaillon.

PHONETIC ENDING.

English Tanton, Danson. French Danton, Tandon, Tanton.

COMPOUNDS.

(*Hard,* fortis) French Dansard. (*Hari,* warrior) Dauntre (= Dauntherl ?) *Roll Batt. Abb.*—English Dancer ?—French Dantier. (*Wine,* friend) Tanduini, *Lib. Vit.*—Fr. Danvin Tennevin.

THE NATION AS THE NAME-GIVER. 311

Then there is a stem *dan*, which Förstemann thinks may be, at least in part, from the name of the Danes. It seems, probable, however, that it is sometimes only a degenerate form of *dand*, and in one or two instances I have so classed it.

SIMPLE FORMS.

Old German Dano, Danno, Denno, Tanno, Tenno, 8th The Danes. cent. Dene, *Lib. Vit.* English DANE, DANA, DANN, DENN, DENNY, DEAN, TANN, TEN. Mod. German DANN, DEHN, TANNE. French DAN, DANNE, DANEY, TAINNE.

DIMINUTIVES.

Old Germ. Tanucho, 9th cent.—Eng. TANNOCK—French DENECHAU. Old Germ. Danila, Tenil, 7th cent.—English DANNELL, DENNELL, TENNELLY—French DANEL, DANELLE, TANLAY.

PATRONYMICS.

Old German Daning, Dening—Eng. DENNING. Eng. DENSON,* DENISON, TENNYSON—French TENNESON.

PHONETIC ENDING.

English DANNAN. French DANIN, DENIN.

COMPOUNDS.

(*And*, life, spirit) English TENNANT—French DENANT. (*Burg*, protection) Old German Danaburg, 10th cent.—French ? DANNEBERG. (*Frid*, peace) Old German Danafrid, 8th cent.—English DANFORD ? (*Gaud*, Goth.) Old German Danegaud, 8th cent.—Mod. German DANKEGOTT ?—French DENÉCHAUD. (*Hard*, fortis) Old Germ. Denihart, 8th cent. —Ang.-Sax. Dæneheard (*found in Dæneheardes hegeræwe,†* *Cod. Dip.* 272)—Eng. DENHARD—French DENARD, DENERT, TENARD. (*Gar*, spear) Old Germ. Thanger, 9th cent.—Eng. DANGER—Modern German DANNECKER—French DENECHER, DENCRE, DENAIGRE, TANGRE. (*Hari*, warrior) Eng. DENYER, DANNER, TANNER—French DENIER, DENNERY, TANIÈRE, TAN-

---

* I do not feel sure of these names. They might be the same as Tanton, &c., in the previous group. See also Benson, Bunsen, &c., p. 236.

† " Dæneheard's hedgerow."

312 THE NATION AS THE NAME-GIVER.

NEUR. *(Man)* Eng. DENMAN, TENNEMAN. *(Red,* counsel) Old Germ. Tennared, 6th cent.—French TANRADE, TENRET. *(Ulf,* wolf) Old German Thanolf, 10th cent.—Ang.-Saxon Denewulf—Eng. DENOLF—French DENEFF, DENAIFFE.

From the tribe of the Ambrones Zeuss and Förstemann derive the word *amber* in proper names—the latter also suggesting that the *b* may be only euphonic and the proper form· *amar,* in which case it might be an allied word to *amal,* p. 143.

SIMPLE FORMS.

<small>The Ambrones.</small> Ang.-Saxon Amber *(found in Ambresbyrig, now Amesbury, Ambresledh, now Ombersly.)* Eng. AMBER, HAMPER, EMBER, IMBER.* French AMPAIRE, EMPAIRE, EMBRY.

DIMINUTIVES.

Old German Ambricho, Embricho, Imbrico, 5th cent.— Eng. AMBRIDGE ?

The Frisian or Friese (Ang.-Saxon Frysa,) appears to give the name to the following. According to Richthoven this people's name is allied to · French *friser,* Eng: *frizzle,* and signifies *comatus,* curled—the wearing of the hair long or curled being considered among the German tribes as a badge of the freeman and the hero. According to Zeuss it is derived from Goth. *fraisan,* tentare, Ang.-Sax. *frása,* periculum, in the sense of valour or courage. In this case, and perhaps in any case, we may include the form *fras.*

SIMPLE FORMS.

<small>Friese, Frisian.</small> Old Germ. Friaso, Friso, Vras, 8th cent. Eng. FREEZE, FRASI. Mod. German FRIESS. French FRISE, FRAYSSE, FRASEY.

---

* Might be referred to the Ymbras of the Traveller's Song, whom Lappenberg supposes to be the Imbers of the Isle of Femern. Thorpe suggests that these Imbers might be a remnant of the Ambrones.

THE NATION AS THE NAME-GIVER. 313

EXTENDED FORM=ENG. FRISIAN.*
French FRISON, FRESSON.

Then there are several names which may be derived from peoples not themselves Teutonic, yet who bordered upon, or might be partially intermixed with, the German tribes. Thus we find that the Anglo-Saxons had several names compounded with Peht or Pict ;† I have suggested a possible reason at p. 295 ; I do not think, with Mr. Kemble, that an intermixture of blood is necessarily to be assumed.

From the Boii, a Celtic tribe who gave the name to Boioaria, now Bavaria, Förstemann derives the stem *boi* in proper names. There appear to be three forms—first, the simple form found in the name of the Boii—secondly, 'the extended form found in German Baviar—and 'thirdly, the further extended form found in Eng. Bavarian.

SIMPLE FORMS.

Old German Boio, Beio, Peio, 7th cent.   Ang.-Saxon The Boii.
Boia.   Eng. BOY, BYE, PYE.   Mod. Germ. BOYE.   French
BOY, BOYÉ, POY, POYÉ.

COMPOUNDS.

(Hard, fortis) Eng. BYARD—French BOYARD, POYARD, POYART. *(Man)* Eng. BOYMAN, PYMAN.

EXTENDED FORM=GERM. BAVIAR.

Old Germ. Baior, Peior, 9th cent.   Eng. BOYER, BYER.
French BOYER, BOYREAU, POYER.

COMPOUND.

(Man) English BEYERMAN.

---

* Possibly another extended form may be found in Eng. FRASER, FREEZOR, French FRASIER, FREEIER.

† Our name PICTURE (Registrar-General's return) seems rather probably to be from this origin, representing an Ang.-Sax. Pecthere or Pehthere.

N 2

314 .THE NATION AS THE NAME-GIVER.

EXTENDED FORM=ENG. BAVARIAN.

Old Germ. Beiarin, 8th cent. French BOIRON, BOYRON,

From the name of the Huns Förstemann derives the following stem, observing however that the root *un* (*unna*, dare, or *un*, negative), is very liable to intermix. It is further to be observed that if Hun, as Grimm suggests, signifies giant, this may also be the meaning in proper names.

SIMPLE FORMS

The Huns. Old German Huno, Huni, Hup, 8th cent. Hun, a king of the Hetware (*Traveller's song*). Honey (*Hund. Rolls*). Eng. HUNN, HONEY. Mod. Germ. HUHN, HUNN.

DIMINUTIVES.

Old German Hunico, 10th cent.—Honoc, *Lib. Vit.*— English HUNNEX—Modern German HÖNICKE, HÖNKE— French HONACHE. Old German Hunichin, 10th cent.— English HUNKING—Mod. Germ. HÜNECKEN. Old German Hunzo, 9th cent.—Eng. HONISS, HUNNS.

COMPOUNDS.

(*Bert*, bright) Old German Hunbert, Humbert, 8th cent. —Ang.-Sax. Hunberht, bishop of Lichfield—Mod. German HUMBERT—French HUMBERT. (*Bald*, bold) Old German Hunibald, 8th cent., Humbold, 9th cent.—Eng. HONEYBALL, HUNIBAL—Modern German HUMBOLDT—French HUMBLOT. (*Frid*, peace) Old German Hunfrid, Humfrid, 8th cent.— Ang.-Sax. Hunfrith, bishop of Winchester—Eng. HUMPHREY —French HONFRAY. (*Ger*, spear) Old Germ. Hunger, 8th cent.—English HUNGER—Mod. German HUNGER—French HONGRE, HONACKER. (*Gaut, goz*, Goth.) Old Germ. Hungoz, 9th cent.—Eng. HUNGATE. (*Hard*) Old Germ. Hunard, 8th cent.—English HUNNARD—Mod. Germ. HÜHNERT—French HONNARD. (*Hari*, warrior) Old Germ. Honher, 8th cent.— English HONNER—Mod. German HONER. (*Man*) Honiman (*Hund. Rolls*).—English HONEYMAN—Mod. Germ. HONIG-MANN, HUNNEMANN. (*Rat*, counsel) Old Germ. Honrad, 9th

THE NATION AS THE NAME-GIVER. 315

cent.—French Honorat. (*Wald*, power) Old Germ. Hunwald, Hunoald, 8th cent.—Hunewald, *Lib. Vit.*—English Hunhold—Mod. Germ. Hunold—French Hunault .

From the name of the Fins Förstemann derives the following stem, found in five Old German names, observing that as the Fins have been neighbours of the Germans ever since the time of Tacitus, it would be surprising if no names had been derived from them. The same remark applies to the Northmen, among whom the name was more common than among the Germans. The word however requires further investigation; Miss Yonge explains it as "white," and referring to Finn as a title of Odin, thinks that it was "an idea borrowed from the Gael by the Norsemen."

SIMPLE FORMS.

Old Germ. Fina. Finn, ancestor of Woden, *Ang.-Sax. geneal.* Fin, a prince of the North Frisians (Beowulf). Old Norse Finnr, Finni. Eng. Finn, Finney.

The Fins.

COMPOUNDS.

(*Bert*, bright) French Finbert. (*Bog*, bow) Old Norse Finbogi—Eng. Finbow. (*Gar*, spear) Old Norse Finngeir—Ang.-Sax. Finger (*found in Fingringahô,* Cod. Dip.* 685)—Eng. Finger. (*Mar*, famous) Eng. Finnimore ?

From the Venedi, Veneti, Winidæ, or Wends may be the following. According to Grimm (*Gesch. d. Deutsch. Spr.*) this people's name, as well as that of the Vandals, is to be referred to Germ. *wenden*, Eng. wend, wander, &c.

SIMPLE FORMS.

Old Germ. Winid, Windo, Wenda, Wento, Wenso, 9th cent. Winta, son of Woden, in the genealogy of the kings

The Wends.

---

* The mound of the Fingerings, "descendents of Finger," now Fingringhoe in Essex.

316 THE NATION AS THE NAME-GIVER.

of the Lindisfari. English WIND, WINDOW, WENT, WINT, VENT, VINT, QUINT. Mod. German WIND, WEND, WENT. French VINIT, VIENT, VINTZ, QUINTY.

PHONETIC ENDING.

Old Germ. Vinidin, 9th cent. Eng. WENDON, VINDIN, QUINTIN. French VINTIN, QUENTIN.

COMPOUNDS.

(*Hari*, warrior) Old German Winidhari, Winidhar, Winithar, 5th cent.—Eng. WINDER, WINTER,* VINTER— Mod. Germ. WINDER, WINTER—French VENTRE, GUINDRE. (*Ram, ran*, raven) Old Germ. Winidram, Winedrannus, 8th cent.—Eng. WINDRAM—French VENDRIN.

Then there is a form *wand*, which may be, at least in some cases, the same as the preceding.

SIMPLE FORMS.

Wand,
Wend?
Old Germ. Wando, Wandi, Wanzo, 8th cent. English WAND, WANT, VANT, VANDY, WANSEY, VANCE. Mod. Germ. WANDE, WANDT. French VANCY.

DIMINUTIVES.

Old Germ. Wendico, 9th cent.—Eng. QUANTOCK—Mod. Germ. WANDTKE.

PATRONYMICS.

Old Germ. Wanding, 8th cent.—Eng. WANDING.

PHONETIC ENDING.

Old Germ. Wanzino. Eng. WANTON, VENSION. French VANDEN, QUANTIN.

COMPOUNDS.

(*Hari*, warrior) Old Germ. Wanther, 8th cent.—English WANDER—French VANTIER, QUANTIER, (*Man*) English WANTMAN.

Then there is a third form from the same root, which may probably be referred to the name of the Vandals.

---

* Might also be from another origin—see p. 141.

THE NATION AS THE NAME-GIVER. 317

SIMPLE FORMS.

The Vandals.

Old German Wandilo, Wandil, Wendil, Wyndele, 5th cent. Ang.-Saxon Windel *(found in Windlesora, now Windsor, &c.,).* English WINDLE, WINTLE. Modern German WANDEL, WENDEL. French VANDALE, VANUTELLE, QUANDELLE.

DIMINUTIVES.

Old German Wandalin (bishop of Chartres), Wantelin, Wendelin, 6th cent.—Modern German WENDLING—French VANTHIELEN. Eng. WENDELKEN.

COMPOUNDS.

(*Hard*, fortis) French VANTILLARD. (*Hari*, warrior) Old Germ. Wandalarius, 6th cent., Βανδαλαριος, Procopius —Eng. VANDELEUR, WINDELER, VANZILLER—Mod. German WENDELER.

Though we cannot doubt that the very common name of SCOTT has been in most cases a surname derived from nationality, yet we find it also in ancient use as a single or baptismal name. Whether in this case also it may, like other names of the same sort, be derived from the nation, or whether, as appears to be the case in the name SCOTTSMITH, we may think of Old Norse *skot*, dart, spear, there are scarcely sufficient grounds for deciding.

SIMPLE FORMS.

Scot.

Old Germ. Scot, 9th cent. Ang.-Sax. Scott *(found in Scottes healh, Cod. Dip. 1,218.)* Scott, *Lib. Vit.*

DIMINUTIVE.
English SCOTTOCK.

PATRONYMIC.
English SCOTTING.

COMPOUNDS.*

(*Bald*, fortis) Eng. SHOTBOLT ? (*Land*) Scotland, *Lib. Vit.*—Scotland, *a Norman in the Acta Sanctorum*—English SCOTLAND. (*Mar* famous) Old Germ. Ecotmar (for Scotmar, according to Förstemann)—Eng. SCOTCHMER.

---

* Besides the names here quoted, Scothard occurs twice as a Frankish name in the Pol. Irm.

318   THE NATION AS THE NAME-GIVER.

I do not think that SPAIN is from the country;
it seems rather to be the same name .as Spegen
which occurs two or three times in the Liber
Vitæ, and which is probably from Ang.-Saxon
spanan, allicere.   So also SWEDEN, which compares with an Old German Swedin, referred by
Förstemann to Old High Germ. *swedan*, to burn.

SWEETSUR evidently means a Sweitser or
Swiss.   But I do not think that PICKARD, p. 178,
means a native of Picardy.   And though JANE-
WAY may be, as Mr. Lower suggests, from an old
word for a Genoese, yet I should rather take it
to be the same as GANNAWAY, from the stem
gan, elsewhere noticed.   ENGLISH and INGLIS
may be the same as the Ang.-Saxon name Ingils
(for Ingisil).   IRELAND may be, like the Old
Germ. names Erland, Airland, &c., the same as
HARLAND, p. 232.   ROMAN also may be from
Rodman, as Robert, Roger, and Roland, from
Rodbert, Rodger, and Rodland.

Lastly, there are one or two names which
seem to refer to a mixture of race.   Such is an
Old Germ. Halbthuring, 9th cent., which seems
to mean a Thuringian on one side.   Also an Old
Germ. Halbwalah, 8th cent., which may mean
half foreigner or half Welsh.   So likewise the
Danish Halfdane, whence the Scottish HALDANE.
But I doubt very much whether Mr. Kemble is
right in thinking that the Anglo-Saxon name
Mûl signifies half-breed ; Miss Yonge at any rate
is certainly wrong in thinking that Ceadwalha,

THE NATION AS THE NAME-GIVER. 319

his brother,had a Cymbric name ; for, as elsewhere shown, it is clearly Teutonic. At the same time it is very probable that the similarity of the name to the Celtic Cadwallader might be the cause of a mutual confusion of the two names.

CHAPTER XVII.

THE SEA AND THE SEA LIFE.

While the Gothic tribes were wanderers in the great Northern Forests, they took their names from the objects that were familiar to them there. The nobler of the savage brutes— the bear, the wolf, the boar—were among the Teuton's favourite types;—the war-game that he loved, and the sword that "was to him as a daughter."

But it was a new life when they came to the water's edge. A new horizon opened to their view—new visions stirred their minds—their destiny took them by the hand—and the bold hunter became the daring viking. Short flights of piracy trained their wings—and the narrow British sea was bridged;—a thousand years to gather head—for it was the wide Atlantic that came next.

On all the German sea-board there were fierce pirates and bold seamen—but the Northmen were the fiercest and the boldest. They harried all shores, and crossed swords with all races. They brought back the gold of Caliphs, and the dark-eyed daughters of Italy. They launched forth into the frozen deep, and saw the whale at his solemn gambols, and met the sea-bear—hoary

THE SEA AND THE SEA LIFE. 321

and grim—drifting on his solitary raft of ice, like
an ancient warrior on his way to Odin's Hall.
And—ere yet the fullness of time was come—
they lifted up a corner of the veil, and peeped
into the grand New World.

Even in death the Viking loved to have his
grave overlooking the sea, that his spirit might
listen to its old familiar voice. Sometimes he
was even buried sitting inside his trusty ship,
with his good sword by his side. More frequently
his barrow was made in the shape of a ship
turned upside down. And sometimes—with a
feeling of poetry not always found in the pro-
ductions of Scalds—that the old sea-rover might
sleep the sounder, they made his bed of the salt
sea-weed.*

From the Goth. *saivs*, Old Sax. and Old High
Germ. *sêo*, Ang.-Sax. *sae*, Eng. "sea," Förstemann
derives the following stem, which is however
liable to intermix with *sig*, victory, p. 172. It
is as might be expected, a stem especially Saxon.

COMPOUNDS.

(*Ber*, bear) Sibar, *Lib. Vit.*—Eng. SEABER, SHEBEARE— Seå, Sew.,
Fr. SEEBER, SEBIRE. (*Bern*, bear) Old Germ. Sebern, 9th cent. Mare.
—Old Norse Sæbiörn—Sberne, *Domesday*—Eng. SEABORN,
SEYBURN, SPORNE—French SEBRON. (*Bert*, bright) Old Germ.
Sebert, 11th cent.—Ang.-Sax. Sæberht—Eng. SEABRIGHT—
Mod. German SEBERT—French SIBERT. (*Burg*, protection)

---

* Graves of this sort—evidently Teutonic—have been discovered in the
Crimea. See the "Antiquities of Kertch and Researches in the Cimmerian Bos-
phorus," by Dr. Duncan M'Pherson. In the course of a discussion on the subject
at a meeting of the Archæological Institute, Mr. Kemble remarked "The layer
of sea-weed in the tomb is a remarkable fact; a similar usage has been noticed in
interments on the shores of the Baltic, and it might have originated in some tradition of water-worship, of which traces occur in the superstitions of Scandinavia."

o 2

322 THE SEA AND THE SEA LIFE.

Old German Seburg, Seopurc, 9th cent.—Seaburch, *Lib.
Vit.*—English SEABURY, SEABROOK—Mod. Germ. SEEBURG—
French SIBOURC. (*Fugel,* fowl) Ang.-Sax. Sæfugel—English
SEFOWL. (*Man*) Old German Seman, 9th cent.—English
SEAMAN—Mod German SEEMANN. (*Rit,* ride) Old Germ.
Seuerit, 9th cent.—English SEARIGHT—French SEURIOT.
(*Wald,* power) Old Germ. Sewald, 11th cent.—Eng. SEA-
WALL, SEWELL ?—Mod. Germ. SEEWALD—French SOUALLE ?
(*Ward,* guardian) Old Germ. Seward, 6th cent.—Ang.-Sax.
Sæward—Eng. SEAWARD, SEWARD, SAWARD—French SUARD.

Another stem of similar meaning may be *und,*
which Förstemann refers to Old High German
unda, fluctus, unda. Hence Old German Undo,
8th cent., and Eng. UNDEY, though *hund,* dog,
is liable to intermix.

The only ancient name from ship, navis,
seems to be a Gothic Scipuar of the 6th cent.
in Procopius, and which answers to our SKIPPER
and SHIPMAN.

The Ang.-Saxon *ceol,* appears to be found in
the names of several Anglo-Saxons, but it is
not easy to say whether it is intended for that
word or for *col,* helmet, p. 226. The only name
from this source among the continental Germans
seems to be a Cheling (*Goldast, rerum Alaman-
nicarum scriptores*).

SIMPLE FORMS.

Keel.
Ship.

Ang.-Saxon Ceol, royal line of Wessex. English KEEL,
KEELY. Mod. Germ. KIEHL. French CHELY ?

PATRONYMICS.

Old German Cheling. English KEELING.

We find in Anglo-Saxon several poetical or
periphrastic expressions for a ship, some of which
seem to occur in English names. Thus we have

THE SEA AND THE SEA LIFE. 323

SEAMARK, which appears to be from Ang.-Saxon *sæmearh*, a sea-horse, a ship. And the name SEAHORSE itself, of English origin, occurs, as Mr. Lower informs us, in New Brunswick. Another Anglo-Saxon expression for a ship was *sæwudu*, "sea-wood," whence seems to be the name SEAWOOD, found in New York.

From the Old Norse *fara*, Ang.-Sax. *faran*, to fare, sail, travel ; Old Norse *fari*, Ang.-Saxon *fara*, voyager, we may take the following, which are however rather apt in some cases to intermix with *fair*, pulcher. A large proportion of the ancient names are Frankish.

SIMPLE FORMS.

Old Germ. FARA, FARO, PHARO, 7th cent. English FAIR, PHAIR, FAIREY, FARRA, PHARAOH, FARROW, FERRY. Mod. Germ. FAHR, FEHR. French FARÉ, FARY, FARAU, FERAY, FERRY.

Fare. Travel.

DIMINUTIVES.

English FARRELL, FERRELL—French FARAL. Old Germ. Farlenus, 8th cent.—Ang.-Sax. Ferling *(found in Ferling-amere, Cod. Dip. 73)*—English FAIRLAN, FURLONG—Mod. Germ. FEHRLEN. Old German Farago, 9th cent.—English FARGO—Modern German FERRACH. French FARACHON—English FIRKIN ?

PATRONYMICS.

French FARENC. English FIRING ?

PHONETIC ENDING.

Old Germ. Farana, 8th cent. English FARREN, FEARON. French FARRAN, FARINE, FERON.

COMPOUNDS.

(And, life, spirit) Old Germ. Ferrand, 11th cent.—Eng. FARRAND, FERRAND—French FERRAND, FERANT. *(Bert, famous)* Old Germ. Farábert, 8th cent.—Eng. FAIRBEARD ? *(Foot, pedes)* Eng. FAIRFOOT—Fr. FÉRAFIAT. *(Gaud, Goth.)*

324 THE SEA AND THE SEA LIFE.

Old Germ. Faregaud, 8th cent.—Eng. FARRAGAT, FORGET—French FARAGUET, FARCOT, FERAGUT, FORGET. (*Gis*, hostage? companion?) Old Germ. Ferigis, 9th cent.—French FARCIS. (*Hari*, warrior) Old Germ. Feriher, 9th cent.—Eng. FARRIER, FARRER, FERRIER—French FERRIER, FERRER. (*Lind*, gentle) Old Germ. Ferlind, 9th cent.—Eng. FORLAND. (*Man*) Old German Faraman, 9th cent.—Fareman, *Hund. Rolls*—Eng. FAIRMAN, FERRIMAN—Modern German FEHRMANN—French FIRMIN? (*Mund*, protection) Old Germ. Faramund, Frankish king, 5th cent.—English FARRIMOND, FARMONT—French FERMOND, FERMENT. (*Ward*, guardian) Old Germ. Faroard, 8th cent.—English FORWARD. (*Weal*, peregrinus) English FAREWELL—French FEROUELLE.

From the above stem *far*, as an extended form comes *farn*; the Goth. *fairni*, Ang.-Saxon *firn*, old, might be suggested, but I should rather prefer to keep to the same sense as found in the previous group, and which is found in the Mod. German *fern*.

Farn. Travel.

SIMPLE FORMS.

Old Germ. Farnus, 7th cent. Forne, (*Domesday*). Eng. FAIRNE, FERN, FERNIE, FORNEY. French FARNE, FERNIE, FORNEY, FOURNY.

DIMINUTIVES.

Old German Fernucus, 8th cent.—French FERNIQUE. French FORNACHON. Eng. FARNELL, FURNELL, FERNILOW—French FERNIL, FOURNEL.

PATRONYMICS.

Ang.-Saxon Fearning (*found in 'Fearninga bròc, Cod. Dip.* 450). French FERNING.

COMPOUNDS.

(*Hari*, warrior) Eng. FERINER, FERNER—French FERNIER. (*Ulf*, wolf) Old Germ. Farnulf, 9th cent.—Eng. FERNYOUGH? (*Wald*, power) Eng. FERNALD. (*Heit*, state, condition) Mod. Germ. FARENHEIT?

THE SEA AND THE SEA LIFE. 325

As another extended form from the same root *far* we may take *fard,* which corresponds with Old Norse *faerd,* Old High German *fart,* Old Saxon *farth,* voyage, expedition.

SIMPLE FORMS.

Fard.
Travel.

Old Germ. Forti. English FARDO, FAIRDAY,* FARADAY, FORD, FORT, FORTY. French FERT, FERTÉ, FORT, FORTEAU.

DIMINUTIVES.

English FARDELL†—French FORTEL.

PHONETIC ENDING.

Fardan (*Domesday*). Eng. FARDEN, FORTIN, FORTUNE? French FORTIN, FORTUNE? FORTUNÉ?

PATRONYMICS.

Old Germ. Ferting, 8th cent. English FARTHING.

COMPOUNDS:

(*Hari,* warrior) Ang.-Sax. Forthere, bishop of Sherborne —English FORDER—French FORTIER. *(Man)* Old German Fartmann, 8th cent.—English FORTYMAN—Mod. German FORTMANN—French FERDMAN. (*Nand,* daring) Old Germ. Ferdinand, king of Castile, 11th cent.—Eng. FERDINAND— French FERDINAND—Ital. FERDINANDI—Spanish FERNANDO, FERNANDEZ.‡ (*Red,* counsel) Forthred, *Lib. Vit.*—English FORDRED.

From the Ang.-Sax. *worian,* vagari, Förstemann derives the following stem.

SIMPLE FORMS.

Wor.
Vagari.

Old German Woro. English WORROW, WORRY, WURR. French VOIRY, VAURY.

DIMINUTIVES.

English WORRELL, WHORLOW—Mod. German WÖRLE— French WERLÉ.

COMPOUNDS.

(*Wald,* power) Old German Worald, 8th cent.—English WORLD.

---

* i.e.=Faird-ay. Otherwise FAIRDAY, FARADAY may be from the stem *far,* with the suffix *dag,* day.

† Might be from the Old German name Farthilt (*hild,* war).

‡ The ending *ez,* in Spanish and Portuguese family names, is a patronymic form, and is supposed by Schmeller *(ueber die endung ez, Spanischer and Portugiesischer familisenamen),* to be of Gothic origin.

326   THE SEA AND THE SEA LIFE.

I have before observed that no animal was held in such high reverence among the Scandinavian races as the bear. And when the Norsemen, penetrating into the depths of the icy sea, found him there before them, in a solitude sublimer than that of the forest—yet grimmer and hardier than before, and a sailor too like themselves—all their old reverence would come on them with increased force. Hence we find as Scandinavian names Sæbiörn (sea-bear), and Snæbiörn (snow-bear). The former I have already referred to—the latter I do not find in English, though the Germans have both SCHNEBERN and SCHNAUBER. But we have the name ISBORN, which, as I take it, has just the same meaning, viz., "ice-bear," and which corresponds with the names Iseburn and Isebur in the Liber Vitæ.

CHAPTER XVIII.

THE RULER AND THE PRINCE.

There are several words having the meaning of birth, race, family, &c., in which is contained the sense of nobility. A manner of expression precisely similar we still use when we speak of a man of birth or a man of family.

A word of the above character is Old High German *chunni*, Ang.-Saxon *cynn*, race, lineage. Hence, in the sense of nobility, is formed Old High German *chuning*, Ang.-Saxon *cyning*, contracted *cyng*, English "king." A word liable to intermix in the following group is Old High German *chuoni*, *kuoni*, Ang.-Saxon *cêne*, English "keen," in the sense of boldness.

SIMPLE FORMS.

Old Germ. Chuno, Cuno, Cono, Couno, Cunni, 8th cent. Cyni, *Lib. Vit.* Eng. CHUNN, CUNIO, CONNE, CONE, CONNY, KENNA, KENNY, KINE, KINNEY, CHINE. Modern German CUNO, KÖNE, KUHN. French CHON, CHONNEAUX, CUNY, COUNE, CONNEAU, CINNA. *[Chun, Cun, Con, Kin. Race.]*

DIMINUTIVES.

Old Germ. Chunulo, 9th cent.—Eng. CONNELL, CUNNELL, CUNLEY, KINNELL, KENNELL—Modern German KOHNLE, KÜHNEL—French CONIL, CONILLEAU. Old Germ. Cinelin, 11th cent.—Eng. CONLAN. Old German Chunico—English KINKEE, KINCH, KENCH—Mod. Germ. KUNICKE, KUHNKE, KÖNICKE. Old Germ. Chunzo, Cuniza, 11th cent.—Ang.-Sax. Cynsy, Archbishop of York—Eng. KINSEY, KINNS, KENISH —French CHONEZ, CONNÉS. Cynicin, *Lib. Vit.*—English KINCHIN—French CINQUIN, CONCHAN.

328 THE RULER AND THE PRINCE.

COMPOUNDS.

(*Bald*, bold) Ang.-Sax. Cynebald, royal line of Wessex—English KINIPPLE ? (*Ber*, bear) English CONYBEAR ? (*Bert*, bright) Old German Chunibert, 7th cent.—Anglo-Saxon Cynebert, bishop of Winchester—Fr. KENNEBERT. (*Burg*, protection) Old Germ. Chunibuirga, 11th cent.—Ang.-Sax. Cyneberga, royal line of Northumbria—Eng. KINNIBURGH. Probably the same as the last is Old German Chunibruch—Eng. KINNEBROOK. (*Drud*, *thryth*, woman ?) Old German Chunidrud, 7th cent.—Ang.-Sax. Cynethryth or Cynedryd, wife of Offa, king of Mercia—Eng. KINDRED—Fr. COINDRET. (*Ger*, spear) Old German Chuneger—Eng. CONGER, CONKER. (*Gest*, hospes) Old German Cunigast, Conigastus, 6th cent.—Eng. CONQUEST ? (*Hard*) Old German Chunihard, 8th cent.—Anglo-Saxon Cyneheard, bishop of Winchester—English KINNAIRD, KENNARD, CUNARD—Modern German KOHNERT, KUHNHARDT, KUHNERT—French CONARD, CONORD, CONORT. (*Hari*, warrior) Old German Chunihari, 8th cent—English CONYER, CONNERY, KINNEAR, KINNER, CHINNERY—Modern German KONER, KUNER—French CONNIER. (*Man*) English KINMAN—Mod. Germ. KÖNEMANN—French ? KUNEMANN. (*Laf*, superstes) Ang.-Sax. Cynlâf (*found in Cynlâfes stân*, *Cod. Dip.* 714)—English CUNLIFFE. (*Mund*, protection) Old Germ. Chunimund, king of the Gepidæ, 6th cent.—Ang.-Sax. Cynemund, bishop of the Magesætas—Eng. KINMONTH—Modern German KÜNEMUND. (*Lac*, play) Old German Chunileihc, 9th cent.—Eng. KINLOCH, KINGLAKE ? (*Niw*, young) Old Germ. Cunnia, 8th cent.—Eng. CUNNEW. (*Rad*, counsel) Old German Chunrad, Cunrad, Conrad, 8th cent. Coenred, *Lib. Vit.*—Eng. CONRATH—Mod. Germ. CONRAD—French CONNERAT, CONRAD, KUNRATH. (*Ric*, power) Ang.-Sax. Cynric, son of Cerdic—English KENRICK—Mod. Germ. KINREICH. (*Wald*, power) Old Germ. Kuniald, Conald, 8th cent.—Ang.-Sax. Cynewald, bishop of Worcester—English CUNNOLD—Modern German KÜHNHOLD—French CUNAULT. (*Wulf*) Old Germ. Chonulf, 7th cent.—Ang.-Saxon Cynewulf, king of Wessex—English CONOFF, CUNIFFE. (*Ward*, guardian) Ang.-Saxon Cyneward, bishop of Wells—English

THE RULER AND THE PRINCE. 329

KENWARD. *(Wig,* war) Kenewi, *Hund. Rolls*—English
KENNAWAY.

From the above root *chun, cun, con, cyn,* is
formed variously the Old High German *chuning,*
Old Sax. *cuning,* Old Fries. *kening,* Ang.-Saxon
cyning, king. Whether our CUNNINGS, KENNING,
CHENNING, and the French CONINX have this
meaning, or whether they are the simple patronymic is uncertain. In the contracted form we
find an Old Germ. Kung, 9th cent., Eng. KING
and CHING, French CONGS and CONGY. The
commonness of the Eng. KING is not accounted
for by anything we find in Old German names.
It is probable that a Celtic word may intermix,
viz., the Irish *cing, cingeadh,* fortis, Gael. *cingeadh,*
fortitudo. Hence Old Celtic names Cingius and
Cingetius. Also the Cingetorix and Vercingetorix
" most valiant ruler" of Cæsar.*

A similar sense of nobility to that found in
the above word signifying " race" is probably contained in the ollowing, which Stark derives from
Old Norse *burdr,* Ang.-Sax. *byrde,* " birth." A
word liable to intermix is *bert,* bright, illustrious.

SIMPLE FORMS.

Old Germ. Burdo. English BURD, BIRD. Mod. Germ. *Burd.
BÜRDE, BURTH. Fr. BURDE, BOURDEAU, BURTHE, BURTHÉ.
Birth.

DIMINUTIVES.

English BURDOCK. English BURDELL—French BOURDEL.
French BOURDELON.

PHONETIC ENDING.

Old German Burdin, 11th cent. Eng. BURDEN. French
BURDIN, BOURDIN.

---

* Gluck, Die bei C. Julius Cæsar vorkommenden Keltischen namen.

P 2

330 THE RULER AND THE PRINCE.

·COMPOUNDS.

(*Heit*, state, condition) Eng. BURDETT*—French BURDET, BOURDET. (*Hari*, warrior) Eng. BURDER—French BOURDIER. (*Land*) French BOURDELANDE.

It is rather probable that the sense of nobility may be contained also in the words signifying "people," such as *leôd, theôd, folc.* Bosworth renders *leôd* as "countryman, man, prince." But in compounds the ordinary sense of "people" may, at least in some cases, obtain. Thus, for instance, in the compounds with *mund, ward,* and *gard,* the idea may be that of "protector of the people." Still, the sense being akin to that of sovereignty, the names would be introduced appropriately here. The Ang.-Sax. *leôd,* Old High German *liut,* was a very common word in ancient names. It is apt to mix with some others, as *laith,* p. 194.

SIMPLE FORMS

Leod. People. Old Germ. Liudo, Liut, Lutto, Luith, 4th cent. English LEUTY, LUTTO, LYDE, LYTH, LEDDY, LITT. Mod. German LUDE, LUTH. French LIOT, LUYT, LUTHE, LITTEAU.

DIMINUTIVES.

Old Germ. Liudila, 8th cent.—English LIDDELOW. Old Germ. Leodechin, Ludechin, 8th cent.—English LUDKIN— Mod. Germ. LÜDECKING.

PHONETIC ENDING.

Old German Liudin, Liutin, 7th cent. English LUDEN, LUTON. French LUDON, LUTON.

COMPOUNDS.

(*Burg*, protection) Old Germ. Liuitburc, 9th cent,—Eng. LUDBROOK. (*Ger*, spear) Old German Liudiger, Leodegar, Ludger, Luger, 6th cent.—Eng. LYDEKKER, LEDGER, LUGAR,

---

* The termination *et* may, as stated at p. 189, be variously derived, but the above name seems to be like the Old German Adelheid, or Adelheit, English Adelaide, "noblehood."

THE RULER AND THE PRINCE. 331

Lucar, Lucre—Mod. Germ. Leutiger—French? Ludger.
(*Gard*, protection) Old German Liudgard, Liucard—English
Ledgard—French Lucard. ' (*Goz*, Goth.) Old German
Luitgoz, Luikoz, 8th cent.—Lucas, *Lib. Vit.*—Eng. Lucas*—
Mod. Germ. Luttkus—French Lucas. (*Hard*) Old Germ.
Luidhard, Leotard, 6th cent.—Eng. Liddard—Mod. Germ.
Luthardt—French Liotard, Leotard, Leutert. (*Hari*,
warrior) Old German Liuthari, prince of the Alamanni, 6th
cent., Leuthar—English Luther—Mod. German Luther—
French Liottier. (*Heit*, state, condition) Old Germ. Liut-
heit, 8th cent.—English Lethead,—French Liottet, Ludet.
(*Hrôd*, glory) Old German Liutrod, 8th cent.—French
Lutteroth. (*Man*) Old Germ. Liudman, 8th cent.—Eng.
Lutman, Lyteman—Modern German Ludtmann. (*Ward*,
guardian) Old Germ. Liudward, 8th cent.—Eng. Ledward.
(*Wig, wic*, war) Old German Liudwig, Liutwic, 6th cent.—
Eng. Lutwidge, Lutwyche—Mod. Germ. Ludwig—French
Ludovic, Ludwig,† Louis—Ital. Luigi. (*Ulf*, wolf) Old
Germ. Liudulf, Litulf, 6th cent.—English Litolff—Mod.
Germ. Ludolf. (*Wald*, power) Old German Liutolt, 7th
cent.—Mod. Germ. Leuthold—French Lieutaut. (*With*,
wood) Old Germ. Leudoidis, 9th cent.—Eng. Ledwith.

As a High German form of the above, the
following may come in here.

SIMPLE FORMS.

Old Germ. Liuzo, Liuz, Liutzo, Liuce, Liuzi, 10th cent.
Luse, Lucy (*Roll Batt. Abb.*). English Luce, Loose, Lucy.
Mod. Germ. Leuze, Lutz, Luz. French Luce, Lucy, Lussy,
Luez, Lutz.

*Liuz.
People.*

DIMINUTIVES.

Old Germ. Liuzila, 8th cent.—Eng. Loosely. French
Lusquin.

COMPOUNDS.

(*Hari*, warrior) French Luzier. (*Mar*, famous) English
Loosemore.

---

* Hitherto, considered to be a Greek or Latin form of Luke.
† "Ludwig dit Louis"—perhaps may be a German, from the alias.

332 THE RULER AND THE PRINCE.

A still more common word in ancient names was Goth. *thiuda*, Ang.-Sax. *théod*, Low German *deot*, people. Several names compounded with it occur in the genealogy of the Kings of Northumbria. Its forms are widely spread, and it is therefore liable to intermix with some other words, as *dod*, p. 273.

Theod, Deot. People.

SIMPLE FORMS.

Old Germ. Theudes, king of the West Goths, 6th cent., Teuto, Tutto, Thiedo, Tito, Tydi, Diedo, Dido, Dudo, Deot. Ang.-Sax. Dudda, Tudda. Tydi, *Lib. Vit.* English Tuita, Tutt, Tutty, Tite, Tidd, Tidy, Thody, Theed, Duddy, Dutt, Duthie, Deed, Deedy, Dyte, Dyett. Mod. German Thiedt, Tiede, Tiedt, Diede, Ditt. French Théot, Thiedy, Tudey, Duté, Duthy, Diette, Ditte, Dida.

DIMINUTIVES.

Old German Theudila, Tutilo, Dudel, 6th cent.—English Tuttle, Duddle—Modern German Tütel, Titel—French Dutil, Tittel, Didelle. Old Germ. Dudecho, 8th cent.—Modern German Duttke—French Dutacq. Old German Dudechin, 11th cent.—Eng. Tutching, Titchen—Modern Germ. Didtchen—French Thiécon. Old Germ. Teodisma, 8th cent.—Fries. Diudesma—French Doussarry.

PHONETIC ENDING.

Old Germ. Theodan, Thiotuni, Dudan, Tutan, 7th cent. Eng. Thoden, Dudin, Teuten. French Thiodon, Tutuny.

PATRONYMICS.

Old German Teuding, Dioting, 8th cent. Eng. Tuting. French Detuncg, Detang.

COMPOUNDS.

(*Bald*, bold) Old German Theudobald, Frankish king, 6th cent., Theobald, Dietbold, Dibald—Ang.-Sax. Theodbald—Tidbald, *Lib. Vit.*—Eng. Theobald, Tidball—Mod. Germ. Theobald, Diebold—Fr. Thibault, Thibaut, Thiéblot, Diebolt. (*Bert*, bright) Old Germ. Theudobert, Frankish king, 6th cent., Theobert—French Thibert. (*Berg*, protection) Old Germ. Theutberg, Teuberga, 8th cent.—French

THE RULER AND THE PRINCE. 333

THIBERGE. (*Gard*, protection) Old German Teutgardis, 8th cent.—French DIEUTEGARD. (*Gaud*, Goth) Old German Teodgot, 8th cent.—French TYTGAT, DIEGOT. (*Hard*) Old Germ. Theodhard, Diethart, Dithard, 8th cent.—Mod. Germ. DIETERT—French DIDARD, DUTARD, TITARD. (*Hari*, warrior) Old German Theodahar, Tudhari, 5th cent.—Ang.-Saxon Theodhere—Eng. THEODORE, TUDOR—Mod. Germ. DIETER—French THEODOR, TUDOR, DIDIER—Ital. TEODORI. (*Ram*, ran, raven) Old Germ. Dietrammus, Teutrannus, 7th cent.—Eng. TEUTHORN—French DIDRON, DEDRON. (*Man*) Old German Tiddman, Dietman, 8th cent.—English TIDDEMAN, TIDMAN, DIETMAN, DETTMAN, DEDMAN—Modern German TIEDEMANN, DETMANN. (*Mar*, famous) Old Germ. Thiudemer, king of the East Goths, 5th cent., king of the Suevi in Spain, 6th cent., Dietmar, Ditmar, 8th cent.—English DETTMER, TIDEMORE—Modern German DETTMER, DITTMER—French? DITTMER. (*Ric*, power) Old Germ. Theodoricus, a Sigamber, 1st cent., king of the East Goths, 5th cent., Deoderich, Diderich, Dietrich—Ang.-Saxon Theodric—English TODRIG, DODDRIDGE, DOTTRIDGE, DEDERICK, DEDRIDGE—Mod. Germ. DEDERICH, DETTRICH—French DIETRICH, DIÉRICKS? (*Wulf*) Old Germ. Theudulf, Diudolf, 7th cent.—French DEDOUVE?

A third word having the meaning of "people" is *folk* or *fulk*, in which may be contained the same sense as in the preceding.

SIMPLE FORMS.

Folk, Fulk. People.

Old German Folco, Fulco, Volko, 9th cent. Fulco, *Domesday*. English FOLK, FULKE, FOUKE, VOAK. Mod. Germ. FOLKE, VOLK. French FOUQUE, FOUCHE, FOUCHÉ, FOUCHY, FAUQUE, FAUCHE.

DIMINUTIVES.

Old Germ. Folchili, 9th cent.—Mod. German FÖLKEL—French FAUCHILLE, FAUCILLE. French FAUCILLON. English FOWKES—French FOUCHEZ.

COMPOUNDS.

(*Bert*, famous) Folcberaht, 8th cent.—Eng. FALLBRIGHT—French FAUBERT. (*Haid*, state, condition) Old German

334   THE RULER AND THE PRINCE.

Folchaid, 8th cent.—English FOLKITT—French FOUQUET, FOUCHET. (*Hard*, fortis) Old Germ. Folchard, 8th cent.—Fulcardus, *Domesday*—English FOLKARD—Modern German VOLKHARDT—French FOUCART. (*Hari*, warrior) Old Germ. Fulchar, Folcheri, 6th cent.—Ang.-Sax. Folchere—English FOLKER, FULCHER—Mod. Germ. VÖLKER—French FOUQUIER, FOUQUERÉ, FOUCHER. (*Man*) Old German Folkman, 8th cent.—Eng. VOLCKMAN*—Mod. Germ. VOLKMANN—French FALCIMAIGNE. (*Ram, ran*, raven) Old German Fulcranus, 7th cent.—French FULCRAN, FULCHIRON, FOUCRON. (*Rad*, counsel) Old German Folcrat, 8th cent.—French FAUCROT. (*Wald*, power) Old German Fulcuald, 7th cent.—French FOUCAULT.

Perhaps a similar sense may be found in the word *odal, udal,* which Förstemann refers to Old High German *uodal*, patria. It was a very common word in ancient names, but I can only trace very few at present.

SIMPLE FORMS.

Odal. Patria.

Old German Odilo, duke in Bavaria, 8th cent., Odilo, surnamed the Holy, Abbot of Clugny, 10th cent., Odal, Udal, &c. English ODELL, UDALL. Mod. Germ. OETTEL. French ODOUL.

DIMINUTIVES.

Old Germ. Odelina, Odeling, 9th cent. Odelin, *Lib. Vit.* Otelinus, *Domesday.* English ODLIN, ODLING. French ODELIN, HOUDELIN, ODILON (BARROT).

COMPOUNDS.

(*Hard*, fortis) Odalhard, 7th cent.—French ODILLARD. (*Helm*, helmet) Old Germ. Odilelm, 8th cent.—Eng. ODLAM ?

Upon the whole I think that the words signifying "land," "country," will also be introduced most appropriately here. The idea seems to be something akin to sovereignty. The most common

---

* Perhaps of German extraction

THE RULER AND THE PRINCE. 335

word with this meaning is Ang.-Sax. *land*, Old High German *lant*, terra ; which is found as early as the 5th cent., and seems to have been especially common in the 7th. Most of the forms in *lan*, and some of those in *lam* probably belong to this stem.

Land.
Terra.

SIMPLE FORMS.

Old German Lando, Landa, Lanto, Lant, Lanno, Lanzo, Lenzi, 8th cent. Eng. LAND, LANDY, LANT, LANCE, LANCEY. Mod. Germ. LAND, LANDT, LANZ. French LANDA, LANTÉ, LANTY, LANNE, LANNEAU, LANCE, LANZI.

DIMINUTIVES.

Eng. LANDELL—French LANDELLE, LANCEL. Old Germ. Lancelin, 11th cent.—French LANCELIN. French LANTIEZ, LANIESSE. Old Germ. Lanzico, 10th cent.—French LANZAC. Old Germ. Landechina, 11th cent.—Eng. LANKIN.

PHONETIC ENDING.

Old Germ. Landina, 8th cent. Eng. LANDEN, LANDON. French LANDON, LANTIN.

PATRONYMICS.

Old Germ. Landing, 8th cent. English LANNING.

COMPOUNDS.

(*Bert*, bright) Old German Landbert, Lambert, 7th cent. —Ang.-Sax. Lambert, Archbishop of Canterbury, A.D. 764— Eng. LAMBERT—Mod. Germ. LAMBERT—French LAMBERT, LAMBRET. (*Burg*, protection) Old German Landburg, 8th cent.—English LAMBROOK—Mod. Germ. LAMBERG—French LANZBERG. (*Frid*, peace) Old Germ. Landfrid, Lanfrid, 8th cent.—Lanfrei, *Lib. Vit.*—Eng. LANDFEAR, LANFEAR—Mod. Germ. LANFRIED—French LANFRAY. (*Hard*) Old German Landohard, 8th cent.—French LANDARD, LANSARD. (*Hari*, warrior) Old German Lanthar, Landar, 6th cent.—English LANDER, LENDER—Mod. Germ. LANDHERR—French LANDIER, LANTIER, LANIER. (*Helm*) Old Germ. Lanthelm, 9th cent.— French LANTHEAUME. (*Had*, war) Old Germ. Lanthad, 9th cent.—French LANTAT. (*Ram, ran*, raven) Old German Lantrannus, 9th cent.—French LANDRON. (*Mar*, famous)

THE RULER AND THE PRINCE.

Old Germ, Landamar, 8th cent.—French LANDEMAR. (*Ric*, power) Old Germ. Landerich, Lantrih, 7th cent.—Landric, *Domesday Yorks*—English LANDRIDGE—French LANDRY, LANZARICK. (*Wine*, friend) Old German Lantwin, 7th cent.—French LANVIN. (*Wig, wi*, war) Old Germ. Lantwih, 9th cent.—Eng. LANAWAY—Mod. Germ LANDWIG. (*War*, defence) Old Germ. Landoar, 8th cent.—English LANWER—Mod. German LANDWEHR. (*Ward*, guardian) Old German Landward, 8th cent.—English LANDLORD ?

Another stem of similar meaning is *gow* (Old High German *gawi*, Mod. German *gau*, country, district)..

Gow, Cow. District.

SIMPLE FORMS.

Old Germ. Gawo, Cawo, 8th cent. Caua, *Lib. Vit.* Eng. GOW, GOWA, COW, COWIE, GOE, COE. Mod. German GAU. French GOUAY, GOUÉ, GOUY, COUÉ. To this stem Förstemann also places the Old German names Geio, Keio, Keyo, 8th cent., and hence might come in English GYE, GUY, GOY, KAY, KEY—Mod. Germ. GEU, GEY—French GUY, GOY.

DIMINUTIVES.

Old Germ. Cauwila, 9th cent.—Eng. COWELL—French GOUEL, GOUILLY, French GOUELLAIN, GOUILLON. Old Germ. Gawiso, 8th cent.—Eng. COISH.

PHONETIC ENDING.

Old Germ. Gawin, 8th cent. English GOWAN, COWAN—French GOUIN, GOYON, GUYON, COUENNE.

PATRONYMIC.

English GOWING, GOING, COWING.

COMPOUNDS.

(*Bald*, fortis) Old German Gawipald, 8th cent.—French GOIBAULT. (*Bert*, bright) Old Germ. Gawibert, Gaipert, 8th cent.—Mod. Germ. KAUPERT—French GUYBERT, COUBART. (*Hard*) Eng. GOWARD, COWARD—French GUYARD, GOYARD, COUARD, COUARDEAU. (*Et*, p. 189) Eng. GUYATT—French GOUET, GOYET. (*Hari*, warrior) English GOWER, GUYER—French GOUHIER, GOUERRE, GOYER. (*Land*) Eng. GOWLAND, COWLAND. (*Man*) Old Germ. Gawiman, 8th cent.—Eng.

THE RULER AND THE PRINCE. 337

COWMAN—Modern German GOEMANN, KAUMANN—French GOUMAIN, COUMON. (*Ric*, power) Old German Gawirich, Goerich, 7th cent.—Eng. COURRIDGE, COURAGE.

One of the most widely-spread stems in ancient names was *athel, adel, ethel, edel,* noble. It is singular that though it was common both among the Franks and the Anglo-Saxons, it is uncommon at present both in French and English. Förstemann and other German writers suppose a frequent contraction in Modern German names of *adal* into *al*—thus Albert for Adalbert, Allard for Adelhard, Allmer ·for Adalmer, &c. But this seems too uncertain a rule to follow, otherwise many names might be added to the list.

SIMPLE FORMS.

Old Germ. Athala, Athal, Adilo, Ethil, Edilo, 5th cent. English EDELL, EDLOW, ETHEL. Mod. Germ. ADAL, EDEL. French ADOUL, EDEL, HADOL.

Athel, Ethel. Noble.

DIMINUTIVES.

Old German Adilin, Edelen, 7th cent. English ADLAN. French ADELON, ADELINE, EDELIN.

PATRONYMICS.

Old Germ. Adalung, Ediling, 8th cent. Mod. German ADELUNG, EDILING. French ETTLING.

COMPOUNDS.

(*Ger,* spear) Old Germ. Adalger, 8th cent.—Ital. ALIGHIERI.* (*Hard*) Old German Adalhard, 8th cent.—Ang.-Saxon Ethelhard, king of Wessex—Adelardus, *Domesday*—Eng. ADLARD—Mod. Germ. ADELHART. (*Helm*) Old Germ. Adalhalm, 8th cent.—Ang.-Sax. Ethelhelm—Eng. ADLAM, HEADLAM? (*Haid*, state, condition) Old German Adalhaid, 9th cent.— English ADDLEHEAD (and the Christian name ADELAIDE). (*Hari*, warrior) Old Germ. Adalhar, 8th cent.

---

* The name of the poet is so derived by Diez: there were, however, also Old German names Alager and Allger. His other name Dante is a contraction of Durante, p. 197, which I ought to have remembered at p. 310.

Q 2

338. THE RULER AND THE PRINCE.

—Ethilheri, *Lib. Vit.*—Eng. EDLERY—Mod. Germ. ADLER, EDELER. *(Funs, fus,* 'eager) Old Germ. Adalfuns, Adalfus, 8th cent.—Eng. ADOLPHUS*—French ALPHONSE—Spanish ALPHONSO. *(Stan,* stone) Old Germ. Adelstein, 9th cent.— Ang.-Sax. Athelstan—English EDELSTEN, EDLESTEN.

From the above word *ethel,* signifying noble, was derived the title of Etheling, given in Anglo-Saxon times to the son of the king. Next to him in rank was the Ealdorman, who had the highest title that could be given to a subject. And our name ALDERMAN, found in Domesday as Aldreman, may not improbably. be referable to this more ancient and higher sense.

A rank of nobility below the Ealdormen were the Thanes, who were divided into two classes, simple Thanes and King's Thanes—a main qualification being the possession of land. This word is found in many ancient names, but as the Ang.-Sax. *thegen* is contracted into *thane,* so the Old High German form *degan* being contracted into *dane,* is apt to mix with another stem, p. 311.

SIMPLE FORMS.

Thegan, Thane. Old German Thegan, Thahan, Tegeno, Degan, 8th cent. English TEGGIN, THAIN, THANE, DEIGHEN, DEGAN, DANE. Mod. Germ. DEGEN, DEIN, TEGEN, THEIN. French DAGIN, DAGNEAU, TEIGNE, TEIGNY, TAINNE.

DIMINUTIVES.

Old Germ. Theginzo, 10th cent.—Eng. DANES—French TAINS. English DAGNALL.

COMPOUNDS.

(Dio, servant) French THENADEY. *(Ger,* spear) Old Germ. Theganger, 9th cent.—English DANGER—French DENAIGRE, DENCRE. *(Hard)* Old Germ. Theganhard, 8th cent.—Mod·

---

* Or, as generally supposed, the Latin form of Adolph.

THE RULER AND THE PRINCE. 339

Germ. THEINERT—French THÉNARD. (*Hari*, warrior) Old Germ. Theganher, 8th cent.—Mod. Germ. THEINER—French THENIER.

The Anglo-Saxon *heretog* or *heretoch* was the leader of an army, and the word corresponds with the High Germ. *herzog*. I find HERTOCKS as an English name of the 17th cent. ; the Germans have HERZOG; and HERCZEGY, apparently French, occurs in the directory of Paris. <small>Heretog, Herzog, General.</small>

A word of similar meaning is Old High Germ. *heroti*, Old Norse *herradr*, leader, general, which is found in some ancient names, though another word *harud*, referred by Zeuss to the tribe of the Harudes, is difficult to separate.

SIMPLE FORMS.
Old German Harud, Herido, 8th cent., Charietto ? 4th cent., Cariatto ? a Frank, 6th cent. Eng. HARROD, HEROD, HARRITT, CHARROTT, CHARITY ? CARRETT. French HERODY, HÉROT, CHAROT, CARRETTE. <small>Herot. General</small>

PHONETIC ENDING
Old Germ. Aruduni, 9th cent. (*with variations*). Eng. HARADON, HARRIDAN.

There is a stem *erl*, found in many ancient names, which is referred by Grimm, Graff, and Förstemann to Old Norse *jarl*, Ang.-Sax. *eorl*, Ang.-Sax. *erl*, English *earl*. I may also mention, however, the Old Norse *erla*, assidue laborare, whence Haldorsen derives the Scandinavian name Erlingr.

SIMPLE FORMS.
Old Germ. Erlo, 9th cent. English EARL, EARLY, ARLE. Mod. Germ. ERLE, HERL. French IRLE. <small>Earl. Comes.</small>

340 THE RULER AND THE PRINCE.

DIMINUTIVES.

Old Germ. Erlicho, 8th cent.—English HURLOCK—Mod. Germ. ERLECKE—French HORLIAC. English ARLISS—Mod. Germ. HARLESS—French HARLEZ.

PATRONYMICS.

Old Germ. Erlunc, 8th cent. Old Norse Erlingr. Eng. URLING. Mod. Germ. ORLING.

COMPOUNDS.

(*Bad*, war) Old German Erlebad, 9th cent.—English HURLBAT. (*Bert*, famous) Old Germ. Erlebert, 8th cent.— English HURLBURT. (*Hari*, warrior) Old German Erleher, Herler, 8th cent.—English HURLER—Mod. Germ. ERLER— French HOURLIER. (*Wine*, friend) Old German Erliwin, bishop of Constance, 8th cent.—English URLWIN—French ARLOUIN.

From the Old High Germ, *hôh*, Mod. Germ. *hoch*, high, in the sense of "exalted," Förstemann derives a stem *hoh*, *hoc*, in proper names. To this I place the following, including one or two names in which the Ang.-Sax. form *hîh*, English "high," seems to be found. The Old Frankish *ch* for *h* occurs in some of the French names. A word very liable to intermix is *hig*, *hog*, Anglo-Saxon *hyge*, *hog*, prudent, thoughtful.

Hoch.
High.

SIMPLE FORMS.

Old Germ. Hocca, 9th cent. Hoce (*Beowulf*). English HOCKEY, HOEY, HOE, HIGH. Mod. German HOCK, HOCH. French HOCQ, HOCHE, CHOQUE.

DIMINUTIVES.

Old German Hohilo, Hoilo, 8th cent. English HOYLE. Mod. Germ. HÖCKEL.

PHONETIC ENDING.

English HOCKEN. French HOCQUIGNY, CHOCHON.

PATRONYMIC.

English HOCKING.

THE RULER AND THE PRINCE. 341

COMPOUNDS.

(*Bert*, bright) Old Germ. Hochbert, Hobert, 8th cent.—English HOBART—Mod. Germ. HOBRECHT. (*Dag*, day) Old Germ. Hodag, 9th cent.—Eng. HOCKADAY—French HOCEDÉ, HOCDÉ. (*Hard*) French HOCART, HOCHARD, HOCHART, CHOCART. (*Hari*, warrior) Mod. German HÖCKER—French HOCHER, CHOQUIER. (*Heid*, state, condition) Eng. HOCKETT, HIGHATT—French HOCQUET, HOCHEID, CHOCQUET. (*Man*) Old German Homan, 9th cent.—English HOCKMAN, HOMAN, OMAN—Mod. German HOHMANN, HOMANN. (*Mar*, famous) Old Germ. Hiemar ?—English HIGHMORE. (*Ric.* power) Old German Hohrich, Horich, 11th cent.—English HORROCKS, ORROCK, ORRIDGE. (*Ward*, guardian) Old Germ. Hohowart, 8th cent.—Old Norse Hâvardr—English HOWARD—French HOCQUART, HOUARD, CHOQUART.

* From the Ang.-Saxon *math*, honor, reverence, Förstemann derives a stem *mad, mat, math*, which also appears in an Old Frankish form as *med*. In the names of women the sense might be that of the Anglo-Saxon *mœth*, a maiden, *mœthie*, modest. A word very liable to intermix is Old High German *maht*, might. Also in some of the simple forms the scriptural name Matthew is difficult to separate.

SIMPLE FORMS.

Old Germ. Matto, Mato, Math, 8th cent. Eng. MADDY, MATTHIE, MEDD, MEAD, METTEE. Mod. German METTE, METTO. French MATTE, MATY, MADY, MATHÉ, MATHIÉ, MATHEY, MÉTAY.

Math, Med. Honour, Reverence.

DIMINUTIVES.

Old German Madacho, 9th cent.—English MADDOCK, MATTOCK—Modern German MADICKE, MATTICKE, METKE—French METGE. Old Germ. Matuas, 8th cent.—Eng. MATTS, METZ—French MATHIS, MATISSE, MATS. English MATKIN, MATCHIN—Mod. Germ. MÄDCHEN. Old German Mathelin, 11th cent.—French MATHLIN, MATTELAIN.

342 THE RULER AND THE PRINCE.

PHONETIC ENDING.

Old Germ. Medana, 9th cent. Eng. MADDEN, MEDDEN, MAIDEN, MEADEN. Fr. MADIN, MATON, MATHAN, METTON.

COMPOUNDS.

(*Hard*) Old Germ. Medard, 6th cent.—French MÉDARD. (*Hari*, warrior) Old German Mather, 9th cent.—English MATHER, MADER, MEADER, MEDARY—Mod. Germ. MADER, MÄTHER, MEEDER—French MATRE, MATTAR, MEDER. (*Grim*, fierce) Old Germ. Mathgrim, 9th cent.—French MATAGRIN. (*Helm*) Old German Madelm, 8th cent.—English MADDAM, MATHAMS, MATTAM, METTAM. (*Lac*, play) Old German Mathlec, 9th cent.—Eng. MEDLOCK. (*Land*) Old German Madoland, 7th cent.—Eng. MATLAND, MEDLAND. (*Man*) Old Germ. Medeman, 9th cent.—Eng. MAIDMAN, MEDDIMAN, METMAN, MEATMAN, MATTHEWMAN ?—Swiss MATTMANN— French MADAMON, METMAN. (*Ric*, power) Old German Madericus, Matrih, 4th cent.—French MATRY, METHORIE. (*Rat*, counsel) French MATTRAT. (*Rid*, ride) Old German Medarid, 6th cent.—French MATHERET. (*Hrod*, glory) French MATROD, MATRAUD. (*Ron*, raven) French MADRON, MATHERON, MATURIN. (*Wald*, power) Old Germ. Meduald, Madolt, 7th cent.—English METHOLD. (*Wine*, friend) English MEDWIN, METHUIN. (*Wig*, *wi*, war) Old German Medoveus, 6th cent.—Eng. MEADWAY—Mod. Dan. MADVIG.

UNCERTAIN NAMES.

English MADDERN. French MATERNE.

The names Matarn and Materni (both of course masculine) appear in the book of the brotherhood of St. Peter at Salzburg in the 8th cent. Förstemann seems to doubt whether they are German : they might, however, be from *arn*, eagle, found as a termination in some other names.

In this chapter will be introduced most appropriately the words having the meaning of power, rule, and authority. The most common word with this meaning is *rick, rich, ridge*, Ang.-Sax. *rice*, power, rule, dominion, or the adjective *rice*,

THE RULER AND THE PRINCE. 343

Old High Germ. *richi, rihi,* powerful. This is a very ancient word in proper names, being found in the 1st cent. in the names of Cruptorix, a Frisian in Tacitus ; Baitorix, a Sigamber in Strabo ; and Theudoricus, also a Sigamber. The ending *rix,* in many Old Celtic names, contains a corresponding and equivalent word.

SIMPLE FORMS.

Old Germ. Rico, Ricco, Richo, Riho, 8th cent. English RICH, RIDGE, RIEKIE, RITCHIE, RYE. Mod. Germ. REICH, RICK, RIECK. French RICQUE, RICHE, RICHY, RICHÉ, RICCI.

Rick, Rich.
Power.

DIMINUTIVES.

Old Germ. Ricilas, prince of the Suevi, 5th cent., Ricilla, Richilo—Eng. RICHLEY, RIGGALL—Mod. German RIEGEL—French RIGAL. Old German Richizo, Rikizo, 10th cent.—English RICHES, RIDGES, RICKS—French RICHEZ, RIQUIEZ. Old Germ. Richinzo—English RITCHINGS.

PHONETIC ENDING.

Old Germ. Richini, Richin, 8th cent. English RICHAN. Mod. Germ. REICHEN. French RICHIN.

COMPOUNDS.

(*Bald,* bold) Old German Richbold, Rihbold, 8th cent.—Eng. RICHBELL, RYBAULD. (*Bert,* bright) Old Germ. Richbert, Rigobert, Rihbert, Rihbret, 7th cent.—Eng. RIBBREAD, 17th cent.—French RIGAUBERT. (*Berg,* protection) Old Germ. Rigaberga, Richbirg, 8th cent.—French RICHEBOURG. (*Gard,* protection) Old Germ. Richgarda, 8th cent.—Eng. RIDGYARD. (*Heid,* state, condition) Old Germ. Richeit, 8th cent.—Eng. RICKETT—French RIQUET. (*Hard*) Old Germ. Ricohard, Frankish prince, 6th cent., Riccard, Richard—Eng. RICHARD, RICKARD, RECORD—Mod. Germ. REICHARDT, RICHARD, RICKERT—French RICHARD, RICARD. (*Hari,* warrior) Old Germ. Richari, prince of the Sueyi, 5th cent., Richer, Riker—Richerus, *Domesday*—Eng. RICHER—Mod. German RICKHER—French RICHER, RICHIER, RICQUIER. (*Helm*) Old Germ. Richelm, 8th cent.—Mod. Germ. REICH-HELM—French RICHÊME, RICHOMME ? (*Leoz,* people ?) Old

344 THE RULER AND THE PRINCE.

German Richloz, 10th cent.—English RECKLESS—French RECLUS. *(Man)* Old German Ricman, Richman, Rihman, 9th cent.—Eng. RICKMAN, RICHMAN, RYMAN—Mod. Germ. REICHMANN, RICKMAN, RIEMANN. *(Mar,* famous) Old Germ. Ricmar, Recomir, Rihmar, 4th cent.—Eng. RYMER—Mod. German RIEMAR—French RECAMIER. *(Mund,* protection) Old Germ. Rihmund, Richmund, 7th cent.—English RICH- MOND—French RICHEMONT. *(Rat,* counsel) Old German Reccared, West Gothic king, 6th cent.—French RECURAT. *(Wald,* power) Old German Ricoald, Richold, Rigald, 7th cent.—English RICHOLD—Mod. German RIEKELT—French RICHAULT, RIGAULT. *(Wealh,* stranger) Old Germ. Ricwal, 9th cent.—English RIDGWELL. *(Wig, wi,* war) Old German Rihwih, Ricwi, 9th cent.—English RIDGEWAY.

Another very common word with this meaning is *wald ;* Goth. *waldan,* Ang.-Saxon *wealdan,* to rule, govern, command, Ang.-Sax. *weald,* power, *wealda,* a ruler. This is also a very ancient stem, being found in the 1st cent. in the names of Cariovalda, a prince of the Batavi, and Catualda, a prince of the Catti. It is very liable, par- ticularly as a prefix, to mix with the stem *wal,* p. 298.

Wald, Walt.
Power.

SIMPLE FORMS.

Old German Waldo, Waldi, Welto, Guelto, 6th cent. Ang.-Saxon Wald *(found in Waldes weg, Cod. Dip.* 1,077*).* Old Norse Valdi. Eng. WALDO, WALDIE, WAUD, WELD, GWILT ? Mod. German WALD, WELDE, WELTE. French VALD, VAUDE, VAUTE, WELD.

DIMINUTIVES.

Old German Waldiko, 8th cent.—Eng. WALDUCK. Old Germ. Waldila, Weltila, 8th cent.—French WELDELL. Old German Waldelin, 7th cent.—Eng. VAUDELIN.

PHONETIC ENDING.

Old German Waldin, 8th cent. Anglo-Saxon Wealden *(found in Wealdenes weg, Cod. Dip.* 1,117*).* Waldinus,

THE RULER AND THE PRINCE. 345.

Domesday. English WALDEN, WELDON, WELTON—Modern Germ. WELDEN, WELTEN—Fr. VALDIN, VALTON, VAUDIN, WELDON.

PATRONYMICS.

Old Germ. Walding, Welting, 8th cent. Eng. WELDING.

COMPOUNDS.

(Hari, warrior) Old Germ. Waldhar, Lombard king 6th cent., Walter, Gualter, Qualter—Ang.-Saxon Wealdhere— Old Norse Valthar—English WALTER, WELDER, VALDER, GWALTER, QUILTER ?—Modern German WALTHER—French WALDER, WALTER, WAUTHIER, VAUTHIER, VAULTIER, VELTER. *(Had,* war) Old German Walthad, 8th cent.—French VALTAT. *(Man)* Old Germ. Waldman, 8th cent.—English WALDMAN—Mod. German WALDMANN—French VELTMAN. *(Ram, ran,* raven) Old German Walderannus, 7th cent.— Walteranus, *Domesday*—Eng. WALDRON—Fr. VALDEIRON, VAUDRON (or from an Old Germ. Waldrun, 11th cent., *run,* companion). *(Rat,* counsel) Old Germ. Waltrat, 7th cent.— French VAUTROT. *(Ric,* power) Old German Waldirih, 7th cent.—French VAUDRY. *(Rand,* shield) French VAUDRAND. *(Schalk,* servant) French VAUDESCAL. *(Wine,* friend) Old Germ. Walduin, 8th cent.—Eng. WALDWIN (christian name).

A third word of similar meaning is *stor, stur,* Ang.-Sax. and Old Norse *stôr,* Old High Germ. *stiuri,* great.

SIMPLE FORMS.

Old Germ. Stur, 9th cent. Old Norse Stôri (surname). Stori, *Domesday Yorks.* English STORR, STORE, STORY, STORAH, STORROW.

Stor, Stur, Great.

DIMINUTIVES.

Old Germ. Sturilio, 7th cent.—French STORELLI. (Old Norse Sturla, Eng. STURLA, Haldorsen derives from *sturla,* angere, in the sense of terrens). English STURROCK. English STORRS—French STOREZ, STOURZA.

COMPOUNDS.

(Bald, bold) French STURBAUT. *(Hari,* warrior) Eng. STORER—French STOHRER.

PHONETIC ENDING.

Eng. STORRON.

R 2

346   THE RULER AND THE PRINCE.

Some other names having the meaning of great, as GROSE, MICKLE, &c., must be understood rather in the sense of large stature.

There is a word *salv*, found in some ancient names, for which Förstemann proposes Old High Germ. *salo*, dark, or the Latin *salvus*. And there is another word *selb*, *self*, for which he proposes Old High Germ. *selbo*, self, ipse. I am inclined to refer both these words, and with more certainty the former, to Old High Germ. *salba*, Ang.-Sax. *salf*, *sielf*, salve, Ang.-Saxon *sealvian*, to anoint. The sense might be either that of healing, or it might be that of conferring regal dignity, of which anointing has been from the most ancient times the symbol. In the latter sense I include them in this chapter.

Salve, Selve. To anoint?

SIMPLE FORMS.

Old Germ. Selbo, Selpo, 8th cent. English SALVE, SELF, SELVES, SELVEY, SILVE, SILVA. French SALVY, SILVY, SILVA, SILVE.

PATRONYMIC.

French SALVAING.

COMPOUNDS.

(Hard) Old Germ. Salvard, Selphard, 9th cent.—French SALVERTE, SYLVERT.

PHONETIC ENDING.

Old Germ. Salvan, 9th cent. English SALVIN. French SALVAN.

CHAPTER XIX.

WISDOM AND KNOWLEDGE.

Names derived from wisdom or learning in the abstract we might fairly presume not to be of the highest antiquity. And there is to a certain extent an evidence in the names·themselves that they are not. The oldest sense in which any word of this class was used was probably that of counsel in war. And yet even this carries us forward to a time when contact with powerful neighbours had taught the rude German tribes that something more than brute force and a headlong rush were necessary to contend against disciplined troops.

The most common stem with this meaning is *rad, rat, red,* Old High German *rat,* Ang.-Saxon *rêd,* Mod. Germ. *rath,* counsel, which occurs, as a prefix and termination, since the 5th cent. A word which might intermix is *rad, ræth,* swift, eager—also Ang.-Sax. *read,* red.

SIMPLE FORMS.

Old Germ. Rado, Radi, Rada, Rato, 6th cent. English RAT, RATTY, REED, REIDY, READY. Mod. German RADE, RATH, RATTI, REDDE, REEDE. French RADÉ, RADI, RATTE, RAT, RATEAU, RATHEAU, RATIÉ, READ, RETY.

Rad, Rat, Red. Counsel.

DIMINUTIVES.

Old Germ. Radacho, Rathago, 9th cent.—Eng. RADDICK —Mod. German RADICKE—French RADIGUE. Old German Ratilo, Radila, 8th cent.—English RATTLE, RADDALL, RED-

348 WISDOM AND KNOWLEDGE.

DALL—Mod. Germ. RADEL, RÄDEL—French RADEL, RATEL. Eng. REDDISH, RADISH—French RADEZ, RATISSEAU. Eng. REDDELEIN, REDLINE.

PHONETIC ENDING.

Old German Raduni, Ratin, Redun, 8th cent. English RADDEN, RATTON, REDDEN. Mod. Germ. RATHEN, REDEN. French RADANNE, RATON, REDON.

PATRONYMICS.

Old German Rading, Rediug, 8th cent.—Eng. REDDING, READING—Mod. Germ. RATTING.

COMPOUNDS.

(*Bald*, bold) Old German Ratbold, 8th cent.—French RATABOUL. (*Brand*, sword) Old German Radbrand, 8th cent.—Eng REDBAND? (*Geil*, elatus) Old Germ. Ratgeil, 8th cent.—English REDGELL, RATTICAL. (*Gaud*, Goth) Old Germ. Ratgaud, 8th cent.—Eng. RETGATE? (*Hari*, warrior) Old Germ. Rathere, Rateri, Rater, Rethere, 6th cent.—Eng. RATTER, RATHER, RATTRAY, READER, REDYEAR—Modern Germ. RADER, RATTER, REDER—French RATHERY, RATHIER, RATTIER, RATTER, REDIER, REDER. (*Heid*, state condition) Old Germ. Radheit, Ratheid, 8th cent.—Eng. REDHEAD—French RADET, RATOTT, REDET. (*Helm*) Old Germ. Rathelm, 8th cent.—Eng. RATTHAM. (*Leib, leif*, superstes) Old Germ. Ratleib, 8th cent.—English RATLIFFE, RADCLIFFE?—Modern German RADLEFF. (*Man*) Old German Radman, Redman, 9th cent.—Eng. REDMAN, REDMAYNE, READMAN—Mod. German RADEMANN, REDMANN. (*Mar*, famous) Old German Radmar, Redmer, 8th cent.—English RADMORE, REDMORE—Mod. Germ. REDMER—French REDMER. (*Mund*, protection) Old German Radmund, Redemund, 7th cent.—Eng. RADMOND, REDMOND. (*Ram, ran*, raven) Old German Ratramnus, 8th cent.—English RATHERAM. (*Wald*, power) Old Germ. Radoald, 8th cent.—French RADOULT. (*War*, defence) Old German Ratwar, 8th cent.—English REDWAR. (*Wig, wi*, war) Old German Ratwig, Ratwih, Redwi, 9th cent.—English RADWAY, REDDAWAY. (*Wine*, friend) Old Germ. Radowin, Redoin, Retwin, 8th cent.—Eng. READWIN

WISDOM AND KNOWLEDGE. 349

—French RATOUIN, RADOUAN. (*Wis*, wise) Old °German Ratwis, Raduis, 8th cent.—French RATOUIS. (*Ulf*, wolf) Old German Radulf, Thuringian duke, 7th cent.—French RADULPHE. (*Wid*, wood) Old Germ. Radoidis, 9th cent.—English REDWOOD.

Another common stem with this meaning is *ragin* (Goth. *ragin*, counsel), which, in accordance with the principle referred to, p. 48, frequently becomes *rain*. A word which might intermix with the latter form is Old Norse *hreinn*, rein deer, whence, according to Haldorsen, the Scandinavian name Hreinn.

SIMPLE FORMS.

Old German Ragan, Ragno, Regin, Raino, 8th cent. Eng. RAGIN, RAGON, REGAN, RAIN, REIN, RAINEY. Mod. Germ. REIN, REYNE. French RAGAN, RAGON, RAGONNEAU, RAGNEAU, REGNIÉ, RAINE, REINE, RAYNA.

Ragin, Regin, Rain. Counsel.

DIMINUTIVES.

Old Germ. Reinco, 11th cent.—Mod. Germ. REINCKE—French RAINGO. Old German Reginzo, Reinzo, 9th cent.—Eng. REGANS, RAINS—Mod. Germ. RENZ. Eng. RECKNELL, REYNAL—French RAINAL.

COMPOUNDS.

(*Bert*, bright) Old Germ. Raganbert, Reinbert, 7th cent.—Eng. RAINBIRD. (*Bald*, fortis) Old Germ. Raganbold, Rainbald, 8th cent.—English RAINBOLD—French RAYMBAULT. (*Frid*, *frith*, peace) Old German Raganfrid, Rainfrid, 7th cent.—English RAINFORD, RAINFORTH—French RAINFRAY. (*Ger*, spear) Old German Ragingar, Raingar, Reginker, 8th cent.—English RANGER, RANAKER*—Mod. Germ. REINIGER. (*Hard*) Old German Raginhart, Regnard, Raynhard, 8th cent.—English REGNART, RENARD, REYNARD—Mod. German REINHARD, REINHART—French REGNARD, REGNART, RAYNARD, RENARD, REINERT. (*Hari*, warrior) Old German Raganhar, Frankish king, 6th cent., Rainher, Rainer—Old

---

* Or to *ran*, rapine, p. 189.

350 WISDOM AND KNOWLEDGE.

Norse Ragnar—English RAYNER—Mod. German REGNER, REINER—Fr. REGNIER, REGNER, RAYNER, REYNIER. (*Had*, war) Old German Reginhad, Rainhad, 8th cent.—English RENAUD—French RAINAUD, RAINOT. (*Helm*) Old German Raganhelm, Rainelm, 8th cent.—Eng. RAYNHAM—French RENEAUME, RENOM. (*Man*) Old Germ. Raynman, 9th cent. —Eng: REINMAN—Mod. Germ. REINMANN. (*Weahl*, stranger) Old Germ. Rainuwalo—Eng. REINWELL—French REYNEVAL. (*Wald*, power) Old Ger. Raginald, Reginold, Rainold, Renald, 6th cent.—Eng. RIGNAULT, REYNOLDS (and the christian name REGINALD)—Modern German REINHOLD, REYNOLD—French REGNAULD, REGNAULT, RENAULD, RENAULT—Ital. RENALDI. (*Ward*, guardian) Old German Raginward, Rainoard, 8th cent.—French RENOUARD. (*Ulf*, wolf) Old Germ. Raginolf, Rainulf, 8th cent.—French RENOUF.

In an age when experience was the only teacher, the man who lived the longest might generally be presumed to know the most. And thus we find that the Ang.-Saxon *frôd* signified both "advanced in years," and also "wise, prudent." This was a common word in ancient names, but is rather scarce at present.

SIMPLE FORMS.

Frôd.
Wise. Old Germ. Frodo, Fruda, Fruoto, 8th cent. Ang.-Sax. Frôda. Old Norse Frôdi. Frodo, *Domesday*. Eng. FROOD, FROUDE, FROWD, FRUDD. French FRIOUD, FROID, FROT, FRUIT.

DIMINUTIVE.

Old German Frutilo, 8th cent.—English (or Germ. ?) FREUTEL.

PHONETIC ENDING.

Old Germ. Frodin, Fruatin, 8th cent.—French FROTTIN.

COMPOUNDS.

(*Gar*, spear) Old German Frodger, Froger, 8th cent.— Eng. FROGER—French FROGER. (*Hari*, warrior) Old Germ. Frothar, Frotar, Fruther, 8th cent.—Fr. FROTTER, FRUITIER, FROIDURE. (*Wealh*, stranger) Old German Fruduwalh, 9th cent.—French FROIDEVAL.

WISDOM AND KNOWLEDGE. 351

From the Ang.-Saxon *wis*, wise, *wisa,* a wise man, leader, *wisiän*, to instruct, lead, govern, are probably the following.

The Old High Germ. *wiz*, Mod. Germ. *weiss*, white, might intermix.

SIMPLE FORMS.

Old German Wiso, Wis, Wizo, Vizo, 7th cent.   English Wise, Wiss, Vize, Vyse, Vice.   Modern German Weise. French Weissé, Visse.

Wise. Sapiens.

DIMINUTIVES.

Old Germ. Wisili, Wisla, 8th cent.—Eng. Whistle?—Mod. Germ. Wiesel.   Old Germ. Wiziko, 10th cent.—Eng. Visick—French Wissocq, Vissac.   Old German Wizikin, 10th cent.—English Whiskin.

PHONETIC ENDING.

Old German Wisun, 9th cent.   French Visonneau.

COMPOUNDS.

(*Gard*, protection) Old German Wisigard, wife of the Frankish king Theodebert, 6th cent., Wisucart—English Viscord, Whiskered?   (*Man*) Old German Wisman, 8th cent.—English Wiseman—Mod. Germ. Wissman—French? Wizemann.   (*Hard*) Eng. Vizard.   (*Hari*, warrior) Eng. Vizer—French Visser, Visier, Vissier.   (*Wald*, power) English Wisewould—Mod. German Weiswald.   Here also Eng. Wisdom, a name of an uncommon class, like Friendship, p. 263.

Another word of the same meaning may be *dis*, *tis*, for which Förstemann proposes Goth. *deis*, wise.   It is not, certain, however, that the Old Norse *dis*, Ang.-Sax. *ides*, woman, goddess, may not come in for part.

SIMPLE FORMS.

Old Germ. Diso, Disso, Disa, Tiso, Tisi, 8th cent.   Eng. Dyce, Dicey, Diss, Dias, Tyas, Tisoe.   Modern German Thies.   French Dizé, Dizy, This, Thisse.

Dis. Wise.

352

WISDOM AND KNOWLEDGE.

DIMINUTIVES.

English TYSACK. French TISSELIN.

PHONETIC ENDING.

English DYSON, TYSON. French DIZAIN, TISON.

COMPOUNDS.

(And, life, spirit) French DISAND, DISANT. *(Hard)* English TIZARD—French DISSARD. *(Hari*, warrior) English TYSER—French TISSIER, TISSAIRE. *(Mar*, famous) English DISMORE. *(Rand*, shield) French TISSERAND.

Another word with the meaning of wisdom or prudence is Old High Germ. *glau, clau*, Ang.-Saxon *gleâw*, which takes the guttural in the Gothic *gluggvus*, Old Norse *klôkr*, Danish and Swedish *klog*, Mod. German *klug*, Dutch *kloek*. Förstemann has only three ancient names, which are all in the Old High German form *glau*, and none of which correspond with the following.

Glow, Clow.
Wise.

SIMPLE FORMS.

Gleu, *Domesday Linc.* English GLOAG, GLOCK, GLEIG, GLEW, CLOGG, CLOAK, CLOW, CLACK, CLEGG? CLAY? Mod. German KLUGE, KLUCK, KLOCKE. French GLUCK, GLOUX, CLECH? CLAYE?

COMPOUNDS.

(Heit, state, condition) English CLAGGETT, CLEGGETT, CLEWETT—French GLOCHET, CLOQUET, CLOUET, CLAYETTE. *(Hari*, warrior) English GLUER, CLUER. *(Man)* Mod. Germ. KLOCKMANN—French CLOQUEMIN.

From the Old High Germ. *lezan*, Mod. Germ. *lesen*, to read, Gothic *leisan*, Old Norse *lesa*, to study, Old Norse *læs, lesinn*, learned, I derive a stem *las, les, lis*, in proper names. The above is, however, only a derived or secondary meaning, the original sense being that of pursuing or collecting, which may be in part that which is found in the following names.

WISDOM AND KNOWLEDGE. 353

SIMPLE FORMS.

Old German Lezzio, 8th cent. Lacy, *Roll Batt. Abb.* Las, Les, Lessi, *Domesday Linc.* English LACY, LESSY, LYS. Mod. Lis. German LESSE. French LEYS, LEZÉ, LAZE, LASSAY, LAS, Learned. LISSE, LIZA, LIZÉ.

DIMINUTIVES.

' French LESACQ, LESAEC, LASEQUE. English LAYZELL, LASSEL—French LASSALLE, LOYSEL.

PHONETIC ENDING.

Old Germ. Lisinia, 9th cent.—Eng. LEASON, LISNEY—French LASSENAY, LASNE, LESENNE, LESNE, LIZON.

PATRONYMICS.

Leising, *Lib. Vit.* Modern German LESSING. French LASSAIGNE.

COMPOUNDS.

(*Hard*) Old German Lisiard, 11th cent.—Eng. LEZARD, LAZARD—Fr. LEZARD, LAZARD, LEYSARD. (*Hari*, warrior) Lessere, *Lib. Vit.*—Eng. LEYSER, LESSER, LEASURE—French LASSIER, LASSERAY, LEZER, LIZERAY. (*Man*) French LASSIMONNE. (*Mar*, famous) English LISSIMORE. (*Rat*, counsel) French LASSARAT, LEZERET. (*Ulf*, wolf) Old Germ. Lisolf—Eng. LE SOUEF—French LASSELVE. (*War*, defence) English LESSWARE—French LASSUÈRE.

As a termination *leis* occurs in five German names of the 8th cent., and Förstemann proposes, though doubtingly, the above derivation. These names are Bertleis (*bert*, illustrious), Guntleis (*gund*, war), Hildeleis (*hild*, war), Witleis (*wit*, wisdom), Vulfleis (*wulf*, wolf). We have a list of names in English with a similar termination which I think tend to confirm this derivation. These are LAWLESS, LEGLESS, RECKLESS, SHARPLESS, BOOKLESS, FAIRLESS, LOVELESS, BARLASS, LANDLESS, and UNGLESS. Of these, LAWLESS has been explained as "regardless of law"—RECKLESS as "void of prudence"—LEGLESS as "wanting

s 2

354 WISDOM AND KNOWLEDGE.

legs"—and BOOKLESS as "destitute of books."
A much better and more natural meaning is
given to almost all of these by the derivation
proposed above. LAWLESS, then, I take it, means
" learned in the law ;" and LEGLESS has nothing
to do with Miss Biffin, but is only another form
of the same. FAIRLESS, as "travel-learned,"
expresses a most natural idea, for so much was
travel regarded as the best means of getting
knowledge, that in the idiom of the German and
Danish languages, "travelled" has become synonymous with "experienced." LANDLESS may have
the same meaning as·FAIRLESS, or it may, though
less probably, be restricted to a knowledge of
one's own country. RECKLESS,* from Ang.-Sax.
reccan, to explain, interpret; and SHARPLESS,
from Ang.-Sax. scearp, sharp, quick, skilful, are
also most natural compounds. BOOKLESS is not
so called from the scantiness of his library, but
from the good use made of what he had. The
Old Norse has the very word, bôklæs, "book-
learned," also "able to read," a much more notable
circumstance in his day than that of being without
books. LOVELESS, alias LOVELACE, is not quite
so obvious. We know that in the Romance days
the lore of love became so intricate as to require
a special court for its adjustment, but this seems
to involve rather too modern a sentiment. Lastly,
BARLAS and UNGLESS,† (ber, bear, and ung or

---

* Another derivation is also proposed for RECKLESS, at p. 344. But we
have also RAGLESS, which seems to come in here.

† With UNGLESS we may perhaps put UNCLES.

WISDOM AND KNOWLEDGE.   355

unc, serpent), referring to the two animals most noted in ancient times for their wisdom, and the former being synonymous with BARWISE, have as natural a meaning as could be desired.   I do not include with the above WANLESS, for it seems to be from Ang.-Saxon *wæn*, a blemish, with the negative termination, which would make it the same as another ·name FAULTLESS.   Some of the other names may be open ·to doubt, indeed I bring forward the subject rather as a question for enquiry.

Such names then as the above, which seem to have more of a direct meaning than is usually found, are among those to which I referred at the beginning of this chapter as indicative of a more recent origin.

From the above word *lis* is formed Ang.-Sax., Old Norse, and Old High Germ. *list*, art, science, from which are derived the following names.

SIMPLE FORMS.

Old Germ. Lista, 9th cent.   English LIST, LESTY, LAST.
Mod. Germ. LIST.

*List.
Scientia.*

DIMINUTIVES.

Old German Listillo, 8th cent.   French LESTELLE.

PHONETIC ENDING.

Old Germ. Listin.   Eng. LISTON.   French LESTIENNE.

PATRONYMICS.

Mod. German LISTING.   French LESTOING.

COMPOUNDS.

(*Hari*, warrior) Old German Listhar, 8th cent.—English LISTER, LESTER—French LISTER, LESTEUR, LASTEYRIE. (*Rad*, rat, counsel) French LESTRADE, LASTRET.

From the Old Norse *læra*, Ang.-Saxon *læran*, to teach, to know ; Old High Germ. *lera*, Ang.-

356 WISDOM AND KNOWLEDGE.

Sax. *lár, lær*, Eng. "lore," learning ; Ang.-Saxon *lareow*, Old Norse *lærari*, teacher, I derive the following. It will be observed that there are very few ancient names from this root, though it is common at present ; and this may perhaps be taken as an additional illustration of the remark which I made at the beginning of this chapter as to the comparatively recent origin of this class of names.

Lore.
Learning.

SIMPLE FORMS.

Old Germ. Lira, Loria, 8th cent. English LARA, LAREY, LARREY, LEAR, LEARY, LERRA, LOREY, LAURIE. French LARRA, LARRÉ, LERRÉ, LIRÉ, LAUR, LAUREY, LAUREAU, LORA, LORÉ, LORY, LOREAU.

DIMINUTIVES.

English LAUREL—French LOREAL, LOREILLE. English LERIGO—French LAROQUE, LORIQUE. Eng. LARKIN, LORKIN —French LORICHON. French LOREZ, LORSA, LARS. French LOREMY.

COMPOUNDS.

Eng. LAROUX, LEREW—French LARRIEU, LARUE, LEREUX = Ang.-Sax. *lareow*, a teacher ? (*Hard*) English LARARD. (*Man*) English LARMAN, LORRIMAN. (*Mar*, famous) Lorimarius, *Domesday*—Eng. LARMER, LORIMER—French LORIMIER, LORMIER, LARMIER. (*Muth*, courage) Eng. LARMUTH, LEARMOUTH. '(*Wealh*, stranger) English LARWILL—French LARUELLE. (*Wig, wi*, war) English LERWAY—French LARROUY, LARIVAY.

From the Ang.-Sax. *scearp*, Old High Germ. *scarf*, Mod. German *scharf*, sharp, quick, acute, there are a few names. Förstemann finds seven from this root in the 8th and 9th cents., but only one corresponding with ours.

Sharp.
Acutus.

SIMPLE FORMS.

English SHARP, SHARPEY, SHARPUS, SCARFE, SCHARB, Modern German SCHARPFF, SCHARF. French CHARPY, CHARFE.

WISDOM AND KNOWLEDGE. 357

DIMINUTIVE.
English SHARPLEY.

PHONETIC ENDING.
Old Germ. Scherfin, 9th cent. Eng. SHARPIN. French CHARPIN.

COMPOUND.
(*Leis*, learned) Eng. SHARPLESS, SURPLICE ?

A common word is *hig, hog, hug,* from Ang.-Sax. *hyge*, Old High Germ. *hugu*, mind, thought, Anglo-Saxon *hygian, hogian*, to study, meditate. The Saxon form, it will be seen, is common in English but not in French. A root very liable to intermix is *hoh, hoch*, high, p. 340.

SIMPLE FORMS.
Old German Hugo, Hug, Huc, Huga, Hughi, Hogo, Chugo, 8th cent. Eng. HUGO, HUG, HUGH, HUIE, HUCK, HOGG, HODGE, HICK, CHICK, CHEEK, CHUCK. Mod. Germ. HUGE, HUGO, HUCKE, HOGE. French HUGO, HUGÉ, HUG, HUC, HUE, HU, HUA.

DIMINUTIVES.
Old Germ. Hugila, Hukili, 9th cent.—English HUGALL, HUCKELL, WHEWELL, HIGLEY, HICKLEY—Modern German HÜGEL—French HUGLA, HUEL, HICKELL. Old German Hugizo, 10th cent.—Eng. HUGHES, HEWISH, HUCKS, HICKS, HODGES—French HUGUES. Hogcin, *Lib. Vit.*—English HODGKIN. Hugelinus, *Domesday*—Hueline, *Lib. Vit.*—Eng. HUELINS, HICKLIN, HICKLING—Fr. HUGUELIN, HIGLIN.

PHONETIC ENDING.
Hygine, *Lib. Vit.* English HUGOUN, HUCKEN, HOGAN, HIGGIN, CHICKEN. French HUGON, HOGAN, HUAN, HOIN, HIENNE.

COMPOUNDS.
(*Bald*, bold) Old German Hugibald, Hubald, 8th cent.—Eng. HUBBLE ?—French HUBAULT—Ital. UBALDO. (*Bert*, bright) Old German Hugubert, Hubert, 7th cent.—English HUBERT—Mod. Germ. HUBERT—French HUBERT. (*Hard*) Old Germ. Hugihart, Hugard, 9th cent.—Eng. HUGGARD, HEWARD—French HUGARD, HUCHARD, HUARD, HUART,

358   WISDOM AND KNOWLEDGE.

Chicard. (*Hari*, warrior) Eng. Hewer, Hewry, Chequer?
—French Huchery. (*Lac*, play) Old Germ. Hugilaih, 8th
cent.—Old Norse Hugleikr—Ang.-Saxon Hygelâc—English
Hillock? Hullock? Ullock?—French Hulek? (*Lind*,
mild) Old German Hugilind, 8th cent.—English Hewland.
(*Man*) Ang.-Sax. Hiccemann (*found in Hiccemannesstân,
Cod. Dip.* 643)—English Hugman, Hughman, Human,
Hodgman, Higman, Hickman—French Humann, Hieck-
mann. (*Gis, kis*, hostage) Eng. Hodgkiss. (*Mot*, courage)
Old Germ. Hugimot, 9th cent.—English Hickmott. (*Mar*,
famous) Old Ger. Hugimar, 10th cent.—Eng. Hogmire, High-
more. (*Not*, bold) French Hugnot,* Hognet. (*Wald*, power)
Old Germ. Hugold, 9th cent.—French Huault. (*Heit*, state,
condition) Hueta, *Domesday*—English Huggett, Huckett,
Hewit—French Hugot, Huet, Huchette, Chiquet.

Another stem of similar meaning I take to be
mun, Old Norse *muni*, the mind, Goth. *munan*,
to think. Grimm, however, refers to Old Norse
munr, pleasure. The names of Odin's two ravens,
Hugin and Munin, whose office it was to bring
him intelligence of all that passed in the world,
are derived respectively from this and the former
root. Mr. Blackwell, in the edition of Mallet's
Northern Antiquities edited by him, has an
amusing speculation upon our two comic in-
separables Huggins and Muggins, which he suggests may possibly be alliteratively corrupted
from the names of Odin's two ravens. This root
is liable to intermix with *man, mon*, p. 57, and
with *mund*, p. 276. Also with Moon, which I
think may be from a mythological origin.

---

* Hence the name of the Huguenots, the origin of which is not yet settled?
The above name Hugnot is evidently not from the sect, but the sect might very
naturally derive, as indeed most sects have done, from the name of a man. The
only other derivation I have seen is a lame one.

WISDOM AND KNOWLEDGE. 359

SIMPLE FORMS.

Old German Muno, Munio, 8th cent. English MUNN, MONEY. French MOUNIE, MUNIÉ.

Mun.
Mind.

PATRONYMICS.

Old Germ. Muning, 8th cent. Eng. MUNNINGS.

COMPOUNDS.

(*Here*, army) Old German Munihari, 6th cent.—French MUNIER, MOUNIER. (*New*, young) Eng. MUNNEW. (*Mund*, protection) Old German Munimund, 7th cent.—English MONUMENT.

From the Old High German *dankjan*, Ang.-Sax. *thencan*, to think, may be the following. Or it may be from the derived sense of German *danken*, English thank.

SIMPLE FORMS.

Old German Thanco, Danco, Thenka, Tenca, 6th cent. English DANKS, DENCH, TANK, TENCH. Mod. Germ. DANK, DENK. French TANC.

Thank.
Thought.

DIMINUTIVES.

Old German Tancila, a Goth, 5th cent., Danchilo—Mod. Germ. DANCKEL—French DANCLA, DANGLA. Eng. TANKLIN.

COMPOUNDS.

(*Hard*) Old Germ. Tanchard, 9th cent.—Eng. TANKARD —Modern German DANKERT—French DANCOURT. (*Hari*, warrior) Old Germ. Thancheri, 9th cent.—English TANKER, TANQUERAY, THACKERAY—Mod. Germ. DENCKER. (*Rat*, red, counsel) Old Germ. Thancharat, Tancrad, 8th cent.— Old Norse Thackrâdr—Eng. TANCRED. (*Wealh*, stranger) Old Germ. Thangwil, 9th cent.—Eng. THACKWELL—French DANGOUELLE. (*Wine*, friend) Old Germ. Tanquin, 8th cent. —French DANQUIN, DANCOINE. (*Wis*, sapiens) French DANGUIS.

Another word having the meaning of thought or meditation may be *chud, chut*, which Förstemann refers, though doubtingly, to Old High German *chûton*, meditari. It might only be another form of *hud* or *hut*.

360 WISDOM AND KNOWLEDGE.

SIMPLE FORMS.

Chut.
Meditari.

Old Germ. Chudo, 8th cent. English CHOOTE, CHOAT. French CHOTTEAU.

COMPOUNDS.

(Hard) French CHOTTARD. *(Hari,* warrior) English CHUTER, CHUTTER.

From the Old High Germ., Mod. Germ., Old Norse *kunst*, Mod. German *kust*, art, science, may be the following. Perhaps the German *gunst*, favor, may intermix.

Const, Cust.
Scientia.

SIMPLE FORMS.

Eng. CONST, COST, CUST. Mod. Germ. KOST. French COSTE, COSTA, COSTEY, COUSTEAU, GOSTEAU.

DIMINUTIVES.

Old Germ. Costila, 6th cent.—English COSTELLO, COST-LOW, COSTALL, COSTLY, GOSTELOW—Fr. COSTILLE, COSTEL. English GOSTLING. Mod. German COSTIS—French COSTAZ, COSTES. Old German Custanzo, 9th cent.—Custance, *Lib. Vit.*—English CUSTANCE.

COMPOUNDS.

(Ger, spear) Eng. COSTEKER. *(Hard)* Old Germ. Custard, 9th cent.—English CUSTARD, GUSTARD—French COSTARD, COUSTARD. *(Hari,* warrior) English COSTER? *(Ulf,* wolf) Old Germ. Custulf, 9th cent.—Eng. COSTIFF.

From the Old Norse *skilia*, to understand, discriminate, apprehend, I take to be the following. An intermixture with *shield*, p. 227, is easy, but I think there is a separate stem, though only one ancient name comes before us.

Skill.
Scientia.

SIMPLE FORMS.

English SKILL. Mod. Germ. SCHILL.

PATRONYMICS.

Ang.-Saxon Scilling, a poet in the Scôp or Bard's song. Eng. SHILLING. Mod. Germ. SCHILLING.

WISDOM AND KNOWLEDGE. 361

COMPOUNDS.

(Ber, bear) English SHILLIBEER ? (*Heit*, state, condition)
Eng. SKILLETT ? SHILLITO ? (*Hari*, warrior) Eng. SKILLER—
Mod. Germ. SCHILLER—French SCELLIER.

From the Goth. *mathl*, concio, sermo ; Ang.-
Sax. *mathelian*, to discourse, harangue, are probably the following. The stem *math*, p. 341, is
however liable in some cases to intermix.

SIMPLE FORMS.

Old Germ. Madalo, 9th cent. Mædle, *Lib. Vit.* English
MADLE, MEDAL, MEDLEY, METHLEY. Mod. Germ. MADEL.

Madal, Mathal. Discourse.

DIMINUTIVES.

Eng. MADLIN, MEDLEN. French MATHLIN, METHLIN.

COMPOUNDS.

(Haid, state condition) Old Germ. Madalhaid, 8th cent.
—French MADOULAUD. *(Hari*, warrior) Old Germ. Madal-
har, 8th cent.—English MEDLAR—Modern German MADLER,
MÄDLER. *(Gaud*, Goth) Old Germ. Madalgaud, 8th cent.—
English MEDLICOTT.

In accordance with the principle of optimism
which prevails in proper names, we may presume
that names derived from the various members of
the body are to be invested with the highest
qualities which pertain to these members. Thus
the hand may be taken to mean dexterity, and
the foot activity. In like manner tongue may
be taken to have the meaning of eloquence,
wisdom, or persuasion. There is only one Old
German name in which it appears, but it enters
into some Old Norse names, as Tungu-Kari,
Tungu-Oddr, &c. Here, though a prefix, it is of
the nature of a surname, as in our APPLE-JOHN.

SIMPLE FORMS.

Old German Tungo. English TONGUE, TONGE, TUNGAY,
DUNGEY.

Tongue. Lingua.

T 2

362   WISDOM AND KNOWLEDGE.

COMPOUNDS.

(*Man*) English TONGMAN. (*Nand*, daring) French TUNGNAND.

In this chapter may be included the names having the meaning of vigilance or watchfulness. From the Ang.-Saxon *wæcan, wæccan*, to watch, Old High German *wak*, vigil, are probably the following. A word liable to intermix is *wag, way*, which I think has the meaning of waving or brandishing.

Wake.
Watchful.

SIMPLE FORMS.

Old German Vaço, Lombard king, 6th cent., Wacho, Wacco. Uach, *Lib. Vit.* Eng. WAKE, WACK. Mod. Germ. WACH. French OUACHÉE, VACHY.

DIMINUTIVES.

Old German Wachilo, 8th cent.—English WAKLEY, WEAKLEY, WEEKLY. Old Germ. Wakis, 6th cent.—Eng. WEEKS—French VAQUEZ. Eng. WAKELIN, WEAKLIN. Old Germ. Wakimus, Gothic leader, 6th cent.—Eng. WAKEM.

COMPOUNDS.

(*Man*) Old Germ. Wachmun, 8th cent.—Eng. WAKEMAN, WAGEMAN.

EXTENDED FORM=ANG.-SAX. *wacor*, WATCHFUL.

Old Germ. Wacar, Waccar, 7th cent. English WAKER. Mod. Germ. WACKER. French VAQUIER.

As a simple form of the stem *ragin*, p. 349, I bring in here the stem *rag*.

SIMPLE FORMS.

Rag.
Counsel.

Old Germ. Ragio, Racco, &c., 8th cent. English RAGG, RACK, RAY. Mod. Germ. RACH, RÄCK. French RAY.

DIMINUTIVES.

Old German Ragilo, Regilo, 7th cent. English REGAL. Mod. Germ. REGEL. French RACLE.

COMPOUNDS.

(*Bald*, audax) Old German Ragibald, 9th cent.—English RAYBAULD—French RAYBAUD. (*Hard*, fortis) Old German Reguhart, Rehhart, 11th cent.—Mod. German RAHARDT--

WISDOM AND KNOWLEDGE. 363

French RACOURT, RAYARD, *(Hari,* warrior) Old German Raghar, Racheri, 6th cent.—English RAREY—Mod. German REYGER, REYHER—French RAGER, RAGARIE, RAYER. *(Had,* war ?) Old German Rachot, 8th cent.—Eng. RACKET, RAGGETT—French RAGOT. *(Helm)* Old German Rachelm, 8th cent.—English RACKHAM. *(Mund,* protection) Old German Ragimund, Raimund, 8th cent.—Eng. RAYMOND, RAYMENT—Mod. Germ. RAIMUND—French RAYMOND. *(Wine,* friend) Old Germ. Racoin, 8th cent.—French RAGOIN. *(Ulf,* wolf) Old Germ. Ragolf, Raholf, Raulf, 8th cent.—Eng. RALPH,* RELPH—Mod. Germ. RALFS.

In this chapter may be included the words in which is contained the meaning of law or judgment. It is rather remarkable that the principal word with this meaning occurs more especially in the names of women, and we can hardly help thinking of that ancient state of society when fatidical women, like Deborah among the Jews, and Albruna among the Germans, seem to have been the real law-givers and judges of the nation. The word in question is the Old High German *tuom, thuom, thum,*† Ang.-Sax. *dôm,* Old English *doom,* judgment.

• SIMPLE FORMS.

Doom. Judgment

Old Germ. Tumo. Tummi, *apparently a Dane, in Saxo.* Ang.-Saxon Diuma, bishop of Mercia. Ang.-Saxon Toma, *found perhaps in Tomanworthig, now Tamworth, Cod. Dip.* 141, *&c.* Tumma, *Lib. Vit.* Tomy, *Roll Batt. Abb.* Eng. TOMEY, TOMB, THUMM, DUME, TOM ? Mod. Germ. THOMA, DUMM, DOHM. Fr. THOMÉ, TOMBE, THOM, DOME, DOMMEY, DOMBEY, DUHOMME, DUMAY.

---

* Derived by Pott, Lower, and others from Radulph. But unless a reason of a different sort can be given, the natural etymological derivation is from Ragolf.

† May not this be the origin of the name of Thumelicus, son of Arminius, 1st cent., for which Grimm proposes Old Norse *thumlungr,* thumb ? The second part of the name might also be from a word of similar meaning, viz., *lag,* law.

364 WISDOM AND KNOWLEDGE.

DIMINUTIVES.

Old Germ. Duomelo, Tomila, Tumila, 9th cent.—English DUMMELOW, DUMBELL, TOMMELL—Modern German DÜMMEL, TÜMMEL—French DOMMEL, THOMEL, TOMBEL. Old German Domlin, 7th cent.—Eng. TOMLIN, DUMLIN, DUMPLIN—Mod. German DÄUMLIN, DÜMLING—French DUMOLIN, DUMOULIN? Anglo-Saxon Domec, (found perhaps in Domeccesige, now Dauntsey, Cod. Dip. 271, &c.)—Modern German DÖMICH—French DOMECQ, DOUMIC. English TOMKIN—Mod. German DÜMICHEN. Eng. TOMSEY, TOMBS—French DOMEZ, DUMEZ, DUMAS?

COMPOUNDS.

(Gis, hostage? companion?) Old Germ. Domigis, Tomichis, 8th cent.—Eng. TOMKIES. (Gisal, same as gis) Old German Domigisil, 6th cent.—French, DOMICILE? (Heid, state, condition) Old German Tomaheid, 9th cent.—English DOMMETT—French DOUMET, THOMET. (Hard, fortis) Old Germ. Domard, 6th cent.—Eng. DUMMERT—Fr. DOMARD, DOMART. (Hari, warrior) Old German Domarius, 7th cent.—Old Norse Domar—Domheri, Lib. Vit.—Eng. DUMMER, TOOMER—Mod. Germ. DOHMEYER—Fr. DOMER, DUMAIRE, DUMERY. (Rit, ride) Old Germ. Dumerit, 6th cent.—French THOMMERET. (Run, wisdom, mystery) Old Germ. Dommoruna,* 7th cent.—French DOMAIRON.

Varying forms of the same stem I take to be the following, as found in Anglo-Saxon dæma, dêma, a judge. Hence the "dempsters," judges of the Isle of Man.

SIMPLE FORMS.

Dam.
Judgment

Old Germ. Tammo, Temmo, Dimo, Diemo, Timo, Temo, 8th cent. Tymmo, a Dane or Northman in Saxo. Demma, Lib. Vit. English DAMM, TAME, TIM. Mod. Germ. DAMM, DEMME, THAMM, TEMM, DIEME, THIMM, TIMM. Fr. DAME, DAMM, DAMÉ, DAMAY, DEMAY, DEMEY, DIMÉ, DIMEY, TAMI, TAMA.

---

* The termination run in female names I have generally taken to be, as Grimm makes it, socia, amica. But in such a name as the above it seems to me that it should rather have the meaning of mysterious, perhaps cabalistic knowledge. So in the case of the wise woman of the Old Germans, Albruna, p. 135.

WISDOM AND KNOWLEDGE. 365

DIMINUTIVES.

Old Germ. Tiemich, 11th cent.—Eng. DIMMICK, DIM-
MOCK, TAMMAGE—Mod. Germ. THIEMKE— French DEMOQUE.
French DAMEL, DEMOLLE, THIMEL, TIMEL. Eng. TAMLYN,
TAMPLIN, TIMLIN—French DAMELON, DEMOLIN, DEMELUN,
DEMOULIN (quasi De Moulin). English DAMES, DEMPSEY,
DIMES, TIMES, TIMS—French DAMEZ, DAMAS, DAMAZY,
DEMOISY.

COMPOUNDS.

(Hard) Old German Tamard, 9th cent.—Mod. German
DAMMERT—French DEMART. (Heid, state, condition) Eng.
TAMIET, DIMMETT—Fr. DAMET, DAMOTTE, DEMOTTE. (Hari,
warrior) Eng. DAMER, DAMORY—Mod. Germ. DAMMER—Fr.
DAMER, DAMOUR (quasi "d'amour"), DEMAR, DEMIER,
DEMORY, DIMIER. (Run, wisdom) English TIMPERON, TAM-
BORINE?—French DAMERON.

Another word of similar meaning may be *stow*,
which Förstemann refers to the Gothic *staua*, a
judge. There are only two ancient names in
which it is found.

SIMPLE FORM.	DIMINUTIVE.	
English STOW.	English STOWELL.	Stow. Judge.

COMPOUNDS.

(Hari, warrior) Old Germ. Stauher, 8th cent.—English
STOWER. (Wald, power) English STOVOLD.

The Ang.-Sax. *lag, lah, leah*, law, is found in
a few ancient names, and in a still greater number of modern ones. There are however some
other words liable to intermix: as *lake*, Anglo-
Saxon *lacan*, to play ; *laug*, Old Norse *laug*,
lavacrum ; perhaps also Ang.-Sax. *leg*, flame.

SIMPLE FORMS.

Old Germ. Lago, Lacco, Leggi,* 9th cent. Eng. LACK,   Lag. Law.
LACKEY, LACKAY, LAW, LAY, LAHEE, LEAH, LEGG, LEGGY,

---

* Förstemann thinks this name may perhaps be a mistake for Seggi. I do
not see any reason for the supposition, and bring it in here.

366 WISDOM AND KNOWLEDGE.

LEE. Mod. German LEGE. French LAGUE, LAC, LACK, LEGÉ, LEGAY.

DIMINUTIVES.

Old German Lagile, 11th cent.—Eng. LAWLEY, LOWLY—French LEGAL, LEGELEY. French LACHELIN. Old Germ. Lagoz, 9th cent.—Eng. LAWES—French LAGESSE.

PHONETIC ENDING.

English LAGGON, LANE. Mod. German LEHN. French LAGNY, LAGNEAU, LAINÉ, LAINE.

COMPOUNDS.

(Hard) English LAYARD. *(Hari,* warrior) Old German Lager, 8th cent.—English LAWYER—Mod. Germ. LACHER—French LAGIER, LAGUERRE, LÉGIER. (Or the above may all be simply the same as English "lawyer"; perhaps, however, in an old meaning of judge). *(Et,* p. 189) English LEGETT—Fr..LAGET, LACQUET, LEGAT. *(Leis,* learned, experienced) Eng. LAWLESS, LOWLESS, LEGLESS. *(Man)** Eng. LACKMAN, LAWMAN, LOWMAN, LAYMAN—Mod. Germ. LACHMAN—Fr.. LAUMAIN, LEHMAN. *(Wald,* power) French LEGAULT.

As a termination *lag* is difficult to separate from other words. The name Wihtlæg in the . genealogy of the Mercian kings from Woden, Eng. WHITELEGG, WHITELAW, seems to belong to it.

The following stem seems to be from Gothic *aivs,* Old High German *éwa,* Anglo-Saxon *jû,* lex, statutum.

Ewe. Lex, Statutum.

SIMPLE FORMS.

Old Germ. Euo, Jo, Evo, 9th cent. English YEO, YEA, EWE, EVE. Mod. Germ. IWE. French EVE, YVE.

DIMINUTIVES.

Old German Ewuli, 9th cent.—English EWELL, EVILL? Old Germ. Eveco, 11th cent.—Mod. Germ. EWICH—French EVEQUE? Old German Evizo, 10th cent.—English EAVES. French YVOSE.

PATRONYMICS.

Euing *(Domesday).* English EWING.

---

* Ang.-Sax. *lahman,* judge.

WISDOM AND KNOWLEDGE. 367

COMPOUNDS.

(*Hard*, fortis) English EWART—Mod. German EWERT—French YVERT. (*Hari*, warrior) Old Germ. Euhar, 9th cent. —Eng. EWER—French AUER. (*Man*) Old Germ. Eoman, Joman, 9th cent.—Eng. YEOMAN, YEAMAN. (*Ric*, power) Old Germ. Euarix (West Gothic king, 5th cent.), Eoricus—Eng. YORICK. (*Wald*, power) Old Germ. Ewald, 8th cent.—English EWALD—Mod. German EWALDT—French JOUALT. (*Ward*, guardian) Old German Euvart, 6th cent.—English YEOWARD. (*Ulf*, wolf) Old Germ. Eolf, 8th cent.—Eng. YEALFE—French YOUF.

The following stem may be referred to Old Norse *thinga*, to deliberate, Old High German *dingón*, to judge. The Old Norse *thing*, corresponding with the Ang.-Sax. *gemôt*, was a council both judicial and deliberative.

SIMPLE FORMS.

English DING, DINGY, TINGEY, TINK. French TINGAY.

*Thing,
Forum,
Conventus.*

DIMINUTIVES.

Anglo-Saxon Dengel, *Cod. Dip.* 981.—English DINGLE, DINGLEY, TINGLE. English TINKLING.

COMPOUNDS.

(*Hari*, warrior) Old Germ. Thincheri, 8th cent.—English TINKER—Mod. Germ. DINGER. (*Man*) English DINGMAN. (*Wealh*, stranger) Eng. DINGWELL—French DINGUEL.

CHAPTER XX.

THE TRUMPET OF FAME.

One of the most ancient stems in Teutonic names is *mar*, (Old High German *mári*, illustrious), which is found in five names of the 1st cent., two of the 2nd, one of the 3rd, and nine of the 4th. Hence it was widely spread, as Förstemann remarks, over all the German tribes. It does not seem, however, to be found in Old Norse names, or to have been common among the Anglo-Saxons. It is most frequent as a termination, and in English names generally takes the Saxon form *more*. As a prefix there are other words liable to intermix, as Anglo-Saxon *mære*, horse, p. 79. Grimm also refers (*Deutsch. Gramm.*) to *mari*, the sea.

Mar, Mer.

Illustrious.

SIMPLE FORMS.

Old Germ. Maro, Mar, Mer, Merio, 9th cent. Ang.-Sax. Mar, (*Cod. Dip.* 981). English MARR, MARRY, MARROW, MERRY. Mod. Germ. MAHR, MARR, MEER. French MÉREAU, MÉRA, MEREY.

DIMINUTIVES.

Old German Maricus, Merica, 9th cent.—Eng. MARIGA, MERRICK—Mod. Germ. MIERCKE, MIRICH—French MÉRIQ. Old Germ Merila, 6th cent.—Eng. MERRELL, MERLE—Mod. Germ. MÄRELL, MEHRLE—French MÉRELLE, MERLY, MARLÉ, MAROLLA, MARIELLE. Old German Merling, 9th cent.— English MARLING, MARLIN—French MARLIN. Old German Mariza, Meriza, 9th cent.—Eng. MARIS, MARRS, MERCY ?— French MARIS. MARIZY.

THE TRUMPET OF FAME. 369

COMPOUNDS.

(*Bod*, envoy) Old German Maroboduus, prince of the Marcomanni, 1st cent.—Mod. German MEERBOTT—French MARBOT. (*Gar*, spear) French MAROGER, MERGER. (*Gaud, Goz*, Goth) Old German Merigoz, 9th cent.—Merigeat, *Lib. Vit.*—Eng. MARGOT—French MÉRIGOUT, MÉRIGOT, MARGOT, MARICOT. (*Gild*, companion?) Old German Margildus, 8th cent.—Eng. MARIGOLD. (*Hard*) Old Germ. Merhart, 9th cent.—French MERARD. (*Lind*, gentle) Old Germ. Merlind, 9th cent.—French MARLAND, MERLAND. (*Man*) English MARMAN, MERRIMAN—French MERMAN, MIRAMON. (*Mund*, protection) English MARMONT, MERRYMENT? (*Wald*, power) Old German Maroald, Merolt, 6th cent.—Modern German MEHRWALD—French MERAULT. (*Wig*, war) Old German Merovecus, Maroveus, 5th cent.—Eng. MARWICK, MARVY—French MARVY. (*Wine*, friend) Old German Maruin, 9th cent.—Mervinus, *Lib. Vit.*—English MARVIN—Mod. Germ. MEERWEIN.

PHONETIC ENDING.

English MARRIAN, MARINE, MERRIN—French MARIN, MARION, MARINIÉ, MARNE.

PHONETIC INTRUSION OF *n*, p. 29.

(*Bald*, bold) French MIRAMBAUT. (*Hari*, warrior) Old Germ. Marnehar, 7th cent.—English MARINER, MARNER—French MARINIER, MARNIER. (*Ulf*, wolf) French MARNEUF.

A still more common word is *bert, pert*, bright, illustrious, corresponding with the Latin *clarus*. It is derived from the Gothic *bairhts*, Old High German *peraht*, Anglo-Saxon *beort, briht*. It was scarce among the Old Saxons, but common among the Anglo-Saxons, Lombards, Franks, and Bavarians. It is not of the same antiquity as the former word, not making its appearance in names before the 6th century. The form *briht* is common in Anglo-Saxon names, as *bright* in English.

U 2

370 THE TRUMPET OF FAME.

Bert, Bright.
Clarus.

SIMPLE FORMS.

Old German Berto, Perhto, 7th cent. Bertha or Bercta, daughter of the Frankish king Charibert, and wife of Ethelbert, king of Kent. Ang.-Saxon Berht or Beort, 7th cent. English BIRT, BURT, BERTIE, BRIGHT, BRIGHTY, PERT, PURT. Mod. Germ. BERT, BERTH, BRECHT. French BERTE, BERTEY, BERTEAU, BERTA, BURT, BURTY, BREHT.

DIMINUTIVES.

Old Germ. Bertilo, Pertilo, 8th cent.—English BIRTLE, BRIGHTLY, PURTELL—Mod. German BRECHTEL, PRECHTEL—French BERTEL, BERTALL. Old Germ. Bertelin, 7th cent.—French BERTELON, BERTHELIN. Anglo-Saxon Byrtsie, *Cod. Dip.* 981—English BIRDSEYE?

PHONETIC ENDING.

Old German Bertin, 7th cent. English BERTIN, PERTON. Mod. Germ. BERTIN. French BERTIN.

PATRONYMICS.

Old Germ. Berting, 8th cent. Eng. BRIGHTING. Mod. Germ. BERTONG.

COMPOUNDS.

(*Hard*) Old Germ. Berthart, 8th cent.—French BURTARD, (*Helm*) Old Germ. Berthelm, 8th cent.—English BERTHAM —French BERTHEAUME. (*Hari*, warrior) Old Germ. Berhthari, Berther, Berter, 7th cent.—French BERTHIER, BERTIER. (*Ram, ran,* raven) Old Germ. Berahtram, Bertram, Bertran, 6th cent.—Eng. BERTRAM—Mod. Germ. BERTRAM—French BERTRON. (*Land,* terra) Old Germ. Bertland, 8th cent.— Eng. BRIGHTLAND. (*Had,* war) Old German Berthad, 8th cent.—French PERTAT. (*Man*) English BRIGHTMAN. (*Mar,* famous) Old Germ. Bertemar—Ang.-Sax. Brihtmar, bishop of Lichfield—Eng. BRIGHTMORE, BIRDMORE—French BERTOMIER. (*Leis,* learned) Old Germ. Bertleis, 8th cent.—Eng. BIRTLES. (*Lac,* play) Old Germ. Bertlaicus—Eng. BIRDLOCK. (*Rand,* shield) Old Germ. Bertrand, 9th cent.—Eng. BERTRAND—Mod. German BERTRAND—French BERTRAND, BERTRANT. (*Ric* power) Old Germ. Perhtrick, Pertrih, 8th cent. —Partriche, *Hund. Rolls*—Eng. PARTRICK? PARTRIDGE? PEARTREE?—French BERTRAY. (*Wald,* power) Old Germ. Berahtold, 7th cent.—French BERTAULT.

THE TRUMPET OF FAME. 371

A third stem of similar meaning is *bram, brem*, (Anglo-Saxon *brême,* renowned, Suio-Goth. *bram*, splendor).

SIMPLE FORMS.

Bram, Brem Renown.

Old Germ. Brimo, 11th cent. Bram, a Dane or North-man in Saxo. Eng. BRAME, BRAMAH, BREEM, BRIM, PRAM, PRIME. Modern German BREHM, PREIM. French BRAME, BRAMMA, PREMY.

DIMINUTIVES.

Eng. BRAMMELL, BRAMBLE, BRAMLEY, BRIMILEY, BRIME-LOW, BRIMBLE.

COMPOUNDS.

(Hard) French BREMARD, PRIMARD. *(Hari,* warrior) Eng. BRAMER, BREMER, PRIMMER—Mod. German BRÄMER—Swed. BREMER—French BRIMEUR, PREMIER ? *(Mund,* protection) English BREMOND—French BREMOND, BRÉMONT, BRIMONT. *(Ric,* power) English BREMRIDGE. *(Wald,* power) French PRIMAULT.

A very common stem is *rod, rot*, which appears since the 5th cent. It was very frequent among the Hessians, Alamanni, and Bavarians, but not so much so among the Saxons. Förstemann refers it to Old Norse *hrôdhr*, glory, and a supposed corresponding Gothic *hrôths*. The aspirated *h* in some cases forms a *c*, as noticed at p. 46. It is probable that *rôd, rôt*, red, also intermixes.

SIMPLE FORMS.

Rod, Rot Glory.

Old German Hrodo, Roado, Chrodo, Rodi, Rudda, Rot, Roth, Ruth, 8th cent. Rudda, *Lib. Vit.* English RODD, ROTH, WROTH, ROUT, ROUTH, ROOT, ROOTH, RUDD, RUTT, RUTTY, RUTH, CROAD, CROTTY, CROWDY. Modern German RHODE, RODDE, ROTH, ROTT, RUTTE, RUTH. French RODE, RODDE, ROTA, ROTH, ROTTA, ROTTÉ, ROTTI, RUDE, RUDEAU, RUTEAU, CROTTÉ.

372

THE TRUMPET OF FAME.

DIMINUTIVES.

Old German Hruodicho, 8th cent.—English RODICK, RUDDICK—Mod. German RODECK. Old German Rutechin, 11th cent.—Eng. RUDKIN—French ROUCHON. Old Germ. Hrodelus, Rodil, Chrodila, 8th cent.—English RUDDELL, ROUTLEY, RUTLEY—Mod. German RÖDEL, RUDEL—French RODEL, ROUDIL, RUDELLE, CROUTELLE. Old Germ. Rodelin —French ROUDILLON, ROULLIN, ROLLIN. English RODDIS, RHODES, ROOTS, ROOTSEY—Fr. RODIEZ, CROUTS, CROUTSCH. Old Germ. Hrodemia, 9th cent.—Eng. RODDAM.

PHONETIC ENDING.

Old Germ. Hrodin, Ruathin, Chrodin, 6th cent. Eng. RODEN, ROTHON, ROTTON, CROTON, CROWDEN. Mod. Germ. RÜDON. French RODIN, RUTTEN.

PATRONYMICS.

Old Germ. Rodinga, 8th cent. English RUDDING. Mod. Germ. RODING.

COMPOUNDS.

(*Bald*, bold) Old German Hrodbald, Robald, 7th cent.— French ROUBAUD. *(Ber*, bear) Old Germ. Hruadbero, 9th cent.—English RODBER. (*Birin, bern*, bear) Old German Roudbirn, 8th cent.—Old Norse Hröthbiörn—English RODBOURN. (*Bert,* bright) Old German Hrodebert, Duke of the Alamanni, 7th cent., Rodbert, Robert, 8th cent.—English ROBERT—Modern German ROBERT, RUPPRECHT—French ROBERT. (*Berg*, protection) Old Germ. Hrotberga, Rodbirg, 6th cent.—French ROBERGE. (*Gar*, spear) Old German Hrodgar, Crodeger, 7th cent.—Anglo-Saxon Hröthgar (*Beowulf*)—Old Norse Hröthgeir—Roeger, *Lib. Vit.*—Roger, *Domesday*—English RODGER, CROAGER—Modern German RÖDGER, ROGER—French ROGER. (*Gard*, protection) Old Germ. Hrodgart, Rutgard, 8th cent.—English RODGARD, RUDGARD. (*Hard*) Old Germ. Hrodhard, Rohard, 7th cent. —English RODYARD—Modern German ROTHARDT—French ROHARD, ROHART. (*Hari*, warrior) Old German Hrodhari, Lombard king, 7th cent., Rotheri, Crother, Rudher—Eng. ROTHERY, RUDDER, RUTTER, CROTHERS—Modern German

THE TRUMPET OF FAME. 373

RODER, RUDER—Fr. RODIER, ROUDIÉRE, RUDDER, RUTTER.
(*Land*, terra) Old German Rodland, Rolland, 8th cent.—
Rolond, *Lib. Vit.*—Eng. ROLLAND—Mod. Germ. ROLLAND
—French ROLAND. (*Laic*, play) Old German Ruodleich,
Rutleich, 8th cent.—Eng. RUTLEDGE, ROUTLEDGE. (*Ram*,
raven) Old Germ. Rothram, Rodrannus, 8th cent.—English
ROTHERAM—French RODRON. (*Man*) Old German Hrod-
man, Ruodman, 8th cent.—English RODMAN, RUDDIMAN,
RUDMAN—Modern German RODEMANN. (*Mar*, famous) Old
Germ. Ruadmar, 7th cent.—Old Norse Hróthmar—French
RUDEMARE. (*Niw*, young) Old Germ. Hrodni, 8th cent.—
Old Norse Hródny—Eng. RODNEY, ROTHNEY. (*Ric*, power)
Old German Hrodric, last of the West Gothic Kings, 8th
cent.—English RODRICK—Mod. German RÜDRICH—Spanish
RODRIGO. (*Wealh*, stranger) Old German Ruadwalah, 8th
cent.—English RODWELL, ROTHWELL, CRUTWELL—French
ROTIVAL. (*Wald*, power) Old Germ. Hrodowald, Lombard
king, 7th cent.—Mod. Germ. RODWALD—French ROUALT.
(*Ward*, guardian) Old Germ. Hrodoward, 8th cent.—French
RODUWART. (*Wig*, *wi*, war) Old Germ. Hrodwig, Ruodwih,
8th cent.—English RUDWICK, RODAWAY, RODWAY—Mod.
Germ. RODEWIG. (*Ulf*, wolf) Old Germ. Hrodulf, king of
the Heruli, 5th cent. ; king of Burgundy, 9th cent.—Ang.-
Sax. Hróthwulf—Eng. RUDOLPH—Mod. German RUDOLPH,
RUDELOFF—French RODOLPHE.

A fifth stem of similar meaning is *rom, rum*,
which Förstemann refers to *hróm, hruam*, glory.
The aspirated *h* forms *c* in a few English names.

SIMPLE FORMS.

Rom, Rum.
Glory.

Old German Hruam, Ruomo, Rumo, 8th cent. Rum,
name of a female serf, *Cod. Dip.* 981. Eng. ROME, ROOM,
RUM, RUMMEY, CROME, CROMEY, CROOM, CRUM.* Modern
German ROHM, RÖHM, ROM. French ROMMY, ROMÉO,
ROMIEU.

---

* This might be from an Old Norse name Krumr, which seems to be from
Dan. *krum*, bent or crooked.

374   THE TRUMPET OF FAME.

DIMINUTIVES.

Old German Rumali. English ROMILLY, RUMLEY, RUM-
BELOW, CROMLEY. Mod. Germ. ROMMEL, RUMMEL. French
ROMMEL, ROUMILLY, RUMMEL.

COMPOUNDS.

(*Bald* bold) Old German Rumbold, 10th cent.—English
RUMBOLD. (*Hari*, warrior) Old Germ. Hrumheri, Rumhar,
6th cent.—Eng. ROMER, RUMMER—Mod. German RAUMER,
REAUMUR, ROMER—French ROUMIER. (*Ulf*, wolf) Old Germ.
Romulf, 6th cent.—French ROMEUF.

The following stem, found in three ancient
names, all in German forms, Förstemann refers
to Lat. *clarus*, Mid. High Germ. *clár*, illustrious.
Some of the following are certainly of German
origin, but others may be doubtful.

Clar, Cler,
Illustrious.

SIMPLE FORMS.

English CLARE, CLARY, CLEAR, CLEARY.   French CLAIR,
CLAREY, CLER, CLERY.

DIMINUTIVES.

Eng. CLARIDGE.   Eng. CLARIS—French CLÉRISSE.

PATRONYMIC.

French CLARENC.

COMPOUNDS.

(*Et*, p. 189) English CLARET—French CLARIAT, CLERET.
(*Mund*, protection) Old Germ. Clarmunt, 9th cent.—English
CLAREMONT—French CLERMONT (or local ?). (*Vis*, wise) Eng.
CLARVIS, CLARVISE.

PHONETIC ENDING.

French CLAIRIN, CLÉRIN.

PHONETIC INTRUSION OF *n*.

(*Bald*, bold) Old German Clarembald, 11th cent.—Eng.
CLARINGBOLD, CLARINGBULL—French CLÉRAMBAULT. (*Burg*,
protection) French CLERAMBOURG.

There is a stem *dal, tal*, which Förstemann
refers to Ang.-Sax. *deal*, illustrious. Another
stem *dale* he separates doubtingly, mentioning
the Goth. *duils*, Ang.-Sax. *dael*, part (better the

THE TRUMPET OF FAME.   375

verb *delan*, to dispense, distribute). A° third word which would suit very well for the sense of some of the compounds is Old Norse *tala*, Ang.-Sax. *talian*, to relate, recount. However, I will not attempt the separation, but introduce the whole group here.

SIMPLE FORMS.
Dal, Del. Illustrious.

Old Germ. Tallo, Dal, Tello, Telo, 8th cent., Daila, Deil, Tail, 5th cent. Tella, *Lib. Vit.* Delee, *Roll Batt. Abb.* Eng. TALL, DALLY, DALLOW, DELL, DELLOW, DALE, DELAY, TEALE. Modern German DAHL, THAL, TELL. Swiss TELL. French DALLÉ, DALLY, TALLE, TEL, DELLE, DELAY, DELEAU.

DIMINUTIVES.
Eng: DALLAS, TALLISS—French DALLOZ, DELESSE. Eng. TALLACK—French DELLAC. Fries. TIALMA—Fr. TALMA.

PHONETIC ENDING.
Old Germ. Thailina, 11th cent. Eng. DALLEN, TALLON. French DALON, DELAN, DELANNEAU, TALLON.

PATRONYMICS.
English DALLING, TELLING, TEELING. Modern German DAHLING. French DELINGE.

COMPOUNDS.
(*Bert*, bright) Old German Dalbert, 8th cent.—Talberct, *Lib. Vit.*—English TALBERT—French DALBERT, TALBERT. (*Bot*, envoy) English TALBOT—French TALABOT, TALBOT, DELABAUD? (*Bon*, slayer) Eng. TELBIN.—French DALIBON. (*Dio*, servant) Eng. DALDY? (*Fer*, travel) Old Germ. Dalferi*—Eng. TELFER—Fr. TAILFER, TAILLEFER, DELOFFRE. (*Fard*, travel) English TALFOURD? TELFORD? (*Ger*, spear) Eng. TALKER?—Fr. DALGER, DELOGER, DELOCRE. (*Hari*, warrior) Old German Dealher, Delheri, 9th cent.—English DALLOR, DELHIER, DELLER, TELLER—Mod. Germ. THALER, DÖLER, TIELER—Fr. DALLERY, DELAIRE, DELERY, TELLIER. (*Hard*) Fr. DALLIARD, TALLARD, TEILLART. (*Man*) Old

---

* This name Förstemann does not seem to be certain about; Dalferi, Dauferi, and Dalferi occur nearly together, and he appears to think that one may be put for the other. Of course I do not put out of question the ordinary derivation of Taillefer, "iron-cleaver."

376 THE TRUMPET OF FAME.

German Dalman, 8th cent.—English DALMAN, TALLMAN—Mod. Germ. DAHLMANN, THALMANN—French DELMON, DALLEMAGNE? TALLEMAN. (*Mar*, famous) English DALLIMORE, DELLAMORE, DELMAR—Mod. Germ. THALMEIER, THALHAMMER?—French DELAMARRE, DELEMER, DELIMIER, DELMER. (*Mag, mac*, might) Eng. TALLEMACH? TALMAGE? (*Mot*, courage) Old Germ. Talamot, 8th cent.—French DELAMOTTE, DELMOTTE, DELAMOTHE. (*Ric*, power) Old Germ. Delricus, 9th cent.—French DALERAC, DELROCQ. (*Rand*, shield) Fr. TALLEYRAND? (*Ward*, guardian) French DELOUARD. (*Wig, wi*, war) Daliwey, *Hund. Rolls*—Eng. DALLOWAY—French DALVI.

There is a stem *blad*, *blat*, which Förstemann, supposing a metathesis, places to the root *bald*, p. 240, but which Stark, as I think, more judiciously, refers to Anglo-Saxon *blæd*, glory. The Ang.-Saxon *blæd*, a blade, leaf, metaphorically a sword (as in English), seems however equally probable. A name Blatspiel, apparently German, in the London directory, seems more naturally referable to the latter, in the sense of "swordplay."

Blad, Blat. Glory.

SIMPLE FORMS.

English BLADE, BLATE, PLATT. French BLAD, BLATTE, BLED, BLET, PLATTE, PLATEAU, PLAIT, PLET.

DIMINUTIVES.

French PLATTEL, PLATEL, BLETEL.

PHONETIC ENDING.

Old Germ. Bladin, 8th cent. English PLATON, PLATTEN. French BLATIN, BLETON.

COMPOUNDS.

(*Hard*) Old Germ. Bladard, 7th cent.—French PLATARD. (*Hari*, warrior) Old Germ. Blathar—Eng. PLATER—French BLADIER, BLATTER, BLETERY, PLAIDEUR? (*Rat*, counsel) French PLATRET.

THE TRUMPET OF FAME. 377

In this place may come in the stem *load, lote, loud*, which Förstemann refers to Old High Germ. *hlût*, loud, which, as in the Greek, had also the sense of illustrious. In support of the latter derivation Abel quotes a line from Ermold Nigel in his poem in praise of Saint Louis.

"Nempe sonat Hluto præclarum, Wicgch quoque Mars est."

Förstemann observes that there is no more difficult root than this in the compass of German names, from its liability to mix with *liud, liut*, people. The initial *h* forms *c* in many names of the Merovingian period, as also in several French and English.

SIMPLE FORMS.

Old Germ. Chlodio, Frankish king, 5th cent.'; Chludius, Lotto.   English LAUD, LOAT, LOTE, LOTT, CLODE, CLOUD, CLOUT.   Mod. German LODE, LOTH, LOTT, KLODE, KLOTH. French LAUDE, LAUDY, LODDÉ, CLAUDE.

Load, Loat. Illustrious.

DIMINUTIVES.

Old German Luotheco, 11th cent.—Eng. LOTCHO.   Eng. LOWDELL—French CLAUDEL.

PHONETIC ENDING.

English LOADEN, LOTON, LOUDON, CLUTTON.   French LAUDON, LOUDUN, LAUTTEN, CLAUDIN.

PATRONYMIC.

English CLOWTING.

COMPOUNDS.

(*Hari*, warrior) Old Germ. Hlodhar, Clothar, 6th cent.—Lothere, King of Kent, A.D. 673, called also Clotherius, *Cod. Dip.* 981—Eng. LOADER, LOWDER, CLOTHIER—Mod. German LÖTHER, LOTTER—Fr. LOEDER, LAUDIER, LAUTIER. (*Hild*, war) Old German Chlotichilda or Clothilda, daughter of the Burgundian king, Chilperic, 5th cent.—French CLOTILDE (christian name). (*Mar*, famous) Old German Chlodomir, son of Chlodwig 1st, 6th cent.—French CLODOMIR. (*Man*)

v 2

378 THE TRUMPET OF FAME.

English LOADMAN, CLOUDMAN, CLOUTMAN—French? LAUTE-
MANN. (*Wig, wi*, war) Old German Lodewig, Chlodowich,
Clodoveus, Clovis, 5th cent.—French CLOVIS.

Another word having the meaning of glory is
Ang.-Sax. and Old High German *wuldar*. This,
in its simple form, is apt to intermix with Walter,
p. 345.

Wulder.
Glory.

SIMPLE FORMS.

English WOLTER. French VOLTIER, WOLTER. Or all
the above may perhaps only be the same as Walter.

COMPOUNDS.

Old German Uulderich, Vulderich, 8th cent. English
WOOLDRIDGE.

In this chapter may be included the names
having the meaning of crown, bracelet, or ornament, in the probable sense of a badge or distinction, as the reward of valour. There is a stem
bowk, bouch, which I take to be from Goth. *baugs*,
Old High Germ. *bauc*, bracelet. And the forms
bug, buck, I also take to be most probably from
the same, on account of the constant tendency to
change the more ancient form *ou* into the simpler
u. A third form is found in the Ang.-Sax. *bedg*,
bedh, bêh, whence I take to be the Eng. "badge."
A word very liable to intermix is *bog, bow*, arcus,
p. 224, from the same general root signifying to
bend.

Bowk,
Bouch.
Bracelet.

SIMPLE FORMS.

Old German Bauco, Paugo, 6th cent. Bucco, Buggo,
Pucco, 8th cent. Ang.-Saxon Bucge, Buga, Beage. Buge,
(*Domesday Notts.*). Eng. BOUCH, BOUCHEY, BEUGO, BUGG,
BEW, BUOK, BUCKIE, BADGE, BEE, (the two latter the Ang.-
Saxon form). Mod. Germ. BAUCH, BAUCKE, PAUCK, BUCK,
BUGGE, PUCHE. French BOUCHÉ, POUCHA.

THE TRUMPET OF FAME. 379

DIMINUTIVES.

Old Germ. Buccelin, General of the Alamanni, 6th cent.
—Eng. BUCKLIN, BUGGELN—French BOUQUILLON, BOUGLON.
English BUCKSEY—French BOUCASSE, BOUCHEZ. English
BUGLEA, BEWLY, BUCKLEY, BUCKLE, PUCKLE—Fr. BOUCLY,
BUCKLÉ, BUCAILLE, BOUGLÉ.

PHONETIC ENDING.

Old Germ. Buchinus, 7th cent. Eng. BUCKNEY, BUGGIN,
PUGIN. French BOUCON, BOUCHON, BOUCHENY, BOUGON,
POUGIN, POUGNY.

COMPOUNDS.

(Hard) French BOUCARD, BOUCART, BOUCHARD, POU-
CHARD. *(Hari,* warrior) Old German Παΰκαρις *(Procop)*—
English BOWKER, BOUCHER—French BOUCHER, BOUCHERIE,
BUCKER, BOUHIER. *(Et,* p. 189) Eng. BOWKETT, BUCKET,
PUCKET—Fr. BOUQUET, BOUCHET, POUCHET. *(Rat,* counsel)
Old German Bougrat, 10th cent.—English BOUCHERETT*—
French BOUGUERET, BOUQUEROT, BOUCHEROT. *(Ron,* raven)
French BOUGRAIN, BOUCHERON. *(Ric,* power) Eng. BUCK-
RIDGE, PUCKRIDGE—French BOUCRY. *(Wald,* power) Old
Germ. Buciowald, 6th cent.—French BOUGAULT, POUGEAULT.
(Ulf, wolf) Old German Baugulf, 8th cent.—Anglo-Saxon
Beowulf ?—English BALFE ?

From the Gothic *mizdô,* Anglo-Saxon *mêd,*
Old High German *mieta,* reward, Eng. "*meed,*"
Förstemann derives a stem *mid, miz,* which may
come in here.

SIMPLE FORMS.

Old German Mieto, Mizo, 8th cent. Mede, *Lib. Vit.*
English MEAD,† MIETTE. French MIDI, MIETTE.

Meed.
Reward.

DIMINUTIVES.

Old Germ. Mitola, 7th cent.—Eng. MIDDLE, MITTELL—
French MIDOL. French MIDOCQ.

---

* Of French origin.

† Or to the stem *math, med,* p. 341.

380 THE TRUMPET OF FAME.

PHONÉTIC ENDING.

English MITTON, MIZON.   French MITON, MIÉTON.

PATRONYMIC.

English MISSING.

COMPOUNDS.

(*Hard*) French MISARD. (*Hari*, warrior) French MIDIÉRE, MISSIER, MIZERY.

CHAPTER XXI.

WEALTH AND PROSPERITY.

Among the words having the meaning of wealth, prosperity, success, the most common root is Old Norse *audr*, Ang.-Saxon *eád*, whence the Gothic *audags*, Ang.-Saxon *eádig*, *eadg*, Old Norse *audgr*, wealthy or prosperous. Förstemann extends this root rather widely, taking in all the forms in *od* and *ot*, for which I think that two other derivations may perhaps in certain cases be proposed, see pp. 194, 217. Most of the English names, it will be seen, are in the Saxon form *ed*, and most of the French in the Gothic form *aud*.

SIMPLE FORMS.

Old German Audo, Oudo, Outo, 7th cent. Old Norse Audr. Ang.-Sax. Edda, Eddi, Eata. Auti, Outi, *Domesday*. Eng. AUGHT, AUGHTIE, OUGHT, AUTH, EADE, EADIE, EDDY, EAT. Modern German OTT. French AUDE, AUDY, AUTIÉ, OUTI, ODE.

DIMINUTIVES.

Old Germ. Audila, 6th cent.—Eng. OUTLAW ?—French AUDILLE. Old Germ. Audac, 6th cent.—French AUDIQUET *(double dimin.)*. English EDKINS. English EDDIS—French AUDIS. Old German Odemia, 8th cent.—Eng. ODAM.

PHONETIC ENDING.

Old Germ. Audin, 7th cent. English AUTON, OUGHTON, EADON. French AUDIN, AUTIN, OUDIN.

PATRONYMICS.

Old German Auding, 8th cent. English OUTING.

COMPOUNDS.

(*Bert*, bright) Old German Audebert, 7th cent.—Modern German ODEBRECHT—French AUDIBERT. (*Brand*, sword)

382 WEALTH AND PROSPERITY.

Old German Autprand, 9th cent.—French AUDEBRAND:
(*Burg*, protection) Old German Autburg, 8th cent.—Anglo-
Saxon Eâdburh—Eng. EDBROOK ? (*Arn, Orn*, eagle ?) Old
German Autorn, 8th cent.—Odierna, *Lib. Vit.*—Hodierna,
temp. William the Conqueror—Eng. ODIERNE. (*Fred*, peace)
Old Germ. Autfrid, 8th cent.—French AUDIFFRED, AUDIF-
FRET. (*Gan*, magic) Old German Audiganus, 9th cent.—
French AUDIGANNE. (*Ger*, spear) Old German Audagar,
Augar, 8th cent.—Ang.-Sax. Edgar—Eng. EDGAR, EDIKER,
AUGER—French AUDIGUIER, ODIGIER, AUGER. (*Hard*) Old
German Authard, 7th cent.—French OUDARD. (*Hari*,
warrior) Old German Autharis, Lombard king, 6th cent.,
Authar—Eng. AUTHER—French AUTHIER, AUTIER, AUDIER·
(*Ram, ran*, raven) Old German Audram, Autrannus, 7th
cent.—Eng. AUTRAM, OUTRAM—French AUDRAN, AUTRAN.
(*Land*) Old Germ. Aotlund, 8th cent.—French AUTHELAND.
(*Mad, med*, reverence) Old German Automad, 8th cent.—
Eng. EDMEAD, EDMETT. (*Man*) Old German Autman, 8th
cent.—English EDMANS—Modern German ODEMANN. (*Mar*,
famous) Old Germ. Audomar, 7th cent.—French AUDEMARS.
(*Mund*, protection) Old Germ. Audemund, 7th cent.—Ang.-
Sax. Eâdmund—English EDMOND—French EDMOND. (*Rad*,
red, counsel) Old Germ. Auderat, Autrad, 8th cent.—Ang.-
Sax. Eâdred, Uhtred—Eng. AUDRITT, OUTRED. (*Ric*, power)
Old German Audricus, Autricus, 7th cent.—Anglo-Saxon
Eâdric—English OUTRIDGE, EDRIDGE—French AUTRIQUE,
AUTEROCHE. (*Weahl*, stranger) Otuel, *Lib. Vit.*—English
EDWELL, EATWELL, OTTIWELL. (*Ward*, guardian) Old Germ.
Audoard, 8th cent.—Ang.-Sax. Eâdweard—Eng. EDWARD—
French AUDEVARD, AUDOUARD, EDOUARD. (*Wig*, war) Ang.-
Sax. Eâdwig—English EDWICK—French AUDOUY. (*Wine*,
friend) Old Germ. Audowin, Audoin, 6th cent.—Ang.-Sax.
Eâdwine—English EDWIN—French AUDOIN. (*Wulf*) Ang.-
Sax. Eadwulf, Eâdulf—Eng. EDOLPH.

A word of similar meaning is Anglo-Saxon
wela, weola, weal, wealth, prosperity. Förstemann separates this stem from another, which he

WEALTH AND PROSPERITY.

383

derives from *wel*, bene, but I think the distinction is scarcely to be made, and class them together.

SIMPLE FORMS.

Old German Wialo, Weala, Welo, 8th cent. English Weale, Wellow, Veale, Wheeley. Mod. Germ. Wiehl. French Weil, Wel, Veil, Viel, Velly, Violleau.

Weal. Prosperity.

DIMINUTIVES.

Old German Weliga. English Wheelock, Whellock, Wellock. French Velic.

PHONETIC ENDING.

English Wheelan. French Veillon.

PATRONYMICS.

Old German Wellunc, 9th cent. English Welling, Wheeling. Mod. Germ. Wehling. French Welling.

COMPOUNDS.

(*Hard*) English Wellard—Modern German Weilert—French Ouellard, Vellard, Veillard, Violard. (*Hari*, warrior) Old Germ. Wielher, 8th cent.—English Wheeler, Weller—Mod. Germ. Weiller—Fr. Veiller, Viollier, (*Land*) Old Germ. Wiolant, Weland,* 8th cent.—Ang.-Sax. Weland—Old Norse Völundr—Eng. Wayland, Weland, Welland—Mod. Germ. Weyland, Wieland. (*Man*) Old Germ. Weliman, 8th cent.—Eng. Wellman—Mod. German Wellmann. (*Rat*, counsel) Old Germ. Wielrat, 8th cent.—Eng. Wheelwright? (*Ulf*, wolf) Old German Weololf—French? Welhoff?

From a similar root is *wol*, which Förstemann refers to Old High German *wolo, wola*, fortuna, bene. As a prefix it may in some cases be formed by syncope from *wolf*.

SIMPLE FORMS.

Old German Wolo, Wola, 9th cent. English Woli, Wolley, Wholey. Mod. German Wohl, Woll. French Vol, Vollée.

Woll. Prosperity.

---

* Grimm thinks that the Weland of Northern mythology may perhaps derive his name from Old Norse *vela*, to deceive, a derivation which would accord with the story of which he is the hero.

384　　WEALTH AND PROSPERITY.

DIMINUTIVES.

Eng. WOLEDGE. French WOILLEZ. French VOILQUIN.

PHONETIC ENDING.

* English WOLLEN. French VOILIN.

COMPOUNDS.

(*Et, p.* 189) Eng. WOLLATT, VOLLET—French VOLLET. *(Hari,* warrior) Eng. VOLLER—French VOLLIER. *(Helm)* Eng. VOLLAM, VOLLUM—French WOILLAUME, VUILLAUME. (*Frid,* peace) Old German Wolafrid, 9th cent.—French VUILLEFROY. *(Mar,* famous) Old German Wolomar, 8th cent.—Mod. Germ. WOLLMER—French VOILLEMIER. *(Mot,* courage) Old German Wolamot, 8th cent.—French VUILLE-MOT. *(Mund,* protection) Old Germ. Wolamunt, 9th cent. —French VOILLEMONT. *(Ric,* power) Old Germ. Wolarih, 8th cent.—Eng. WOLRIGE. *(Work,* opus)* Eng. WHOLE-WORK ?

From the Goth. *ufjô,* abundance, Förstemann thinks may perhaps be derived the root *uf, ôf,* remarking, however, that the root *ub,* (Old Norse *ubbi,* fierce) is liable to intermix. There is, moreover, another derivation suggested by the name of the Mercian king Offa or Uffa. His ancestor of the same name, who ruled over the continental Angeln, "was blind till his seventh, and dumb till his thirteenth year ; and though excelling in bodily strength, was so simple and pusillanimous that all hope that he would ever prove himself worthy of his station was abandoned." *(Thorpe.)* This description naturally suggests to us as the etymon of his name, the Anglo-Saxon *uuf,* owl, English "oaf," blockhead. It does not, however, seem to me necessary to assume with Mr. Thorpe that it was any resemblance to his Anglian

---

* This is found as the termination of some ancient names.

WEALTH AND PROSPERITY. 385

ancestor that gave the name to the Mercian Offa ; I should rather suppose that the ignoble origin (if such it were) of the name had passed out of mind, and that it was assumed in accordance with the common principle of taking the name of an ancestor.

SIMPLE FORMS.

Old Germ. Uffo, Offo, 8th cent. Ang.-Saxon Offa, king of Mercia. English OFFEY, OUGH. Mod. Germ. OFF.

Off, Uff.
Abundance.

DIMINUTIVES.

Old German Ofilo, 7th cent. „English OFFILL, UFFELL, OFFLOW, OFFLEY. Mod. Germ. OEFFELE.

PHONETIC ENDING.

Old German Offuni, 8th cent. English OFFEN. French OFIN, OFFNY.

COMPOUNDS.

(*Hard*) English OFFORD. (*Hari*, warrior) Eng. OFFER. (*Man*) French OFFMAN.

For the following stem, on which Förstemann remarks as very obscure, he suggests Ang.-Sax. *tass*, acervus, congeries frugum.

SIMPLE FORMS.

Old German Taso, *Lombard king*, 6th cent., Tasso, Dasso. Eng. DASSY. Mod. Germ. DASSE. French DASSY, TASSY. Ital. TASSO ?

Tass.
Acervus.

DIMINUTIVES.

Old German Tassilo, *Bavarian king*, 6th cent., Dassilo, Dessilo—Eng. TASSELL—Mod. Germ. DASSEL—Fr. TASSEL, TASSILY, DESOLLE. French TASSELIN.

COMPOUNDS.

(*And*, life, spirit) English DASENT ?—French DESSANT ? DESAINT ? (*Et, p.* 189) English DASSETT—French DASSET, TASSOT. (*Hard*, fortis) English DESSERT—French TASSERT, DESERT. (*Hari*, warrior) French DASSIER. (*Man*) English TASMAN—Mod. Germ. DESSMANN, TESSMAN. (*Rat*, counsel) Old Germ. Tasrad, 9th cent.—French DESRAT. (*Ger*, spear) English TASSIKER ? TASKER ?—French TASCHER ?

w 2

386 · WEALTH AND PROSPERITY.

The idea of inheritance seems to be found in the ·root *arb*, *arp*, which Förstemann refers to Gothic *arbja*, Old Norse *arfi*, heir, Gothic *arbi*, Old Norse *arfr*, Ang.-Sax. *erfe*, hereditas. I do not feel sure, however, that we ought not to take the most ancient meaning of the root, as found in Sansc. *arv*, to destroy, to desolate. Zeuss and Grimm mention. also Gothic *airps*, Anglo-Saxon *eorp*, fuscus. (In Ang.-Saxon and Old Norse this word had also the meaning of wolf, a suitable sense for proper names.)

Arb, Arp. Inheritance.

SIMPLE FORMS.

Old German Arbo, Arpo, Erbo, Erpo, Herbo, Herpo, Herfo, 8th cent. Arpus, a prince of the Catti in Tacitus, 1st cent., probably comes in here. Old Norse Erpr. Eng. HARP, HERP. Modern German ARVE, ERB, ERPF, HARPE. French ARBEAU, ARBEY.

DIMINUTIVES.

Old Germ. Erfilo—Mod. Germ. ERPEL—French HERBEL, HARBLY. French HERBELIN. French HERBECQ. French HARBEZ.

PHONETIC ENDING.

Old German Erbona, Arbun, 8th cent.—English ARBON, ARPIN—French ARPIN, HERBIN, HERPIN.

COMPOUNDS.

(*Gast*, guest) Arbogastes, a Frankish general under the Emperor Gratian, 4th cent.—French ARBOGAST. (*Hard*) Old German Arphert, 9th cent.—French ARFORT. (*Hari*, warrior) Old German Erphari, 8th cent.—English ARBER, ARBERY, HERPER, HARPER ?—Modern German HERPFER ?—French ARBRE, ARVIER, HERVIER. (*Mund*, protection) Old German Erpmund, 10th cent.—French ARBOMONT. (*Ulf*, wolf) Old Germ. Erpulf, 8th cent.—French ARVEUF.

Another stem of similar meaning·may be *laib*, *laiv*, which Förstemann refers to Gothic *laifs*,

WEALTH AND PROSPERITY. 387

superstes. The meaning, however, may be, as Förstemann suggests, simply that of son. A root liable to intermix is *liub, leof,* p. 264.

SIMPLE FORMS.

Old Germ. Leifi. English LAVEY, LABY, LEVEY. Mod. Germ. LEFF. French LABÉ, LABIE, LEBEY, LEBEAU, LEVÉ, LEVEAU.

Laib, Laiv. Superstes.

DIMINUTIVES.

English LAVELL, LEVELL—French LABELLE, LAVALLE, LAVALLEY, LEBEL. French LABICHE, LEBOCQ. French LEFLON. English LAVIS, LEVIS—French LEBIEZ.

PHONETIC ENDING.

Old German Leibin, Laifin, 9th cent.—English LAVIN, LEVIN—Mod. Germ. LEBIN—Fr. LAVENAY, LAFON, LEBAN.

COMPOUNDS.

(Ern, eagle) English LABERN—French LAVERNE. *(Et, p.* 189) English LEVETT—French LABITTE, LAFITTE, LEVITE. *(Hard)* Modern German·LEPERT—French LEVARD. *(Hari,* warrior) Old Germ. Leibher, 8th cent.—Eng. LAVER, LABOR —Mod. Germ. LAIBER—French LAVIER, LABOUR, LABORIE. *(Ram, ran,* raven) Eng. LABRAM—French LAVIRON. *(Rat,* counsel) Old Germ. Leibrat, 8th cent.—English LEVERET— French LEVRAT, LEBRET. *(Ric,* power) English LAVERICK, LEVERIDGE—Fr. LABRIC, LEBRECK. *(Wald,* power) French LAVAULT, LEBEAULT. *(Ulf,* wolf) Old German Laibulf, 8th cent.—French LEBUFFE, LEBŒUF.

The sense of acquisitiveness may perhaps be found in the root *arg, arc, erc,* which Graff refers to Old High German *arc, arac,* avarus, though Förstemann thinks that some older meaning may lie at the bottom of it.

SIMPLE FORMS.

Old Germ. Argo, Archo, Araho, Ercho, 9th cent. Eng. ARCH, URCH, ARGUE. Mod. Germ. ERCHE, ERCK. French ARGY, ARAGO.

Arg, Arc. Acquisitive.

DIMINUTIVES.

Old Germ. Argila, 7th cent. English ARKELL, ARCULUS *(Birm.)*

388 WEALTH AND PROSPERITY.

COMPOUNDS.

(And, life, spirit) Old Germ. Argant, 11th cent.—Eng. ARGENT—French ·ARGAND. *(Bald,* bold) Eng. ARCHBOLD, ARCHBELL. *(Bud,* envoy) Old Germ. Argebud, 7th cent.— Eng. ARCHBUTT. *(Hard)* Old Germ. Archard, 10th cent. —Eng. ARCHARD, ORCHARD, URQUHART. *(Hari,* warrior) Old German Argar, Erchear, 8th cent.—Archere, *Roll Batt. Abb.*—Eng. ARCHER—Mod. Germ. ERKER—French ARCHEREAU. *(Rat,* counsel) Old Germ. Archarat, 8th cent.—Eng. ARKWRIGHT? *(Mund,* protection) Old German Argemund, 7th cent.—English ARGUMENT.

CHAPTER XXII.

THE OUTER MAN.

Names derived from personal characteristics, such as stature, complexion, &c., must no doubt have in many cases been originally surnames. Bede, in his Ecclesiastical History, gives us one of the earliest instances of surnames of this sort. There were two Hewalds, both missionaries to the Old Saxons, one of whom was called for the sake of distinction black Hewald, and the other white Hewald, from the different colour of their hair. This brings us back to the year 692. But such names appear also to have been often given baptismally, and though in some cases we may suppose that they were an actual description of the infant, yet in the majority of cases I conceive that they were simply adopted as being names in use.

The sense of personal beauty enters into a considerable number of names. From the Old High Germ. *scôni*, Mod. Germ. *schon*, Ang.-Sax. *sceone*, *scêne*, are the following.

SIMPLE FORMS.

Old German Sconea, 9th cent. English SKONE, SHONE, SKEEN, SKINEY, SHEEN, SHINE, SHINN. Mod. Germ. SCHON. French SCHONE.

Shone, Sheen. [Beautiful.

COMPOUNDS.

(*Burg*, protection) Old Germ. Sconiburga, Sconburg, 10th cent.—French SHOENBERG. (*Hari*, warrior) Old Germ. Sconhari, 8th cent.—English SHONER, SHINER, SHINNER—Mod. Germ. SCHÖNER—French ? SCHENER. (*Man*) Eng. SHENIMAN.

390

THE OUTER MAN.

The sense of personal beauty is in some instances closely allied to that of brightness. Thus the above root is related to Eng. "shine" and "sheen." And the Old Norse *dægilegr*, pulcher, is probably connected with *dag*, day, *dagian*, to shine. Again, the sense of brightness is used metaphorically to express glory or fame, as in the root *bert*, bright, p. 369. But though these two senses are naturally liable to intermix, I am inclined to think that the more general meaning is that of personal beauty. In the former edition I took the root *dag*, day, to be derived from the personification of Northern mythology. But Grimm ·*(Deutsch. Gramm.)* suggests whether its meaning may not be that of brightness or beauty. The latter sense I take as the most suitable, and introduce the group in. this place.

SIMPLE FORMS.

Dag, Tag, Brightness, Beauty. Old German Dag, Dago, Daga, Dacco, Tacco, 6th cent. English DAGG, DACK, DECK, DAY, TAGG, TEGG, TAY. Mod. German DAAKE, DÄGE, DECK, TAG, TACK. French DAGA, TAQUO, DECQ, DEGAY.

DIMINUTIVES.

Old German Dagalo, Tacilo, 7th cent.—English DAGLEY, DAILY, TACKLE, TACKLEY, TEKELL—Mod. German DEGEL, TAGEL—Fr. DEGALLE, DEGOLA, DECLE, DECHILLY, DECLA, DAILLY. Old Germ. Dacolenus, 7th cent.—French DACLIN, DECLINE, DEGLANE. English DAYKIN. Eng. DAYES, DAZE, DAISY—French DAGES, DACES.

COMPOUNDS.

(*And*, life, spirit) Old Germ. Dachant, 8th cent.—French DAGAND. (*Bald*, bold) Old German Tagapald, Dacbold, 8th cent.—Daegbald, *Lib. Vit.*—English DAYBELL—Mod. Germ.

THE OUTER MAN.   391

TABOLD.   (*Bern*, bear) Old German Tagapern, 9th cent.—
English TAYBURN.   (*Bert*, bright) Old German Dagobert,
Frankish king, 7th cent.—Mod. German DABBERT—French
DACBERT, DEGOBERT.   (*Birg*, protection) Old German Taga-
birga, 9th cent.—Eng. TACKABARRY.   (*Gest*, hospes) French
DAGEST. (*Grim*, fierce) Old German Dagrim, 9th cent.—
French DAGRIN, DAGRON.*   (*Hari*, warrior) Old German
Daiher, 9th cent.—Dacher, *Lib. Vit.*—English DAGGER,
DACKER, DAYER, DAIRY—Modern German TÄGER—French
DAGUERRE, DAGOURY, DACHERY, DEGORY, DECKER, DECORI.
(*Hard*) English TAGART, TEGART—Mod. German DECKERT—
French TACHARD, DÉCHARD.   (*Helm*) Old Germ. Dachelm,
9th cent.—English DACOMBE—French DECHAUME.   (*Med*,
reverence) French DAGOMET.   (*Man*) Eng. TACKMAN, DAY-
MAN—Mod. German TAGMANN.   (*Mund*, protection) Old
German Dagamund, 9th cent.—English DAYMONT.   (*Rand*,
shield) French DEGRAND, DECRAND. (*Rat*, counsel) Old Germ.
Dacarat, 8th cent.—French DECRET.   (*Wine*, friend) Old
Germ. Dagoin, 8th cent.—French DAGOIN, DACQUIN.   (*Ulf*,
wolf) Old German Dagaulf, Thuringian duke, 6th cent.—
Mod. Germ. DAULF—French DEGOF, DECUVE.

PHONETIC INTRUSION OF *n*.

(*Hard*) Old Germ. Tagenard, 9th cent.   Fr. TAGNIARD.

I take the stem *glas, glis*,† also to have the
meaning of shining, smoothness, and hence of personal beauty.   In the former edition I referred
our name GLASS to glass, vitrum, but I now
think it necessary to look deeper, and to take the
root from which that word is derived.   The sense
contained is that of brightness, smoothness, and
polish, and the root is found in Old High Germ.

---

* Or these two names, and especially the latter, may be the same as the
Dæghrefn of Beowulf—*refn*, raven, being in French names frequently contracted
into *ron*.

† Perhaps to the same stem may be put English GLOSS, CLOSE, French
CLOSSE, CLOEZ, English CLOSER, French CLOSIER, &c.

392　THE OUTER MAN.

glizan, Mod. German *gleiszen*, to shine, Old Norse *glœsa*, to polish, Old High German *glas, glis*, brightness, English glaze, gloss, glisten.

Glass, Glis.
Brightness
Beauty.

SIMPLE FORMS.
Old German Glis, 10th cent. English GLASS, GLASSEY, GLAZE, CLASS. Mod. Germ. GLASS, GLEISS, KLASS. French GLAS, GLAISE, GLAZE.

DIMINUTIVE.
English GLASKIN.

PHONETIC ENDING.
English GLASSON, GLISSAN, CLASSON. French GLASSON, CLASSEN.

COMPOUNDS.
(*Hard*) Eng. GLAZARD. (*Hari*, warrior) Old German Glisher, 8th cent.—Eng. GLAZIER, GLAISHER—Mod. German GLÄSER—French GLAESER. (*Wald*, power) Eng. CLISSOLD.

Again, the sense of brightness sometimes merges into that of whiteness. Thus the Anglo-Saxon *blanc*, Old High Germ. *blanch*, white, seem to have their root in Old Norse *blanka*, to shine. And the Ang.-Sax. *blâc*, pale, is derived from the verb *blîcan*, to shine. Hence, as the Eng. "fair" means both light-complexioned and also beautiful, so I think in the above two roots there may be something more contained than the mere sense of white or pale.

Blank.
White,
Beautiful?

SIMPLE FORMS.
Old Germ. Blanca, 10th cent. English BLANK, BLANCH, BLENKY, BLINCO, PLANK, PLANCHÉ, PLINCKE. Mod. Germ. BLANK, BLANG, BLENK, PLANCK. French BLANC, BLANQUE, BLANCA, BLANCHE, BLANGY, PLANQUE, PLANCHE.

PHONETIC ENDING.
English BLENKIN.* French BLANCHIN.

---

* Hence BLENKINSOP as a local name, "Blenkin's hope," (Ang.-Sax. *hôp*, mound).

THE OUTER MAN. 393

COMPOUNDS.

(Et, p. 189) English BLANCHETT—French BLANQUET, BLANCHET, PLANQUET. (*Hard*) Old Germ. Blancard, Blanchard, 11th cent.—English BLANCHARD—Modern German BLANCKARDT—French BLANCARD, BLANCHARD, BLANGEARD, PLANCHARD. (*Hari*, warrior) English BLANCKER—French BLANQUIER, PLANKER, PLANCHER. (*Man*) Eng. BLANKMAN. (*Ron*, raven) Eng. BLENKIRON, BLINCKHORN—French BLANCHERON. (*Ward*, guardian) French BLANQUART.

From the Anglo-Saxon *blícan*, to shine, Old High Germ. *bleih*, Ang.-Sax. *blác*, pale, I derive the following stem, which is cognate with the last, losing the nasal. There are several Old German names, but only one corresponding with ours.

SIMPLE FORMS.
Eng. BLICK, BLEAK, BLEACH, BLAKE, BLAKEY, BLACOW, BLIGH. French BLECH.

Blake, Blick. Pale, Beautiful?

COMPOUNDS.
(Hari, warrior) Old German Blicker, 8th cent.—English BLAKER, BLEACHER—Mod. Germ. BLECHER—French BLÉQUIER. (*Man*) Blaecmon, *Lib. Vit.*—Eng. BLAKEMAN.

Of a similar meaning maybe the word *flad*, *flat*, for which Grimm supposes a Gothic *flêths*, Old High Germ. *flât*, in the sense of brightness, cleanness. Traces of these two senses are found respectively in the Mid. High German *vlaetec*, shining, and Mod. German *unflath*, filth. As a termination it is peculiar to the names of women, and in Ang.-Sax. takes the form *fled*, as in Adelfleda, Wynfleda, &c. The Old Norse *fliôd*, a beautiful or elegant woman, may be cognate.

SIMPLE FORMS.
English FLATT, FLETT, FLATAU. Mod. German FLATHE. French FLAD, FLAUD.

Flad, Flat. Fair.

X 2

394 THE OUTER MAN.

DIMINUTIVE.
PHONETIC ENDING.

Eng. FLATTELY. Eng. FLITTON. French FLATON.

COMPOUNDS.

(Hari, warrior) English FLATTER, FLATTERY. *(Man)* English FLATMAN. *(Rod,* glory) Old German Fladrudis, 8th cent.—French FLATRAUD.

Another word having the meaning of beauty may be *wan, wen.* Förstemann suggests Gothic *vêns,* opes, or Old High Germ. *wân,* spes, opinio. Graff also refers to Old High Germ. *wan,* deficiens, imperfectum, and *wâni,* poverty. The most suitable root, as it seems to me, in most cases, is Old Norse *vænn,* formosus, elegans, to which I here place it.

Wan, Wen.
Beautiful.

SIMPLE FORMS:

Old Germ. Wan, Wano, Vano, Wenni, 8th cent. Eng. WANE, WENN, VANE, VANN, VENN. Fr. VANEY, GUÉNEAU.

DIMINUTIVES.

Old Germ. ·Wanilo, Venilo, 8th cent.—Eng. WANNELL, VENNELL—French VANELLI, VENELLE. Old Germ. Wanicho, Wenniko, 9th cent.—Eng. VANNECK—Mod. Germ. WANNICK —French VANEGUE. Old German Wannida, Wanito, 9th cent.—Eng. WANNOD—French VANETTI.

PHONETIC ENDING.

Old Germ. Wanini, 8th cent. French VANIN, VANONI.

PATRONYMICS.

Old Germ. Waning, Wening, 7th cent. Eng. WENNING, VENNING. Mod. Germ. WENING.

COMPOUNDS.

(And, life, spirit) Old Germ. Weniant, 9th cent.—French VENANT. *(Bald,* bold) Old German Wanbald, 9th cent.— French GUÉNÉBAULT. *(Ger,* spear) Old German Wanegar, 8th cent.—French VANACKÈRE—Mod. German WENIGER. *(Hari,* warrior) Eng. VANNER, VENNER—French WANNER, VANNIER. *(Hard)* French VANARD, VENARD, GUENARD. *(Laug,* lavacrum ?) Old Germ. Wanlog, 8th cent.—English WENLOCK. *(Man)* English WENMAN, WAINMAN ? *(Muth,* courage) English WENMOTH. *(Rat,* counsel) Old German

THE OUTER MAN. 395

Wanrat, 9th cent.—Eng. WAINWRIGHT?—French GUÉNERAT. (*Wald*, power) French VENAULT, GUENAULT.

· The names derived from complexion or colour of the hair are liable to some uncertainty on account of the curious manner in which certain of the words denoting colour intermix in their roots. To call black white has passed into a proverb, yet, as Mr. Wedgwood has shown, it is probable that the original meaning of black *was* white or pale. Again, the two colours, blue and yellow, which have stood in hostile array on so many hustings, can scarcely be separated in their roots. The Old Norse *blår* Haldorsen renders both as flavus and cæruleus ; the Italian *biavo*, blue, is explained by Florian as pale straw-coloured ; the Dutch *blond* is applied to the livid hue of a bruise, as well as to the yellowish colour of the hair ; and the Old French *bloi* is explained by Roquefort as blond, jaune, bleu, et blanc. Hence, as Mr. Wedgwood observes, it becomes difficult to separate Mid. Lat. *blavus*, blue, from Latin *flavus*, yellow.

So far then as the root *black* appears to be baptismal, we cannot be sure that it does not intermix with the two previous roots *blank* and *blake*.

SIMPLE FORMS.

Blache, Blac, *Domesday*. Eng. BLACK, BLACKIE. French. BLAQUÉ.

Black. Niger?

COMPOUNDS.

(*Hari*, warrior) Eng. BLACKER—Fr. BLACHIER, BLACHER. (*Man*) Blæcman, genealogy of the kings of Northumbria—Blacheman, *Domesday*—Eng. BLACKMAN.

396 THE OUTER MAN.

Between blue and ·yellow we have scarcely a choice, if we take a positive colour at all. In the few Old Germ. names in which it occurs Förstemann proposes the latter sense as the more natural. But there is a wider sense which might perhaps be taken. The Anglo-Saxon *bleo*, blue, signifies also bloom, beauty, and the root appears to be found in the Old High Germ. *bluen*, Ang.-Saxon *blewan*, *blowan*, to blow, bloom, flourish. A similar sense is found in many other names.

Blue, Blow. Bloom?

SIMPLE FORMS.

Old Germ. Blawa, Bloa, 8th cent. Eng. BLEW, BLEAY, BLOW. French BLEU, BLOU, BLEÉ.

COMPOUNDS.

(Hari, warrior) English BLEWER, BLOWER.

There is a word *bleon*, found in several Old German names, which Grimm takes to be related to, and have the same meaning as Ang.-Sax. *bleo*, bloom, colour. To this may belong the following.

Blain. Bloom?

SIMPLE FORMS.

Old Germ. Bleon, Pleon, 8th cent. Eng. BLOWEN, BLAIN, BLANEY, PLAIN. French BLAIN, BLEIN, BLIN, PLAIN, PLANUS.

COMPOUNDS.

(Hari, warrior) English PLANNER—French BLENNER, PLANIER, PLANER. *(Rice*, powerful) French PLANRY.

It is probable that the word *bland*, *blond*, which is found in some German forms both in ancient and modern names, has the same meaning, as the Ital. *biondo*, French *blond*, fair or flaxen. Diez suggests that this may be a nasalised form of Old Norse *blaudr*, Danish *blöd*, soft, weak, in the sense of a soft tint. Mr. Wedgwood connects it with Pol. *blady*, pale, Ital. *biado*, *biavo*, pale,

THE OUTER MAN. 397

straw-coloured. Förstemann refers in the following names to the Ang.-Sax. *blanden-feax,* which he renders flavi-comus. But Bosworth renders it only grey-haired, from *blanden,* to mix (*i.e.* black and white). There may be an intermixture of these two meanings, but the former seems the more probable.

SIMPLE FORMS.

Old German Bland, 10th cent. English BLAND, PLANT. *Bland.*
French BLOND, BLONDEAU, BLONDÉ, BLANZY, PLANTY. *Fair, Flaxen.*

DIMINUTIVES.

Old Germ. Blandila (with the variation Brandila). Eng. BLINDELL, BLONDELL. French BLONDEL.

PHONETIC ENDING.

Eng. BLANDEN. French BLANDIN, BLONDIN, PLANTIN.

COMPOUNDS.

(Hard) French PLANTARD. (*Hari,* warrior) French PLANTIER.

.From the Ang.-Sax. *deorc,* dark, in the sense of complexion, I take to be the following. Hence the name of the Maid of Orleans, commonly called Joan D'Arc, but properly Joan Darc. There are some ancient names, but not any corresponding with ours.

SIMPLE FORMS.

Eng. DARK, DARCH. French DARQUÉ, DARCHE, DERCHE. *Dark.* *Fuscus.*

DIMINUTIVE.

French DARCLON.

PHONETIC ENDING.

Eng. DARKIN, DARGAN? French DERQUENNE.

COMPOUNDS.

(Hari, warrior) English DARKER—French DARQUIER. *(Man)* English DARKMAN.

Of a similar meaning may be the word *darn,, tarn,* which Förstemann refers to Ang.-Sax. *derne,*

398 THE OUTER MAN.

occultus, Old High German *tarnjan*, dissimulare,
&c., supposing as the most ancient meaning that
of dark complexion. Here again there are no
ancient names to correspond with ours.

Darn, Tarn.
Dark.

SIMPLE FORMS.

Eng. DERN, TARN. French DARNAY, DERNL.

DIMINUTIVES.

Eng. DARNELL, DARNLEY. French DARNIS.

COMPOUNDS.

(*Aud*, prosperity) French TARNAUD. (*Hari*, warrior)
English TARNER.

The stem *white* is very difficult to separate
from other stems. In Ang.-Saxon there are names
beginning with *whit* or *hwit*, as if from white,
albus, and others beginning with *wiht*, as if from
wiht, a man. These sometimes seem to interchange; thus the nephew of Cerdic is called both
Whitgar and Wihtgar. The corresponding Old
Germ. form is generally *wid* or *wit*, as in Witgar
and Widgar, and the probability seems to be that
all these names are the same. Förstemann refers
to *wit*, wide, and *wid*, wood. The commonness of
our name WHITE is I apprehend owing to its
being in most cases a surname derived from complexion.

So BROWN we can scarcely doubt to have
been in most cases a surname. Yet it was by no
means uncommon as a baptismal name, and it is
not quite certain as to its meaning. Förstemann
thinks that there may be an intermixture of *brûn*,
brown, and of Old High German *brunno*, Anglo-
Saxon *brunn*, *burn*, Scott. " burn," brook, (in the

THE OUTER MAN. 399

sense of impetuosity?) I also think, see p. 127, of Old Norse *brûn*, the eyebrow.

But even taking the sense of "brown," there may be something more to be said. The sense in proper names is in so many cases the deepest-lying one, that I am led to enquire what is the root of brown. Clearly, as it seems to me, that suggested by Mr. Wedgwood, "the colour of things burnt, from Gothic *brinnan*, German *brennan*, to burn." The sense of burning seems to be that in the Ang.-Sax. *brûn-ecg*, an appellation of a sword. This is rendered by Bosworth "brown-edged," but should it not be rather "bright or burnished edge?" So the Mod. Germ. has *bruniren*, to burnish. The Ang.-Sax. *brand*, English brand, a sword, shews a similar sense from the same root. Our name then, BROWN-SWORD, I take to have the meaning of "bright-sword." And a similar sense, or perhaps rather that of fiery or impetuous, may at any rate inter-mix in the following names.

SIMPLE FORMS.

Old Germ. Brun, Bruno, Bruni, 8th cent. Ang.-Saxon Brûn.* Brôn, *Lib. Vit.* Old Norse Brûni. Eng. BROWN, BRUNE. Mod. German BRAUN, BRUNN, BRÜNO. Fr. BRUN, BRUNO, BRUNEAU, BRUNY.

Brown. Fuscus?

DIMINUTIVES.

Old Germ. Brunicho, 8th cent.—Mod. Germ. BRUNCK—French BRUNACHE. Eng. BROWNELL, BROWNLOW—French BRUNEL, PRUNEL.

---

* Brûn, bydel, in a charter of manumission, *Cod. Dip.* No. 1353. Brown, the beadle, "what a nineteenth century sound?" Mr. Turner oddly enough translates it "the brown beadle."

400 THE OUTER MAN.

PHONETIC ENDING.

Old Germ. Brunin. Eng. BRUNNEN.

PATRONYMICS.

Old German Bruning, 8th cent. Bruningus, *Lib. Vit.*
Eng. BROWNING.

COMPOUNDS.

(*And*, life, spirit) French BRUNANT. (*Et*, p. 189) English
BROWNETT—French BRUNET, PRUNET. (*Hard*) Old German
Brunhard, 9th cent.—Modern German BRUNNERT—French
BRUNARD. (*Ger*, spear) Old German Brunger, 8th cent.—
English BRUNKER. (*Hari*, warrior) Old German Brunheri,
Brunher, 9th cent.—Fr. BRUNER, BRUNNER, BRUNNARIUS,
PRUNIER. (*Ric*, power) Old German Brunric, 9th cent.—
Eng. BROWNRIGG ?

The stem *dun* may be either referred to Ang.-
Sax. *dunn*, brown, or to Old Norse *duna*, thunder.
The latter seems to me the more probable, as
there are other names with the same meaning,
elsewhere referred to.

It is probable that GREY, like BROWN and
WHITE, has been in most cases a surname. But
it is also found in many baptismal names, and
there is another sense, which seems to be closely
allied, and which may perhaps intermix. The
Old Norse *grár*, grey, signifies also malignus ;
and the Germ. *grauen*, to turn grey, signifies also
to detest, and to be afraid of. So also the Old
High Germ. *gris*, grey, seems to contain the root
of Ang.-Sax. *grislíc*, Eng. grisley, The particle
gr seems to be formed from a natural expression
of horror or aversion. There may then be contained in some of the names from this root a
similar sense to that referred to at p. 192.
Nevertheless, judging from the ancient names,

THE OUTER MAN. 401

the meaning in some cases is certainly nothing more than grey. The following may be referred to the Ang.-Sax. *grêg*, Old Fries. *gre*, Old High German *graw*.

Gray.
Griseus.

SIMPLE FORMS.

Old Germ. Grao, Grawo. Gray, *Roll Batt. Abb.* Eng. GREGG, GREY, GREW, CRAY, CREW. Mod. German GRAU. French GRÉGY, GRAU.

DIMINUTIVES.

English GRAYLING. French GREILING.

COMPOUNDS.

(*Ber*, bear) Eng. GRUEBER ? (*Man*) Old Germ. Graman, 8th cent.—Eng. GRUMMAN—Mod. Germ. GRAMANN—French GRAMAIN. (*Wald*, power) Old German Graolt—French GRAULT.

Another word of the same meaning is Old High Germ. *gris*, Lat. *griseus*, French *gris*. The Old Norse *gris*, porcellus, whence apparently the name Grîs of several Northmen in the Landnamabok, might intermix.

Gris,
Grey.

SIMPLE FORMS.

Old German Grisus, Crisso, 8th cent. Gressy, Cressy, Gracy ? *Roll Batt. Abb.* English GRICE, GRACE ? GRACEY ? CRESSY. French GRIESS, GRESY, GRÉSY.

DIMINUTIVES.

English GRISSELL, GRESLEY, CRESSALL—French GRISOL, GRESLÉ, GRAESLE. French GRISELIN, GRESLON.

PHONETIC ENDING.

French GRIESSEN, GRISON, CRESSON.

COMPOUNDS.

(*Hard*) French GRISARD. (*Hari*, warrior) French GRISIER, GRESSIER. (*Land*) French GRESLAND. (*Wald*, power) Eng. GRISOLD, GRESWOLD.

A stem which may perhaps come in here is *more* or *moor*, respecting which Förstemann remarks—" a not uncommon but an uncer-

Y 2

402

THE OUTER MAN.

tain stem, for which I scarcely dare venture to think of the Old High German *môr*, Æthiops." Yet if there were names derived from the Huns, I do not quite see why not from the Moors, whose name must have been familiar to most of the German peoples. At the same time, it will perhaps be safer to take the more general sense of dark or swarthy complexion. Though I do not feel quite sure that it may not' be in some cases a degenerate form of *mord*, p. 258, as we find in the Diplomata of Pardessus a person variously called Mora and Morta. On the whole, however, I feel inclined to bring in the stem here.

Mor, Moor Dark.

SIMPLE FORMS.

Old German Maur, Mauri, Mor, Moro, Mora, Moor, 6th cent. Eng. MORE, MOREY, MAURY, MORROW, MOORE. Mod. Germ. MOHR. French MAUR, MAUREY, MORÉ, MOREAU.

DIMINUTIVES.

Old Germ. Maurilo, 8th cent.—English MORELL—Mod. Germ. MÖHRLE—French MAUREL, MOREL. Old German Mauroleno, Morlenus, 7th cent.—English MORLING—French MORILLON, MOURLON. Old German Mauremia, 9th cent.— French MORIAMÉ.

PHONETIC ENDING.

Old German Morino, 8th cent. Morin, *Hund. Rolls.* English MORAN, MOORHEN. Mod. Germ. MOHRIN. French MAURIN.

PATRONYMICS.

Old German Mauring, 8th cent. Mod. Germ. MORING. French MAURENQUE.

COMPOUNDS.

(*Bert*, famous) Old Germ. Maurbert, Morbraht, 8th cent. —Eng. MOREBREAD? (*Hard*, fortis) Old German Morhard, 8th cent.—Modern German MOHRHARD—French MORARD. (*Hari*, warrior) Old Germ. Maurhar, 8th cent.—Mod. Germ. MAURER—French MAURIER. (*Lac*, play) Old Germ. Maurlach, 8th cent.—English MORLOCK—French MOURLAQUE.

(*Helm*) French Morihalm. (*Man*) English Moreman, Moorman—Modern German Möhrmann. (*Ward*) English Morward.

Snow is I think more probably from a mythological origin than from anything relating to complexion. It was the name of a mythical king of Denmark, one of whose daughters was also called Mïöll, which signifies freshly fallen snow. The latter was a common female name among the Northmen, and hence may perhaps be our Miall, Miell, Meall. In addition to the two Old German names, Sneoburg and Sneward, cited by Förstemann as compounded with *sneo*, snow, I adduce two others, Snahard and Snædisa, from the Liber Vitæ. The latter signifies " snownymph" or " snow-woman," and may be compared with our Snowman (*Suff. Surn.*)

There are several names which seem to be derived from the curling of the hair, and at the bottom of some of which may lie a heroic sense. For among the ancient German tribes the wearing of the hair long or curled was considered a badge of the noble or the hero. In Anglo-Saxon *locc-bora* signified " a hair-bearer, a noble," and *locc-bore* " one entitled by her rank to wear long hair, a lady," (*Bosworth*). The tribe of the Suevi was noted, according to Tacitus, for wearing their hair fastened up into a peculiar curl or knot. This peculiarity I have suggested, p. 304, as the origin of their name. A similar origin is suggested by Grimm and Richthoven for the name

404 THE OUTER MAN.

of the Frisians (or Frieses), viz., the Old Friesic *frisle,* a curl, of which the simple form is found in English *frizz,* to curl, *frieze,* a rough woollen cloth, and the French *friser.* The latter is probably of German origin, as it is not found in the Italian language. Other derivations have however been proposed for this people's name, as that by Zeuss referred to at p. 312.

From the Old Norse *krusa,* to curl, may perhaps be the following. The North. English word *cruse* or *crowse,* which has the meaning of forward or "bumptious," may possibly be from this origin, preserving a trace of the heroic sense. A word liable to intermix is *grouse,* elsewhere noticed· in this chapter.

Cruse.
Curled.

SIMPLE FORMS.
English CRUSE, CRUSO. German KRUSE. Dan. KRUSE. French CRUICE, CREUSE, CREUZÉ, CREUCY, CROUSSE, CROUSI, CRUZ, CRUSSY.

DIMINUTIVES.
English CRUSSELL. French CRUZEL.

COMPOUNDS.
(Hard) French CREUSARD. *(Hari,* warrior) French CRUSSIÉRE.

From the Ang.-Sax. *crisp,* curled, may be the following. But the Latin *crispus* may have an equal claim, for there is nothing in any of these forms essentially German.

. Crisp.
Curled.

SIMPLE FORMS.
English CRISP, CRIPPS ?

DIMINUTIVES.
English CRESPEL. French CRESPEL.

PHONETIC ENDING.
Crispina, daughter of Rollo, duke of Normandy, 10th cent. Eng. CRISPIN, CRESPIN. French CRISPIN, CRESPIN.

THE OUTER MAN. 405

From the Danish *krolle*, Old English "crull," English "curl," may be the following.

SIMPLE FORMS.

Curly, *Roll Batt. Abb.* English CROLL, CROLY, CURLL. Mod. Germ. KROLL, KRULL.

Croll.
Curled

PATRONYMIC.

English CURLING.

Under this head may in some cases be included the name HARDING. As a general rule the stem *hard* is to be referred to Ang.-Sax. *heard*, English hardy. But the Hardings (in Ang.-Sax. Heardingas) are celebrated in ancient poems as a heroic race, and Grimm has observed (*Deutsch Myth.* 317, 321) that there was a Gothic hero race called Azdingi, and an Old Norse Haddingjar. He remarks that the Gothic *zd*, the Ang.-Saxon *rd*, and the Old Norse *dd* interchange, so that Heardingas, Azdingi, and Haddingjar may all be different forms of the same word. And the root may be found in the Old Norse *haddr*, a lock or curl, giving the sense of "crinitus, capillatus, cincinnatus," which, as before observed, was the attribute of the hero.

From the German *gross*, great, in the sense of large stature, and from an extra High German form *grauss*, as noticed at p. 49, may be the following. Förstemann however refers this stem to Anglo-Saxon *greosan*, horrere, in the sense of *metuendus*.

SIMPLE FORMS.

Old Germ. Grozo, Grauso, Gros, Cros, 6th cent. English GROSE, GROUSE, CROSS. Mod. Germ. GROSS. French GROSSE, GRUSSE, CROSSE, CROZE.

Gross,
Grouse.
Great.

406 THE OUTER MAN.

DIMINUTIVES.

French Groseille, Gruselle. French Grosselin.

COMPOUNDS.

(*Hard,* fortis) Eng. Grosert—French Grossard, Crossard. (*Hari,* warrior) English Groser, Croser—French Grossier, Crozier. (*Man*) Eng. Grossman, Crossman.

Another word having the meaning of great is probably *mic* or *muc*, which Förstemann takes to be the simple form of Gothic *mikilo,* Sco. *mickle* and *muckle.*

Mic, Muc. Great.

SIMPLE FORMS.

Old Germ. Micca, 3rd cent. Mucca, *Lib. Vit.* English Michie, Mico, Much. Mod. Germ. Mucke, Mugge. French Michy, Miché, Mougé.

COMPOUNDS.

(*Hard,* fortis) Old Germ. Michard, 11th cent.—Modern Germ. Mückert—French Micard. (*Wald,* power) English Muckelt—French Micault, Michault. (*Wine,* friend) French Micouin.

Mickle, Muckle. Great.

EXTENDED FORM MICKLE, MUCKLE.

Eng. Mickle, Muckle. Mod. Germ. Mückel. French Micol.

COMPOUNDS.

(*Hard,* fortis) French Micquelard. (*Hari,* warrior) French Micollier. (*Man*) Mod. German Michelmann— French Mukleman. (*Mar,* famous) English Michelmore? (*Rat,* counsel) English Micklewright? Mucklewrath? (*Manchester.*)

From the Ang.-Saxon *thic,* Old Norse *thyckr, digr,* Mod. Germ. *dick,* stout, thick, may be the following.

Dick, Thick. Stout.

SIMPLE FORMS.

Old Germ. Thicho. Old Norse Thyckr, Digr *(surnames).* English Thick, Dick, Dickie, Tigg, Tick. Mod. German Dick, Tieck.

DIMINUTIVES.

Ang.-Sax. Diccel *(found in Diccelingas, now Ditchling, Cod. Dip.* 314)—Eng. Diggle, Tickle.

THE OUTER MAN. 407

PHONETIC ENDING.
Old Germ. Tichhan, 9th cent. Eng. DICKIN.°

COMPOUNDS.
(Et, p. 189*)* English THICKET. *(Hard)* Mod. German DICKERT—French DICHARD, DIGARD. *(Hari,* warrior) Eng. DICKER, DIGORY—French DICHARRY. *(Man)* Eng. DICKMAN, DIGMAN, DITCHMAN—Mod. Germ. DIKMANN.

Of a similar meaning I take to be the stem *buss,* as shewn in Old Norse *bússa,* a stout woman, *bússa,* a broad ship, *busi,* a short, broad knife.

SIMPLE FORMS.
Old German Buaso, Puaso, 8th cent. Sivard Buss, a Northman ? *(Domesday Linc.)* Eng. Buss, BUSSEY. Mod. Germ. Boos, Buss. French BUSSE, BUSSY, PUSSY.

Buss.
Stout.

DIMINUTIVES.
Old German Busilo, 8th cent. English BUSSELL. Mod. Germ. BÖSEL.

PATRONYMIC.
English BUSSING.

COMPOUNDS.
(Hard) English BUSZARD—French BUSSARD. *(Hari,* warrior) French BUSSER, BUSSIÉRE. *(Man)* Eng. BUSSMAN—Mod. Germ. BUSSMANN—French BUISMAN.

I take the stem *boss* (for which Förstemann finds no other derivation than the Old High German *bôsi,* Mod. Germ. *böse,* wicked, which he admits to be an unsatisfactory one) to be the same as *buss.* But it suggests as possible a rather different meaning, though from a common origin, viz., the Dutch *bosse, busse,* a boss or knob of a buckler, French *bosse,* a bunch, hump, or knob. Again, as Mr. Wedgwood observes, the words signifying a lump or protuberance have commonly also the sense of striking, knocking, of which he gives many examples. And we have Dutch

408 THE OUTER MAN.

bossen, Ital. *bussare,* French *bousser,* to knock, Bav. *bossen,* to strike so as to give a dull sound. Either this, or the sense of the boss of a buckler, are meanings which might obtain, along with that first mentioned.

Boss
Burly ?

SIMPLE FORMS.

Old German Boso, Bosso, Poso, 6th cent. English Boss, Bossey. Mod. German Boss, Pose. French Bos, Bosse, Bossy, Posso.

DIMINUTIVES.

Old German Bosico, 9th cent.—French Possac. Old Germ. Poasilo, 8th cent.—Eng. Bosley—French Boselli. French Possesse, Posez.

COMPOUNDS.

(*Hari,* warrior) Old German Bozhar, 8th cent.—English Bosher—French Boussiere, Bossuroy. (*Hard*) English Bossard—French Bossard, Poussard. (*Helm*) Old Germ. Boshelm, 11th cent.—Eng. Bossom. (*Man*) Eng. Bosman. (*Wald,* power) Old Germ. Buzolt, 8th cent.—Mod. German Bosselt—French Posselt. (*Ulf,* wolf) Old Germ. Possulf, 8th cent.—French Poussif ?

I take the stem *bost, bust,* to have the same meaning as *boss* and *buss,* viz., that most probably of bulkiness or burliness. This is shewn in our word "bust," the original meaning of which, Mr. Wedgwood observes, was the trunk or body of a man ; also in the Old Norse *bústinn,* burly.* There are only two ancient names in which it is found, viz., Boster and Postfred, both 9th cent. Both these names Förstemann thinks may be corruptions, but the evident occurrence of the word in the following names makes it probable that this is not the case.

---

* Mr. Lower, on the name BUIST, gives the same meaning, referring to the Scotch *buist,* thick and gross.

THE OUTER MAN.   409

SIMPLE FORMS.
Eng. Boast, Busst, Buist, Post.   French Bost.   Bost, Bust. Burly.

DIMINUTIVES.
Eng. Bostel, Postle—French Postel.   Eng. Bostock.

PHONETIC ENDING.
English Bustin, Poston.

COMPOUNDS.
(*Hard*) English Bustard, Pustard.   (*Ric,* power) Eng. Bostridge.   (*Wald,* power) French Bustault.

From the Old Norse *kortr,* Old Fries. *kort, kurt,* short, and the corresponding High German form *kurz,* may be the following.   The Latin *curtus,* French *courte,* may intermix.

SIMPLE FORMS.
Old German Corso, 8th cent.   English Corse, Course, Curtze, Cort, Court, Curt.   French Course, Coursy, Corta, Court, Courty, Courteau, Curty.   Cort, Corse. Short.

DIMINUTIVES.
English Courcelle.—French Coursel, Cortel.   French Curtelin.

PHONETIC ENDING.
Curson, Curtenay, *Roll Batt. Abb.* Eng. Corsan, Curson, Curtain, Courtenay.   Modern German Kohrssen.   French Corsain, Courson, Courtin.

COMPOUNDS.
(*Hari,* warrior) English Corsar, Courser, Courtier— French Cortier, Courtier.   (*Rand,* shield) French Coursserant.   (*Rat,* counsel) English Courtwright.

There are many words containing the meaning of physical strength, though in some cases it is not easy to separate this meaning from that of courage, valour, or fierceness.

From the Gothic *magan,* posse, I take to be derived the following stem, with which, however, the Gothic *meki,* sword, may, as suggested by Förstemann, intermix.

z 2

410   THE OUTER MAN.

Magan.
Posse.

SIMPLE FORMS.

Old German Mago, Macco, Maho, Maio, Megi, 6th cent. Eng. MAGGY, MAY, MAYO, MEGGY, MEE, MAYHEW? Mod. Germ. MACK, MEYE. French MAY, MACHU? MAHEU?

DIMINUTIVES.

Old German Megilo, Meilo, 8th cent.—English MAYALL, MALE—French MAILLEY. Eng. MAYLIN—French MAYLIN. Old Germ. Megizo, 10th cent.—Eng. MAIZE, MAISEY.

COMPOUNDS.

(Hari, warrior) Old Germ. Megiher, Magher, 8th cent.— English MAGER, MAYER—Modern German MAGER—French MAHIER, MAYER. *(Had,* war?) Old German Magodius, 11th cent.—Magot, *Lib. Vit.*—English MAGGOT. *(Man)* Eng. MAYMAN. *(Ron,* raven) Old German Megiran, 8th cent.— Eng. MEGRIN—French MAGRON, MACRON, MAYRAN. (*Wald,* power) Old German Magoald, 8th cent.—Modern German MACHOLD, MAYWALD—French MAHAULT. *(Wine,* friend) Old Germ. Magwin, Macwin, 7th cent.—French MACQUIN. (*Ward,* guardian) French MACQUARD, MACQUART.

From the above root *mag* is formed Ang.-Sax. *mægin,* English *main,* vis, robur, from which we may take the following.

Magin.
Vis, Robur.

SIMPLE FORMS.

Old German Magan, Main, 8th cent. English MAINE. Mod. Germ. MÄCHEN, MEHNE. French MAGNÉ, MAGNEY.

COMPOUNDS.

(Bald, fortis) Old Germ. Meginbold, 8th cent.—French MAGNABÁL. *(Burg,* protection) Old Germ. Meginburg, 8th cent.— French MAINBOURG. *(Fred,* peace) Old Germ. Maginfrid, 8th cent.—French MAINFROY. *(Gald)* Old German Megingald, 10th cent.—French MAINGAULT. *(Ger,* spear) Old Germ. Meginger, 9th cent.—English MANGER. (*Gaud,* Goth) Old Germ. Megingaud, 8th cent.—French MAINGOT. *(Hard,* fortis, durus) Old German Maginhard, Mainard, 7th cent.—English MAYNARD—Mod. German MEINERT—French MAGNARD, MAYNARD. *(Hari,* warrior) Old Germ. Maganhar, Mayner, 7th cent.—Mod. Germ. MEINER—French MAGNIER, MAYNIER.

THE OUTER MAN. 411

From the root *mag* is also formed Old, High German *maht*, Mod. Germ. *macht*, Anglo-Saxon *miht*, English *might*.

SIMPLE FORMS.
Old Germ. Maht, 9th cent. English MIGHT.

COMPOUNDS.
(*Hari*, warrior) Old Germ. Mahtheri, Macther, 8th cent. —English MIGHTER—French MACTIER. (*Hild*, war) Old German Mahthildis, 8th cent.—English MATILDA (*christian name*).

Among the words having the meaning of nimbleness or activity must be included several which are derived from simple roots signifying to fly, to run, to move, to go. From the Ang.-Sax. *fligan, flogan*, Old Norse *fliug*, to fly, may be the following. Or we may perhaps take the active sense, to put to flight. Or again, the meaning of dart or arrow, as found in the Anglo-Saxon *flá*, French *fleche*, both from this root, may intermix.

SIMPLE FORMS.
Old German Flacco, Flecco,* (ancestor of the Nesselrode family). Ang.-Saxon Flagg, (*found in Flegges gávan, Cod. Dip.* 578). English FLAGG, FLACK, FLEGG, FLECK, FLUCK, FLOOK, FLY, FLEA. Fr. FLEIG, FLECK, FLICK, FLICHY, FLÉ.

DIMINUTIVES.
Mod. Germ. FLÖGEL, FLÜGEL. French FLECHELLE.

COMPOUNDS.
(*Et*, p. 189) Eng. FLEWITT—French FLACHAT, FLIQUET, FLOQUET. (*Hard*) Fr. FLICOURT, FLOCARD. (*Hari*, warrior) Eng. FLYGER, FLYER, FLUER. (*Man*) English FLEEMAN— Modern German FLUEMANN.

Maht. Might.

Flag, Fleg. To Fly.

---

* The Old Norse *fleckr*, Old High Germ. *flecco*, Old English *fleck*, a mark or spot, may intermix. It would not be unnatural for a child to derive its name from some peculiar mark with which it might happen to be born.

412

THE OUTER MAN.

From the Anglo-Saxon *winge*, Mod. German *schwinge*, English wing, in the sense of swiftness, may be the following.

Wing, Wink. Ala.

SIMPLE FORMS.

Old German Winc, Vinco, 9th cent. Old Norse Vingi, (messenger of Atli or Attila in the Volsungasaga). English WING, WINCH, VINGOE, VINK. Modern German WINCK, SCHWINGE. French VINCQ, WENK.

COMPOUNDS.

(Hari, warrior) Wingere, *Lib. Vit.*—Eng. WINGER.

Of a similar meaning may be the word *floss*, Old Norse *flos*, plumula vestium, whence *flosi*, plumatus, also volans, from which Haldorsen derives the Old Norse name Flosi. There is only one Old German name, Flozzolf, in which it appears, and Förstemann gives no opinion on it.

Floss. Plumatus.

SIMPLE FORMS.

Old Norse Flosi. English FLOSS. French ? FLOSI.

From the Ang.-Sax. *wadan*, Old High Germ. *watan*, to go, probably in the sense of celerity, Förstemann derives the stem *wad, wat.* The Anglo-Saxon *hwæt*, keen, bold, might intermix, though there does not seem any trace of it in the ancient names. Grimm derives the name of the mythical hero Wada or Wato, from his having, as elsewhere referred to, *waded* over the Grœnasund.

Wad, Wat. Vadere.

SIMPLE FORMS.

Old Germ. Wado, Waddo, Watto, Vato, 6th cent. Ang.-Sax. Wada. Old Norse Vadi. Eng. WADE, WADEY, WADD, WADDY, WATT, WEDD. Modern German WADT, WEHDE. French VADÉ, WATTEAU, VEDY.

DIMINUTIVES.

Old Germ. Wadila, Watil, Vatili, 7th cent.—Ang.-Sax. Weatla—English WADDLE, WATTLE, WATLEY, WEDDELL—

THE OUTER MAN. 413

Mod. Germ. WEDELL—French WATEL, VATEL, VEDEL. Old
Germ. Vadiko, Veduco, 3rd cent.—Eng. WADGE? WEDGE?
Old Germ. Waddolenus, Watlin, 7th cent.—Eng. WADLING,
WATLING—French WATELIN, English WADKIN, WATKIN.
English WATTS—Fries. WATSE.

PHONETIC ENDING.

Old Germ. Vatin, 9th cent. Eng. WADDEN, WATHEN—
French WATIN, VATTON.

COMPOUNDS.

(Gis, hostage) Old German Watgis, 8th cent.—English
WATKISS. *(Gar,* spear) Old German Wadegar, 8th cent.—
English WADDICAR, WATKER. *(Hard)* Old Germ. Wadard,
8th cent.—French VATARD. *(Hari,* warrior) French VATIER.
(Leof, dear) Eng. WADDILOVE. *(Mar,* famous) Old German
Vadomarius, Prince of the Alamanni, 4th cent.—English
WADMORE, WATMORE, WHATMORE—Fr. VATTEMARE. *(Man)*
English WADMAN, WHATMAN, WETMAN. *(New,* young) Old
Germ. Vettani, Wattnj, 8th cent.—English WATNEY. *(Ric,*
power) Old Germ. Wadirih, 9th cent.—French VATRY.

From the Goth. *thragjan,* Ang.-Sax. *thregjan,*
to run, Förstemann derives the following stem,
the sense of which, in the Ang.-Sax. *thræc,* merges
in that of bravery or strength. A cognate Celtic
word seems to be the Obs. Irish *traig,* foot.

SIMPLE FORMS.

Old Germ. Trago, 8th cent. Eng. DRAGE, DRAKE, DRAY,
TRAY. Mod. Germ. DREY. French DRACQ, DRACH, DRÉGE,
DRÉO.

Drag, Trag.
To Run.

DIMINUTIVES.

Old German Dregil, 9th cent. English TRAIL. French
TRÉCOLLE.

PHONETIC ENDING.

Eng. DRAGON, DRAIN, TRAIN. French TRAGIN, TRAJIN,
DRAIN.

COMPOUNDS.

(And, life, spirit) Old Germ. Traganta, 8th cent.—French
TRÉGONT. *(Hard)* French TRÉHARD. *(Hari,* warrior) Eng.
TRAHAR, TRAER—Mod. German TREYER—French TRAGER,
TRAYER. *(Fuss,* foot) French DREYFUS? TREIFOUS?

THE OUTER MAN.

From the Old Norse *bif*, motus, Old Saxon *bivon*, Ang.-Sax. *bifian*, Old High German *biben*, tremere, Förstemann derives the following stem. The sense may probably be that of nimbleness or activity, as in the Old Norse *pipr*, velox, from the same root.

Bib, Biv, Pip. Active.

SIMPLE FORMS.

Old German Bibo, Bebo, Bevo, Pippi, Pipa, 8th cent. Ang.-Sax. Bebba, Pybba. Eng. BIBB, BIBBY, BEBB, PIPE, PIPPY. Mod. Germ. PIPPE. French BIBUS, BIFFE.

DIMINUTIVES.

Ang.-Sax. Piple (found in the name of his grave, Piples beorh, *Cod. Dip.* 774). English BIBLE, BEVILLE, PEPLOE—French BIBAL.

PHONETIC ENDING.

Old Germ. Bibbin, Bivinus, Pippin, 7th cent. Ang.-Sax. Pippen *(found in Pippenes fenne, Cod. Dip.* 1,360). English BEVAN, BIFFIN, PEPIN, PIPPIN. French PEPIN.

COMPOUNDS.

(Hard) English BEFFORD, PEPPARD—Modern German BIPPART, PIPPERT—French BEBERT, BÉFORT, BIBERT, BIVERT, PIPARD, PIVERT. *(Wald,* power) French PIFFAULT, BIBAUT, BIFFAUT.

Clever. Active.

I think that English CLEVER, CLEAVER, and French CLIVER may be the same as our word "clever," though more probably in its original sense, which, I take it, was that of personal activity. We may trace this in the Old English word *clever*, to climb (still retained in Cumberland), from the Old Norse *klifra*, Dutch *klaveren*, *kleveren*, to clamber.* Something of the transition sense seems to be found in the expression of a

---

* I am glad to find this etymology, which I suggested in the previous edition, confirmed by the authority of Mr. Wedgwood.

THE OUTER MAN. 415

horse being "clever at his fences." The English CLEVERLY might be a diminutive, but seems more probably a disused adjective form.

From the Old Norse *klifa*, to climb (of which the above word *klifra* is a frequentative), may be the Eng. CLIVE, CLIFF, and CLEVELEY. Perhaps CLIFT may be added to this group; the Cumberland dialect has *clifty*, active. *Clive, Cliff. Active.*

There are several words in which the sense of activity or sprightliness is allied to that of budding or sprouting. Again, the sense of a sprout or shoot frequently merges into that of spear or dart, as mentioned at p. 207. Thus the Gothic *sprauto*, active, Eng. *spruce* and *sprightly*, Ang.-Saxon *spreot*, sprout, shoot, also spear, pike, Old High German *spriuzan*, English *sprout*, are all from the same root. In the former sense I take the following. *Sprout, Spruce. Sprightly.*

SIMPLE FORMS.
Old Germ. Sprutho, 8th cent. English SPROUT, SPRATT, SPROAT, SPRITT, SPRUCE, SPRICE. Mod. Germ. SPROTTE.

Again, the Old Norse *sprækr* and *spræklegr*, Prov. Eng. *spragg*, *sprack*, *spry*, smart, active, are allied to Ang.-Sax. *sprec*, a shoot. *Sprack, sprightly.*

SIMPLE FORMS.
Spraga, *Lib. Vit.* Eng. SPRAGG, SPRACK, SPARK, SPRECK, SPRIGG, SPRAY, SPRY.

DIMINUTIVES.
Spraclingus, *Lib. Vit.* English SPRACKLIN.

Here also, probably from Old Norse *spræklegr*, come in Sprakaleg, brother of Sweyn, King of Denmark, Eng. SPRECKLEY. Also perhaps Eng.

416   THE OUTER MAN.

SPURCE and SPURGEON, the nearest form to which seems to be the Sansc. *spurj*, to spout, not a bad etymon, by the way, for the name of the well-known preacher.

Another word in which we may perhaps take the bursting forth of water as an emblem of liveliness and activity is *bun*, for which Förstemann finds no suitable etymon, and for which I suggest the Old Norse *buna*, scaturire.

SIMPLE FORMS.

Bun .
To burst
forth.

Old German Bunno, Bunni, Bun, 8th cent. Buna, *Lib. Vit.* English BUNK, BONNEY. French BOUNEAU.

PHONETIC ENDING.

Old Germ. Punin, 8th cent. English BUNYAN. French BUNON.

PATRONYMIC.

English BUNNING. Modern German BÜNNING.

COMPOUNDS.

(*Et*, p. 189) English BUNNETT, PUNNETT—French BUNET, PUNIET. (*Hari*, warrior) English BUNYER. (*Wald*, power) English PUNELT.

From the Old High German *ilan*, festinare, Förstemann derives the following stem. Hence, I take it, the name Ylbod, quoted by Mr. Lower, from the records of Lewes Priory, in the sense of a speedy messenger.

SIMPLE FORMS.

Ile. '
To hasten.

Old Germ. Ilo. Ylla, *Lib. Vit.* Eng. ILEY, EEL, ELEY. Mod. Germ. IHL, IHLE.

COMPOUNDS.

(*Hari*, warrior) Old German Illehere, 8th cent.—English IHLER. (*Man*) English ILLMAN.

From the Old High German *fendo*, foot, are the following.

THE OUTER MAN. 417

SIMPLE FORMS.

Fand, Fant
Foot.

Old German Fanto, Fendio, 8th cent., Modern German FENDT.

DIMINUTIVES.

Old German Fandila, 7th cent.—Eng. FENDALL. Eng. FENDICK.

PHONETIC ENDING.

English FENTON. French FANTON.

COMPOUNDS.

(*Hard*) French FANDARD. (*Hari*, warrior) Eng. FENDER. (*Helm*) Eng. FANTOM, FENTUM. (*May*) Eng. FENTIMAN.

As foot in proper names has the meaning of nimbleness, so hand we may presume to have the meaning of dexterity or skilfulness. The English word handy is in fact formed on just the same principle. A word very liable to intermix is *and*, life, spirit.

SIMPLE FORMS.

Hand, Hant.
Manus.

Old German Hanto, 9th cent. English HAND, HANDEY, HENDY, HENTY. Mod. Germ. HANDT. French HANDUS.

DIMINUTIVES.

English HANDEL, HANDLEY. Modern German HANDEL. French HENDLÉ.

PHONETIC ENDING.

Old Germ. Hantuni, 8th cent. Eng. HANTON, HENDEN, HENTON.

It is difficult to say in what sense the following are derived. The word seems evidently to be, as Förstemann suggests, the Old High Germ. and Old Sax. *wamba*, Ang.-Sax. *wamb*, the belly. Was it by accident that Scott, in the grand story of Ivanhoe, gave a name like this to the jester ?

SIMPLE FORMS.

Wamb.
Belly.

Old German Wamba, king of the West Goths 7th cent., English WAMBEY.

PHONETIC ENDING.

Old Germ. Wambanis (*Genitive*). Eng. WAMPEN.

A 3

418 THE OUTER MAN.

Most of the other names apparently derived from parts of the body, as NECK, CHIN, ARM, THUMM, MOUTH, SHIN, &c., are to be otherwise derived.

There are no inconsiderable number of names which are derived from the period of life. From the Ang.-Sax. *ald, ield*, Old High Germ. *alt, old*, Eng. old, are the following.

Ald, Alt. Old.

SIMPLE FORMS.

Old Germ. Aldo, Alto, 7th cent. Alda, *Lib Vit*. Eng. ALLDAY, ALLT, ALLTY, ELT, OLD, YELD. Mod. Germ. ALT.

DIMINUTIVES.

Aldhysi, Haldisa, *Lib. Vit.* Eng. ALDIS, OLDIS.

PHONETIC ENDING.

Old German Aldini, Altun, 8th cent. English ALDEN, ALTON, ELDEN, ELTON. Mod. Germ. ALTEN. French ALDON.

PATRONYMICS.

Old German Alding, 8th cent. Eng. OLDING. French OLDING.

COMPOUNDS.

(*Bert*, bright) Old Germ. Aldebert, Oldebert, Olbert, 8th cent.—Eng. ALDEBERT—French ALDEBERT, OLBERT. (*Brand*, sword) Old German Altbrand, 8th cent.—French ALBRAND. (*Gan*, magic) Old German Altiganus, 9th cent.—French ALECAN, ALKAN. (*Gar*, spear) Old German Aldegar, 7th cent.—Eng. OLDACRE—French OLACHER. (*Hari*, warrior) Old German Althar, 9th cent.—Aldberi, *Lib. Vit.*—English ALDER—Mod. Germ. ALDER, ALTER. (*Helm*) Old German Althelm, 8th cent.—Ang.-Sax. Aldhelm—English ALDHAM, ELTHAM. (*Roc*) Old German Altroch, 9th cent.—French ALTAROCHE. (*Man*) Old Germ. Aldman, Altman, 8th cent. Aldmon, *Lib. Vit.*—Eng. ALTMAN, OLDMAN—Mod. German ALTMANN. (*Rad*, counsel) Old German Aldrad, 8th cent.— English ALDRED, ELDRED. (*Rit*, ride) Old Germ. Aldarit— English ALDRITT—French ALTERIET. (*Ric*, power) Old Germ. Alderich, Olderich, Altrih, 6th cent.—Eng. ALDRICH,

THE OUTER MAN. 419

ALDRIDGE, ELDRIDGE, OLDRIDGE, ALTREE, OLDRY—French ALTAIRAC. (*Thius*, servant) Old Germ. Aldadeus, 8th cent. —English ALDERDICE?

From the Ang.-Sax. *gamol*, Old Norse *gamal*, Old High German *kamol*, old, are the following. Förstemann has twelve names from this root, but only one corresponding with ours.

SIMPLE FORMS.

English GAMBLE, GEMBLE, GEMMILL, CAMMELL. French CHAMEL?

Gamol. Old.

DIMINUTIVES.

English GAMBLING, GAMLIN. French GAMBELON. Ital. GAMBALUNGA.

COMPOUNDS. -

(*Hari*, warrior) Old Germ. Kamalhere, 8th cent.—Eng. GAMBLER, CAMALARY (*Boston*)—Mod. Germ. KAMLER.

A not uncommon name among the Northmen was Eylífr, which seems to be from Old Norse *eylífr*, ever-living.* It was undoubtedly baptismal, for one of the men in the Landnamabok is surnamed " the young." Hence may be English AYLIFFE, perhaps French ELOFFE. A similar name seems to be the Langlif in the Liber Vitæ.

From the Old High German *jung*, *junc*, Ang.-Sax. *jong*, *jung*, *gung*, *ging*, English *young*, are the following.

SIMPLE FORMS.

Old Germ. Jungo, Junggi, 10th cent. English YOUNG. Mod. Germ. JUNG, JÜNKE. French JUNG, YUNC.

Young, Jung Juvenis.

DIMINUTIVES.

English GINGELL. French JUNCAL, GUNCKEL.

COMPOUNDS.

(*Aud*, prosperity) French GINAUD. (*Hari*, warrior) Eng. YOUNGER, GINGER—Mod. Germ. JUNGHER—Fr. JONCHERY,

---

* Another derivation perhaps might however be suggested—see p. 210.

420 THE OUTER MAN.

(or all these same as English younker ?) *(Man)* Old Germ. Yungman, 9th cent.—English YOUNGMAN—Modern German JUNGMANN. Old Germ. Jungericus, Gothic king, 4th cent.—Mod. Germ. JÜNGERICH.

There is a stem *jun*, which Förstemann thinks may perhaps be the older form of *jung*, supposing a contraction of *juvan* (Latin juvenis).

SIMPLE FORMS.

Jun.
Young?

Old. Germ. Juno, Junno, 8th cent. Eng. JUNE, JUNIO.* French JUNY, JOUNNEAUX.

COMPOUNDS.

(Hard) Old Germ. Joonard, 11th cent.—French JONNARD, JONNART. *(Hari,* warrior) Eng. JUNNER—French JONIÉRE. *(Wald,* power) French JOUNAULT.

There is a stem *new, ny*, which Grimm and Weinhold take to be from the Old High German *naw, niwi*, Ang.-Saxon *new*, Dan. and Swed. *ny*, Sanscrit *nava*, new. The meaning they take to be that of "young," as in the Greek ; and in the names of women, to which as a termination, this root is confined, Grimm supposes a Goth. *nivi*, in the sense of virgin. Förstemann considers that the form *ny* is more particularly a Bavarian, and perhaps also a Lombard form. It is, however, also Scandinavian.

SIMPLE FORMS.

Niv, New,
Ny.
Young.

Old German Niwo, Nivo, Nivi, Nevo, Nibo, 7th cent. English NEW, NEWEY, NAY, NEVE, NIAVI. Mod. German NEUE, NEY. French NEU, NEY, NÉE, NÈVE, NAEF, NAVEAU, NIVEAU.

DIMINUTIVES.

English NEWICK. English NEWLING—French NOULIN.

PHONETIC ENDING.

English NEWEN, NEVIN, NAVIN.

---

* A Boston surname—English ?

THE OUTER MAN. 421

COMPOUNDS.

(*Cum, quum*, guest, stranger) Neucum (*Domesday*)—Eng. NEWCOME, NEWCOMB. (*Ger*, spear) French NEWIGER, NÉGRE? (*Hard*) Old Germ. Niviard, Nivard, 6th cent.—Mod. Germ. NEUWERT—French NIVARD, NIVERT, NIBART, NIARD. (*Hari*, warrior) French NIVIÉRE, NAVIER. (*Leof*, dear) English NEWLOVE.* (*Man*) Eng. NEWMAN—Mod. Germ. NIEMANN —French NEYMAN. (*Rat*, counsel) Old Germ. Niwirat, 9th cent.—Old Norse Nyráthr—Mod. Germ. NEURATH—French NEYRET. (*Reid*, ride) Old Norse Nereidr—English NEROD. (*Ric*, power) Old Germ. Niwerich—French NEYREY, NAVRY. (*Wald*, power) French NIBAULT, NAVAULT.

There is a stem *bob, bov, bop*, &c., which Förstemann refers to Germ. *bube*, Dutch *boef, boeve*, boy. The word *bube* is not found in the German language prior to the 13th cent., but there is no doubt about the antiquity of the root, which is cognate with Lat. *pupus, pupillus*, &c. Mr. Wedgwood observes that " the origin seems the root *bob, bub, pop, pup*, in the sense of something protuberant, stumpy, thick, and short." If this, however, be the case, it suggests that the meaning in proper names might be akin to '*boss, buss*, &c., p. 408.

SIMPLE FORMS.

Bob, Bop. Boy. *

Old German Bobo, Bobbo, Boppo, Poppo, Bubo, Pupo, Poupo, Poapo, Popi, Bovo, Bova, Boffo, 6th cent. Anglo-Saxon Bubba. Boffa, *Lib. Vit.* English BOVEY, BOVAY, BOFF, BOFFEY, BUBB, BUBA, POPE, POPPY, POVEY, PUPP. Mod. German BOBBE, BOPP, BUBE, POPP, PUPPE. French BOBÉE, BŒUF.

DIMINUTIVES.

Old German Bobilo, Bovilo, Popila, Popili, 8th cent.— Eng. BOVILLE, POPLE, POFLEY—Mod. Germ. BOBEL, POPEL

---

* New, in the sense of young, gives a sufficiently expressive meaning to this name, without supposing a gay Lothario in the case.

422 THE OUTER MAN.

—French Bouville, Povel, Pupil, Populus. Mod. Germ. Pupke—French Bubeck. English Bobkin, Popkin—Mod. German Popken. Old German Bobolin, 6th cent.—French Popelin. Eng. Poplett, Puplet—Fr. Boblet, Bouvelet.

PHONETIC ENDING.

Old German Bobin, 6th cent. English Bobbin, Buffin, Poupin. French Bobin, Boffin, Bouvin, Buffon, Popon.

COMPOUNDS.

(*And*, life, spirit) French Bobant. (*Et*, p. 189) Pobbidi, *Lib. Vit.*—English Bobbitt—French Bobot, Buffet, Popet. (*Hard*) Buffard, *Roll Batt. Abb.*—Eng. Bobart, Poupard, Poupart—Mod. Germ. Bobardt—Fr. Bouvard, Popard. (*Hari*, warrior) Eng. Bouvier, Bouverie, Buffrey— French Bobiére, Bouvier, Bouvry, Buffier, Pupier. (*Ulf*, wolf) English ? Popoff—French Boboeuf. (*Wald*, power) French Buffault.

From the Ang.-Saxon *cnapa*, German *knabe*, boy, may be the following. The suggestion of Mr. Wedgwood (see last page) that the origin of Old Germ. *bube*, Eng. *boy*, is "the sense of something protuberant, stumpy, thick, and short," is strongly confirmed by this root, which is cognate with English *knob*, a lump. And therefore, as in the case of the last root, the meaning might possibly be like that of *boss*, see p. 408.

SIMPLE FORMS.

Knab, Knap. Boy.
Old German Hnabi, 8th cent. English Knapp, Nabb, Knope. Mod. German Knabb, Knapp. French Naba ? Naef ?

DIMINUTIVE.
English Napkin.

PATRONYMIC.
English Knapping.

COMPOUND.
(*Man*) English Knapman.

From the Goth., Old High Germ., Old Norse *barn*, Anglo-Saxon *bearn*, child, may be the following.

THE OUTER MAN. 423

SIMPLE FORMS.
English BARNEY. French BARNAY.
DIMINUTIVE,
French BARNICH.

COMPOUNDS.

(*Hard*) Old Germ. Barnard, 9th cent.—Eng. BARNARD—
Mod. Germ. BARNHARD. (*Et*, p. 189) English BARNETT—
French BARNET. (*Hari*, warrior) French BARNIER. (*Wine*,
friend) Old Germ. Barnuin, 9th cent.—French BARNOUVIN.

*Barn.
Child.*

There is a stem *kim, chim,* which Förstemann
refers to Old High German *kim, chim,* germen.
None of the ancient names correspond with ours.

SIMPLE FORMS.
English KIMM. French CHIMAY.

DIMINUTIVES. .
French CHIMEL. English CHIMLEN.

COMPOUNDS.

(*New, ny,* young) English CHIMNEY—French CHIMÈNE.
(*Hari,* warrior) French CHEMERY.

*Kim, Chim.
Germen.*

Another stem of somewhat similar meaning
may be *sab, sap, saf, sav.* Förstemann refers to
a supposed Goth. *safjan,* adduced by Grimm, in
the sense of the Lat. *sapere.* It is not, however,
easy to see any suitable meaning for proper names
in that root, and I would rather, in the absence
of any better explanation, take the Ang.-Sax. *sap,*
Old High Germ. *saf,* Eng. "sap," in the sense of
youth, growth, viridity.

SIMPLE FORMS.

Sabas, a Goth, 4th cent. · Saba,* also called Saebeorht,
an Anglo-Saxon prince (*Bede's Ecc. Hist.*) English SABEY,
SAPP, SAFE. French SAPY, SAPIA, SAVY, SAUVE? SAUVÉ?
SAUVEY?

*Sab, Sav,
Sap,
Youth,
Viridity.*

424 THE OUTER MAN.

DIMINUTIVES.

Old German Sabulo, Savalo, 7th cent.—English SABLE, SAFFELL, SAVELL, SAVEALL—Fr. SAUVEL. Eng. SABBAGE, SAVIDGE, SAVAGE—French SAPICHA, SAUPIQUE, SAUVAGE. Eng. SAPLIN—French SABLON, SAVELON..

PHONETIC ENDING.

Eng. SABINE, SAPHIN. French SABBINI, SAPIN, SAVIGNY, SAVIN.

COMPOUNDS.

(*Aud*, prosperity) Old Germ. Sapaudus, 9th cent.—Fr. SABAUD. Perhaps also to this Old German Sapato—French SABOT, SAVIT. *(Hard)* English SAFFORD—Mod. German SAVERT—Fr. SABART, SAVARD, SAVART. (*Hari*, warrior) Eng. SAPPER—Mod. Germ. SAPHIR (see p. 4)—Fr. SAUPHAR, SAUVIER, SAUVEUR? (*Ron*, raven) Eng. SAFRAN—French SABRAN, SAVARIN, SOUVERAIN? (*Ric*, power) Old German Sabaricus, Savarich, Safrach (Gothic leader, 4th cent.), Saffarius—Savari, *Lib. Vit.*—Eng. SAVERICK, SAVORY, SAFFERY —French SAVARY, SAFFRAY, SAUFFROY.

Probably to the above group may be placed Eng. SAPTE, which shews the Old Norse, Danish, and Mod. Germ. form *saft*, taking a *t*.

The following stem may be referred to the Mod. Germ. *grob*, Dan. *grov*, coarse, clumsy. But I think that the original meaning may probably have only been that of large stature. Compare English *gross*, in a similarly changed sense—also Eng. *plump*, which in German and Danish means coarse. Förstemann has only one Old German name Griubinc, which he does not explain.

SIMPLE FORMS.

Grob, Grove.
Stout?

Anglo-Saxon Grobb, *(found in Grobbes den, Cod. Dip.* 1066). Eng. GROBE, GROVE, GRUBB, GRUBY, CROPP? Mod.

---

* Mr. Kemble considers Saba to be only a familiar or abbreviated form of Saebeorht.

THE OUTER MAN.

425

German Gröbe, Grobe. French Grub, Gruby, Crobey, Croppi?

DIMINUTIVES.

Mod. Germ. Gröbel. French Grouvelle.

COMPOUNDS.

(*Hari*, warrior) Eng. Grover, Cropper? (*Man*) Eng. Groffman.

B 3

CHAPTER XXIII.

THE INNER MAN.

As the baptismal name was conferred by the fond parent, and the surname by the impartial world—so there is more truth in the latter than in the former. They represent the honest opinion which a man's neighbour had of him, and are complimentary or otherwise, as the case may be. There are forty-two men in the Landnamabok of Iceland having Helgi (holy), as a baptismal name, but only three that had acquired it as a surname. And of the former there was one who had the surname of Gudlaus—"Holy the Godless." What a bitter satire!

Seeing then, as will be manifest from the following, how great is the preponderance of baptismal names, we cannot in any degree admit the evidence of proper names as a test even of the accredited virtue of ancient times.

Beginning with the name of "Holy" already referred to—so easy to assume and so difficult to deserve—we have the following. This word however is liable to intermix with two others, Ang.-Sax. *hál,* sound, hale, and *hæle,* hero.

Halic, Halley. Holy.

SIMPLE FORMS.

Old German Halicho, Halec, 8th cent. Eng. HOLLICK, HALLEY. Mod. Germ. HALLICH, HEILIG. French HAILIG, HALLEY, HALLU, HÉLY.

DIMINUTIVE.

English HALLILEY, HOLLALEY. French ALELY.

THE INNER MAN. 427

COMPOUNDS.

(*Bert*, bright) Old Germ. Halacbert, Helihpret, 8th cent.
—Halgeberct, *Lib. Vit.*—Eng. HALLOWBREAD, HALBERT?
(*Dag*, day) Old Germ. Halegdag, 9th cent.—Eng. HALLIDAY,
HOLLIDAY. (*Ger*, spear) Old Germ. Heligher, 9th cent.—
Eng. HOLKER—French HOLACHER. (*Man*) Eng. HOLEYMAN,
HOLLIMAN—Mod. Germ. HEILIGMANN. (*Rat*, red, counsel)
Old Germ. Halegred, 9th cent.—French ALIGROT. (*Wig*, *wi*,
war) Old Germ. Heilagwih, 9th cent.—English HALLOWAY,
HOLLOWAY—French HALEVY.

From the Ang.-Sax. *dugan*, Old High Germ.
tugan, to be virtuous, good, honourable ; Anglo-
Saxon *theaw*, Old High German *dau*, morals,
behaviour, are probably the following.

SIMPLE FORMS.

Old Germ. Tugus, Tukko, Docca, Tocca, Dauo, 8th cent.
Old Norse Toui. Ang.-Sax. Tuk, *in a grant to the monastery
of Croyland, A.D.* 1,051. Tocca, *Lib. Vit.* English TUGGY,
TUCK, TUKE, TUCKEY, DUCK, DOKE, DOCK, DUKE, TOW, TOE,
DOW, DOWEY, DOE, DEW, DEWEY. Modern German TOCK,
TUCH, DUCKE, DAU, DEWE. French TOCHE, DOCHE, DUC,
DOUÉ, DIEU.

(margin: Dug, Dow. Virtue.)

DIMINUTIVES.

Old German Dauwila, Dewila, 9th cent.—Eng. DOWELL,
DEWELL, DULY, TOWELL—Fr. DUCEL, DUGELAY, DOUELLE,
DOUILLY. Old Germ. Dugiliu, 8th cent.—Eng. DUCKLING,
DOWLING—French DULONG. Eng. DEWICK—French DUICK.

PHONETIC ENDING.

Old Germ. Dawin, 8th cent. Eng. DUGGIN, DUDGEON,
DEWEN. French DUGENNE, DUQUIN.

PATRONYMICS.

English DOCKING, DEWING. French DUCOING.

COMPOUNDS.

(*Et, p.* 189) English DUCKETT, DOGGETT—Fr. DUQUET,
DOUET, TUGOT. (*Hard*) Eng. DUGARD, TOWART, TEWART—
French DUGARD, TOUGART, TOUCART. (*Hari*, warrior) Eng.
DUCKER, DOCKER, TUCKER, TOKER, DOWER, DEWAR, TOWER
—Mod. German DÜKHER, TUCHER—Fr. DUCHER, DUCOROY,

428

THE INNER MAN.

Douare. *(Land)* Eng. Dowland—Fr. Dugland. *(Man)* Old Germ. Dugiman, Tugeman, 9th cent.—Eng. Tugman, Duckman—French Dewamin, Dumain. *(Mar, famous)* Old German Daumerus, 6th cent.—Eng. Dugmore. *(Ulf, wolf)* Old Germ. Tugolf, Touwolf, Daulf, 7th cent.—Fr. Dewulf. *(Wald, power)* Eng. Dugald—French Tugault, Douault. *(Wealh, stranger)* Eng. Dugwell, Tugwell, Tuckwell.

DOUBTFUL NAMES.

Eng. Dugood, Toogood, Towgood. Perhaps from Ang.-Sax. *duguth,* virtuous, honourable.

From the Ang.-Sax. *dafan,* Gothic *gadaban,* convenire, Ang.-Sax. *dêfe,* fit, proper, Förstemann derives the stem *dab, daf, dap,* to which also I place *dav,* referred by him to the preceding root. The scriptural name David may probably intermix in some of the following.

Dab, Daf. Seemly.

SIMPLE FORMS.

Old Germ. Davo, 9th cent. Eng. Dabb, Dapp, Daffy, Tapp, Tappy, Davy, Devey. Fr. Dabeau, Dabée, Dappe, Dapy, Daffy, Davy, Devy, Devay, Taveau.

DIMINUTIVES.

Old German Dafila, Davila, 7th cent.—English Davall, Deffell—French Daval, Deville, Tavel. Eng. Taplin, Devlin—French Dablin. Old Germ. Tabuke, 11th cent. Eng. Davock, Davidge, Devick—Fr. Davach, Devicque.

PHONETIC ENDING.

English Daven, Devon, Tappin. Fr. Davin, Devenne, Taffin, Tapin.

COMPOUNDS.

(Hard) Eng. Dafford—Fr. Dabert, Devert, Tavard. *(Ram, ran,* raven) Eng. Tabram, Daviron—French Dabrin, Daveron. *(Ric, power)* Old Germ. Daperich, 10th cent.— French Dafrique. *(Wald, power)* Old Germ. Tavold, 10th cent.—French Davault.

From the Gothic *triggws,* Old Norse *triggr,* Ang.-Sax. *treowe,* Old High German *driu,* Mod.

THE INNER MAN. 429

Germ. *treu*, Eng. "true," may be the following. But this stem is very apt to intermix with *driuqan*, militari, p. 195.

SIMPLE FORMS.

Old Germ. Driwa. Old Norse Tryggo, King of Norway. English Trigg, Trickey, Tree, Troy, Try, Dry. French Triché, Triau, Try, Driou.

Trigg, Try. True.

COMPOUNDS.

(*Bert*, bright) French Triebert, Trubert. (*Et*, p. 189) Eng. Trickett, Drewett—French Triquet, Tricot. (*Hard*) French Tricard. (*Hari*, warrior) Eng. Trigger, Tricker, Dryer—French Triger, Drier. (*Leof*, dear) Eng. True-love. (*Wald*, power) French Druault.

DOUBTFUL NAMES.

English Truefitt. French Triefus, Dreyfus. Perhaps from Ang.-Sax. *fôt*, Old High Germ. *fuaz*, Mod. Germ. *fuss*, English foot.

There is a word *just*, found in some German compounds, which Förstemann seems to think may be from the Latin. However, the French *jouste*, tilt, tournament, of which the Old Flemish *just*, impetus (whence also Eng. "jostle"), seems to be the origin, may be mentioned. None of the ancient names correspond with the following.

SIMPLE FORMS.

English Just, Justey. French Juste, Jost.

Just.

COMPOUNDS.

(*Mund*, protection) English Justamond (*wrangler* 1750). (*Wald*, power) French Justault.

There is a stem *fid*, which Förstemann thinks, unless the few ancient names be corruptions either of *frid*, peace, or of *faid*, hostility, may be from the Latin *fidus*, faithful. The following names

430 THE INNER MAN.

go to shew that there is such a stem, but the Ang.-Saxon *fittan,* to sing, also to dispute, might also be proposed.

Fid.
Faithful.

SIMPLE FORMS.

Old German Fidis, 11th cent. English FIDDEY, FIDOE, FITT. French FITTE, FITY.

DIMINUTIVES.

Old Germ. Fidolus, 6th cent.—Eng. FIDELL—Mod. Germ. FIDALL—French FIDELE? Eng. FITKIN.

COMPOUNDS.

(*Hari,* warrior) Eng. FITTER—French FIDERY. (*Man*) English FIDDAMAN, FITMAN. (*Mund,* protection) English FIDDAMENT.

From the Ang.-Sax. *sôth,* true, Eng. " sooth," of which the Gothic form would be *sanths,* and the Old High German *sand,* (though neither of these are preserved,) Förstemann derives the stem *sand, sants.* The Anglo-Saxon *sand,* messenger, seems a word which might intermix, and which indeed in some cases I have taken in preference. Förstemann includes also *sod* as a Saxon, and *sad* as a West Frankish and Lombard form.

Sand, Sad.
True

SIMPLE FORMS.

Old German Sando, Sadi, 8th cent. English SANDOE, SANDY, SANT, SANTY, SADD, SODO, SODDY. Mod. German SAND, SANDT. French SANDEAU, SANTI.

DIMINUTIVES.

Old German Sanzo, 9th cent.—English SANS, SANDS, SANDYS—Mod. Germ. SANTZ—French SANCE, SANDOZ. Eng. SANDELL, SANTLEY—French SANZEL. French SANDELION.

COMPOUNDS.

(*Hari,* warrior) Old German Sandheri, Santher, 8th cent. —Eng. SANDER,* SANTER—Mod. Germ. SANDER, SANTER— French SANDRÉ, SANTERRE. (*Man*) English SANDMAN.

---

* Most of the English writers, and some of the German, as Pott, make Sander a contraction of Alexander

THE INNER MAN. 431

(*Ric*, power) Old Germ. Sandrih, 9th cent.—French SANTRY. (*War*, defence) English SANDWER. (*Ulf*, wolf) Old German Sandolf—Mod. Germ. SANDHOFF.

PHONETIC ENDING.
Eng. SANDEN, SODDEN. Mod. Germ. SANDEN.

PHONETIC INTRUSION OF *r*.
(*Hari*, warrior) Old Germ. Sandrehar, 8th cent.—French SANDRIER.

From the Ang.-Sax. *sïdu*, Old High German *situ*, Mod. German *sitte*, manners, morals, may be the following. The sense, according to the usual rule in proper names, must be that of good manners or morals.

SIMPLE FORMS.
Old German Sito, Sita, 9th cent. Sido, king of Suevia in Tacitus. English SIDE, SIDEY, CITY. Modern German SITTE. Dutch SEYDE. French SITT.

Sid, Sit. Manners.

DIMINUTIVES.
Old German Situli, 8th cent.—Ang.-Sax. Sidel *(found in Sidelesham, Cod. Dip. 464)*—Eng. SIDDELL—Mod. Germ. SEYDEL—French SIDOLI, SITTELL, SEDILLE. Old German Sitilin, 8th cent.—French SEDILLON. English SIDDONS.

PHONETIC ENDING.
Eng. SIDDEN, SITTON, SIDNEY. French SIDNEY.

COMPOUND.
(*Ger*, spear) English SIDGEAR.

Of somewhat similar meaning may be the following, which Förstemann refers to Old Norse *skicka*, ordinare, and the noun *schick*, used in many Low German dialects in the sense of order.

SIMPLE FORMS.
Old Germ. Scih, 11th cent. English SHICK, SKY. Mod. Germ. SCHICK.

Shick. Order, propriety.

DIMINUTIVE.
English SHICKLE.

432 THE INNER MAN.

From the Old High Germ. *ercan*, Áng.-Sax., *eorcen*,[*] genuine, pure, Förstemann derives the following stem.

Ercen.
Pure.

SIMPLE FORMS.

Old German Ercan, 10th cent. Mod. German HERKEN. French ARQUIN.

COMPOUNDS.

(*Bald*, bold) Old Germ. Ercanbald, Arcambald, Archambald, 8th cent.—Eng. ARCHAMBAUD—French ARCHAMBAULT —Ital. ARCIMBOLDI (*of Milan*). (*Hard*) Old Germ. Ercanhart, 8th cent.—French ARCHINARD. (*Heid*, state, condition) Old Germ. Ercanheid, 9th cent.—Eng. HARKNETT. (*Hari*, warrior) Old German Erkanher, 8th cent.—Mod. German HERKNER—French ERCKENER.

There are several words having the meaning of life, zeal, spirit, though the sense is often difficult to separate from that of bodily activity. From the Old High Germ. *ando*, zelus, Förstemann derives the following stem, which is, however, very liable to intermix with two others, *hand*, manus, and Ang.-Sax. *ent*, giant.

And, Ant.
Life, spirit.

SIMPLE FORMS.

Old German Ando, Anto, 7th cent. Ang.-Saxon Anta, (*found in Antan hláw, Cod. Dip.* 150). Eng. AND, ANDOE. Mod. Germ. ENDE. French ANTY.

DIMINUTIVES.

Old German Antecho, 10th cent.—French ANTIQ. Old German Andala, 5th cent.—English ANTILL, ANTLEY. Old Germ. Andolenus, 8th cent.—English ANDLAN.

COMPOUNDS.

(*Helm*) English ANTHEM—French ANTHEAUME. (*Hari*, warrior) Old German Antheri, Anter, 9th cent.—French ANTIER. (*Rad*, counsel) Old German Andrad, 8th cent.— Eng. ANDRADE, HANDRIGHT. . (*Ric*, dominion) Old German Andarich, 5th cent.—English ANTRIDGE—Mod. German ENTRICH.

---

[*] Perhaps the stem *aro*, p. 387, may be a simple form of the above.

THE INNER MAN. 433

From the Old High German *zila*, English *zeal*, are the following.

SIMPLE FORMS.

Old German Zilo, Zello, 8th cent. Eng. ZEALL, ZEALEY. Mod. Germ. ZIEHLE. French ? ZELLE.

Zeal.

COMPOUNDS.

(*Ger*, spear) Old German Cilger, 10th cent.—French ZELGER. (*Hari*, warrior) French ZEILLER, ZELLER. (*Man*) Old German Ciliman, 8th cent.—English SILLIMAN ?—Mod. German ZILLMANN.

From the Old High German *gern*, eager, are probably the following.

SIMPLE FORMS.

Old German Cherno, Kerne. Gurnay, *Roll Batt. Abb.* English GURNEY, CHIRNEY, CURNO, CORNEY. Mod. German GERN, KERN. French JOURNÉ, CORNAY.

Gern, Kern, Eager.

DIMINUTIVES.

English GURNELL, CORNELL—French CORNELY, CORNILLEAU. Eng. CURNICK, CORNICK. French CORNICHON. Mod. Germ. GERNLEIN—French CORNILLON.

PATRONYMICS.

English CORNING. Mod. Germ. GERNING.

COMPOUNDS.

(*Bert*, famous) French CORNIBERT. (*Hard*, fortis) Eng. GURNARD—Mod. Germ. GERNHARDT. (*Hari*, warrior) Eng. GURNER, KIRNER, CORNER—Mod. Germ. GERNER, KÖRNER—French CURNIER. (*Man*) Old Germ. Gerneman, 9th cent.—Eng. CORNMAN—Mod. Germ. KERNMANN. (*Wald*, power) Old Germ. Gernolt, 9th cent.—French JOURNAULT.

There are several words which have the meaning of joy, mirth, cheerfulness. From the Old High Germ. *mandjan*, gaudere, *mendi*, gaudium, Förstemann derives the following stem. As a termination it is very liable to intermix with *man*, homo. The form *mance, mence*, seems to be High German.

C 3

434

THE INNER MAN.

Mand,
Mance.
Joy.

SIMPLE FORMS.

Old German Manto, Manzo, Manso, 8th cent. English MANT, MANDY, MENDAY, MANNSE, MENCE. Mod. German MANDT, MENDE, MANZ, MENSE. Fr. MANTEAU, MANCEAU, MANSEY.

DIMINUTIVES.

Mantel, *Domesday*—Mauntel, Mancel, *Hund. Rolls.*— Eng. MANDLE, MANTLE—Mod. Germ. MENTZEL, MENZEL— —Fr. MANDELL, MENTEL, MANCEL. Eng. MENDES—French MANDOUCE, MENDEZ, MANSOZ—Spanish MENDEZ, MENDOZA.

PHONETIC ENDING.

Old Germ. Mantoni (*genitive*), 9th cent. Eng. MANTON. French MANDON, MANTION, MENTION, MANSON ? MANSION ?

COMPOUNDS.

(*Hard*) French MANSARD. (*Hari*, warrior) Eng. MANDER, MANCER, MENSER.

The word *spil* is not quite certain. Förstemann gives it the meaning of joy (which it had in Old Norse), in preference to that of play, as in the German *spielen*. The Gothic *spillon*, Old Norse *spiala*, to relate, discourse, is also suitable.

Spil.
Joy.

SIMPLE FORMS.

Eng. SPILL. Mod. Germ. SPIEL. French ? SPILL.

PATRONYMIC.

English SPILLING.

COMPOUNDS.

(*Hard*) Old Germ. Spilihard, Spilhard, 8th . cent.—Eng. SPILLARD. (*Hari*, warrior) Eng. SPILLER, SPELLAR—Mod. Germ. SPIELER—French ? SPILLER. (*Man*) Eng. SPILLMAN, SPELMAN— Mod. Germ. SPIELMANN.

The stem *glad* also seems to me rather uncertain. It might be from *glad*, lætus, or it might be from Old Norse *gledia*, to polish, Mod. German *glatt,* Danish *glat*, Dutch *glad*, smooth, polished. In that case the sense might probably

THE INNER MAN. 435

be that of · personal beauty, as referred ,to in chapter 22.

SIMPLE FORMS.

Old Germ. Cletto, 8th cent. Eng. GLAD, CLAD, GLIDE, GLEED. Mod. German GLADE.

Glad.
Lætus ?

DIMINUTIVES.

English GLADDELL, GLEADALL. Eng. GLADDISH—Mod. German GLADISCH.

PHONETIC ENDING.

English GLADDEN, GLIDDON. French GLATIGNY.

PATRONYMICS.

English GLADDING. French GLADUNG, CLADUNG.

COMPOUNDS.

(*Hard*) French GLATARD. (*Man*) English GLADMAN. (*Wine*, friend) Gladewinus, *Domesday*—English GLADWIN. (*Wis*, sapiens) Gledewis, *Lib. Vit.*—Eng. GLADWISH ?

There is a stem *fag*, which Förstemann takes to be the simple form of Ang.-Sax. *fægen*, Eng. fain, as shewn in Goth. *fahêds*, joyfulness.

SIMPLE FORMS.

Old German Facco, 9th cent. Feg, Fech, *Domesday.* Fag, *Hund. Rolls.* English FAGG, FAKE, FAY, FAHEY. Mod. German FACK, FECKE. French FAGE, FÈGE, FÈCHE, FAYE, FAHY.

Fag.
Joyful.

DIMINUTIVES.

Old German Fachilo, Fagala, 11th cent. English FAIL. French FAGEL, FAYOLLE, FAILLE.

COMPOUNDS.

(*Et*, p. 189) Eng. FAGGOTS*—French FAGET, FAQUET, FAYET. (*Hard*) French FAGARD, FAYARD. (*Hari*, warrior) Old Germ. Fagher—Eng. FAKER—French FAGUER.

EXTENDED FORM=ENG. FAIN.

Eng. FAGAN, FACHNEY, FEHON. French FAJON, FAIN.

Fagin,
Fain.

COMPOUNDS.

(*Hard*) French FEINERT. (*Hari*, warrior) French FAGNIER, FECHNER, FEINER.

---

* May possibly represent the Gothic *fahêds*, joyfulness.

436 THE INNER MAN.

From the Ang.-Saxon *gamian,* to play, sport, English "game," may be the following. Or the meaning may rather be that of joyfulness, as in Old High German *gaman,* Anglo-Saxon *gamen,* gaudium.

Gam, Cam.
Gaudium.

SIMPLE FORMS.

Old German Gammo, Cammo, 7th cent. Gam, Game, (*Domesday*). English GAME, CAMM. Mod. German GAMM, KAMM. French GAME, GAIME, CAM, JAM, JAME, JAMEAU.

DIMINUTIVES.

Eng. GAMMAGE, CAMMEGH—French GAMACHE. French GAMICHON.

COMPOUNDS.

(*Hard*) Old German Gamard, 7th cent.—Mod. German GAMMERT—French GAMARD, GAIMARD, CAMARD. (*Hari,* warrior) Old German Gamer, 9th cent.—Eng. GAMER (17th cent.)—Mod. Germ. KAMMER—French CAMIER. (*Rit,* ride) Old Germ. Gamarit, 8th cent.—French CAMARET. (*Wald,* power) French JAMAULT.

Gamen.
Gaudium.

EXTENDED FORM=ANG.-SAX. GAMEN.

Old German Gaman. English GAMMON. Mod. German GAMANN. French GAMEN, JAMIN, CAMIN.

From the Old Norse *gæla,* exhilirare, Old High German *geil,* elatus, Anglo-Saxon *galan,* to sing,* may be the following.

Gale.
Elatus.

SIMPLE FORMS.

Old German Gailo, Gelo, Geli, Cailo, 8th cent. Gale, Calle, *Hund. Rolls.* English GALE, GALEY, GALL, GALLY, GALLOW, CALE, CALEY, CALLOW, GELL, JELL, JELLEY, KELL, KELLY, KELLOW. Modern German GAYL, GEHL, KEHL. French GALLE, GALLÉ, GALLY, GELLE, GELLÉ, JAL, JALEY, CAILLE, CAILLEAU.

---

* Förstemann separates the two stems, *gale* and *gall,* which, however, as being, I take it, from the same root, and moreover in modern names impossible to separate, I put together.

THE INNER MAN.

DIMINUTIVES.

Old Germ. Geliko, Jeliko, 10th cent.—English JELLICOE, KELLOCK—Mod. Germ. GEILICH. English JELLIS, JEALOUS, GALLOWS ? KELSEY—French GALISSE, GELLEZ, CAILLIEZ. Eng. CALKIN—French GALICHON. Eng. GALILEE—French CAILLELAU—Ital. GALILEO ?

PHONETIC ENDING.

Old Germ. Gailin, 8th cent. Galun, *Hund. Rolls.* Eng. GALLON, GELLAN. Fr. GALINO, GALON, JAILLON, CAILLON, CALLON.

PATRONYMICS.

French GELLYNCK—Ital. GALLENGA.

COMPOUNDS.

(And, life, spirit) Galaunt, *Hund. Rolls.*—Eng. GALLAND, GALLANT, KELLAND—French GALAND, GALANT, JAILLANT, CAILLANT. *(Bert,* bright) French GALABERT, JALLIBERT. *(Bot.* envoy) Eng. GALBOT—French GAILHABAUD, CAILLE-BOTTE, CALLEBAUT. *(Burg,* protection) Old Germ. Cheilpurc, 9th cent.—French GALLIBOUR, GALIBOURG. *(Drud,* dear) Old Germ. Kaildrud, 8th cent.—French GAILDRAUD. *(Fred,* peace) Old Germ. Galafred, 9th cent.—Ang.-Saxon Galfrid, Gaufrid—English GEOFFRY—French GALOFFRE, JEOFFROY, GAULOFRET. *(Ger,* spear) English GALLAGER—Mod. Germ. GALLIGER—French GALICHER. *(Hard)* Gallard, *Hund. Rolls.*—English GAYLEARD, GALLARD, GELLARD, KELLORD— Mod. Germ. KAHLERT—French GAILLARD, JAILLARD, CAIL-LARD. *(Hari,* warrior) Eng. GAYLER, GALLERY, GELLER— Mod. Germ. KEHLER—French CALLIER, CAILLER, CAILLIER, CALLERY. *(Lind,* mild) Old German Geilindis, 8th cent.— Eng. GALINDO. *(Rat,* counsel) Old Germ. Gailrat, Keylrat, 8th cent.—Fr. JALLERAT, CALARET. *(Sind,* via) Old Germ. Geilsind, 8th cent.—French GALLISSANT. *(Wald,* power) French CAILLAULT. *(Wig, wi,* war) Old German Geilwih, Keilwih, 8th cent.—Galewey, Galaway, *Hund. Rolls.*—Eng. GALLOWAY, CALLAWAY, KELLAWAY—Fr. JALVY, CAILLOUÉE.

From the Ang.-Saxon *singan,* to sing, *sang, sanc,* song, may be the following. Förstemann mentions also Ang.-Sax. *sinc,* treasure.

438

THE INNER MAN.

Sang, Sing.
Cantare.

SIMPLE FORMS.

Old Germ. Sancho, 8th cent.   English SANG, SANKEY, SHANK ? SHANKEY ?   Mod. Germ. SANCKE, SENKE.

DIMINUTIVES.

Eng. SINGLE—French SENGEL, SINGLY.   Fr. SANCHEZ, SINGES.

COMPOUNDS.

(*Hari*, warrior) Old German Singar, 8th cent.—English SINGER, SINKER—Fr. SINGER, SINGERY.   (*Ward*, guardian) ·French SANGOUARD.   (*Wine*, friend) Eng. SANGWIN—French SANGOUIN.

Another stem of similar meaning seems to be *gid*, Ang.-Sax. *gidd*, a poem, *giddian*, to sing.

Gid.
Cantare.

SIMPLE FORMS.

Old Germ. Giddo, 9th cent.   Cyda, *Lib. Vit.*   English GIDDY, KIDDY, KIDD, KITT, KITTY, KITTO, CHITTY ?   Fr. GIDE, GITEAU.

DIMINUTIVES.

Old Germ. Chitell ?—English GIDLEY, GIDLOW, KIDDLE, KITTLE, CHIDELL ? CHITTLE ?—French GIDEL.   English CHITTOCK.

PHONETIC ENDING.

Eng. GIDDEN, KIDNEY.   French GITTON.

COMPOUNDS.

(*Ger*, spear) English KIDGER.   (*Hard*) French GITTARD. (*Man*) Eng. GIDMAN, KIDMAN.   (*Wine*, friend) Old German Gydoin, 11th cent.—French GIDOIN.   (*Ward*, guardian) Fr. GIDOUART.

There is a word *nun*, *non*, found in several ancient names, on which Förstemann gives no opinion, and for which I think of Old Norse *nunna*, to sing, or perhaps rather, to hum.   I take it that both this, and the preceding stems have something of the meaning of the Scotch *lilt*, which, as rendered by Jamieson, is "to sing cheerfully."   More particularly, I think, to sing

THE INNER MAN. 439

without words, an especial mark of gaiety and light-heartedness. So in the fine Old Scotch ballad of "The Flowers of the Forest," the sense of the desolation that had come upon the land is expressed by a contrast not easily surpassed in its simple pathos.

> " I've heard a lilting at our ewe milking—
> Lasses a' lilting before the break of day,
> But now there's a moaning in ilka green loaning,
> For our braw foresters are a' wed awa."

It would be difficult in the compass of a line to bring out a more perfect picture of rural happiness and content than the " lasses a' lilting," and before the break of day too, when man is generally more disposed to go about his work in grim silence.

SIMPLE FORMS.

Nun.
Cantillare.

Old German Nunno, Nonno, Nunni, 7th cent. Nun, kinsman of Ina, king of Wessex. English NUNN, NUNNEY, NOON. Mod. Germ. NONNE. French NONY.

DIMINUTIVES.

Old German Nunnil. English NUNLEY.

PATRONYMIC.   COMPOUND.

Eng. NOONING. (*Hari*, warrior) Eng. NUNNERY.

Pleg.
Play.

From the Ang.-Sax. *plegan*, to play, appear to be formed a number of names in our own early annals. There was a Plegmund, 19th Archbishop of Canterbury, and in the *Liber Vitæ* are a Plecga, Plegheri, Plegheard, Pleghelm, Plegbrecht, and Pleguini. This stem in the *Altdeutsches Namenbuch* mixes up with another, *blic*, which Grimm and Förstemann refer to *blic*, fulmen. But whatever might be the original meaning of the stem, I think it is clear that the Anglo-Saxons in

440 THE INNER MAN.

their names thought of it in the above sense. Corresponding with the two first names in the *Liber Vitæ* are our PLAY and PLAYER. Possibly, however, the sense may be taken to be that of the play of battle, so often dwelt on by the Ang.-Saxon poets.

From the Old High Germ. *blíde*, Ang.-Sax. *blíthe*, Eng. blythe, Förstemann derives a number of names. But another root, *blad, blat*, p. 376, is liable to intermix.

Blythe.
Hilaris.

SIMPLE FORMS.
Old Germ. Bledas, Blida, Plida, 5th cent. Eng. BLYTH, BLIGHT, BLEDY. Mod. German BLEDE, BLEDOW. French BLED ? BLET ?

DIMINUTIVES.
Old Germ. Blidilo, 9th cent. Eng. PLEYDELL. French BLETEL ?

PHONETIC ENDING.
Old Germ. Blidina, 8th cent. Eng. BLETHYN, PLEADEN. French BLETON.

COMPOUNDS.
(*Gaud*, Goth) Old German Blidgaud, 8th cent.—English BLOODGOOD. (*Ger*, spear) Old Germ. Blidegar, Plidger, 7th cent.—Eng. PLEDGER. (*Mar*, famous) Old Germ. Blidmar, Blimmar, 8th cent.—Eng. PLIMMER.

From the Anglo-Saxon *bliss*, joy, *blissian*, to rejoice, exult, may be the stem *bliss*, with which we may also put *bless*. But the Ang.-Sax. *blíse*, a blaze, is a word liable to intermix.

Bliss.
Joy?

SIMPLE FORMS.
Blesio, apparently German, found on an ancient inscription in the Netherlands. English BLISS. French BLESS,. BLESSEAU.

DIMINUTIVE
Eng. BLESSLEY.

PATRONYMIC.
Mod. Germ. PLESSING.—Fr. BLESSING.

THE INNER MAN.   441

COMPOUNDS.

(*Et*, p. 189) English Blisset, Blessed.   (*Hard*) English Blizzard.   (*Hari*, warrior) French Blesser, Plessier.

Of an opposite meaning may be the following, which seem to be from Gothic *saurga, saurja*, Ang.-Saxon *sorg, sorh*, Dutch *zorg*, Eng. *sorrow*. Though possibly the original sense may have been rather that of anger.

SIMPLE FORMS.

Sorg.
Sorrow?

English Surgey, Sourk, Soar, Sour.   Mod. Germ. Sorg. French Sourg, Sirguey, Zorgo, Soreau, Soury.

COMPOUNDS.

(*Et*, p. 189) Eng. Surgett, Sirkett, Circuit.   *(Hari*, warrior) French Zircher, Zurcher.   *(Ulf,* wolf) Old Germ. Sergulf, 10th cent.—French Surcouf.

From the Old Norse *driúpr*, Mod. Germ. *trübe*, sorrowful, may be the following.   But as the root-meaning seems to be that rather of "overcast," possibly the sense in proper names might be that of dark complexion.   Förstemann gives no opinion upon it.

SIMPLE FORMS.

Troub.
Sorrow?

Old Germ. Trubo.   Eng. Truby, Troup, Droop.   Mod. Germ. Traub, Trübe.   French Traubé, Troupeau, Trouvé, Trufy, Drubay, Druveau.

DIMINUTIVES.

French Trouble, Trupel.   French Trouplin, Troplong.

COMPOUNDS.

(Hari, warrior) French Troupier, Truffier.

Then there are a few names which seem to be derived from joke or facetiousness.   From the Old Norse *skop*, Old High German *scopf*, jocus, English *scoff*, Förstemann derives the following.

D 3

442. THE INNER MAN.

Scop, Scof.
Jocus.

SIMPLE FORMS.

Old German Scopo, Scoppo, 9th cent. Scupi, *Lib. Vit.* Scope, *Lord Mayor of London, A.D.* 1403. Eng. SHOPP, SHOPPEE, SCOBIE. Mod. Germ. SCHOPPE, SCHÖPF.

DIMINUTIVES.

Old Germ. Scopilius. English SCOBELL, SHOVELL.

COMPOUNDS.

(*Hari*, warrior) English SHOVER, SHOPPERIE*—French SCOFFIER.

From the Ang.-Sax. *husc, hucs*, irony, " chaff," whence probably English *hoax*, I take to be the following names, with which I find nothing to correspond in the *Altdeutsches Namenbuch.*

Husc.
Irony.

SIMPLE FORMS.

English HUSK, HUX. Mod. German HOSKE. French ? HUSCH, HUX.

PATRONYMICS

English HOSKING. English HUSKISSON.

PHONETIC ENDING.

English HOSKIN, HUXEN. French HUSQUIN.

COMPOUNDS.

(*Hari*, warrior) English HUSHER, USHER.

From the Ang.-Sax. *gilp*, strepitus, jactantia, may be the following.

Gilp.
Jactantia

SIMPLE FORMS.

Eng. GILBY, KILBY. French GILBÉ, GELPY, KILBÉ.

DIMINUTIVES.

Mod. Germ. GELPKE. French GILBLAIN.

PHONETIC ENDING.

English GILPIN, KILPIN.

Scimph.
Jocus.

From the Old High German *scimph*, jocus, Förstemann derives the name Scemphio, 8th cent. Hence may be English SCAMP, quoted by Lower. May not the above be the origin of our word scamp ?

There is a word *salt, salz*, of which I find no

---

* A Boston surname—English ?

THE INNER MAN. 443

trace in ancient names, but to which Pott, in the Modern German name Salz, gives the meaning of salax. I also think of Old Norse *salt*, the sea, as a possible word.

SIMPLE FORMS.

Eng. SALT, SAULT, SOLTAU. Mod. Germ. SALZ. French SAULT, SOULT, SALZE.

Salt, Salz. Salax.

DIMINUTIVES.

French SALSAC, SALZAC.

COMPOUNDS.

(*Hard*) French SALZARD. (*Hari*, warrior) Eng. SALTER —French SELTIER, SELZER. (*Man*) Mod. Germ. SALTZMANN.

Perhaps of a similar meaning may be the root *brass*, Old Norse *brass*, salax ; unless, as seems to be the case in some instances, it is to be referred to the metal.

SIMPLE FORMS.

English BRASS, BRASSEY. French BRASA, BRAZY.

Brass. Salax ?

DIMINUTIVES.

French BRASSAC. English BRASSELL, BRAZILL ?

COMPOUNDS.

(*Hard*) French BRASSART. (*Hari*, warrior) Eng. BRASIER, BRAZIER—French BRASSIER, BRASSERIE.

From the Old Norse *ginna*, to seduce, *gan*, magic, are probably the following. A large proportion of the ancient names from this root seem to have been those of women, and the general sense is probably only that of seductiveness or fascination. But in one case, where we find Ganna as the name of a fortune-teller or witch, we must take the direct sense of magic.* A stem liable to intermix is *gagan, gain*, p. 175.

---

* Perhaps to this stem we may put the female name Genovefa, 6th cent., and the present Christian name Genovefa in Germany and Généviève in France. If the name be German, it might mean "weaver of spells." Miss Yonge, however, argues for a Celtic origin, as also do Leo and Mone. But Grimm (*Gesch. d. Deutsch. Spr.*) assumes the Germanhood of the name, which compares with others having the same termination.

THE INNER MAN.

Gan.
Magic,
Fascination.

SIMPLE FORMS.

Old Germ. Ganna, 1st cent. Canio, *Lib. Vit.* English GANN, GANNOW, CANN, CANNEY, GENNA, GINN, GUINEAU. French GANNE, GANNEAU, GANIÉ, JAN, JANNY, GEN, GENY, GENEAU, GIN.

DIMINUTIVES.

Eng. CANNEL—French GANIL, GENELLE, CANAL. .Eng. JENKIN—Mod. Germ. JENICHEN—French JANQUIN, GENNEQUIN, JENNEQUIN. French GÉNIQUE, JANAC. French JANLIN.

PHONETIC ENDING.

Old Germ. Ginnana, 8th cent. Eng. GANNON, CANNON. French GENIN, JANIN, CANON.

PATRONYMICS.

Old Germ. Gening, 8th cent. Eng. JANNINGS, JENNINGS, CANNING.

COMPOUNDS.

(*Bert*, famous) Old German Gimbert, 8th cent.—English GIMBERT—French GIMBERT. (*Bod*, *bot*, messenger) Old Germ. Genobaud, Frankish prince, 3rd cent.—Fr. JEANPOT. (*Had*, war) Old German Genad, 8th cent.—Eng. JENNOTT—Mod. Germ. GENET—French GENETTE. (*Hard*) Old Germ. Ganhart, Genard, 7th cent.—French GANARD, GENARD, CANARD. (*Hari*, warrior) Old German Genear, Ginheri, 8th cent.—Eng. GENNER, JENNER, JENNERY, CANNAR, CANARY—Modern German GENER—French GANIER, JANNAIR, GINIER, CANIER. (*Man*) English GINMAN. (*Rid*, ride) Old German Generid, 8th cent.—English JEANNERET—French GÉNÉRAT. (*Ric*, power) English JENRICK—Mod. German GENNERICH—French JEANRAY. (*Wig*, *wi*, war) Eng. GANNAWAY, JANAWAY, GINVEY, JENVEY—French GENEVEÉ. (*Wald*, power) French CANAULT.

Of a similar meaning is probably the word *span, spen,* &c., Anglo-Saxan *spanan, spenan,* to allure, *spôn,* allured, *spônere,* enticer, allurer. As in the former case, the Old German names (of which one only corresponds with ours) seem to be all or mostly those of women.

THE. INNER MAN. 445

SIMPLE FORMS.

Span, Spon.
Allicere.

Speinn, Spegen, *Lib. Vit.* Eng. SPAIN, SPON, SPINNEY ? Mod. Germ. SPOHN. French SPONI, SPINN ?

DIMINUTIVES.

Old Germ. Spenneol ? 9th cent.—Eng. SPANIEL ?

COMPOUNDS.

(*Hari,* warrior) Eng. SPOONER*—Mod. Germ. SPANIER ? —French SPENNER ? (*Leof,* dear) Eng. SPENLOVE, SPENDLOVE.

From the Ang.-Sax. *masc, max,* Mod. Germ. *masch,* English "mesh," a noose, may be the following, perhaps in something of a similar sense to the foregoing.

SIMPLE FORMS.

Mash, Max.
Allicere ?

Old Germ. Masca, 8th cent., Maxus, 9th cent. . English MASH, MAXSE, MAXEY, MOXEY. Modern German MASKE, MASCH, MESKE.

DIMINUTIVE.

English MASKELL.

PHONETIC ENDING.

English MACHINE, MAXON, MOXON.

COMPOUNDS.

(*Hari,* warrior) Eng. MESHER—French MASCAR. (*Man*) English MASHMAN.

There is a stem *gog, cog, coc,* which may perhaps, though very uncertainly, come in here. The sense may be that of English *cog,* Spanish *cocar,* to cajole, Danish *kogle,* Dutch *kokelen,* to juggle. The root of this seems to be found in German *kugel,* Dutch *kogel,* a ball, the simple form of which is seen in North. English *cog,* a roundish lump. But there are several other derivations which might be proposed, as—1*st,* cock, the bird—2*nd,* the cuckoo, in Persian *koku,* Indian *kuka,* Welsh *cog,* Old High Germ. *gaug,*

---

* Or from Anglo-Saxon *spónere,* enticer, seducer.

446

THE INNER MAN.

Swed. *gök*, and that there are names from the cuckoo is shewn at p. 105—3rd, the Ang.-Saxon *geôc*, courage, p. 244.

Cog, Cock.
To cajole?

SIMPLE FORMS.

Old Germ. Gogo, Cogo, Coco, 6th cent.   Cuga, *Lib. Vit.* Gaugy, *Roll Batt. Abb.*   Eng. GOGAY, COCK.   Mod. German KOCH.   French COQ, COQUEAU, COCHE.

DIMINUTIVES.

Eng. COCKLE, COGHILL—Mod. Germ. GOGEL, GOCKEL—French GOCHEL, COQUILLE.   Eng. COGLIN, COCKLIN—Mod. German KÖCHLIN—French COCLIN, COQUELIN, COCHELIN. Eng. GOGGS, COCKS—French COGEZ, COCCOZ.

PATRONYMICS.

English COCKING.   Mod. Germ. GÖCKINGK.

COMPOUNDS.

(*Et,* p. 189) Eng. COCKETT—French COQUET.   (*Hard*) Mod. Germ. KÖCKERT—French COCARD, COCHARD.   (*Hari*, warrior) Eng. COGGER, COCKER—Mod. German KÖCHER— French COCHERY.   (*Man*) Eng. COCKMAN, COACHMAN ?

PHONETIC ENDING.

Eng. GOGGIN, COGGIN, COCKIN.   French COQUIN, COCHIN, COGNY.

PHONETIC INTRUSION OF *n.*[*]

(*Hard*) Old Germ. Guginhart, 11th cent.   Fn. COGNARD, COCHINART.

From the Old Norse *locka*, to seduce, beguile, may be the following.   Hence seems to be the name of Loki, the mischief-maker among the gods in Northern mythology.   The Ang.-Sax. *locc*, a curl, might also be proposed in the sense referred to at p. 403.

Lock.
To beguile?

SIMPLE FORMS.

Locchi, *Lib. Vit.*   Eng. LOCK, LOCKIE.   French LOCQUÉ, LOCHE.

---

[*] Possibly hence also the Swiss Guggenbühl, (for Guggenbald ?)

THE INNER MAN. 447

COMPOUNDS.

(Hard) Old Germ. Lokard, Lochard, 9th cent.—Eng. LOCKHART—Fr. LOCARD, LOCHART. *(Hari,* warrior) Ang.-Sax. Locar, *Cod. Dip.* 819—English LOCKER. *(Et,* p. 189) English LOCKETT—French LOCQUET. *(Rat,* counsel) French LOCRET. *(Man)* Eng. LOCKMAN—Mod. Germ. LOCHMANN.

From the Ang.-Sax. *prût,* proud, may be the following. But in Old Norse *prûdr* seems rather to have meant courteous or polite, which is probably a preferable sense for men's names.

SIMPLE FORMS.

Proud. Polite?

Toui, surnamed Pruda, a Northman at the Court of Canute. English PRUDAY, PROUD, PROUT, PROWSE. Mod. Germ. PRUTZ? French PRUEDE, PROUT, PROUTEAU, PRUCE.

PATRONYMIC.

English PROUTING.

UNCERTAIN NAMES.

English PRUDENCE.

There was an Ang.-Sax. priest called Prudens, *Cod. Dip.* 971. This name seems most probably Latin.

Eng. PROUDFOOT.

Finding another name PUDDEFOOT, I think the *r* may be only intrusive. PUDDEFOOT seems to be from *bud,* a messenger.

From the Ang.-Saxon, Old High Germ. *wild,* ferus, silvaticus, are probably the following. The stem, however, is very apt to mix up with *wald* and *will.*

SIMPLE FORMS.

Wild. Ferus.

Old German Wilto, 9th cent. English WILT, WILD, WILDEY, WILDAY, GWILT. Modern German WILD, WILDT. French VILDÉ.

DIMINUTIVE.

Eng. WILDISH.

PATRONYMIC.

Eng. WILDING.

COMPOUNDS.

(Hard) French VILTARD, VILLETARD. *(Hari,* warrior) Old Germ. Wildehar, 8th cent.—English WILDER, QUILTER. *(Man)* Eng. WILDMAN.

448 THE INNER MAN.

From the Ang.-Sax. *haest*, hot, hasty, Förstemann derives the following stem, which is however liable to intermix with *ast*, p. 216.

Hast.
Hasty.

SIMPLE FORMS.

Eng. HAST, HASTIE. French HESTEAU.

DIMINUTIVE.

English HASTILOW.

COMPOUNDS.

(*Hari*, warrior) French HASTIER—Eng. HESTER. (*Ric*, power) Eng. HASTRICK. (*Wald*, power) Old Germ. Heistald —French HAISTAULT.

From the Old High Germ. *rasti*, Mod. Germ. *rast*, Anglo-Saxon *rest*, English *rest*, requies, Förstemann derives the stem *rast*, *rest*. I am also inclined to add the forms *rost* and *rust*, found in Fries. *rost*, Dutch and Low German *rust*, Mod. Germ. *rüst*, English roost. Though for the form *rust* the German *rüsten*, to arm, may also be proposed. Förstemann has only the three following names. In the *Liber Vitæ* I find also a Restoldus.

Rest.
Requies.

SIMPLE FORMS.

Old German Rusto, Rust, 9th cent. Eng. ROST, RUST. Mod. Germ. ROST, RUST. French ROST, ROSTY, ROSTEAU.

DIMINUTIVES.

Eng. RASTALL, RESTELL—Mod. Germ. RÖSTEL. English RUSTICH. French ROSTOLAN.

PHONETIC ENDING.

Eng. RUSTON. French RESTON, ROSTAN.

PATRONYMICS.

Old German Resting, 8th cent.—Mod. Germ. RUSTING. French ROSTANG.

COMPOUNDS.

(*Ric*, power) Eng. RASTRICK, RESTORICK.

From the Ang.-Saxon *fersc*, *fresc*, Old High German *frisc*, Mod. German *frisch*, we may take

THE INNER MAN. 449

the following. But whether in the sepse of innocence or purity, or in the sense of spirit and liveliness, or thirdly, in the sense of *novus* or *juvenis*, I must leave undetermined. The stem does not appear in the *Altdeutsches Namenbuch,* and curiously enough, it is in the name of the Italian family of the Frescobaldi that it appears most distinctly in a German form. I find, however, that Mr. Taylor has got Freshings in his table of Teutonic settlements in France and England.

SIMPLE FORMS.

Freso.
Fresh.

Ferse,* *Domesday.* English FRESH, FRISKEY, FURZE. Mod. Germ. FRISCH. French FRESCO.

DIMINUTIVES.

French FRESCAL. Modern German FRISCHLIN—French FRESLON.

COMPOUNDS.

(Bald, fortis) Ital. FRESCOBALDI. *(Hari,* warrior) Old German Friskaer,† 9th cent.—English FRESHER, FURZER. *(Hard)* French FRESSARD, FROISSARD.

From the Old Norse *idja,* to labour, Förstemann derives the following stem.

SIMPLE FORMS.

Ide, Ite.
To labour

Old Germ. Ido, Ito, Hiddo, Hitto, 8th cent. Ang.-Sax. Ida, king of Bernicia. Eng. HIDE, HITT. Mod. German IDE.

DIMINUTIVES.

Old German Idala, 8th cent.—English IDLE. French ITAQUE. French ITASSE, YTASSE (or to *idis, itis,* nymph, woman ?)

PHONETIC ENDING.

Old German Idinus, 8th cent. English IDEN, HIDDEN. French ITENEY.

---

* The Ang.-Sax form *fersc.* I am not sure, however, that this, as well as English FURZE and FURZER, should not be put to Friese, p. 312.

† Förstemann makes this Fris-kaer, placing it to Friese, p. 312. According to my placing, it would be Frisk-aer=Friskhar.

E 3

450

THE INNER MAN.

COMPOUNDS.

(*Hari*, warrior) Old German Ithar, Iter, Hither, 7th cent.
Eng. HIDER. Mod. Germ. ITTER. French HITIER, YTIER.

In this chapter may be included the stem *act*, which Förstemann refers to Old High German *ahtôn*, Old Norse *akta*, to think. But I should rather take the sense to esteem, respect, which this root also has.

Act, Ect.
To esteem.

SIMPLE FORMS.

Old German Hecto, 9th cent. Mod. Germ. HECHT.

COMPOUNDS.

(*Hari*, warrior) Old German Aecther, 7th cent.—Ecther, *Lib. Vit.*—English HECTOR—French HECTOR. (*Ric*, power) Old German Huctrich, king of the Alamanni—English UTTRIDGE ?

From the Gothic *svêrs*, honoratus, Old High Germ. *suâri*, gravis, Förstemann derives a stem found in a few ancient names.* The connection between the two senses is found in our own expression, "a man of weight."

Swar.
Honoratus

SIMPLE FORMS.

Eng. SWEARS, SWIRE, SQUARE, SQUAREY.

PATRONYMICS.

Old Germ. Suaring, 8th cent. English SWEARING.

COMPOUNDS.

(*Hari*, warrior) English SWEARER ?

---

* One of these is Swarnagal (heavy nail) a name found in the 8th cent. in the *Verbrüderungsbuch von St. Peter zu Salzburg.* This seems to suggest an older origin for the curious class of names at p. 220 than I have there supposed.

CHAPTER XXIV.

THE STATION IN LIFE.

Though a larger proportion of the names in this chapter have been originally surnames than in any of the preceding, yet even in this department of the subject there are not a few that are baptismal.

The first place is naturally due to the most ancient of all occupations, that of the tiller of the soil. There is an Old German word *sass*, Mod. German *sasz*, signifying settler, inhabitant, from which, in the opinion of Adelung, the Saxons derive their name. Hence may be the following, but of course the stem *sax*, p. 200, may intermix. A Saxon or Low Germ. form may be *sat*.

SIMPLE FORMS.

Old Germ. Sazo, Sasso, 9th cent. English SASS, SATOW. Mod. Germ. SASS. French SASSE, SASSY.

Sass, Sat. Settler.

COMPOUNDS.

(*Hari*, warrior) Eng. SATTER*—French SASSIER, SASSÉRE, SEZERIE, SATORY. (*Rat*, counsel) Eng. SETRIGHT—French SAZERAT. (*Ric*, power) French SAZERAC.

From the Old High German *buur, bouer, pawer*, Mod. Germ. *bauer*, Ang.-Sax. *bure*, Dutch *buur, boer, bouwer*, English "boor," countryman, seem to be the following. But the stem *burg*, p. 279, is liable to intermix.

---

* Or from Ang.-Sax. *sætere*, seducer, whence Sæter, the god who gave the name to Saturday.

452

THE STATION IN LIFE.

Boor, Bower.
Countryman.

SIMPLE FORMS.

Power, *Roll Batt. Abb.* English BOORE, BOWER, POORE, POWER. Modern German BAUER. French BOUR, BOURÉ, BOUREAU, POURE, POURREAU.

DIMINUTIVES.

English BURRELL—French BOURREL, BOURLA. English BURLING—French BOURRILLON.

COMPOUNDS.

(*Hard*) French BOURARD. (*Man*) English BOORMAN, BOWERMAN, POORMAN—Mod. German BAUERMANN.

Of the ancient occupation of the hunter we find considerable trace in baptismal names. From the Old High Germ. *jagon,* Mod. German *jagen,* Old Norse and Swedish *jaga,* to hunt, I take to be the following names, many of which have variously been derived by English and German writers from the scriptural names John, Jacob, and Joachim. Can our word "jockey" be derived from this root?

Jag, Jack.
Hunter.

SIMPLE FORMS.

Old Germ. Jacco, 11th cent., Joco, 9th cent. Eng. JACK, JAGO. Modern German JÖCK. French JACQUE, JACQUÉE, JACQUEAU.

DIMINUTIVES.

Jachelinus, Jagelinus (*Domesday*)—Eng. JACKLIN—Mod. Germ. JECKLIN—Fr. JACQUELIN. Eng. JACKALL, JEKYLL—Mod. Germ. JACKEL, JECKEL—Fr. JEKEL. Eng. JOCKISCH, JACKS, JAX—French JACCAZ, JACQX.

PHONETIC ENDING.

French JAQUIN, JEGON. Mod. Germ. JOCHEN. French JAQUIN, JOKIN.

COMPOUNDS.

(*Hard*) English JAGGARD—French JACQUART. (*Hari,* warrior) Old Germ. Jager, Jahheri, 9th cent.—Eng. JAGGER—Mod. Germ. JAEGER, JÖCHER—French JAGER, JACQUIER, JAQUIERY, JAHYER, JAYR. (*Et,* p. 189) English JACKETT,

THE STATION IN LIFE. 453

JAGGED, JAGET. *(Man)* English JACKMAN—Mod. German JAGEMANN—Fr. JACQUEMAIN, JACQUEMIN. *(Mar,* famous) French JACQUEMAR, JACQUEMIER. *(Wald,* power) French JACQUAULT.

From the Old Dutch *perssen,* to hunt, Mr. Talbot derives the name PERCIVAL. The root may also mean to constrain, compel, being the same as English " press." Hence it is liable to intermix with the stem *bris,* p. 186. There is only one Old Germ. name, on̈ which Förstemann gives no opinion.

SIMPLE FORMS.

Old German Purso, 8th cent. English PEARSE, PERCY, PURSE, PURSEY, PRESS? PRESSEY? French PERS.

Perse. To hunt?

DIMINUTIVES.

Percelay *(Roll Batt. Abb.)*—English PURCELL. PURSLOW, PARCELL, PARSLEY—French PERSIL. Eng. PERSAC. French PERSOZ.

COMPOUNDS.

(Hard) Eng. PURSSORD. *(Hari,* warrior) Eng. PURSER. *(Leof,* dear) Eng. PURSELOVE, and probably as a corruption, PURSEGLOVE. *(New,* young) English PRESSNEY—Fr. PRESNE. *(Wealh,* stranger) English PERCIVAL? PRESSWELL?—French PARSEVAL? PERSEVAL? *(or local from ville, town.)*

One of the most common stems is *bod, bud, pot, put,* which I take to be from Ang.-Sax. *boda,* Old Norse *bodi,* Mod. German *bode,* Danish *bud,* envoy or messenger. The older German writers gave it the meaning of ruler or leader, and Förstemann doubts whether it is to be explained in the sense of præbere, offerre, or of jubere, as both are to be found in the root from which it is derived. I am inclined to think, from the nature of the

454 THE STATION IN LIFE.

compounds in which it is found, that its general sense is that which I have mentioned. It is rather apt in some cases to mix up with *bald*, fortis.

Bod, Bud, Pot. Envoy.

SIMPLE FORMS.

Old German Bodi, Boddo, Botto, Budo, Buddo, Butta, Poto, Potho, 8th cent. Also probably Baudo, Boudus, Boutus, 4th cent. Ang.-Sax. Putta. Eng. BODDA, BODY, BOTT, BOOT, BOOTY, BOOTH, BUDD, BUDDO, BUTT, PUDDY, PUTT, POTT, POTTO, (*Alderman of Cambridge, 17th cent.*) Mod. Germ. BODE, BOTE, BOTH, BOOTH, BUTTE, POTT, POTH. Danish BUDDE. French BODO, BODEAU, BOTTI, BOTHEY, BOUDEAU, BOUTHEY, BOUTY, BOUT, BUTTI, BUTHEAU, POTEAU, POTEY, POTHÉ, PUTEAU.

DIMINUTIVES.

Old Germ. Bodilo, Potilo, Podal, Putilo, 7th cent.—Old Norse Budli—Ang.-Sax. Pottel (*found in Pottelestreôw, Cod. Dip.* 441)—English BODELL, BODLEY, BODILY, BOADELLA, BOTTLE, BOTLY, BUDDLE, BOODLE, BUTTEL, POTTLE, POODLE —Modern German BUDDEL—French BOUTEL, POTEL. Old Germ. Poticho, Putico, 8th cent.—Ang.-Sax. Puttoc—Eng. PUDDICK, PUTTICK, BUDGE—Mod. Germ. BODECK, BUDICH, BUDKE, BUDGE—French POTAGE? Old Germ. Bodekin, 11th cent.—Eng. BODKIN—Fr. BODICHON. Old Germ. Bodolenus, Butilin, Budelin, Bodalung, 6th cent.—English BUTLIN, BUTLING, BUDLONG—Modern German BÖHTLINGK—French BOTTELIN, BOUTELON, BUDILLON. French BODASSE, BUTTEZ,

PHONETIC ENDING.

Old Germ. Baudin, 6th cent. Ang.-Sax. Potten (*found in Pottenstreow, Cod. Dip.* 1,283). Boden, *Roll Batt. Abb.* English BODEN, BOTTEN, BUDDEN, BUTTON, POTTEN. Mod. German BODEN. French BODIN, BOTTIN, BUDIN, BUTTIN, POTIN.

PATRONYMICS.

Old German Poting. Anglo-Saxon Buttingc (*found in Buttingc gráf, Cod. Dip.* 126, &c. Pudding, *Lib. Vit.* Eng. BOTTING, BUDDING, PUDDING. Mod. Germ. BÖDING, BÜTTING. French BOUTUNG.

THE STATION IN LIFE.   455

COMPOUNDS.

(Cum, guest, stranger) Eng. BUDDICOMBE, PUDDICOMBE—French? BUDDICOM. *(Fer,* travel) Eng. PUDDIFER, POTIPHER, BOETEFEUR*—French POTEFER. *(Foot,* pedes) Eng. PUDDEFOOT, PROUDFOOT? *(Ger,* spear) Old Germ. Baudachar, 7th cent.—Eng. BODICKER, BODGER, PODGER, POTICARY?—Mod. Germ. BOTTGER. *(Hard)* Old German Podard, 5th cent.—French BODARD, BODART, BOUDARD, BOUTARD, POTARD. *(Hari,* warrior) Old German Botthar, 7th cent.—Boterus, *Domesday*—English BUTTER, BUTTERY, POTTER, POTTIER—Modern German BUDER, BUTTER, PUTTER—French BODER, BODIER, BOUDIER, BOTTIER, BOUTIER, POTHIER, POTIER, POTERIE. *(Gis,* hostage) Old Germ. Boutgis, Boggis, Duke of Aquitania, 6th cent.—English BOGGIS. *(Man)* English BODMAN, BUTIMAN, BEAUTYMAN, POTTMAN, PUTMAN—Mod. Germ. BODEMANN, PÜTTMANN. *(Mar,* famous) Old German Baudomir, 7th cent.—Eng. BODMER, BUDMORE, BUTTEMER, PODMORE—Modern German BOTHMER, BODEMEYER—French BOTTEMER. *(Mund,* protection) Old Germ. Baudemund, 7th cent.—French POTEMONT. *(Rad,* counsel) Old German Boderad, 9th cent.—French POITRAT. *(New,* young) Old German Baudonivia, 7th cent.—English PUDNEY—French POTONIÉ. *(Ric,* power) Old German Buttericus, Bauderich, Poterich, 7th cent.—English BUTTERICK, BUDDRICH—Mod. German BÖDRICH—French BOUTARIC. *(Rid, rit,* ride) Old German Bodirid, Buotrit, 7th cent.—English BOTWRIGHT, BOATWRIGHT? *(Wald,* power) Old German Baudowald—French BOUDAULT. *(Run,* companion) Old Germ. Bauderuna, 7th cent.—French BOUTRON, POTRON. *(Wine,* friend) Old German Butwin, 8th cent.—English POTWINE—French BODEVIN, BOUDEVIN, PODEVIN, POTEVIN, POTVIN.

UNCERTAIN NAMES.

English BUTTRESS, PEWTRESS. French BOUTRAIS.

There is a stem *ras,* for which Förstemann suggests Old Norse *rása,* to run, Eng. "race." This, though not found as the termination of any ancient names, seems likely to obtain in the above. And an Old German Hraspod, 9th

---

* Also BOUTFLOWER and BUTTERFLY as corruptions?

456 THE STATION IN LIFE.

cent., may be the converse. Possibly HUNTRESS *(Folks of Shields)* may be from the same ending, with *hund*, dog, or *hunta*, hunter.

Of a similar meaning may be the root *sind*, *sint*, which Förstemann refers to Old High Germ. *sind*, way, observing that the sense may rather be that of the derivative *gisindi*, comitatus, satellites. This stem is apt to mix up with Old High Germ. *swind*, Ang.-Sax. *swith*, vehement, but I think that it is too strongly defined to be entirely merged.

Sind, Send.
Envoy.

SIMPLE FORMS.

Old German Sindo, Senda, 8th cent. Sindi, *Domesday.* Eng. SENT. Mod. Germ. SINT. French CENT.

DIMINUTIVES.

Old German Sindico, 8th cent.—French SYNDIC. Old Germ. Sindila, 6th cent.—Eng. SENDALL. Old Germ. Sinzo, 11th cent.—Mod. Germ. SINZ—French SINS.

PHONETIC ENDING.

Old Germ. Sinduni, 8th cent. Eng. SINDEN, SINTON.

COMPOUNDS.

(*Bert*, bright) Old Germ. Sindbert, Simpert, 8th cent.— Eng. SIMBERD. (*Hard*) Old German Sindard, 7th cent.— French SINTARD. (*Berg*, protection) Old Germ. Sindeberga, 7th cent.—French SENTUBERY. (*Hari*, warrior) Old Germ. Sinthar, Sintar, 7th cent.—Eng. SINDREY, SINDER, CENTRE— French CENDRE. (*Rat*, counsel) Old German Sindarat, 7th cent.—French CINTRAT.

From the Old High German *scalc*, servant, seem to be the following. This stem was most common among the Alamanni and Bavarians, less so among the Franks and Saxons.

Shalk.
Servant.

SIMPLE FORMS.

Old German Scalco, Scalh, 8th cent. English SHAWKEY, SHALLOW, SHALLEY. Modern German SCHALK, SCHELCK. French ? SCHALL.

THE STATION IN LIFE. 457

COMPOUNDS.
(*Man*) Old Germ. Scalcoman—Eng. SHAWMAN?

And from the Old High Germ. *sculta*, servant, may be.

SIMPLE FORMS.
Old German Sculd, 9th cent.   English SHOULT, SHOLTO. Mod. Germ. SCHULDT.

COMPOUNDS.
(*Hari*, warrior) Eng. SHOULDER?—French? SCHOLDER?

Another stem of the same meaning, more common as a termination, is Goth. *thius*, Anglo-Saxon *theow*, Old High Germ. *dio*, whence may be the following.

SIMPLE FORMS.
Old Germ. Dio, 9th cent.   Eng. DEY, DYE, TYAS, THEW. Mod. Germ. THIE.   French DIEY, DIÉ, DHIOS.

Dye, Thy. Servant.

DIMINUTIVES.
Eng. DIACK.   French DIACHE, THIAC.

COMPOUNDS.
(*Hard*) French DIARD.   (*Hari*, warrior) English DYER, THYER.   (*Loh*, grove) Old German Thioloh, 9th cent.—Eng. DIALOGUE.   (*Mad, met*, reverence) Old Germ. Deomad, 9th cent.—English DEMAID—French DEMAIT, DHOMET.   (*Man*) Old Germ. Dioman—Eng. DEMON—Mod. Germ. DIEMANN —French DEMANNE.   (*Nand*, daring) French DIANAND. (*Mund*, protection) Old Germ. Thiomunt, 9th cent.—Eng. DIAMOND—French DEMANTE.

From the Old High German *gisal*,* hostage, are probably the following, though the Old Norse *gisli*, dart, may intermix.   I do not feel sure, however, that the sense of the Mod. Germ. *gesell*, companion, is not the prevailing one.   In modern

---

* In Anglo-Saxon names it frequently appears in the form *gils*, and hence I take to be the christian name Giles, most oddly, according to my view, derived from Ægidius, respecting which Miss Yonge seems to be the first to hint a doubt. Pott's alternative suggestion of the Latin Julius is not much better.

F 3

458   THE STATION IN LIFE.

names it is generally contracted into *gil*, as we find also to have been sometimes the case in ancient names.

Gisil, Gill. Hostage?

SIMPLE FORMS.

Old Germ. Gisal, Kisal, 7th cent., Gillo, Gilla, 10th cent. Eng. KISSELL, CHISEL, GILL, GILLEY, GILLOW, KILL, KILLEY. Mod. Germ. GEISEL, KIESEL, GILL, KILLE. French GESEL, GILLE, GILLY.

DIMINUTIVES.

Old Germ. Gislin, 7th cent.—French GHISLAIN, GESLIN. Eng. GILLOCH, KILLICK. French GILQUIN.

PHONETIC ENDING.

Old Germ. Gillin, 9th cent. Eng. GILLEN. Mod. Germ. KILLIN. French GILAN.

PATRONYMICS.

Old Germ. Gisolung, 9th cent. Anglo-Saxon Gyseling, *(found in Gyselingham, now Gislingham, Suffolk.)* Eng. GILLING. Mod. Germ. KISSLING.

COMPOUNDS.

(*Bald*, bold) Old German Gisalbald, 8th cent.—French GILBAULT. (*Bert*, bright) Old German Gisalbert, 7th cent., Gilbert, 8th cent.—English GILBERT—Mod. German GISSELBRECHT, GILBERT—French GILBERT. (*Bod*, envoy) English GILBODY. (*Brand*, sword) Old Germ. Gislebrand, 8th cent.— Eng. GILLIBRAND. (*Fred*, peace) Old German Gisalfrid, 9th cent.—Eng. GILFORD, GILFRED (*christian name*). (*Hard*) Old Germ. Giselhard, 8th cent.—Eng. GILLARD—French GILLARD—Italian GILARDI. (*Hari*, warrior) Old German Gisilhar, Kisalheri, 8th cent.—Eng. GILLER, KILLER—Mod. German GESSLER, KESSLER — French GIESELER, GILLIER. (*Had*, war) Old German Gislehad, Kisalot, 9th cent.— English CHISLETT, GILLETT—French GHILLET. (*Helm*) Old German Gisalhelm, 8th cent.—English GILLIHOM, GILLIAM. (*Ran*, raven) Old Germ. Gislaran, 8th cent.—Fr. GILLERON. (*Man*) Old German Gisleman, 9th cent.—English GILLMAN, KILLMAN. (*Mar*, famous) Gisalmar, 7th cent., Gilmar, 8th cent.—English GILMORE—Mod. German KILLMER—French GILMER.

THE STATION IN LIFE. 459

Then there is a stem *gis,* which Förstęmann takes to be the simple form of the above word *gisal.* Besides the High German form *kis,* there is also a Lombard form *chis.*

SIMPLE FORMS.

Old German Giso, Gizo, Kiso, Cisso, 7th cent. •Perhaps Geeso, 6th cent. Anglo-Saxon Cissa, King of the South Saxons, 6th cent. Chese, *Hund. Rolls.* Eng. KISS, CHEESE? Mod. Germ. GEISS, GIESE, KISS, TSJISSE (*Friesic*). French GHYS, GIESÉ, GUIZOT ? CHESSÉ ? CHIÈZE ?

Gis, Kis. Hostage?

DIMINUTIVES.

Gesecg, *genealogy of the kings of the East Saxons*—Eng. KISSICK.—Mod. Germ. GISECKE. Old German Gisoma, 9th cent.—Eng. JESSMAY.

PHONETIC ENDING.

English CHESSEN, CHESNEY. French GISSIEN, CHESNEY, CHESNEAU.

PATRONYMICS.

Old German Gising. English GISSING. Mod. German GIESING.

COMPOUNDS.

Old German Gisbert, 8th cent.—Mod. Germ. GISBRECHT —French GESBERT, GISBERT. (*Helm*) French GESSIAULME, GESSIOMME—Eng. CHISHOLM ? (*Man*) Old Germ. Guesman ? 8th cent.—English CHISMAN, CHESMAN, CHEESEMAN ?—Mod. Germ. GIESEMANN.

Names derived from trade were naturally of rare occurrence in ancient times. There is an Old German Coufman, 9th cent., which may be from Old High German *koufman,* Modern German *kaufmann,* merchant. I do not think, however, (see p. 248) that this is altogether certain, though it is in its favour that the corresponding Anglo-Saxon *ceâpman* and *côpeman* are also represented by English CHAPMAN and COPEMAN, the latter corresponding with a Copaman in the *Liber Vitæ.*

460 THE STATION IN LIFE.

In the name of a grave *(Ceapan hláw)*, we find an Ang.-Sax. Ceapa, which seems to be from *ceápa*, a merchant, and with which corresponds Eng. CHEAPE.

Names derived from handicraft, as a general rule, are of more recent origin, and have been well explained by Mr. Lower, to whose work the reader may be referred for further information respecting them. At the same time I hold to the opinion that a great number of the names apparently so derived are nothing more than accidental coincidences. Such are many ending in *er*, such as ANGLER, CARTER, COLLIER, CLOTHIER, HARPER, MARINER, MARKER, RINGER, SLATER, STOKER, TASKER, TURNER, WALKER, &c., most of which are referred to elsewhere. Nevertheless, I will not dispute that in some cases two different origins may obtain for the same name. Thus it is very probable that the common name of WALKER is sometimes from Ang.-Sax. *wealcere*, a fuller.

So also I take it that many of the names ending in *wright*, as ARKWRIGHT, ALLWRIGHT, BOAT-WRIGHT, CARTWRIGHT, CHEESEWRIGHT, GOODWRIGHT, HARTWRIGHT, SIEVEWRIGHT, WAIN-WRIGHT, WOOLWRIGHT, are compounds either of *rat*, counsel, or of *rit*, ride, both common as ancient terminations. In some of these cases again two different origins may obtain, but we must be guided very much by the probabilities of the case. Thus BOATWRIGHT, CARTWRIGHT,

THE STATION IN LIFE. 461

and WAINWRIGHT would be natural enough as names derived from trade. But the term " wright " would I think hardly be properly applied to makers of cheeses, or manufacturers of wool. Again, ARKWRIGHT has been explained as a maker of meal chests. But it would not be reasonable to suppose that a division of labour such as does not even obtain at present, prevailed in the more primitive days of old, so that any one man was exclusively employed in making chests.

So also many of the names ending in *man*, as ALEMAN, BELLMAN, CLOUTMAN, COLEMAN, GINMAN, HARTMAN, HENMAN, HONEYMAN, POTMAN, SALEMAN, &c., I do not conceive to be derived from trade or occupation.

The commonness of the name of SMITH is to be accounted for by the fact that anciently the term was not confined to iron work, but was applied to everything which required " smiting." Thus the poet was a " verse-smith," though he had only to " cudgel his brains." Though no doubt generally a surname, it may be in some few cases baptismal. There was an Old German Smido, 9th cent., and we have the names SMITHY and SMYTHA—here we seem to have the three endings *a*, *i*, and *o*, the characteristics of baptismal names. Perhaps Eng. SMITHER, SMITER, French SMYTTÉRE, Mod. Germ. SCHMIEDER, may be a compound, *hari*, warrior. The names of Germany shew some further signs of connection with an ancient name-stem in the diminutives

462   THE STATION IN LIFE.

SCHMIEDECKE, SCHMIEDEL, and SCHMIDLIN, and in the apparently patronymic form SCHMEDDING. In the case of these names the meaning may simply be that of smiting, and most probably in a warlike sense.

Our name BROWNSMITH* is, I take it, the opposite to blacksmith, and signifies the smith who did the bright or burnished work. SHEAR-SMITH might have the same meaning, from Ang.-Saxon *scir*, bright, but is more probably the same as the German SCHAARSCHMIDT (Anglo-Saxon *scer*, plough-share). SCOTTSMITH I have referred to at p. 317 as similar to ARROWSMITH. GROSSMITH I should be inclined to explain as the opposite to the German *kleinschmidt*, " small smith," i.e., maker of locks, &c. Our WILDSMITH seems to be the same as the German WALD-SCHMIDT, which appears to be from *wald*, forest. For other Smiths, English and German, see Lower and Pott.

As ALDERMAN, p. 338, is most probably to be explained in its ancient and higher sense, so also CONSTABLE, if we refer it to an office at all, must be looked upon (see Lower) in a similar light. But, as I have elsewhere shewn, it may also be derived from a name of christian import not uncommon among the early Frankish converts.

---

* So also BROWNSWORD, p. 399. But what the meaning of GREENSMITH is, also of GREENSWORD and of GRUNEISEN (green iron), the latter name, I take it, of German origin, I do not know.   Dr. Doran ("Names and Nicknames" in the Universal Review) mentions an Irish chieftain called Eochod "of the sharp green sword."

THE STATION IN LIFE. 463

BISHOP is a name about the origin of which there is some difficulty. We first find it in the name of a heathen (Biscop) in the genealogy of the kings of the Lindisfari, and I have suggested a possible explanation at p. 182. It occurs more commonly among the Anglo-Saxons in christian times, and oddly enough, all the men so called in the *Liber Vitæ* are ecclesiastics. Possibly, for a young man intended for the church, it might be thought to be rather an auspicious name. It is possible then that Bishop may have been a heathen name, continued in christian times, but doubtless in a changed sense.

CHAPTER XXV.

ALL FLESH IS AS GRASS.

Something akin to the above sentiment lies at the root of a number of our names. Grass itself (Old High Germ. *gras, cras*, Ang.-Sax. *græs*, by transposition *gærs*,) is adduced by Förstemann as the root of several ancient names. He suggests however as probable a lost verb *grasan*, virere, crescere.

Grass, Gars.
Gramen.

SIMPLE FORMS.

Old German Garsia, 8th cent. English GRASS, GRASSIE. Mod. German GRAESSE. French GRASS, GRASSI, GRASSO, GARCE, GARCEAU, GARCIA.

DIMINUTIVES.

Eng. GRASSICK. French GRASSAL.

COMPOUNDS.

(*Et*, p. 189) English GRASSET—French GRASSET. (*Hard*) French GRASSART. (*Man*) English GRASEMAN—Mod. Germ. GRASSMANN.

Of a similar meaning I take to be the stem *green*, which, though in most English names it is probably local, is undoubtedly in some cases baptismal. The various forms of the annexed are found in Old High Germ. *gruon*, Ang.-Saxon *groen, grên*, Eng. "green." The German *kron*, English "crown," might intermix, though this does not seem to be the case as far as the ancient names are concerned.

ALL FLESH IS AS GRASS. 465

SIMPLE FORMS.

Grone, Green. Flourishing.

Old German Grun, Gruna, Cruan, Chrona, *(daughter of the Burgundian king Chilperich, 5th cent.)* Greno, *Domesday.* English GRONOW, GREEN, GREENY, CREAN, CRONEY, CROWN ? Mod. German GROHN, GRUN, GRÜN, KRÖN. French GRUNE, GREINN, CRON, CRONEAU.

DIMINUTIVES.

Eng. GRENELL—French GRUNELLE. Grensy, *Roll Batt. Abb.*—Eng. GREENISH, GREENHOUSE—French GRENUZ.

PATRONYMICS.

Grenesune *(Domesday).*—English GREENSON. English GREENING, GRUNING—Mod. Germ. GRÖNING, GRÜNING.

COMPOUNDS.

(Hard) Old Germ. Cronhart, Cruanhart, 9th cent.—Mod. German GROHNERT, GRUNERT, GRÜNERT—French GRENARD. *(Hari,* warrior) English GREENER, GRUNER—Mod. German GRÜNER, GRÖNER, KRONER—French GRONIER, CRONIER, GRENIER, CRENIER. *(Man)* Eng. GREENMAN.

From the Old High German *blôma*, Modern German *blume*, flower, Förstemann derives the following stem ; though we may perhaps take the wider sense of blooming or flourishing.

SIMPLE FORMS.

Bloom, Plume. Flower.

Old German Pluoma. English BLOOM, BLOOMY, PLUME, PLUM. Mod. German BLUME, BLUM. Mod. Danish BLOM. French BLOME, BLUM.

DIMINUTIVES.

Eng. BLOMELEY, PLUMLEY—Mod. Germ. BLÜMEL.

COMPOUNDS.

(Hard) Mod. Germ. BLUMHARDT—Dutch BLOMMAERT— French BLOMARD, PLUMARTIN *(Dimin. ?) (Hari,* warrior) English BLOOMER, PLUMER, PLOMER—Mod. Germ. BLUMER— French PLUMIER, PLUMERAY. *(Ric,* power) English PLUM-RIDGE ? PLUMBRIDGE ?

From the Ang.-Sax. *blosm*, blossom or flower, is our name BLOSSOM. The root-meaning, as re-

G 3

466 ALL FLESH IS AS GRASS.

marked by Mr. Wedgwood, is to shine, to glow, as shewn in Old Norse *blossa*, to flame, &c. Hence Eng. BLOSS and BLOSSETT.

The Latin *flos, floris*, French *fleur*, appears, like some other Romanic words, to have been adopted to a certain extent into the Teutonic name-system, particularly among the Franks. Whether our name FLOWERDAY may be referred to such origin and derived from the common ending *dag*, day, brightness, beauty, I should not like to assume in the absence of any corresponding ancient name.

Grimm, in his *Frauennamen aus blumen*, read before the Academy at Berlin, discourses with his usual fulness of learning on the names derived from flowers and plants among various nations. The Hebrews, whose national career gave a cast of sternness and gloom to their sentiment, exhibit only two—Tamar, signifying a palm-tree, and Susannah, signifying a lily. The hieroglyphics of ancient Egypt reveal to us three—the lotus as a man's name, the ivy and the palm as names of women. The nomenclature of the Romans was somewhat wanting in names of this class, while that of the fanciful and elegant-minded Greeks was richer than any other.

The ancient German tribes, full of rude and fierce energy, despised the gentle associations of trees and flowers. If they thought of the lime-tree or the ash, it was not of their beauty or their pleasant shade, but of the spear and the shield

ALL FLESH IS AS GRASS. 467

which their wood was good to make. Their idea of woman was not as the angel to smooth the stern side of life, but as the ministering spirit of the war-god to incite the warrior on his course. Hence the objects of comparison which seem to us so natural—the ivy and the clematis as the emblems of endearing dependance—the violet "half hidden to the eye" as the emblem of modest sweetness—had no place in their imaginations. And as a general rule, the names of women were as fierce and ungentle as those of men.

But with the Minnesingers of the middle ages a softer feeling arose, and names derived from flowers began to be in use. It is probably from this period that names such as the following, more common in German than in English, date their origin. Eng. ROSEBLADE, German ROSENBLATT and ROSENBLÜT (rose-leaf)—Eng. ROSINBLOOM (rose-flower)—Germ. ROSENGARTEN (rose-garden), ROSENHAGEN (rose-hedge), ROSENZWEIG (rose-branch), ROSENSTIEL, ROSENSTOCK, ROSENSTENGEL (rose-stem), ROSENKRANZ (rose-crown), ROSENWEBER (weaver of roses, *i. e.*, into garlands). Perhaps also such as English ROSETHORN, ROSTERNE ; English HAWTHORN, HAGDORN, Germ. HAGEDORN ; Eng. PRIMEROSE, English SWEETAPPLE, German GÜLDENAPFEL, &c. But such as the English PEPPERCORN, Mod. Germ. PFEFFERKORN, and German HABERKORN, KLÖVEKORN, &c., must be from some different origin, perhaps feudal tenure or custom.

468 ALL FLESH IS AS GRASS.

From the Romanic tongues, probably about the period of the middle ages, come such names as French HYACINTHE; Eng. VIOLETT, Modern Germ. VIOLET, French VIOLETE; Eng. BLANCH-FLOWER, &c. A pretty poem of the middle ages celebrates the loves of two children called Rose and Blanchefleur, who, dying, were buried in one grave, from which sprung the mingled lily and sweet-briar.

There are, however, a few names of the earlier period which seem to be derived from trees or plants. In some cases, as that of the ash and the lime-tree, a particular reason 'may obtain, apart from any sylvan associations. In other cases it is not so easy to see the reason why. Thus the Old Norse name Humbl, whence probably Eng. HUMBLE,* and perhaps French HUMMEL, seems to be from *humall*, the hop-plant, though as to the reason for its adoption we are quite in the dark. It is not difficult to account for such a name as THORNE, which seems to be ancient. As an Anglo-Saxon name it occurs in the name of a place —Thorninga byra, "the hillock of the Thornings," *i. e.*, descendants of Thorn. As a Scandinavian name Thorny occurs in Saxo.† The sense might be that of spear, as in many other names of the same class already referred to.

Thystell, which occurs as the surname of a

---

* Might, however, also be from Hunibald, Humbald, p. 314.

† The female name Thorny in the Landnamabok is not, as I before thought, from *thorn*, but more probably a compound of Thor and *ny*, young, which as a termination seems exclusively feminine.

ALL FLESH IS AS GRASS.

469

Northman in the Landnamabok, may probably be explained on something of the same principle as that of the Scotch motto " Noli me tangere." THISTLE is an English name, though not common.

To the other words signifying shoot or branch —in most cases probably in the sense of spear—may be added the root *stoff, stuf, stub*, from Old Norse *stufr, stubbr*, Anglo-Saxon *styb*, branch or shoot. We have the word *stove* in this sense in Cumberland ; Leicestershire has *stovin*. Förstemann has no trace of this stem.

Stof, Stuf, Stub. Branch.

SIMPLE FORMS.

Ang.-Sax. Stuf, nephew of Cerdic. Old Norse Stufr, a poet in the Laxdæla-saga. English STUBBE, STOBIE, STOBO, STOP, STIFF. Mod. German STOFF, STÜVE. French STOUF, STOFFE, STUVÉ, STUPPY.

DIMINUTIVES.

Eng. STOVEL, STOFFELL, STIFFEL. Mod. Germ. STIEBEL. French STOFFELL, STIVAL.

PATRONYMICS.

Ang.-Sax. Stopping, *(found in Stoppingas, Cod. Dip. 83.)* Eng. STUBBING, STEBBING.

COMPOUNDS.

(Hard) Eng. STOBART, STUBBERT, STUPART, STIBBARD—French STEVART. *(Hari,* warrior) English STUBER, STUBBER, STOPHER, STOVER—Mod. Germ. STÜBER—French STOFFER.

EXTENDED FORM=ANG.-SAX. *STOVN*, LEICEST. *STOVIN*.

English STOVIN, STIFFIN. French STOBIN, STEUBEN, STEFFEN.

Another word having the meaning of shoot or branch—and in this case probably in nothing more than its simple sense—is *quist*, which Professor Leo, in a communication to *Notes and Queries*, refers to Swed. *quist*, branch. The Old

Quist. Branch.

470   ALL FLESH IS AS GRASS.

Norse *quistr*, and the Dutch *quast* have also the same sense ; the Mod. German *quaste* means tuft or tassel. Hence English HASSELQUIST, LINDQUIST, and ZETTERQUIST, signifying respectively " hazel-branch," " lime-branch," and " aspen-branch." It seems probable that these names do not date beyond the middle ages.

Then there are some other names which seem, to say the least, doubtful. As for instance the Old German Balsimia—English BALSAM, French BALSEM (INE)—which Grimm takes to be from the balsam-plant. But Förstemann, in his work published subsequently, places in apposition the names Baldisma and Baltisma, and it seems probable that the whole are only diminutives from the root *bald*, fortis.

Another doubtful name is LILY. There is an Old German Liula, 8th cent., and a later Liela, which Grimm takes to be from the *vitis alba* or *clematis.* Then there is also an Ang.-Sax. Lilla, but while the Old German names are those of women, the Anglo-Saxon is that of a man. The question then is in the first place whether these various names are the same ; and in the second place whether in any case the above is the right meaning. Or might the Ang.-Sax. *lilie*, English " lily," obtain in any of these names ?

LILL.   SIMPLE FORMS.
Lily ?   Old German Liula, Liela, 8th cent.   Anglo-Saxon Lilla.
Eng. LILL, LILLO, LILY, LELY.   French LILLO, LELLY, LELY.
                         COMPOUNDS.
               English LILLYMAN, LILLIMAN.

ALL FLESH IS AS GRASS. 471

The English OLIVE, OLIFF, and the French OLIVE, OLIVA, OLIFFE, might be from the olive tree. The names Oliva and Olefia occur in the " Polytyque de l'Abbé Irminon" in the 8th cent. But the Scandinavian name Olaf, borne by several kings of Denmark, Norway, and Sweden, and with which correspond Old German names Olaf, Olef, and Olof, 8th cent., might intermix. The word also appears in some German compounds, as Olevildis, 9th cent., (*hild,.* war). To these might be put the Olifard in the *Roll Batt. Abb.* and in the *Liber Vitæ*, present French OLIVERT. It is hard to say whether all or any of these latter names are from the olive.

Doubtful also are English OAKE, OAKEY, AIKIN, AIKMAN. There are Old German names Aiko, Oiko, Occo, Eckan, and Eckeman, for which Graff and Förstemann propose *aki*, disciplina, *ekka*, edge, &c., see p. 209. Nevertheless, the oak, as the emblem of stability and strength, would be very natural for men's names, and it does not seem to me at all certain that the above are not so derived.

I do not think that MAPLE is from the tree ; neither does the derivation from *ma belle* seem a sufficient one. The names Mabilia and Mabic in the *Lib. Vit.* appear to be diminutives, and the stem-name is also found there as Map. Hence English MABB, MABBUTT, &c., and the French MABILLON, another diminutive. As to the etymology, I can give no opinion. If the name Mabilia

472 ALL FLESH IS AS GRASS.

may be dissevered from the others, I should be inclined to refer it to the Latin amabilis.

Our name ROWNTREE (the mountain ash) is probably derived from some of the superstitions connected with that tree. ROINTRU is also a French name, derived, it may be, from some of the many Scotch settlers who have left traces of their nationality in the names of that country. Whether our ROWEN is from the same origin or from a Saxon Rodwin, (whence in the female form Rowena), may be uncertain. Miss Yonge is surely in error in saying that there is " nothing Teutonic" about Rowena : it would be derived from Rodwina as naturally as Robert and Roland from Rodbert and Rodland. The female form Rodwina does not, however, occur in the *Altdeutsches Namenbuch,* though the man's name Rodwin is common.

IVY, Mr. Lower thinks, may be derived from the old holiday games, in which Ivy was a female character. IVYMEY, which may be "ivy-maiden," may perhaps be from this source, as also IVYLEAF. But IVY itself, along with IVE and IFE, and a Mod. Germ. IVE, seems to be from an Old Germ. Ivo, Ang.-Sax. Iffi, the probable etymon of which if it be not from the root *ab,* p. 60, is Old Norse *ŷfa,* to rage. Indeed, IVYMEY itself may be taken to be a diminutive form from this stem, corresponding with an Old Germ. Ivamus, 11th cent.

Our name JESSAMINE seems to be a corruption of another name, JESSIMAN, which again may

THE STATION IN LIFE.

be the same as an Old Germ. Gezzeman, the root of which is doubtful. Our name NUTT I take to be the same as Knut, which we incorrectly make a dissyllable in Canute. So ALMOND, FILBERT, MEDLAR, POPPY, GARLICK, &c., I take to be ancient names. I even doubt the old song which says

> "Johnny Figg was a grocer, white and red,"

so far as it may be adduced for the explanation of our name, which I refer, as at p. 249, to an ancient stem.

H 3

CHAPTER XXVI.

THE STUFF A MAN IS MADE OF.

Though the gentle associations of trees and flowers seem to have been but little in favour among our fierce ancestors, yet there is another class of names derived from metals, which, as more in accordance with the character of their ideas, hold a larger place in their nomenclature. Among these iron, as the symbol of hardness and strength, was naturally the most common, and probably the most ancient. There are three forms, 1st, the Gothic *eisarn*, Old High German *isarn*, Anglo-Saxon *isern*. This is the original form from which are derived respectively the later forms *isan* and *iren* in Old High German and Anglo-Saxon. The first in some names might also be the adjective, Old High German *isern*, Mod. Germ. *eisern*, ferreus. So in the *Chron. of Limburck* there is a Heinrich der Isern, Henry the Iron.

Ison, Isarn.
Iron.

SIMPLE FORMS.

Old German Isinus, 8th cent., Isarn, 10th cent., Isarna, one of the Anses in Jornandes. English Ison, Izon, Iron, Isern. Mod. Germ. Eisen. French Eysen.

COMPOUNDS.

(Bert, bright) Old German Isanbert, Isambert, 8th cent. Mod. German Isanbart—French Izambert. *(Burg,* protection) Old German Isanburg, Irinbric, 8th cent.—English Ironbridge—Mod. Germ. Isenberg. *(Hard)* Old German Isanhard, Isnard, 8th cent.—English Isnard—Mod. German

THE STUFF A MAN IS MADE OF. 475

EISENHARDT—French ISNARD. *(Man)* Old Germ. Isanman, 9th cent.—English IRONMAN. *(Wald,* power) Old German Isinolt, 9th cent.—French ESNAULT. *(Ulf,* wolf) French ESNOUF.*

SURNAME.

Ironside was the surname both of our own Edmund and also of Björn, king of Sweden. IRONSIDE is a present English name.

Then there is another form *is,* which if we take it to be, on the principle which I have assumed throughout this work, the older form of *isarn* and *ison,* must represent the Sansc. *ayas,* Gothic *aiz,* which at first probably meant copper, but on the discovery of iron was transferred to that metal.† But in a few names, as ISBORN, p. 326, *is,* glacies, may probably intermix.

SIMPLE FORMS.
Old Germ. Iso, Isi, 8th cent.   Eng. EYES, ICE.

Ise.
Iron?

DIMINUTIVES.
Old Germ. Islo, Isula, 8th cent.—English ICELY—Mod. Germ. EISELE—French EISELÉ.   Eng. ISELIN—Mod. Germ. EISELN—French ISELIN, YSLIN.

COMPOUNDS.
(Bert, bright) Old German Isabert, Isbert, 7th cent.— French ISBERT. *(Burg,* protection) Old German Hisburg— Eng. ISBURG. *(Hard)* English ISARD, IZARD—Mod. Germ. ISERT—French IZARD, YZARD. *(Hari,* warrior) Old Germ. Isheri, Iser, 8th cent.—Eng. ? HEISER—Mod. Germ. EISER— French ISAR. *(Man)* Old German Isman—Ang.-Sax. Hyseman *(found in Hysemannes thorn, Cod. Dip.* 714)—English HEASMAN ?—Mod. Germ. EISEMANN. *(Mar,* famous) Old Germ. Ismar, 9th cent.—Eng. ISMER. *(Odd,* dart) Old Norse Isodd—Eng. IZOD. *(Ward,* guardian) Old German Isevard, Isoard, 10th cent.—French ISOARD.

---

* Förstemann has only the form Isulf. The form Isernuulf occurs in the Liber Vitæ.

† Max Müller, Lectures on the Science of Language. Second series.

476 THE STUFF A MAN IS MADE OF.

From the Old High German *stahal*, Modern German *stahl*, Ang.-Sax. *stŷl*, English "steel," are the following.

Stal, Steel.
Chalybs.

SIMPLE FORMS.

Old German Stahal, Stal, 8th cent. Old Norse Stâli, (surname). English STEEL, STEAL, STALEY. Mod. German STAHL. French STAL.

COMPOUNDS.

(*Hard*) Old Germ. Stahelhart, Stallard, 8th cent.—Eng. STALLARD. (*Man*) Eng. STEELMAN, STALMAN—Mod. Germ. STAHLMANN.

PHONETIC ENDING.

English STEALIN, STALON, STALLION. Modern German STÄHELIN. French STALIN.

DOUBTFUL NAMES.

English STEELFOX, STELFOX. Most probably a corruption of Steelfax, from the colour of the hair. The traces of Fox as an ancient name-stem are not such as to warrant us in thinking of a compound like the Old Germ. Stahalolf (steel wolf).

BRASS and COPPER seem both somewhat doubtful. The former, as at p. 443, might be referred to Old Norse *brass*, salax; the latter might be a corruption of COWPER, (Old Norse *kaupari*, North. English "couper," dealer); or a compound from the stem *cop*, p. 248. The correspondence of a Mod. Germ. KUPFER is however so far in favour of the metal.

As iron and steel seem to have been synonyms of hardiness and strength, so gold may probably have been a synonym of affection. Thus in an Old Friesic song quoted by Halbertsma, a lover addresses his mistress as "goune Swobke," "golden Swobke." Thus babies are said to be

THE STUFF A MAN IS MADE OF. 477

"as good as gold." A similar expression occurs in a Modern Greek lullaby (Fauriel, "*Chants populaires de la Grèce Moderne*"), where a child is addressed as "a golden little boy." There was an Alfgar, or Wulfgar, bishop of Lichfield, surnamed *se gyldena*, "the golden"—perhaps, Mr. Kemble suggests, from his munificence, or as I think equally probable, from his goodness. Old High German forms of *gold*, as found in the annexed, are *golt, kold, kolt.* ...

SIMPLE FORMS.

Gold. Aurum.

Ang.-Sax. Golde (*woman's name*). Eng. GOLD, GOLDIE, GOULD, GOULT, GOULTY, COLD, COLT. French GAULT.

PHONETIC ENDING.

Old German Coldin, 9th cent. English GOLDEN (*or an adjective ?*)

PATRONYMICS.

English GOLDING, GOLDINGAY.

COMPOUNDS.

(*Birin, pirin,* bear) Old German Goldpirin, 9th cent.— English GOLDBOURN. (*Ber,* bear) French GOLDBER. (*Hard*) English COLTHARD. (*Hari,* warrior) English GOLDER, COLTER—French GAULTIER. (*Man*) Eng. GOLDMAN, COLDMAN, COLTMAN—Mod. Germ. GOLDMANN. (*Ney,* young) Old German Golni ? 10th cent.—Eng. GOLDNEY. (*Red,* counsel) Old German Goltered, 10th cent.—Eng. COULTHRED. (*Ric,* power) Old Germ. Goldericus, 9th cent.—English GOLDRICK, GOLDRIDGE, COLDRICK. (*Run,* companion) Old German Goldrun, Coldrun, 10th cent.—Coldrun, *Lib. Vit.*—English CALDERON—French CAUDRON—Span. CALDERON. (*Wine,* friend) English GOLDWIN.

To the same stem Förstemann places the following, suggesting, however, the Old High German *geltan*, reddere, valere. Whether of the two is the root-meaning is difficult to decide, but it is not improbable that there may be a mixture.

478 THE STUFF A MAN IS MADE OF.

Gild.

SIMPLE FORMS.

Old German Gildo, *Comes Africa*, 5th cent.—Gildia, *a Goth*, 6th cent.—Geldis, 9th cent. Ulf Cilt, *Domesday*. English Guild, Gilt, Kilday, Kilt, Kilto, Kilty. Span. Gildo.*

PATRONYMICS.

Old German Gelding, Gilting, 8th cent. Eng. Gilding, Gelding, Kelting.

COMPOUNDS.

(*Hard*, fortis) Old Germ. Gildard, Ghelthard, 6th cent.— Eng. Gildert, Geldert. (*Hari*, warrior) Old Germ. Gelther —English Gilder, Kilderry.† (*Man*) Mod. Germ. Giltemann. (*Ulf*, wolf) Old Germ. Geldulf, Keltolf, 7th cent.— Eng. Kilduff.† (*Wig*, war) Old German Geltwi—English Gildawie.

From the Old Norse form *gull*, gold, may perhaps be the following. The Old Norse *gull*, gold, is sometimes prefixed to Scandinavian names, as in Gull-Thorir, Gull-Haraldr, "Gold-Thorir," "Gold-Harold." I thought before, that— Ivar being a Scandinavian name—our Gulliver might be Gull-Ivar, "Gold Ivar," a name like these. But as the name does not stand alone in that form, I now think the above scarcely probable.

Gul.
Gold.

SIMPLE FORMS.

Eng. Gull, Gully, Cull, Culley. Mod. Germ. Güll. French Goulay.

DIMINUTIVES.

English Gullick. Mod. Germ. Gülich.

PHONETIC ENDING.

English Gullen, Cullen.

---

* The Spaniards have also Hermenegildo, from the Old German name Herminigild, found in the 6th cent. in the name of a son of the West-Gothic king Leuvigild, of a bishop of Oviedo in the 9th cent., a Spanish abbot in the 10th. The prefix is Armin or Ermin, p. 146.

† Kilderry and Kilduff are Boston surnames, and seem to be English. They may come in here, though they have rather a Celtic sound.

THE STUFF A MAN IS MADE OF. 479

COMPOUNDS.

(*Bert*, bright) English GULBERT. (*Et*, p. 189) English GULLET—French GOULETTE. (*Fred*, peace) Gulfered, Gulfer, *Domesday*—Eng. GULLIFORD, GULLIVER.

We do not find any trace of silver in ancient names. There is an Old Germ. Selphar 8th cent., and an Old Norse Solvar, but perhaps these, along with English SILVER, Mod. Germ. SILBER, may be placed to the stem *salv, self*, p. 346. Another derivation may however be traced in the Silebuhr in the *Liber Vitæ*, which points to a stem *sil*, referred to, but not explained by Förstemann. At the same time, the present German names SILBERARD, SILBERMAN, &c., rather seem to point to an ancient name-stem.

From the Old High German *stain*, Old Norse *steinn*, Ang.-Sax. *stân*, Dutch *steen*, Eng. "stone," in the sense of hardness and firmness, are the following. The stem is more common in Old Norse names than in Old German.

SIMPLE FORMS.

Stane. Stone.

Old Germ. Steina, 10th cent. Old Norse Steinn, Steini. English STAIN, STEEN, STONE, STONY, STONAH, STANNAH— French STEIN.

DIMINUTIVES.

English STENECK—Mod. German STEINECKE. English STENNELL, STONEL.

PATRONYMICS.

Old Germ. Steining, 10th cent. Eng. STENNING.

COMPOUNDS.

(*Biörn*, bear) Old Norse Steinbiörn—English STAINBURN. (*Burg*, protection) Old German Stemburga, for Steinburga— English STEAMBURG, STEMBRIDGE, STONEBRIDGE. (*Ger*, spear) Old Germ. Staniger, 9th cent.—French STEINACHER. (*Hard*) Old German Stainhard, Stanard, 8th cent.—Stannard,

480 THE STUFF A MAN IS MADE OF.

Domesday—Eng. STANNARD, STONARD, STONEHEART—Mod. Germ. STEINHART. (*Hari*, warrior) Old Germ. Steinher, 8th cent.—Old Norse Steinhar—Eng. STAINER, STONER, STONIER —Mod. Germ STEINER. (*Man*) Eng. STONEMAN—Mod. Germ. STEINMANN. (*Wald*, power) Old Germ. Stainold, 8th cent. —English STONHOLD.

Miss Yonge, who considers the names derived from iron, steel, stone, &c., as weapon names, takes in also the following Old Norse names as derived from *hallr*, stone. But the Old Norse *halr*, vir liber et-liberalis, may perhaps intermix.

Hall. Stone?

SIMPLE FORMS.

Old Germ. Halo, 8th cent. Old Norse Hallr. English HALL, HALLEY. Mod. Germ. HAHL, HALL. French HALLÉ, HALLEY.

COMPOUNDS.

(*Burg*, protection) Old Norse Hallbiorg—English HALL-BOWER—French HALLBERG. (*Grim*, fierce) Old Norse Hallgrimr—Eng. HALLGREEN—French HALLEGRAIN. (*Steinn*, stone) Old Norse Hallsteinn—Eng. HAILSTONE.

From the Old High Germ. *proz*, gemma, may be the following.

Proz. Gemma,

SIMPLE FORMS.

Old Germ. Brozo, 9th cent. Eng. BROS. Mod. German BROSE. French BROSSE.

DIMINUTIVES.

Old German Prozila, 9th cent.—Mod. German BRÖSEL—French BROSSEL.

COMPOUNDS.

(*Hard*) French BROSSARD. (*Hari*, warrior) English PROSSER—French BROSSIER.

Wood can hardly be included among names of this class. If the meaning be not, as I have previously suggested, in some cases that of spear, the sense of *sylva* is more suitable than that of *lignum*.

THE STUFF A MAN IS MADE OF. 481

In what sense Cork, which appears in several English names, as CORKING, CORKLING, CŎRKER, CORKERY, CORKMAN, &c., all seemingly in Teutonic forms, is to be taken I cannot say, nor can I find any other etymon, if the stem be German, as it seems, than English *cork*. Unless possibly we may take it to be the same as CARK and KARKER (Carker, *Lib. Vit.*), and think of Ang.-Sax. *cearcian*, to chirp, in a sense similar to that of many names in chapter 23.... Corc was an Old Celtic name, but such an origin would not account for the above forms.

Though Iron, Steel, Gold, Stone, &c., seem natural for the names of men, as indicating, in a sense more or less metaphorical, the stuff they were made of, yet even the proverbial partiality of a shoemaker would hardly account in this way for the name of LEATHER. And at p. 195 I have indicated another origin for this name; while the names LEATHERBY, LEATHERHEAD, LEATHER-DALE, LEATHERBARROW, are local, derived as I think from the personal name. The last name, LEATHERBARROW, is probably from a hill so called on the banks of Windermere.

I 3

CHAPTER XXVII.

THE CHRISTIAN ERA.

I do not propose here to refer to that large class of names taken from the holy men of Scripture or from the saints of the church, which followed on the introduction of Christianity, further than so far as in the case of some of them a different origin may, more or less strongly, be suggested.

Thus such names as BOAZ, ENOCH, LOT, might be referred to the Old German names Boezzo, Enneco, Lotto, from roots referred to respectively at pages 408, 289, 377. And the names EVE, HAGAR, and RUTH, to the Old Germ. names Ivo, Hahger, and Ruth, all names of men. So JUDE, MARK, SAUL, JOB, are capable, as elsewhere noticed, of a different interpretation. Something depends on the character of the name, and the probability of its adoption. For instance —such names as BOAZ, SAUL, LOT, scarcely seem to have any particular claim on the sympathies of a convert.

But the doubt becomes much stronger in the case of names upon which a Christian would naturally be disposed to look with horror or contempt. Who—for instance—would be called HEROD, after the child-slayer — or PHARAOH, after the stiff-necked king—or JUDAS, after the arch apostate—or CAIN, after the first murderer —or OGG, after the king of Basan—or BALAAM,

THE CHRISTIAN ERA. 483

after the temporizing prophet? ESAU, the reckless yet open-hearted, may excite our sympathy, but scarcely our admiration. The name of PILATE recalls the most melancholy story in the history of a man. And scarcely even the strong patriotism of a Saxon mother would seek for its type in the unpitying JAEL. While other names there are, such as POTIPHAR, which have nothing to kindle reverence, and nothing to excite aversion.

Yet the whole of the above are family names in England or in France. And I have elsewhere suggested a different origin for all of them except Esau, Judas, and Jael. The first corresponds with an Old German Eso, from the root *ans, as,* divus, p. 119, the second, a French name, may perhaps, along with JUDICE and JUDISSÉ, be a diminutive from the stem Jud, p. 305—the last may be the same as GALE, p. 436.

But though such names might not be voluntarily assumed—yet there are no doubt cases—though I hold them to be rare—in which a name has been thrust upon a man against his will. And there is in Paris a J. ISCARIOT (the first name for aught I know may be Judas), which can scarcely be derived otherwise than from the traitor.*

---

* Curiously enough—while these sheets are passing through the press—an article in the Athenæum offers a probable explanation of this name. "The Marquess (Michael Imperiale of Genoa) wrote a book to prove that Judas had been very unfairly dealt with by his contemporaries and posterity; and dying, Imperiale left a sum to be expended in masses for the benefit of the soul of Iscariot. Those who sided with him named their boys Michael, and some would have called their by the name of the traitor, had not the Church authorities stepped in and stopped the scandal." So then the name after all does seem to have been voluntarily assumed, and all that we can say is that "there is no accounting for tastes."

484 THE CHRISTIAN ERA.

Though it is certain that we have as family names the Scriptural JOHN, THOMAS, BENJAMIN, DANIEL, SIMON, &c., I strongly doubt JACK, TOM, BEN, SYME, or SIMM being, at least in all cases, the corresponding diminutives. I include also in my objection the supposed diminutives of Teutonic names, as BILL, BOBBY, DICK, HARRY, &c. And I not only doubt the supposed diminutives of female Scriptural names, as NANNY, BETTY, SALLY, and MOLL; but in some instances the names themselves.

It does not seem at all probable that we should have names taken from the three sacred persons of the Trinity. There are indeed English names GOD and GODHEAD, the former that of a writer about the 17th century. But these belong to an ancient root, whether god, deus, or good, bonus, is not altogether certain, but at any rate anterior to Christianity. In like manner, and not originally in a Christian sense (though a Christian sense might afterwards come to be attached to them), I take Eng. LOVEGOD, LOVE-GOOD, Mod. German LIEBEGOTT, GOTTLIEB. So also the French names DIEU and LEDIEU I explain differently pp. 427, 194.

The name CHRIST, which is English, French, and German, might, according to the opinion of Förstemann, be from the second person of the Trinity. However, I have made a suggestion respecting it, p. 133. The Gothic *kriustan*, to gnash, may also be suggested. But, whatever

THE CHRISTIAN ERA. 485

might be the original meaning of the word, I
cannot but admit that the Frankish converts
must have looked upon it as referring to Christ.
In the London Directory for 1832, I find the
name MESSIAH, which, along with a French
MEZIA, I place to a root of uncertain meaning
quoted elsewhere.

The following names apparently must be referred to the Ang.-Saxon Iob, Jove, but whether
in a heathen or a Christian sense I cannot say.
Förstemann gives no explanation of the ancient
names.

SIMPLE FORMS.   Job.
Old German Joppo, 9th cent. English JOB, JOVE, JOPP,   Jove.
JUBB. Mod. German JUPPE. French JOB, JOBBÉ, JOUVE,
JUBÉ.

DIMINUTIVES.
Old German Jovila, 7th cent.—French JOVEL, JUVILLE.
English JOBLING, JOPLING—French JUBELIN, JUBLIN,

COMPOUNDS.
(*Hard*) French JOVART. (*Hari*, warrior) Eng. JOBBER,
JUBBER.

There was an Ang.-Sax. priest called Spiritus,
Cod. Dip. 762, which I before took to be from
the third person of the Trinity, and to be perhaps
the origin of Eng. SPIRIT. But I now take the
Saxon Spiritus to be only a slight corruption of
a Gothic Spirithius. We find the name in the
corresponding Old High Germ. form of Spiridio
(*dio*, *thius*, servant). So also an Anglo-Saxon
Electus, *Cod. Dip.* 98, which I before took to be
from the Latin, and to signify "elect" as a name
of Christian import, may only be the same as a
Goth. Electeus, and an Old High Germ. Electeo,

486 THE CHRISTIAN ERA.

from the stem referred to at p. 142. But it is very possible in both these cases also that the heathen idea may have been superseded by a Christian one. There is a present German name HEILIG-GEIST, but I am much inclined to think that it is only a corruption of some ancient name ending in *gast* (hospes), as perhaps Haldegast(es), which we find in the 3rd cent.

In this place, and as a name of Christian import, I think that we may in many, if not in most cases, class CONSTABLE. In the two Frankish registers whose titles I have elsewhere quoted, the names Constabulus, Constabulis, Constabula, Constabila, occur rather frequently both among men and women. I take the word to be derived from the Latin *constabulire*, and, like another name Firmatus found along with them, to signify "established in the faith."

In the *Traditiones Corbejenses* occurs in the 9th cent. the Old Saxon name Horobolla, which Grimm *(Gesch. d. Deutsch. Sprach.)* conjectures to have the meaning of "earthen vessel," in reference to a common Christian simile. Whatever may be the meaning of the name (which Förstemann takes to be that of a woman, though this is not certain), it may possibly be suggested as the origin of our ARABELLA, for which no sufficient etymon has as yet been proposed—Miss Yonge's suggestion of a corruption of the Old Norse female name Arnhildur not having even the ordinary recommendation of verbal resemblance.

THE CHRISTIAN ERA. 487

Names probably dating from crusading times are French JERUSALEM and NAZARETH. More uncertain are Eng. and French SARASIN, Germ. SARRAZIN ; the name Sarzinus occurs in the *Pol. Rh.* Saladin, Mr. Lower observes, was an English surname temp. Ed. 1st. It is not an uncommon name in France at present. Perhaps English TURK, French TURC, Germ. TÜRK, may be a name of the same class. It would rather seem, however, from names of places in the Cod. Dip., that Turca was an Ang.-Saxon name. Mr. Lower conjectures Turk to be an abbreviation of Turketil, which derives some confirmation from the name Turk' (*sic*) in the Liber Vitæ.

While the Eng. CHRISTMAS and PENTECOST, and the French NOEL are probably derived from nothing more than persons having been born at the time of these Christian festivals, the names Pask, Pash, &c., seem, at least in some cases, to have a deeper root. The word occurs in German compounds in some names of the 8th and 9th cents. ; Förstemann refers it to the Hebrew *pascha*, and indeed I do not know of anything else from which it can be derived. At the same time, seeing the remote origin of names, any argument based on this ground is necessarily inconclusive.

SIMPLE FORMS.

Old Germ. Pasco. Eng. PASCOE, PASK, PASH. French Pask. Passover. PASCHE.

COMPOUNDS.

(*Hard*) French PASCARD. (*Man*) English PAXMAN ? (*Wald*, power) French PASCAULT.

488   THE CHRISTIAN ERA.

Our names TIFFIN and TIFFANY, French TIEFFIN and TIPHAINE, corresponding with a Tephonia in the Lib. Vit., seem to be from the Old French *tiephaine*, the feast of the Epiphany, (*Pott*, 699).

Though the English DEVOLL is I think to be otherwise accounted for, yet the Germans have both TEUFEL itself, and also many names formed from it, as TEUFELSKIND (Devil's child) ; TEUFELSKOPF (Devil's head) ; SCHLAGENTEUFEL (Fighting devil) ; JAGENTEUFEL (Hunting devil) ; and the most curious of all, DUSENDTEUFEL (Thousand devils).

The French have DIEUDONNÉ, DIEULAFAIT, DIEULEVEUT, and DIEUTEGARDE. The last would seem to bring before us a pious mother, watching over her new-born babe, and looking forward, perhaps in a troublous time, to the dangers and trials of the days to come. So at first I took it, till I was compelled to yield the pleasing theory to the claims of an Old Frankish name Teutgard(is).

CHAPTER XXVIII.

THEY CALL THEIR LANDS AFTER THEIR OWN NAMES.

A large proportion of the names of persons are derived from the names of places. Again—a large proportion of the names of places are derived from the names of persons—Dodd acquires a property, and it is called " Dodd's worth "—Grim builds a village, and it is called "Grim's by." Then Doddsworth and Grimsby give surnames to other men in after times—it may be to the very descendants of the original owners.

So that the nomenclature to some extent runs in a circle, and we have names, such as MONT-GOMERY, in which we are able to trace at least four distinct revolutions of the wheel. First—Gomerie,* the man, fixes his dwelling on the hill, and the place is called after him Mont-Gomerie. Secondly—Mont-Gomerie, the place, gives name to Roger de Montgomery the man. Thirdly—Montgomery the man, following the fortunes of the Conqueror, founds and calls after his own name, Montgomery, in Wales. Fourthly—Montgomery the place, again in its turn gives surnames to men. And if we could suppose that some of the places called Montgomery, in America, are named after a man and not after a town, we should be able to add a fifth.

---

* The Old German Gomerih, p. 59

J 3

490 THEY CALL THEIR LANDS

In many instances we find the original name still hovering round the locality called after it. Thus, when I find that WINDER is not an uncommon name in Westmorland, it confirms me in the opinion that Windermere may be the lake or "mere" of a man called Winder. Walking through Handsworth, in Staffordshire, and seeing the name of HAND upon the shops, I said to myself "Handsworth is the *worth* or estate of a man called Hand, and these may be the descendants of that man."

It is a very characteristic nomenclature—that of the Teutonic settler. Thoroughly matter-of-fact—he plants his dwelling in the cleft of the mountain, with the towering peak above, and the rushing torrent below, and he calls it—"Eagle's nest?"—not a bit of it—"Brown's seat," or "Dobb's cot." It is characteristic of individuality and independence—individuality of right—independence of character. The map of England, dotted over with the possessive case, is a standing protest against communism. And there are many names of places, formed from a single name, which show where one man has held his own in solitary self-reliance among the lonely valleys and dreary mountains.

The chapter of local surnames must always be a large one, though the tendency of my theories is very considerably to reduce it.

In the first place, there are many simple names, such as BANK, BECK, BOWER, CROSS,

AFTER THEIR OWN NAMES. 491

DALE, FRITH, GILL, HEDGE, HILL, ING, MOSS, ORCHARD, PITT, POOL, RIDGE, SLADE, STREET, WALL, &c., which I take, more or less certainly, to be from ancient baptismal names of altogether different meaning.

In the second place, there are no small number of names which, though their apparent meaning is the real one, are yet from ancient baptismal names, and whatever may have been the original sense, are certainly not from locality. Such is HOUSE, of which the meaning can hardly be anything else than house, domus. Some of the ancient compounds, as Huseburg, Husimunt, Husward, all signifying "protection (or protector) of the house," are intelligible enough, though it is not very clear as to the sense of the simple form.

SIMPLE FORMS.

House. Domus.

Old Germ. Huss, Husi, Huozo, 8th cent. Eng. HOUSE, HUSSEY? Mod. Germ. HAUSE. French HOUSSE, HOUSEAU, HOUZE, HOUZEAU.

DIMINUTIVES.

Old Germ. Husicho, 9th cent.—Eng. HUSSICK, HOUSEGO. Eng. HUSSELL—French HOUSEL. French HOUSSEZ. Old Germ. Husito, 8th cent.—French HOUSSET.

PATRONYMICS.

Old Germ. Husinc, 8th cent. Mod. Germ. HUSUNG.

COMPOUNDS.

(*Burg,* protection) Old Germ. Huseburg—French HUSBROCQ. (*Hard*) Eng. HOUSSART—French HOUSARD. (*Man*) Old Germ. Huozman, 11th cent.—Eng. HOUSEMAN—Mod. Germ. HAUSSMANN—French HOUSSEMAINE.

A similar word appears to be *inn*, which Förstemann refers to Ang.-Sax. *inn*, domus. But

492   THEY CALL THEIR LANDS

the verb *innian,* to entertain, may be suggested. To the ancient names in the *Altdeutsches Namenbuch* may be added an Inuald in the *Liber Vitæ.*

Inn.
Domus.

SIMPLE FORMS.

Old German Inno, 9th cent.   Anglo-Saxon Ina, king of Wessex. Hyni, *Lib. Vit.* Eng. HINE? Mod. Germ. IHN. French HINÉ?

COMPOUNDS.

(Frid, peace) Old Germ. Infrid, 9th cent.—Infrith, *Lib. Vit.*—French INFROIT. *(Man)* Eng. INMAN, HINMAN. *(Mar,* famous) French INEMER. *(Ward,* guardian) Eng. INWARD.

The Gothic *haims,* Ang.-Saxon *hâm,* English " home," is found in a number of ancient names, but it is difficult to separate from another stem *ham,* which seems to be of a different meaning, though perhaps related.

Hame.
Home.

SIMPLE FORMS.

Old Germ. Haimo, Aymo, 7th cent.   Ang.-Sax. Hâma. English HOME, AMEY? Mod. Germ. HEIM. French HAIM, AMEY? AIMÉ?

DIMINUTIVES.

Old Germ. Heimezo, 11th cent.—Eng. HAYMES, AMES— French AYMES. Old Germ. Haimelin, 10th cent.—English HAMLIN—French HAMELIN.

COMPOUNDS.

(Gar, spear) Old German Heimger, 9th cent.—French HAMGER. *(Hard,* fortis) Old Germ. Heimard, Aimard, 8th cent.—French AIMARD. *(Hari,* warrior) Old Norse Heimir? —English HAMER, HOMER, OMER—French HÉMAR, AYMER, OMER. *(Mund,* protection) Old German Haimund, Hemmund, 8th cent.—Eng. HEMMENT—French AYMONT, OMOND. *(Rad,* counsel) Old German Haimrad, 8th cent.—French AMURAT. *(Ric,* power) Old German Haimirich, Heinrich, Heinrih, 8th cent.—Eng. HENRY—Mod. Germ. HEINRICH—

AFTER THEIR OWN NAMES. 493

French HENRI. (*Ward*, guardian) Old German Heimwart, 9th cent.—English HOMEWARD. (*Wid*, wood) Old German Haimoidis, 10th cent.—Eng. HOMEWOOD ? (*Helm*) French AMIAUME.

There are also several ancient names derived from *wood*, perhaps in the sense of a sacred grove. Though as before suggested, the sense of spear may in some cases obtain. The following seem to be from Goth. *vidus*, Old High German *witu*, Ang.-Sax. *wudu*, English "wood." But Old High German *wit*, amplus, is liable to intermix ; also Anglo-Saxon *wiht*, a man, *hwit*, white, and *wit*, knowledge, understanding.

SIMPLE FORMS.

Wid, Wood. Sylva.

Old German Wido, Wieda, Witto, Guido, Quido, 6th cent. Ang.-Sax. Wudda, A.D. 688. Gwido, *Lib. Vit.* Eng. WIDOW, WEED, VIDY, WITHY, WITH, WITTY, WOODEY, WOOD. Modern German WEEDE, WITH, WITTE. French VIDEAU, VIDÉ, VITEAU, VITÉ, VITTE, VITTU, VIDUS (*Gothic?*), GUIDÉ, GUIDOU. Ital. GUIDO, GUIDI.

DIMINUTIVES.

Old German Widucho, Wituch, Widego, 8th cent.— Uiduc, *Lib. Vit.*—Eng. WHYTOCK, WEDGE, VETCH—Mod. German WITTICH—French VIDOCQ. Old German Widilo, Witili, Wital, 8th cent.—English WHITELL, WHITLEY, WOODALL—Mod. German WEIDEL—French VIDEL, VITEL. Old German Widulin, Witalinc, 8th cent.—Eng. WHITLING, WOODLIN—Modern German WITTLING—French VIDALON, VIDALENC. Old Germ. Widomia, 9th cent.—Eng. WHITMEE. Old German Witiza, West Gothic king, 8th cent.—English WHITSEY—French VITTIZ, GUIDEZ.

PHONETIC ENDING.

Old Germ. Widen, Wittin, 6th cent. English WITTON, WEEDIN, WOODEN. Mod. Germ. WITTEN. French VIDON, VITON, GUIDON, GUITTON.

494 THEY CALL THEIR LANDS

PATRONYMICS.

Old Germ. Wieding. Eng. WEEDING, WHITING, WOODING. Mod. Germ. WEDDING, WIETING.

COMPOUNDS.

(*Cock,* p. 27) Eng. WOODCOCK—French VITCOCQ. (*Bert,* bright) Old German Witbert, Witpret—Witbred (*Hund. Rolls*)—Eng. WHITBREAD ? (*Bern,* bear) Old Germ. Witubern, 9th cent.—Eng. WHITBURN. (*Gar,* spear) Old German Witgar, Widger, Witker, 9th cent.—Ang.-Saxon Wihtgar, Nephew of Cerdic—English WIDGER, WOODGER, WHITECAR, WHITTAKER ? (*Hait,* "hood") Old German Withaidis, 9th cent.—Eng. WHITEHEAD, WHITEHEAT, WOODHEAD. (*Hard,* fortis) Old Germ. Withard, Witard, 8th cent.—Eng. WHITEHART, WOODARD—French VIDARD, GUITARD. (*Ron,* raven) Old Germ. Widrannus, 8th cent.—Eng. WITHERON, WHITEHORN ?—Mod. Germ. WIETHORN—French VIDRON. (*Hari,* warrior) Old German Withar, Witar, 8th cent.—Wither (*Domesday*)—Eng. WHITER, WHITEAR, WITHER, GWYTHER, WOODYER, WOODER(SON)—Mod. German WITTER—French VITTIER, WITIER, GUITTER. (*Ring,* combat) Old German Witering, 8th cent.— English WITTERING, WITTEWRONG. (*Haus,* house) Old Germ. Withaus, 8th cent.—Eng. WHITEHOUSE ? WIDEHOSE ? WOODHOUSE ?—Mod. Germ. WITTHAUS. (*Lag,* law) Old Germ. Witlagius, Witleg, 9th cent.—Ang.-Saxon Wihtlæg—Eng. WHITELEGG, WHITLAW. (*Laic,* play) Old Germ. Widolaic, 8th cent.—Eng. WEDLAKE, WEDLOCK, WHITELOCK ?—Mod. German WEDLICH—French ? WITLICH. (*Leis,* learned) Old German Witleis, 8th cent.—French VITALIS.* (*Man*) Old German Widiman, Witman, 9th cent.—Eng. WIDEMAN, WHITEMAN, WOODMAN—Mod. Germ. WIDMANN, WEITMANN—French ? WIDEMAN. (*Mar,* famous) Widiomar (Gothic king, 4th cent.), Widmar, Witmar—Uitmer, *Lib. Vit.*—Eng. WHITMORE—Mod. Germ. WIDMER —French ? WIDMER. (*Rat,* counsel) Old German Widerad, Witerat, 6th cent.—English WITHERED, WHITETHREAD, WHITEROD, WHITEWRIGHT. (*Ric,* power) Old German

---

* This seems more naturally from *wit*, wisdom.

AFTER THEIR OWN NAMES. 495

Witirich (Goth. king, 4th cent.) Witirih—Eng. WITHERICK, WHITRIDGE—Modern German WITTRICH—French VITRAC, VITRY, GUITRY.

Lund. Grove.

The Old Norse *lundr*, grove, seems to enter into some ancient names. Hence may be Eng. LUND, LUNDY, LOUND, LUNT, and French LUOND, LUNDY, perhaps LUNETEAU. But there is but small evidence in these of a baptismal origin.

Scog, Scow. Grove.

Another word also found in some ancient names is Old Norse *skôgr*, Dan. "*skov*," North Eng. "shaw," a wood. From this appear to be Eng. SCOW, SHAW, and SHOE, as simple forms—SKOGGIN and SCAWEN as an extended form—and perhaps SHOOBERT and SHOOBRICK as compounds.

In the third place, the coincidence or the resemblance between some of the endings of ancient names and local terminations must be reckoned in diminution of the names apparently derived from places. Thus the ending *burg*, *bury*, *brook*, *brick*, may be sometimes from *birg*, *birc*, protection, very common as the termination of ancient names, and not from the local *bury* or *borough*. I am inclined to think that *bridge*, in a few names such as DRAWBRIDGE, IRONBRIDGE, BRASSBRIDGE, is also from the same origin. Though the name WOODBRIDGE would be derived naturally enough from a locality, yet there were no iron bridges in the days when surnames were given, and I doubt whether a brass bridge exists even in the brain of Dr. Fairbairn.

So *burn* is sometimes from *bern*, a bear, and

496 THEY CALL THEIR LANDS

not from *burn*, a brook. *Head* is sometimes from *haid*, state, condition, and not from the local word. *Ing* I take as a general rule to be the patronymic, and not from *ing*, a meadow. So *gate, gill, house, cot, lake, land, more, wall, wick, with, wood,* in certain cases I have throughout these pages taken to be from ancient terminations.

In like manner I take it that present German names ending in *hof* are in some cases from the ancient endings *olf, ulf,* wolf, and not always from the local *hof,* court. That this is so, will I think be clear from the following comparative list of ancient German and present German names, all of which latter are classed by Pott as local. But it must be remembered that Pott's work was written before the Altdeutsches Namenbuch had brought many of these ancient names to light.

Old Germ.	Mod. Germ.	Old Germ.	Mod. Germ.
Botolf	Potthoff	Jungolf	Junghoff
Burgolf	Berghoff	Lindolf	Lindhof
Duomolf	Dumhoff	Morolf	Morhof
Ekkulf	Eckhoff	Sandolf	Sandhoff
Eudolf	Uhthoff	Steinolf	Steinhoff
Fisculf	Fischhof	Sundarolf	Sundrehof
Geldulf	Kalthoff	Thiholf	Teichhof
Grasulf	Grashoff		

In the fourth place, a very considerable number of the names of places are simply the names of men, unqualified by any geographical term whatever. Mr. Kemble (*Saxons in England*) was the first in this country to point out that

AFTER THEIR OWN NAMES. 497

many names of places, as Halling and Cooling in Kent, Patching in Surrey, Brightling in Sussex, were in Anglo-Saxon a nominative plural—Hællingas, Culingas, Peaccingas, Byrhtlingas, signifying respectively, " the Hallings," " the Coolings," " the Packings," " the Brightlings." These then are the names of family communities, being, as Latham observes, " political or social, rather than geographical terms."

In the names of places in Germany, especially in Bavaria, the nominative plural in *ingas* is comparatively rare, and we have most commonly a form in *ingen* or *ingum*, which, according to Förstemann, is a dative plural, but according to Max Müller,* an old genitive plural. Hence Göttingen, Tübingen, Leiningen, Grüningen, Harlingen, from the families of the Göttings, Tübings, Leinings, Grünings, and Harlings. Also very commonly a form in *inga* or *inge*, which may be either a dative singular or a genitive plural ; in the opinion of Förstemann sometimes the one and sometimes the other. In Anglo-Saxon names of places the form *ingum* also occurs, though not frequently. Thus Godalming in Surrey was anciently Godelmingum, a settlement of the sons or descendants of Godhelm. Sometimes the same place in various charters appears in both the forms *ingas* and *ingum*. Thus Malling in Kent was in Anglo-Saxon variously Meallingas and

---

* Lectures on the Science of Language. Second Series.

K 3

498   THEY CALL THEIR LANDS

Mallingum. Mr. Taylor, in "Words and Places," has carried this subject still further, and instituted a comparison, of the highest interest and importance, between the Teutonic settlements as indicated by these forms in England, Germany, and France.

In the last-named country there appears to be found a different—perhaps a later form. We have Les Henrys, Les Bernards, Les Roberts, Les Guillets, Les Guillemottes, Les Girards, Les Arnauds, &c., all of which, like the foregoing, seem to contain the names of family communities.

But I go further than this, and take the ground that many names of places, both in France and England, are nothing more than the name of a single man. When we find in France something like 6,000 places called after saints, without any geographical term whatever, as St. Omer, St. Leonard, &c., it naturally occurs to us that just on the same principle places might be called after men who were not saints. No one I think would doubt that the places called Fitz James, Robinson, David, Taillefer, are simply from the names of men. And as certainly do I take to be from the same origin Angelard, Audembert, Arnoult, Audiracq, Bertric, Bertrand, Blanchard, Brunembert, Folcarde, Folckling, Francillon, Ferando, Gandolphe, Guillaume, Guiscard, Godisson, Girouard, Godinand, Jacque, Jacquelin, Josse, Josselin, Jossenard, Humbert, Lambert, Méro-

AFTER THEIR OWN NAMES. 499

bert, Willeman. These, which I have selected from Duclos' "*Dictionnaire général des villes, bourgs, villages, hameaux et fermes de la France,*" are all simply Teutonic names of men. In some cases there is a *le* or *la* prefixed, as Le Frank, Le Guidault, Le Bernard, Le Guildo, La Godefroy, La Caroline. There is one place called Fille-Guécélard, while we have also Guécélard by itself. Some names, however, as Les Allemands, Les Juifs, Les Innocents, Les· Boutilliers, Les deux freres, Le Bras-de-fer, Le Grenadier, may perhaps only be derived from the signs of taverns.

So also in England, many names of parishes and places, such as Landulph in Cornwall, Biddulph in Staffordshire, Goodrich in Herefordshire, Haytor in Devon, Hicks in Gloucestershire, Burnard, Guthrie, Jellybrands, Lockhart, Osburn, Sibbald, and Thorbrand in Scotland, I take to be simply from the names of men. In some cases as that of Coldred in Kent, and Catmere in Berks, we can perceive one of the principles upon which such names have arisen. Thus the former place was in Anglo-Saxon Colrêdinga gemaêre, "the boundary of the descendants of Colred," and the latter was Catmêres gemaêre, "Catmere's boundary." The inconvenient length of these titles has caused the whole to be dropped except the name of the individual. Thus then, even if our names CATOMORE and CATMORE are directly from the place, yet the place itself is simply the name of an Anglo-Saxon. And as such, it furnishes the

500 THEY CALL THEIR LANDS

link between our names and the Catumerus of Tacitus.

Many of the local terminations, such as *ton*, *ham*, *bury*, &c., speak for themselves—I subjoin a list of those most commonly occurring which seem to require an explanation.

By. Dan. *by*, a village or small collection of houses. This is the word which, more than any other, distinguishes the Danish settlements from the Saxon.

Den. Ang.-Sax. *den*, a valley. Leo thinks the word adopted from the Celtic.

Force. Old Norse *fors*, a waterfall. Hence WILBERFORCE, probably from the name Williber or Williberg, the latter anciently rather common.

Garth. Ang.-Saxon *geard*, Old Norse *gardr*, a place *guarded* by a fence, a farm-stead. Liable to intermix with *gard* as an ancient ending of personal names.

Gate. In the South of England an opening, Ang.-Sax. *geat*, but in the North also a road or way, Old Norse *gata*. Liable to intermix with an ancient termination *gaud* or *gat*, which Förstemann takes to mean Goth.

Gill. Old Norse *gil*, a small ravine, not necessarily, as sometimes stated, containing water. Liable to intermix with an ancient termination *gil*, which is probably a contraction of *gisal*, hostage.

Holt. Ang.-Sax. and Old Norse *holt*, a grove. Though this word is sometimes found in ancient names, see p. 281, yet as a termination there is no reason to think it in any case other than local.

Hope, Op. Anglo-Saxon *hopu*, a mound. Or sometimes in the Danish districts probably from Old Norse *hôp*, a recess.

How. Old Norse *haugr*, a mound, in particular a grave-mound.

AFTER THEIR OWN NAMES. 501

Hurst. Anglo-Saxon *hyrst*, a grove.

Over. Anglo-Saxon *ôfer*, shore, border.

Shaw. Old Norse *skôgr*, Danish *skov*, a wood. Hence BRADSHAW = BROADWOOD. Though this word is found in a few ancient personal names, yet as a termination we may take it to be in all cases local.

Sted. Ang.-Sax. *stede*, Danish *sted*, a fixed place, a " farm-. stead," a " house-stead."

Stow. Ang.-Sax. *stow*, a place.

Ster. Old Norse *stadr*, same as *sted* above, confined to the Norwegian districts of the North of Scotland.

Thorp. Anglo-Saxon and Old Norse *thorp*, German *dorf*, a village. Frequently, both in England, Germany, and Denmark, corrupted into *drup* or *trup*.

Thwaite. Norwegian *thveit*, Dan. *tved*, a clearing in a forest, Ang.-Sax. *thwitan*, to cut. Most common in Cumberland and Westmorland.

Toft. Ang.-Sax. *toft*, Old Norse *tôft*. Its present meaning seems to be a small home field. But the original sense appears to have been that of a spot where a decayed messuage has stood, "area domus vacua," Haldorsen has it. The Norwegian and Swedish form *tômt*, from *tômr*, empty, seems to point to this.

Wick. Ang.-Sax. *wîc*, a dwelling-place. Also a bay, which is the usual, if not the invariable Scandinavian sense. Apt to intermix with *wig*, *wic*, war, a common ending of ancient names.

With. Old Norse *vidr*, a wood. It is confined to the Danish part of England, and corresponds with *wood* in the Saxon. Sometimes confounded with *worth*, an altogether different word. *With* or *wood* is also a common termination of ancient personal names.

Worth, Worthy. Ang.-Sax. *worth*, *worthig*, an estate, farm, field.

502   THEY CALL THEIR LANDS

The names of France do not appear, as far as I can judge, to contain such a variety of local terminations as those of England. The most common are *ville* and *cour*—also *iére*, the etymology of which I cannot explain. It is very frequently formed from a personal name. Thus from Robert, Bernard, Josserand, we have as names of places Robertiére, Bernardiére, Josserandiére.

As a prefix *bois* and *mont* are very common, and very frequently combined with a personal name. Thus in the *Annuaire de Paris* we have BOISGARNIER, BOISGAULTIER, BOISGELIN, BOISGONTIER, BOISGUILBERT, BOISGUYON, BOIS-RENAUD; and in the same volume we have GARNIER, GAULTIER, GELIN, GONTIER, GUILBERT, GUYON, RENAUD, from which the above local names have been formed. So we have MONT-GERARD, MONTGOLFIER, MONTGOBERT, MONTAU-FRAY, MONTANGERAND, MONTMORENCY, MONT-AURIOL, MONTALEMBERT—and the corresponding GERARD, GOLFIER, GOBERT, AUFRAY, ANGERAND, MORENZO, AURIOL, and ELAMBERT, most, if not all, of which, as well as the foregoing, are of Teutonic origin.

There are some names, such as Eng. WATER-FALL, German WASSERFALL, which it is difficult to know whether to ascribe to a local origin or not. They might belong to a class of nnmes like the Eng DRINKWATER, DRAWWATER (both of which Mr. Lower finds in the Hundred Rolls), and the Germ. KALTWASSER, GUTWASSER, SPAR-

AFTER THEIR OWN NAMES. 503

WASSER (Coldwater, Goodwater, Savewater). But another German name STOBWASSER (Dustwater), reminding us of the Staubbach, seems to point more to a local name.

The number of English names derived from places has in my opinion been greatly overrated. As an approximation, I should be disposed to estimate them at about one third of the whole.

CHAPTER XXIX.

OLD SAXONS AND ANGLO-SAXONS.

It may seem a curious fact that we have more of Old Saxon than we have of Ang.-Saxon names. I use the word Old Saxon in its wide sense, and I mean to say that we have at the present day more of those names such as the early invaders—Angles, Saxons, Jutes, or Frisians— brought over with them to this country, than we have of those regular compound names which were current in the height of the Anglo-Saxon power. And further—that if we turn to the ancient seats from which those early settlers came, we shall find that still the same names are current there. There is a people—or rather a remnant of a people—who once owned a large portion of the German sea-board—now much broken up and intermixed, but still in some in-sulated places holding their nationality with little change—very near relatives of ours—though few know more of them than the name. Of all the ancient dialects none has a more close connection with the Anglo-Saxon than the Old Friesic—of all the modern dialects perhaps none has such strong points of resemblance to the English as the New Friesic. On all the wide continent of Europe they alone use the word "woman" like

OLD SAXONS AND ANGLO-SAXONS. 505

ourselves. "It is generally," observes Mr. Latham, " the first instance given of the peculiarity of the Frisian language. 'Why can't they speak properly, and say *kone?*' says the Dane. '*Weib* is the right word,' says the German. 'Who ever says woman? cry both." *(Ethnology of the British Islands.)*

Mr. Halbertsma, in the article written by him in Bosworth's "Origin of the English and Germanic languages," observes that there are few of the early Saxon names which are not in use among the present Frisians, though by time a little corrupted or abbreviated. The same writer remarks upon the connection between Friesic names[*] and those in use in England, quoting a few examples, which might be greatly increased by a reference to Outzen's Glossary, and to Wassenberg's "Eigennaamen der Friesen."

How then is the fact to be accounted for that while we have so many of these names which were common to all the Germanic races, and which are still found so numerously on the shores from which our early settlers came, we have comparatively very few of the regular Anglo-Saxon compound names, such as Athelstan, Athelhard, Ethelbald, Ethelred, &c.? It occurs to me as rather probable that the pure Ang.-Saxon system of compound names might be somewhat of a fashion, confined for the most part to the nobler classes (whose names of course it is that appear

---

[*] Such as Watse, Ritse, Rodse, Gibbe, &c

L 3

506 OLD SAXONS AND ANGLO-SAXONS.

chiefly before us in history), and not pervading the mass of the people, who still held on mainly to the old names to which they had been accustomed. Hence, the Saxon nobility being in part extinguished, and in part Normanized at the Conquest, a reason may be found for the scantiness of names of this class at the present day.

But in fact we find, all through Anglo-Saxon times, many names which were German but not Anglo-Saxon, and Mr. Kemble, in his valuable treatise on " The Names, Surnames, and Nicnames of the Anglo-Saxons," has, I think, dealt with them from rather too exclusive a point of view. Some of these names he thinks can only be explained by reference to Cymric or Pictish roots—such, for instance, as Puch, Padda, Uelhisc, Theabul, Pechthelm, and Pehthat. The two former are only variations of German forms, pp. 378, 166—the third compares with a Williscus, p. 123—the fourth seems only a corruption of Theobald—and the two last, though probably from the name of the Picts, are yet formed on a common Teutonic principle as noticed in chap. 16.

Others, such as Podda, Dudda, Bubba, Tudda, Odda, Obe, Offa, Ibe, Beda, Becca, Beonna, Acca, Hecca, Lulla, he thinks were probably nicnames. But, as I have shewn throughout these pages, names of this class pervade the whole system of Teutonic nomenclature, and they are just the sort that are especially common in Friesland at the present day. The remarks of Mr. Haig upon

OLD SAXONS AND ANGLO-SAXONS. 507

this subject are so much in accordance with my own views that I re-produce them here. "I believe that these simple names are the most ancient, that they belong originally to periods beyond the reach of history. They prevail in the dawn of our annals, as the compounds do in their noon; and it seems to me quite as probable that many of them were given from motives of association with the memory of persons who had gone before, as that they were given on account of personal peculiarities. Thus in the 8th century, when almost all the sovereigns in the Heptarchy bore compounded names, one of these simple names appears almost alone, and that belonging to the most illustrious prince of his time, Offa. His name had been originally Winifrid, but he received that of Offa, in memory of one who had ruled over the Angles, his ancestors, before their coming into Britain; a name which had already been borne by a King of the East Saxons, and perhaps for a similar reason, for he also counted an Offa among his ancestors."

It occurs to me, then, as possible, in the case of some of these personages who appear before us with a regular compound name and also with a simple name—the latter being in Mr. Kemble's opinion a nicname—that it may have been in fact the real original name, and the former only assumed in accordance with the prevailing fashion. Instances of these double names are Athelwold, also called Mol, king of Northumbria; Aldwine,

508 OLD SAXONS AND ANGLO-SAXONS.

also called Wor, bishop of Mercia; Hrôthwaru, also called Bucge; and Adelberga, also called Tata.

There is another class of names to which something of a similar principle may apply. We find an archbishop of Canterbury whose name was Eadsige, but who was also called Æti, and signs by that name. So there was a bishop of Selsey who was generally called Sicgga, but whose name seems to have been properly Sigefrith. And there was an Ælfwine, bishop of Lichfield, who was also called Ælle—a Torhthelm, bishop of Leicester, who is called by nearly every contemporary authority Totta—an Eadwine, duke of the Northumbrians, who also appears as Eda. Mr. Kemble considers all these short names to be merely contractions, answering in fact to our Tom, Bob, Bill. I do not doubt that this may in some instances have been the case, but seeing that these short names are in reality older Teutonic names than the others, I would just suggest the possibility of a simple name being in some cases—as for instance, when a man had received an accession of dignity—lengthened out to correspond with his increased importance. The following remarks by Dr. Doran* bear upon this point. "Length, too, is supposed to have added dignity to a name. Diocles, the man, expanded into Diocletian, the emperor; a parvenu, on acquiring wealth, developed from

---

* "Notes on Names and Nicnames." Universal Review, May, 1860.

OLD SAXONS AND ANGLO-SAXONS. 509

Simon into Simonides ; and when the lady, whose name signified Brown (Bruna), became Queen of France, she added a train to that cognomen as ladies at court do to their dresses, and thenceforth swept loftily across records and registers as Queen Brunehault." In such a manner might perhaps Sicgga become Sigefrith, and Eada Eadwine. This is a theory, however, that must be stated with caution and reserve.

CHAPTER XXX.

THE SCANDINAVIAN VIKINGS.

It must already have been made apparent to the reader, of how high importance, in the explanation of Teutonic names, are the languages of the Scandinavian North. We find many names, borne by Germans, which cannot be explained by a reference to any German dialect, and of which we find the etymons in the Old Norse. The reason of this is two-fold. In the first place, it cannot fail to be the case that any ancient language, with a scanty literature, must have had many words which have not come down to modern times. This is the case with all the ancient German dialects ; and the Old Norse, which amid the stern and desolate rocks of Iceland has preserved a treasure of ancient lore more abundant than the rest, being a language closely cognate, then comes in to their assistance.

In the second place, following out the theory which I have already laid down, that anciently names were bestowed, at least to a considerable extent, not with any reference to their meaning, but simply as having been borne by men who had gone before, it follows that in many cases they have survived dialects, and may often be carried back to a time when the two great branches of the German and the Scandinavian were as yet unsevered.

THE SCANDINAVIAN VIKINGS. 511

In any case it will be apparent that etymology alone would cause us vastly to over-rate the amount of the Scandinavian element in our nomenclature, and that we must take other circumstances into 'consideration in attempting to form even an approximate estimate.

In the year 787, according to the Ang.-Saxon Chronicle, the first three ships of the Northmen visited our shores. And the reeve of the shire, little knowing what manner of men they were, rode over to take them, and there they slew him. " These were the first ships of Danish men which sought the land of the English nation." But the Icelandic records take notice of earlier Scandinavian invasions of Britain, and the opinion of some of our ablest ethnologists is in favour of this belief. Mr. Latham, referring to the statements of the Ang.-Saxon Chronicle, makes the following remarks:—"For the fact of Danes having wintered in England A.D. 787, they are unexceptionable. For the fact of their never having done so before, they only supply the unsatisfactory assertion of a negative. . . . . The present writer believes that there *were* Norsemen in Britain anterior to 787, and also that these Norsemen *may* have been the Picts."

The extent of the Scandinavian colonization of England, and the characteristic features which distinguish it, have been described by Mr. Worsaae in his work on the Danes and Norwegians in England. Its head-quarters were in Lincoln-

512 THE SCANDINAVIAN VIKINGS.

shire, and that part of Yorkshire round the estuary of the Humber. It extended across the island to Chester, and as far north as Cumberland, where it might probably be met by a more purely Norwegian stream from the Isle of Man—Cumberland and Westmorland being more Scandinavian than Northumberland and Durham. The Watling Street formed a boundary to the south-west, which it rarely passed. To some—though, as it seems to me, not to any very marked extent—names of Scandinavian origin are more prevalent in this district than in the rest of England.

There are two classes of names which we may fairly ascribe to the influence of the Northern invasions. The first class consists of names which are in themselves Scandinavian rather than German —that is, names which we find to have been borne by Northmen and not by Germans. The second class consists of names which though in themselves as much German as Scandinavian, yet do in point of fact appear to have been introduced into this country by the Northmen. Neither of these two classes are numerous, and there remains a much larger class in which we cannot attempt to draw any distinction.

In the first class are to be included many of the compounds of Thor, as noticed at p. 128. Also Ketell and its compounds, as English THURKETTLE and ASHKETTLE, and French TURQUETIL and ANQUETIL. Likewise English TURKLE and ROSKELL, from the Old Norse Thorkell and

THE SCANDINAVIAN VIKINGS.

Hrosskel, contractions, as Grimm thinks, of Thorketell and Hrossketel. And English BLUNKELL, which seems to be a similar contraction of the Old Norse Blundketell. ULPH and ORME, as contrasted with WOLF and WORM, exhibit the Scandinavian form as compared with the German. Though the elision of *w* in the final syllable of names was common in some German dialects, it was not so at the beginning. The well-known Danish name Sweyn (English SWAIN and SWAINSON), is one not found among the Germans. Among other names which may be ascribed to the Northmen are English OTTER, OLIFF, HACON, GUNNER, BROTHER, HAVELOCK, DOLPHIN, STURLA, SCHOOLEY,* all of which appear in our early history.

In the second class of names are such as HAROLD, which, though in itself as much German as Scandinavian, yet, as Mr. Kemble has observed, does not make its appearance in our annals until introduced by the Northmen. I include also HOWARD, which also then first makes its appearance. So that there may be a foundation of strict truth for Lord Dufferin's remark in a lecture on the Northmen, that "some sturdy Haavard, the proprietor of a sixty-acre farm, but sprung from that stock the nobility of whose blood has become proverbial, may be successfully opposing a trifling tax at Drontheim, while an illustrious kinsman of his house is the representation of England's majesty at Dublin."

---

* The Old Norse Skûll, from *skyla*, to protect .

M 3

514 THE SCANDINAVIAN VIKINGS.

Among our Irish names are also to be found some trace of the Scandinavian colonization. We have Mc.Auliffe (Olaf), Mc.Gary (Geiri), Mc.Oscar (Asgeir), Mc.Vicar (Vikar), Mc. Swiney (Sweyn), Mc.Caskill (Askell). "Even to the present day," observes Mr. Worsaae, "we can follow, particularly in Leinster, the last traces of the Ostmen through a similar series of peculiar family names, which are by no means Irish, but clearly original Norwegian names; for instance, Mac Hitteric or Shiteric (son of Sigtryg), O'Bruadair (son of Broder), Mac Ragnall (son of Ragnvald), Roaill (Rolf),* Auleef (Olaf), Manus (Magnus), and others. It is even asserted that among the families of the Dublin merchants are still to be found descendants of the old Norwegian merchants formerly so numerous in that city. The names of families adduced in confirmation of this, as Harrold (Harald), Iver (Ivar), Cotter or Mac Otter (Ottar), and others which are genuine Norwegian names, corroborate the assertion."

It does not seem probable that we have many Scandinavian names derived indirectly through the Normans. For even in Normandy names of Scandinavian origin seem to be much less common than they are with us, though it may be owing in part to the greater tendency of the language to disguise or corrupt them. A notable instance is the name of the first duke of Normandy, changed from Hrolf into Rollo.

---

* Rather Hroald?

THE SCANDINAVIAN VIKINGS. 515

In Norway and Denmark at the present day the ancient names are more commonly used as christian than as surnames. They have OLUF, HARULD, KNUD, IVER, STEEN, ESKILD, ELSE, ARNOLD, GUNDE, HILLE, TERKEL, and TORBEN, some of which are more corrupted from their original forms than they are with us.

CHAPTER XXXI.

A CHAPTER OF FRAGMENTS.

There are several groups which I have found it difficult to bring in under any of the heads into which I have divided this work. And there are some others, overlooked in their proper places, which, along with the first-named, will be introduced here.

There is a class of words which seem to have the force of an intensitive, such as *all*, omnis, which is common as a prefix. But though we can account for such names as compounds, there is an evident difficulty with regard to the simple forms, and unless we can suppose the word to have had the sense of the Celtic *all*, magnus, celsus, eximius, we must, I think, assume such forms in the first instance to have been contractions of compound names.

All
Omnis.

SIMPLE FORMS.

Old German Allo, Alla, 5th cent. English ALLO, ALOE, ALLEY, AWL. Mod. Germ. ALLE. French ALÉ, ALLIÉ.

COMPOUNDS.

(Bert, illustrious) Old Germ. Alabert, 9th cent.—Anglo-Saxon Aluberht—Eng. ALBERT, ALLBRIGHT—Mod. German ALBRECHT—French ALABERT, ALBERT. (*Frid*, peace) Old German Alafrid, 8th cent.—English ALLFREY. (*Ger*, spear) Old German Alager, 10th cent.—Ang.-Sax. Algar—English ALGER—Modern German ALKER—French ALGIER, ALÁGRE. (*Hard*, fortis) Ang.-Sax. Ealhard—English ALLARD—Mod. German ALERT—French ALLARD—Ital. ALARDO. (*Hari*, warrior) Old German Alaher, 8th cent.—Ang.-Sax. Ealhere

A CHAPTER OF FRAGMENTS. 517

—French ALLAIRE. (*Mag*, might[*]) Eng. ALLMACK. (*Man*) Old Germ. Alaman, 11th cent.—Eng. ALLMAN—Mod. Germ. AHLMANN. (*Mar*, famous) Old Germ. Alamar, 9th cent.— Eng. ALMAR—Mod. Germ. ALLMER. (*Moth*, *moz*, courage) Old Germ. Alamoth, 6th cent.—French ALLEMOZ. (*Mund*, protection) Old Germ. Alamunt—English ALMOND. (*Noth*, bold) Ang.-Sax. Ælnoth—Eng. ALLNUTT—French ALINOT. (*Ric*, power) Old German Alaric (Gothic king, 5th cent.), Alarih—French ALRICQ, ALLERY. (*Run*, companion) Old German Alarun, 8th cent.—French ALLERON. (*Ward*, guardian) Old Germ. Aloard, 8th cent.—Eng. ALLWARD— Mod. Germ. AHLWARDT—French ALLOUARD. (*Wid*, wood) Old German Aluid, 9th cent.—Eng. ALLWOOD. (*Wig*, war) Old Germ. Alawig, Alawih, 8th cent.—Ang.-Sax. Alewih— Eng. ALLAWAY, ALLVEY—French ALLEVY. (*Wine*, friend) Old German Allowin, 7th cent.—English ALWIN—French ALAVOINE.

Of the same meaning I take to be *fil*, which Förstemann calls " a yet unexplained root, in which we can scarcely venture to think of *filu* (multus)."[†]   There does not appear to me to be any difficulty other than that which exists in the previous case.   The Saxon form *ful* intermixes in a few instances.

SIMPLE FORMS.

Old Germ. Filla, 8th cent.   English FILL, FILLEY, FILE, FULL.   Mod. Germ. FÜLL.   French PHILY, FIALA, FEUILLE.

Fil, Ful. Multus.

DIMINUTIVES.

Eng. FULLECK—French FILOCQUE.   Eng. FILKIN.

PATRONYMICS.

Old German Filing.   English FILLING.

---

[*] We only find one Old Germ. name in which this appears as a termination. Of course there may be others, which have not come down to us, and of which the above seems very probably to be one. See also TALLEMACH, p. 376.

[†] In the name Feologild, of the 16th archbishop of Canterbury, it appears as if from *feolo*, yellow, and it is very probable that the Anglo-Saxons did take it in that sense.

518 A CHAPTER OF FRAGMENTS.

COMPOUNDS.

(Bcud, bot, pot, messenger) Old German Philibaud, .7th cent.—Eng. FILPOT*—French PHILIPPOT, PHILIPPOTEAUX. *(Bert,* illustrious) Old German Filibert, 7th cent.—English FILBERT—Mod. Germ. FILBERT—French PHILIBERT. *(Hard,* fortis) Eng. FULLERD—French FILARD, FEUILLARD. *(Hari,* warrior) Eng. FILER, FILLARY—Fr. PHILERY. *(Liub,* dear) Old Germ. Filuliub, 9th·cent.—Eng. FULLALOVE. *(Man)* Old Germ. Filiman, 9th cent.—English FILEMAN—Mod. German FIELMANN—French FILLEMIN. *(Mar,* famous) Old German Filomar, 5th cent.—Eng. FILLMER, PHILLIMORE, FULLMER—Mod. Germ. FILLMER. *(Dio, thew, thius,* servant) Old Germ. Feletheus, king of the Rugii, 5th cent.—English FILLDEW, FELTOE, FELTUS, FELTHOUSE? FIELDHOUSE? *(Gar,* spear) English FULLAGAR.

Perhaps of a similar meaning may be *gans,* (German *ganz,* totus, integer.) Or it may be, as Förstemann thinks not improbable, only another form of *gand,* p. 74. The name of the Vandal king Genserich, Grimm derives from gänserich, a gander. It may, however, only be from this stem, with the common termination *ric,* power. There is, however, uncertainty about the correct form, see p. 204.

Gans.
Totus.

SIMPLE FORMS.

Old Germ. Genzo. Mod. Germ. GENTZ, GANS. French CANCE, CANCY.

DIMINUTIVES.

Old German Gansalin—Mod. German GÄNZLEN—French CANCALON.

COMPOUNDS.

(Hari, warrior) Old German Gentsar, 9th cent.—French GANTZÈRE. *(Man)* English GANSMAN.

---

* Generally assumed to be a diminutive of Philip—which may be the case—the French having several similar forms, as ROBERTET and HENREQUET,

A CHAPTER OF FRAGMENTS. 519

Possibly to the above may belong the Cauncy or Chauncy in the Roll of Battle Abbey, English CAUNCE, CHANCE, CHANCEY, French CHANCEAU.

I have referred, p. 66, to the ending *heit*, English *hood*, as in Adalheid, &c. This, as an ending, may be reasonably explained, but when we find apparently the same word as a prefix and even as a simple form, it becomes difficult to say in what manner we should interpret it. Weinhold *(Deutschen Frauen)* refers to Old High Germ. *haitar*, serenus.

SIMPLE FORMS.

Old Germ. Haito, Haido, Haida, Eid, 8th cent. English HEIGHT, HAYDAY, ADE, ADIE. Mod. Germ. HAID, HEYDT. French AIDÉ.

Hait.
Hood.

DIMINUTIVES.

Old Germ. Heidilo, Aitla, 8th cent.—English HATELY—Mod. Germ. HEIDEL—French CHÂTEL. English HAYDOCK.

PHONETIC ENDING.

Old Germ. Heidin, 9th cent. English HAYDON. Mod. Germ. HEYDEN, HAYDN. French ADIN.

COMPOUNDS.

(*Hari*, warrior) Old German Haitar, 9th cent.—English HAYTER—Mod. German HEITER—French HETIER. (*Rad*, counsel) Old Germ. Aitrada, 9th cent.—Eng. HATRED.[*]

What the meaning of *horn* is in men's names seems very doubtful. If from horn, *cornu*, there are two senses of which we might think—first, that of a sharp point, like so many of the names in chapter 13—secondly, that of those feats of the drinking-horn on which the Northmen especially so much prided themselves. But Förstemann, in the name Hornung, (he has not the simple form

---

[*] If it be pronounced like our word *hatred*.

520 A CHAPTER OF FRAGMENTS.

Horn,) refers to Ang.-Sax. *hornung*, spurius, filius naturalis. I am inclined to think, however, that Hornung is nothing more than the patronymic of Horn ; the form in which it is found in Anglo-Sax. names of places, as Horningaden and Horningamære, "the valley of the Hornings" and "the boundary of the Hornings," seems inconsistent with any other supposition. Unless, therefore, Horn itself may be taken to mean illegitimate, that meaning ought not to be given to the patronymic Horning. Horn was the hero of one of the most popular of the early romances.

SIMPLE FORMS.

Horn. Anglo-Saxon Horn, *found in Hornesbeorh,** *Cod. Dip.*
Cornu ? 1309. Aldwin Horn, *a tenant before Domesday.* English HORN. Mod. Germ. HORN, French HORNE.

DIMINUTIVES.

English HORNIDGE—Mod. German HORNECK, HORNIG. Mod. Germ. HÖRNLEIN.

PATRONYMICS.

Old German Hornung, 8th cent. Ang.-Saxon Horning, *found in Horningeshæth, now Horningsheath in Sussex.* English HORNING. Mod. Germ. HORNUNG.

COMPOUNDS.

(Hard) Mod. Germ. HORNHARD. *(Hari,* warrior) Eng. HORNER ? *(Man)* Eng. HORNMAN, HORNIMAN—Mod. Germ. HORNEMANN.

If the word *horn* may be taken to have the meaning of illegitimate, there is another word, *belis,* also occurring in men's names, which according to Grimm, has the opposite meaning. It is found in the name of Belisarius, the Gothic general under the emperor Justinian, and there

---

* The surname HORNSBY is from a similar origin (Dan. *by,* village).

A CHAPTER OF FRAGMENTS. 521

are eight other instances of the same name, with some unimportant variations, in the Altdeutsches Namenbuch. Grimm *(Gesch. d. Deutsc. spr.)* refers to Gothic *valis*, legitimate, and makes Belisar = a Gothic Valishar (*hari*, warrior). The following modern names are with some diffidence introduced here.

SIMPLE FORMS.

English BELLISS,* BELLIES, BELLOWS, PALLACE. Mod. Belis. Legitimate. Germ. PALLAS. French PELOSSE, PALISSE.

COMPOUNDS.

(*Hari*, warrior) Old German Belesar, 6th cent. English BELSER, PALLISER. French BELLISCER, BELSEUR, PELISSIER. Ital. BELISARIO.

I doubt very much the explanation of our name LOVECHILD as meaning, an illegitimate person. Luuecild is an early name in the *Liber Vitæ*—it seems to be more probably an epithet of affection.

The Eng. TWISS, TWICE, corresponding with an Old Germ. Zuizo, 9th cent., (High Germ. z = Ang.-Sax. t,) appears to have the meaning of geminus, twin. So also English TWAY, TWINE, whence the patronymic TWINING. Perhaps also TWIGG, with which appears to correspond an Anglo-Saxon Tuica, found in Tuicanham, now Twickenham. Or the last may have the sense of spear, like many other words of the same class elsewhere referred to. TWYMAN, however, I should rather compare with the Old Norse *tweggiamaki*, a double man, i.e., of twice the ordinary size or strength.

---

* See also p. 269.

N 3

522 A CHAPTER OF FRAGMENTS.

Our name LAMMAS might be supposed to be derived from the season, like CHRISTMAS, NOEL, &c. But Lammasse occurs in the Hundred Rolls without prefix ; LAMAS is also a French name ; and there was a king of Lombardy in the 5th cent. called Lamisso or Lamissio—the name, according to the old chroniclers, being derived from *lama*, water, on account of his having in childhood been rescued from a pond.

The following stem seems somewhat obscure —Förstemann refers to Old High German *mez*, modus, or *maz*, cibus.

Mass.
Mess.

SIMPLE FORMS.

Old Germ. Mazzo, Masso, 8th cent. Ang.-Sax. Mœssa,* *found in Mœssanuyrth, Cod. Dip.* 721. English MASSIE, MESSIAH. Mod. Germ. MASS, MESS. French MASSE, MASSÉ, MASSEAU.

DIMINUTIVES.

Old Germ. Massila, *father of Maldra or Masdra, king of the Suevi*, 5th cent., Mezli, 9th cent.—Massilia, *Lib. Vit.*— English MASSALL, MEASEL—Mod., Germ. MASSL, MÄSSEL. Old Germ. Mazelin, bishop of Wurzburg, 11th cent.—English MASLIN—French MASSILLON, MAZELIN.

PHONETIC ENDING.

Old Germ. Massana, *wife of the Lombard king Cleph*, 6th cent. English MASSINA, MESSEENA, MASSON. Mod. Germ. MASSEN. French MASSENA,† MASSON.

PATRONYMICS.

Old Germ. Messinc. Eng. MESSING. French MESENGE.

COMPOUNDS.

(*Hard*) French MASSART. (*Hari*, warrior) Eng. MASSURE, MEASURE—Mod. German MESSER—French MAZIER,

---

* And Mæssings, found in Mæssingaham, now Massingham.

† " Mr. D'Israeli (Coningsby, 2, 203) says that Massena, as well as other French marshals, was a Hebrew, and that his real name was Manasseh. He was a native of Nice. Now in the Piedmontese dialect, *masena* signifies a child. . . Is there any foundation for Mr. D'Israeli's statement ?" *E. G. R. in Notes and Queries. Vol.* 10, *p.* 147.

A CHAPTER OF FRAGMENTS. 523

Messier, Mezière. (*Man*) English Mashman—Mod. Germ. Massman—French Massemin.

PHONETIC INTRUSION OF *n*.
(*Bert*, famous) Eng. Massingberd—French Masimbert.*

The stem *wag, way*, is difficult to separate from the stem *wac*, p. 362. But it seems to me that there is a separate word, probably having the meaning of waving or brandishing, as in the Wægbrand (Wave-sword) in the genealogy of the kings of Northumbria.

SIMPLE FORMS.
Old Germ. Wago, Waggo, 9th cent. Waga, second from Woden in the genealogy of the Mercian kings. Wege (*Domesday*). English Wagg, Wegg, Vague, Way. Mod. Germ. Wage, Wege. French Vaghi, Végé, Veé, Wey.

Wag, Way. Wave, brandish.

DIMINUTIVES.
English Waylen. French Wegelin.

PHONETIC ENDING.
Old Germ. Vagan, 8th cent. Old Norse Vagen. English Wain. French Vagney, Vaganay, Weyn.

COMPOUNDS.
(*Gaud*, Goth) English Waygood. (*Hari*, warrior) Old Germ. Wagher, 8th cent.—English Wager—Mod. German Wager, Weger. (*Man*) English Wagman, Wayman—Mod. Germ. Weymann—French? Wegman. (*Bert*, famous) Old Germ. Wagpraht, 9th cent.—English Weybret.

Respecting the root *aus, aur*, I quote the following remarks of Förstemann. "We must assume such a German root with the meaning of light, brightness; and see it in the German form of the Sanscrit root *usch*, as we also find it in the Latin *aurum, aurora, uro;* in the Greek $\dot{\eta}\dot{\omega}s$, and

---

* There is an Old Frankish name Masembold, 8th cent., similarly formed from this stem.

A CHAPTER OF FRAGMENTS.

in the Ang.-Sax. *eðrendel,* a star. Here appears the simple form of the root, of which we have an extension in *aust, auster* (oriens)."

Aus, Aur.
Brightness.

SIMPLE FORMS.

English ORE, OUSEY. French AUREAU, AURAY, AURY, OURY, ORY, AUSSY, USSE.

DIMINUTIVES.

Old Germ. Ausilas, 6th cent.—English AURIOL, ORIEL—French AUZOLLE, AUREILLE, ORIOLLE. Old German Orizo, 10th cent.—English ORRISS.

PHONETIC ENDING.

Old German Orein, 11th cent. English ORRIN. French AUZON.

COMPOUNDS.

(*Bert,* famous) Old German Auripert, 7th cent.—French AUSBERT. (*Gan,* magic) English ORGAN—French AUREGAN. (*Gar,* spear) English ORGER—French AURIGER. (*Hari,* warrior) Old German Ausari, 9th cent.—French AUSSIÈRE. (*Wald,* power) Old German Ausvold, Ausold, 9th cent.—English HOUSEHOLD?

In the *Haupts zeitschrift* of Weinhold he refers to the name Ochon, of a king of the Heruli, 6th cent., deriving it from the Goth. *auhns,* oven, in the older meaning of fire. Should this derivation obtain, the English OVEN, as well as the Modern German OKEN, and the French OCHIN, may be similarly explained.

A stem of uncertain meaning is *gad,* which Förstemann refers to a lost verb *gadan,** in the sense of uniting. But various other words are so liable to intermix that I will not attempt to give any general meaning to the group.

---

* Hence, I presume, the Mod. Germ. *gatten,* to unite, *gatte,* spouse, &c.

A CHAPTER OF FRAGMENTS. 525

Probably the form *cat* would come in more properly here than as introduced at p. 168.*

SIMPLE FORMS.

Gad.

Old Germ. Gaddo, Gatto, Geddo, Getto, 7th cent. Eng. GADD, GATTY, GEDD, GET, GETTY, CADDY. Mod. German GADE, GEDE, KADE. French GADY, GADÉ, GATEAU, GATHÉ, GETTE, CADEAU.

DIMINUTIVES.

English CADDICK—Modern German GAEDCKE. English CADELL. French GATILLON, CADILHON.

COMPOUNDS.

(*Hari*, warrior) English GETTER—French CADIER. (*Leof*, dear) English GATLIFFE, GETLIVE. (*Man*) Anglo-Saxon Cædmon—English CADMAN, GETTMAN. (*Niw*, young) Old Germ. Gatani, 8th cent.—Eng. GEDNEY. (*Walah*, stranger) Old German Kaduwalah, Cadualus, 8th cent.—Ceadwalha,* king of Wessex—English CADWELL.

PHONETIC INTRUSION OF *l*.†

(*Hari*, warrior) Old German Gadelher, 11th cent.—Mod. Germ. KETTLER—French GATELLIER.

---

* Ought, perhaps, rather to be brought in here than along with *hath*, war, p. 109.

† As well as the form *gadel*, there is also a form *gader*, which might account for such names as English GATHERGOOD, (in the 13th cent. found as Gadregod).

CHAPTER XXXII.

CONCLUSION.

I might—ere taking leave of the subject— amuse the reader by many instances of the curious relation in which names sometimes stand to avocations. Thus of nine MASH's in the London directory, five are dealers in potatoes. PORTE, CLARET, and CHAMPAGNE are wine-merchants in Paris, VERJUS is a doctor, and VIRGILE keeps the hotel Byron. On the other hand CLOVIS and ODIN are tailors, SALADIN is a hair-dresser, MILORD is a grocer, and MINERVE sells lemonade. Madame THAIS watches over the morals of a religious order; Madame MIZERY keeps an hotel, and I dare say makes people very comfortable.

Again—as I have throughout these pages advocated the opinion that many curious-sounding names are only corruptions of ancient names, so I may give a few instances of others which we might have had. We have many which seem to be from beverages—we might also have had ICE-AND-CREAM—the Old Germ. Isancrim (Iron-fierce.) We have GOODENOUGH, and I have taken it to be from an Old Frankish name Godenulf— so we might have had Badenough, from an Old German Badanulf. The termination *wif*, woman, common in ancient female names, might have

CONCLUSION. 527

given us, without any corruption, EGG-WIFE, ANGEL-WIFE, SILLY-WIFE, and COLD-WIFE.* The Old Germ. names Austrigosa and Wisegoz (Ostrogoth and Visigoth) would naturally have become EASTER-GOOSE and WISEGOOSE.

Many other examples I might introduce, but I prefer to close the subject with a more serious train of thought. My aim has been to vindicate the antiquity, and to assert the nobility, of our common English names. I have endeavoured to show that very many of those which seem the meanest and the most vulgar, are in reality the most ancient—that, philologically speaking, the Norman territorial seigneurs are the parvenus—the Babbs and the Bubbs and the Dadds, the Raggs, the Ruggs, and the Wiggs, the Potts, the Juggs, and the Tubbs, the grand old nobility. And in the names of our great rivals by sea and land, I have sought to trace the forgotten relationship of two thousand years.

An eminent modern scholar, the late Dr. Donaldson, has remarked of English names, that "though generally very much corrupted in orthography and pronunciation, they often preserve forms of words which have been lost in the vernacular language of the country, and so constitute a sort of living glossary." This is true, but it is not the whole truth. They contain words which have been lost in the whole cycle of Teutonic languages — they contain senses which have perished, though the words are still extant—

528 CONCLUSION.

they contain all forms of ancient dialects, and all forms of transition between one dialect and another.

Nor is their value less as a record of past modes of thought. There is not one of them but had a meaning once—they are a reflex of a bye-gone age—a commentary on the life of our fore-fathers.

ADDITIONS AND CORRECTIONS.

P. 24.   The ending *ma* in Friesic names, which I have taken to be a diminutive, is considered by Pott and Ruprecht to be the same as *man*.   In that case it would not be the same as the ending *ma*, *mia*, &c., in Old Frankish names with which I have compared it, as many of these names are feminine.

P. 26.   The name Erasmus I have taken to be a latinized form of a Friesic Erasma.   But in default of finding it in any case in the latter form, the derivation of Pott from the Greek Erasmios must perhaps be preferred.

P. 105.   HOULET, HULETT, &c., might also be the same as a Hugolot in the Liber Vitæ, a diminutive or compound of *hug*, p. 357.

P. 125.   I have to apologise for the name CRIMSON.   I found it in Mr. Bowditch's index, and concluded that there was such a name.   Subsequently, referring to the text, I found that it ran—" we have *no* Crimson !"

P. 135.   The name Albruna, of the wise woman of the old Germans, (from *alf*, *elf*, and *rún*, wisdom or mystery, p. 364) was probably derived from her supposed character of soothsayer.   From the same origin comes Oberon, the name of the fairy king.   We have AUBERON as a Christian name, but I do not know it as a family name.

P. 151.·   NEFFLEN is, I think, a German, not an English name.

P. 256.   NESTLE, NESTLING, &c. Grimm, (*Gesch. d. Deutsch. Sprach.*) refers, in the case of an Old German name Nestica, to *nest*, torques, *nestila*, fibula.

P. 261.   FRIDAY might also be derived from an Ang.-Saxon Frigedæg, (found in Frigedæges trêow, Cod. Dip. 1221).   So FREBOUT, also FREEBODY, might be the

o 3

530　ADDITIONS AND CORRECTIONS.

same as an Old German Friobaudes, 6th cent., from *fri*, liber. Hence also FRIAR and FRIARY, Modern German FREIER, from an Old German Friher, 8th cent. And FREEMAN, corresponding with a Friumon in the Liber Vitæ.

P. 262.　SIEVEWRIGHT would be better placed along with SEARIGHT, to an Old German Seuerit, p. 322, from Goth. *saivs*, Ang.-Sax. *sae*, mare.

P. 263.　The introduction of the name GWYNN here may be liable to misconstruction. I merely mean to ask the question whether—comparing it with an Old German Guuine—a Teutonic name can in any case be mixed up with the Celtic.

P. 310.　DANDELYON. The family of this name became extinct in the reign of Edward IV.

P. 313.　The name PICTURE might be from Pictor as a latinization of painter.

P. 317.　The most certain instance of Scot as a baptismal, and not as a descriptive name, is a Scot Agumdessune (for Agemundessune ?) in the Liber Vitæ.

P. 349.　Our name RECKNELL is more probably the same as the German RECKNAGEL, p. 221.

P. 382.　The Ang.-Sax. Uhtred ought not, I think, to come in here ; the stem *act*, p. 450, is more suitable.

P. 397.　The authority for the statement that the name of the Maid of Orleans was properly Darc, not D'Arc, is her latest French biographer, whose name I do not at present remember, and whose information was derived from an examination of ancient documents.

P. 425.　Pott has GROVE and GROVEMANN as Low German names.

P. 464.　Our name GRASSICK corresponds with a Garsic in the Liber Vitæ, Ang.-Saxon *gærs*, another form of *græs*.

INDEX OF FRENCH NAMES.

Abault, 61
Abavid, 61
Abbadie, 61
Abbé, 60
Abbette, 61
Abert, 61
Abit, 61
Acar, 210
Acart, 210
Accault, 210
Aclocque, 210
Adde, 287
Adée, 287
Adeline, 337
Adelon, 337
Adhemar, 288
Adin, 519
Admant, 288
Adolphe, 72, 288
Adoul, 337
Adour, 288
Aeschimann, 217
Agasse, 193
Agenet, 210
Agis, 193
Agmand, 210
Agon, 211
Agoult, 210
Agram, 210
Agron, 210
Aidé, 519
Aigle, 94
Aigoin, 210
Aiguillé, 94, 154
Aillard, 154
Ailleret, 154
Ailly, 154
Aimard, 492
Aimé, 492
Ajalbert, 154
Ajasse, 193
Alabert, 516
Alâgre, 516
Alavoine, 517
Albaret, 135
Albenque, 135
Albert, 516
Albin, 134
Albo, 134
Albrand, 299, 418
Alby, 134
Aldebert, 418
Aldon, 418
Alé, 516
Alecan, 418

Alely, 426
Alfred, 135
Algier, 516
Aligrot, 427
Alinot, 517
Alix, 142
Alkan, 418
Allain, 238
Allard, 516
Allaire, 517
Allaiz, 300
Allaume, 38
Alleaume, 38
Allemoz, 517
Allengry, 239
Alleron, 517
Allery, 517
Allevy, 517
Allié, 516
Allien, 238
Allonier, 239
Allouard, 517
Alphonse, 338
Alquier, 142
Alricq, 517
Altairac, 419
Altaroche, 418
Alteriet, 418
Amade, 284
Amadeuf, 284
Amblard, 143
Amail, 143
Amédée, 284
Amelin, 143
Ameling, 143
Amette, 284
Amey, 492
Amis, 284
Amiaume, 493
Amory, 130
Ampaire, 312
Amurat, 492
Anceau, 119
Anceaume, 119
Ancel, 119
Ancelin, 119
Ancement, 120
Andraud, 300
Andro, 300
Andry, 300
Anery, 289
Anfray, 289
Angé, 212
Angel, 213
Angelier, 213

Angerand, 502
Angevin, 212
Angibert, 292
Angibout, 292
Anglement, 213
Anglade, 213
Anglard, 213
Angouard, 293
Anguy, 212
Anicker, 289
Anjubault, 292
Anne, 289
Anné, 289
Année, 289
Anquetil, 52, 512
Ansart, 119
Anselin, 119
Anselme, 119
Ansmann, 120
Ansmant, 120
Ansel, 119
Antheaume, 432
Antier, 432
Antiq, 432
Antraygues, 300
Anty, 432
Appay, 60
Appert, 61
Aran, 95
Arago, 387
Arbogast, 50, 386
Arbeau, 386
Arbey, 386
Arbomont, 386
Arbre, 386
Archambault, 12, 432
Archereau, 388
Archinard, 432
Ardier, 250
Ardouin, 251
Arfort, 386
Argand, 388
Argy, 387
Arioli, 95
Arlouin, 340
Armandeau, 147
Armandet, 147
Armengaud, 50 146
Armenté, 147
Armeny, 146
Armet, 147
Armez, 147
Arnault, 95
Arnold, 95
Arnou, 95

532 INDEX OF FRENCH NAMES.

Arnould, 95
Arondel, 152
Arpin, 386
Arquin, 432
Arrault, 95
Arranger, 95
Arrivetz, 95
Arrondeau, 95
Artault, 251
Arteil, 250
Artus, 250
Arveuf, 386 ·
Arvier, 386
Ascoli, 216
Asperti, 119
Astel, 216
Astier, 216
Astorgis, 303
Astruc, 216
Asse, 89, 119
Assegond, 119
Asselin, 119
Assell, 119
Assuerus, 120
Atloff, 288
Atys, 288
Aubard, 135
Aubé, 134
Aubel, 134
Aubery, 135
Aubez, 134
Aubier, 135
Aubigny, 134
Aubin, 134
Aubineau, 134
Aubouer, 135
Aubouin, 135
Aubriet, 135
Aubrun, 135
Auchard, 142
Aude, 381
Audebrand, 382
Audemars, 382
Audevard, 52, 282
Audibert, 52, 381
Audier, 382
Audiffred, 382
Audiffret, 382
Audiganne, 382
Audiguier, 52, 382
Audille, 381
Audin, 381
Audis, 381
Audiquet, 381
Audouard, 52, 382
Audoin, 382
Audouin, 52
Audouy, 382
Audran, 382
Audy, 381
Auer, 290
Aufray, 502
Auger, 382

Auray, 524
Aureau, 524 ·
Auregan, 524
Aureille, 524
Auriger, 524 ·
Ausbert, 524
Aussière, 524
Auspert, 119
Auteroche, 382
Autheland, 382
Authier, 382
Autié, 381
Autin, 381
Autier, 382
Autran, 382
Autrique, 382
Auzolle, 524
Auzon, 524
Avare, 290
Avart, 290
Aveline, 290
Avi, 290
Avisseau, 290
Avisse, 290
Avizard, 290
Avizart, 290
Avizeau, 290
Aycard, 210
Ayel, 154
Aymer, 210, 492
Aymes, 492
Aymont, 210, 492
Ayrault, 95
Azard, 169
Azan, 169
Aze, 169
Azema, 169
Azémar, 169
Azibert, 169
Azille, 169
Azimon, 169

Babault, 291
Babé, 291
Babeau, 291
Babeuf, 291
Babin, 291
Bablin, 291
Babonneau, 291
Babouard, 291
Baboulène, 291
Babuleau, 291
Bac, 172
Baccaud, 172
Bach, 172
Bachiment, 172
Bacqua, 172
Bacquart, 172
Bacque, 172
Bacquet, 172
Badel, 166
Bader, 166
Badier, 166

Badou, 166
Bady, 166
Baffert, 291
Bagard, 172
Bagary, 172
Bagier, 172 ·
Baglan, 172
Bague, 172
Bail, 192
Bailla, 192
Bailliard, 192 ·
Bailière, 192
Baillieu, 192
Bailly, 172, 192
Baissin, 181
Balay, 192
Balcoq, 27
Baldé, 241
Baldeveck, 242
Balery, 192
Baldi, 241
Ballard, 192
Balle, 192
Balleret, 192
Balloche, 192
Bally, 192
Ballu, 192
Balsan, 242
Balsemine, 241
Baltar, 131, 241
Baltard, 241
Baltazard, 241
Balzac, 241
Banc, 182
Bance, 235
Bancelin, 235
Banié, 175
Bannielle, 175
Bannier, 175
Banouard, 175
Bangy, 182
Bansard, 236
Baraban, 70
Barault, 61
Barachin, 61
Bard, 222]
Bardé, 222
Bardeau, 222
Bardelle, 222
Bardillon, 222
Bardon, 222
Bardonneau, 222
Bardy, 222
Barelle, 61
Barnay, 423
Barnet, 423
Barnich, 423
Barnier, 423
Barnouvin, 423
Baroin, 62
Barratte, 62
Barre, 61
Barré, 61

INDEX OF FRENCH NAMES.

533

Barrean, 61
Barret, 62
Barris, 61
Barteau, 222
Bartel, 222
Barry, 61
Bassaget, 181
Basse, 181
Basseé, 181
Basso, 181
Basta, 183
Bastard, 183
Baster, 183
Bastie, 183
Bastier, 183
Bataille, 166
Batard, 167
Batault, 167
Batel, 166
Bathery, 167
Bathilde, 167
Batté, 166
Battu, 166
Baud, 241
Baudeau, 241
Baudement, 241
Baudeuf, 242
Baudichon, 241
Baudier, 241
Baudin, 242
Baudouin, 242
Baudrand, 241
Baudrit, 241
Baudro, 242
Baudron, 241
Baudry, 241
Bauduer, 241
Bavard, 291
Bebert, 414
Bec, 222
Béchade, 222
Bechman, 222
Beck, 222
Becker, 222
Becklé, 222
Becquemie, 222
Becquet, 222
Becquey, 222
Bedard, 167
Bedé, 166
Bedeau, 166
Bedel, 166
Bedier, 167
Bedmar, 167
Bednec, 166
Bedouin, 167
Bedu, 166
Béfort, 414
Belac, 269
Belaize, 269
Belet, 269
Belhomme, 269
Belin, 270

Belissent, 270
Bellamy, 24, 192
Bellart, 269
Bellavoine, 270
Belleau, 192
Bellée, 192
Bellemar, 192
Bellemain, 269
Bellemare, 269
Bellenot, 269
Belletre, 219
Bellhomme, 192
Belli, 192
Bellicard, 269
Bellier, 269
Belligard, 269
Belliscer, 521
Belloc, 269
Bellu, 192
Belment, 269
Belnot, 269
Belseur, 521
Belz, 269
Bena, 176
Benard, 177
Bence, 177, 235
Benech, 176
Benecke, 176
Benda, 235
Bender, 236
Bengel, 182
Benier, 177
Benz, 177, 235
Ber, 68
Berard, 69
Beral, 69
Beranger, 70
Berault, 69
Bercher, 69
Beer, 68
Berge, 279
Bergeau, 279
Berger, 69, 279
Bergerat, 279
Berguerand, 279
Berheaume, 69
Berich, 69
Berille, 69
Berillon, 69
Beringer, 70
Berjeault, 279
Berl, 69
Berly, 69
Bermard, 69
Bermond, 69
Bermont, 69
Bernard, 26, 71
Bernardet, 26
Bernardin, 26
Bernault, 71
Berne, 70
Bernelle, 70
Berney, 70

Bernier, 71
Berot, 69
Berquier, 279
Berquin, 69
Berryer, 69
Berta, 370
Bertall, 370
Bertault, 370
Berte, 370
Berteau, 370
Bertel, 370
Bertey, 370
Bertheaume, 370
Berthelin, 370
Berthier, 370
Bertier, 370
Bertin, 370
Bertomier, 370
Bertrand, 370
Bertrant, 370
Bertray, 370
Bertron, 370
Bestault, 183
Best, 183
Bestel, 183
Bessard, 181
Bessay, 181
Besse, 181
Beslay, 181
Besson, 181
Bessona, 181
Bessoneau, 181
Betail, 166
Bethery, 167
Betou, 166
Bette, 166
Bevaire, 91
Bibal, 414
Bibaut, 414
Biber, 91
Bibert, 414
Bibus, 414
Bical, 177
Bichard, 178
Bicheron, 178
Bidault, 167
Bied, 166
Biére, 68
Biffaut, 414
Biffé, 414
Bigé, 177
Bigeard, 178
Bigey, 177
Bigle, 177
Bigot, 178
Bigre, 178
Billard, 269
Billault, 270
Bilbault, 269
Bilco, 269
Bilhet, 269
Bilken, 269
Bille, 269

534 INDEX OF FRENCH NAMES.

Billecoq, 27
Billet, 269
Billequin, 269
Billey, 269
Billez, 269
Billiard, 269
Billiére, 269
Billing, 269
Billion, 270
Billoteau, 219
Bina, 176
Binant, 177
Binard, 177
Binda, 235
Binder, 236
Bineau, 176
Biney, 176
Bing, 178
Bingé, 178
Binier, 177
Binnecher, 177
Binoch, 176
Binz, 177
Biron, 70
Bisard, 181
Biseau, 181
Bissay, 181
Bissen, 181
Bitcher, 178
Bivert, 414
Blacher, 395
Blachier, 395
Blad, 376
Bladier, 376
Blain, 396
Blaive, 184
Blanc, 392
Blanca, 392
Blancard, 393
Blanchard, 393
Blanche, 392
Blancheron, 393
Blanchet, 393
Blanchin, 392
Blandin, 397
Blangeard, 393
Blangy, 392
Blanquart, 393
Blanque, 392
Blanquet, 393
Blanquier, 393
Blanzy, 397
Blaque, 395
Blatin, 376
Blatte, 376
Blatter, 376
Blavier, 184
Blavin, 184
Blech, 393
Bled, 376, 440
Bleé, 396
Blein, 396
Blenner, 396

Blequier, 393
Bless, 440
Blesseau, 440
Blesser, 441
Blessing, 440
Blet, 376, 440
Bletel, 376, 440
Bletery, 376
Bleton, 376, 440
Bléquier, 393
Bleu, 396
Blevanus, 184
Blève, 184
Blin, 396
Bloo, 214
Blocaille, 215
Blomard, 465
Blome, 465
Blond, 397
Blondé, 397
Blondeau, 397
Blondel, 397
Blondin, 397
Bloquel, 215
Bloquiére, 215
Blou, 396
Blum, 465
Bobant, 422
Bobée, 421
Boblet, 422
Bobiére, 422
Bobin, 422
Boboeuff, 422
Bobot, 422
Boch, 224
Bochard, 225
Bochin, 225
Bochmer, 225
Bodard, 455
Bodart, 455
Bodasse, 454
Bodeau, 454
Boder, 455
Bodevin, 455
Bodichon, 454
Bodier, 455
Bodin, 454
Bodo, 454
Boffin, 422
Boeuf, 421
Bognard, 225
Bognier, 225
Bohard, 225
Bohné, 225
Boimer, 225
Boin, 225
Boiron, 314
Boisgarnier, 502
Boisgaultier, 502
Boisgelin, 502
Boisgontier, 502
Boisguilbert, 502
Boisguyon, 502

Boisrenaud, 502
Bola, 281
Boler, 281
Boll, 281
Bollack, 281
Bollé, 281
Bolley, 281
Bompart, 176
Bon, 175
Bonnafous, 176
Bonald, 176
Bonamy, 24, 177
Bonaparte, 55, 176
Bonardi, 176
Bonasseaux, 175
Bondeau, 235
Bondy, 235
Bonfils, 176
Bonheur, 176
Bonichon, 175
Boniface, 176
Bonier, 176
Boninc, 175
Bonnaire, 176
Bonnard, 176
Bonnardet, 176
Bonnaud, 175
Bonnay, 175
Bonne, 175
Bonneau, 175
Bonnefons, 176
Bonnell, 175
Bonnelye, 175
Bonnemain, 176
Bonnement, 176
Bonnery, 176
Bonni, 175
Bonningue, 175
Bonnissent, 176
Bonno, 175
Bonny, 175
Bonnyaud, 175
Bonomé, 177
Bonpard, 176
Bonté, 235
Bonys, 175
Bonzé, 175, 235
Borda, 229
Borde, 229
Bordery, 229
Bordier, 229
Bordmann, 229
Bos, 408
Boselli, 408
Bossard, 408
Bosse, 408
Bossuroy, 408
Bossy, 408
Bost, 409
Bottelin, 454
Bottemer, 455
Bothey, 454
Botti, 454

INDEX OF FRENCH NAMES. 535

Bottier, 455
Bottin, 454
Boucard, 379
Boucart, 379
Boucasse, 379
Bouchard, 379
Bouché, 378
Boucheny, 379
Boucher, 379
Boucherie, 379
Boucheron, 379
Boucherot, 379
Bouchet, 379
Bouchez, 379
Bouchon, 379
Boucly, 379
Boucon, 379
Boucry, 379
Boudard, 455
Boudault, 455
Boudeau, 454
Boudevin, 455
Boudier, 455
Bougault, 379
Bouglé, 379
Bouglon, 379
Bougon, 379
Bougrain, 379
Bougueret, 379
Bouhier, 379
Bouillac, 281
Bouillard, 281
Bouillé, 281
Bouillerie, 281
Bouillien, 281
Bouillier, 281
Bouilly, 281
Boulan, 281
Boulas, 281
Boulay, 281
Bouligaud, 281
Boulier, 281
Boullard, 281
Boullery, 281
Boulloche, 281
Boulmier, 281
Boulo, 281
Boulu, 281
Bouneau, 416
Bouquerot, 379
Bouquet, 379
Bouquillon, 379
Bour, 452
Bourard, 452
Bourdeau, 329
Bourdel, 329
Bourdelande, 330
Bourdelon, 329
Bourdet, 330
Boudier, 330
Bourdin, 329
Bouré, 452
Boureau, 452

Bourg, 279
Bourges, 279
Bourgery, 279
Bourla, 452
Bourrel, 452
Bourrillon, 452
Bourquard, 279
Boussiere, 408
Bont, 454
Boutard, 455
Boutaric, 455
Boutel, 454
Boutelon, 454
Bouthey, 454
Boutier, 455
Boutrais, 455
Boutron, 455
Boutung, 454
Bouty, 454
Bouvard, 422
Bouvelet, 422
Bouvier, 422
Bouville, 422
Bouvin, 422
Bouvry, 422
Boy, 313
Boyard, 313
Boyé, 313
Boyer, 313
Boyreau, 313
Boyron, 314
Brachard, 185
Bracher, 185
Brack, 185
Bracq, 184
Brag, 130
Brahy, 184
Brainne, 185
Brame, 371
Bramma, 371
Brand, 198
Brandao, 198
Brandau, 198
Brandely, 198
Brandès, 199
Brandy, 198
Braquelonne, 185
Braquemin, 185
Brasa, 443
Brassac, 443
Brassart, 443
Brasserie, 443
Brassier, 443
Braud, 218
Brault, 185
Bray, 184
Brayer, 185
Brayoud, 185
Brazier, 53
Brazy, 443
Bréard, 185
Bréau, 184
Brechard, 185

Brechemin, 185
Breck, 184
Brée, 184
Bregand, 185
Brégeard, 185
Bregere, 185
Bregevin, 185
Breht, 370
Bremard, 371
Bremond, 371
Bremont, 371
Bresillon, 186
Bressand, 186
Bresse, 186
Bresseau, 186
Bressel, 186
Bresser, 186
Bressy, 186
Bret, 185
Bretar, 185
Breteau, 185
Bretel, 185
Bretocq, 185
Breucq, 193
Breyer, 185
Breysse, 186
Brezol, 186
Briant, 185
Briard, 185
Bricaire, 185
Bricard, 185
Brichard, 185
Bricon, 185
Bride, 185
Brideau, 185
Brigaud, 185
Brimeur, 371
Brimont, 371
Brioude, 185
Brique, 184
Brisac, 186
Brise, 186
Brissard, 186
Brissaud, 186
Brisay, 186
Brizard, 186
Broc, 193
Broca, 90
Brocard, 194
Brocq, 90
Brodin, 218
Brodu, 218
Broet, 218
Brondel, 198
Bronder, 199
Brossard, 480
Brosse, 480
Brossel, 480
Brossier, 480
Brot, 218
Brousse, 186
Brucy, 186
Bruezier, 186

536 INDEX OF FRENCH NAMES.

Brugière, 194
Bruhière, 194
Brun, 399
Brunache, 399
Brunant, 400
Brunard, 400
Bruneau, 399
Brunel, 399
Bruner, 400
Brunet, 400
Brunnarius, 400
Brunner, 400
Bruno, 399
Bruny, 399
Bruzelin, 186
Bubeck, 422
Bucaille, 379
Bucker, 379
Bucklé, 379
Buddicom, 455
Budillon, 454
Budin, 454
Buffault, 422
Buffet, 422
Buffier, 422
Buffon, 422
Buisman, 407
Bulard, 281
Bulla, 281
Bulle, 281
Bulleau, 281
Bullier, 281
Bully, 281
Buloz, 281
Bunet, 416
Bunon, 416
Bunzel, 235
Burc, 279
Burchard, 279
Burckel, 279
Burde, 329
Burdet, 330
Burdin, 329
Burgal, 279
Burgard, 279
Burq, 279
Burt, 370
Burtard, 370
Burthé, 329
Burthe, 329
Burty, 370
Burvevin, 279
Bussard, 407
Busse, 407
Busser, 407
Bussière, 407
Bussy, 407
Bustault, 409
Butheau, 454
Buttez, 454
Butti, 454
Buttin, 454

Cabé, 285
Cadeau, 525
Cadier, 525
Cadilhon, 525
Caffort, 248
Cagin, 174
Cagnard, 174
Cahen, 174
Caillant, 437
Caillard, 437
Caillault, 437
Caille, 436
Cailleau, 436
Caillebotte, 437
Caillelau, 437
Cailler, 437
Caillier, 437
Cailliez, 437
Caillon, 437
Caillouée, 437
Cain, 174
Calaret, 437
Callebaut, 437
Callery, 437
Callier, 437
Callon, 437
Calvo, 83
Cam, 436
Camard, 436
Camaret, 436
Camier, 436
Camin, 436
Campy, 171
Canal, 444
Canard, 101, 444
Canault, 444
Cancalon, 518
Cance, 518
Cancy, 518
Canda, 74
Candelle, 74
Candre, 74
Candy, 74
Canier, 444
Canivet, 201
Canneva, 201
Canon, 444
Cantel, 74
Cantier, 74
Cantillon, 74
Caraman, 203
Cardon, 277
Careau, 202
Carel, 202
Carey, 202
Carlin, 202
Carment, 203
Carnot, 203
Carod, 203
Carol, 59
Carraz, 202
Carré, 202
Carrette, 339

Carriére, 203
Cart, 276
Cartault, 277
Carteau, 276
Carteret, 277
Carthery, 277
Cartier, 53, 277
Carton, 277
Carquin, 202
Castaing, 296
Castaldi, 296
Castan, 296
Castel, 296
Casterat, 296
Castier, 296
Castrique, 296
Casty, 296
Cat, 168
Catal, 168
Catala, 168
Catau, 168
Catillon, 168
Catty, 168
Catu, 168
Cauchard, 307
Cauche, 307
Cauchy, 307
Caudron, 477
Causin, 309
Caussade, 309
Caussat, 309
Causse, 309
Cauzard, 309
Cauzique, 309
Cavel, 285
Cazalong, 205
Caze, 205
Cazel, 205
Cellard, 308
Cellerin, 308
Cellier, 308
Celesse, 308
Cels, 308
Cendre, 456
Cent, 456
Cérémonie, 230
Cesac, 272
Ceysson, 272
Cezard, 272
Cezille, 272
Chabault, 168
Chabot, 168
Chabrand, 199
Chadinet, 168
Chadirac, 168
Chaft, 219
Chamel, 419
Champagne, 526
Champeau, 171
Champlon, 171
Champy, 171
Chanceau, 519
Chandel, 74

INDEX OF FRENCH NAMES. 537

Chanteau, 74
Chanterac, 75
Chantier, 74
Chantrot, 74
Chapt, 219
Charavay, 233
Charey, 231
Charfe, 356
Charier, 232
Chario, 231
Charle, 59
Charmond, 50, 233
Charmont, 50, 233
Charmotte, 233
Charoin, 233
Charot, 339
Charpin, 357
Charpy, 356
Chartier, 250
Charton, 251
Charue, 231
Charvey, 233
Charvin, 233
Chassard, 307
Chastaing, 296
Châtel, 519
Chatelin, 168
Chaumer, 60
Chaussée, 307
Chaussier, 307
Chaussy, 307
Chefter, 219
Chely, 322
Chemery, 423
Cheneveau, 201
Chereau, 223
Cheri, 223
Chesneau, 459
Chesney, 459
Chessé, 459
Chevy, 285
Chicard, 358
Chièze, 459
Chilman, 163
Chimay, 423
Chimel, 423
Chimène, 423
Chipier, 286
Chippard, 285
Chiquet, 358
Chobillon, 227
Chocart, 341
Chochon, 340
Chocquet, 341
Chomeau, 59
Chon, 327
Chonez, 327
Chonneaux, 327
Chopard, 227
Choqier, 307
Choquart, 341
Choque, 307, 340
Choquet, 341

Choquier, 341
Chorey, 223
Chottard, 360
Chotteau, 360
Choupe, 227
Christ, 133, 484
Christel, 133
Christy, 133
Ciceri, 272
Cinna, 327
Cinquin, 327
Cintrat, 456
Ciza, 272
Clabaut, 183
Clabbeck, 183
Cladung, 435
Clarenc, 374
Claret, 526
Clarey, 374
Clair, 374
Clairin, 374
Claparéde, 183
Clapeyron, 183
Clapier, 183
Clapisson, 183
Clariat, 374
Classen, 392
Claude, 377
Claudel, 377
Claudin, 377
Clavé, 183
Claveau, 183
Clavel, 183
Claverie, 183
Clavey, 183
Clavier, 183
Clavrot, 183
Claye, 352
Clayette, 352
Clech, 352
Clenchard, 199
Cler, 374
Clérambault, 374
Clerambourg, 374
Cleret, 374
Clérin, 374
Clérisse, 374
Clermont, 374
Clery, 374
Cliver, 414
Clodomir, 46, 50, 377
Cloquemin, 352
Cloquet, 352
Clotilde, 46, 377
Clouet, 352
Clovis, 46, 378, 526
Cocard, 446
Coccoz, 446
Cochard, 446
Coche, 446
Cochelin, 446
Cochery, 446
Cochin, 446

Cochinart, 446
Coclin, 446
Coderet, 116
Codini, 116
Codron, 116
Coffard, 248
Coffin, 249
Coffineau, 249
Coffy, 248
Cogez, 446
Cognard, 446
Cogny, 446
Coiffard, 248
Coindret, 328
Colbert, 226
Colére, 226
Coli, 226
Colinard, 226
Collange, 226
Collard, 226
Colle, 226
Colleau, 226
Collery, 226
Collichon, 226
Collier, 53, 226
Collman, 226
Colombert, 226
Com, 59
Côme, 296
Comont, 60
Commeny, 297
Commun, 297
Conard, 328
Conchan, 327
Congs, 329
Congy, 329
Conil, 327
Conilleau, 327
Coninx, 329
Conneau, 327
Connerat, 328
Connés, 327
Connier, 328
Conord, 328
Conort, 328
Conrad, 328
Conseil, 163
Conté, 163
Conti, 163
Conter, 164
Continant, 164
Contour, 164
Copeau, 248
Copel, 248
Coppez, 248
Coq, 446
Coqueau, 446
Coquelin, 446
Coquot, 446
Coquille, 446
Coquin, 446
Cora, 202
Coralli, 202

Γ 3

538 INDEX OF FRENCH NAMES.

Corich, 202
Cornay, 433
Cornely, 433
Cornichon, 433
Cornibert, 433
Cornilleau, 433
Cornillon, 433
Corsain, 409
Corta, 409
Cortel, 409
Cortier, 409
Coru, 202
Cosmène, 310
Cosne, 310
Cosnuau, 310
Cosquin, 309
Cosse, 309
Cossé, 309
Cosseret, 310
Cossin, 309
Costa, 360
Costard, 360
Costaz, 360
Coste, 360
Costel, 360
Costes, 360
Costey, 360
Costille, 360
Coté, 115
Coteau, 115
Cotel, 115
Coteret, 116
Cothrune, 116
Cotta, 115
Cottance, 115
Cottard, 116
Cotte, 115
Cottey, 115
Couard, 336
Couardeau, 336
Coubart, 336
Couder, 116
Coudert, 116
Coudoin, 117
Coudy, 115
Coué, 336
Couenne, 336
Coumon, 337
Coune, 327
Course, 409
Coursel, 409
Courson, 409
Coursserant, 409
Coursy, 409
Court, 409
Courteau, 409
Courtier, 409
Courtin, 409
Courty, 409
Cousin, 309
Coussy, 309
Coustard, 360
Cousteau, 360

Coutance, 115
Coutanseau, 115
Coutard, 116
Couteau, 52, 115
Coutem, 115
Coutier, 116
Coutin, 117
Coutray, 116
Coutrot, 116
Couty, 115
Coutz, 115
Couzineau, 309
Coville, 248
Coze, 309
Cozic, 309
Cozzi, 309
Cramm, 97
Crenier, 465
Crepé, 188
Crepeau, 188
Crepelle, 188
Crepy, 188
Crespin, 404
Crespel, 404
Cresson, 401
Creucy, 404
Creusard, 404
Creuse, 404
Creuzé, 404
Cria, 170
Cribier, 188
Crispin, 404
Croco, 253
Crobey, 425
Crochard, 253
Crochet, 253
Cron, 465
Croneau, 465
Cronier, 465
Croppi, 425
Croquart, 253
Crossard, 406
Crosse, 405
Crotté, 371
Croué, 253
Crousse, 404
Crousi, 404
Croutelle, 372
Crouts, 372
Croutsch, 372
Croze, 405
Crozier, 406
Cruice, 404
Cruq, 253
Crussiére, 404
Crussy, 404
Cruz, 404
Cruzel, 404
Cucu, 105
Cudey, 115
Cufay, 248
Cuit, 115
Cumenge, 297

Cumon, 297
Cunault, 328
Cuny, 327
Cuqu, 105
Curnier, 433
Curtelin, 409
Curty, 409

Dabeau, 428
Dabée, 428
Dabert, 428
Dablin, 428
Dabrin, 428
Dacbert, 50, 391
Daces, 390
Dachery, 391
Daclin, 390
Dacquin, 391
Dado, 291
Daffy, 428
Dafrique, 428
Daga, 390
Dagand, 390
Dages, 390
Dagest, 391
Dagin, 338
Dagneau, 338
Dagoin, 391
Dagomet, 391
Dagoury, 391
Dagrin, 391
Dagron, 391
Daguerre, 391
Dailly, 390
Dalbert, 375
Dalcrac, 376
Dalger, 375
Dalibon, 375
Dallé, 375
Dallemagne, 376
Dallery, 375
Dalliard, 375
Dalloz, 375
Dally, 375
Dalon, 375
Dalvi, 376
Damas, 365
Damay, 364
Damazy, 365
Dame, 364
Damé, 364
Damel, 365
Damelon, 365
Damer, 365
Dameron, 365
Damet, 365
Damez, 365
Damm, 364
Damotte, 365
Damour, 365
Dan, 311
Dancoine, 359
Dancourt, 359

INDEX OF FRENCH NAMES.

539

Dancla, 359
Dandou, 310
Danel, 311
Danelle, 311
Dancy, 311
Dangla, 359
Dangouelle, 359
Danguis, 359
Danin, 311
Danne, 311
Danneberg, 311
Danquin, 359
Dansard, 310
Danse, 310
Dantier, 310
Danton, 310
Danty, 310
Danvin, 310
Danzel, 310
Dappe, 428
Dapy, 428
Darche, 397
Darclon, 397
Dard, 209
Dardenne, 209
Dardie, 209
Dardier, 209
Dargaud, 208
Dargenne, 208
Daridan, 209
Darier, 208
Darnay, 398
Darnet, 208
Darnis, 398
Darqué, 397
Darquier, 397
Darralde, 208
Darru, 208
Darte, 209
Dary, 208
Dasset, 385
Dassier, 385
Dassy, 385
Davach, 428
Davault, 428
Daval, 428
Daveron, 428
Davin, 428
Davy, 428
Déchard, 391
Dechaume, 391
Dechilly, 390
Decker, 391
Decla, 390
Decle, 390
Decline, 390
Decori, 391
Decq, 390
Decrand, 391
Decret, 391
Decuve, 391
Dedouve, 333
Dedron, 333

Degalle, 390
Degay, 390
Deglane, 390
Degobert, 50, 391
Degof, 391
Degola, 390
Degory, 391
Degrand, 391
Delabaud, 375
Delaire, 375
Delamothe, 376
Delamotte, 376
Delamarre, 376
Delan, 375
Delanneau, 375
Delay, 375
Delcau, 375
Delemer, 376
Delery, 375
Delesse, 375
Delimier, 376
Delinge, 375
Dellac, 375
Delle, 375
Delmer, 376
Delmon, 376
Delmotte, 376
Deloffre, 375
Delocre, 375
Deloger, 375
Delouard, 376
Delrocq, 376
Demait, 457
Demanne, 457
Demar, 365
Demart, 365
Demante, 457
Demay, 364
Demelun, 365
Demey, 364
Demier, 365
Demolin, 365
Demolle, 365
Demoisy, 365
Demoque, 365
Demotte, 365
Demory, 365
Demoulin, 365
Denaigre, 311, 338
Denaiffe, 312
Denant, 311
Denard, 311
Denechau, 311
Denéchaud, 311
Denecher, 311
Dencre, 311, 338
Deneff, 312
Denert, 311
Denier, 311
Denin, 311
Dennery, 311
Dentu, 310
Denullein, 310

Derche, 397
Derni, 398
Derquenne, 397
Desaint, 385
Desert, 385
Desrat, 385
Dessant, 385
Dessolle, 385
Detang, 332
Detuncg, 332
Devay, 428
Devenne, 428
Devert, 428
Devicque, 428
Deville, 428
Devy, 428
Dewamin, 428
Dewulf, 428
Dhios, 457
Dhomet, 457
Diache, 457
Dianand, 457
Diard, 457
Dichard, 407
Dicharry, 407
Didu, 332
Didard, 333
Didelle, 332
Didier, 333
Didron, 333
Dié, 457
Diebolt, 332
Diegot, 333
Diéricks, 333
Diesch, 229
Dietrich, 333
Diette, 332
Dieu, 427
Dieudonné, 488
Dieulafait, 488
Dieuleveut, 488
Dieutegard, 333
Dieutegarde, 488
Diey, 457
Digard, 407
Dilhac, 189
Dillé, 189
Dillery, 189
Dillet, 189
Dillon, 190
Dilly, 189
Dimé, 364
Dimey, 364
Dimier, 365
Dinguel, 367
Disand, 352
Disant, 352
Discry, 229
Dissard, 352
Ditto, 332
Dittmer, 333
Dizain, 352
Dizé, 351

540 INDEX OF FRENCH NAMES.

Dizy, 351
Dobbé, 103
Dobel, 103
Dobelin, 103
Doche, 427
Dodard, 273
Dodé, 273
Dodeman, 273
Dodin, 273
Dodo, 273
Doermer, 208
Domairon, 364
Domard, 364
Domart, 364
Dombey, 363
Dome, 363
Domecq, 364
Domer, 364
Domez, 364
Dommel, 364
Dommey, 363
Domicile, 364
Donay, 129
Doncker, 130
Donne, 129
Donné, 129
Donnellan, 130
Dor, 208
Dorchies, 208
Doré, 208
Doreau, 208
Dorel, 208
Dorin, 208
Dorvault, 208
Dory, 208
Dothée, 273
Dotin, 273
Douare, 428
Douault, 428
Doubey, 103
Doudau, 274
Doudeau, 273
Doudelle, 274
Doué, 427
Douet, 427
Douelle, 427
Douilly, 427
Doumet, 364
Doumic, 364
Dournel, 190
Doussamy, 26
Doussan, 274
Doussarry, 332
Dousse, 273
Doussoulin, 274
Doutey, 273
Dozière, 273
Dozon, 273
Drach, 413
Drache, 100
Dracq, 100, 413
Drain, 413
Drége, 413

Dréo, 413
Dreyss, 242
Drevault, 196
Dreyfus, 413, 429
Drier, 429
Driou, 429
Dromery, 243
Drou, 195
Drouard, 196
Drouen, 196
Droulin, 195
Drouyn, 196
Droz, 249
Druault, 429
Drubay, 441
Drucquer, 196
Drude, 270
Druey, 195
Drugeon, 196
Drumond (note), 243
Druveau, 441
Dubeau, 103
Duc, 427
Ducel, 427
Ducher, 427
Ducoing, 427
Ducoroy, 427
Dugard, 427
Dugelay, 427
Dugenne, 427
Dugland, 428
Duhomme, 363
Duick, 427
Dulong, 427
Dumain, 428
Dumaire, 364
Dumas, 364
Dumay, 363
Dumery, 364
Dumez, 364
Dumolin, 364
Dumoulin, 364
Duquet, 427
Duquin, 427
Durand, 197
Durandard, 197
Durandeau, 197
Durant, 197
Dureau, 208
Durel, 208
Durey, 208
Durney, 190
Durr, 208
Duru, 208
Dutacq, 332
Dutard, 333
Duté, 332
Duthy, 332
Dutil, 332
Duveau, 103

Eberli, 76
Eberlin, 76

Ebert, 61
Ebrard, 76
Echanbard, 211
Echement, 210
Echinard, 211
Echivard, 210
Edard, 288
Edel, 337
Edelin, 337
Edmond, 382
Edouard, 382
Egalin, 209
Egalon, 154
Egasse, 193
Egaze, 193
Egle, 154
Egly, 154
Egon, 211
Egrot, 210
Eisele, 475
Elambert, 239, 502
Elcké, 142
Ellies, 300
Elmerick, 143
Elmire, 299
Ellouin, 299
Elluis, 299
Eloffe, 419
Embry, 312
Eme, 253
Emelin, 143
Emeric, 254
Emericque, 254
Emmel, 143
Emmery, 254
Emmon, 254
Empaire, 312
Emy, 253
Enault, 289
Enard, 289
Encelain, 213
Enfré, 289
Eng, 292
Engel, 213
Enguehard, 292
Enique, 289
Eune, 289
Enouf, 289
Enslen, 119
Entragues, 300
Erambert, 95
Erard, 95
Erckener, 432
Ernie, 95
Ernouf, 95
Ernoult, 95
Erouard, 95
Erouart, 95
Escalin, 216
Escaré, 217
Escayrac, 217
Esnault, 475
Esnouf, 475

INDEX OF FRENCH NAMES. 541

Esquille, 216
Esser, 119
Essique, 119
Estavard, 216
Este, 216
Estelle, 216
Estocq, 216
Etéy, 287
Ethée, 287
Ettling, 337
Eude, 282
Eudeline, 282
Eve, 366
Eveque, 366
Everickx, 76
Evrard, 76
Evratt, 76
Eychenne, 211
Eymond, 210
Eyraud, 210
Eysen, 474

Fagard, 435
Fage, 435
Fagel, 435
Faget, 435
Fagnier, 435
Faguer, 435
Faby, 435
Fain, 435
Faille, 307, 435
Fajon, 435
Falcimaigne, 334
Fallou, 307
Fandard, 417
Fané, 234
Fannière, 234
Fannon, 234
Fano, 234
Fanton, 417
Faquet, 435
Farachon, 323
Faraguet, 324
Faral, 323
Farau, 323
Farcis, 324
Farcot, 324
Faré, 323
Farenc, 323
Farine, 323
Farne, 324
Farran, 323
Fary, 323
Fastier, 252
Fastou, 251
Fastré, 252
Fath, 62
Faubert, 333
Fauche, 333
Fauchille, 333
Fauoille, 333
Faucillon, 333
Fauleau, 307

Faulle, 307
Faulon, 307
Fauque, 333
Fayard, 435
Faye, 435
Fayet, 435
Fayolle, 435
Fèche, 435
Fechner, 435
Fège, 435
Feiner, 435
Feinert, 435
Fenaille, 234
Fenelon, 234
Férafiat, 323
Feragut, 324
Ferant, 323
Feray, 323
Ferdinand, 325
Ferdman, 325
Ferment, 50, 324
Fermery, 215
Fermin, 215
Fermond, 50, 324
Fernie, 324
Fernier, 324
Fernil, 324
Ferning, 324
Fernique, 324
Feron, 323
Ferouelle, 324
Ferrand, 323
Ferrer, 324
Ferrier, 324
Ferry, 323
Fert, 325
Ferté, 325
Fessard, 247
Fessy, 246
Feste, 251
Fester, 252
Festu, 251
Feuillard, 518
Feuille, 517
Feydeau, 256
Feytou, 256
Fiala, 517
Ficatier, 257
Ficher, 249
Fidele, 430
Fidery, 430
Fieschi, 247
Figeau, 249
Figuier, 249
Filard, 518
Fillemin, 518
Filocque, 517
Finbert, 315
Fink, 104
Firmin, 324
Fissart, 247
Fisteberg, 251
Fisq, 247

Fitte, 430
Fity, 430
Fix, 247
Fixon, 247
Fixary, 247
Fizeau, 246
Fizel, 247
Flad, 393
Flachat, 411
Flambert, 220
Flammgar, 220
Flan, 220
Flanneau, 220
Flaton, 394
Flatraud, 394
Flaud, 393
Flé, 411
Flechelle, 411
Fleck, 411
Fleig, 411
Flichy, 411
Flick, 411
Flicourt, 411
Fliquet, 411
Flocard, 411
Flohn, 220
Floquet, 411
Flosi, 412
Focillon, 93
Foissac, 246
Foissy, 246
Foncier, 246
Forget, 324
Forme, 215
Fornachon, 324
Forney, 324
Fort, 325
Forteau, 325
Fortel, 325
Fortier, 325
Fortin, 325
Fortune, 325
Fortuné, 325
Fossard, 246
Fosse, 246
Fossier, 246
Fossy, 246
Foucart, 334
Foucault, 334
Fouche, 333
Fouché, 333
Foucher, 334
Fouchet, 334
Fouchez, 333
Fouchy, 333
Foucron, 334
Foucrot, 334
Foulley, 93
Fouque, 333
Fouqueré, 334
Fouquet, 334
Fouquier, 334
Fournel, 324

542 INDEX OF FRENCH NAMES.

Fourny, 324
Foussard, 246
Fousse, 246
Foussier, 246
Fraimbault, 215
Franc, 306
Francè, 306
Francey, 306
Franche, 306
Francia, 306
Francillon, 306
Franco, 306
Frankaert, 306
Franque, 306
Franquelin, 306
Franquin, 306
Franz, 306
Frasey, 312
Frasier, 313 (note)
Fraysse, 312
Frebault, 261
Frecal, 449
Frecault, 132
Frech, 132
Fredeau, 261
Frederick, 261
Fredière, 261
Fredoille, 261
Frelon, 261
Fremancour, 216
Fremeaux, 215
Fremery, 215
Fremier, 215
Fremin, 215
Fremineau, 215
Frémont, 215
Fremunger, 216
Frémy, 215
Frepat, 261
Frescal, 449
Fresco, 449
Fresier, 313 (note)
Freslon, 449
Fressard, 449
Fresson, 313
Freté, 261
Freteau, 261
Friand, 263
Friant, 263
Fricault, 132
Fricq, 132
Friéde, 261
Friker, 132
Frioud, 350
Frise, 312
Frison, 313
Fritel, 261
Froger, 350
Froid, 350
Froidure, 350
Froideval, 350
Froissard, 449
Fromain, 215

Froment, 215
Fromillon, 215
Frommé, 215
Frot, 350 .
Frotter, 350
Frottin, 350
Fruit, 350
Fruitier, 350
Fulchiron, 334
Fulcran, 334
Fusch, 247
Fusier, 246
Fusil, 246
Fusy, 246

Gabalda, 286
Gabaret, 286
Gabé, 285
Gabin, 285
Gadé, 525
Gady, 525
Gagin, 174
Gagnard, 174
Gagne, 174
Gagné, 174
Gagneau, 174
Gagner, 174
Gagnery, 174
Gagnière, 174
Gagny, 174
Gaide, 206
Gaignaud, 174
Gailhabaud, 437
Gaildraud, 437
Gaillard, 437
Gaimard, 436
Gaime, 436
Gain, 174
Gainard, 174
Gairel, 202
Gaissard, 205
Gaitte, 206
Galabert, 437
Galand, 437
Galant, 437
Galle, 436
Gallé, 436
Gallibour, 437
Galibourg, 437
Galicher, 437
Galichon, 437
Galino, 437
Gallissant, 437
Galisse, 437
Galoffre, 437
Galon, 437
Gally, 436
Gamache, 436
Gamard, 436
Gambelon, 419
Game, 436
Gâmen, 436
Gamichon, 436

Ganard, 101, 444
Gand, 74
Gandell, 74
Gandillon, 74
Gandier, 74
Gandolphe, 72, 75
Gandoin, 75
Ganié, 444
Ganier, 444
Ganil, 444
Ganivet, 201
Ganne, 444
Ganneau, 444
Ganter, 74
Gantzère, 518
Gapy, 285
Garand, 203
Garault, 204
Garay, 202
Garce, 464
Garceau, 464
Garcia, 464
Gard, 276
Gardey, 276
Gardère, 277
Gardin, 277
Gareau, 202
Garella, 202
Garey, 202
Garibal, 203
Gariel, 202
Garin, 204
Garlin, 202
Garnier, 502
Garnot, 203
Garré, 202
Garrel, 202
Garrelon, 202
Garrier, 203
Garvin, 204
Garzend, 204
Gasc, 205
Gasché, 205
Gaslonde, 296
Gassart, 296
Gasselin, 296
Gastal, 296
Gasté, 296
Gastier, 296
Gastine, 296
Gasty, 296
Gateau, 525
Gatechair, 206
Gatellier, 525
Gatillon, 525
Gathé, 525
Gattebon, 206
Gaudermen, 29, 117
Gaudibert, 115
Gaudiveau, 116
Gauduchon, 115
Gaulofret, 437
Gault, 477

INDEX OF FRENCH NAMES. 543

Gaultier, 477, 502
Gaussen, 309
Gaussiran, 310
Gautrot, 116
Gauzey, 309
Gavalda, 286
Gavault, 286
Gavarni, 285
Gaveau, 285
Gavel, 285
Gavelle, 285
Gaytte, 206
Gaze, 205
Gazel, 205
Gazelius, 205
Gebel, 285
Gelin, 502
Gelle, 436
Gellé, 436
Gellez, 437
Gellynck, 437
Gelpy, 88, 442
Gen, 444
Genard, 444
Gendrot, 74
Gendry, 75 ·
Geneau, 444
Genelle, 444
Générat, 444
Genette, 444
Geneveé, 444
Genin, 444
Génique, 444
Gennequin, 444
Gente, 74
Gentil, 74
Gentillon, 74
Genty, 74
Geny, 444
Geraude, 203
Gerard, 26, 203, 502
Gerault, 204
Geray, 202
Gerbaud, 203
Gerbault, 39, 203
Gerbaut, 203
Gerbet, 203
Gerbert, 203
Gerdolle, 276
Gerdy, 276
Gerente, 203
Gérez, 202
Germain, 203
German, 203
Germond, 203
Gerrier, 203
Gery, 202
Gervaise, 204
Gesbert, 459
Gesel, 458
Geslin, 458 ·
Gessiaulme, 459
Gessiomme, 459

Geste, 296
Gestelli, 296
Geston, 296
Gette, 525
Gheerbrant, 199, 203
Ghillet, 458
Ghislain, 458
Ghys, 458
Gibault, 286
Gibert, 285
Giblin, 285
Giboin, 286
Gibon, 285
Gibory, 28 6
Gibou, 285
Giboz, 285
Gibus, 285
Gide, 438
Gidel, 438
Gidoin, 438
Gidouart, 438
Giesé, 458
Gieseler, 458
Gif, 285
Giffard, 285
Gilan, 458
Gilbault, 458
Gilbé, 442
Gilbert, 458
Gilblain, 442
Gillard, 458
Gille, 458
Gilleron, 458
Gillier, 458
Gilly, 458
Gilmer, 458
Gilquin, 458
Gimbert, 444
Gin, 444
Ginaud, 419
Ginier, 444
Girard, 203
Girardin, 26, 203
Girauld, 204
Girbal, 203
Girier, 203
Girod, 203
Girou, 202
Girouard, 204
Giry, 202
Gisbert, 459
Gissien, 459
Giteau, 438
Gittard, 438
Gitton, 438
Giverne, 285
Giverny, 285
Gladung, 435
Glaeser, 53, 392
Glaise, 392
Glas, 392
Glasson, 392
Glatard, 435

Glatigny, 435
Glaze, 392
Glochet, 352
Gloux, 352
Gluck, 352
Gobert, 502
Gochel, 446
Godde, 115
Godeau, 115
Godefroid, 116
Godefroy, 116
Godel, 115
Godelier, 29, 117
Godfrin, 116
Godillon, 115
Godin, 117
Godineau, 117
Godquin, 115
Godry, 116
Göer, 202
Goibault, 336
Goldber, 477
Golfier, 502
Gom, 59
Gomant, 60
Gombault, 50, 164
Gombrich, 60
Gomer, 60
Gomme, 59
Gon, 163
Gondal, 163
Gonde, 163
Gondhard, 164
Gondolo, 163
Gondouin, 164
Gondret, 164
Gonelle, 163
Gonsse, 163
Gontard, 164
Gonthier, 164
Gontier, 164, 502
Gorand, 203
Gorez, 202
Gorre, 202
Gorrisse, 202
Gossard, 309
Gossart, 309
Gosse, 309
Gosselin, 100, 309
Gosset, 309
Gossin, 309
Gossiome, 310
Gosteau, 360
Gottung, 115
Gouay, 336
Goudal, 115
Goudard, 116
Goudchau, 115
Goudeau, 115
Goudemant, 116
Goudoin, 117
Goué, 336
Gouel, 336

544 INDEX OF FRENCH NAMES.

Gouellain, 336
Gouerre, 336
Gouet, 336
Gouhier, 336
Gouillon, 336
Gouilly, 336
Gouin, 336
Goulay, 478
Goulette, 479
Goumain, 337
Gousse, 99, 309
Goussery, 309
Gout, 115
Gouté, 115
Gouthierre, 116
Goutmann, 116
Gouy, 336
Goy, 336
Goyard, 336
Goyer, 336
Goyet, 336
Goyon, 336
Graesle, 401
Gramain, 401
Grass, 464
Grassal, 464
Grassart, 464
Grasset, 464
Grassi, 464
Grasso, 464
Grau, 401
Grault, 401
Greel, 196
Grellier, 196
Grégy, 401
Grehier, 170
Greiling, 401
Greinn, 465
Gremé, 125
Gremeau, 125
Grenard, 465
Grenier, 465
Grenuz, 465
Gresland, 401
Greslé, 401
Greslon, 401
Gressier, 401
Gresy, 401
Grésy, 401
Grière, 170
Griess, 401
Griessen, 401
Grigault, 170
Grigi, 170
Grill, 196
Grilly, 196
Grim, 125
Grimal, 125
Grimar, 125
Grimault, 50, 125
Grimbert, 125
Grimblot, 125
Grimoard, 125

Grimoin, 125
Grimont, 125
Grisard, 77, 401
Griselin, 401
Grisier, 401
Grisol, 77, 401
Grison, 401
Gronier, 465
Grossard, 406
Grosse, 405
Grosselin, 406
Groseille, 406
Grossier, 406
Grouvelle, 425
Grub, 425
Gruby, 425
Grumay, 59
Grune, 465
Grunelle, 465
Grusse, 405
Gruselle, 406
Guala, 298
Gude, 115
Gudin, 117
Guenard, 394
Guenault, 264, 395
Gueneau, 263
Guéneau, 394
Guénébault, 394
Guenée, 263
Guénerat, 264, 395
Guenu, 263
Guenin, 264
Guérand, 203
Guérard, 203
Guerbet, 203
Guerico, 202
Guerin, 204
Guérin, 305
Guerineau, 204
Guermont, 203
Guerne, 305
Guernet, 203
Guernier, 305
Gueroult, 204
Guerre, 202
Guerrier, 203
Guerry, 202
Guersant, 204
Guessard, 244
Guestier, 296
Gueurel, 202
Guiard, 165
Guibald, 165
Guibaud, 165
Guibert, 165
Guichard, 165
Guiche, 164
Guichot, 165
Guidé, 493
Guidez, 493
Guidon, 493
Guidou, 493

Guiet, 165
Guieu, 164
Guilaine, 123
Guilbaut, 123
Guilbert, 123, 502
Guiler, 124
Guilet, 124
Guilhem, 124
Guilhermy, 124
Guilhery, 124
Guillard, 124
Guillaume, 124
Guille, 123
Guillemain, 124
Guillemant, 124
Guillemont, 124
Guillemot, 124
Guilles, 123
Guillié, 123
Guillochin, 123
Guillon, 123
Guillot, 26
Guillotin, 26
Guimbal, 264
Guindre, 316
Guinery, 264
Guinier, 264
Guitard, 494
Guitter, 494
Guitton, 493
Guitry, 494
Guizot, 47, 459
Gunckel, 419
Gutel, 115
Gutman, 116
Guttin, 117
Gutron, 116
Guy, 336
Guyard, 336
Guybert, 336
Guyon, 336, 502

Habay, 60
Habert, 61
Habdey, 61
Habez, 61
Habich, 60
Habit, 61
Haby, 60
Hache, 209
Hacq, 209
Hacquart, 210
Hacquin, 211
Hadamar, 168
Hadingue, 168
Hadol, 168, 337
Hadrot, 168
Hagard, 210
Hage, 209
Hagene, 211
Haguenoer, 211
Hailig, 426
Haim, 492

INDEX OF FRENCH NAMES.

545

Hain, 211
Hainfray, 211
Haistault, 448
Halevy, 427
Halinbourg, 239
Hallberg, 480
Hallé, 480
Hallegrain, 480
Halley, 426, 480
Hallu, 426
Hamger, 492
Hamelin, 492
Hamoir, 130
Handus, 417
Hanne, 289
Hannebert, 289
Hannequin, 289
Hannicque, 289
Hannier, 289
Hanno, 289
Hannong, 289
Hannz, 119
Hans, 119
Hany, 289
Happe, 60
Happert, 61
Happey, 60
Happich, 60
Harand, 232
Harang, 232
Harbez, 386
Harbly, 386
Hardelé, 250
Hardi, 250
Hardier, 250
Hardoin, 251
Hardon, 251
Hardouin, 251
Hardy, 250
Harel, 231
Hariel, 231
Harlay, 231
Harlé, 231
Harlet, 232
Harlez, 340
Harmand, 232
Harmant, 232
Harmier, 232
Harnault, 95
Haro, 231
Hart, 250
Hartard, 250
Hartmann, 251
Harry, 231
Hassan, 307
Hasse, 307
Hastier, 448
Hatté, 168
Haudebourg, 280
Haudibert, 280
Hault, 282
Haye, 209
Hazard, 169

Hebert, 61
Hecklé, 209
Hector, 450
Hedelin, 168
Hedou, 168
Hedouin, 169
Hellion, 238
Hély, 426
Hémar, 492
Henard, 289
Henault, 289
Hendlé, 417
Henique, 289
Henne, 289
Hennebert, 289
Hennecart, 289
Hennecy, 289
Hennel, 289
Hennequin, 289
Henning, 289
Henno, 289
Henoc, 289
Henrequet, 518 (note)
Henri, 493
Henriot, 26
Henriquet, 26
Hérard, 232
Herbault, 39, 232
Herbecq, 386
Herbel, 386
Herbelin, 386
Herber, 232
Herbert, 232
Herbette, 232
Herbin, 386
Herbut, 232
Herce, 79
Herczegy, 339
Herdevin, 251
Héreau, 231
Herel, 231
Hériché, 231
Heriez, 231
Herincq, 232
Hering, 232
Herlan, 231
Hermagis, 147
Hermain, 232
Herman, 232
Hermand, 232
Hermé, 147
Hermel, 147
Hermeline, 147
Hermes, 147
Hermet, 233
Hermier, 147, 232
Hermy, 147
Herny, 95
Herody, 339
Herold, 233
Hérot, 339
Herou, 231
Herouard, 233

Herouin, 233
Heroult, 233
Hérpin, 386
Herr, 231
Herrincq, 232
Herrissé, 231
Herry, 231
Herse, 79
Hersent, 233
Herterich, 251
Hervier, 386
Hervieu, 233
Hervy, 233
Hesse, 307
Hesteau, 216, 448
Hesz, 307
Hetier, 519
Heudé, 282
Heudebert, 282
Heudel, 282
Heudier, 282
Heudin, 282
Heuré, 83
Hevre, 76
Heymen, 210
Hibert, 61
Hickell, 357
Hieckmann, 358
Hienne, 357
Higlin, 357
Hilaire, 162
Hilber, 162
Hildebrand, 162, 199
Hilger, 162
Hillairet, 163
Hiller, 162
Hilpert, 162
Himely, 140
Hiné, 492
Hingue, 292
Hinque, 292
Hitier, 450
Hipp, 60
Hiver, 76
Hocart, 341
Hocdé, 341
Hocedé, 341
Hochard, 341
Hochart, 341
Hoche, 340
Hocher, 341
Hocheid, 341
Hocq, 340
Hocquart, 341
Hocquet, 341
Hocquigny, 340
Hogan, 357
Hognet, 358
Hoin, 357
Holacher, 282, 427
Hole, 282
Hollande, 282
Hollier, 282

Q 3

546   INDEX OF FRENCH NAMES.

Honache, 314
Honfray, 314
Hongre, 314
Honacker, 314
Honnard, 314
Honorat, 315
Hontang, 84
Hordequin, 217
Horliac, 340
Horne, 520
Horteloup, 218
Hortus, 217
Houard, 341
Hoube, 227
Houdaille, 280
Houdart, 280
Houde, 280
Houdelin, 334
Houdemare, 280
Houdouin, 280
Houelleur, 53
Houlard, 106
Houlet, 105
Houlié, 105
Houllier, 106
Houplon, 227
Houppe, 227
Hour, 83
Hourlier, 340
Housard, 491
Houseau, 491
Housel, 491
Housse, 491
Houssemaine, 491
Housset, 491
Houssez, 491
Houze, 491
Houzeau, 491
Hozdez, 217
Hu, 357
Hua, 357
Huan, 357
Huard, 357
Huart, 357
Huault, 358
Hubac, 227
Hubard, 227
Hubault, 357
Hubel, 227
Hubert, 357
Hublin, 227
Huc, 357
Huchard, 357
Huchery, 358
Huchette, 358
Hudault, 280
Hude, 280
Hudelo, 280
Hudibert, 280
Hue, 357
Huel, 357
Huet, 358
Hug, 357

Hugard, 357
Hugé, 357
Hugelin, 357
Hugla, 357
Hugnot, 358
Hugo, 357
Hugon, 357
Hugot, 358
Huguelin, 357
Hugues, 357
Hulbert, 105
Hulek, 358
Hulot, 105
Humann, 358
Humbert, 314
Humblot, 314
Hummel, 468
Hunault, 315
Huppé, 227
Hurard, 83
Hurault, 83
Hureau, 83
Huré, 83
Hurel, 83
Hurey, 83
Hurez, 83
Hurier, 83
Husbrocq, 491
Husch, 442
Husquin, 412
Hutteau, 280
Hux, 442
Hyacinthe, 468

Ibert, 61
Ignard, 211
Igouf, 210
Imard, 254
Imbault, 254
Imbert, 254
Imbs, 254
Imer, 254
Inemer, 492
Infroit, 492
Ingé, 292
Ingel, 213
Inger, 292
Inghelbrecht, 213
Ingisch, 292
Ingold, 293
Ingouf, 293
Ingrain, 292
Ingray, 292
Irle, 339
Isambert, 50
Isar, 475
Isbert, 475
Iscariot, 483
Iselin, 475
Isnard, 475
Isoard, 475
Itaque, 449
Itasse, 449

Iteney, 449
Ivorel, 76
Ivry, 76
Izambert, 474
Izard, 475

Jaccaz, 452
Jacquart, 452
Jacquault, 453
Jacque, 452
Jacquée, 452
Jacqueau, 452
Jacquelin, 452
Jacquemain, 453
Jacquemar, 453
Jacquemier, 453
Jacquemin, 453
Jacquier, 452
Jacqx, 452
Jaffa, 285
Jager, 452
Jahyer, 452
Jaillant, 437
Jaillard, 437
Jaillon, 437
Jal, 436
Jaley, 436
Jallerat, 437
Jallibert, 437
Jalvy, 437
Jam, 436
Jamault, 436
Jame, 436
Jameau, 436
Jamin, 436
Jan, 444
Janac, 444
Janin, 444
Janlin, 444
Jannair, 444
Janny, 444
Janquin, 444
Janus, 143
Japy, 285
Jaquiery, 452
Jaquin, 452
Jarland, 203
Jarrier, 203
Jarry, 202
Jauge, 244
Jaugeard, 245
Jaugey, 244
Javel, 285
Jayr, 202, 452
Jazeraud, 205
Jeanpot, 444
Jeanray, 444
Jegon, 452
Jekel, 452
Jennequin, 444
Jeoffry, 437
Jerusalem, 487
Jèze, 205

INDEX OF FRENCH NAMES. 547

Job, 485
Jobbé, 485
Jokin, 452
Jonchery, 419
Joniére, 420
Jonnard, 420
Jonnart, 420
Jordery, 139
Jordy, 139
Josse, 309
Josseau, 309
Josseaume, 310
Josselin, 309
Josscrand, 310
Josset, 309
Jossier, 309
Jossu, 309
Jotrat, 306
Joualt, 367
Jouard, 245
Jouault, 245
Joubert, 245
Jouet, 245
Jougaud, 245
Jouhaud, 245
Jouisse, 244
Joumar, 245
Jounault, 420
Jounneaux, 420
Jourdan, 140
Jourde, 139
Jourdier, 139
Jourdy, 139
Journault, 433
Journé, 433
Jousse, 309
Jousselin, 309
Jousserand, 310
Jouve, 485
Jouvin, 306
Jovart, 485
Jovel, 485
Jozan, 309
Jozeau, 309
Jubé, 485
Jubelin, 485
Jublin, 485
Jude, 305
Judeau, 305
Judice, 483
Judissé, 483
Judlin, 305
Jue, 244
Jué, 244
Juéry, 245
Juge, 244
Jugier, 245
Jugla, 244
Jui, 244
Juigné, 245
Juin, 245
Julia, 244
Juncal, 419

Jung, 419
Juny, 420
Juquin, 245
Justault, 429
Juste, 429
Juteau, 305
Jutier, 306
Juttel, 305
Juville, 485

Kennebert, 328
Kilbé, 442
Kleber, 183
Krier, 53, 170
Kunemann, 328
Kunrath, 328
Kuntzlé, 163
Kunzé, 163

Labé, 387
Labelle, 387
Labiche, 387
Labié, 387
Labitte, 387
Laborie, 387
Labour, 387
Labric, 387
Lac, 366
Lachelin, 366
Lack, 366
Lacquet, 366
Ladé, 195
Ladret, 195
Laduron, 195
Laederich, 195
Lafitte, 387
Lafon, 387
Lagesse, 366
Laget, 366
Lagier, 366
Lagneau, 366
Lagny, 366
Lague, 366
Laguerre, 366
Laine, 366
Lainé, 366
Laitié, 194
Laity, 194
Lamart, 26
Lamartine, 26
Lamballe, 86
Lambelin, 86
Lambert, 335
Lambie, 86
Lambla, 86
Lamblin, 86
Lambret, 335
Lamfroy, 86
Lampy, 86
Lamquin, 86
Lamy, 86
Lance, 335
Lancel, 335

Lancelin, 335
Landa, 335
Landard, 335
Landelle, 335
Landemar, 336
Landier, 335
Landon, 335
Landron, 335
Landry, 336
Lanfray, 335
Lanier, 335
Laniesse, 335
Lanne, 335
Lanneau, 335
Lansard, 335
Lantat, 335
Lanté, 335
Lantheaume, 335
Lantier, 335
Lantiez, 335
Lantin, 335
Lanty, 335
Lanvin, 336
Lanzac, 335
Lanzarick, 336
Lanzberg, 335
Lanzi, 335
Larivay, 356
Larmier, 356
Laroque, 356
Larouy, 356
Larra, 356
Larré, 356
Larrieu, 356
Lars, 356
Larue, 356
Laruelle, 356
Las, 353
Laseque, 353
Lasne, 353
Lassaigne, 353
Lassalle, 353
Lassarat, 353
Lassay, 353
Lasselve, 353
Lassenay, 353
Lasseray, 353
Lassier, 353
Lassimonne, 353
Lassuère, 353
Lasteyrie, 355
Lastret, 355
Latard, 195
Laterrade, 195
Latour, 195
Latry, 195
Latte, 195
Laude, 377
Laudier, 377
Laudon, 377
Laudy, 377
Laulhé, 284
Laull, 284

INDEX OF FRENCH NAMES.

Laumain, 366
Laur, 356
Laureau, 356
Laurey, 356
Lautemann, 378
Lautier, 377
Lautten, 377
Lavalle, 387
Lavalley, 387
Lavault, 387
Lavenay, 387
Laverne, 387
Lavier, 387
Laviron, 387
Lazard, 353
Laze, 353
Leban, 387
Lebeau, 387
Lebeault, 387
Lebel, 387
Lebey, 387
Lebiez, 387
Lebocq, 387
Lebœuf, 387
Lebreck, 387
Lebret, 387
Lebuffe, 387
Ledagre, 195
Ledé, 194
Ledier, 195
Ledieu, 194, 484
Ledo, 194
Ledoux, 194
Leduc, 194
Leflon, 387
Legal, 366
Legat, 366
Legault, 366
Legay, 366
Legé, 366
Legeley, 366
Legier, 366
Lehman, 366
Lelly, 470
Lely, 470
Lender, 110
Lendormi, 100, 110
Lené, 274
Lenègre, 274
Lenique, 274
Lenté, 110
Leo, 87
Leonard, 87
Leotard, 331
Leppe, 265
Leppich, 265
Lereux, 356
Lerré, 356
Lesacq, 353
Lesaec, 353
Lesenne, 353
Lesne, 353
Lestelle, 355

Lesteur, 355
Lestienne, 355
Lestoing, 355
Lestrade, 355
Letac, 194
Letaille, 194
Létalle, 194
Letang, 194
Le Thière, 195
Letho, 194
Letocq, 194
Letoile, 194
Letteron, 195
Lettu, 194
Leutert, 331
Levard, 387
Levé, 387
Leveau, 387
Levêque, 265
Levick, 265
Levier, 265
Levite, 387
Levrat, 387
Lewy, 87
Leys, 353
Leysard, 353
Lezard, 353
Lezé, 353
Lezer, 353
Lezeret, 353
Libault, 265
Libec, 265
Libert, 265
Liboz, 265
Liebherre, 265
Liefquin, 265
Lieppe, 265
Lieutaut, 331
Lillo, 470
Linard, 274
Lindemann, 110
Linder, 110
Linet, 104
Linge, 109
Lingé, 109
Linget, 109
Link, 87
Linnée, 274
Linotte, 104, 274
Lion, 87
Liontz, 87
Liot, 330
Liotard, 331
Loittet, 331
Loittier, 331
Lioult, 87
Lippert, 265
Lips, 265
Liré, 356
Lisse, 353
Lister, 355
Litteau, 330
Livio, 265

Liza, 353
Lizé, 353
Lizeray, 353
Lizon, 353
Locard, 446
Loch, 131
Lochart, 446
Loche, 446
Locque, 131, 446
Locquet, 446
Locret, 446
Loddé, 377
Loeder, 377
Lolly, 284
Loque, 131
Lora, 356
Loré, 356
Loreal, 356
Loreau, 356
Loreille, 356
Loremy, 356
Lorez, 356
Lorichon, 356
Lorimier, 356
Lorique, 356
Lormier, 356
Lorsa, 356
Lory, 356
Louauld, 87
Loué, 87
Loudun, 377
Louin, 87
Louis, 331
Loup, 265
Louva, 265
Louveau, 265
Louvel, 265
Louvier, 265
Lovy, 265
Loysel, 335
Lubac, 265
Lucard, 331
Lucas, 331
Luce, 331
Lucy, 331
Ludet, 331
Ludger, 331
Ludon, 330
Ludovic, 331
Ludwig, 331
Luez, 331
Luling, 284
Lully, 284
Lunardi, 139
Lunaud, 139
Lundy, 495
Luneau, 139
Lunel, 139
Luneteau, 495
Luona, 495
Luppé, 265
Lusquin, 331
Lussy, 331

INDEX OF FRENCH NAMES. 549·

Luthe, 330
Luton, 330
Lutteroth, 331
Lutz, 331
Luyt, 330
Luzier, 331

Mabillon, 471
Machu, 410
Macquard, 410
Macquart, 410
Macquin, 410
Macron, 410
Mactier, 411
Madamon, 342
Madin, 341
Madoulaud, 361
Madron, 342
Mady, 341
Magnabal, 410
Magnard, 410
Magné, 410
Magney, 410
Magnier, 410
Magron, 410
Mahault, 410
Maheu, 410
Mahier, 410
Mailley, 410
Mainbourg, 410
Mainfroy, 410
Maingault, 410
Maingot, 410
Malamy, 179
Malapert, 179
Malaquin, 178
Malaret, 179
Malbot, 179
Maleco, 178
Malingue, 178
Mallac, 178
Mallard, 179
Malle, 178
Mallé, 178
Malo, 178
Malory, 179
Malrait, 179
Malsang, 180
Maltaire, 180
Malteaux, 180
Malzac, 180
Malzar, 180
Manalt, 58
Manceau, 434
Mancel, 434
Mandell, 434
Mandon, 434
Mandouce, 434
Maneau, 58
Manec, 58
Manfray, 58
Mangal, 58
Maningne, 58

Manley, 58
Mann, 58
Mannier, 58
Mansard, 434
Mansey, 434
Mansion, 434
Manson, 434
Mansoz, 434
Manteau, 434
Mantion, 434
Many, 58
Marbot, 369
Marc, 80
Marché, 80
Marchire, 80
Marcillon, 80
Marcol, 80
Maricot, 369
Marcq, 80
Marcuard, 80
Marcus, 80
Margot, 369
Marielle, 368
Marin, 369
Marinié, 369
Marinier, 369
Marion, 369
Maris, 368
Marizy, 368
Marland, 369
Marlé, 368
Marlin, 368
Marne, 369
Marneuf, 369
Marnier, 369
Maroger, 369
Marolla, 368
Marquery, 80
Mars, 143
Marvy, 369
Mascar, 448
Masimbert, 48, 523
Massart, 522
Masse, 522
Massé, 522
Masseau, 522
Massemin, 523
Massena, 522
Massillon, 522
Masson, 522
Matagrin, 342
Materne, 342
Mathan, 342
Mathé, 341
Matheret, 342
Matheron, 342
Mathey, 341
Mathié, 341
Mathis, 341
Mathlin, 341, 361
Matisse, 341
Maton, 342
Matraud, 342

Matre, 342
Matrod, 342
Matry, 342
Mats, 341
Mattar, 342
Matte, 341
Mattelain, 341
Mattrat, 342
Maturin, 342
Maty, 341
Maubert, 180
Maudemain, 181
Mauduit, 181
Mauger, 181
Maulde, 180
Maull, 178
Maur, 402
Maurel, 402
Maurenque, 402
Maurey, 402
Maurier, 402
Maurin, 402
May, 410
Mayer, 410
Maylin, 410
Maynard, 410
Maynier, 410
Mayran, 410 ·
Mazelin, 522
Mazier, 522
Mèdard, 342
Meder, 342
Melaye, 179
Melick, 179
Melier, 180
Mélique, 179
Mellé, 179
Menault, 58
Mendez, 434
Meneau, 58
Menel, 58
Menier, 58
Menne, 58
Mentel, 434
Mention, 434
Meny, 58
Méra, 368
Merard, 369
Merault, 369
Méreau, 368
Mérelle, 368
Merey, 368
Merger, 369
Mérigot, 369
Mérigout, 369
Mériq, 368
Merland, 369
Merly, 368
Merman, 369
Mesenge, 522
Messier, 522
Métay, 341
Metge, 341

550 INDEX OF FRENCH NAMES.

Methlin, 361
Methorie, 342
Metman, 342
Metton, 342
Mezia, 485
Mezière, 523
Micard, 406
Micault, 406
Michault, 406
Miché, 406
Michy, 406
Micol, 406
Micollier, 406
Micquelard, 406
Micouin, 406
Midi, 379
Midiére, 380
Midocq, 379
Midol, 379
Miéton, 380
Miette, 379
Mildé, 283
Miley, 179
Milhomme, 179
Milisch, 179
Mill, 179
Millange, 179
Millard, 179
Millaux, 179
Mille, 179
Miller, 53, 180
Millery, 180
Milly, 179
Milord, 180, 526
Milsent, 180
Minachon, 266
Minard, 266
Minart, 266
Miné, 266
Minel, 266
Minerve, 143, 144, 526
Mineret, 266
Mineur, 266
Minich, 266
Minier, 266
Minne, 266
Minnette, 266
Mirambaut, 369
Miramon, 369
Misard, 380
Missier, 380
Miton, 380
Mizery, 380, 526
Modelonde, 237
Molay, 178
Moitié, 237
Moitier, 237
Moitry, 237
Mole, 92, 178
Molique, 178
Moll, 92, 178
Mollard, 179
Mollé, 178

Monard, 58
Monde, 276
Mondebard, 276
Mondière, 276
Mondin, 276
Mondo, 276
Monfrat, 58
Monneau, 58
Monnier, 58
Monny, 58
Montagne, 276
Montagny, 276
Montalembert, 502
Montangerand, 502
Montaufray, 502
Montault, 276
Montauriol, 502
Montée, 276
Montel, 276
Montgerard, 502
Montgobert, 502
Montgolfier, 502
Montier, 276
Montmorency, 502
Morard, 402
Morda, 258
Mordaque, 258
Mordret, 258
Moré, 402
Moreau, 402
Morel, 402
Morenzo, 502
Moriamé, 402
Morihalm, 403
Morillon, 402
Morsaline, 258
Mort, 258
Mortemard, 259
Mortemart, 259
Mortier, 258
Mortieu, 258
Morziére, 258
Mosson, 238
Mossy, 237
Motard, 237
Moteau, 237
Motelle, 237
Motheron, 237
Mothu, 237
Motte, 237
Motté, 237
Mougé, 406
Mouillard, 179
Mounie, 359
Mounier, 359
Mourceau, 258
Mourlaque, 402
Mourlon, 402
Mourzelas, 258
Mousac, 237
Mouson, 238
Mousse, 92, 237
Moussel, 237

Mousseron, 237
Moussey, 237
Mossu, 237
Moussy, 237
Moustier, 238
Mousty, 238
Moutard, 237
Moutie, 237
Moutier, 237
Moutry, 237
Mouzard, 237
Mozin, 238
Mukleman, 406
Mundel, 276
Munié, 359
Munier, 359
Musard, 237
Mussey, 237
Musson, 238
Mustel, 238
Mutel, 237

Naba, 422
Nadaud, 275
Nadault, 275
Naef, 420, 422
Nagel, 220
Nalbert, 220
Nallard, 220
Nancy, 239
Nant, 239
Nanta, 239
Nanteau, 239
Nanteuil, 239
Nantier, 239
Nantiez, 275
Natier, 275
Natte, 275
Natter, 275
Naud, 240
Naudeau, 240
Naudier, 240
Naudy, 240
Naury, 300
Navault, 421
Naveau, 420
Navier, 421
Navry, 421
Nebout, 255
Née, 420
Neél, 220
Négre, 421
Nely, 220
Nenard, 239
Nenning, 239
Néollier, 220
Nesseler, 256
Nestlé, 256
Nestlen, 256
Netter, 255
Neu, 420
Nève, 420
Newiger, 421

INDEX OF FRENCH NAMES. 551

Ney, 420
Neyman, 297, 421
Neyret, 421
Neyrey, 421
Niard, 255, 421
Nibart, 255, 421
Nibault, 255, 421
Nibelle, 151
Nicaise, 126
Nicard, 126
Nicaud, 126
Nick, 126
Nicour, 126
Nidelay, 256
Niédré, 255
Nisard, 255
Nitot, 255
Nivard, 421
Niveau, 420
Nivelleau, 151
Nivert, 421
Niviere, 421
Nizard, 255
Nizey, 255
Nizolle, 256
Nodé, 240
Nodier, 240
Nodler, 240
Noel, 487
Nony, 439
Norbert, 301
Norest, 301
Nourigat, 301
Nortier, 301
Nory, 300
Notaire, 54, 240
Notre, 240
Notte, 240
Nottelle, 240
Noulin, 420
Novel, 151
Nozière, 240

Oberlé, 76
Obry, 76
Ochin, 524
Ode, 381
Odelin, 334
Odigier, 382
Odilon, 334
Odillard, 334
Odin, 52, 121, 526
Odoul, 334
Ofin, 385
Offman, 385
Uffny, 385
Og, 193
Ogé, 193
Oger, 193
Ogier, 193
Olacher, 418
Olbert, 418
Olding, 418

Olefia, 471
Oliffe, 471
Oliva, 471
Olive, 471
Olivert, 471
Omer, 492
Omond, 492
Oriolle, 524
Orsay, 79
Orsel, 79
Orth, 217
Ortiguier, 217
Ortolan, 217
Osmont, 120
Osselin, 119
Ostard, 302
Ouachée, 362
Oualle, 298
Ouarnier, 305
Oudard, 382
Oudin, 381
Ouellard, 383
Oulif, 71
Oulman, 106
Oury, 83
Oustria, 302
Outi, 381
Ouvrard, 76
Ouvré, 76
Ozouf, 120

Pacaud, 172
Pacault, 172
Paccard, 172
Pacilly, 172
Pacquement, 172
Pacquier, 53, 172
Pader, 166
Pagelle, 172
Paillard, 192
Paille, 192
Paillerie, 192
Pailleur, 192
Pailley, 192
Pailliart, 192
Palisse, 521
Pallanque, 192
Pallu, 192
Palmier, 192
Panart, 175
Panay, 175
Panchaud, 182
Panckouke, 182
Panel, 175
Panhard, 175
Panisse, 175
Pannier, 175
Pansin, 236
Pansu, 235
Pantel, 235
Panthou, 235
Pantiche, 235
Pantou, 235

Papau, 291
Papault, 291
Pape, 291
Paper, 291
Papillon, 291
Papin, 291
Pappert, 291
Papy, 291
Paquel, 172
Parade, 62
Paradis, 62
Pardaillon, 222
Pardon, 222
Pariseau, 61
Parisse, 61
Parly, 61
Parra, 61
Parrette, 62
Parseval, 453
Party, 222
Pascard, 487
Pascault, 487
Pasche, 487
Passard, 181
Passe, 181
Passy, 181
Pasté, 183
Pasteau, 183
Pastier, 183
Pastré, 183
Pasty, 183
Pataille, 166
Patard, 167
Patay, 166
Paté, 166
Pathe, 166
Pathi, 166
Pathier, 167
Patoche, 166
Patry, 167
Patte, 166
Pattu, 166
Paty, 166
Paultre, 241
Pautrat, 241
Pavard, 291
Pavin, 291
Pavy, 291
Pech, 222
Pecquery, 222
Pecquet, 222
Pelabon, 219
Pelcot, 269
Pelez, 269
Péligri, 269
Pelissier, 521
Pellagot, 269
Pellard, 269
Pelle, 192
Pellé, 192
Pellecat, 269
Pellegrin, 269
Pellenc, 192

552 INDEX OF FRENCH NAMES.

Pelleteret, 219
Pellin, 270
Pellier, 269
Pellu, 192
Pelman, 269
Pelosse, 521
Pelté, 219
Peltier, 219
Peltret, 219
Peltzer, 219
Pelvey, 270
Penabert, 177
Penant, 177
Penaud, 177
Pencé, 177
Penel, 177
Penicaud, 177
Peniére, 177
Penigot, 177
Pennequin, 177
Penquier, 182
Pensard, 236
Pensé, 235
Peny, 176
Pepin, 414
Perard, 69
Perault, 69
Pére, 68
Periche, 69
Perichon, 69
Perigault, 69
Perilla, 69
Perjeaux, 279
Perlin, 69
Pernelle, 70
Perny, 70
Perocheau, 69
Perody, 69
Perol, 69
Perreau, 68
Perrelle, 69
Perrier, 69
Perrin, 70
Perronin, 69
Perrot, 69
Pers, 453
Perseval, 453
Persil, 453
Persoz, 453
Pestel, 183
Pestre, 183
Pesty, 183
Pertat, 370
Petard, 167
Petel, 167
Petry, 167
Pettex, 166
Pettier, 167
Peuvrelle, 91
Peyre, 68
Peyredieu, 69
Philibert, 518
Philery, 518

Philippot, 518
Philippoteaux, 518
Phily, 517
Pical, 177
Picaud, 178
Picault, 178
Pichard, 178
Pichaud, 178
Picher, 178
Pichery, 178
Pichi, 177
Pichou, 177
Pick, 177
Pickard, 178
Picory, 178
Picque, 177
Picquet, 178
Pidault, 167
Piefer, 91
Pielard, 291
Piella, 219
Pielle, 219
Piffault, 414
Pigault, 178
Pigeard, 178
Pigeat, 178
Pigeau, 178
Pigeory, 178
Pigeron, 178 ·
Pilate, 269
Pillard, 269
Pillas, 269
Pille, 269
Pillette, 269
Pilley, 269
Pillien, 270
Pilot, 269
Piolé, 219
Piolenc, 219
Pilte, 219
Pin, 176
Pinau, 176
Pinaud, 177
Pinault, 177
Pinchon, 178
Pineau, 176
Pinel, 177
Pingard, 178
Pingeon, 178
Pinhard, 177
Pinsard, 236
Pinseau, 177, 235
Pinsonneau, 236
Pinson, 236
Pipard, 414
Pipre, 91
Pirnier, 71
Piron, 70
Pissard, 181
Pissin, 181
Piver, 91
Pivert, 414
Plaideur, 376

Plain, 396
Plait, 376
Planchard, 393
Planche, 392
Plancher, 393
Planer, 396
Planier, 396
Planker, 393
Planque, 392
Planquet, 393
Planry, 396
Plantard, 397
Plantier, 397
Plantin, 397
Platret, 376
Planty, 397
Planus, 396
Platard, 376
Plateau, 376
Platel, 376
Platret, 376
Platte, 376
Plattel, 376
Plessier, 441
Plet, 376
Plivard, 184
Plocque, 214
Ploquin, 215
Plou, 214
Plougoulm, 215
Plouin, 215
Plouvier, 184
Ployer, 215
Plumartin, 465
Plumeray, 465
Plumier, 465
Pluquin, 215
Pochard, 225
Podevin, 455
Pogé, 224
Poggiale, 224
Poignard, 225
Pol, 281
Polac, 281
Polart, 281
Pold, 241
Polffer, 281
Polleau, 281
Pollisse, 281
Poly, 281
Pon, 175
Ponceau, 235
Poncel, 235
Pond, 235
Ponnelle, 175
Ponsard, 236
Ponsery, 236
Ponson, 236
Pont, 235
Ponteau, 235
Ponthieu, 235
Ponti, 235
Pontier, 236

INDEX OF FRENCH NAMES. 553

Popard, 422
Popelin, 422
Popet, 422
Popon, 422
Populus, 422
Port, 229
Porta, 229
Porte, 526
Portevin, 229
Posez, 408
Possac, 408
Posselt, 408
Possesse, 408
Posso, 408
Postel, 409
Poitrat, 455
Potage, 454
Potard, 455
Poteau, 454
Potefer, 455
Potel, 454
Potemont, 455
Poterie, 54, 455
Potevin, 455
Potey, 454
Pothé, 454
Pothier, 455
Potier, 455
Potin, 454
Potonié, 455
Potron, 455
Pottier, 53, 54
Potvin, 455
Poucha, 378
Pouchard, 379
Pouchet, 379
Pougeault 379
Pougin, 379
Pougny, 379
Foulain, 281
Poulin, 281
Foullard, 281
Poulle, 281
Poure, 452
Pourreau, 452
Poussard, 408
Poussif, 408
Povel, 422
Poy, 313
Poyard, 313
Poyart, 313
Poyé, 313
Poyer, 313
Prand, 198
Pray, 184
Prax, 185
Preau, 184
Preault, 185
Préclin, 185
Pregniard, 185
Premier, 371
Premy, 371
Presne, 453

Prétard, 185
Preté, 185
Pretre, 185
Preyer, 185
Primard, 371
Primault, 371
Prodin, 218
Prot, 218
Proteau, 218
Prothaut, 218
Prout, 447
Prouteau, 447
Pruce, 447
Pruede, 447
Prunel, 399
Prunet, 400
Prunier, 400
Prunzelle, 186
Pulin, 281
Pulle, 281
Puniet, 416
Pupier, 422
Pupil, 422
Pussy, 407
Puteau, 454

Quandelle, 317
Quantier, 316
Quantin, 316
Queck, 164
Quenard, 264
Quenault, 264
Quenay, 263
Queneau, 263
Quenelle, 263
Quenemer, 264
Quenessen, 263
Quentin, 316
Querrey, 278
Quetil, 128 (note)
Quezin, 244
Quickerat, 165
Quierot, 165
Quillac, 123
Quillard, 124
Quillé, 123
Quillier, 124
Quilleret, 124
Quilleri, 124
Quillet, 124
Quin, 263
Quinard, 264
Quinault, 264
Quincey, 263
Qui eau, 263
Quinier, 264
Quinty, 316
Quyo, 164

Raba, 187
Raban, 97
Rabeau, 187
Rabeuf, 187

Rabier, 187
Rabigot, 187
Rabillon, 187
Rabineau, 97
Rabon, 97
Rabot, 89
Rabotte, 89
Rabou, 187
Rabouin, 187
Raby, 187
Racle, 362
Raccurt, 363
Radanne, 348
Radé, 347
Radel, 348
Radet, 348
Radez, 348
Radi, 347
Radigue, 347
Radouan, 349
Radoult, 348
Radulphe, 349
Raffard, 187
Raffin, 97
Rafflin, 187
Rafford, 187
Raftier, 228
Raffy, 187
Ragan, 349
Ragarie, 363
Rager, 363
Ragneau, 349
Ragoin, 363
Ragon, 349
Ragonneau, 349
Ragot, 363
Rainal, 349
Rainaud, 350
Rainbeaux, 137
Raine, 349
Rainfray, 349
Raingo, 349
Rainot, 350
Rambert, 97
Randier, 228
Randouin, 228
Rangheard, 230
Ranoe, 189
Raoul, 52
Rapé, 187
Raphel, 187
Rapilly, 187
Rapin, 97
Rapineau, 97
Rapp, 187
Rat, 347
Rataboul, 348
Rateau, 347
Ratel, 348
Ratheau, 347
Rathery, 348
Rathier, 348
Ratié, 347

R 3

554 INDEX OF FRENCH NAMES.

Raton, 348
Ratott, 348
Ratouin, 349
Ratouis, 349
Ratte, 92, 347
Ratter, 348
Rattier, 348
Rattisseau, 348
Raucour, 253
Ravanne, 97
Ravard, 187
Ravault, 187
Raveau, 187
Raveaud, 187
Ravel, 187
Raveneau, 97
Ravier, 187
Ravon, 97
Ravou, 187
Ray, 362
Rayard, 363
Raybaud, 362
Rayer, 363
Raymbault, 349
Raymond, 363
Rayna, 349
Raynard, 349
Rayner, 350
Read, 347
Rebard, 188
Rebel, 188
Rebillon, 188
Rebold, 188
Recamier, 344
Reclus, 344
Recurat, 344
Redaut, 254
Reder, 348
Redet, 348
Redier, 348
Redmer, 348
Redon, 348
Regimbeau, 137
Regnard, 349
Regnart, 349
Regnauld, 350
Regnault, 350
Regner, 350
Regnié, 349
Regnier, 350
Reine, 349
Reinert, 349
Renard, 349
Renauld, 350
Renault, 350
René, 104, 189
Reneaume, 350
Renel, 189
Renesson, 189
Rennecon, 189
Renny, 189
Renom, 350
Renouard, 350

Renouf, 350
Reston, 448
Rety, 347
Reveil, 188
Revel, 188
Revelin, 188
Reverd, 188
Revu, 188
Reynier, 350
Reyneval, 350
Ribail, 188
Ribault, 188
Ribier, 188
Ribiére, 188
Rible, 188
Riboni, 188
Ribou, 188
Ribun, 188
Ricard, 343
Ricci, 343
Richard, 343
Richault, 344
Riche, 343
Riché, 343
Richebourg, 343
Richême, 343
Richemont, 344
Richer, 343
Richez, 343
Richier, 343
Richin, 343
Richomme, 343
Richy, 343
Ricque, 343
Ricquier, 343
Ridde, 254
Rideau, 254
Ridel, 254
Ridière, 254
Riette, 254
Riedle, 354
Riedling, 254
Rif, 188
Riffaud, 188
Riffault, 188
Rigal, 343
Rigaubert, 343
Rigault, 344
Ringard, 230
Ringel, 230
Ringier, 53, 230
Ripard, 188
Ripault, 188
Ripaut, 188
Riquet, 343
Riquiez, 343
Rist, 193
Ritaud, 254
Rivain, 188
Rivard, 188
Rivau, 188
Rivaud, 188
Rivay, 188

Rivé, 188
Rivelin, 188
Riviere, 188
Robbe, 187
Robert, 372
Robertet, 518 (note)
Roberge, 372
Robi, 187
Robichon, 187
Robier, 187
Robiquet, 187
Roblin, 187
Robquin, 187
Rocauld, 253
Rocault, 253
Rochard, 253
Roche, 252
Rocher, 253
Rocque, 253
Rocquelin, 253
Rode, 371
Rodde, 371
Rodel, 372
Rodier, 373
Rodiez, 372
Rodin, 372
Rodolphe, 373
Rodron, 373
Roduwart, 373
Rogé, 253
Rogeau, 253
Roger, 372
Roget, 253
Rogez, 253
Rogue, 253
Roguelin, 253
Rohard, 253, 372
Rohart, 372
Rohault, 253
Roland, 373
Rollin, 372
Roméo, 373
Romeuf, 374
Romieu, 373
Rommel, 374
Rommy, 373
Ronce, 228
Ronceray, 228
Rond, 228
Rondeau, 228
Rondelle, 228
Rondy, 228
Ronze, 228
Ronzier, 228
Roquebert, 253
Roques, 253
Roquette, 253
Roscher, 79
Rosémon, 79
Roslin, 79
Rosly, 79
Rossel, 79
Rosselin, 79

INDEX OF FRENCH NAMES. 555

Rosser, 79
Rossi, 79
Rost, 448
Rostan, 448
Rostang, 448
Rosteau, 440
Rostolan, 448
Rosty, 448
Rota, 371
Roth, 371
Rotta, 371
Rotté, 371
Rotti, 371
Rotival, 373
Roualt, 373
Roubaud, 372
Roucolle, 252
Rouchon, 372
Roudiére, 373
Roudil, 372
Roudillon, 372
Roullin, 372
Roumier, 374
Roumilly, 374
Rouvier, 187
Roubo, 187
Rouffe, 187
Rouher, 253
Rouveau, 187
Rouvel, 187
Rovillain, 187
Rubé, 187
Rubelle, 187
Rubier, 187
Rubio, 187
Ruby, 187
Rudder, 373
Rude, 371
Rudeau, 371
Rudelle, 372
Rudemare, 373
Rummel, 374
Rupp, 187
Ruprich, 187
Ruteau, 371
Rutten, 372
Rutter, 373

Sabart, 424
Sabaud, 424
Sabbini, 424
Sablon, 424
Sabot, 424
Sabran, 424
Sacareau, 171
Sacquin, 171
Sacre, 171
Saffray, 424
Saillard, 308
Saillenfest, 308
Saillofest, 308
Sailly, 308
Sala, 308

Saladin, 526
Salard, 308
Salathé, 308
Salesse, 308
Salfray, 308
Saligny, 308
Saligot, 308
Salin, 308
Salle, 308
Sallé, 308
Salleron, 308
Sallier, 308
Salmon, 308
Salsac, 443
Salvaing, 346
Salvan, 346
Salverte, 346
Salvy, 346
Salzac, 443
Salzard, 443
Salze, 443
Sance, 430
Sanchez, 438
Sandeau, 430
Sandelion, 430
Sandoz, 430
Sandré, 430
Sandrier, 431
Sanegon, 170
Sangouard, 438
Sangouin, 438
Sannier, 170
Santerre, 430
Santi, 430
Santry, 431
Sanzel, 430
Sapia, 423
Sapicha, 424
Sapin, 424
Sapy, 423
Saqui, 171
Sar, 230
Saramon, 230
Sarasin, 487
Sarger, 230
Sari, 230
Sarra, 230
Sarrault, 230
Sarre, 230
Sarrette, 230
Sarrion, 230
Sasse, 451
Sassére, 451
Sassier, 451
Sassy, 451
Satory, 451
Sauffroy, 424
Saul, 138
Sault, 443
Saunac, 99
Sauphar, 424
Saupíque, 424
Sauvage, 424

Sauve, 423
Sauvé, 423
Sauvel, 424
Sauveur, 424
Sauvey, 423
Sauvier, 424
Savard, 424
Savart, 424
Savarin, 424
Savary, 424
Savelon, 424
Savigny, 424
Savin, 424
Savit, 424
Savy, 423
Sax, 200
Say, 171
Sayer, 171
Sazerac, 451
Sazerat, 451
Scat, 191
Scatti, 191
Scellier, 361
Schall, 456
Schefter, 219
Schener, 389
Schilte, 227
Scholder, 457
Schone, 389
Scoffier, 442
Sebault, 172
Sebillon, 262
Sebire, 321
Sebron, 321
Secrot, 173
Sedille, 431
Sedillon, 431
See, 172
Seeber, 321
Seeger, 173
Segard, 173
Segaut, 172
Sège, 172
Seguier, 173
Seguin, 173
Segur, 173
Séguret, 173
Selabelle, 308
Selin, 308
Selle, 308
Sellerin, 308
Sellier, 308
Seltier, 443
Selzer, 443
Sem, 262
Semé, 75, 262
Semel, 262
Semelé, 262
Semey, 75, 262
Semichon, 75, 262
Senac, 170
Senard, 170
Sené, 170

556 INDEX OF FRENCH NAMES.

Seneca, 170
Senelle, 170
Sengel, 438
Senillon, 170
Sennegon, 170
Senocq, 170
Sentubery, 456
Serail, 230
Serard, 230
Serdou, 198
Seré, 230
Serieu, 230
Seroin, 230
Serra, 230
Serre, 230
Serrier, 230
Sert, 198
Sery, 230
Sester, 293
Sestier, 293
Seuriot, 322
Sevelinges (De), 262
Sevilla, 262
Sevry, 262
Seyffert, 173
Seyssel, 272
Sezerie, 451
Shoenberg, 389
Sibert, 173, 321
Sibot, 173
Sibourc, 322
Sicard, 173
Sicbel, 172
Sichel, 172
Sidney, 431
Sidoli, 431
Siegel, 172
Siegrist, 173
Siemers, 173
Siess, 272
Siéver, 262
Siglé, 172
Signet, 173
Silva, 346
Silve, 346
Silvy, 346
Simard, 262
Simart, 262
Simier, 262
Simil, 262
Simond, 173
Simus, 262
Singer, 438
Singery, 438
Singes, 438
Singly, 438
Sins, 456
Sintard, 456
Sipière, 362
Sirguey, 441
Sisco, 272
Sister, 293
Sitt, 431

Sittell, 431
Sive, 261
Six, 200
Smyttére, 461
Sobbel, 304
Soinard, 99
Soinoury, 99
Sol, 138
Solard, 138
Sole, 138
Soleret, 138
Solier, 138
Sombert, 99
Sommaire, 141
Sommerard, 141
Sommervogel, 94
Sonder, 302
Sorbet, 230
Soreau, 441
Sorel, 230
Sorieu, 230
Sorré, 230
Soto, 266
Soualle, 322
Souchard, 267
Souchay, 267
Soucherad, 267
Soucherard, 268
Soucheret, 267
Soucherre, 268
Souday, 301
Souden, 301
Soudier, 301
Sougère, 268
Sougit, 267
Souin, 99
Soule, 138
Soulé, 138
Soulery, 138
Soult, 443
Soupault, 304
Soupe, 304
Soupé, 304
Soupeau, 304
Soupir, 304
Souply, 304
Sourd, 198
Sourdeau, 198
Sourdeval, 198
Sourdière, 198
Sourg, 441
Soury, 441
Soussi, 266
Soutif, 301
Souty, 301
Souverain, 424
Spada, 199
Spenner, 445
Spicq, 207
Spill, 434
Spiller, 434
Spinn, 445
Spire, 206

Spiro, 206
Sponi, 445
Staar, 245
Stach, 213
Stal, 476
Stalin, 81, 476
Steffen, 476
Stein, 479
Steinacher, 476
Sterckeman, 245
Steuben, 469
Stevart, 469
Stival, 469
Stobin, 469
Stocq, 213
Stoffe, 469
Stoffell, 469
Stoffer, 469
Stohrer, 345
Storelli, 345
Storez, 345
Stouf, 469
Stourza, 345
Stricker, 245
Stuppy, 469
Sturbaut, 345
Stuvé, 469
Suasso, 266
Suard, 322
Succaud, 267
Suchel, 267
Sue, 267
Suet, 266
Suin, 99
Summer, 141
Supply, 304
Suquet, 267
Surcouf, 441
Susse, 266
Sybille, 262
Sylvert, 346
Syndic, 456
Systermann, 293

Tachard, 391
Taffin, 428
Tagniard, 391
Tailfer, 375
Taillefer, 375
Tainne, 311, 338
Tains, 338
Talabot, 375
Talbert, 375
Talbot, 375
Tallard, 375
Tallon, 375
Talle, 375
Talleman, 376
Talleyrand, 376
Talma, 24, 375
Tama, 364
Tami, 364
Tanc, 359

INDEX OF FRENCH NAMES. 557

Tandon, 310
Tandou, 310
Tangre, 311
Tanière, 311
Tanlay, 311
Tanneur, 311
Tanniere, 53, 311
Tanrade, 311
Tanton, 310
Tapin, 428
Taquo, 390
Tarabon, 208
Taragon, 208
Taratre, 209
Tard, 209
Tardu, 209
Tardy, 209
Taré, 208
Targant, 208
Taride, 209
Tarlay, 208
Tarnaud, 208, 398
Tarratte, 209
Tartary, 209
Tartter, 209
Tascher, 53, 385
Tassel, 385
Tasselin, 385
Tassert, 385
Tassily, 385
Tassot, 385
Tassy, 385
Taté, 271
Tavard, 428
Taveau, 428
Tavel, 428
Taze, 291
Teigne, 338
Teigny, 338
Teillart, 375
Tel, 375
Tellier, 375
Tenaillon, 310
Tenard, 311
Tencé, 310
Tenneson, 311
Tennevin, 310
Tenret, 312
Terray, 208
Terre, 208
Terreur, 208
Terrier, 208
Terseur, 242
Tetard, 291
Tête, 271
Thais, 526
Thenadey, 338
Thénard, 339
Thenier, 339
Theodor, 333
Théot, 332
Thiac, 457
Thibault, 332

Thibaut, 332
Thiberge, 333
Thibert, 332
Thiéblot, 332
Thiedy, 332
Thiécon, 332
Thierré, 268
Thierry, 268
Thimel, 365
Thiodon, 332
Thirault, 268
Thirouin, 268
Thiry, 268
This, 351
Thisse, 351
Thom, 363
Thomé, 363
Thomel, 364
Thomet, 364
Thommeret, 364
Tieffin, 488
Tillé, 189
Tilliard, 189
Tillier, 189
Tilman, 190
Tilmant, 190
Tillon, 190
Tillot, 190
Tilly, 189
Timel, 365
Tiné, 129
Tinel, 130
Tingay, 367
Tiphaine, 488
Tireau, 268
Tisci, 229
Tison, 352
Tissaire, 352
Tisselin, 352
Tisserand, 352
Tissier, 352
Titard, 333
Tittel, 332
Tixier, 229
Toche, 427
Tombe, 363
Tombel, 364
Tonne, 129
Tonnellé, 130
Torin, 208
Toty, 273
Toucart, 427
Tougart, 427
Tourault, 129
Tournachon, 190
Tournaillon, 190
Tournaire, 190
Tournal, 190
Tournay, 190
Tourne, 190
Tourneur, 190
Tournery, 190
Tousac, 274

Tout, 273
Toutan, 274
Toutay, 273
Touvée, 103
Touvy, 103
Touzeau, 273
Touzé, 273
Touzel, 274
Touzelin, 274
Touzin, 274
Trabold, 196
Tracy, 242
Trager, 413
Tragin, 413
Trajin, 413
Trappe, 196
Trassard, 242
Traubé, 441
Trayer, 413
Trays, 242
Treboul, 196
Trécolle, 413
Treffil, 196
Trégont, 413
Tréhard, 413
Treifous, 413
Trens, 242
Tress, 242
Tressan, 242
Tressard, 242
Triau, 429
Tribou, 196
Tricard, 429
Triché, 429
Tricot, 429
Triebert, 429
Triefus, 429
Triger, 429
Triquet, 429
Troly, 141
Troplong, 441
Tross, 249
Trote, 270
Trotté, 270
Trottier, 271
Trotrot, 271
Trou, 195
Trouble, 441
Troude, 270
Troupeau, 441
Troupier, 441
Trouplin, 441
Trousseau, 249
Trousel, 249
Trouve, 441
Trubert, 196, 429
Truc, 195
Trudon, 271
Truelle, 195
Truffier, 441
Trufy, 441
Trupel, 441
Trusson, 249

558 INDEX OF FRENCH NAMES.

Trutey, 270
Trutin, 271
Try, 429
Tudey, 332
Tudor, 333
Tugault, 428
Tugot, 427
Tunna, 129
Tungnand, 362
Turc, 487
Turell, 208
Turgis, 208
Turquetil, 129
Turgot, 128
Tutuny, 332
Tytgat, 333

Ude, 282
Ulliac, 105
Ulman, 106
Urier, 83
Usse, 524

Vachy, 362
Vadé, 412
Vaganay, 523
Vaghi, 523
Vagney, 523
Valant, 298
Valci, 298
Vald, 344
Valdeiron, 345
Valdin, 345
Valerand, 298
Valerant, 298
Valet, 298
Valfort, 88
Valfroy, 298
Valhere, 298
Valiè, 298
Vallée, 298
Valleran, 298
Vallery, 298
Vallez, 298
Vallier, 298
Valls, 298
Valmer, 298
Valtat, 345
Valton, 345
Vanackère, 394
Vanard, 394
Vancy, 316
Vandale, 317
Vanden, 316
Vanegue, 394
Vanelli, 394
Vanetti, 394
Vaney, 394
Vanin, 394
Vannier, 394
Vanoni, 394
Vanthielen, 317
Vantier 316

Vantillard, 317
Vanutelle, 317
Vaquez, 362
Vaquier, 362
Varache, 278
Varagniac, 305
Varaine, 279
Varangot, 305
Varangue, 278
Varay, 278
Varé, 278
Varichon, 278
Varin, 305
Varinay, 305
Varinont, 278
Varnier, 305
Varrall, 278
Vart, 277
Vassal, 244
Vassard, 244
Vasse, 244
Vasselin, 244
Vasseur, 244
Vasson, 244
Vassy, 244
Vatard, 413
Vatel, 413
Vattemare, 413
Vatier, 413
Vatton, 413
Vatry, 413
Vaude, 344
Vaudescal, 345
Vaudin, 345
Vaudrand, 345
Vaudron, 345
Vaudry, 345
Vaultier, 345
Vaury, 325
Vaute, 344
Vauthier, 345
Vautrot, 345
Vedel, 413
Vedy, 412
Veé, 523
Végé, 523
Veil, 383
Veillard, 383
Veiller, 383
Veillon, 383
Velic, 383
Vellard, 383
Velly, 383
Velpeau, 88
Velter, 345
Veltman, 345
Venant, 394
Venard, 394
Venault, 395
Venelle, 394
Vendrin, 316
Ventre, 316
Verbruggé, 278

Verchère, 74
Verdel, 277
Verdery, 277
Verdié, 277
Verdier, 277
Verge, 73
Vergé, 73
Vergeon, 74
Vergnaud, 74
Vergne, 74
Vergnot, 74
Verière, 278
Verillon, 278
Vérité, 257
Verjus, 526
Vermon, 278
Vernaud, 305
Vernay, 305
Vernaz, 305
Verneau, 305
Vernel, 305
Verneret, 305
Vernert, 305
Vernet, 305
Verney, 305
Vernier, 305
Véro, 278
Verry, 278
Vertu, 257
Vessier, 244
Vestier, 303
Vestraete, 303
Viard, 165
Viareingue, 278
Viault, 165
Vibert, 165
Vicart, 165
Vicaire, 165
Vicel, 165
Vichard, 165
Vicherat, 165
Viclin, 165
Vicq, 164
Vidalenc, 493
Vidalon, 493
Vidard, 494
Videcocq, 27
Vidé, 493
Videau, 493
Videl, 493
Vidocq, 493
Vidon, 493
Vidron, 494
Vidus, 493
Viel, 383
Vient, 316
Viette, 165
Viey, 164
Vigé, 164
Vigerie, 165
Vigier, 165
Vigla, 165
Vilbaut, 123

INDEX OF FRENCH NAMES. 559

Vilcère, 123
Vilcocq, 27
Vilde, 447
Villachon, 123
Villain, 123
Villard, 124
Ville, 123
Villé, 123
Villegri, 123
Villemain, 124
Villemont, 124
Villemot, 124
Viller, 124
Villerie, 124
Villerm, 124
Villeret, 124
Villette, 124
Villetard, 447
Villiame, 124
Villiaume, 124
Villmar, 124
Villy, 123
Viltard, 447
Vimar, 165
Vinay, 263
Vinbourg, 264
Vincey, 263
Vinche, 263
Vincke, 263
Vincq, 412
Vinit, 316
Vinson, 263
Vintin, 316
Vintz, 316
Violard, 383
Violete, 468
Violleau, 383
Viollier, 383
Virgille, 526
Virot, 257
Virquin, 74
Visier, 351
Visonneau, 351
Vissac, 351
Visse, 351
Visser, 351
Vissier, 351
Visto, 303
Vitalis, 494
Vité, 493
Viteau, 493
Vitél, 493

Vitococq, 494
Viton, 493
Vitrac, 494
Vitry, 495
Vitte, 493
Vittier, 494
Vittiz, 493
Vittu, 493
Voilin, 384
Voillemier, 384
Voillemont, 384
Voilquin, 384
Voiry, 325
Vol, 383
Volf, 71
Vollée, 383
Vollet, 384
Vollier, 384
Voltier, 378
Voulquin, 93
Vuillaume, 384
Vuillefroy, 384
Vuillemot, 384

Wal, 298
Walder, 345
Walferdin, 88
Wallart, 298
Walles, 298
Walter, 345
Walz, 298
Wanner, 394
Warée, 278
Warengue, 278
Warin, 305
Warinier, 305
Warmé, 108
Warnet, 305
Waro, 278
Waroquier, 278
Warre, 278
Watel, 413
Watelin, 413
Watin, 413
Watteau, 412
Wauthier, 435
Wegelin, 523
Wegman, 523
Weissé, 351
Weil, 383
Wel, 383
Weld, 344

Weldell, 344
Weldon, 345
Welling, 383
Welhoff, 383
Wenk, 412
Werlé, 325
Wernlé, 305
Wey, 523
Weyn, 523
Wiart, 165
Wibaille, 63
Wicart, 165
Wicot, 165
Wideman, 494
Widmer, 494
Wigy, 164
Wilbrod, 123
Willard, 124
Willaume, 124
Willerme, 124
Willemin, 124
Willemot, 124
Winnen, 264
Wissocq, 351
Witier, 494
Witlich, 494
Wizemann, 351
Woillaume, 72, 384
Woillez, 384
Woillot, 72
Wolter, 378
Wulveryck, 72

Youf, 367
Yslin, 475
Ytasse, 449
Ytier, 450
Yunc, 419
Yve, 366
Yvose, 366
Yvert, 367
Yzard, 475

Zeiller, 433
Zelger, 433
Zelle, 433
Zeller, 433
Zircher, 441
Zorgo, 441
Zurcher, 441

INDEX OF ENGLISH NAMES.

Abba, 60
Abbe, 60
Abbey, 60
Abbiss, 61
Abbott, 61
Abdy, 39, 61
Abson, 61
Achard, 209
Ache, 209
Achlin, 209
Acken, 211
Acorn, 210
Acre, 210
Acron, 210
Acroyd, 210
Addicott, 288
Addiss, 288
Addy, 287
Addlehead, 337
Ade, 519
Adie, 519
Adier, 288
Adkin, 288
Adlam, 337
Adlan, 337
Adlard, 337
Adler, 96
Admans, 288
Adolph, 72, 238
Adolphus, 338
Agan, 211
Agar, 210
Agg, 209
Aggas, 193
Aggis, 193
Aglin, 154
Agombar, 211
Ague, 209
Aguilar, 154
Aikin, 211, 471
Aikman, 210, 471
Ailger, 154
Ailman, 154
Air, 89, 94
Airey, 94
Airy, 89
Akass, 193
Ake, 209
Akey, 209
Alban, 134
Albany, 134
Albert, 516
Albery, 135
Aldebert, 418
Alden, 28, 418
Alder, 418

Alderdice, 419
Alderman, 338, 462
Aldham, 418
Aldis, 418
Aldiss, 64, 65
Aldred, 418
Aldrich, 41, 418
Aldridge, 41, 419
Aldritt, 418
Ale, 154
Aleman, 154, 461
Alfred, 41, 135
Alger, 516
Alice, 300
Alker, 142
Allain, 238
Allan, 238
Allard, 516
Allaway, 517
Allbright, 516
Allbut, 299
Allcard, 142
Allchin, 299
Allday, 418
Alley, 516
Allfrey, 516
Allgood, 299
Allick, 142
Allies, 300
Allix, 142
Allmack, 517
Allman, 517
Allnutt, 517
Allo, 516
Allt, 418
Allty, 418
Allvey, 517
Allward, 517
Allwood, 517
Allwright, 460
Almár, 517
Almiger, 143, 225
Almond, 473, 517
Aloe, 516
Alp, 134
Alpenny, 134
Alpha, 134
Alsager, 300
Altman, 418
Alton, 418
Altree, 419
Alvary, 135
Alvert, 135
Alvey, 134
Alvis, 134
Alwin, 517

Amber, 312
Ambleman, 143
Ambler, 143
Ambridge, 312
Ames, 492
Amett, 284
Amey, 492
Amiss, 284
Amor, 130
Amory, 130
Ampleman, 143
Ancrum, 289
And, 100, 432
Anderson, 32
Andlan, 432
Andoe, 100, 432
Andrade, 432
Ang, 212
Angel, 213
Angelo, 213
Angleman, 213
Angler, 213, 460
Angley, 213
Anglin, 213
Anguish, 293
Angwin, 212
Anhault, 289
Anne, 65, 289
Anning, 289
Anniss, 289
Anns, 119
Ansell, 119
Anselme, 119
Anser, 119
Anslow, 119
Anster, 274
Anstey, 274
Anthem, 432
Antill, 432
Antley, 432
Antridge, 432
App, 60
Appach, 60
Applin, 61
Appold, 61
Apsey, 61
Arabella, 486
Arber, 386
Arbery, 386
Arbon, 386
Arch, 387
Archambaud, 11, 432
Archard, 388
Archbell, 388
Archbold, 388
Archbutt, 388

INDEX OF ENGLISH NAMES. 561

Archer, 388
Arculus, 387
Arden, 251
Arding, 250
Ardouin, 251
Argent, 388
Argue, 387
Argument, 276, 388
Ariell, 95
Arkell, 387
Arkwright, 41, 388, 400
Arle, 95, 339
Arliss, 340
Arm, 418
Armat, 147
Armeny, 146
Armgold, 147
Armiger, 147
Arminger, 8, 146
Armine, 146
Armory, 147
Armour, 147
Arms, 147
Arn, 95
Arnaman, 95
Arney, 95
Arno, 95
Arnold, 95
Arnulphe, 95
Arnum, 95
Arpin, 386
Arrend, 96
Arrowsmith, 462
Arter, 250
Arundel, 152
Asay, 119
Asberry, 119
Asbridge, 119
Ascough, 217
Ash, 142, 216
Ashbold, 217
Asher, 217
Ashkettle, 11, 128, (note,) 512
Ashlin, 216
Ashman, 217
Ashmore, 217
Ashpart, 217
Ashwin, 217
Ashwith, 217
Ashwood, 217
Aslin, 119
Aslock, 120
Ask, 142, 216
Askey, 216
Askwith, 42
Asman, 120
Aspern, 119
Asperne, 39
Asqwith, 37, 217, 223
Ass, 89, 119
Assey, 119
Aste, 216

Astle, 216
Astor, 216
Astray, 216
Astwood, 216, 223
Atack, 288
Atkey, 288
Atkin, 288
Atkiss, 40, 288
Atley, 288
Atmore, 288
Attey, 19
Attle, 288
Attoe, 287
Attride, 288
Attridge, 288
Atts, 288
Attwood, 288
Atty, 287
Aubery, 135
Audritt, 382
Auger, 382
Aught, 381
Aughtie, 381
Aukward, 142
Auleef, 514
Auriol, 524
Austell, 302
Auth, 381
Auther, 382
Auton, 381
Autram, 382
Aveline, 290
Aveling, 290
Aver, 290
Avery, 290
Avila, 290
Avill, 290
Avis, 290
Aviz, 290
Awl, 516
Ayer, 210
Aylard, 154
Ayle, 154
Ayley, 154
Ayliffe, 210, 419
Ayling, 154
Aylmer, 154
Aylward, 154
Aylwin, 154
Ayscough, 39

Babb, 291
Babbage, 291
Babe, 291
Babell, 291
Baber, 291
Babin, 291
Baby, 291
Bacchus, 143
Back, 172
Backer, 172
Backhouse, 144
Bad, 166

Badder, 166
Baddeley, 166
Badge, 378
Badger, 89
Badgery, 90
Badock, 166
Badkin, 166
Badman, 167
Bagg, 172
Baggett, 172
Bagley, 48, 172
Baglin, 172
Baguley, 172
Bail, 192
Bailey, 48, 172, 192
Balaam, 192, 482
Balchin, 241
Balder, 131, 241
Baldey, 240
Baldhead, 241
Baldick, 241
Baldridge, 241
Baldry, 41, 241
Baldwin, 42, 242
Balfe, 73, 379
Ball, 192
Ballard, 192
Baller, 192
Balley, 192
Balling, 192
Ballock, 192
Balls, 241
Balmer, 192
Balsam, 26, 241, 470
Baltic, 241
Balyer, 192
Bance, 235
Bancker, 182
Band, 235
Bander, 236
Banderet, 236
Bang, 182
Banger, 175
Banghart, 182
Bank, 182, 490
Bankart, 182
Bankier, 182
Bann, 175
Banner, 175, 234
Bannick, 175
Banny, 175
Banter, 87
Banting, 236
Bantock, 235
Banton, 236
Banyard, 175
Bard, 222
Bardelle, 222
Bardin, 222
Barding, 222
Bardolf, 72
Bardolph, 222
Bardouleau, 222

s 3

562 INDEX OF ENGLISH NAMES.

Bardy, 222
Barebone, 70
Barefoot, 158
Barehard, 69
Barlas, 354
Barlass, 353
Barley, 22, 61
Barling, 61
Barlow, 22, 61
Barmore, 69
Barnacle, 158
Barnard, 423
Barnett, 423
Barney, 423
Barr, 22, 61
Barrass, 61
Barrell, 22
Barrett, 61, 62
Barreyman, 62
Barrow, 22, 61
Barry, 22, 61
Barter, 222
Bartie, 222
Bartlett, 222 (note)
Bartman, 222
Bartram, 222 (note)
Barwise, 68, 69, 355
Baseke, 181
Basil, 181
Basin, 181
Bask, 181
Bass, 181
Bastard, 12, 183
Baste, 183
Bastick, 183
Basting, 183
Baster, 183
Bastow, 183
Bastray, 183
Bath, 166
Batho, 166
Bather, 166
Batkin, 166
Batley, 166
Batt, 166
Batting, 166
Battle, 166
Batty, 166
Baud, 240
Baugh, 291
Bavarian, 314
Bavin, 291
Beacall, 222
Beach, 222
Beachman, 222
Beadle, 166
Beadman, 167
Beagle, 48
Beakem, 222
Beale, 48
Bear, 68
Bearbenn, 70
Beater, 166

Beath, 166
Beatley, 166
Beatty, 166
Beau, 224
Beautyman, 455
Beaver, 90, 91
Bebb, 414
Beck, 222, 490
Beckett, 222
Beckman, 222
Bed, 166
Beddard, 167
Bedding, 166
Beddoe, 166
Bede, 166
Bee, 47, 378
Beecher, 222
Beechey, 222
Beer, 68
Begg, 47, 64, 222
Beetle, 166
Befford, 414
Beldam, 241
Belfry, 269
Bell, 192
Bellamy, 192
Beller, 269
Bellett, 269
Bellew, 192
Bellies, 521
Belliss, 269, 521
Bellman, 269, 461
Bellmain, 269
Bellment, 269
Bellmore, 192, 269
Belly, 192
Bellord, 269
Bellow, 192
Bellows, 521
Belser, 521
Belsey, 269
Belt, 240
Beltram, 241
Belward, 270
Ben, 484
Bence, 235
Bench, 182
Bender, 236
Bendelow, 235
Bending, 236
Bendle, 235
Bendy, 235
Benger, 177
Benjamin, 484
Benkin, 22, 177
Benmore, 177
Benn, 21, 22, 176
Bennell, 21, 176
Benner, 177
Benney, 176
Bennicke, 176
Benning, 177
Bennoch, 176

Benns, 177
Bense, 177
Benson, 236
Bent, 235
Bentall, 235
Bentinck, 236
Benton, 236
Bentwright, 236
Berger, 69
Beringer, 70
Bernard, 40, 70
Bernhard, 40
Bernold, 71
Berrett, 69
Berridge, 69
Berrier, 69
Berrill, 69
Berringer, 70
Bertham, 370
Bertie, 370
Bertin, 370
Bertram, 41, 370
Bertrand, 41, 370
Berward, 69
Besley, 181
Bessel, 181
Bessemer, 181
Bessett, 181
Best, 183
Bethell, 166
Bethray, 167
Betkin, 166
Betteley, 166
Bettell, 166
Betteridge, 167
Betty, 65, 166, 484
Beugo, 378
Bevan, 414
Beville, 414
Bew, 47, 378
Bewley, 48
Bewly, 379
Beyerman, 313
Bibb, 414
Bibby, 414
Biber, 91
Bible, 414
Bick, 77, 84, 177
Bicker, 178
Bickle, 177
Bickley, 177
Biddick, 166
Biddulph, 42, 72, 167
Bidgood, 40
Biffin, 414
Bigelow, 177
Bigg, 47, 64, 77, 177
Biggar, 178
Bigman, 178
Bilke, 13, 269
Bill, 17, 269, 484
Billamore, 269
Billet, 13, 269

INDEX OF ENGLISH NAMES.

563

Billeter, 219
Billham, 269
Billiard, 13, 269
Billin, 270
Billing, 269
Billingay, 269
Billis, 269
Billman, 269
Billow, 13, 17, 269
Billy, 17, 269
Billyeald, 270
Binden, 236
Binder, 236
Bingey, 178
Binney, 176
Binns, 177
Birch, 106
Bird, 92, 329
Birdlock, 370
Birdmore, 370
Birdseye, 370
Birne, 70
Birner, 70
Birney, 70
Birt, 370
Birtle, 370
Birtles, 370
Biscoe, 181
Bisgood, 181
Bishop, 182, 463
Bisney, 181
Biss, 181
Bissell, 181
Bissmire, 181
Bitch, 84, 177
Bithrey, 167
Black, 395
Blacker, 395
Blackie, 395
Blackman, 395
Blacow, 393
Blade, 376
Blain, 396
Blake, 393
Blakeman, 393
Blaker, 393
Blakey, 393
Blanch, 392
Blanchard, 393
Blanchett, 393
Blanchflower, 468
Blancker, 393
Bland, 396
Blapden, 397
Blaney, 396
Blank, 392
Blankman, 393
Blate, 376
Bleach, 393
Bleacher, 393
Bleak, 393
Bleay, 396
Bledy, 440

Blenky, 392
Blenkin, 392
Blenkinsop, 392 (note)
Blenkiron, 393
Blessed, 441
Blessley, 440
Blethyn, 440
Blevin, 184
Blew, 396
Blower, 396
Blick, 393
Bligh, 393
Blight, 440
Blinckhorn, 393
Blinco, 392
Blindell, 397
Bliss, 440
Blissett, 441
Blizzard, 441
Block, 214
Blockey, 214
Blogg, 214
Blomeley, 465
Blondell, 397
Bloodgood, 440
Bloom, 465
Bloomer, 465
Bloomy, 465
Bloss, 466
Blossett, 466
Blossom, 465
Blow, 214, 396
Blowen, 215, 396
Blower, 215, 396
Bluck, 214
Blunkell, 513
Blyth, 440
Boadella, 454
Boag, 224
Board, 229
Boarder, 229
Boardman, 229
Boardwine, 229
Boast, 409
Boatwright, 455, 460
Bonz, 482
Bobart, 422
Bobbin, 422
Bobbitt, 422
Bobby, 484
Bobkin, 422
Bock, 224
Bodda, 454
Bodell, 454
Boden, 454
Bodgener, 225
Bodger, 455
Bodily, 454
Bodicker, 455
Bodkin, 454
Bodley, 454
Bodman, 455
Bodmer, 455

Body, 454
Boetefeur, 455
Boff, 421
Boffey, 421
Bogard, 225
Bogg, 224
Boggis, 455
Boggon, 225
Bogie, 224
Bogle, 224
Bogman, 225
Bogue, 47
Bold, 240
Bolden, 29, 242
Boldero, 131, 242
Boldery, 241
Bolding, 241
Boling, 281
Bollin, 281
Bollman, 281
Bolt, 240
Bolter, 241
Boltwood, 242
Bomgarson, 176
Bonar, 176
Bonbright, 176
Bond, 225
Boney, 175
Boniger, 37, 170
Bonken, 175
Bonnell, 175
Bonner, 176
Bonnick, 175
Bonning, 175
Bonny, 175
Bonnyman, 176
Bonser, 236
Bonsey, 175, 235
Bonter, 236
Boodle, 454
Bookless, 353, 354
Bool, 280
Boore, 452
Boorman, 452
Boot, 454
Booth, 454
Booty, 454
Border, 229
Bosher, 408
Bosley, 408
Bosman, 408
Boss, 408
Bossard, 408.
Bossey, 408
Bossom, 408
Bostel, 409
Bostock, 409
Bostridge, 409
Bothy, 224
Botly, 454
Bott, 454
Botten, 454
Botting, 454

564 INDEX OF ENGLISH NAMES.

Bottle, 454
Botwright, 455
Bouch, 378
Bouchey, 378
Boucher, 379
Boucherett, 379
Boudrow, 242
Boughtwhore, 241
Boully, 280
Boulting, 241
Boutflower, 455 (note)
Bouverie, 422
Bouvier, 422
Bovay, 421
Bovey, 421
Boville, 421
Bow, 224
Bowdry, 241
Bowe, 47
Bowell, 224
Bowen, 225
Bower, 452, 490
Bowerman, 452
Bowker, 379
Bowkett, 379
Bowl, 280
Bowler, 281
Bowman, 225
Bowmer, 225
Box, 32
Boy, 313
Boyer, 313
Boyman, 313
Bracher, 185
Brack, 184
Bradnell, 221
Bradshaw, 501
Bragan, 185
Bragg, 130
Bragger, 130
Braham, 371
Brain, 185
Brainard, 185
Brake, 184
Brakeman, 185
Bramble, 371
Brame, 371
Bramer, 371
Bramley, 371
Brammell, 371
Brand, 198
Brandard, 199
Brander, 199
Brandis, 199
Brandish, 199
Brandle, 198
Brandling, 199
Brandram, 199
Brandreth, 199
Brandrick, 199
Brandy, 19, 198
Brant, 198
Brasier, 443

Brass, 443, 476
Brassbridge, 495
Brassell, 443
Brassey, 443
Bray, 184
Brayer, 185
Brayman, 185
Brazier, 53, 443
Brazill, 443
Braznell, 221
Breach, 184
Breakell, 185
Breaker, 185
Bream, 106
Breazard, 186
Breecher, 185
Breem, 371
Breeze, 185
Bremer, 371
Bremond, 371
Bremridge, 371
Brent, 198
Breslin, 186
Bressey, 185
Brett, 185
Brettell, 185
Brew, 193
Brewer, 194
Brewes, 185
Breysic, 186
Briand, 185
Briant, 185
Brick, 184
Brickell, 185
Bricker, 185
Brickman, 185
Bridge, 184
Bridgeman, 185
Bridgen, 185
Bridger, 185
Bridges, 185
Brier, 185
Brigg, 184
Briggs, 185
Bright, 106, 370
Brighting, 370
Brightland, 370
Brightly, 370
Brightman, 370
Brightmore, 370
Brightwine, 42
Brighty, 370
Brigman, 185
Brim, 371
Brimble, 371
Brimelow, 371
Brimiley, 371
Brisco, 186
Brise, 185
Brisk, 186
Brisley, 186
Brisman, 186
Brissey, 185

Brittell, 185
Britnell, 221
Britter, 185
Brix, 185
Brixey, 23, 185
Broad, 218
Broadwood, 501
Brocard, 194
Brock, 90, 193
Brockmann, 194
Broderick, 218
Brodie, 218
Brodhead, 218
Broke, 193
Broker, 194
Brond, 198
Brook, 193
Brooker, 194
Brooking, 193
Brookman, 194
Brookson, 193
Bros, 480
Brother, 218, 293, 513
Brotherson, 293
Brown, 126, 398, 400
Brownell, 399
Browning, 400
Brownlow, 399
Brownett, 400
Brownrigg, 400
Brownsmith, 462
Brownsword, 462 (note)
Bruce, 185
Brune, 399
Brunker, 400
Brunner, 400
Bruzand, 186
Bruzaud, 186
Buba, 421
Bubb, 421
Buck, 85, 378
Bucket, 379
Buckie, 378
Buckle, 379
Buckley, 379
Bucklin, 379
Buckney, 379
Buckridge, 379
Bucksey, 379
Budd, 454
Budden, 454
Buddicombe, 455
Budding, 454
Buddle, 454
Buddo, 454
Buddrich, 455
Budge, 454
Budlong, 454
Budmore, 455
Buffin, 422
Buffrey, 422
Bugg, 47, 110, 378
Buggeln, 379

INDEX OF ENGLISH NAMES.

565

Buggin, 379
Buglea, 48, 379
Builder, 219
Buist, 408 (note), 409
Bulck, 281
Bulfinch, 104
Bulger, 281
Bull, 82, 280
Bullaker, 281
Bullard, 281
Bullen, 281
Buller, 281
Bulley, 280
Bulling, 281
Bullion, 281
Bulliss, 281
Bullmore, 281
Bullock, 281
Bullstrode, 3
Bulman, 281
Bulmer, 281
Bulwer, 281
Bundle, 235
Bundock, 235
Bundy, 235
Bunn, 416
Bunnett, 416
Bunney, 416
Bunning, 416
Bunsall, 235
Bunse, 235
Bunsen, 236 (note)
Bunt, 102
Bunten, 236
Bunter, 236
Bunting, 102, 236
Bunyan, 416
Bunyer, 416
Burchard, 279
Burchell, 279
Burd, 239
Burdekin, 93
Burdell, 329
Burden, 329
Burder, 330
Burdett, 330
Burdock, 329
Burge, 279
Burger, 279
Burgess, 279
Burgwin, 279
Burke, 279
Burley, 69
Burling, 452
Burn, 70
Burnell, 70
Burness, 70
Burnidge, 70
Burning, 70
Burnish, 24, 70
Burnman, 69
Burrell, 452
Burt, 106, 370

Buss, 407
Bussell, 407
Bussey, 407
Bussing, 407
Bussman, 407
Busst, 409
Bustard, 102, 409
Buszard, 407
Butiman, 455
Butlin, 454
Butling, 22, 454
Butolph, 72
Butt, 454
Buttel, 454
Buttemer, 455
Butter, 455
Butterfly, 455 (note)
Butterick, 455
Buttery, 455
Button, 454
Buttress, 455
Buzzard, 102
Byard, 313
Bye, 47, 313
Byer, 313
Bynner, 177
Byron, 70

Cable, 285
Caddick, 525
Caddy, 525
Cade, 206
Cadell, 525
Cadman, 525
Cadwell, 169, 525
Cahan, 174
Cain, 174, 482
Cains, 174
Calderon, 42, 477
Cale, 436
Caley, 436
Calf, 83
Calkin, 437
Calkling, 307
Callaway, 437
Callow, 436
Camalary, 419
Camel, 89
Camm, 436
Cammegh, 436
Cammell, 419
Camp, 171
Campkin, 171
Camplin, 171
Campling, 171
Canary, 444
Candall, 74
Cande, 74
Candelin, 74
Candy, 74
Caney, 174
Cann, 444
Cannar, 444

Cannel, 444
Canney, 444
Canniffe, 201,
Canning, 444
Cannon, 444
Cant, 74
Canty, 74
Cantelo, 74
Cantle, 74
Cantor, 74
Capstick, 227
Carnry, 203
Caravan, 204
Card, 276
Carden, 277
Carder, 277
Cardwell, 277
Carew, 202
Carey, 202
Cark, 481
Carl, 59
Carland, 203
Carless, 59
Carley, 59
Carlin, 202
Carling, 202
Carloss, 59
Carman, 203
Carr, 202
Carrett, 329
Carrick, 202
Carrier, 203
Carroll, 59
Carroway, 204
Cart, 276
Cartell, 276
Carter, 53, 277, 460
Carthew, 277
Carton, 277
Cartridge, 277
Cartwright, 277, 460
Carty, 276
Case, 205
Casement, 205
Casey, 205
Cash, 205
Cashman, 205
Cashow, 205
Cask, 205
Casky, 205
Cassell, 296
Castang, 296
Castello, 296
Caster, 296
Castle, 296
Castley, 296
Caston, 296
Cate, 206
Cater, 206
Catmore, 499
Catmur, 168
Cato, 168, 206
Catomore, 168, 499

566 INDEX OF ENGLISH NAMES.

Catt, 168
Cattey, 168
Cattle, 168
Cattley, 168
Cattlin, 22, 168
Catto, 168
Caulk, 307
Caulking, 307
Caunce, 519
Cause, 309
Causer, 309
Causey, 309
Cayzer, 205
Cazaley, 205
Centre, 456
Chad, 168
Chadborn, 168
Chadbot, 168
Chaddock, 168
Chadman, 168
Chadwick, 169
Chadwin, 169
Chaffinch, 104
Chalk, 307
Chalker, 307
Chalkey, 307
Chalklen, 307
Chalkling, 307
Champ, 171
Chance, 519
Chancey, 519
Chant, 74
Chanter, 74
Chantrey, 74
Chapman, 459
Chard, 250
Charie, 231
Charity, 339
Charker, 232
Charles, 59
Charman, 46, 232
Charrott, 339
Chart, 250
Charter, 250
Chataway, 169
Chatwell, 169
Chaucer, 307
Cheape, 460
Cheek, 357
Cheese, 459
Cheeseman, 459
Cheesewright, 460
Cheever, 285
Chenning, 329
Chequer, 358
Cherrill, 202
Cherry, 231
Chesman, 459
Chesney, 459
Chessen, 459
Chick, 357
Chicken, 357
Chidell, 438

Child, 162
Children, 42, 46, 162
Childers, 162
Chill, 162
Chilly, 162
Chillmaid, 46, 163
Chillman, 46, 163
Chimlen, 423
Chimney, 423
Chin, 418
Chine, 327
Ching, 329
Chinnery, 328
Chipman, 285
Chipp, 45, 285
Chippen, 285
Chipper, 285
Chirney, 432
Chisel, 458
Chisholm, 459
Chislett, 458
Chisman, 459
Chittle, 438
Chittock, 438
Chitty, 438
Choat, 360
Choote, 360
Christ, 133, 134, 484
Christmas, 487, 522
Christo, 133
Christy, 133
Chrystal, 133
Chubback, 227
Chuck, 357
Chunn, 327
Chuter, 360
Chutter, 360
Circuit, 441
City, 431
Clack, 352
Clad, 435
Claggett, 352
Claplin, 183
Clapp, 183
Clapper, 183
Clapson, 183
Clare, 374
Claremont, 374
Claret, 374
Claridge, 374
Claringbold, 39, 374
Claringbull, 39, 374
Claris, 374
Clarvis, 374
Clarvise, 374
Clary, 374
Class, 392
Classon, 392
Clavey, 183
Clay, 352
Clear, 374
Cleary, 374
Cleaver, 414

Clegg, 352
Cleggett, 352
Clench, 199
Cleveley, 415
Clever, 414
Cleverly, 415
Clewett, 352
Cliff, 415
Clift, 415
Clinch, 199
Cling, 199
Clingo, 199
Clink, 199
Clinkard, 199
Clissold, 392
Clive, 415
Cloak, 352
Clode, 377
Clogg, 352
Close, 391 (note)
Closer, 391 (note)
Clothier, 377, 460
Cloud, 46, 377
Cloudman, 378
Clout, 377
Clouting, 377
Cloutman, 378, 461
Clow, 352
Cluer, 352
Clutton, 377
Coachman, 446
Cob, 248
Cock, 446
Cocker, 446
Cockett, 446
Cockin, 446
Cocking, 446
Cockle, 446
Cocklin, 446
Cockman, 446
Cocks, 446
Cod, 106
Codd, 115
Codley, 17
Codling, 115
Cody, 115
Coe, 336
Coffey, 248
Coffman, 248
Coffin, 249
Cogger, 446
Coggin, 446
Coghill, 446
Coglin, 446
Coish, 336
Colbran, 226
Colbreath, 226
Colburn, 226
Cold, 477
Coldman, 81, 477
Coldrick, 477
Cole, 226
Colenso, 24, 226

INDEX OF ENGLISH NAMES. 567

Coleman, 226, 461
Coley, 226
Coll, 17
Colla, 17, 19, 226
Collamore, 226
Collar, 226
Collard, 226
College, 226
Colley, 226
Collick, 226
Collier, 53, 226, 460
Colling, 226
Collins, 24, 226
Colman, 226
Colmer, 226
Colt, 81, 477
Coltart, 81
Colter, 81, 477
Colthard, 477
Coltmann, 81, 477
Combe, 59, 296
Combridgr, 59
Comer, 60
Comley, 60
Commin, 63, 297
Comont, 60
Comrie, 60
Conder, 164
Condron, 164
Condry, 164
Condy, 163
Cone, 327
Conger, 328
Conker, 328
Conlan, 327
Conne, 327
Connell, 327
Connery, 328
Conny, 327
Conoff, 328
Conquest, 328
Conrath, 328
Consell, 163
Const, 360
Constable, 462, 486
Conybear, 328
Conyer, 328
Coode, 101, 115
Coolbreath, 226
Coote, 52, 101, 115
Cooze, 309
Copeman, 248, 459
Copelin, 248
Copestake, 227
Copley, 248
Copp, 248
Coppard, 248
Copper, 476
Coppernoll, 221
Coppin, 249
Coppock, 248
Copsey, 23, 248
Corbett, 98

Corbin, 98
Corbould, 202
Corby, 98
Core, 202
Corker, 481
Corkery, 481
Corking, 481
Corkling, 481
Corkman, 481
Cornell, 433
Corner, 433
Corney, 433
Cornick, 433
Corning, 433
Cornman, 433
Corsan, 409
Corsar, 409
Corse, 409
Cort, 409
Cory, 202
Cose, 309
Cosier, 309
Cossack, 309
Cossart, 309
Cossey, 309
Cosson, 309
Cost, 360
Costall, 360
Costeker, 360
Costello, 360
Coster, 360
Costiff, 360
Costlow, 360
Costly, 360
Cotman, 116
Cott, 115
Cottam, 115
Cotter, 116, 514
Cottle, 115
Cotton, 117
Coulthred, 477
Cound, 163
Counsell, 163
Count, 163
Counter, 164
County, 163
Countze, 163
Courage, 337
Courcelle, 409
Ceurridge, 337
Course, 409
Courser, 409
Court, 409
Courtenay, 409
Courtier, 409
Courtnell, 221
Courtwright, 409
Cousin, 296, 309
Coutts, 115
Covell, 248
Coveny, 249
Covert, 248
Covey, 248

Cow, 336
Cowan, 336
Coward, 12, 336
Cowell, 336
Cowie, 336
Cowing, 336
Cowland, 336
Cowman, 337
Cowper, 476
Craig, 97
Craigie, 97
Craik, 97
Crake, 97
Crakell, 97
Cram, 97
Cray, 401
Creah, 170
Creak, 170
Creaker, 170
Crealey, 196
Cream, 125
Creamer, 125
Crean, 465
Cree, 170
Creech, 170
Creelman, 196
Creer, 170
Crespel, 404
Crespin, 404
Cressall, 401
Cressy, 401
Crew, 401
Cribb, 188
Crickmay, 25, 170
Crilly, 196
Crimson, 125
Criper, 188
Crippen, 188
Cripps, 404
Crisp, 404
Crispin, 404
Croad, 46, 371
Croager, 46, 372
Crock, 252
Crocker, 253
Crockett, 253
Croker, 253
Croll, 405
Croly, 405
Crome, 372
Cromey, 372
Cromley, 374
Croney, 465
Crook, 46
Croon, 373
Cropp, 424
Cropper, 425
Croser, 406
Cross, 405, 490
Crossman, 406
Crotch, 46
Crothers, 372
Croton, 372

568 INDEX OF ENGLISH NAMES.

Crotty, 371
Crowden, 372
Crowdy, 371
Crowe, 97
Crown, 465
Crowson, 97
Crucknell, 221
Crum, 373
Cruse, 404
Cruso, 404
Crussell, 404
Crutwell, 373
Cryer, 53, 170
Cryme, 125
Cubbidge, 248
Cubby, 248
Cubitt, 144, 248
Cubley, 248
Cuckoo, 105
Cudd, 115
Caddon, 117
Cuddy, 115
Cufman, 248
Cuff, 248
Cuffey, 248
Cuffley, 248
Cufflin, 248
Cull, 478
Cullen, 478
Culley, 478
Cumber, 234
Cumberbatch, 234
Cumberbeach, 234
Cumberpatch, 234
Cumming, 297
Cumper, 234
Cunard, 328
Cundell, 163
Cundy, 163
Cuniffe, 328
Cunio, 327
Cunley, 327
Cunliffe, 328
Cunnell, 327
Cunnew, 328
Cunnings, 329
Cunnold, 328
Cupid, 143, 144
Cupit, 144, 248
Curling, 405
Curll, 405
Curnick, 433
Curno, 433
Curson, 409
Curt, 409
Curtail, 409
Curtze, 409
Curwen, 204
Cust, 360
Custance, 24, 360
Custard, 360
Cutlove, 40
Cutmore, 116

Cutright, 116
Cuttell, 115
Cutting, 115
Cutto, 19

Dabb, 428
Dack, 390
Dacker, 391
Dacombe, 391
Dadd, 291
Daddy, 291
Dade, 291
Dadmun, 292
Dafford, 428
Daffy, 428
Dagan, 338
Dagg, 390
Dagger, 391
Dagley, 48, 390
Dagnall, 338
Daily, 390
Dainty, 310
Dairy, 391
Daisy, 390
Daldy, 375
Dale, 375, 491
Dallas, 375
Dallen, 375
Dallimore, 376
Dalling, 375
Dallor, 375
Dallow, 375
Dalloway, 376
Dally, 375
Dalman, 376
Damer, 365
Dames, 365
Damm, 364
Damory, 365
Dana, 311
Dance, 310
Dancer, 310
Dancey, 310
Dand, 310
Dandelyon, 12, 310
Dando, 310
Dandy, 45, 310
Dane, 311, 338
Danes, 338
Danford, 311
Danger, 311, 338
Daniel, 484
Danks, 359
Dann, 311
Dannan, 311
Dannell, 311
Danner, 311
Danson, 310
Dapp, 428
Daracott, 208
Darch, 397
Dardy, 208
Dargan, 208, 397

Dark, 397
Darker, 397
Darkies, 208
Darkin, 397
Darkman, 397
Darley, 208
Daly, 48
Darnell, 398
Darnley, 398
Darr, 208
Darrell, 208
Darrigon, 208
Darrow, 208
Dart, 209
Darter, 209
Dartnell, 221
Darwin, 208
Dasent, 385
Dassett, 385
Dassy, 385
Date, 291
Datt, 291
Daunt, 310
Davall, 428
Daven, 428
Davidge, 428
Daviron, 428
Davock, 428
Davy, 428
Day, 390
Daybell, 390
Dayer, 391
Dayes, 390
Daykin, 390
Dayman, 391
Daymont, 391
Daze, 291, 390
Dazey, 291
Deal, 101
Dean, 311
Dear, 268
Dearbird, 268
Dearlove, 268
Dearman, 268
Dearth, 209
Deary, 27, 268
Deck, 390
Dederick, 333
Dedman, 333
Dedridge, 333
Deed, 332
Deedy, 332
Deer, 85
Deffell, 423
Deighen, 338
Delay, 375
Delhier, 375
Dell, 375
Dellamore, 376
Deller, 375
Dellow, 375
Delmar, 376
Demaid, 457

INDEX OF ENGLISH NAMES. 569

Demon, 457
Dempsey, 365
Dench, 106, 359
Dendy, 310
Denhard, 311
Denison, 45, 311
Denman, 312
Denn, 311
Dennell, 311
Denning, 311
Denny, 311
Denolf, 312
Denson, 311
Denyer, 311
Dern, 398
Derwin, 268
Dessert, 385
Dettman, 333
Dettmer, 333
Devey, 428
Devick, 428
Devlin, 428
Devoll, 488
Devon, 428
Dew, 427
Dewar, 427
Dewell, 427
Dewen, 427
Dewey, 427
Dewick, 427
Dewing, 427
Dey, 457
Diabogue, 457
Diack, 457
Diamond, 457
Dias, 351
Dicey, 351
Dick, 406, 484
Dicker, 407
Dickie, 406
Dickin, 407
Dickman, 407
Dietman, 333
Diggle, 406
Digman, 407
Digory, 407
Digweed, 42
Dilger, 189
Dilke, 189
Dill, 189
Diller, 189
Dilley, 189
Dillicar, 189
Dillick, 189
Dillimore, 190
Dillman, 190
Dillmet, 190
Dillon, 190
Dillow, 189
Dillwyn, 190
Dilnut, 41
Dimes, 365
Dimmett, 365

Dimmick, 365
Dimmock, 365
Dine, 31
Dineley, 130
Ding, 367
Dingle, 367
Dingley, 367
Dingman, 367
Dingwell, 367
Dingy, 367
Dining, 31, 130
Dinn, 129
Dinning, 130
Disher, 229
Dishman, 229
Dismore, 352
Diss, 64, 65, 351
Ditchman, 407
Dix, 229
Dixie, 229
Dobel, 103
Dobie, 103
Doblin, 103
Dock, 427
Docker, 427
Docking, 427
Dodd, 45, 273
Doddridge, 273, 333
Dodman, 273
Doe, 427
Doggett, 84, 427
Doke, 427
Doll, 63
Dolland, 40
Dolling, 63
Dolphin, 184, 513
Dommett, 364
Donelan, 130
Donn, 129
Donnell, 129
Donney, 129
Donno, 129
Donnor, 128
Doody, 273
Door, 208
Doran, 208
Dorbon, 208
Dorey, 208
Dorman, 208
Dormer, 208
Dorrell, 208
Dorton, 209
Dotchin, 273
Dotry, 273
Dottridge, 273, 333
Doubt, 273
Doubty, 273
Doudney, 274
Dove, 103
Dovey, 103
Dow, 427
Dowd, 273
Dowden, 274

Dowdle, 274
Dowdiken, 274
Dowding, 274 p
Dowdy, 273
Dowell, 427
Dower, 427
Dowey, 427
Dowland, 428
Dowling, 22, 427
Dowse, 273
Dowsing, 274
Dowson, 274
Dozell, 273
Dozy, 273
Drabble, 196
Drage, 100, 413
Dragon, 413
Drain, 413
Drake, 100, 413
Drawbridge, 495
Drawsword, 236
Drawwater, 502
Dray, 413
Draysey, 242
Dresser, 242
Drew, 195
Drewell, 195
Drewery, 196
Drewett, 429
Drinkwater, 502
Droop, 441
Drought, 270
Drowdy, 270
Drown, 196
Druce, 249
Druggan, 196
Drum, 243
Drummer, 243
Drummey, 243
Drummond, 243 (note)
Drury, 196
Dry, 429
Dryer, 429
Dubbins, 103
Duck, 100, 427
Ducker, 427
Duckett, 427
Duckling, 100, 427
Duckman, 428
Duddle, 273, 332
Daddy, 273, 332
Dudgeon, 427
Dudin, 332
Duga, 100
Dugald, 428
Dugard, 427
Duggin, 100, 427
Dugmore, 428
Dugood, 428
Dugwell, 428
Duke, 427
Duly, 427
Dumbell, 364

T 3

570 INDEX OF ENGLISH NAMES.

Dume, 363
Dumlin, 364
Dummelow, 364
Dummer, 364
Dummert, 364
Dumplin, 364
Dunavin, 130
Dunger, 130
Dungey, 361
Dunkin, 22
Dunn, 21, 22, 129
Dunnell, 21, 129
Dunning, 130
Dunstone, 130
Durand, 197
Durell, 208
Durley, 208
Durman, 208
Durre, 208
Duthie, 332
Dutt, 273, 332
Dyce, 351
Dye, 457
Dyer, 457
Dyett, 332
Dyson, 352
Dyte, 332

Eade, 381
Eadie, 381
Eadon, 381
Eager, 210
Eagle, 94, 154
Eagling, 154
Eames, 254
Earee, 94
Earheart, 95
Earl, 339
Early, 339
Earney, 95
Earwig, 94
Earwaker, 112 (note)
Earratt, 94
Earth, 139
Earthy, 139
East, 302
Easter, 302
Easterbrook, 303
Easterday, 303
Eastman, 302
Eastmure, 302
Easto, 302
Easty, 302
Eat, 381
Eatwell, 382
Eaves, 366
Ebbetts, 61
Ebbidge, 60
Eber, 76
Ebert, 61
Eborall, 76
Edbrook, 382
Eddis, 381

Eddy, 381
Edell, 337
Edelsten, 338
Edgar, 40, 382
Edge, 209
Ediker, 382
Edkins, 381
Edlery, 338
Edlesten, 338
Edlow, 337
Edmans, 382
Edmead, 382
Edmett, 382
Edmond, 382
Edolph, 382
Edridge, 382
Edward, 382
Edwell, 382
Edwick, 382
Edwin, 382
Eel, 416
Egg, 209
Egley, 154
Ego, 209
Elbow, 134
Elden, 418
Eldred, 418
Eldridge, 419
Element, 276, 299
Eley, 416
Elgar, 299
Elgood, 299
Elk, 142
Elkin, 299
Ell, 17, 299
Ella, 17, 19, 299
Ellacot, 299
Ellard, 299
Ellen, 238
Ellenor, 239
Ellery, 299
Elley, 17, 299
Ellice, 300
Elliker, 299
Elliman, 299
Ellion, 238
Ellis, 300
Ellmaker, 143
Ellwood, 299
Elmore, 299
Elphee, 134
Elphick, 134
Else, 300
Elsegood, 300
Elsey, 300
Elt, 418
Eltham, 418
Elton, 418
Elve, 134
Elvery, 135
Elves, 134
Elvidge, 134
Elvis, 134

Elvy, 134
Elwin, 299
Ember, 254, 312
Emblem, 143
Emblin, 143
Emblow, 143
Emeler, 143
Emeny, 254
Emerick, 254
Emery, 254
Emly, 143
Emlyn, 143
Emmett, 110, 284
Emms, 254
Emus, 284
Engall, 213
England, 213
Engleburtt, 213
Engleheart, 213
English, 318
Enniss, 289
Enoch, 289, 482
Enock, 289
Enough, 289
Enright, 289
Enscoe, 119
Ensell, 119
Enser, 119
Enzer, 119
Epp, 60
Erasmus, 26
Erickson, 32
Erinine, 146
Erratt, 94
Erskine, 79
Esau, 483
Eslin, 119
Essel, 119
Este, 216
Estle, 216
Esty, 216
Ethel, 337
Ether, 282
Etheridge, 282
Etridge, 288
Etty, 287
Eve, 366, 482
Evelyn, 22, 290
Ever, 76
Everall, 76
Everard, 76
Evered, 76
Everett, 76
Every, 76
Evezard, 290
Evill, 366
Ewald, 367
Ewart, 366
Ewe, 85, 366
Ewell, 366
Ewer, 366
Ewing, 366
Eye, 209

INDEX OF ENGLISH NAMES. 571

Eyes, 475

Fachney, 435
Faddy, 62
Faed, 256
Fagan, 435
Fagg, 435
Faggots, 435
Fahey, 435
Fail, 307, 435
Fair, 323
Fairbeard, 323
Fairey, 323
Fairday, 325
Fairfoot, 323
Fairfoul, 93
Fairlan, 323
Fairless, 353, 354
Fairlie, 467
Fairman, 324
Fairne, 324
Fairweather, 139
Faith, 256
Faithy, 256
Fake, 435
Faker, 435
Fall, 307
Fallbright, 333
Fallon, 307
Fallow, 307
Fanline, 234
Fann, 64, 234
Fanner, 234
Fanning, 64
Fannon, 234
Fanny, 64, 234
Fantom, 417
Faraday, 325
Fardell, 325
Farden, 325
Fardo, 325
Farefowl, 93
Farewell, 324
Fargo, 323
Farmont, 324
Farnell, 324
Farra, 323
Farragat, 324
Farrand, 323
Farrell, 323
Farren, 323
Farrer, 324
Farrier, 324
Farrimond, 324
Farrow, 323
Farthing, 325
Fast, 251
Fastaff, 72, 252
Faster, 252
Fastin, 251
Fastolf, 72
Father, 293
Fatman, 62

Fatt, 62
Fatty, 62
Faullon, 93
Faultless, 355
Faunce, 246
Fay, 435
Fearon, 323
Feasal, 247
Feast, 251
Feaster, 252
Fechter, 257
Feddon, 256
Fees, 246
Fehon, 435
Fellow, 307
Felthouse, 518
Feltoe, 518
Feltus, 518
Feltuss, 42
Fendall, 417
Fender, 417
Fendick, 417
Fenlon, 234
Fenton, 417
Fenn, 64, 234
Fennell, 234
Fenner, 234
Fenning, 64
Fentiman, 417
Fentum, 417
Ferdinand, 325
Feriner, 324
Fermin, 215
Fern, 324
Fernald, 324
Ferner, 324
Fernie, 324
Fernilow, 324
Fernyough, 324
Ferrand, 323
Ferrell, 323
Ferrier, 324
Ferriman, 324
Ferry, 323
Fester, 252
Fetman, 62
Fett, 62
Fetter, 293
Fetterman, 293
Ficker, 249
Ficklin, 249
Fickling, 249
Fiddaman, 430
Fiddament, 430
Fiddey, 430
Fidell, 430
Fidge, 249
Fidoe, 430
Fieldhouse, 518
Figg, 249
Filbert, 473, 518
File, 517
Fileman, 518

Filer, 518
Filkin, 517
Fill, 517
Fillary, 518
Filldew, 518
Filley, 517
Filling, 517
Fillmer, 518
Filpot, 518
Finbow, 315
Finch, 104
Fineweather, 139
Finger, 315
Fink, 104
Finn, 315
Finney, 315
Finnimore, 315
Firing, 323
Firkin, 323
Firminger, 216
Fish, 106, 247
Fishline, 247
Fisk, 106, 247
Fisken, 247
Fist, 251
Fister, 252
Fitkin, 430
Fitman, 430
Fitt, 430
Fitter, 430
Fix, 247
Fixson, 247
Fiz, 21 (note), 246
Fize, 246
Fizard, 247
Flack, 411
Flagg, 411
Flambard, 220
Flane, 220
Flatau, 393
Flatman, 394
Flatt, 393
Flattely, 394
Flatter, 394
Flattery, 12, 394
Flawn, 220
Flea, 411
Fleck, 411
Fleeman, 411
Flegg, 411
Flett, 393
Flewitt, 411
Flint, 131
Flitton, 394
Flook, 411
Floss, 412
Flowerday, 466
Fluck, 411
Fluer, 411
Fly, 411
Flyer, 411
Flyger, 411
Fog, 136

572 INDEX OF ENGLISH NAMES.

Foggo, 136
Folk, 333
Folkard, 334
Folker, 334
Folkitt, 334
Ford, 325
Forder, 325
Fordred, 325
Forget, 324
Forland, 324
Forney, 324
Fort, 325
Fortin, 325
Fortune, 325
Forty, 325
Fortyman, 325
Forward, 324
Foskey, 247
Foss, 246
Fossey, 246
Fossick, 246
Fouke, 333
Fowell, 10, 93
Fowkes, 333
Fowle, 10, 93
Fox, 247
Foxell, 247
Foxen, 247
Foxery, 247
Frame, 215
France, 306
Franco, 306
Francourt, 306
Frank, 306
Frankel, 306
Franklin, 306
Frasi, 312
Fraser, 313 (note)
Fread, 261
Freak, 132
Freck, 132
Fred, 261
Frederick, 41, 261
Freebody, 261
Freeborn, 261
Freeborough, 261
Freebout, 261
Freebridge, 261
Freeland, 261
Freeling, 261
Freelove, 261
Freem, 215
Freestone, 42, 261
Freeth, 261
Freeze. 312
Freezor, 313 (note)
Fremlin, 205
Fremont, 215
French, 306
Fresh, 449
Fresher, 449
Frethy, 261
Freutel, 350

Fricke, 132
Fricker, 132
Frickey, 132
Frid, 261
Friday, 261
Friend, 263
Friendship, 263, 351
Frisian, 313
Friskey, 449
Frith, 261, 491
Froger, 350
Fromunt. 215
Frood, 350
Frost, 135
Frostick, 136
Frostman, 136
Froude, 350
Frowd, 350
Frudd, 350
Fuel, 10, 93
Fuggel, 93
Fuggle, 10
Fulcher, 334
Fulke, 333
Full, 517
Fullalove, 518
Fulleck, 517
Fullerd, 518
Fullmer, 518
Furlong, 323
Furnell, 324
Furze, 449
Furzer, 449
Fuss, 246
Fussell, 246
Fussey, 246
Fuszard, 246
Fux, 247

Gabb, 285
Gable, 285
Gadban, 208 (note)
Gadd, 525
Gade, 206
Gadlan, 206
Gaff, 285
Gaffery, 285
Gaffin, 285
Gagan, 174
Gahan, 174
Gain, 174
Gainer, 174
Gainey, 174
Gains, 174
Gaiter, 206
Galbot, 437
Gale, 436, 483
Galey, 436
Galilee, 437
Galindo, 437
Gall, 436
Gallager, 437
Galland, 437

Gallant, 437
Gallard, 437
Gallery, 437
Gallon, 437
Gallow, 436
Galloway, 437
Gallows, 437
Gally, 436
Galt, 76
Gamble, 419
Gambler, 419
Gamlin, 419
Gambling, 419
Game, 436
Gamer, 436
Gammage, 436
Gammon, 436
Gande, 74
Gandell, 74
Gander, 74, 100
Gandy, 74
Gann, 444
Gannaway, 318, 444
Gannon, 444
Gannow, 444
Gansman, 518
Gant, 74
Ganter, 74
Gapp, 285
Garbett, 203
Garbrand, 203
Garbutt, 39, 203
Gard, 276
Garden, 276
Gardie, 276
Gare, 20, 202
Garell, 202
Garey, 202
Garforth, 39, 203
Garing, 202
Garland, 40, 203, 276
Garlick, 203, 473
Garling, 202
Garman, 203
Garment, 41, 203
Garnett, 203
Garrard, 203
Garras, 202
Garraway, 204
Garrett, 41
Garrick, 20, 202
Garrod, 203
Garrold, 204
Garrow, 202
Garstin, 42
Garter, 277
Garvey, 204
Garwood, 37, 204, 223
Gash, 205
Gashry, 205
Gaskell, 205
Gast, 296
Gaster, 296

INDEX OF ENGLISH NAMES. 573

Gastin, 203, 296
Gastineau, 296
Gasting, 296
Gataker, 206
Gate, 206
Gathergood, 525 (note)
Gatliffe, 525
Gatty, 525
Gaussen, 309
Gavelle, 285
Gavey, 285
Gayleard, 437
Gayler, 437
Gazard, 205
Gaze, 205
Gazelle, 205
Gearing, 202
Geary, 202
Geazey, 205
Gebhard, 285
Gedd, 525
Gedney, 525
Geere, 202
Geldert, 478
Gelding, 478
Gell, 436
Gellan, 437
Gellard, 437
Geller, 437
Gemble, 419
Gemmill, 419
Gender, 74
Genna, 444
Genner, 444
Gent, 74
Gentery, 75
Gentle, 74
Gentry, 75
Geoffry, 437
Gerard, 203
Gerduck, 276
Gerhold, 204
Gerich, 202
Gerish, 202
Gerkin, 202
Gerloff, 203
German, 203
Germany, 203
Get, 525
Getler, 525
Getlive, 525
Gettman, 525
Getty, 525
Gibb, 44, 285
Gibbard, 285
Giberne, 285
Giblen, 285
Gibbon, 285
Gibbs, 285
Gibby, 285
Gidden, 438
Giddy, 438
Gidley, 438

Gidlow, 438
Gidman, 438
Gieve, 44, 285
Giffard, 285
Giffin, 285
Gilbert, 458
Gilbody, 458
Gilby, 442
Gildawie, 478
Gilder, 478
Gildert, 478
Gilding, 478
Gilford, 458
Gilfred, 458
Gill, 458, 491
Gillard, 458
Gillen, 458
Giller, 458
Gillett, 458
Gilley, 458
Gilliam, 458
Gillibrand, 39, 199, 458
Gillihom, 458
Gilling, 458
Gillman, 458
Gilloch, 458
Gillow, 458
Gilmore, 458
Gilpin, 442
Gilt, 478
Gimber, 148
Gimbert, 444
Gingell, 419
Ginger, 419
Ginman, 444, 461
Ginn, 444
Ginneau, 444
Ginvey, 444
Gipp, 44
Gippert, 285
Gipps, 285
Gipsy, 285
Girl, 202
Girling, 202
Gissing, 459
Gist, 296
Given, 285
Glad, 435
Gladdell, 435
Gladden, 435
Gladding, 435
Gladdish, 435
Gladman, 435
Gladwin, 435
Gladwish, 435
Glaisher, 395
Glaskin, 392
Glass, 392
Glassey, 392
Glasson, 392
Glaze, 392
Glazard, 392
Glazier, 53, 392

Gleadall, 435
Gleed, 435
Gleig, 352
Glew, 352
Gliddon, 435
Glide, 435
Glissan, 392
Gloag, 352
Glock, 352
Gloss, 391 (note)
Gluer, 352
Gond, 115 (note)
Goat, 85
Goater, 116
God, 106, 115, 484
Godbold, 115
Godbolt, 115
Goddam, 115
Goddard, 116
Godden, 28, 115 (note), 117
Godding, 49, 115
Goddy, 115
Godfrey, 115
Godhead, 116, 484
Godkin, 115
Godier, 116
Godliman, 30, 117
Godman, 49, 116
Godmund, 116
Godrich, 49
Godrick, 116
Godschall, 116
Godsell, 116
Godskall, 116
Godso, 114
Godsoe, 23, 114, 115
Godward, 117
Godwin, 49, 117
Goe, 336
Gogay, 446
Goggin, 446
Goggs, 446
Going, 336
Gold, 81, 477
Goldbourn, 477
Golden, 477
Golder, 477
Goldfinch, 104
Goldie, 477
Golding, 477
Goldingay, 477
Goldman, 81, 477
Goldney, 41, 477
Goldrick, 477
Goldridge, 477
Goldwin, 477
Gomery, 59
Gomm, 59
Goudish, 163
Good, 101, 115
Goodacre, 116
Goodair, 116

574 INDEX OF ENGLISH NAMES.

Goodall, 115
Goodday, 115
Goodear, 116
Gooden, 117
Goodenough, 29, 117, 526
Goodere, 116
Goodered, 116
Goodess, 115
Goodey, 115
Goodheart, 116
Gooding, 49, 115
Goodlake, 116, 164
Goodland, 116
Goodliffe, 116
Goodluck, 11, 164
Goodman, 49, 116
Goodnow, 116
Goodram, 116
Goodrich, 49
Goodrick, 116
Goodridge, 116
Goodsall, 116
Goodwill, 117
Goodwin, 49, 117
Goodwright, 116, 460
Goodyear, 116
Gook, 105
Goose, 99, 309
Gooseman, 310
Goosey, 309
Gooze, 309
Gorbell, 203
Gorbold, 203
Gore, 202
Gorebrown, 39, 203
Goren, 204
Goring, 202
Gorman, 203
Gorway, 204
Gosbell, 309
Goshawk, 96
Gosheron, 310
Gosland, 310
Goslee, 310
Goslin, 309
Gosling, 100, 309
Gosmer, 310
Gosnell, 298
Gospell, 309
Goss, 309
Gossett, 309
Gostelow, 360
Gostling, 360
Goswell, 310
Goswold, 310
Goth, 308
Gothard, 116
Gott, 115
Gotto, 115
Gougou, 105
Gould, 477
Goult, 477

Goulty, 477
Gow, 336
Gowa, 336
Gowan, 336
Goward, 336
Gower, 336
Gowing, 336
Gowland, 336
Gowk, 105
Goy, 336
Gozar, 309
Gozzard, 309
Grace, 401
Gracey, 401
Graseman, 464
Grass, 464
Grasset, 464
Grassick, 464
Grassie, 464
Graygoose, 100
Grayling, 401
Gream, 125
Greek, 170
Greele, 196
Greely, 196
Greer, 170
Green, 465
Greener, 465
Greenhouse, 465
Greening, 465
Greenish, 465
Greenman, 465
Greensmith, 462 (note)
Greenson, 465
Greensword, 462 (note)
Greeny, 465
Gregg, 170, 401
Grenell, 465
Gresley, 401
Greswold, 401
Grew, 401
Grey, 401
Grice, 77, 401
Grier, 170
Grigg, 170
Grill, 196
Grimaldi, 125 (note)
Grimbold, 125
Grimble, 125
Grime, 125
Grimley, 125
Grimm, 125
Grimmer, 125
Grimmet, 125
Grimmond, 125
Grimson, 125
Grisold, 401
Grissell, 77, 401
Grist, 134
Grobe, 424
Gronow, 465
Groom, 10, 59
Groombridge, 41, 59

Groffmann, 425
Grose, 45, 48, 346, 405
Groser, 406
Grosert, 406
Grossmith, 462
Grote, 45, 48, 49
Grouse, 49, 102, 405
Grover, 425
Grossman, 406
Grove, 424
Grubo, 424
Gruby, 424
Grueber, 401
Grumble, 11
Grumley, 60
Grumman, 401
Grummant, 60
Grummer, 60
Gruner, 465
Gruneisen, 462 (note)
Gruning, 465
Guelpa, 88
Guelph, 46
Guest, 296
Guestling, 296
Guilan, 123
Guild, 478
Guillaume, 124
Guille, 122
Gulbert, 479
Gull, 478
Gullen, 478
Gullet, 479
Gullick, 478
Gulliford, 479
Gulliver, 478, 479
Gully, 478
Gum, 10
Gumboil, 11, 50, 164
Gumm, 59
Gumma, 59
Gummoe, 59
Gundey, 163
Gundick, 163
Gundry, 164
Gunn, 163
Gunnell, 163
Gunner, 155, 164, 513
Gunnery, 39, 164
Gunning, 163
Guns, 163
Gunson, 32, 163
Gunston, 164
Gunter, 155, 164
Gunther, 155, 164
Gurnard, 433
Gurnell, 433
Gurner, 433
Gurney, 433
Gurr, 202
Gurwood, 42, 204
Gustard, 360
Gut, 115

INDEX OF ENGLISH NAMES. 575

Guthrie, 164
Gutman, 116
Gutterman, 117
Guy, 336
Guyatt, 336
Guyer, 336
Gwalter, 47, 345
Gwillam, 47
Gwillan, 47
Gwilt, 344, 447
Gwyer, 165
Gwynn, 263
Gwyther, 494
Gye, 336

Hack, 209
Hackaday, 39
Hackman, 210
Hacon, 211, 513
Hadaway, 169
Haddo, 19
Haddock, 106, 168
Hadkiss, 40, 168
Hadley, 168
Hadlow, 168
Hadnutt, 168
Hadow, 19, 168
Hadrot, 168
Hadwen, 169
Haedy, 168
Hagan, 155
Hagar, 210, 482
Hagdorn, 467
Hagel, 209
Hagen, 211
Haggard, 209
Haggie, 209
Haig, 209
Hail, 209
Hailing, 209
Hailstone, 480
Hain, 211
Halbert, 427
Haldane, 318
Halfacre, 135
Halfhead, 135
Halfman, 135
Halfpenny, 134
Halfyard, 11
Hall, 480
Hallbower, 480
Halley, 426, 480
Hallgreen, 480
Halliday, 427
Halliley, 426
Hallingman, 239
Hallowbread, 427
Halloway, 427
Hambling, 143
Hamer, 492
Hamlet, 40
Hamlin, 492
Hamling, 143

Hammer, 130
Hammill, 143
Hammond, 210
Hamper, 312
Hance, 119
Hancock, 27
Hand, 417, 490
Handel, 417
Handcy, 417
Handley, 417
Handright, 432
Hang, 212
Hanger, 289
Hankey, 289
Hankin, 289
Hanlon, 289
Hanman, 289
Hanmer, 289
Hann, 17, 101, 289
Hanna, 17, 101, 289
Hannay, 19
Hannell, 101, 289
Hanney, 17, 289
Hanny, 101
Hanrott, 289
Hansard, 119
Hansom, 119
Hanson, 32
Happey, 60
Haradon, 339
Harbar, 232
Harber, 232
Harbert, 232
Harboard, 232
Harbord, 232
Harbour, 232
Harbud, 232
Hard, 250
Hardacre, 250
Hardaway, 251
Harden, 251
Harder, 250
Harding, 250, 405
Hardham, 250
Hardiment, 251, 276
Hardoff, 251
Hardman, 251
Hardwick, 251
Hardwidge, 251
Hardy, 250
Hardyear, 250
Hare, 89, 231
Hargill, 40, 232
Hargood, 40, 232
Harker, 40, 232
Harknett, 432
Harland, 232, 318
Harle, 157, 231
Harley, 231
Harling, 157, 231
Harlot, 40, 232
Harlott, 12
Harlow, 231

Harman, 40, 46, 232
Harme, 147
Harmer, 147, 232
Harmond, 233
Harmony, 146
Harnard, 95
Harnett, 41
Harney, 95
Harnor, 95
Harnott, 41
Harold, 233, 513
Harp, 7, 386, 460
Harper, 386
Harral, 231
Harre, 89, 231
Harridan, 339
Harridge, 231
Harries, 231
Harris, 231
Harritt, 339
Harrod, 339
Harrold, 514
Harrow, 89, 231
Harry, 89, 231, 484
Harryman, 232
Hart, 85, 250
Hartell, 250
Harter, 250
Hartie, 250
Harting, 250
Hartland, 251
Hartman, 461
Hartnall, 251
Hartnell, 221
Hartnett, 251
Harton, 251
Hartridge, 251
Hartry, 251
Hartstonge, 250 (note)
Hartwright, 251, 460
Harvest, 95
Harvey, 42, 233
Harvig, 42
Harward, 233
Harwin, 233
Harwood, 233
Hase, 21, 89
Hasell, 21, 169
Haskell, 216
Hasluck, 120
Hass, 89, 307
Hassan, 307
Hasselquist, 470
Hast, 448
Hastie, 448
Hastilow, 448
Hastrick, 448
Hately, 519
Hathaway, 169
Hathway, 42, 169
Hatley, 168
Hatred, 519
Hatrick, 168

576 INDEX OF ENGLISH NAMES.

Hatt, 14, 168
Hattemore, 168
Hatten, 22
Havard, 290
Havelock, 40, 160, 513
Haviland, 290
Haw, 209
Haward, 155
Hawke, 96
Hawken, 96
Hawthorn, 467
Hay, 209
Hayday, 19, 519
Haydock, 519
Haydon, 519
Hayman, 210
Haymes, 492
Haysman, 169
Hayter, 519
Hayzen, 169
Hazard, 169
Haze, 169
Head, 168
Headache, 168 (note)
Heading, 168
Headlam, 337
Headrick, 168
Hearing, 232
Hearl, 231
Hearly, 231
Hearse, 79
Heart, 250
Hearty, 250
Heasman, 475
Heath, 168
Heaven, 140
Heaver, 76
Heaverman, 76
Hebb, 60
Hebbert, 61
Heber, 76
Hebson, 32, 61
Heck, 209
Heckle, 209
Hector, 450
Heddy, 168
Hedge, 209, 491
Hedgman, 210-
Hedley, 168
Heggie, 209
Heifer, 76
Height, 519
Heiser, 475
Helfrich, 275
Hellmore, 163
Helm, 225
Helper, 275
Helps, 275
Hemberg, 225
Hembery, 225
Hembrow, 225
Hemment, 492
Hemmer, 130

Henden, 417
Hender, 300
Hendy, 417
Henfrey, 289
Henn, 289
Hennell, 289
Hennessy, 289
Henney, 289
Henniker, 289
Henman, 289, 461
Henning, 289
Henniss, 289
Henry, 492
Henton, 417
Henty, 417
Heppey, 60
Herbert, 38, 232
Herbet, 232
Herd, 250
Herdman, 251
Herepath, 232
Heringaud, 232 (note)
Hermon, 232
Herne, 95
Herniman, 95
Herod, 339, 482
Herp, 386
Herper, 386
Herrick, 231
Herridge, 231
Herries, 231
Herring, 106, 232
Hersant, 42, 233
Hersey, 79
Hertocks, 339
Hesse, 307
Hessey, 307
Hession, 307
Hesson, 307
Hester, 448
Hetley, 168
Hett, 168
Hettich, 168
Heward, 357
Hewer, 358
Hewish, 357
Hewit, 358
Hewland, 358
Hewry, 358
Hezel, 169
Hibbert, 61
Hibbitt, 61
Hibson, 61
Hick, 157, 210, 357
Hickley, 357
Hicklin, 357
Hickling, 157, 357
Hickman, 358
Hickmott, 41, 358
Hickock, 210
Hicks, 357
Hidden, 449
Hide, 449

Hider, 450
Higgin, 357
High, 340
Highatt, 341
Highmore, 341, 358
Higley, 357
Higman, 358
Hilber, 162
Hildebrand, 39, 162, 199
Hilder, 162
Hilding, 162
Hildreth, 163
Hildrup, 163
Hildyard, 162
Hilgers, 162
Hill, 162, 491
Hillam, 38
Hillary, 39, 162
Hilliam, 38
Hilliard, 162
Hillman, 163
Hillock, 358
Hillson, 162
Hilly, 162
Hillyer, 162
Hilmer, 163
Hilridge, 163
Hilt, 162
Hincks, 3, 78
Hinge, 292
Hingeston, 78
Hinch, 292
Hinchey, 292
Hinchliff, 292
Hinchcliff, 292
Hine, 492
Hinman, 492
Hinxman, 78, 80
Hipkin, 61
Hipp, 60
Hipson, 32
Hipwood, 61
Hitt, 449
Hoadley, 168
Hobart, 341
Hoblin, 227
Hobman, 227
Hockaday, 341
Hocken, 340
Hockett, 341
Hockey, 340
Hocking, 340
Hockman, 341
Hocknell, 221
Hodd, 168|
Hodge, 357
Hodges, 357
Hodgkin, 257
Hodgkiss, 358
Hodgman, 358
Hoe, 340
Hoey, 340
Hogan, 357

INDEX OF ENGLISH NAMES.

577

Hogg, 76, 357
Hogmire, 358
Holder, 282
Holderried, 282
Holding, 282
Hole, 282
Holeman, 282
Holeyman, 427
Holker, 282, 427
Holl, 282
Hollaley, 426
Holland, 282
Holler, 282
Hollick, 426
Holliday, 427
Holliman, 427
Holling, 282 (note)
Hollingsworth, 282 (note)
Holloway, 427
Holt, 282
Holter, 282
Holtman, 282
Holy, 227
Homan, 58, 341
Home, 492
Homer, 492
Homeward, 493
Homewood, 493
Honey, 314
Honeyball, 314
Honeyman, 314, 461
Honis, 314
Honner, 314
Hoof, 227
Hoofman, 227
Hoofnail, 221
Hoole, 105, 282
Hoop, 227
Hope, 227
Hopkin, 227
Hopman, 227
Hord, 217
Horder, 218
Horn, 520
Horner, 520
Hornidge, 520
Horniman, 520
Horning, 520
Hornman, 520
Hornsby, 520 (note)
Horrocks, 341
Horsell, 79
Horsenail, 221
Horsey, 79
Horskins, 79
Horsman, 79
Hort, 217
Hoskin, 442
Hosking, 442
Hoste, 302
Houlet, 105
House, 491

Housego, 491
Household, 524
Houseman, 491
Houssart, 491
Howard, 42, 155, 341, 513
Howle, 105
Howley, 105
Howman, 290
Hoyle, 340
Hubback, 227
Hubbard, 227
Hubble, 227, 357
Hube, 227
Hubert, 357
Huck, 357
Huckell, 357
Hucken, 357
Huckett, 358
Hucks, 357
Hudd, 280
Huddert, 280
Huddle, 280
Huddy, 280
Hudkin, 280
Huelins, 357
Hug, 357
Hugall, 357
Huggard, 357
Huggett, 358
Hugh, 357
Hughes, 357
Hughman, 358
Hugman, 358
Hugo, 357
Hugoun, 357
Huie, 357
Hulbert, 105
Hulett, 105
Hullah, 282
Hullock, 358
Human, 358
Humble, 468
Humphrey, 40, 314
Hund, 84
Hundy, 84
Hungate, 314
Hunger, 314
Hunhold, 314
Hunibal, 314
Hunking, 314
Hunn, 314
Hunnard, 314
Hunnex, 314
Hunns, 314
Hunt, 84
Hunting, 84
Huntress, 456
Hurdle, 217
Hurlbat, 340
Hurlburt, 340
Hurler, 340
Hurlock, 340

Hurrell, 83
Hurry, 83
Husher, 442
Husk, 442
Huskisson, 442
Hussell, 491
Hussey, 491
Hussick, 491
Hutt, 280
Hutting, 280
Huttman, 280
Hutty, 280
Hux, 442
Huxen, 442
Hymes, 254

Ibbett, 61
Ibison, 61
Ice, 475
Icely, 475
Iden, 449
Idle, 449
Ife, 472
Igo, 210
Ihler, 416
Iley, 416
Illman, 163, 416
Image, 254
Imber, 312
Imbert, 254
Inch, 292
Inchbald, 292
Inchboard, 11, 292
Inches, 292
Ing, 292, 491
Ingelow, 213
Ingle, 213
Ingledew, 39, 213
Inglesent, 213
Inglis, 318
Ingoe, 292
Ingold, 292
Ingram, 41, 292
Ingrey, 292
Ingwell, 428
Inkson, 292
Inman, 492
Inward, 492
Ireland, 318
Iremonger, 146
Iron, 474
Ironbridge, 474, 495
Ironman, 475
Ironside, 158, 475
Irvin, 233
Irwin, 233
Isard, 475
Isborn, 326, 475
Isburg, 475
Iscariot, 483
Iselin, 475
Isern, 474
Ismer, 475

U 3

578   INDEX OF ENGLISH NAMES.

Isnard, 475
Isnell, 221
Ison, 474
Ive, 472
Iver, 514
Iverson, 32
Ivory, 76
Ivy, 472
Ivyleaf, 472
Ivymey, 24, 472
Izard, 475
Izod, 475
Izon, 474

Jack, 452, 489
Jackall, 452
Jackett, 452
Jacklin, 452
Jackman, 452
Jacks, 452
Jael, 483
Jaget, 453
Jaggard, 452
Jagged, 453
Jagger, 452
Jago, 452
Janaway, 444
Jane, 174
Janes, 174
Janeway, 318
Jannings, 444
January, 174
Jarman, 203
Jarrold, 204
Jarvie, 204
Jary, 202
Jax, 452
Jealous, 437
Jeanneret, 444
Jeary, 202
Jebb, 44, 285
Jeff, 285
Jekyll, 452
Jell, 436
Jelley, 436
Jellicoe, 21, 437
Jelliss, 21, 437
Jenkin, 444
Jenner, 444
Jennery, 444
Jennings, 444
Jennott, 444
Jenrick, 444
Jenvey, 444
Jephson, 32
Jerrold, 204
Jervis, 204
Jerwood, 204
Jessamine, 472
Jessiman, 472 ·
Jessmay, 24, 459
Jesson, 32
Jeula, 244

Jew, 244
Jewell, 244
Jewery, 245
Jewett, 245
Jewin, 245
Jewiss, 244
Jipp, 44,
Job, 482, 485
Jobber, 485
Jobling, 485
Jockisch, 452
Jodwin, 306
John, 484
Jooth, 305
Jopling, 485
Jopp, 485
Jordan, 140
Jortin, 140
Joskyn, 309
Josland, 310
Jove, 485
Jowett, 245
Jubb, 485
Jubber, 485
Judas, 482, 483
Judd, 305
Jude, 482
Judge, 244
Judkin, 305
Judson, 305
Judwine, 306
Jugg, 244
Juggins, 244
Juggo, 244
Jukes, 244
June, 420
Junio, 420
Junner, 420
Juo, 244
Jurd, 139
Just, 429
Justamond, 429
Justey, 429
Jutson, 305
Jutting, 305

Kalkman, 307
Kalvo, 83
Karker, 481
Kay, 336
Kays, 205
Keast, 296
Kebel, 285
Keel, 322
Keeling, 322
Keely, 322
Kell, 436
Kelland, 437
Kellaway, 437
Kelloch, 437
Kellord, 437
Kellow, 436
Kelly, 436

Kelsey, 437
Kelting, 478
Kemp, 171
Kemplen, 171
Kench, 327
Kendray, 75
Kendrick, 75
Kenish, 327
Kenna, 327
Kennard, 328
Kennaway, 329
Kennell, 327
Kenning, 329
Kenny, 327
Kenrick, 328
Kenward, 329
Keppel, 285
Kerley, 202
Kerman, 203
Kerr, 202
Kerrell, 202
Kerridge, 202
Kesten, 296
Kettle, 128 (note)
Key, 336
Kibb, 285
Kibbe, 45
Kibbey, 285
Kidd, 438
Kiddle, 438
Kiddy, 438
Kidger, 438
Kidman, 438
Kidney, 438
Kilby, 442
Kilday, 478
Kilderry, 478
Kill, 458
Killduff, 478
Killer, 458
Killey, 458
Killick, 458
Killman, 458
Kilpin, 442
Kilt, 478
Kilto, 478
Kilty, 478
Kimm, 423
Kinch, 327
Kinchin, 327
Kindred, 328
Kine, 327
King, 329
Kinglake, 328
Kinipple, 328
Kinkee, 327
Kinloch, 328
Kinman, 328
Kinmouth, 328
Kinnaird, 328
Kinnear, 328
Kinnebrook, 328
Kinnell, 327

INDEX OF ENGLISH NAMES.

579

Kinner, 328
Kinney, 327
Kinniburgh, 328
Kinns, 327
Kinsey, 23, 327
Kipp, 44, 285
Kipling, 285
Kirner, 433
Kiss, 459
Kissell, 458
Kissick, 459
Kitt, 438
Kittle, 438
Kitto, 438
Kitty, 438
Knapman, 422
Knapp, 422
Knapping, 422
Knife, 201
Knipe, 201
Knitt, 255
Knope, 422
Knyvett, 201, 224

Labern, 387
Labor, 387
Labram, 387
Laby, 387
Lack, 365
Lackay, 365
Lackey, 365
Lackman, 366
Lacy, 353
Ladd, 195
Lady, 194
Ladyman, 195
Laggon, 366
Lahee, 365
Laid, 194
Laidman, 195
Lamb, 86
Lambert, 335
Lambey, 86
Lamboll, 86
Lambrook, 335
Lamelin, 86
Lamert, 86
Lammas, 522
Lamp, 86
Lampee, 86
Lamping, 86
Lampkin, 86
Lamprey, 86
Lampson, 86
Lanaway, 336
Lance, 335
Lancey, 335
Land, 335
Landell, 335
Landen, 335
Lander, 335
Landfear, 335
Landless, 353, 354

Landlord, 336
Landon, 28, 335
Landridge, 336
Landy, 335
Lane, 366
Lanfear, 335
Lankin, 335
Lanning, 335
Lant, 335
Lanwer, 336
Lara, 356
Larard, 356
Larey, 356
Larkin, 356
Larman, 356
Larmer, 356
Larmuth, 356
Laroux, 356
Larrey, 356
Larwill, 356
Lassel, 353
Last, 355
Late, 194
Later, 195
Lateward, 195
Lath, 195
Lathall, 194
Lathangue, 194
Lathy, 194
Latimer, 195
Latliff, 195
Latta, 195
Latter, 195
Lattey, 195
Laud, 377
Laurel, 356
Laurie, 356
Lavell, 387
Laver, 387
Laverick, 387
Lavey, 387
Lavin, 387
Lavis, 387
Law, 365
Lawes, 366
Lawley, 366
Lawless, 353, 354, 366
Lawman, 366
Lawyer, 366
Lay, 365
Layard, 366
Layman, 366
Layzell, 353
Lazard, 353
Leader, 195
Leah, 365
Lean, 274
Leaning, 274
Leap, 265
Lear, 356
Learmouth, 356
Learra, 356
Leary, 356

Leason, 353
Leasure, 353
Leath, 194
Leathart, 195
Leather, 195, 481
Leatherby, 481
Leatherbarrow, 481
Leatherdale, 481
Leatherhead, 481
Leathley, 194
Leddy, 330
Ledgard, 331
Ledger, 330
Ledward, 331
Ledwith, 331
Lee, 366
Leeding, 194
Leete, 194
Lefroy, 265
Legett, 366
Legg, 365
Leggy, 365
Legless, 353, 354, 366
Lely, 470
Lender, 335
Lennard, 87
Lent, 110
Leo, 87
Leonard, 87
Leopard, 87, 265
Leowolf, 87
Lepper, 265
Lerew, 356
Lerigo, 356
Lerway, 356
Le Souef, 353
Lesser, 353
Lessware, 353
Lessy, 353
Lester, 355
Lesty, 355
Lethead, 331
Letley, 194
Leuty, 330
Levell, 265, 387
Lever, 265
Leveret, 387
Leveridge, 387
Levett, 387
Levey, 387
Levin, 387
Levinge, 265
Levis, 387
Lew, 87
Lewen, 87
Lewey, 87
Leyser, 353
Lezard, 353
Libbis, 265
Liberty, 265
Liddard, 331
Liddelow, 330
Lief, 264

580 INDEX OF ENGLISH NAMES.

Life, 264
Lill, 470
Lilliman, 470
Lillo, 470
Lillyman, 470
Lily, 470
Lind, 110
Lindegreen, 109
Lindeman, 110
Linder, 110
Lindo, 110
Lindquist, 470
Line, 274
Liney, 274
Ling, 109
Lingard, 109
Lingen, 109
Lingo, 109
Lining, 274
Link, 87
Linn, 274
Linnegar, 274
Linnell, 274
Linnet, 104, 274
Linney, 274
Lion, 87
Lipp, 265
Liptrot, 265
Lisney, 353
Lissimore, 353
List, 355
Lister, 355
Liston, 355
Litolff, 331
Litt, 330
Livemore, 265
Livesey, 265
Livey, 31
Livick, 265
Living, 31, 265
Loaden, 377
Loader, 377
Loadman, 378
Loat, 377
Lock, 446
Locke, 2, 131
Locker, 447
Lockett, 447
Lockie, 19, 131, 446
Lockhart, 4, 447
Lockman, 447
Loft, 131
Lollard, 284
Looney, 139
Loose, 331
Loosely, 331
Loosemore, 331
Lorey, 356
Lorimer, 356
Lorkin, 356
Lorriman, 356
Losh, 88
Lot, 482

Lotcho, 377
Lote, 377
Loton, 377
Lott, 377
Loud, 46
Loudon, 377
Lound, 495
Loup, 264
Love, 20, 265
Lovechild, 521
Loveday, 39, 265
Lovegod, 484
Lovegood, 484
Lovekin, 265
Lovelace, 354
Loveland, 265
Loveless, 353, 354
Lovell, 265
Loveman, 265
Lover, 265
Loveridge, 265
Lovesey, 265
Lovesy, 23
Loveys, 265
Lovick, 20, 265
Loving, 265
Lowance, 87
Lowdell, 377
Lowder, 377
Lowe, 87
Lowen, 87
Lowless, 366
Lowly, 366
Lowman, 366
Lowson, 32
Lowy, 87
Lubbock, 265
Luby, 265
Lucar, 330
Lucas, 331
Luce, 331
Lucre, 331
Lucy, 65, 331
Ludbrook, 330
Luden, 330
Ludkin, 330
Lugar, 330
Lulman, 284
Lull, 284
Lully, 284
Lumb, 86 (note).
Lump, 86 (note)
Lumpkin, 86 (note)
Lumpy, 86 (note)
Lund, 495
Lundy, 495
Lune, 139
Lunt, 495
Lush, 88
Lusk, 88
Luther, 331
Lutman, 331
Luton, 330

Lutto, 330
Lutwidge, 331
Lutwyche, 331
Lyde, 330
Lydekker, 330
Lynch, 87
Lyons, 87
Lys, 353
Lyteman, 331
Lyth, 330

Mabb, 471
Mabbutt, 471
Machine, 445
Maddam, 342
Madden, 342
Maddern, 342
Maddock, 341
Maddy, 341
Mader, 342
Madle, 361
Madlin, 361
Mager, 410
Maggot, 410
Maggy, 410
Mahood, 66
Maiden, 342
Maidman, 342
Maine, 410
Maisey, 410
Maize, 410
Malady, 180
Male, 410
Maliff, 179
Malkin, 178
Mall, 178
Mallard, 102, 179
Malley, 178
Malling, 178
Mallock, 178
Mallory, 179
Malt, 180
Malthouse, 179
Malthus, 42, 179
Maltman, 181
Maltwood, 181
Mancer, 434
Manchee, 58
Manchin, 58
Mander, 434
Mandle, 434
Mandy, 434
Manfred, 40, 58
Manger, 58, 410
Mangles, 58
Manhood, 66
Manigault, 58
Manlove, 40, 58
Manly, 58
Mann, 21, 57, 58
Mannakay, 21, 58
Mannell, 58
Mannico, 21, 58

INDEX OF ENGLISH NAMES. 581

Manning, 58
Mannix, 58
Mannse, 434
Manship, 66
Mant, 434
Mantle, 434
Manton, 434
Manus, 514
Many, 58
Maple, 471
Mara, 79
March, 80
Marcher, 80
Marcus, 80
Mare, 79
Margot, 369
Mariga, 368
Marigold, 12, 369
Marine, 369
Mariner, 369, 460
Maris, 368
Mark, 80, 482
Marker, 80, 460
Markey, 80
Marklile, 80
Marklove, 80
Markwick, 80
Marlin, 368
Marling, 368
Marman, 369
Marner, 369
Marmont, 369
Marner, 369
Marr, 368
Marramore, 80
Marrs, 368
Marrian, 369
Marrow, 368
Marry, 368
Mars, 143, 144
Marvin, 369
Marvy, 369
Marwick, 369
Mary, 79
Maryman, 80
Mash, 445, 526
Mashman, 445, 523
Maskell, 445
Maslin, 522
Massall, 522
Massie, 522
Massina, 522
Massingberd, 48, 523
Masson, 32, 522
Massure, 522
Matchin, 341
Mathams, 342
Mather, 342
Matilda, 411
Matkin, 341
Matland, 342
Mattam, 342
Matthewman, 342

Matthie, 341
Mattock, 341
Matts, 341
Maule, 178
Maury, 402
Mawney, 138
Maxey, 445
Maxon, 445
Maxse, 445
May, 410
Mayall, 410
Mayer, 410
Mayhew, 410
Maylin, 410
Mayman, 410
Maynard, 48, 410
Mayne, 48
Mayo, 410
Mc. Auliffe, 514
Mc. Cambridge, 59 (note)
Mc. Caskill, 514
Mc. Gary, 514
Mc. Hitterick, 514
Mc. Oscan, 514
Mc. Otter, 514
Mc Ragnall, 514
Mc. Shitterick, 514
Mc. Swiney, 514
Mc. Vicar, 514
Mead, 341, 379
Meaden, 342
Meader, 342
Meadway, 342
Meall, 403
Mearing, 79
Measel, 522
Measure, 522
Meatman, 342
Medal, 361
Medary, 342
Medd, 341
Medden, 342
Meddiman, 342
Medland, 342
Medlar, 361, 473
Medlen, 361
Medley, 361
Medlock, 342
Medlicott, 361
Medwin, 342
Mee, 410
Meech, 200
Meek, 200
Meeker, 200
Meekey, 200
Meeking, 200
Meers, 79
Megen, 47
Meggy, 410
Megrin, 410
Meller, 180
Melliard, 180
Mellis, 179

Mellish, 24, 179
Mello, 179
Mellodew, 180
Mellow, 179
Mellowday, 180
Melody, 12, 180
Mence, 434
Menday, 434
Mendes, 434
Menne, 58
Mennie, 58
Mennow, 58
Menser, 434
Mercy, 368
Merle, 368
Merrell, 368
Merrick, 368
Merriman, 80, 369
Merrin, 369
Merry, 368
Merryment, 369
Mesher, 445
Messeena, 522
Messiah, 485, 522
Messing, 522
Methold, 342
Methley, 361
Methwin, 342
Metman, 342
Mettam, 342
Mettee, 341
Metz, 341
Miall, 403
Michie, 406
Mico, 406
Michelmore, 406
Mickle, 346, 406
Micklewright, 406
Middle, 379
Miell, 403
Miette, 379
Might, 411
Mighter, 411
Mildert, 283
Mildmay, 25, 282
Mildred, 283
Mile, 17
Miley, 17, 179
Milk, 179
Millard, 180
Miller, 53, 180
Millie, 179
Millicent, 42, 180
Millige, 179
Millikin, 179
Millinge, 179
Millis, 23, 179
Mills, 23
Milo, 17, 179
Minard, 266
Mince, 266
Minchin, 266
Miner, 266

582 INDEX OF ENGLISH NAMES.

Minke, 266
Minn, 106, 266
Minnet, 266
Minney, 27, 266
Minnow, 106, 266
Minns, 266
Minoch, 266
Missing, 380
Mist, 136
Mister, 136
Mittell, 379
Mitton, 380
Mizon, 380
Moat, 237
Mode, 237
Model, 237
Moder, 237
Moderate, 237
Moist, 238
Mole, 92, 178
Moll, 65, 92, 178, 484
Mollard, 179
Molley, 178
Molling, 178
Moncur, 58
Monger, 58
Money, 58, 359
Montgomery, 485
Monument, 276, 359
Mood, 237
Moody, 237
Moon, 8, 138
Mooney, 3, 138
Mootham, 237
Moran, 402
Morday, 258
Morde, 258
Mordue, 258
More, 402
Morebread, 402
Morell, 402
Moreman, 403
Morey, 402
Morling, 402
Morlock, 402
Moore, 402
Moorhen, 402
Moorman, 403
Morrow, 402
Morse, 258
Morsel, 258
Morsman, 259
Mort, 258
Mortal, 258
Mortar, 258
Mortram, 258
Morward, 403
Mose, 237
Moser, 237
Mosey, 237
Moslin, 237
Moss, 237, 491
Mossman, 237

Mostran, 238
Mote, 110, 237
Moth, 110, 237
Mother, 293
Motion, 238
Motley, 237
Mott, 237
Mottow, 237
Mottram, 237
Mouat, 237
Mould, 180
Moulder, 180
Mouldick, 180
Moulding, 180
Moult, 180
Mound, 276
Mount, 276
Mountain, 276
Mouse, 92, 237
Mousell, 237
Mouser, 237
Mouth, 237, 418
Moutrie, 237
Mouttell, 237
Mouzon, 238
Moxey, 445
Moxon, 445
Much, 406
Muckelt, 406
Muckle, 406
Mucklewrath, 406
Muddiman, 237
Muddock, 237
Muddle, 237
Mudlin, 237
Mudridge, 237
Munday, 276
Mundell, 276
Munden, 276
Mundy, 276
Munn, 359
Munnew, 359
Munnings, 359
Munting, 276
Murdoch, 258
Mursel, 258
Murt, 258
Murta, 258
Murtard, 258
Murtha, 258
Musick, 237
Muspratt, 237
Mussard, 237
Mussell, 237
Must, 238
Mustard, 238
Muster, 238
Mustill, 238
Musto, 238
Mustolph, 42
Mustoph, 238
Musty, 238
Mutimer, 41

Mutlow, 237
Mutter, 237
Mutton, 238
Muzzy, 237
Mynn, 266
Myrtle, 258

Nabb, 422
Nadall, 256
Nadauld, 275
Nagle, 10, 220
Nail, 10, 220
Nalder, 256
Naldrett, 256
Nance, 239
Nann, 239
Nannery, 239
Nanny, 239, 484
Nans, 239
Nanson, 32, 239
Napkin, 422
Narrowcoat, 301
Natkins, 275
Natt, 275
Navin, 420
Nay, 420
Naylor, 220
Neate, 255
Neck, 126, 418
Need, 258
Needle, 256
Needler, 256
Nefflen, 151
Negus, 255
Nenner, 239
Nerod, 421]
Nestle, 256
Nestling, 256
Nettle, 256
Neve, 420
Neville, 151
Nevin, 420
New, 420
Newey, 420
Newcome, 297, 421
Newcomb, 421
Newen, 420
Newick, 420
Newling, 420
Newlove, 421
Newman, 297, 421
Nex, 126
Niavi, 420
Nibbs, 8
Nibbett, 255
Nibloe, 151
Nice, 255
Nick, 126
Nickerson, 126
Nicklen, 126
Niess, 255
Nightingale, 104
Nisbet, 255

INDEX OF ENGLISH NAMES. 583

Nivoley, 151
Nix, 126
Nixie, 126
Noad, 240
Nobbs, 8
Noble, 151
Noddle, 240
Nodder, 240
Noding, 240
Noel, 522
Noon, 439
Nooning, 439
Norcott, 301
Norfor, 301
Norgate, 301
Norlan, 301
Norman, 301
Norquest, 301
Norramore, 301
Norrie, 300
North, 300
Northard, 240
Northcott, 301
Northeast, 301
Northey, 240, 300
Northmore, 301
Noser, 240
Notman, 240
Nott, 240
Notter, 54
Nottidge, 240
Novell, 151
Nunley, 439
Nunn, 439
Nunnery, 439
Nunney, 439
Nutt, 240, 473
Nuttall, 240
Nutter, 240
Nutting, 240
Nuttman, 240
Nusser, 240

Oake, 471
Oakey, 471
Oborn, 156
O'Bruadair, 514
Odam, 381
Oddy, 217
Odell, 334
Oden, 120
Odierne, 382
Odlam, 334
Odlin, 334
Odling, 334
Offen, 385
Offer, 385
Offey, 385
Offill, 385
Offley, 385
Offlow, 385
Offord, 385
Ogborn, 193

Ogg, 193, 482
Ogier, 193
Oiley, 154
Oldacre, 418
Old, 418
Oldis, 418
Olding, 418
Oldman, 418
Oldridge, 419
Oldry, 419
Oliff, 471, 513
Oliphant, 88
Olive, 471
Oman, 341
Omer, 492
Onslow, 119
Orchard, 388, 491
Ord, 217
Ordish, 217
Ordward, 218
Ordway, 218
Ore, 524
Organ, 524.
Orgar, 217
Orger, 524
Oriel, 524
Orman, 59
Orme, 108
Ormerod, 148
Orridge, 341
Orrin, 524
Orriss, 524
Orrock, 341
Orth, 217
Osborn, 119
Osburn, 39
Osgood, 119
Osman, 120
Osmer, 120
Osmond, 120
Ost, 302
Ostell, 302
Ostermoor, 303
Ostrich, 102, 303
Oswald, 42, 120
Oswin, 120
Osyer, 119
Ott, 194
Otter, 91, 513, 194
Ottey, 194
Ottiwell, 382
Otway, 194
Ough, 385
Ought, 381
Oughton, 381
Ousey, 524
Outing, 381
Outlaw, 12, 381
Outram, 41, 382
Outred, 382
Outridge, 382
Ouvry, 76
Oven, 524

Over, 76
Overacre, 76, 112 (note)
Overall, 76
Overed, 76
Overett, 76
Overmore, 76
Overy, 76
Ovey, 290
Ower, 290
Owle, 105
Owler, 106
Owley, 105
Owst, 302
Oyster, 302
Oysterman, 303

Pack, 172
Packard, 172
Packer, 53, 172
Packett, 172
Packman, 172
Paddick, 166
Paddle, 166
Padley, 166
Paddy, 166
Padman, 167
Padmore, 167
Pail, 192
Paillard, 192
Pairo, 68
Painter, 87
Palairet, 192
Paler, 192
Paley, 192
Palfrey, 81, 192
Palfriman, 81
Paling, 192
Pallace, 521
Palliser, 521
Palmer, 192
Palsy, 241
Pan, 143
Pander, 87
Pann, 175
Pannell, 175
Pannier, 175
Pant, 31
Panter, 87, 236
Panther, 87, 236
Panting, 31, 236
Pantlin, 235
Panton, 236
Pantry, 236
Pape, 291
Papillon, 291
Paraday, 61
Paradise, 62
Paragreen, 69
Paragren, 69
Paramour, 12, 69
Parcell, 453
Pardar, 222
Pardew, 62

584 INDEX OF ENGLISH NAMES.

Parding, 222
Pardoe, 19, 222
Pardon, 12, 222
Parfrey, 61
Paris, 61
Parish, 61
Parkin, 22, 61
Parman, 62
Parr, 22, 61
Parramore, 69
Parrell, 61
Parrot, 62
Parry, 61
Parsey, 61
Parsley, 453
Part, 222
Parter, 222
Partrick, 370
Partridge, 102, 370
Pascoe, 487
Pash, 487
Pask, 487
Pass, 181
Passman, 181
Passmer, 181
Passey, 181
Paste, 183
Patmore, 167
Patridge, 167
Patry, 167
Patte, 166
Pattie, 166
Pattle, 166
Pattman, 167
Patullo, 166
Paulding, 241
Pavey, 291
Pavier, 291
Paxman, 487
Pay, 101
Pea, 101
Peabody, 39
Peach, 222
Peachy, 222
Peacock, 101
Peak, 222
Pear, 68
Pearl, 69
Pearman, 69
Pearse, 453
Peartree, 370
Peascod, 181
Peat, 166
Peatie, 166
Pechell, 222
Pecker, 222
Peckett, 222
Pedder, 166
Pedley, 166
Peede, 166
Peel, 219
Peeling, 219
Peer, 68

Peevor, 91
Peffor, 91
Pegg, 64, 65
Pelham, 269
Pell, 192
Pellett, 269
Pellew, 192
Pelly, 192
Pendall, 235
Pender, 236
Pendered, 236
Penk, 182
Penkett, 182
Penman, 177
Penn, 176
Pennant, 41, 177
Pennell, 177
Penner, 177
Pennick, 176
Penny, 176
Pennycad, 177
Pennymore, 177
Penson, 236
Pentecost, 487
Pentelow, 235
Pentin, 236
Pepin, 414
Peploe, 414
Peppard, 414
Peppercorn, 467
Percival, 453
Perch, 106
Percher, 69
Percy, 453
Perdue, 69
Peregrine, 69
Perkin, 69
Perley, 69
Perner, 69
Pero, 68
Perown, 69
Perram, 69
Perriam, 69
Perrigo, 69
Perrin, 70
Perrott, 69
Persac, 453
Pert, 370
Perton, 370
Perwort, 69
Pest, 183
P. ster, 183
F ther, 166
'ethick, 166
Peto, 166
Petley, 166
Petrick, 167
Petrie, 167
Pett, 166
Petter, 166
Petty, 166
Peverall, 91
Pevrell, 91

Pewtress, 455
Phair, 323
Pharaoh, 323, 482
Phillibrown, 39
Phillimore, 41, 518
Physic, 21
Physick, 247
Pick, 77, 177
Pickard, 178, 318
Pickell, 177
Picker, 178
Pickett, 178
Pickman, 178
Pidduck, 166
Pigg, 64, 77, 177
Piggott, 178
Pigram, 178
Pilate, 483
Pilbeam, 219
Pilford, 269
Pilgrim, 12, 269
Pill, 13, 17, 269
Pilley, 17, 269
Pillman, 269
Pillow, 13, 17, 269
Pilon, 270
Pilot, 269
Pinard, 236
Pinch, 178
Pincheon, 178
Pinder, 236
Pingo, 178
Pink, 178
Pinkert, 178
Pinkey, 178
Pinn, 176
Pinnock, 176
Pinny, 176
Pino, 176
Pipe, 414
Piper, 91
Pippin, 414
Pippy, 414
Pitcher, 178
Pitt, 491
Pittock, 166
Plain, 396
Planché, 392
Plank, 392
Planner, 396
Plant, 396
Plater, 376
Platon, 376
Platt, 376
Platten, 376
Play, 440
Player, 440
Pleaden, 440
Pledger, 440
Plevin, 184
Pleydell, 440
Plimmer, 440
Plincke, 392

INDEX OF ENGLISH NAMES.

585

Plomer, 465
Plough, 214
Ploughman, 215
Pluck, 214
Plucknett, 215
Plugg, 214
Plum, 465
Plumbridge, 465
Plume, 465
Plumer, 465
Plumley, 465
Plumridge, 465
Plunkett, 215 (note)
Pocock, 101
Podger, 455
Podmore, 455
Poe, 101
Pofley, 421
Pogmore, 225
Poignard, 225
Polden, 242
Pole, 281
Poleman, 281
Pollard, 281
Polley, 281
Pollo, 281
Pollock, 281
Polwin, 281
Pond, 235
Ponder, 236
Ponson, 236
Pony, 175
Poodle, 454
Pool, 491
Poole, 280
Pooley, 281
Poore, 452
Poorman, 452
Pope, 421
Popkin, 422
Pople, 421
Poplett, 422
Popoff, 422
Poppy, 421, 473
Port, 229
Portman, 229
Portwine, 229
Post, 409
Postle, 409
Poston, 409
Poticary, 455
Potiphar, 483
Potipher, 455
Potman, 461
Pott, 454
Potten, 454
Potter, 53, 54, 455
Pottier, 455
Pottle, 454
Pottman, 455
Potto, 454
Potwine, 455
Poulter, 241

Poupard, 422
Poupart, 422
Poupin, 422
Povey, 421
Power, 12, 452
Powter, 241
Powder, 241
Prain, 185
Pram, 371
Prangnell, 221
Pratt, 2
Pray, 184
Preacher, 185
Preslin, 186
Press, 453
Pressey, 453
Pressney, 453
Presswell, 453
Præter, 185
Pretty, 185
Prettyman, 185
Prickle, 185
Priddy, 185
Pride, 185
Prigg, 184
Prime, 371
Primerose, 467
Primmer, 371
Prisley, 186
Priseman, 186
Prissey, 186
Prissick, 186
Pritt, 185
Prosser, 480
Protheroe, 218
Protyn, 218
Proud, 447
Proudfoot, 447, 455
Prout, 447
Prouting, 447
Prowse, 447
Pruday, 447
Prudence, 447
Pruse, 186
Pucket, 379
Puckle, 379
Puckridge, 379
Puddefoot, 447, 455
Puddick, 454
Pubdicombe, 455
Puddifer, 455
Pudding, 454
Puddy, 454
Pudney, 455
Pugin, 379
Pull, 281
Pullan, 281
Pullar, 281
Pulley, 281
Pulling, 281
Pulman, 281
Punelt, 416
Punnett, 416

Punter, 236
Puplet, 422
Pupp, 421
Purcell, 453
Purchase, 12, 69
Purches, 69
Purdie, 39
Purgold, 69, 279
Purkis, 69
Purland, 69
Purling, 69
Purnell, 70
Purney, 70
Purrier, 69
Purse, 453
Purser, 453
Purseglove, 3, 453
Purselove, 453
Pursey, 453
Purselow, 453
Purssord, 453
Purt, 370
Purtell, 370
Purvis, 69
Pustard, 409
Pustin, 409
Putman, 455
Putt, 454
Puttick, 454
Pye, 313
Pyeman, 313

Quail, 102, 298
Qualey, 298
Quallet, 298
Quantock, 316
Quaritch, 47
Quarman, 278
Quarrell, 47, 278
Quarrier, 47, 278
Quarry, 278
Quash, 244
Queen, 63, 263
Quennell, 263
Quick, 164
Quickly, 165
Quier, 165
Quiggle, 164
Quilke, 123
Quill, 47, 122
Quillan, 47
Quilliams, 47, 63, 124
Quillinan, 41, 47, 124
Quillish, 123
Quillman, 124
Quilter, 345, 447
Quin, 47, 63, 263
Quince, 263
Quincey, 263
Quiney, 263
Quiner, 264
Quinlin, 263
Quint, 316

V 3

586 INDEX OF ENGLISH NAMES.

Quintin, 316
Quomman, 63, 297
Quy, 164

Raban, 97
Rabbit, 89
Rabone, 97
Raby, 187
Rack, 362
Racket, 363
Rackhal, 363
Radcliffe, 348
Raddall, 347
Radden, 348
Raddick, 347
Radish, 348
Radmond, 348
Radmore, 348
Radway, 348
Raffell, 187
Raffold, 187
Rafter, 228
Raftery, 228
Ragg, 362
Raggett, 363
Ragin, 349
Ragless, 354 (note)
Ragon, 349
Rain, 85, 349
Rainbird, 349
Rainbold, 349
Rainbow, 137
Rainey, 349
Rainford, 349
Rainforth, 349
Rains, 349
Ralph, 72, 363
Ram, 85
Ramm, 97
Rampling, 228
Ramridge, 97
Ranaker, 349
Rance, 228
Rancour, 230
Rand, 228
Randle, 228
Randolph, 42, 72, 228
Ranger, 48, 189, 349
Raniker, 189
Rann, 189
Rannie, 189
Ransom, 228
Rantem, 228
Raper, 187
Rapkin, 187
Rapp, 187
Rarey, 363
Rastall, 448
Rastrick, 448
Rat, 347
Ratcliff, 40
Rather, 348
Ratheram, 348

Ratliffe, 348
Ratt, 92
Ratter, 348
Rattham, 348
Rattical, 348
Rattle, 347
Ratton, 348
Rattray, 348
Ratty, 347
Raven, 97
Ravenor, 97
Ravenshear, 97
Ravey, 187
Ray, 362
Raybauld, 362
Rayment, 363
Raymond, 363
Rayner, 48, 350
Raynham, 350
Reader, 348
Reading, 348
Readman, 348
Readwin, 348
Ready, 347
Reavell, 188
Reckless, 344, 354
Recknell, 349
Record, 343
Redband, 348
Reddall, 347
Reddaway, 348
Redden, 348
Reddelein, 348
Redding, 348
Reddish, 348
Redgell, 348
Redhead, 348
Redline, 348
Redman, 40, 348
Redmayne, 348
Redmond, 348
Redmore, 348
Redmont, 41
Redout, 254
Redwar, 348
Redwood, 349
Redyear, 348
Reed, 347
Reffel, 188
Regal, 362
Regan, 349
Regans, 349
Reginald, 350
Regnart, 349
Reidy, 347
Rein, 349
Reinman, 350
Reinwell, 350
Relph, 363
Remnant, 41
Renard, 48, 349
Renaud, 350
Rendel, 228

Render, 228
Renn, 104, 189
Rennell, 189
Rennie, 104, 189
Rennison, 189
Renno, 104, 189
Renter, 228
Rentle, 228
Rentmore, 228
Repuke, 188
Restell, 448
Restorick, 448
Retgate, 348
Revere, 188
Revill, 188
Reynal, 349
Reynard, 349
Reynolds, 350
Rhodes, 372
Ribb, 188
Ribbeck, 188
Ribread, 343
Rich, 343
Richan, 343
Richard, 343
Richbell, 343
Richer, 343
Riches, 23, 343
Richley, 343
Richman, 344
Richmond, 344
Richold, 344
Rickard, 343
Rickett, 343
Rickman, 344
Ricks, 23, 343
Riddell, 254
Riddick, 254
Ridding, 254
Ride, 254
Rideout, 254
Rider, 254
Ridey, 254
Ridge, 343, 491
Ridger, 254
Ridges, 343
Ridgeway, 344
Ridgwell, 344
Ridgyard, 343
Ridhard, 254
Riding, 254
Ridlon, 254
Riekie, 343
Riff, 188
Riggall, 343
Rignault, 350
Rind, 140
Rinder, 140
Rindle, 140
Ring, 230
Ringer, 53, 230, 460
Ringgold, 230
Rink, 230

INDEX OF ENGLISH NAMES. 587

Riper, 188
Ripere, 188
Ripkey, 188
Ripley, 188
Rippin, 188
Rist, 133, 134
Ritchie, 343
Ritchings, 343
River, 188
Rivers, 188
Riviere, 188
Roach, 252
Roaf, 187
Roaill, 514
Ronke, 252
Robb, 187
Robbie, 187
Robert, 372
Robley, 187
Roblow, 187
Robolin, 187
Rochez, 253
Rock, 252
Rockey, 252
Rockett, 253
Rodaway, 373
Rodber, 372
Rodbourn, 372
Rodd, 371
Roddam, 372
Roddis, 372
Rode, 46
Roden, 372
Rodgard, 372
Rodger, 40, 372
Rodick, 371
Rodman, 373
Rodney, 41, 373
Rodrick, 373
Rodway, 373
Rodwell, 373
Rodyard, 372
Roff, 187
Roffie, 187
Roger, 46
Roget, 253
Roker, 253
Rolf, 72
Rolfe, 253
Rolland, 373
Roman, 318
Rome, 373
Romer, 374
Romilly, 374
Rondeau, 228
Roof, 187
Rook, 46, 252
Rooke, 98
Rooker, 253
Room, 373
Roope, 187
Rooper, 187
Root, 371

Rooth, 371
Roots, 372
Rootsey, 372
Rope, 187
Roper, 187
Rosbert, 79
Roscoe, 79
Roseblade, 467
Rosery, 79
Rosethorn, 467
Rosier, 79
Rosinbloom, 467
Roskell, 79
Rosling, 79
Rosoman, 79
Ross, 79
Rosser, 79
Rost, 448
Rosterne, 467
Rotch, 46
Roth, 371
Rotheram, 373
Rothery, 372
Rothon, 372
Rothney, 373
Rothwell, 373
Rottenfysche, 107
Rottenheryng, 107
Rotton, 372
Rough, 187
Round, 228
Roupell, 187
Rout, 371
Routh, 371
Routley, 372
Routledge, 373
Rowen, 472
Rowntree, 472
Rubb, 187
Ruby, 187
Rubery, 187
Rubidge, 187
Ruck, 252
Rucker, 253
Rudd, 371
Ruddell, 372
Rudder, 372
Ruddick, 372
Ruddiman, 373
Rudding, 372
Rudgard, 372
Rudkin, 372
Rudman, 373
Rudolph, 373
Rudwick, 373
Rue, 252
Ruff, 187
Ruffle, 187
Ruffy, 187
Rugg, 252
Rugman, 253
Rum, 373
Rumball, 38

Rumbelow, 374
Rumble, 38
Rumbold, 38, 374
Rumley, 374
Rummer, 374
Rummey, 373
Rundle, 228
Runicles, 22
Rust, 448
Rustich, 448
Ruston, 448
Ruth, 371, 482
Rutledge, 373
Rutley, 372
Rutt, 371
Rutter, 372
Rutty, 371
Rybauld, 343
Rye, 343
Ryman, 344
Rymer, 344

Sabbage, 424
Sabey, 423
Sabine, 424
Sable, 424
Sack, 171
Sackelld, 171
Sacker, 171
Sackman, 171
Sadd, 430
Safe, 423
Saffell, 424
Saffery, 424
Safford, 424
Safran, 424
Sager, 171
Sago, 171
Sailor, 308
Sala, 308
Salamon, 308
Sale, 308
Saleman, 308, 461
Salkeld, 171 (note)
Sall, 65
Sallaway, 308
Salles, 308
Sally, 484
Salmon, 308
Salt, 45, 443
Salter, 443
Salve, 346
Salvin, 346
Sam, 75
Sampkin, 75
Sandell, 430
Sanden, 431
Sander, 430
Sandman, 430
Sandoe, 430
Sands, 430
Sandwer, 431
Sandy, 430

588 INDEX OF ENGLISH NAMES.

Sandys, 430
Saner, 170
Sang, 438
Sangwin, 438
Sankey, 438
Sans, 430
Sant, 430
Santer, 430
Santley, 430
Santy, 430
Saphin, 424
Saplin, 424
Sapp, 423
Sapper, 424
Sapte, 424
Sarah, 230
Sarasin, 487
Sarch, 231
Sare, 230
Sarel, 230
Sargood, 230
Sarratt, 230
Sass, 451
Satchell, 171
Satow, 451
Satter, 131, 451
Sauce, 266
Saul, 138, 482
Sault, 443
Savage, 424
Saveall, 424
Savell, 424
Saverick, 424
Savidge, 424
Savory, 424
Saward, 322
Saxe, 200
Saxl, 201
Say, 171
Sayer, 171
Scaddan, 191
Scadlock, 191
Scaffold, 219
Scamp, 442
Scarfe, 356
Scarman, 223
Scarnell, 221
Scarr, 223
Scarrow, 223
Scharb, 356
Schooley, 513
Scobell, 442
Scobie, 442
Scolding, 148, 228
Score, 223
Scotchmer, 317
Scotland, 317
Scott, 317
Scottock, 317
Scotting, 317
Scottoh, 19
Scottsmith, 317, 462
Scow, 495

Scullion, 12
Scurry, 223
Sea, 172
Seaber, 321
Seaborn, 321
Seabright, 321
Seabrook, 322
Seabury, 322
Seage, 172
Seago, 172
Seahorse, 323
Seaman, 322
Seamark, 323
Seamer, 173
Sear, 230
Search, 231
Seare, 173
Searight, 322
Seavy, 261
Seawall, 322
Seaward, 322
Seawen, 495
Seawood, 323
Secker, 173
Sedger, 173
Sedgwick, 173
Seffert, 173
Sefowl, 94, 322
Segar, 173
Seguin, 173
Self, 346
Sell, 308
Sellar, 308
Selley, 308
Sellick, 308
Selling, 308
Sellis, 308
Sellon, 308
Selman, 308
Selves, 346
Selvey, 346
Selway, 308
Semy, 75
Sendall, 456
Senlo, 170
Sent, 456
Seppings, 262
Serbutt, 230
Serle, 230
Sermon, 230
Serrell, 230
Setright, 451
Sew, 267
Seward, 42, 322
Sewell, 322
Sewey, 267
Sex, 200
Sexey, 200
Sexmer, 201
Seyburn, 321
Seyfried, 173
Seymour, 7, 173
Shadbolt, 168

Shaddock, 168
Shade, 191
Shadrake, 168
Shadwell, 191
Shaft, 219
Shafter, 219
Shafto, 219
Shakeshaft, 236
Shakespere, 236
Shalley, 456
Shallow, 456
Shank, 438
Shankey, 438
Shark, 231
Sharkey, 231
Sharkley, 231
Sharp, 356
Sharpey, 356
Sharpin, 357
Sharpus, 356
Sharpless, 354, 357
Sharpley, 357
Shaw, 495
Shawkey, 456
Shawman, 223, 457
Sheaf, 148
Shearsmith, 462
Sheath, 191
Sheather, 191
Shebeare, 321
Sheen, 389
Sheer, 223
Sheniman, 389
Sherman, 223
Sherrell, 223
Sherry, 223
Shether, 191
Shick, 431
Shickle, 431
Shield, 148, 227
Shierbrand, 199, 223
Shillibeer, 361
Shilling, 360
Shillito, 361
Shin, 418
Shine, 389
Shiner, 389
Shinn, 389
Shinner, 389
Shipman, 322
Shirk, 231
Shirkey, 231
Shiverick, 262
Shlange, 108
Shoe, 495
Sholto, 457
Shone, 389
Shoner, 389
Shoobert, 495
Shoobrick, 495
Shopp, 442
Shoppee, 442
Shopperie, 442

INDEX OF ENGLISH NAMES. 589

Shore, 223
Shorey, 223
Shorman, 223
Shotbolt, 317
Shoulder, 457
Shoult, 456, 457
Shovell, 442
Shover, 442
Shurey, 223
Sibbald, 172
Sibbick, 262
Sibel, 262
Sibert, 173
Sibery, 262
Sibley, 262
Sibson, 262
Sibthorp, 262
Sickens, 172
Sickle, 172
Sicklemore, 30, 173
Sicklen, 172
Sickling, 172
Sickman, 173
Siddell, 431
Sidden, 431
Siddons, 431
Side, 431
Sidey, 431
Sidgear, 431
Sidney, 431
Sier, 173
Sievewright, 262, 460
Sievier, 262
Siffken, 262
Siggers, 173
Siggs, 8, 172
Sigley, 172
Sigmund, 7, 173
Sigournay, 173
Sigourney, 30
Sigrist, 173
Sike, 172
Silliman, 433
Silva, 346
Silve, 346
Silver, 479
Sim, 21
Simco, 21, 262
Simberd, 456
Simkin, 262
Simkiss, 262
Simm, 262, 484
Simmell, 262
Simmonds, 173
Simmons, 7
Simon, 484
Sindrey, 456
Sinden, 456
Sinder, 456
Singer, 438
Single, 438
Sinker, 438
Sinton, 456

Sipless, 262
Sipling, 262
Sipp, 261
Sipthorp, 262
Sirkett, 441
Sisley, 272
Sisterson, 293
Sitton, 431
Sivrac, 262
Six, 200
Size, 272
Sizeland, 272
Sizen, 272
Sizer, 272
Skate, 191
Skatliff, 191
Skeen, 389
Skeet, 191
Skelding, 148, 228
Skelt, 227
Skill, 360
Skiller, 361
Skillett, 361
Skiney, 389
Skipper, 322
Skipwith, 37
Skoggin, 495
Skone, 389
Skoulding, 148, 228
Sky, 431
Slack, 257
Slade, 201, 491
Sladen, 201
Slader, 201
Slagg, 257
Slate, 201
Slater, 201, 460
Slay, 257
Slee, 257
Sleeman, 258
Slegg, 257
Slewey, 257
Slewman, 258
Slight, 201, 257
Slow, 257
Slowey, 257
Slowman, 258
Sly, 257
Slybody, 257
Slyman, 258
Slyoff, 258
Smelt, 106, 270
Smith, 461
Smither, 461
Smiter, 461
Smithy, 461
Smytha, 461
Snagg, 108
Snake, 108
Snare, 246
Snarey, 246
Snipe, 102
Sneezy, 256

Snelgar, 245
Snell, 245
Snelling, 245
Snook, 108
Snow, 136
Snowball, 137
Snowman, 403
Snugg, 108
Soane, 99
Soar, 441
Sodden, 431
Soddy, 430
Sodo, 430
Solberry, 138
Sole, 138
Soley, 138
Solly, 230
Soltau, 443
Sorlie, 230
Sorter, 198
Sortwell, 198
Soul, 138
Souper, 304
Sour, 441
Sourk, 441
South, 301
Southard, 301
Souther, 302
Southey, 301
Southon, 301
Southward, 301 (note)
Spade, 200
Spademan, 200
Spader, 200
Spadey, 200
Spain, 317, 445
Spaniel, 445
Spar, 104
Spark, 415
Sparling, 104
Sparrow, 104
Sparrowhawk, 96
Speak, 207
Speakman, 207
Spear, 206
Spearing, 206
Spearman, 206
Speck, 207
Speed, 207
Speight, 200
Spellar, 434
Spelman, 434
Spendlove, 445
Spenlove, 445
Sperling, 104
Sperwin, 206
Spice, 207
Spike, 207
Spikeman, 207
Spill, 434
Spillard, 434
Spiller, 434
Spilling, 434

590 INDEX OF ENGLISH NAMES.

Spillman, 434
Spinney, 445
Spiring, 206
Spirit, 485
Spite, 207
Spitta, 207
Spitty, 207
Spon, 445
Spooner, 445
Sporne, 321
Sprack, 415
Spracklin, 415
Spragg, 415
Spratt, 207
Spray, 415
Spreck, 415
Spreckley, 415
Sprice, 415
Sprigg, 415
Spritt, 415
Sproat, 207, 415
Sprout, 207, 415
Spruce, 415
Spry, 415
Spurge, 416
Spurgeon, 416
Spyer, 206
Square, 450
Squarey, 450
Stack, 213
Stackard, 213
Stackler, 213
Stackman, 213
Stag, 213
Staggall, 214
Stagg, 85
Stagman, 213
Stain, 479
Stainburn, 479
Stainer, 480
Staker, 213
Staley, 476
Stalon, 476
Stallard, 476
Stallion, 81, 476
Stalman, 476
Stand, 252
Standing, 252
Stanger, 214
Stank, 214
Stannah, 479
Stannard, 480
Stark, 245
Starker, 245
Starkey, 245
Starkman, 245
State, 252
Stead, 252
Steady, 252
Steal, 476
Stealin, 476
Steamburg, 479
Stebbing, 469

Stedman, 252
Steed, 252
Steedman, 252
Steel, 476
Steelfox, 476
Steelman, 476
Steen, 479
Steggall, 214
Stelfox, 476
Stembridge, 479
Steneck, 479
Stennell, 479
Stenning, 479
Stent, 252
Sterckeman, 245
Stericker, 245
Stibbard, 469
Stick, 213
Sticker, 213
Stickle, 214
Stickler, 214
Stickman, 213
Stidolph, 72, 252
Stiff, 469
Stiffel, 469
Stiffin, 469
Stinchman, 214
Sting, 214
Stinger, 214
Stirk, 245
Stith, 252
Stitt, 252
Stobart, 469
Stobie, 469
Stobo, 469
Stock, 213
Stocker, 213
Stockill, 213
Stockman, 213
Stocqueler, 214
Stoffell, 469
Stoker, 213, 460
Stonah, 479
Stonard, 480
Stone, 479
Stonebridge, 479
Stoneheart, 480
Stonel, 479
Stoneman, 480
Stoner, 480
Stonhold, 480
Stonier, 480
Stony, 479
Stop, 469
Stopher, 469
Storah, 345
Store, 345
Storer, 345
Stork, 245
Storr, 345
Storron, 345
Storrow, 345
Storrs, 345

Story, 345
Stovell, 469
Stover, 469
Stovin, 469
Stovold, 365
Stow, 365
Stowell, 365
Stower, 365
Straker, 245
Street, 171, 491
Streeten, 171
Streeter, 171
Strettell, 171
Stride, 171
Strude, 190
Strudwick, 191
Struthers, 191
Strutt, 48, 190
Stubbe, 469
Stubber, 469
Stubbert, 469
Stubbing, 469
Stuber, 469
Stuck, 213
Stuckey, 213
Stupart, 469
Sturge, 106, 245
Sturgeon, 106
Sturla, 345, 513
Sturrock, 345
Such, 267
Suck, 267
Suckey, 267
Sucker, 268
Suckermore, 268
Suckley, 267
Suckling, 267
Suckman, 267
Sudden, 301
Suett, 266
Sugar, 268
Sugarman, 268
Sugg, 76, 267
Suggett, 267
Suit, 266
Summer, 140
Summersell, 94
Sumpter, 301
Sun, 8, 138
Sunday, 301
Sunrise, 139
Sunshine, 139
Sunter, 301
Supple, 304
Surgett, 441
Surgey, 441
Surplice, 357
Susans, 45
Suse, 45, 266
Sutcliff, 267
Suthery, 301
Sutliff, 267
Swaap, 304

INDEX OF ENGLISH NAMES. 591

Swabb, 304
Swabey, 304
Swain; 513
Swainson, 513
Swale, 104
Swallow, 104
Swanberg, 99
Swann, 99
Swannack, 99
Swannell, 99
Swanwick, 99
Swearer, 450
Swearing, 450
Swears, 450
Sweat, 266
Sweden, 318
Sweeby, 304
Sweet, 45, 266
Sweetapple, 467
Sweeten, 45
Sweeting, 267
Sweetlove, 267
Sweetman, 267
Sweetsur, 318
Swenwright, 99
Swire, 450
Swonnell, 99
Sword, 198
Sworder, 198
Sycamore, 30, 173
Sykes, 172
Syme,. 262, 484
Syster, 293

Tabram, 428
Tackabarry, 391
Tackle, 390
Tackley, 390
Tackman, 391
Tadd, 291
Taddy, 291
Tadloo, 291
Tadman, 292
Tagart, 391
Tagg, 390
Tait, 271
Talbert, 375
Talbot, 39, 375
Talfourd, 375
Talker, 375
Tall, 375
Tallack, 375
Tallemach, 376
Talliss, 375
Tallman, 376
Tallon, 375
Talmage, 376
Tamborine, 365
Tame, 364
Tamiet, 365
Tamlyn, 365
Tammage, 365
Tamplin, 365

Tancred, 41, 359
Tandy, 45, 310
Tank, 359
Tankard, 359
Tanker, 359
Tanklin, 359
Tann, 311
Tanner, 53, 311
Tannock, 311
Tanqueray, 359
Tansell, 310
Tansey, 310
Tant, 310
Tanton, 310
Taplin, 428
Tapp, 428
Tappin, 428
Tappy, 428
Targett, 128
Tarn, 398
Tarner, 398
Tarr, 208
Tarratt, 209
Tarry, 208
Tarryer, 208
Tart, 209
Tarter, 209
Tasker, 53, 385, 460
Tasman, 385
Tassell, 385
Tassiker, 385
Tate, 271
Tatlock, 292
Tattle, 291
Tatuin, 292
Tay, 390
Tayburn, 391
Teale, 101, 375
Tear, 268
Tearoy, 268
Teat, 271
Teather, 292
Tedd, 291
Tedder, 292
Tedman, 292
Teeling, 375
Tegart, 391
Tegg, 390
Teggin, 338
Tekell, 390
Telbin, 375
Telfer, 375
Telford, 375
Teller, 375
Telling, 375
Ten, 311
Tench, 106, 359
Tendall, 310
Tennant, 311
Tennelly, 311
Tenneman, 312
Tennyson, 45, 311
Tent, 310

Ternouth, 208
Terrier, 208
Terry, 208
Tetlow, 291
Teuten, 332
Tewart, 42, 427
Thackeray, 359
Thackwell, 359
Thain, 338
Thane, 338
Theed, 332
Theobald, 332
Theodore, 333
Teuthorn, 333
Thew, 457
Thick, 406
Thicket, 407
Thistle, 469
Thoden, 332
Thody, 332
Thomas, 484
Thorburn, 128
Thorgate, 128
Thorold, 129
Thoroughgate, 128
Thoroughgood, 11, 128
Thoroughwood, 129
Thotman, 129
Throssell, 103
Thrush, 103
Thumm, 363, 418
Thunder, 128
Thurber, 128
Thurgar, 128
Thurgood, 11, 128
Thurkettle, 129, 512
Thurkle, 129
Thurmott, 129
Thurston, 129
Thyer, 457
Tick, 406
Tickle, 406
Tidball, 332
Tidd, 332
Tiddeman, 333
Tidemore, 333
Tidman, 333
Tidy, 332
Tiffany, 488
Tiffin, 488
Tigg, 406
Tileman, 190
Tilgman, 190
Tilke, 189
Till, 189
Tilleard, 189
Tiller, 189
Tilley, 189
Tillick, 189
Tillier, 189
Tilling, 189
Tillman, 190
Tillott, 189

592 INDEX OF ENGLISH NAMES.

Tim, 364
Times, 365
Timlin, 365
Timperon, 365
Tims, 365
Tingey, 367
Tingle, 367
Tink, 367
Tinker, 367
Tinkling, 367
Tinley, 130
Tinling, 130
Tinney, 129
Tinning, 130
Tisoe, 351
Titchen, 332
Titcomb, 297
Tite, 271, 332
Titmus, 104
Tizard, 352
Toby, 103
Todd, 45, 273
Toddy, 273
Todman, 273
Todrig, 333
Toe, 427
Toker, 427
Tolcher, 184
Tolken, 184
Tolkien, 184
Tom, 363
Tomb, 363, 484
Tombs, 364
Tomey, 363
Tomkies, 364
Tomkin, 364
Tomlin, 22, 364
Tommell, 364
Tomsey, 364
Ton, 129
Tonge, 361
Tongman, 362
Tongue, 361
Tonner, 128
Toodle, 274
Toogood, 428
Toomer, 364
Toot, 273
Tootal, 274
Toothaker, 274
Toovey, 103
Torr, 127
Torry, 127, 208
Totman, 273
Tottell, 273
Totten, 273
Tottey, 273
Tournay, 190
Tovey, 103
Tow, 427
Towart, 427
Towell, 427
Tower, 427

Towgood, 428
Tozier, 273
Trace, 242
Tracy, 242
Traer, 413
Trahar, 413
Traies, 242
Trail, 141, 413
Train, 413
Traiser, 242
Trapp, 196
Trass, 242
Travel, 196
Tray, 413
Treasure, 242
Treble, 196
Tree, 429
Tremble, 11, 243
Tress, 242
Tricker, 429
Trickett, 429
Trickey, 429
Trigg, 429
Trigger, 429
Tripp, 196
Trist, 249
Trister, 249
Tristram, 249
Trodden, 271
Troke, 195
Troll, 141
Trood, 270
Trott, 270
Trotter, 271
Trottman, 271
Troughton, 271
Troup, 441
Trout, 106, 270
Trow, 195
Trowell, 195
Trower, 196
Trowse, 249
Troy, 429
Truby, 441
Truce, 249
True, 195
Truefitt, 429
Truelove, 429
Trueman, 196
Trumbull, 243
Trump, 243
Trumper, 243
Trumpy, 243
Trush, 103
Truss, 249
Trussell, 249
Try, 429
Tubb, 103
Tubby, 103
Tuck, 100, 427
Tucker, 427
Tuckey, 427
Tuckwell, 428

Tudor, 333
Tuffnell, 220
Tuggy, 427
Tugman, 428
Tuke, 427
Tuita, 332
Tulk, 184
Tun, 129
Tunaley, 130
Tungay, 361
Tunn, 106
Tunnay, 129
Tunnell, 130
Tunno, 129
Tunny, 106, 129
Tunstan, 130
Tupp, 103
Turk, 487
Turnbull, 3, 243
Turnell, 190
Turner, 190, 460
Turney, 190
Turnley, 190
Turrell, 208
Turtle, 103
Tutching, 332
Tuting, 332
Tutt, 332
Tuttle, 332
Tutty, 332
Tway, 521
Twice, 521
Twigg, 521
Twine, 521
Twining, 521
Twiss, 521
Twyman, 521
Tyas, 131, 351, 457
Tysack, 352
Tyser, 352
Tyson, 352
Tyus, 131

Udall, 334
Udy, 282
Uffell, 385
Ulier, 106
Ullock, 358
Ullmer, 106
Ulman, 106
Ulp, 71
Ulph, 71
Uncle, 294
Uncles, 354 (note)
Undey, 322
Ungless, 354
Unit, 286
Unna, 286
Unwin, 286
Urch, 387
Ure, 83
Urie, 83
Urling, 340

INDEX OF ENGLISH NAMES.

593

Urlwin, 340
Urquhart, 388
Urwick, 83
Urwin, 83
Usher, 442
Uttridge, 450

Vague, 523
Valder, 345
Valiant, 298
Valler, 298
Vallily, 298
Vallis, 298
Valpy, 88
Vance, 316
Vandeleur, 317
Vandy, 316
Vane, 394
Vann, 394
Vanneck, 394
Vanner, 394
Vant, 316
Vanzller, 317
Varick, 278
Varnell, 305
Varnish, 24, 305
Varrell, 278
Vassall, 244
Vasser, 12, 244
Vaudelin, 344
Veale, 383
Venn, 394
Vennell, 394
Venner, 394
Venning, 394
Vension, 316
Vent, 316
Venus, 143
Verco, 73
Verge, 65, 73
Verger, 74
Vergoose, 278
Verity, 7, 257
Verling, 278
Vermon, 278
Verner, 305
Verney, 305
Vest, 303
Vestal, 303
Vesterman, 303
Vesty, 303
Vetch, 154, 493
Vibert, 165
Vick, 164
Vicary, 165
Vice, 351
Vickridge, 165
Vidy, 493
Vigor, 165
Vinall, 263
Vindin, 316
Vine, 263
Vinegar, 12, 264

Vinen, 264
Viney, 263
Vingoe, 412
Vink, 412
Vint, 316
Vinter, 316
Violett, 468
Virgin, 65, 73, 74
Virgo, 65, 73
Virtue, 257
Viscord, 351
Vise, 351
Visick, 351
Vizard, 351
Vizer, 351
Voak, 333
Volckman, 334
Vollam, 384
Voller, 384
Vollet, 384
Vollum, 384
Vowell, 93
Vowles, 93
Vulliamy, 71
Vyse, 351

Wack, 362
Wadd, 152, 412
Wadden, 413
Waddicar, 413
Waddilove, 413
Waddle, 412
Waddy, 412
Wade, 152, 412
Wadey, 412
Wadge, 413
Wadkin, 413
Wadling, 413
Wadman, 413
Wadmore, 413
Wageman, 362
Wager, 523
Wagg, 47, 523
Wagman, 523
Wain, 523
Wainman, 394
Wainwright, 395, 461
Wake, 362
Wakelin, 362
Wakem, 24, 362
Wakeman, 362
Waker, 362
Wakley, 362
Waland, 298
Walden, 28, 345
Waldie, 344
Waldman, 345
Waldo, 340
Waldron, 42, 345
Walduck, 344
Waldwin, 345
Wale, 102, 298
Walcy, 298

Walford, 88
Walk, 298
Walker, 298, 460
Walkey, 298
Walking, 298
Walkley, 298
Walklin, 298
Wolkman, 298
Walko, 298
Wall, 298, 491
Wallace, 298
Wallack, 298
Waller, 298
Wallet, 298
Wallfree, 298
Walliker, 298
Wallis, 23
Walliss, 298
Wallower, 298
Wallraven, 298
Walls, 23, 298
Walrond, 41, 298
Walter, 47, 345
Wambey, 417
Wampen, 417
Wand, 316
Wander, 316
Wanding, 316
Wane, 394
Wanless, 354
Wannell, 394
Wannod, 394
Wansey, 316
Want, 316
Wantman, 316
Wanton, 12, 316
Warbolt, 278
Warbrick, 278
Ward, 277
Wardell, 277
Warder, 277
Wardman, 277
Wardy, 277
Ware, 278
Waring, 278
Warland, 278
Warlock, 278
Warman, 278
Warmer, 39, 278
Warne, 305
Warner, 305
Warnett, 305
Warnock, 305
Warraker, 278
Warre, 278
Warrell, 47, 278
Warren, 278, 305
Warrenburg, 305
Warrener, 305
Warrier, 47, 278
Warring, 278
Warry, 278
Warter, 277

W 3

594   INDEX OF ENGLISH NAMES.

Warwicker, 278
Wash, 244
Washer, 244
Washman, 244
Wasman, 244
Wasp, 107
Wass, 244
Wassell, 244
Waste, 244
Wastell, 244
Wastling, 22
Waterfall, 502
Wathen, 413
Watker, 413
Watkin, 413
Watkiss, 40, 413
Watley, 412
Watling, 413
Watmore, 413
Watney, 413
Watt, 32, 152, 412
Wattle, 412
Watts, 32, 413
Waud, 344
Way, 10, 47, 523
Wayland, 152, 383
Waygood, 523
Waylen, 523
Wayman, 523
Weakley, 362
Weaklin, 362
Weale, 383
Wearey, 278
Wearg, 73
Webling, 63
Wedd, 412
Weddell, 412
Weddon, 120
Wedge, 154, 413, 493
Wedlake, 40, 224, 494
Wedlock, 12, 224, 494
Weed, 493
Weedin, 493
Weeding, 494
Weekly, 362
Weeks, 362
Wegg, 10, 523
Weible, 63
Weir, 278
Weland, 152, 383
Welcome, 123, 297
Weld, 344
Welder, 345
Welding, 345
Weldon, 345
Welford, 88
Welland, 383
Wellard, 383
Weller, 383
Wellflin, 88
Welling, 383
Wellman, 383
Wellock, 383

Wellow, 383
Welp, 88
Welpley, 88
Welton, 345
Wendelken, 317
Wendon, 316
Wenlock, 394
Wenman, 394
Wenmoth, 394
Wenn, 394
Wenning, 394
Went, 316
Werge, 73
Werk, 73
Werner, 305
Werrett, 257
Werritt, 7
Wesson, 244
West, 303
Westall, 303
Wester, 303
Westerday, 303
Westerman, 303
Westfall, 303
Wetman, 303, 413
Weybret, 523
Whalebelly, 107
Whatman, 413
Whatmare, 413
Wheelan, 383
Wheeler, 53, 383
Wheeley, 383
Wheeling, 383
Wheelock, 383
Wheelwright, 383
Wheen, 263
Whellock, 383
Whenman, 264
Whenn, 263
Whewell, 357
Whibley, 63
Whichelo, 165
Whigam, 165
Whincopp, 39
Whipday, 63
Whipp, 62
Whippy, 62
Whish, 121
Whisker, 122
Whiskered, 351
Whiskin, 351
Whiskyman, 122
Whistle, 351
Whitbread, 494
Whitburn, 494
White, 398, 400
Whitear, 494
Whitecar, 494
Whitehart, 494
Whitehead, 494
Whiteheat, 494
Whitehorn, 494
Whitehouse, 494

Whitelaw, 366, 494
Whitelegg, 366, 494
Whitell, 493
Whitelock, 494
Whiteman, 494
Whiter, 494
Whiterod, 494
Whitethread, 494
Whitewright, 494
Whitheron, 494
Whiting, 106, 494
Whitley, 493
Whitling, 493
Whitmee, 24, 493
Whitmore, 494
Whitridge, 495
Whitsey, 493
Whittaker, 494
Whittock, 154
Wholey, 383
Wholework, 384
Whorlow, 325
Whytock, 493
Wibby, 62
Wiche, 164
Wichett, 165
Wick, 164
Wicker, 165
Wickey, 164
Wickson, 165
Wicking, 165
Wickman, 165
Widehose, 494
Wideman, 494
Widger, 494
Widow, 47, 493
Wigg, 164
Wiggett, 165
Wigle, 164
Wigman, 165
Wigmore, 165
Wigram, 165
Wigson, 165
Wilberforce, 500
Wilbourn, 123
Wilbraham, 123
Wilbur, 123
Wilcock, 27
Wilcomb, 123
Wild, 447
Wilday, 447
Wilder, 447
Wildey, 447
Wildgoose, 100
Wilding, 447
Wildish, 447
Wildman, 447
Wildsmith, 462
Wilford, 123
Wilfred, 123
Wilgoss, 123
Wilke, 123
Wilkie, 21, 123

INDEX OF ENGLISH NAMES. 595

Wilkin, 22
Will, 22, 31, 47, 122
Willam, 38
Willament, 124
Willan, 47, 123
Willard, 124
Willer, 124
Willett, 124
Willey, 21, 122
William, 38, 47
Williams, 47, 124
Williment, 276
Willin, 123
Willing, 31, 123
Willink, 123
Willis, 23, 32, 123
Willmer, 124
Willmot, 41
Willmott, 124
Willock, 123
Willoe, 122
Wills, 23, 123
Wilt, 447
Willthew, 42
Wimble, 48, 264
Winbolt, 264
Winbridge, 264
Winch, 263, 412
Wincup, 264
Wind, 316
Windeler, 317
Winder, 316, 490
Windle, 317
Window, 316
Windram, 316
Windred, 264
Wine, 263
Winegar, 264
Wineman, 264
Winer, 264
Wing, 412
Wingate, 264
Winger, 412
Wingood, 264
Winlo, 263
Winlock, 264
Winmen, 264
Winn, 47, 263
Winney, 263
Winning, 263
Winship, 263
Winson, 263
Winston, 264
Wint, 316
Winter, 140, 316
Wintle, 317
Wipkin, 63
Wippell, 7, 63
Wire, 165

Wirgman, 74
Wisdom, 351
Wise, 351
Wiseman, 351
Wisewould, 351
Wish, 121
Wishart, 121
Wisher, 122
Wishman, 122
Wiss, 351
Witcher, 165
With, 493
Wither, 494
Withered, 494
Witherick, 495
Withy, 493
Wittering, 494
Wittewrong, 494
Wittich, 154
Witton, 493
Witty, 493
Woledge, 384
Wolf, 71, 513
Wolfem, 71
Wolfram, 72
Woli, 383
Wollatt, 72, 384
Wollen, 384
Wolley, 383
Wolper, 72
Wolrige, 384
Wolsey, 71
Wolter, 378
Woodall, 493
Woodard, 494
Woodbridge, 495
Woodcock, 494
Wooden, 493
Wooderson, 494
Woodey, 493
Woodger, 494
Woodhead, 494
Woodhouse, 494
Wooding, 494
Woodlin, 493
Woodman, 494
Woodyer, 494
Woolbert, 71
Woolcott, 71
Wooldridge, 378
Woolfolk, 71
Woolfreys, 71
Woolgar, 71
Woolger, 71
Woolhead, 71
Woollams, 72
Woollard, 71
Woolley, 72
Woolmer, 72

Woolnoth, 72
Woolrych, 72
Woolston, 72
Woolwright, 460
Worry, 325
Workey, 78
Workman, 74
Worknot, 74
Worin, 513
World, 325
Wormald, 108
Wormbolt, 108
Worme, 108
Worrell, 325
Worrow, 325
Wren, 104, 189
Wrentmore, 228
Wrinkle, 230
Write, 254
Writt, 254
Wright, 254
Writer, 254
Wroth, 371
Wurr, 325
Wyard, 165
Wyatt, 165
Wyberg, 165
Wybrow, 165
Wye, 164
Wyfolde, 63
Wyman, 165
Wymer, 165

Yea, 366
Yealfe, 367
Yeaman, 367
Yeatman, 306
Yeld, 418
Yem, 253
Yeo, 366
Yeoman, 367
Yeoward, 367
Yesterday, 303
Yett, 305
Yewd, 282
Yorick, 367
Yost, 302
Youd, 282
Young, 419
Younger, 419
Youngman, 420
Youngmay, 25
Youring, 83
Yowden, 282

Zealey, 433
Zeall, 433
Zetterquist, 470

INDEX OF GERMAN NAMES.

Aar, 94
Abbe, 60
Abendrot, 139
Abendstern, 139
Abich, 60
Acke, 209
Acker, 210
Adal, 337
Ade, 287
Adelhart, 337
Adelung, 337
Adler, 338
Adolf, 288
Adolph, 72
Ahlmann, 517
Ahlwardt, 517
Ahr, 94
Aicher, 210
Albel, 134
Albrecht, 516
Alder, 418
Alert, 516
Alf, 134
Alker, 516
Alle, 516
Allehn, 238
Allmer, 517
Allner, 239
Alt, 418
Alten, 418
Alter, 418
Altmann, 418
Ameis, 284
Amelung, 143
Anderburg, 300
Angelé, 213
Anke, 212
Anselm, 119
Anser, 119
Anshelm, 227 (note)
Appe, 60
Arnhold, 95
Arnold, 95
Artelt, 251
Arve, 386
Asche, 216
Ascher, 217
Asel, 119
Asser, 119
Avemann, 290

Babe, 291
Backe, 172
Bade, 166
Bader, 166
Büder, 166

Badicke, 166
Bage, 172
Bahr, 68
Bald, 241
Baldauf, 242
Baldenius, 242
Balding, 241
Ball, 192
Baltz, 241
Baltzer, 241
Balz, 241
Banck, 182
Bandel, 235
Bandke, 235
Bang, 182
Banger, 175
Bannwart, 175
Banse, 235
Barde, 222
Bardel, 222
Bärecke, 69
Barnhard, 423
Bart, 222
Barten, 222
Barth, 222
Barther, 222
Barthmann, 222
Basch, 181
Büsel, 181
Baske, 181
Bass, 181
Bassmann, 181
Bath, 166
Bauch, 378
Baucke, 378
Bauer, 452
Bauermann, 452
Beckel, 222
Beckh, 222
Beede, 166
Beer, 68
Beerin, 70
Behl, 192
Behn, 176
Behrens, 70
Belke, 269
Bellin, 270
Benckert, 182
Bendell, 235
Bender, 286
Beneken, 177
Benicke, 176
Bennemann, 177
Bennert, 177
Benning, 177
Bennold, 177

Bense, 235
Bente, 235
Bentingck, 236
Benzel, 235
Ber, 68
Berger, 69
Berghoff, 496
Bermann, 69
Bernard, 70
Berner, 71
Bernicke, 70
Berning, 70
Berringer, 70
Bert, 370
Berth, 370
Bertin, 370
Bertong, 370
Bertram, 370
Bertrand, 370
Bese, 181
Beste, 183
Bethe, 166
Bethke, 166
Bettack, 166
Bette, 166
Bever, 91
Bieber, 91
Bieck, 177
Biercher, 69
Bigge, 177
Bihn, 176
Bila, 269
Bilger, 269
Bilhardt, 269
Bilke, 269
Bille, 269
Biller, 269
Billing, 269
Bilmer, 269
Binder, 236
Binnecke, 176
Bippart, 414
Blanckardt, 393
Blang, 392
Blank, 392
Blankennagel, 221
Blecher, 393
Blede, 440
Bledow, 440
Blenk, 392
Block, 214
Blockmann, 215
Blum, 465
Blume, 465
Blümel, 465
Blumer, 465

INDEX OF GERMAN NAMES.

597

Blumhardt, 465
Bobardt, 422
Bobbe, 421
Bobel, 421
Bochmann, 225
Böck, 224
Bode, 454
Bodeck, 454
Bodemann, 455
Bodemeyer, 455
Boden, 454
Böding, 454
Bödrich, 455
Boehner, 176
Böge, 224
Bogenhardt, 225
Bögert, 225
Bogner, 225
Bohl, 281
Bohling, 281
Bohn, 175, 225
Bohnhardt, 176
Böhtlingk, 454
Boldt, 241
Bölicke, 281
Bölke, 281
Boll, 281
Bollert, 281
Bollmann, 281
Boltche, 241
Bonn, 175
Bonne, 175
Bonnecke, 175
Boos, 407
Booth, 454
Bopp, 421
Bösel, 407
Bösewetter, 139
Boss, 408
Bosselt, 408
Bote, 454
Both, 454
Bothmer, 455
Bottger, 455
Boye, 313
Brach, 184
Brackmann, 185
Brämer, 371
Brandeis, 199
Brandel, 198
Brändlein, 199
Brandroth, 199
Brandt, 198
Braun, 399
Brecht, 370
Brechtel, 370
Brehm, 371
Breis, 186
Brese, 186
Brocke, 193
Brocker, 194
Brockmann, 194
Broockmann, 194

Brose, 480
Brösel, 480
Bruch, 193
Bruchhardt, 194
Bruckmann, 194
Brückmann, 185
Bruder, 218, 293
Brüderlein, 293
Brunck, 399
Brunn, 399
Brunnert, 400
Brüno, 399
Bry, 184
Bube, 421
Buck, 378
Buddel, 454
Buder, 455
Budge, 454
Budich, 454
Budke, 454
Bugge, 378
Buhl, 281
Buhler, 281
Buhlmann, 281
Bull, 281
Bund, 235
Bünning, 416
Bunsen, 236
Bunte, 235
Bunting, 236
Buol, 281
Burckhardt, 279
Bürde, 329
Burger, 279
Bürger, 279
Burghold, 279
Burke, 279
Burth, 329
Buss, 407
Bussmann, 407
Butte, 454
Butter, 455
Bütting, 454

Cahn, 174
Campe, 171
Christ, 133
Christel, 133
Conrad, 328
Coppel, 248
Cosmar, 310
Costis, 360
Cuno, 327

Daake, 390
Dabbert, 391
Düge, 390
Dahl, 375
Dahling, 375
Dahlmann, 376
Damm, 364
Dammer, 365
Dammert, 365

Danckel, 359
Dank, 359
Dankegott, 311
Dankert, 359
Dann, 311
Dannecker, 311
Darold, 208
Dasse, 385
Dassel, 385
Date, 291
Dau, 427
Daulf, 391
Däumlin, 364
Deck, 390
Deckert, 391
Dederich, 333
Degel, 390
Degen, 338
Dehn, 311
Dein, 338
Demme, 364
Dencker, 359
Denk, 359
Dessman, 385
Detmann, 333
Dette, 291
Dettmer, 333
Dettrich, 333
Dewe, 427
Dick, 406
Dickert, 407
Didtchen, 332
Diebold, 332
Diede, 332
Diehr, 268
Diemann, 457
Dieme, 364
Dieter, 333
Dietert, 333
Dikmann, 407
Dill, 189
Dillemann, 190
Dillert, 189
Dilling, 189
Dinger, 367
Disch, 229
Ditt, 332
Dittmer, 333
Dixmann, 229
Dode, 273
Dohm, 363
Dohmeyer, 364
Döler, 375
Dömich, 364
Donn, 129
Dooer, 208
Dorand, 197
Dormann, 208
Dormeier, 208
Dörwald, 268
Droge, 195
Drey, 413
Drude, 270

598 INDEX OF GERMAN NAMES.

Drucker, 196
Drue, 195
Drumann, 196
Drute, 270
Ducke, 427
Dükher, 427
Dulcken, 184
Dulk, 184
Dumhoff, 496
Dumichen, 364
Dümling, 364
Dumm, 363
Dümmel, 364
Durand, 197
Dusendteufel, 488
Duttke, 332

Ebbecke, 60
Ebbrecht, 61
Eber, 76
Eberhard, 76
Ebermann, 76
Eckardt, 210
Ecke, 209
Eckhoff, 496
Eckholdt, 210
Edel, 337
Edeler, 338
Ediling, 337
Egel, 154
Eger, 210
Egge, 209
Eisele, 475
Eiseln, 475
Eisemann, 475
Eisen, 474
Eisenhardt, 475
Eiser, 475
Elbe, 134
Elben, 134
Ellenberg, 239
Ellert, 299
Emele, 143
Emerich, 254
Emmel, 143
Emmert, 254
Ende, 432
Ender, 300
Enge, 292
Engel, 213
Engelhardt, 213
Engelin, 213
Englebrecht, 213
Englemann, 213
Englen, 213
Engler, 213
Enger, 292
Engert, 292
Engwald, 292
Ensle, 119
Entrich, 432
Erb, 386
Erche, 387

Erck, 387
Erd, 139
Erdmann, 251
Erhardt, 95
Erker, 388
Erle, 339
Erlecke, 340
Erler, 340
Ermel, 147
Ermen, 146
Ermisch, 147
Erpel, 386
Erpf, 386
Esch, 216
Escher, 217
Eschmann, 217
Eschrich, 217
Essich, 119
Estrich, 216
Ette, 287
Evers, 76
Ewaldt, 367
Ewert, 367
Ewich, 366
Eyl, 154

Fack, 435
Fahl, 307
Fahne, 234
Fahr, 323
Farenheit, 324
Füster, 252
Fechter, 257
Fecke, 435
Feder, 293
Fehr, 323
Fehrlen, 323
Fehrmann, 324
Fendt, 417
Ferrach, 323
Fest, 251
Fetter, 293
Fichte, 257
Fick, 249
Fidall, 430
Fiege, 249
Fielmann, 518
Filbert, 518
Fillmer, 518
Fisch, 247
Fischart, 247
Fischhof, 247, 496
Fix, 247
Flathe, 393
Flögel, 411
Fluemann, 411
Flügel, 411
Folke, 333
Fölkel, 333
Fortmann, 325
Francke, 306
Frank, 306
Franklin, 306

Freche, 132
Frede, 261
Freitag, 261
Fretter, 261
Freund, 263
Freutel, 350
Frick, 132
Fricker, 132
Friderich, 261
Fried, 261
Friedel, 261
Friess, 312
Frisch, 449
Frischlin, 449
Füchsel, 247
Füll, 517

Gabe, 285
Gabel, 285
Gabold, 286
Gade, 525
Gaedcke, 525
Gaide, 206
Galliger, 437
Gamann, 436
Gamm, 436
Gammert, 436
Gans, 518
Gante, 74
Ganter, 74
Günzlen, 518
Gapp, 285
Gast, 296
Gau, 336
Gause, 309
Gavel, 285
Gayl, 436
Gebel, 285
Geber, 285
Gebhardt, 285
Gede, 525
Gehl, 436
Gehr, 202
Gehrer, 203
Geilich, 437
Geisel, 458
Geiss, 459
Gelpke, 442
Génedl, 74
Genderich, 75
Gener, 444
Genet, 444
Gennerich, 444
Gent, 74
Gentz, 518
Gepp, 285
Gerbert, 203
Gerboth, 203
Gerhard, 203
Gerhold, 204
Gericke, 202
Gering, 202
Gerlach, 203

INDEX OF GERMAN NAMES. 599

Germann, 203
Gern, 433
Gerner, 433
Gernhardt, 433
Gerning, 433
Gernlein, 433
Gerold, 204
Gerwin, 204
Gessler, 458
Geu, 336
Gey, 336
Gherken, 202
Giese, 459
Giesemann, 459
Giesing, 459
Gilbert, 458
Gill, 458
Giltemann, 478
Gisbrecht, 459
Gisecke, 459
Gisselbrecht, 458
Glade, 435
Gladisch, 435
Gläser, 392
Glass, 392
Gleiss, 392
Gockel, 446
Göckingk, 446
Göde, 115
Gödecke, 115
Gödel, 115
Godehard, 116
Goemann, 337
Göethe, 309
Gogel, 446
Göhr, 202
Goldmann, 477
Gomm, 59
Gören, 204
Görich, 202
Göring, 202
Göschen, 309
Gose, 309
Göseken, 309
Gosling, 309
Göss, 309
Gossman, 310
Gothe, 309
Gottel, 115
Gotter, 116
Gottfried, 116
Gotthardt, 116
Götting, 115
Gottleib, 116
Gottlieb, 484
Götze, 115
Graesse, 464
Gramann, 401
Grashoff, 496
Grassmann, 464
Grau, 401
Grimm, 125
Grimmel, 125

Grimmer, 125
Gröbe, 425
Grobe, 425
Gröbel, 425
Grohn, 465
Grohnert, 465
Gröner, 465
Gröning, 465
Gross, 405
Grun, 465
Grün, 465
Grüner, 465
Grunert, 465
Grünert, 465
Grüning, 465
Gude, 115
Guibert, 165
Guldenapfel, 467
Gülich, 478
Güll, 478
Gummrich, 60
Gundel, 163
Günther, 164
Gunz, 163
Günzel, 163
Guter, 116
Gütermann, 117
Gutte, 115
Güttel, 115
Guttman, 116
Guttwein, 117
Gutwasser, 502

Haberkorn, 467
Hachmann, 210
Hacke, 209
Hückel, 209
Hackert, 210
Hadank, 168
Hüdel, 168
Hädicke, 168
Haertel, 250
Hagart, 210
Hagedorn, 467
Hügelen, 209
Hagen, 211
Hager, 210
Hagner, 211
Hahl, 480
Haid, 519
Hall, 480
Hallich, 426
Halm, 225
Hamelmann, 143
Hammer, 130
Handel, 417
Handt, 417
Hänelt, 289
Hanewald, 289
Hanisch, 289
Hanke, 212
Hanne, 289
Hanneken, 289

Hannemann, 289
Hannicke, 289
Harder, 250
Hardt, 250 ?
Hardweck, 251
Häricke, 231
Harke, 231
Härle, 231
Härlin, 231
Harless, 340
Harmann, 232
Harpe, 386
Harprecht, 232
Harring, 232
Hartmann, 251
Hürtnagel, 221, 251
Harting, 250
Hartrot, 251
Hartung, 250
Hartz, 250
Harward, 233
Hass, 307
Hatt, 168
Haube, 227
Hause, 491
Haussmann, 491
Haydn, 519
Hayer, 210
Haymann, 210
Heb, 60
Hecht, 450
Heckmann, 210
Hedde, 168
Hedrich, 168
Heer, 231
Heering, 232
Hehr, 231
Heidel, 519
Heilig, 426
Heiliggeist, 486
Heiligmann, 427
Heim, 492
Heinhardt, 211
Heinrich, 492
Heiter, 519
Helf, 275
Helfrich, 275
Helm, 225
Helmar, 163
Hemmer, 130
Henne, 289
Hennert, 289
Hennemann, 289
Hennicke, 289
Henning, 289
Herber, 232
Herbert, 232
Herbothe, 232
Herde, 250
Herden, 251
Herel, 231
Herger, 232
Herken, 432

600 INDEX OF GERMAN NAMES.

Herkner, 432
Herl, 231, 339
Herm, 147
Hermann, 232
Herold, 233
Herpfer, 386
Herr, 231
Herring, 232
Herrle, 231
Herrmuth, 233
Herth, 250
Hertrich, 251
Herwig, 233
Herzog, 339
Hess, 307
Hetz, 169
Hetzel, 169
Heyden, 519
Heydt, 519
Heye, 209
Heyne, 211
Hilbert, 162
Hild, 162
Hildebrand, 162
Hilger, 162
Hill, 162
Hiller, 162
Hillmann, 163
Hillmer, 163
Hilt, 162
Hiltmann, 163
Hiltrup, 163
Himmel, 140
Hinck, 292
Hobrecht, 341
Hoch, 340
Hock, 340
Höckel, 340
Höcker, 341
Hoffmann, 227
Hoge, 357
Hohman, 341
Hold, 282
Holder, 282
Holle, 282
Holler, 282
Hollmann, 282
Holt, 282
Homan, 341
Honer, 314
Hönicke, 314
Honigmann, 314
Hönke, 314
Höpke, 227
Höpken, 227
Hörder, 250
Horn, 520
Horneck, 520
Hornemann, 520
Hornhard, 520
Hornig, 520
Hörnlein, 520
Hornung, 520

Hoske, 442
Hubert, 357
Hucke, 357
Hudemann, 280
Hufnagel, 221
Huge, 357
Hügel, 357
Hugo, 357
Huhn, 314
Hühnert, 314
Hulde, 282
Humbert, 314
Humboldt, 314
Hunecken, 314
Hunger, 314
Hunn, 314
Hunnemann, 314
Hunold, 315
Hupe, 227
Husung, 491
Hüthel, 280
Hutte, 280

Ibe, 60
Icke, 210
Ide, 449
Ihl, 416
Ihle, 416
Ihm, 253
Ihn, 492
Imm, 253
Immich, 254
Imse, 254
Ingel, 213
Isanbart, 474
Isenberg, 474
Isert, 475
Itter, 450
Ive, 472
Iwe, 366

Jackel, 452
Jaeger, 452
Jagemann, 453
Jagenteufel, 488
Jechlin, 452
Jeckel, 452
Jenichen, 444
Jochen, 452
Jöcher, 452
Jöck, 452
Jordan, 140
Jüde, 305
Jung, 419
Jüngerich, 420
Jungher, 419
Junghoff, 496
Jungmann, 420
Jünke, 419
Juppe, 485
Jütte, 305

Käbe, 285

Kade, 525
Kahlert, 437
Kalb, 83
Kalfs, 83
Kalker, 307
Kalthoff, 496
Kaltwasser, 502
Kamler, 419
Kamm, 436
Kammer, 436
Kant, 74
Kanter, 74
Karl, 59
Karmann, 203
Karthin, 277
Kasch, 205
Kaske, 205
Kast, 296
Katt, 168
Kaumann, 337
Kaup, 248
Kaupert, 336
Keber, 286
Kehl, 436
Kehler, 437
Kehr, 202
Kehrer, 203
Kemp, 171
Kendel, 74
Kerhle, 202
Kern, 433
Kernmann, 433
Kerwin, 204
Kessler, 458
Kettler, 525
Kiehl, 322
Kiesel, 458
Kille, 458
Killin, 458
Killmer, 453
Kinreich, 328
Kiss, 459
Kissling, 458
Klaber, 183
Klapp, 183
Klass, 392
Klencke, 199
Kling, 199
Klink, 199
Klinkhardt, 199
Klocke, 352
Klockmann, 352
Klode, 377
Kloth, 377
Kloverkorn, 467
Kluck, 352
Kluge, 352
Knabb, 422
Knapp, 422
Kniep, 201
Koch, 446
Köcher, 446
Köchlin, 446

INDEX OF GERMAN NAMES. 601

Köckert, 446
Kohl, 226
Kohlhardt, 226
Kohlmann, 226
Kohlig, 226
Köhling, 226
Kohnert, 328
Kohnle, 327
Kohrssen, 409
Koll, 226
Koller, 226
Kollmeyer, 226
Komm, 59
Köne, 327
Könemann, 328
Koner, 328
Könicke, 327
Konter, 164
Kopisch, 248
Kopp, 248
Körner, 433
Koss, 309
Kost, 360
Kott, 115
Kotting, 115
Krieger, 170
Kriegk, 170
Krimmer, 125
Kroll, 405
Krön, 465
Kroner, 465
Krull, 405
Kruse, 404
Kubbe, 248
Kuckkuck, 105
Kude, 115
Kuhn, 327
Kühnel, 327
Kuhnert, 328
Kuhnhardt, 328
Kühnhold, 328
Kuhnke, 327
Kumm, 59
Kunde, 163
Künemund, 328
Kuner, 328
Känicke, 327
Künsel, 163
Kunte, 163
Kunth, 163
Kuntke, 163
Kunz, 163
Kupfer, 476
Kupfernagel, 221
Kutter, 116

Lachman, 366
Lacher, 366
Laiber, 387
Lambert, 335
Lamberg, 335
Lamle, 86
Lamm, 86

Lampe, 86
Land, 335
Landherr, 335
Landt, 335
Landwehr, 336
Landwig, 336
Lanfried, 335
Lanz, 335
Laue, 87
Lebin, 387
Leder, 195
Leding, 194
Leff, 387
Lege, 366
Lehn, 366
Leine, 274
Leiter, 195
Lende, 110
Lenhard, 87
Leonhard, 87
Lepert, 387
Leppoc, 265
Lepsius, 265
Lesse, 353
Lessing, 353
Lethe, 194
Lette, 194
Leuchs, 88
Leue, 87
Leuthold, 331
Leutiger, 331
Leuze, 331
Lewald, 87
Leyde, 194
Lieb, 265
Liebegott, 484
Liebel, 265
Lieber, 265
Liebert, 265
Liebetrut, 265
Liebich, 265
Liebig, 265
Liebmann, 265
Linck, 87
Linde, 110
Lindhof, 496
Linn, 174
Liphard, 265
Lippe, 265
Lippel, 265
Lippert, 265
List, 355
Listing, 355
Lochmann, 447
Lode, 377
Löhle, 284
Loth, 377
Löther, 377
Lott, 377
Lotter, 377
Lubbe, 265
Lubbecke, 265
Lude, 330

Lüdecking, 330
Ludolf, 331
Ludtmann, 331
Ludwig, 331
Luth, 330
Luthardt, 331
Luther, 331
Luttkus, 331
Lutz, 331
Luz, 331

Mächen, 410
Machold, 410
Mack, 410
Mädchen, 341
Madel, 361
Mader, 342
Madicke, 341
Madler, 361
Mädler, 361
Mager, 410
Mahl, 178
Mahr, 368
Maldt, 180
Malle, 178
Mandt, 434
Manecke, 58
Manfried, 58
Mangold, 58
Manhardt, 58
Mann, 58
Mannchen, 58
Manneck, 58
Mannel, 58
Mannert, 58
Mannikin, 58
Manz, 434
March, 80
Märell, 368
Mark, 80
Märker, 80
Markloff, 80
Markwardt, 80
Marr, 368
Martyrt, 258
Masch, 445
Maske, 445
Mass, 522
Müssel, 522
Massen, 522
Massl, 522
Massman, 523
Mäther, 342
Matticke, 341
Maurer, 402
Maywald, 410
Meeder, 342
Meer, 368
Meerbott, 369
Meerwein, 369
Mehne, 410
Mehrle, 368
Mehrwald, 369

X 3

602   INDEX OF GERMAN NAMES.

Meiner, 410
Meinert, 410
Mende, 434
Mennel, 58
Mense, 434
Mentzel, 434
Menzel, 434
Meske, 445
Mess, 522
Messer, 522
Metke, 341
Mette, 341
Metto, 341
Meye, 410
Michelmann, 406
Mielecke, 179
Mielert, 180
Miercke, 368
Milch, 179
Milcke, 179
Milde, 283
Miller, 180
Mirich, 368
Mode, 237
Model, 237
Moder, 237
Mohl, 178
Mohr, 402
Mohrhard, 402
Mohrin, 402
Möhrle, 402
Möhrmann, 403
Monschein, 139
Mordt, 258
Mordtmann, 259
Morgenrot, 139
Morgenstern, 139
Morhof, 496
Moring, 402
Mörtz, 258
Mortzschke, 258
Most, 238
Moster, 238
Mosthal, 238
Moth, 237
Mozart, 237
Mucke, 406
Mückel, 406
Mückert, 406
Mudder, 293
Müdel, 237
Mugge, 406
Mund, 276
Munding, 276
Mundt, 276
Muntz, 276
Mushacke, 237
Mushard, 237
Müslein, 237
Muss, 237
Muth, 237
Muthreich, 237
Mütter, 237

Mutterlein, 293
Mütz, 237
Mützell, 237

Nädelin, 256
Nadell, 256
Nadler, 256
Nagel, 220
Nagler, 220
Nahl, 220
Näning, 239
Nanne, 239
Nänny, 239
Nanz, 239
Nath, 275
Nebel, 151
Neidl, 256
Nendel, 239
Nenne, 239
Nessel, 256
Nesselrath, 256
Nessler, 256
Neue, 420
Neurath, 421
Neuwert, 421
Ney, 420
Nibel, 151
Nick, 126
Nied, 255
Nieder, 255
Niedhardt, 255
Niedling, 256
Niemann, 297, 421
Niepoth, 255
Niete, 255
Nippolt, 255
Nitze, 255
Nitzert, 255
Nizze, 255
Nonne, 439
Nord, 300
Nordmann, 301
Nordmeyer, 301
Normann, 301
North, 300
Nötel, 240
Noth, 240
Notter, 240
Nuding, 240
Nutt, 240
Nutzer, 240

Oberlin, 76
Odebrecht, 381
Odemann, 382
Oeffele, 385
Oertling, 217
Oester, 302
Oettel, 334
Off, 385
Oken, 524
Orling, 340
Ort, 217

Ortel, 217
Orteln, 217
Orth, 217
Ortlieb, 218
Ost, 302
Ostermann, 303
Ostermeier, 303
Osterrath, 302
Ostertag, 303
Ostmann, 302
Oswald, 120
Ott, 381.

Packe, 172
Padel, 166
Pahl, 192
Paldamus, 241
Pallas, 143, 521
Panse, 235
Pantke, 235
Pape, 291
Pappe, 291
Pass, 181
Pätel, 166
Pathe, 166
Püthe, 166
Pattke, 166
Pauck, 378
Peck, 222
Pedel, 166
Peel, 219
Pelegnard, 269
Pellgram, 241
Penn, 176
Pennicke, 176
Pesel, 181
Pethke, 166
Petter, 166
Pfanner, 234
Pfau, 101
Pfefferkorn, 467
Pich, 177
Pick, 177
Pickel, 177
Pickhardt, 178
Piehl, 219
Pielert, 219
Pielke, 269
Piper, 91
Pippe, 414
Pippert, 414
Planck, 392
Plessing, 440
Plöger, 215
Plucker, 215
Plügge, 214
Pogge, 224
Poggel, 224
Pöhler, 281
Pohlert, 281
Pohlmann, 281
Polgar, 281
Polte, 241

INDEX OF GERMAN NAMES. 603

Pölten, 242
Popel, 421
Popken, 422
Popp, 421
Pose, 408
Poth, 454
Pott, 454
Potthoff, 496
Prechtel, 370
Preim, 371
Preiss, 186
Prutz, 447
Puche, 378
Pupke, 422
Puppe, 421
Putter, 455
Püttmann, 455

Quaritch, 278
Quile, 123
Quilling, 123
Quin, 263

Raben, 97
Rabener, 97
Rack, 362
Räck, 362
Rade, 347
Radel, 348
Rädel, 348
Rader, 348
Rademann, 348
Radicke, 347
Radleff, 348
Raffel, 187
Rahardt, 362
Rahn, 189
Raimund, 363
Ralfs, 363
Ralphs, 72
Rampf, 228
Rand, 228
Randolff, 228
Ranke, 230
Ranter, 228
Rath, 347
Rathen, 348
Ratter, 348
Ratti, 347
Ratting, 348
Rauch, 253
Raumer, 374
Reaumur, 374
Recknagel, 221
Redde, 347
Reden, 348
Reder, 348
Redmann, 348
Redmer, 348
Reede, 347
Regel, 362
Regenbogen, 137
Regner, 350

Reibe, 187
Reiber, 188
Reich, 343
Reichardt, 343
Reichen, 343
Reichhelm, 343
Reichmann, 344
Reiff, 187
Rein, 349
Reincke, 349
Reiner, 350
Reinhard, 349
Reinhart, 349
Reinhold, 350
Reiniger, 349
Reinmann, 350
Rencker, 230
Renter, 228
Renz, 349
Reyger, 363
Reyher, 363
Reyne, 349
Reynold, 350
Rhode, 371
Richard, 343
Rick, 343
Rickert, 343
Rickher, 343
Rickman, 344
Ridder, 254
Rieck, 343
Riedl, 254
Riegel, 343
Rickelt, 344
Riemann, 344
Riemar, 344
Riffel, 188
Rinck, 230
Ringe, 230
Ringel, 230
Ringer, 230
Ringert, 230
Ringwald, 230
Ritt, 254
Ritter, 254
Robert, 372
Rocke, 253
Rodde, 371
Rodeck, 372
Rödel, 372
Rodemann, 373
Roder, 373
Rodewig, 373
Rödger, 372
Roding, 372
Rodnagel, 221
Rodwald, 373
Roger, 372
Rogge, 253
Rohloff, 253
Rohm, 373
Röhm, 373
Rolf, 72

Rolland, 373
Rom, 373
Romer, 374
Rommel, 374
Rosenblatt, 467
Rosenblüt, 467
Rosengarten, 467
Rosenhagen, 467
Rosenkranz, 467
Rosenstengel, 467
Rosensteil, 467
Rosenstock, 467
Rosenweber, 467
Rosenzweig, 467
Rosnagel, 221
Rost, 448
Röstel, 448
Roth, 371
Rothardt, 372
Rothschild, 227 (note)
Rott, 371
Rübe, 187
Rücke, 253
Rücker, 253
Ruckert, 253
Rudel, 372
Rudeloff, 373
Ruder, 373
Rudolph, 373
Rüdon, 372
Rudrich, 373
Ruhe, 253
Rummel, 374
Rundnagel, 221
Rüppell, 188
Rupprecht, 372
Rust, 448
Rusting, 448
Ruth, 371
Rutte, 371

Saarmann, 230
Sach, 171
Sachs, 200
Sacke, 171
Sager, 171
Sahl, 308
Sahm, 75
Sahr, 230
Sallmann, 308
Saltzmann, 443
Salz, 45, 443
Sancke, 438
Sand, 430
Sanden, 431
Sander, 430
Sandhoff, 431, 496
Sandt, 430
Sann, 170
Santer, 430
Santz, 430
Saphir, 424
Sarrazin, 487

604   INDEX OF GERMAN NAMES.

Sass, 451
Sause, 266
Savert, 424
Sax, 200
Scar, 223
Schaarschmidt, 462
Schade, 191
Schalk, 456
Schar, 223
Scharf, 356
Scharpff, 356
Schat, 191
Scheer, 223
Schelck, 456
Scheurbrand, 223
Schick, 431
Schiermann, 223
Schildt, 227
Schill, 360
Schiller, 361
Schilling, 360
Schinnagl, 221
Schlagenteufel, 488
Schlauch, 257
Schlech, 257
Schmedding, 462
Schmidlin, 462
Schmieder, 461
Schmiedecke, 462
Schmiedel, 462
Schnauber, 326
Schnebern, 326
Schnell, 245
Schon, 389
Schöner, 389
Schönwetter, 139
Schöpf, 442
Schoppe, 442
Schuldt, 457
Schürmann, 223
Schurr, 223
Schwabe, 304
Schwäble, 304
Schwann, 99
Schwanecke, 99
Schweppe, 304
Schwerdt, 198
Schwinge, 412
Sebert, 321
Sebode, 173
Seeburg, 322
Seemann, 322
Seewald, 322
Sehr, 230
Selke, 308
Selle, 308
Sello, 308
Semm, 75
Senke, 438
Senne, 170
Senner, 170
Senhert, 170
Seppe, 261

Serre, 230
Seydel, 431
Seyer, 173
Seyfrid, 173
Seymer, 173
Sicher, 173
Sichert, 173
Sick, 172
Sickel, 172
Siebe, 261
Siebecke, 262
Siebert, 173
Siebold, 172
Sieg, 172
Siegfried, 173
Sieger, 173
Sieghardt, 173
Siegmann, 173
Siegmund, 173
Sieke, 172
Sieveking, 262
Sigel, 172
Sigg, 172
Sigle, 172
Siglen, 172
Silber, 479
Silberard, 479
Silbermann, 479
Simund, 173
Sint, 456
Sinz, 456
Sitte, 431
Sohl, 138
Sorg, 441
Spaeth, 200
Spanier, 445
Sparwasser, 502
Spät, 200
Speck, 207
Speckmann, 207
Speer, 206
Spiel, 434
Spieler, 434
Spielmann, 434
Spiess, 207
Spohn, 445
Spöring, 206
Sprotte, 415
Stacke, 213
Stackemann, 213
Stade, 252
Stähelin, 476
Stahl, 476
Stahlmann, 476
Stang, 214
Stark, 245
Stecker, 213
Steckert, 213
Steding, 252
Stedmann, 252
Stegemann, 213
Steinecke, 479
Steiner, 480

Steinhart, 480
Steinhoff, 496
Steinmann, 480
Sterk, 245
Sterker, 245
Stichert, 213
Stich, 213
Stickel, 214
Stiebel, 469
Stiegler, 214
Stobwasser, 503
Stock, 213
Stöckel, 214
Stöckhardt, 213
Stockmann, 213
Stoff, 469
Strauss, 48, 190
Streit, 171
Streiter, 171
Stucke, 213
Stüber, 469
Stüve, 469
Suckard, 267
Summer, 141
Sundelin, 301 (note)
Sundrehoff, 496
Sündrehoff, 302
Suppe, 304
Susman, 267
Süss, 266
Sybel, 262

Tabold, 391
Tack, 390
Tade, 291
Taddel, 291
Tag, 390
Tagel, 390
Täger, 391
Tagmann, 391
Tanne, 311
Taube, 103
Teichhof, 496
Tegen, 338
Tell, 375
Temm, 364
Tessmann, 385
Teufel, 488
Teufelskind, 488
Teufelskopf, 488
Thal, 375
Thaler, 375
Thalhammer, 376
Thalmann, 376
Thalmeier, 376
Thamm, 364
Thein, 338
Theiner, 339
Theinert, 339
Theobald, 332
Theuer, 268
Thie, 457
Thiedt, 332

INDEX OF GERMAN NAMES.

Thiemke, 365
Thier, 268
Thies, 351
Thimm, 364
Thoma, 363
Thürnagel, 221
Tieck, 406
Tiede, 332
Tiedemann, 333
Tiedt, 332
Tieler, 375
Till, 189
Tillmann, 190
Tilo, 189
Timm, 364
Tischer, 229
Titel, 332
Tock, 427
Tode, 273
Todt, 273
Tödtmann, 273
Tonne, 129
Tott, 273
Trappe, 196
Traswalt, 242
Traub, 441
Traum, 243
Trautman, 271
Treyer, 413
Troche, 195
Tröder, 271
Trübe, 441
Trüger, 196
Trummer, 243
Tsjisse, 459
Tuch, 427
Tucher, 427
Tümmel, 364
Turhold, 208
Türk, 487
Tütel, 332

Uhle, 105
Uhr, 83
Uhthoff, 496
Ulbricht, 105
Ullmann, 106

Vater, 293
Vetter, 293
Vetterlein, 293
Violet, 468
Vogel, 93
Volhardt, 334
Volk, 333
Völker, 334
Volkmann, 334

Wach, 362
Wacker, 362
Wackernagel, 221
Wadt, 412
Wage, 522

Wager, 523
Wahl, 298
Wahler, 298
Wahlert, 298
Wahlman, 298
Wahlmar, 298
Wahren, 305
Walcker, 298
Wald, 344
Waldmann, 345
Waldschmidt, 462
Walke, 298
Wall, 298
Waller, 298
Wallick, 298
Walther, 345
Wande, 316
Wandel, 317
Wandt, 316
Wandtke, 316
Wannick, 394
Warburg, 278
Warlick, 278
Warnecke, 305
Warner, 305
Wart, 277
Warth, 277
Wartman, 277
Wass, 244
Wasserfall, 502
Wassmann, 244
Wedding, 494
Wedell, 413
Wedlich, 494
Weede, 493
Wege, 523
Wegel, 165
Wegelein, 165
Weger, 523
Wegerich, 165
Wehde, 412
Wehling, 383
Wehr, 278
Wehrlen, 278
Wehrmann, 278
Weidel, 493
Weiger, 165
Weih, 164
Weiher, 165
Weilert, 383
Weiller, 383
Wein, 263
Wyinberg, 264
Weinen, 264
Weinger, 264
Weinhardt, 264
Weinhold, 264
Weinkopf, 264
Weinmann, 264
Weise, 351
Weiswald, 351
Weitmann, 494
Welde, 344

Welden, 345
Welf, 88
Wellmann, 383
Welte, 344
Welten, 345
Wend, 316
Wendel, 317
Wendeler, 317
Wendling, 317
Weniger, 394
Wening, 394
Went, 316
Werck, 73
Werker, 74
Werne, 305
Werner, 305
Wernert, 305
Wessel, 244
Westermann, 303
Westphal, 303
Weygold, 165
Weyland, 383
Weymann, 523
Wibel, 63
Wibking, 63
Wich, 164
Wichman, 165
Wick, 164
Wickardt, 165
Widmann, 494
Widmer, 494
Wiebe, 62
Wiegel, 165
Wiehl, 383
Wieland, 383
Wiemann, 165
Wiemer, 165
Wiesel, 351
Wiethorn, 494
Wieting, 494
Wiggele, 165
Wiggert, 165
Wild, 447
Wildt, 447
Wilhelm, 124
Wilke, 123
Willberg, 123
Willcomm, 297
Wille, 123
Willer, 124
Willert, 124
Willet, 124
Willich, 123
Williez, 123
Willing, 123
Willisch, 123
Willkomm, 123
Willmann, 124
Wilmar, 124
Wilz, 123
Winck, 412
Wind, 316
Winder, 316

606 INDEX OF GERMAN NAMES.

Winecke, 263
Winheer, 264
Winke, 263
Winne, 263
Winning, 263
Winter, 316
Wippel, 63
Wissman, 351
With, 493
Witte, 493
Witten, 493
Witter, 494

Witthaus, 494
Wittich, 493
Wittling, 493
Wittrich, 495
Wohl, 383
Wolf, 71
Wolfer, 72
Woll, 383
Wollmer, 384
Worle, 325
Wulfert, 71

Wunsch, 121
Wünscher, 122
Wurm, 108

Zaiser, 272
Zeiz, 272
Ziehle, 433
Zillmann, 433
Zuck, 267
Zucker, 268
Zuckert, 267

FRENCH NAMES

Anquetil, 128
Chanteclaire, 74
Chantoiseau, 74
Cloez, 391

Closier, 391
Closse, 391
Dietsch, 229

Drumond, 243
Frasier, 313
Frezier, 313

CPSIA information can be obtained
at www.ICGtesting.com
Printed in the USA
LVHW100551290322
714679LV00002B/57